Secrets

Volumes 11 & 12

Secrets

The Best in Women's Erotic Romance
Volumes 11 & 12

Red Sage Publishing, Inc.
Seminole, FL

Secrets Volume 11

Masquerade © 2005 by Jennifer Probst
Ancient Pleasures © 2005 by Jess Michaels
Manhunt © 2005 by Kimberly Dean
Wake Me © 2005 by Angela Knight

Secrets Volume 12

Good Girl Gone Bad © 2005 by Dominique Sinclair
Aphrodite's Passion © 2005 by Jess Michaels
White Heat © 2005 by Leigh Wyndfield
Summer Lightning © 2005 by Saskia Walker

ISBN 0-7394-6056-0

Published by Red Sage Publishing, Inc.
P.O. Box 4844
Seminole, FL 33775

TABLE OF CONTENTS:

Jennifer Probst

Jess Michaels

Kimberly Dean

Angela Knight

Volume 11

Secrets

Satisfy your desire for more.

Secrets

Volume 11

Masquerade

by Jennifer Probst

To My Reader:

I loved writing *Masquerade.* Start with a delicious concept: masked strangers and a bargain to be truthful. Add in the mystery of never revealing their faces, and the stark intimacy of sharing every secret fantasy. The result is a steamy romance that breaks down all barriers. I feel that readers can relate to this couple who have to battle their fear of vulnerability in order to win the ultimate prize: love.

The setting takes place in the sensual world of Italy, Lake Como. I remember looking at the eccentric mansions around the lake and spinning this tale. I truly hope you enjoy the journey and I look forward to sharing more stories. Please go to my website, www.jenniferprobst.com, and write to me. I welcome all feedback from readers.

Chapter One

Hailey Ashton closed the door to her best friend's office and sat down on the chair opposite his desk. Her fingers trembled slightly with excitement as she slid the gold embossed invitation across the polished wood. "I'm going to meet the man of my dreams."

Michael Rivers raised one brow at her declaration and picked up the invitation. "I didn't know you were looking for one." His chocolate brown eyes held a gleam of intrigue and his fingers raked through wheat strands of hair. One lock fell stubbornly over his forehead in rebellion. It was the only part of his appearance not ruthlessly groomed and neat.

She gave a sigh. "Who isn't? Women were raised on stories of knights and dragon slayers. No wonder we get depressed when a man can't do his own laundry."

He grinned and glanced at the card. "A masquerade ball?"

Hailey leaned over. "It's the annual party our boss sponsors. I've heard stories about them but I've never gone."

"Yeah, I remember seeing one of these in my mailbox. It's more like a weekend event than a party. Employees are invited but mostly the rich and famous attend. He picks a different theme each year. This one's being held in some private villa in Italy. Must be nice." Michael narrowed dark brown eyes. "Don't tell me. You've targeted some Duke of England to take you away from all this."

"Very funny. I don't care about money and you know it. I just thought this would be different." She paced the lush wine carpet. "Sometimes I feel like my life is closing in on me. I do everything right. I exercise at the gym, I don't eat red meat, I make sure I get eight hours sleep. Even the men I date are boring. Do you know I can't remember the last time a man kissed me good night and my knees buckled? Usually I can't wait to get back to my own apartment. Lord, I have more fun with you watching a DVD and eating popcorn. Isn't that sad?"

"Tragic," he said wryly.

"Sorry, I didn't mean it like that." She sighed and pushed back her heavy mane of red hair. "I want to break out of my routine and meet someone I've always wondered about."

Michael studied her, then shifted in his chair. The leather creaked gently beneath his weight. "Are you looking for a general man of your dreams, or have you narrowed the search to one?"

Unfortunately, he knew her well enough to realize she was hiding something. "I'd confess but you'll probably yell."

He muttered something under his breath. "Tell me."

"Promise you won't lecture?" she asked.

He groaned. "I promise. Spill it."

"Our boss."

His face plainly showed his disbelief. "You're kidding me. Ciro Demitris? He's not only the boss of this company, Hailey. He owns a software empire all over the world and he's richer than Midas. You've never even met him. Hell, most people in the organization never caught a glance of the guy."

She raised her chin. "I've seen his pictures in magazine articles! I'd know what he looks like if I saw him."

Michael shook his head. "You think this man is the answer to your rut? He'd eat you for breakfast and not look back."

Her voice turned to ice. "Thanks for the confidence in me."

"Oh, hell, you know what I meant. The rumors about him should make you think twice. Why do you think he throws these parties each year? He's an eccentric who likes to play with people's minds. He does this for his own entertainment."

"You know nothing about him personally, and neither do I. But this party can change that. I know you don't think I'm glamorous enough to hold my own, but with a mask on I can be the woman I always wanted. I can be beautiful and exciting and mysterious."

His tone softened as he stared at her. "You are, Hailey. You just don't see it."

She stopped pacing and looked down at her sensible oatmeal colored business suit and pumps. As always, she dressed to be a businesswoman, and she realized that somehow, along the way, the real woman inside had gotten lost. How could she explain to anyone, even her best friend? She walked back over to the chair and sank down. Then tried to put her feelings into words.

"I'm thirty years old, Michael. I've never been married, never had children, and until lately, I never thought I'd miss it. But I feel trapped. I'm afraid to do anything different if it doesn't fit with my daily schedule. I live for my work, but I know there has to be more out there. This is my chance. And even if nothing happens between us, at least I know I tried. Can you understand?"

A strange array of emotions passed over his carved features, then cleared. He smiled. "Yeah, I think I understand. But these parties are way out of your league. Demitris is known for his erotic themes. I've heard stories about drunken orgies, people playing out their sexual fantasies. Anything goes when a person steps through the door. He's made a reputation of being entirely discreet, and offering his guests the same." Michael paused. "I'm worried."

Hailey faced her best friend and realized she couldn't tell him the whole truth. He was the only man she felt close to, but she had never confessed her upbringing to him. She wasn't one to blame her sexual repressions on her parents, though their deeply-held belief sex was wrong had created problems since her teens.

She'd spent most of her life being reminded of her mother's mistake. Namely her. One drunken night had produced her parents' only child, and after they were forced to marry, they turned to religion. Sex was wrong. Sex meant loss of control. Sex meant diseases and pregnancy and a man controlling every part of a woman's existence. Sex meant fewer choices. Her parents made sure she would never have an opportunity for any reckless behaviors. Of course, she had rebelled.

Then realized her parents were right.

Hailey firmly shook off the memories and refocused on Michael. She ached for an experience to finally propel her out of her rut. She wanted to be free to express her sexuality without fear. The idea of shedding her clothes and her prim ways left her with a tingle of heat that bloomed in her belly. An odd combination of wanting and shame mingled together. She battled with an inner voice that taunted, its familiar sensual tone urging her to throw away constraints.

The voice came sometimes in the middle of the night, a swirl of sexual images of naked men sucking at her breasts, thrusting their fingers deep inside of her as she screamed for release. The last three months the dreams were relentless. She would wake in the middle of the night, bucking her hips upward into empty space, the tension pounding through her body until she moaned in agony and waited for the feeling to pass. With an iron willed control, she never let herself go, never pleasured herself. She believed in controlling her life to the last detail, which included her sexuality. Much easier to deny the wanting than pass over the edge of no return. Because the voice that came to her deep in the darkness always reminded her once she plummeted into her sexual fantasies, she'd never come back.

But the voice was growing stronger. She had always been able to keep the echo to a low murmur. Now, the roar crashed through her mental barriers at night and left her aching for so much more.

She admitted to obsessing a bit over Ciro Demitris. Once she had seen his picture, looked into those deep, brooding eyes, something had happened to her. The article in *Fortune* magazine sketched him as a private eccentric who lived an isolated life. She wanted him to be the one to do all the things she fantasized about. She didn't want to be afraid anymore of losing control.

The thought teased at the fringes of her mind for weeks, and when she received the invitation, she knew the time had come to take a chance.

Her life was perfect on paper. Strong financial background. Solid career. The ability to choose any path she craved. Yet, she felt unfulfilled and empty as she moved through her days. She admitted she was now more scared of being trapped in her ideal life than she was of embarking on a reckless affair.

No, she couldn't tell Michael, her sweet, supportive friend.

"I'll be fine." She said the words firmly but a quiver in her belly screamed she was a liar.

He nodded, obviously deciding to accept her decision. "Okay. So, what's the plan?"

"I already know where I can rent my costume and mask. The party starts Thursday night, and ends Sunday. Everyone unmasks at dawn on the final night. The map was enclosed with the invitation so I know how to get there." She brightened. "Why don't you come with me? This party could help you, too."

He winced. "Boy, you're full of complements this morning. I happen to be satisfied with my dull life."

"You need a woman, old friend. I think your last date was six months ago, almost the same time mine was," she teased.

"Sorry, the Bulls game is on. No glamour queen can compete."

"You're still hung up on her, aren't you?" she asked softly.

He stiffened, then consciously relaxed his fingers around the invitation. "My faithless ex-wife is off having a grand old time with her boyfriend. I never give her a second thought."

"It's been two years, Michael."

He gave a lopsided grin, full of his usual charm. "She never let me watch the basketball games. How could I possibly miss her?"

She let him coax a smile from her. "Okay, I give. I should know by now you'll never be one of these tortured heroes like Heathcliff in *Wuthering Heights*. I've got to stop forcing that role on you."

"Deal," he said. He glanced at his watch. "I've got a meeting at ten. Davidson has a new software program he's still working kinks out of and my head's on the block. Our charming boss will fire me in a heartbeat if I don't get it working. Hmmm, maybe if you two hit it off you can put in a good word for me."

"Cute, real cute." She paused, then bit her lip as she tried to broach the subject. "Michael, I've got to ask you for one small favor."

He rubbed his fingers against his temple as if anticipating a headache. Wheat colored strands of hair ruffled under the motion, then settled back into place. "Why am I afraid to ask?"

"Well, since it's a masquerade ball, and you so intelligently pointed out I don't really know what our boss looks like, I need to know what he'll be wearing."

He blinked. "There will be hundreds of people in that mansion. All in masks and costumes. How am I supposed to get this information?"

"Oh, come on, you've got the inside on all the top people in this firm. We both know this party is presented as a social occasion, but it's still about business. Executives are going to want to get the ear of Ciro

Demitris. I bet there are people who'll know exactly what his costume is. I just need you to be one of them."

"You don't ask for much. Got any money to grease their palms?"

She grinned cheekily. "Just use your charm. That's why you've been promoted to director, isn't it?"

"And your smart comebacks are why you're still a lowly manager."

She made a face, then rose from the chair and walked towards the door. "So, this wonderful manager can count on her best friend to do a little detective work, right?"

The phone beeped insistently and interrupted his comeback. He reached for the receiver and mouthed, "You owe me."

She laughed and left the office.

Hailey stared at the woman in the full length mirror and caught her breath. It was her. But it wasn't.

The woman's hair had been left loose instead of fastened into her usual tight bun. Gleaming red strands poured wildly down her shoulders. Her blue eyes were framed by dark, lush lashes and took on a hint of mystery behind the brightly colored peacock mask. Her lips had been lined and colored with deep red lipstick, making them appear full and enticing. Her conservative suits and baggy sweat pants had been replaced with a midnight blue silk dress. The material covered every inch of her body but slashed down the front in a deep V, exposing the ripe white curves of her breasts. Delicate high heeled sandals enhanced her height. A simple strand of diamonds clasped around her neck, and the light caught and shimmered on the stones, emphasizing the smooth naked skin beyond.

The longer she stared at her reflection, the more she felt as if a change was taking place deep inside of her. Tonight was the opportunity to explore hidden parts of herself she had denied. She dated many men before, but always approached the relationship with a brick wall firmly erected to hide her feelings. Usually after the third date, the man realized he wasn't going to get "lucky" and moved on. Hailey admitted a portion of fault. She never gave them a chance to get to know her. She offered intelligent conversation, occasional humor, and a simple elegance that was part of her nature. Never any raw emotions or vulnerability. God, how she wanted that now. How she wanted to experience a man who could think of nothing but touching her skin, giving pleasure. A man who was so forceful there would be no thought to holding back. Poised on the edge of a cliff, Hailey wanted more than anything to take a deep breath and jump. But she was still afraid.

Therefore, Ciro Demitris was the perfect man. A man who might give her the push she so desperately needed.

After she read his biography in Fortune, Ciro Demitris had visited her every night in her dreams. Nights filled with darkness and passion and release. Erotic adventures that caused her to wake up in a tangle of damp sheets. She realized this party was the opportunity of a lifetime.

She intended to find the man behind the public image. He was confident about his abilities and could have any woman he wanted. He showed a cool demeanor to the world, but Hailey suspected he felt a number of things kept carefully hidden.

The magazine article painted him as a corporate mogul who traveled the globe and dated a variety of beautiful women.

Hailey was more interested in the private man, the one who gave to charities and avoided long term commitments, possibly because of a broken heart. Like Michael.

The thought made her glance nervously at the phone. She needed to leave within the hour and he still hadn't called. There was no way her plan could work if she didn't know what her boss wore.

The phone rang.

She snatched it up. "Did you get the information?"

A deep laugh rumbled over the receiver. "No hello? No singing 'Hail to the Hero' when I risked my life to get you the identity of his top secret costume? No payoff?"

She sighed impatiently. "You're impossible. I promise when I come back from the weekend I will personally fall before your feet and thank you. But first give me the information."

"Hmmm, this sounds too good to pass up. Will you clean my house, too?"

"Michael!"

"Okay, okay. Our little tycoon will be the Phantom of the Opera this evening. Fitting, too. The guy seems to be part mystery, part monster."

"Thank you. You don't know how much this means to me," she said.

The line hummed with sudden silence. When he spoke, his voice was quiet. "I think I do. I hope you find what you're looking for."

"I hope so, too," she whispered. "Bye. I'll call you on Sunday when I get back."

"I'll be waiting."

The phone clicked.

Michael replaced the receiver and glanced at his packed suitcase. Tension twisted his gut when he realized there would be no turning back. The plan was set. He had imparted the identity of the costume, and now Hailey was poised to meet the man who would turn her sexual fantasies into reality.

The only thing she didn't know was, the man would be Michael Rivers, not Ciro Demitris.

The thought of finally touching her the way he craved made him grow hard. Yes, he was her best friend. But he wanted so much more, and every time he dared to push the line, he watched her back off with a polite wariness that stopped him like a bucket of ice water. She would never give him a chance. He had lived with the knowledge for almost a year now, and he finally had the opportunity to change his future. Their future.

Two years ago, they were working on the same project together and formed a tentative friendship. An attraction always zinged beneath the surface, but he had been married, and committed to his wife.

Until his wife left him. Admitted to an affair and walked off without a glance back.

Things began to fall apart at work and in all aspects of his life. He refused to admit he needed help, but Hailey had saved his ass on many occasions and never asked a question. Before long, they were spending more time together. Drinks after work; planning sessions spent in the dim light of the conference room; long lunches over a bottle of wine. He finally opened up and told her everything. She held his hand as he cried for the first time. She supported him through lonely evenings and made him laugh again.

Michael took a deep breath and thought over the past year they spent together. He couldn't pinpoint the moment he fell in love with her. He believed it was a gradual deepening of emotion, like a warm summer breeze rather than a crashing thunderstorm.

Before long, they were having movie nights together with a tub of popcorn, feet propped up on the table clad in comfortable sweatpants. They took tennis lessons and teased each other over their bumbling inaccuracies and lack of coordination. He didn't remember when he stopped grieving over his wife and looked toward the future. A future he wanted to share with Hailey.

He'd watched her date a variety of men with a knot in his gut, but she never stayed away too long. The man would always demand a certain level of intimacy, and Hailey would come back to Michael, her safe, comfortable friend. But whenever he felt courageous enough to take their relationship to the next level, the walls would come up, and he always backed off.

He knew she would never let him be her lover.

She was too comfortable in their routine and too afraid of taking a chance and ruining their friendship. He knew she enjoyed the safety of their relationship and the guarantee she'd never be asked for more. But now he wanted Hailey enough to take a leap—even if it meant losing her forever.

Michael knew she was afraid to let go. Her body screamed sex, but her aura kept men firmly away. He wanted to be the man to tap into those hidden aspects of Hailey, but he'd had no way to get what he wanted.

Until now.

He'd noticed a change in her the past few weeks. A restless gleam within those Carribean blue eyes, a distraction in her work. He watched her talk with other men and found she was more open, more flirtatious. Like a juicy fruit on the vine, Hailey was ready to be picked . . . savored . . . licked. And now, after all the years of celibacy, she had finally reached her explosion point. Rage wrenched at him when he heard of her plan. He knew he would lose her. She was finally ready to take a chance and explore her sexuality. And she had not chosen him. She had picked out a stranger with a heartless reputation who would use her and throw her away.

Michael did not intend for that to happen. If his lady wanted to be seduced, he planned to give her exactly what she wanted.

On his terms.

The stage was set. He'd studied Demitris' photo and carefully changed enough of his appearance to his satisfaction. Contact lenses turned his brown eyes to a mossy green. A dark rinse turned his hair black, and he'd slicked the strands away from his face in the style that made Ciro famous for female fantasies. One diamond earring now pierced his left ear. His cloak and mask would cover the rest.

He knew more than his appearance needed to be changed.

Michael shook his head when he thought of the past year and his behavior. He always played the protector, not the seducer. This weekend would give him the opportunity to slip into a more dominant role. Demitris was a loner. Probably a control freak. Used to getting women and weary of the games they played. He would take all of those emotions and use them for the role. Hailey confessed she wanted to be free to become a different woman.

He intended to be a different man.

Hailey expected the millionaire and wouldn't search for similarities to her safe, dull friend. He felt confident she wouldn't recognize him. The rest he'd leave to fate.

He got up from the bed and switched off the lights. He knew Hailey would never give him the opportunity to please her. The need was always a distant glimmer in her blue eyes, a need he intended to satisfy tonight. And when it was all over, and he unmasked, if she turned him away at least he would have the memory of her to warm the cold nights ahead. The memory of her breasts in his mouth, his penis thrust deep inside her heat, her cries of pleasure echoing in his ear. Anything was worth that.

Anything.

He turned and closed the door behind him.

She reached the mansion after sundown. White washed stucco gleamed under the first splash of moonlight. Hailey breathed in the fragrant air and lifted her head to catch the warm breeze scented with roses and a hint of lemon. Two decks hooked around the first and second story, offering visitors an enthralling view of Lake Como. She picked her way over the cobblestone pathways. The sounds of laughter and music caressed her ears and called to her as if in a dream. She paused and took in the scene before her.

People gathered on the decks and throughout the gardens, sipping champagne. Exotic masks and brilliant costumes filled her vision and added to the dreamlike quality. And she realized for the first time, she could explore the real Hailey Ashton, who was safely hidden behind her mask and would not have to be exposed until the final night.

She grabbed a glass of champagne and made her way deeper into the gardens, seeking a moment to gather her composure. He could be anywhere, and she wondered where to start her search. Maybe she'd make her way through the crowds on the first floor, then move to . . .

Someone was watching her.

Hailey spun around. She searched through the thick shadows of the garden. Her skin tingled and burned, as if touched by the sun. She heard the music in the background, the dim shouts of laughter and gaiety as people swarmed around the villa, and then her eyes caught on a flash of white which pierced through the darkness.

He stood on the balcony overlooking the garden. A black cloak covered his body. His hair was slicked back from his forehead, the strands inky black and blending with the darkness. Catlike eyes gleamed through the carved holes of the stark white mask.

Hailey sucked in her breath as a current of raw, sexual energy sizzled in the air. Most of his face was covered, leaving only his mouth and eyes exposed. But as her gaze met his, Hailey felt his isolation as he stood alone, watching her. Dressed as the Phantom, he was a man who kept to the shadows, presenting a civilized veneer to the world which masked the violence. Hailey knew then she gazed upon Ciro Demitris.

Minutes ticked by. Frozen by the sheer power of the electricity stretching between them, Hailey waited, torn between the need to flee and the need to stay.

Then he turned and disappeared from the balcony.

Hailey shuddered. The tension eased, and she began to re-gather her control. This was what she had come for, but the reality of his presence shook her to the very core.

Without pausing to think, she headed determinedly through the garden. She found the staircase and made her way to the second floor, assuming he would still be up there. She passed couples lounging on the steps. A woman with her gown pulled down to the waist laughed as the man beside her dribbled champagne over her breasts and licked at her nipples. Her moans mingled with the strains of the music. Hailey rushed past them, her face burning, and walked down the dimly lit hallway. The chattering voices and music grew faint when she finally found the balcony where her host had stood. The doors were flung open, and Hailey glimpsed the twisting pathways of the garden in the distance. The bedroom was decorated in wood and burgundy tones. A king size bed dominated the room. A dozen plump pillows set off the sheen of wine satin sheets, and cherry wood antique furniture subtly blended into the background.

A vivid tapestry hung on the far wall, a naked Venus offering her body to an array of suitors. Her breasts and belly gleamed as she thrust her head back, her lips parted, her eyes greedy with need as she was pleasured on a soft bed of grass.

He wasn't there.

Hailey sighed and turned away. Maybe he decided to join the party in the ballroom. She still didn't know how she would approach him, what she would say . . .

"You shouldn't have come."

A deep masculine voice cut through the air. Steel sheathed in silk. Satin dragged over skin. A gravelly tone, yet oddly familiar. Vivid images flashed before her as Hailey felt that voice pour over her ears like warm honey. Her body responded as if the heavy liquid had been dripped over the naked breasts, hips, thighs . . .

Her hand paused on the knob. Halfway tempted to flee, she forced herself to turn and reminded herself this man was whom she had traveled miles to meet.

He stepped out of the shadows. His black cloak whispered around his body as he moved toward her. Hailey ignored her rapidly beating heart and strove to sound cool and confident.

"I'm sorry, I didn't know anyone was in here," she said as he drew closer. "I was so intrigued by the villa I decided to do a little exploring."

Those eyes narrowed, and Hailey realized they were not just dark brown, but also green, an odd combination that made his gaze even more haunting. His lips turned downward in something that resembled a sneer. "Forgive me for assuming we'd start by being honest. I've forgotten how easy it is for women to lie."

She flinched in both surprise and embarrassment. Hailey forced her chin upward. "I don't lie. And I resent your assumptions about my character. You don't even know who I am."

"I know you came looking for me," he said softly. "I know we're about to start the game a man and woman play when they're attracted to one another. But it's not time yet." He turned as if to dismiss her. "I'm not ready to join the others. You shouldn't have come," he repeated.

An outraged squeak escaped her lips at his raging arrogance. "You flatter yourself, Phantom. I came up here for my own reasons. Now that you've satisfied my curiosity, I can leave." Hailey spun on her heel and opened the door. The music drifted through the crack and filled the room.

"So, you did lie."

She stiffened. "I suppose I did. But you're safe from me. I'm not interested in playing games."

His voice was rough and demanding. "Then what did you want?"

Hailey refused to turn around, refused to meet those mocking eyes. "I saw a man who was lonely, separate. I came up here to find out what could cause someone to feel like that." She paused. "Now I know."

She shut the door behind her. On the stairs, the bare breasted woman thrust upward to receive the ministrations of her lover. The man flicked his fingers over one juicy red nipple, then bent his head.

Hailey rushed past them and stopped in the ballroom. Tears burned behind her eyelids but she refused to give in. She had been wrong. She'd wanted to meet Ciro Demitris, but he was way beyond her, too ensnared in these wicked sexual games that she couldn't play. Michael was right, she thought. She was way out of her league.

Hailey grabbed a glass of champagne and took a few healthy swallows. Though repulsed by his arrogant statements, the pounding heat between her thighs was still too real. He excited her, his command, his masculinity, the raw heat shimmering in those brown-green eyes.

He wouldn't frighten her off. She would stay and use the party to force away her repressions and allow her to express some freedom.

She tried to fight the vivid picture swirling in her mind of what she could do with the Phantom. Tried to ignore how badly she wanted to be the bare breasted woman being pleasured.

Her heels clicked on the highly polished floors as she explored the mansion. A twelve piece orchestra took up the front part of the room, and couples danced to the music of Glen Miller and Frank Sinatra. Men in dark suits and tuxedos escorted women dressed in black velvet and red satin, hidden by a variety of masks that enticed as much as they concealed. A mingling rush of perfumes filled the air.

A crystal chandelier shimmered above marble floors and illuminated the rich tapestry and paintings that framed the walls. A circular staircase reminded her of the old Southern style in *Gone with the Wind,* when Rhett Butler first spotted the beautiful Scarlett.

The champagne helped. As the sweet fire of alcohol swept through her blood, Hailey relaxed. One man's arms led to another's as she danced with a long line of suitors, and looked into faces hidden by masks. Another stranger drew her into his arms and led her onto the dance floor. She opened her mouth to protest, but as the music swelled, she gave herself to the moment. Something inside of her loosened and broke through her normal reserve. As the hours ticked toward midnight, the music changed to a Salsa and pounded and pulsed in a more demanding rhythm. Hailey swung from partner to partner. She threw back her head and relished the freedom of the moment, and then she was pulled toward a broad chest and held in an iron grip.

His gaze burned with a masculine demand behind a gleaming white mask. Hailey stumbled, and her fingers gripped the sleek folds of his cloak as she fought for balance. He drew her closer until every carved muscle of his body pressed against hers, the thrust of his erection against the softness of her belly. Her breasts felt suddenly heavy, tender. Her nipples rose against the blue dress in a demand to be freed. Hailey shuddered.

A smile touched his lips. His jaw held rough stubble and gave him a more dangerous air. The diamond in his left ear caught the light and glimmered with icy brilliance. "Why did you come?"

"Curiosity. You haven't satisfied it yet." Fear flamed to life. Hailey wondered if he spotted the emotion in her face. "I'm not part of your fantasy, Phantom. I'll dance with you, but I won't play your games."

"Then you're lying to yourself, my dear. The moment you put on the mask and stepped through the gates you told me you wanted to play." His fingers trailed the length of her spine in a gentle caress, which contradicted the hardness in his eyes. "That's why you're here."

"And why are you here?" she asked. "You sit in judgment, hiding behind a cloak and a mask while you watch and wait. It's easy to be cynical of life when you refuse to be in it, Phantom. Perhaps that's your own secret fear."

Another man reached out to grab her. Demitris twisted her around to avoid the outstretched arms, and his black cloak swirled around their legs as she was led to the other side of the room.

"You've got a sharp tongue," he said.

"And you're arrogant."

Did his face reflect surprise or was that a trick of the light? Hailey wondered if there was anyone who surprised him. Had he lived so long in the shadows, he didn't know anything else existed?

"I don't know if I believe you," he said. "It could be clever words and a clever act. Lies mesh too easily with truth when people play games, and women know that better than anyone."

"You're also a chauvinist," she told him pleasantly.

"Maybe you decided to play with fire because you feel safe behind a mask."

Hailey nodded. "Maybe you're right."

"Who are you?" he demanded.

She stared at him, trying to see past through the carved mask. She had come tonight to learn to be a different person, but suddenly, she wanted to give him the truth of who she was. For once, safe behind her mask, she wanted to reveal herself to him in a way she never had before. The possibility of such surrender made fear curl and tighten in her stomach. Along with excitement.

"My name is Hailey."

"What do you want?"

She took a deep breath and plunged. "I want to know you. The person behind the mask, the person inside. And I want you to know me."

"People never reveal their true selves. They conceal and lie until they don't know who they are anymore." His tone held distance, pain.

"They only want what they perceive, and when they find the truth, they leave."

"I want to know you," she repeated.

He gripped her arm and dragged her off the dance floor. He turned her around and pointed to a couple on the stairs who writhed in delight. The man had shoved up the woman's gown, and her legs lay open to any observer, her sex pink and wet as the man slid his finger over her. Her cries were swallowed up in the roar of the crowd.

Hailey felt the strength of his rock-hard penis strain against her buttocks. Felt his fingers clamp around her arms. She tried to mask her response; her mind fought the knowledge her body already embraced. She wanted this man, wanted to be claimed by him.

"Do you see them, Hailey?" His voice sounded like roughened gravel. He slowly pulled her back against him. Lifted her up an inch. Then rocked into her with slow, subtle motions. "That's what you came here for tonight. And I intend to give you everything you want. But first we must set up the rules of the game."

"What rules?"

"You'll tell me everything. No lies, no half truths, no denials. You must lay yourself open as that woman's legs, and let me do whatever I want to you. You'll answer every one of my questions. Obey my every command for the time you're here. And on the last night, I'll let you choose. You can walk away without ever seeing my face. Or you can unmask and I will do the same."

Her body shook. Her gaze was trained on the couple. She struggled to draw air into her lungs. "I have to give you everything?" Hailey repeated.

"Everything."

She paused. Then craned her head around to face him. "Why make a bargain with me? There are plenty of women here who'll do whatever you want without hesitation."

A half smile settled on his full lips. "Because you came looking for me. You made me want you."

She closed her eyes and tried to clear her head. Tried to think of the implications of such a bargain. "I did no such thing and you still didn't answer the question. You want more than just one night of sex. You want . . ."

"I want it all."

Her eyes flew open. He pulled her harder against him and forced her to feel his erection. Forced her to breathe in the masculine scents of musk and spice and soap, to cradle his iron hard thighs. Forced her to imagine his lips taking his pleasure over her body, imagine each demanding thrust of his tongue.

"Aren't you tired of hiding? When was the last time you exposed yourself to a lover—gave him a glimpse of your inner soul without the fear he'll walk away? One year ago? Five years ago? Ever?"

She tried to turn away from the raw words but he grasped her chin between his fingers. "I want to know who you are. Use your mask to hide your face and feel safe, but give me the truth. I'm tired, too." His voice grew weary, distant. "I want to see beyond the surface just this once. We have the opportunity of a lifetime right before us. We can both be ourselves and still be safe."

"And you?" Hailey met his gaze head on. "What about you, Phantom? Am I to remain vulnerable while you give nothing?"

"I will answer any question you ask. Give you every fantasy you have ever wanted. Isn't that enough?"

Still, she hesitated.

"I promise I won't hurt you. Everything we do together will be for your pleasure. But there will no halfway. All or nothing."

At that moment, everything broke free within her. Her fantasy had been granted. She could explore the hidden parts of her sexuality with a man she desired. She could open herself up to this person in all the ways she had hidden over the years. Another man would finally know who she was—her body and soul. After being locked away in emotional isolation for her whole life, Ciro Demitris had offered the key to freedom.

But, God, what a price.

An icy chill raced down her spine and threw her into a panic. The taunting voices of her parents took hold—warning her to step back before it was too late. The image of her own night of personal heartbreak passed before her eyes. She would get hurt. He could use her and laugh and she would be alone again, except this time without pride, steeped in humiliation. What if she showed him everything she was and it wasn't enough? What if he played a cruel game for his amusement? He could strip both her body and soul bare, and she'd be helpless against him.

The thoughts tangled in her mind like a whirling cyclone.

Then, Hailey realized she had nothing more to lose.

She was already alone and afraid to venture into any intimate relationships. This was her time to take a chance and believe in herself. She was so tired of being fearful of every twist and turn life tossed her way. She had done everything her parents had asked; she had been a good girl. But tonight was an opportunity to let her body fly, to selfishly take pleasure and revel in it. She could not walk away from this gift thrown at her feet.

"I need your answer. Will you give yourself to me until the masquerade is over?"

His hips continued the slow rocking, and liquid heat pulsed between her legs. She arched backward in a blatant invitation, and gave him her answer.

"Yes. I'll do what you ask."

His breath hissed behind her. Without words, he took her hand and led her up to the bedroom she had found him in. He shut the heavily carved door, shutting out the noise of the party, and in the sudden silence, stared at her.

She was stunningly beautiful, Michael thought. She stood in the center of the room, her shimmering blue dress reaching to the floor, fiery red waves of hair spilling down her back. Her long white fingers clenched and unclenched in both anticipation and fear. With her he could satisfy the burning craving in his loins, knew his desire would finally be sated. She was his for the next three nights and would obey his every command. He would not have only her body, as he dreamed of, but he had a chance to touch her inner soul.

"Do you want me to undress?"

A smile touched his lips at her faintly trembling voice. "I'd like to ask you a few questions first. When was the last time you had a man take you?"

"It's been a few years."

He lifted an eyebrow in surprise, then took a few graceful steps toward her. "Your choice?"

"Yes."

"Why?"

She hesitated, and then continued, "My parents believed sex was wrong. I grew up on the notion that the act was something behind closed doors, something to be ashamed of."

"Go on," he urged, taking the time to light a cigarette.

"I heard stories from others, stories of wild encounters that left women helpless for more. I was scared. I never wanted to lose any control over my life, afraid I'd become a man's play toy and then be left behind. I decided it would be easier to ignore sex and go after the things that were safe."

He took a deep pull on the cigarette and blew out the smoke in a lazy circle. "Do you ever pleasure yourself?"

A blush stained her cheeks. "No."

"But you'll leave these reservations behind for our bargain?"

She nodded. "If you command me to."

He smiled then, a dangerous, masculine smile that promised every temptation and satisfaction she had ever dreamed of. "Good. I admire control in a woman. The proper control can extend sexual pleasure for hours on end. Take your dress off."

Her fingers fumbled slightly on the back zipper. The tab slid down and the hiss cut through the silence. The material pooled at her feet. She wore a black garter belt and sheer black stockings with heels. A black lacy bra molded her breasts. Her breathing became heavier, but she managed to stand quietly before him. The smoke drifted through the room and mixed with the remnants of incense. "I want you to keep your gaze on me at all times. Listen to what I ask. When you hear the bell signaling the end of the night, you'll put your clothes back on and leave without another word. I'll meet you back here tomorrow night. Agreed?"

"Yes." She barely whispered the word.

"Take off your bra. I just want to look at you." She unclasped the garment and dropped it on the floor. Her white breasts were heavy and ripe, tipped with pale pink nipples. Minutes ticked by as he drank his fill. A delicate flush washed over her body, almost as if she felt his hot gaze on her like a touch. "You were made to have a man love you. Take your hands and caress yourself. That's right, feel the pointed tips of your nipples. Now imagine my own hands upon you, my tongue licking at them, biting them. I would spend a long time just working your breasts, Hailey, refusing to touch any other part of your body. Now slide your underwear down and leave your garter and stockings on."

He watched her chest rise and fall in tortured breathing. Carribbean blue eyes blazed at him, a mixture of shame, anger, and wanting, but she never took her gaze from his. The panties slid down her legs. Fiery red curls beckoned him from across the room, and his cock throbbed to thrust inside her tight, wet heat. He stroked himself lazily as he watched her, enjoying the anticipation of what was to come.

"Now slide your hand down your belly. That's right. Place your palm between your legs. Do you feel the heat?"

She hissed out a yes.

"Are you aroused?"

She shuddered. "Yes."

"Good. Let's test this will power, shall we?" He paused in front of her and studied the graceful curve of her neck, the slight color on her cheeks. Her lower lip trembled slightly, as if hating to give up her control but determined to stick to the bargain.

He softened his tone. He knew she was afraid and wanted to calm her. "You remind me of one of the paintings on the wall, with your red hair and lush body. I need to see more of you, baby. You belong to me for the next three nights, and I intend on enjoying every inch of you. Part your legs."

She paused for one moment. Then widened her stance.

Michael sucked in his breath at the sight of her delicate pink lips, slick with moisture. He ground out his cigarette and forced himself to stay where he was until he gained control. God, how he wanted to stick his tongue up her wetness and taste her. Spread her legs wider and thrust into her clingy heat until her screams echoed in his ears. He laughed low with pleasure. And he would. But not tonight. Tonight was about foreplay, and he intended to enjoy the torture. He had waited over a year for her; one more night would only heighten the climax.

Slowly, he closed the distance between them. Like a predator in flight, he circled around her and let the folds of his cape brush against her naked buttocks. He watched her shudder, watched her fight for the control she was so proud of, and knew the lesson she must learn tonight was surrender.

He stood behind her and placed both palms on her shoulders. Breathed in the scent of vanilla and sweet smelling soap, breathed in the heady scent of female arousal. He let his fingers slide through the thick strands of her hair with slow, easy motions, letting the waves brush gently against her bare back.

He did this for a long time, until he sensed her muscles begin to relax. Then he cupped a fistful of the silky fire and used the ends like a paintbrush over her body, as if preparing a canvass. With quick, teasing strokes, he touched her nipples, then moved away. Caressed the side of her breasts, then traced her cleavage. Tickled the sensitive underside of her neck. Then let her hair drop from his fingers as he placed his palms on her naked skin.

"There are times for control, and times for surrender. Your stubbornness has become your prison. Do you remember how good it feels to have a man's hands over you?"

He kept his touch light as he studiously avoided touching her nipples. Following the path he had traced before, now he used his own fingers to caress her body while he kept up a slow, circling motion that urged a moan from deep in her throat. Her head slipped back to allow him more access. "That's it, let go and let me touch you any way I want, let me show you what you've been missing . . ."

Hailey felt like she was slowly going out of her mind. Her nipples grew taut and swollen, aching for the touch of his fingers. Her heart thundered like a pack of thoroughbreds, and a honeyed warmth throbbed between her thighs, and made her knees grow weak. Her lids slid closed as she allowed herself to sink into the sensation. Long, tapered fingers touched her breasts, then gently plucked at her nipples, circling round and round as he urged her arousal to climb higher. She craved his tongue on the hard tips of her breasts, craved his fingers plunging inside her dampening heat. Yet, still he continued to only softly touch, lingering briefly, before moving on.

Warm hands slid down her stomach, explored her belly button, the crease of her thigh, the curve of her hips. They stroked over her buttocks as his foot urged her legs further apart for his exploration. Seething tendrils of sensation nipped at her control and left only the touch of him and the need for more. For years, she had been able to fight her desires, but tonight, as she felt his hot gaze on the private part of her, the wildness was unleashed. His fingers separated the cheeks of her buttocks and slipped between them to test her heat. A rush of wetness met him, and Hailey bit down on her lower lip to keep from crying out. Still, he didn't stop there, didn't allow her a moment of sanity, but pushed her further as he whispered in her ear the things he would do to her, with his tongue and lips and teeth and cock. The cool folds of his cloak swirled around her open legs until he stood before her, his gleaming eyes taunting the control she had built for herself. Never pulling his gaze from hers, he knelt, dragging his palms from her buttocks to the V between her legs. With gentle motions, he parted her swollen lips and exposed her completely.

"What do you want?"

She shook her head hard, as if to deny her own wanting. "Oh, please," she gasped. "I need . . ."

"Not yet. You're not ready enough."

A choked sob rose from her throat. Every part of her throbbed, and she let herself beg him for more as her hips rocked forward in a demanding motion. He soothed her with his voice, but his touch stoked the fire, as his index finger slid over the swollen nub just once, then stretched inside of her, the tight channel making way for him as a rush of wetness met his entry.

Hailey knew she had never wanted anyone as badly as she wanted him in that moment, and within the loss of control came surrender, an acceptance of her female sexuality she had never felt peace with.

Michael was overcome by the need to possess her completely. The fantasies he had spun over the past year faded away, replaced by the reality of her sheer beauty and honesty. He knew then it was not only Hailey being taught a lesson in control. He ached to end the masquerade right now and make love to her without his mask. Instead, he pressed his face to her stomach until the impulse passed.

He murmured against the smooth skin of her belly, breathed in the musky scent of her as he removed his finger. Her entire body pulsed like an instrument about to be played, and he felt stretched to the limits of his control. Her blue eyes were wild, drugged with passion. She gasped for breath, her nipples hard little points straining for his mouth, her clitoris so swollen just a brief touch of his tongue could make her come.

He couldn't remember another time he had wanted a woman more, couldn't remember when he'd reveled in such an abandoned response from just his touch. Halfway tempted to rip off his clothes and take her right now, he hesitated a moment.

A bell rang out.

Silence filled the room, broken only by the sounds of their breathing.

Michael struggled, wresting back his control. "You may put your clothes on." He paused. "We'll meet again tomorrow."

Hailey blinked at him in confusion. Now? He wanted her to leave now when she was consumed with passion, so close to fulfillment? Was this torment part of his game? To make her crave him more?

She pulled her clothes back on and dressed without a word. Then she walked past him and out the door.

She followed everyone through the massive archways and waited her turn to board the ferry. The damp, musky scent of her arousal rose to her nostrils. The other guests bumped against her as they obeyed the rules of the party. At dawn, every guest was escorted back to their various hotels. No one was allowed to return to the villa until the following night.

Hailey felt eyes upon her as she was about to step off the dock. As she settled down in the boat, she looked up and directed her gaze to the second floor balcony off the right corner of the villa.

A masked figure was barely visible, but she caught a glimmer of white which gleamed from the distance. The shadows closed around him and fought to reclaim their territory. When the ferry chugged through the calm waters, the figure turned and disappeared from the balcony, and Hailey wondered briefly if the whole night had only been an illusion.

But as the ferry headed towards her hotel, she realized she had been flung over the edge of her sexuality. There was no going back. The thoughts of what her Phantom was going to do to her burned through her body with shame and hard edged desire.

There would be no sleep tonight.

Only anticipation for tomorrow.

Chapter Two

"Good evening."

She stepped into the room and shut the door behind her. Her palms dampened with nervous perspiration. Her stomach slid and rolled like she was on a roller-coaster, the sensations caused by excitement—not fear. She forced herself to return his greeting. "Good evening, Phantom."

He wore the black cloak. His mask tonight was smaller, still blinding white, but of a smoother material that fit snugly over his eyes and nose, and left more of his mouth free. His lips were full and perfectly sculpted, with a savage curl to the lower one that told her he could be cruel when he chose. "Did you dream about me, Hailey?"

"Yes."

He walked towards her then, with a slow, masculine grace. Moss green eyes gleamed with sexual appreciation as he took in her figure. The long tight sheath shimmered with gold sparkles, emphasizing the curve of her hips and the thrust of her breasts. "I'm glad," he said softly. "Will you walk with me?"

She drew back in surprise, then nodded. "Of course."

He led her through the party and out to the garden. The sweet scents of citrus and roses saturated the air with a potency that made her feel slightly drunk. Hailey maneuvered her way over the cobblestones and when she stumbled, he reached for her hand. His fingers interlaced with hers in a union that staked his claim. She expected a rush of intimidation. Instead, she experienced more excitement.

He allowed the silence of the night to soothe and relax her. The faint sounds of Frank Sinatra's *Summer Wind* stroked her ears as he stopped at a stone bench hidden within the lush tangle of trees and flowers. She sat beside him. He turned her hand over and his thumb began to press and massage the sensitive skin of her palm. An involuntary sigh whispered from her lips.

He smiled. "Where do you live?"

"New York, born and bred."

"And what do you love about New York?"

She gave a chuckle. "Never ask that to a native. We love a good bagel, good baseball, and a good argument."

"So, you never wanted to leave?"

A memory teased the fringes of her mind and brought a touch of sadness. Almost as if he felt the change in her, his touch moved to each of her fingers, rubbing and pressing, soothing from the base to the fingertip. She opened her mouth to make a lighthearted remark and move on, but then she remembered her promise. Hailey took a deep breath and started talking.

"I almost left once. After my parents died, I found myself wanting to experience a different life. One of my own making. I had no other relatives so I was alone. The crowds I was accustomed to made me even more lonely. I almost packed everything up and moved down South, but then I remembered an old friend of my father's who worked in Manhattan. I decided to look him up."

"You didn't want to run away. You were strong enough to try and find who you were in the same place where you lost yourself."

His statement made her head swing around to face him. The words touched something deep within her. "Yes. That's exactly what I wanted."

"Did your father's friend help you?"

She nodded. "He was kind. He worked for a small computer firm and got me a job. I took the opportunity to learn everything about the business and made my way to manager. Now I have security. Money. Safety."

"Do you have everything you were looking for?"

Hailey thought of the long nights alone, staring out at the city chaos and longing to be one of them. She thought of Michael, her best friend, whom she used to protect herself from the unknown. "No," she said softly. "But I'm still trying."

His thumb pressed into the pulse at her wrist and felt the slow steady beat of her heart. Then he trailed his fingers up and down her arm, brushing the sensitive area behind her elbow. Comfort blended with sensuality and caused an inner battle within. His voice spun an intimacy of longtime friends. His touch spun a web of raw edged desire and pure want.

"Sometimes it's easier to blame your past. Parents seem to have this control over children. And when they're gone, we realize there are no more obstacles to stop us from what we really want." He paused. "What did your parents keep you from?"

She sighed into the night and let the words spill from her lips. "Everything. Life. My mother got pregnant young and my father was forced to marry her. They never let me forget I was a mistake. Especially after they found religion." She shook her head at the memories. "My weekends were spent in church and confession. I was never able to date, or go to parties, or be a normal kid. I always dreamed of making my own choices. I wanted freedom so desperately, but when I didn't have my parents anymore, nothing made sense."

"You have to find your own sense."

Something changed in the air. She sucked in her breath as she felt the comfort twist to desire, and his fingers tightened around her arm. Their brief talk had pulled down the barriers she erected last night, and the trembling began deep in the pit of her belly as she realized tonight her Phantom would stake his claim.

"I want to ask you a question," he said softly. "Were you excited when you thought of what we had done in that room?"

He accepted her nod as an answer.

"And did you pleasure yourself in your bed last night?"

Her voice came out in a whisper. "No."

His fingers reached out to touch her face. Slowly traced around the gold mask she wore. His thumb roughly pressed over her mouth, parted her lips, and dragged his flesh across her lower teeth. She tasted his skin and wanted more. He lowered his head. His warm breath caressed her as he continued speaking. "Before I take you back upstairs, I want the truth. What stops you from taking your own pleasure? I can't believe you'd turn away from your own sexuality for all these years. Your parents are gone, Hailey. What else are you afraid of?"

She didn't want to answer, but his fingers gently stroked her cheek, her hair, her jawline. She was vulnerable to him when he was kind, and the knowledge gleamed in his eyes, reminding her that at the end of the masquerade he would have more of her than any other man.

She had never spoken of that night to anyone. But now, with her face safely hidden, she decided to tell the truth. "My parents didn't allow me to go away to school, so I went to the local community college so I could live at home. I was nineteen when I met him. He was in my Biology class and I found him beautiful. Blonde hair, blue eyes, and a smile that made me melt. I had never strayed from my parent's rules, but that weekend when he asked me out, I couldn't say no."

She took a deep breath and continued. "I lied to my mother and snuck out to meet him. We went to one of those college parties I heard so much about. I remember the drinking, and the pot, and the wild sex going on in the rooms. I was overwhelmed but excited. I felt ready to take a chance and try to experience being a normal teenager.

"After a few drinks, he took me into one of the rooms. We just talked at first, then started kissing. I never felt like that before. All geared up and wanting something I was so afraid of. But then he started moving faster, and too soon his clothes were off, and I was confused. I just wanted to kiss, but he kept going and . . .

She trailed off. Raised her chin. Then forced the words out. "We had sex. I didn't want to, but don't really remember fighting him. Things happened so fast and it was over and I felt . . . used. He put on his pants and thanked me for the good time. Then left the room.

"I heard laughter from outside and knew he was telling his friends how he got lucky. I ran all the way home and never saw him again."

His hand was gentle as he stroked her hair. There was a protective gleam in his eyes she found comforting. "So your first experience confirmed what your parents had been telling you all along."

She gave a bitter laugh. "Yes. I was afraid to go back and run into him. I was afraid I would be pregnant and end up exactly like my mother. That's when I decided they were right. Sex took away control, and I promised myself I would never feel like that again."

The emotions warred inside of her, until every secret fear she battled spilled helplessly from her lips. "Don't you see?" she whispered. "I don't want any man to have that power over me. At least I'll be safe."

"You'll be alone."

"But safe," she repeated fiercely.

Warm hands cupped her cheeks. His lips stopped inches from hers. "Turning away from your womanhood is giving you a false sense of control. You let that asshole win. You've let your parents win.

"Use me and fight back, Hailey." His words dripped over her like hot molasses. His eyes dared her to meet his lips halfway. "You're a beautiful, sexual woman who had a horrible experience. I can show you how to take your pleasure from a man without feeling shame. When I'm done with you, you'll beg for more, as a woman to a man. And you'll feel empowered—not degraded. Do you want me?"

Her voice broke. "Yes."

"Come with me." He stood and put out his hand. He was cloaked in darkness; a phantom image outlined sharply in the light of a full moon, almost a mirage of the dream that had come to her night after night. But his eyes glittered hard with passion and need, the cruel curl to his lip softened as he urged her to make the choice. And she saw so much more in that moment. She saw the man who would give her everything she had looked for if only she had the courage to go with him.

She didn't hesitate as she stood and took his hand.

He led her back through the garden, up the stairs, into the room they shared the night before. Shut the door. Then faced her. "Do you want me?" he asked again.

The dam broke open. Hailey stumbled two steps and reached for him, standing on tiptoes to meet his lips. She repeated her answer with a deep sense of hunger, her rush of breath mingling with his. "Yes."

"Kiss me."

His lips took hers, his tongue slid within the damp, honeyed cave to engage in a sensual game of plunge and retreat. He tasted of smoke and fine brandy and hot male wanting. His tongue tangled around hers, his lips closing in a gentle suction as he took her fully into his mouth. They drank of each other with greed. His teeth sank into the plump lower lip and bit down carefully. A hot wave of sensation seized her between her legs. A sob caught in her throat. She wanted him to take her like an animal, wanted to open herself up to every fantasy he ever had; and as if he knew what she was thinking, he drew back slightly and lowered the zipper of the gold sheath.

The fabric pooled around her feet. She wore nothing underneath.

Hot eyes devoured every inch of her skin. Plump white breasts were swollen, tipped by tight pink nipples. The smooth skin of her belly trembled slightly, sloping into a mass of fiery red curls that hid her lips from him. Cherry red toenails curled into the burgundy carpeting in anticipation of what was to come.

Michael swore softly under his breath. All the questions had been answered. He fought the need to rip off his mask and take her in his arms to give her comfort. He fought the rage that urged him to find the man who had hurt her and make him pay. But he did none of that. He knew this was a chance to give her something back—something that had been taken from her too young. And he knew in that moment he had never loved anyone as much as he loved Hailey Ashton.

He wanted to give her an ecstasy she had never experienced before. He wanted to free her of demons and watch her smile. He wanted to possess every part of her body and soul—and still knew when she met his unmasked face she might turn away. This woman had shared painful truths about herself. He respected her strength, and her honesty, and swore by the time she walked away, she would never deny her sexuality again.

"Come with me." He led her over to the window and positioned her in front of him. The sleek folds of his cloak caressed her naked buttocks and thighs. She felt his erection press against her, and she gripped the edge of the windowsill as the waves of heat sliced through her body. Her gaze blindly sought out the lights in the distance. The balmy night air washed over her skin, and the sounds of the party rose upward in waves of music and laughter and moans of satisfaction. In other rooms tonight, other sexual games were being played out. Hailey felt the sheer excitement of being one of them, reveling in her nakedness and in the man who was about to take her.

"Close your eyes," he demanded in a low, gravelly tone. "I want you to feel everything I do to you. You're not allowed to turn around or to touch me. Do you understand?"

"Yes."

Large hands slipped around her waist and skated upward to cup her heavy breasts. His thumbs rubbed over her nipples, and the sensitive peaks tingled, pearling into hard points. One foot nudged her legs apart, widening her stance, so she was open to him. He spoke into her ear. His teeth pulled at the lobe as his tongue darted around the sensitive shell in hot, quick licks.

"I'm going to do everything to you tonight. I'm going to make you beg and plead and cry for me before I give you what you want."

Every part of her body was being touched, tasted, his tongue in her ear, his fingers on her breasts, his hard cock rubbing against her buttocks in a teasing motion that made a moan spill from her lips. His palm slid down her belly and cupped the junction of red curls. He separated her plump lips slowly, and she felt the rush of air against her hard, throbbing clitoris in a maddening caress. His thumb caressed the miniature bud with a slow, steady rhythm, then stopped when her hips bucked upward against his hand in a plea for release. His teeth bit her neck, sucked hard, and one finger entered her, his flesh soaked by her wetness. She felt the excitement within her build, and she craved an orgasm, but every time he brought her to the edge he stopped, until she begged him in broken pleas.

Pleasure. Pain. Wanting. Need.

"I won't let you come until I'm inside of you, baby. Not until you scream for me to take you."

Both of his hands slipped down her body and pried her legs further apart. While one thumb teased her pulsing bud, he used his other hand to plunge three fingers into her, moving in and out with a ferocious pace until she did as she asked, screaming wildly for him to take her, and then his rock-hard penis was freed from his cloak as he bent her forward and rammed his organ into her tight, clinging heat.

She climaxed immediately. Multiple waves of ecstasy washed over her, through her. She felt her breasts sway freely in the night breeze, and her head arched upward as her hips rocked against the hard swell of flesh that invaded her body. He pumped himself in her over and over, not letting her first orgasm pass until another one took hold, and then she sobbed for the pleasure to stop, it was too much, but he kept going on and on. His member was long and iron hard, and he slid himself almost all the way out before pounding back, so deep inside she felt her G-spot tickled and teased until she came again. Then he let himself go, and he exploded deep inside of her. Hailey sobbed with pure release, and he held her and stroked her until she quieted. He closed the window and guided her over to the bed.

Like a child, he laid her upon the burgundy satin sheets, and stripped off his own cloak to rest beside her. Silence bathed the room. She listened to his deep breathing, her head on his chest, his arms pulling her tight against him.

She finally felt able to speak. "That wasn't fair."

A deep chuckle rumbled through his chest. "You had about forty-eight orgasms. How wasn't that fair?"

She lifted her head to look at him. His eyes gleamed behind the white mask. "I didn't get to look at you. Touch you. Am I going to get a shot at torturing you?"

The distant air he normally exuded faded away. His hands played with her long red curls and his face softened with humor. "I don't think that was in the agreement."

"Maybe we need an amendment."

"Ah, but then you wouldn't get the final goal. I get your full cooperation. Then at the end you can make your own decision."

She felt him distancing again, and she wondered why she felt so sad. She was a grown woman and knew this game was about sex. Then why did she feel as if she wanted to know this man, not as the Phantom, but as Ciro Demitris? She dismissed the thought as foolish but still felt compelled to launch some inquiries.

"You said you believe people only show the surface. Do you know why?"

The corner of his lips twitched slightly. "Do I get a guess or do you just tell me the answer?"

"Wise ass," she muttered.

He laughed then, and pulled her back into his embrace when she would have grouchily turned away. "Tell me."

"It's so much easier to give people what they expect. Do you remember what it was like to be a child, Phantom?"

"Barely."

"I do. I remember I used to run everywhere because I was so excited to see what part of life came next. Then my mother told me it wasn't ladylike to run. People expected me to behave a certain way, and I got a reward when I was quiet and dignified. So I became what they wanted."

He stroked her hair back from her forehead. His voice was thoughtful. "Do you miss running?"

She gave a deep sigh. "I miss the other part."

"What part?"

"Wanting to see what happens next. After a while, it became so much easier to walk. There was nothing exciting to run for."

They were silent for a while, but his hands soothed and stroked. His body heat comforted and Hailey relaxed deeper into the smooth, cool sheets. "Once you stopped running, what else gave you pleasure? Do you have anything you're passionate about in life?"

The faint sounds of the orchestra drifted through the window. The flickering of the candle lent an air of intimacy as she spoke. "I enjoy many things. Reading, movies, good food and good wine. Opera."

"La Traviata."

She rolled over to face him and laughed in delight. "Yes, my favorite. A little dramatic for a man, I always thought."

"Now who's being a chauvinist?"

She placed an impulsive kiss on his lips. "You're right."

"Have you ever been married?"

"No."

"Children?"

"No." She felt a twinge of sadness.

He seemed to catch her response. "Do you want children?"

"I want a dozen. But I want the whole picture, including the husband and house and happy marriage."

He reached out to touch her cheek. "Why do women always want to settle down and men always want to run away?"

Hailey smiled. "I don't believe that. I think everyone wants to meet his or her true soul mate. Once that happens, a person makes a choice to either take a chance or stay safe. Women sometimes settle for somebody less than a true love because they're afraid no one else will come along. And men just get scared of what will happen if they do meet their true love."

"Not fear, Hailey. Maybe some men realize the real thing isn't out there."

She let his words simmer for a moment before answering. "Do you do this often, Phantom?" she asked. "Bargain with a woman for everything, then walk away?"

He stiffened beneath her. "No."

"Why did you?"

"Maybe I was tired of running myself." She opened her mouth to respond, but he continued, his words growing fierce. "You say you want a husband and children. A soul mate. You may want these things but they come at a price, Hailey Are you willing to lose this control and take a chance? Or is it still easier to just live in the fantasy?"

She wondered at his anger, but he suddenly rolled over and pinned her beneath him. Within moments, his face cleared. The humor was back. "Why do I feel we switched roles? Are you using my temporary weakness to plunder my secrets?"

Her eyes widened. "I don't think your weakness was all that temporary." His erection demandingly pressed against her inner thigh. "I thought men needed a little bit more, er, time."

He grinned wickedly. "You were lied to. Your education about a man's true abilities has just begun. But first I want you to drink something for me."

He left the bed and brought back a glass of sparkling white liquid in a heavily cut glass. She looked at him questioningly.

"It's a slight aphrodisiac," he explained. "Quite harmless. The drink will heighten your senses and lengthen your pleasure. Here, let me," he murmured.

He filled his mouth with the liquid, leaned over, and slowly let the spiked wine trickle from his lips into her mouth. The sharp, fruity essence slid down her throat in a sensual caress, and she felt her body quicken again. He put the glass on the bedside table, then rose from the bed.

Hailey watched him with heavily lidded eyes, enjoying his nakedness. He moved with a muscled grace uncommon to men, his chest and shoulders broad, his buttocks firm, his legs long and lean. His heavy erection jutted out before him with dominant pride, and the remembrance of feeling him pulse inside her made her hot again. Whipcord strength rippled from every carved muscle as he made his way through the room. When he returned to the bed, he had a corded silk rope, and two vials of oil. Already the effect of the wine coursed through her. The cool satin sheets slid over her naked skin. She made a noise low in her throat as she stretched out on the bed. Her sex throbbed with slow, heavy pulses and her flesh felt hot as she watched him approach.

He knelt between her thighs, his erection brushing against her tight red curls. She moaned and opened her legs, inviting him to take her again. Her lips were flushed pink and wetness gleamed in the dim glow of the light. "Phantom," she whispered urgently.

A sharp longing cut through him. Damn it, he wanted her to say *his* name, wanted her to know it was him giving her such intense pleasure. He pushed the thought away and concentrated on the moment. For now, she belonged to him, and he intended to enjoy their time together. He knew she was already feeling the effect of the wine, and anticipation shot through him at having her at his will. "What do you want, sweetheart?" he asked.

"I want you to take me again. I want you deep and hard inside me."

"I intend to. But not yet. I have some other plans." He took the rope and gently tied both of her wrists to the bedpost, so her arms were bound above her head. Her breasts arched upward in a gift he intended to enjoy slowly.

"What are you doing?"

He smiled at her sultry tone. "I want to enjoy every inch of your body, Hailey, in every way possible. I intend to taste you and play with you a little more. This will be our second episode of the evening."

She tugged at the silken ropes, and he knew her absolute helplessness only added to her desire. He reached over and uncapped a small vial of oil. The heady scents of incense and herbs rose in the air. Slowly, he poured the oil onto his fingers. Then he coated the tips of both nipples with careful precision, avoiding the heavy weight of her breasts. When each point gleamed, he placed a dab on the swell of her belly right above her pubic hair. Then his knees widened her legs further apart. He took the vial and tipped it right above her clitoris, watching the golden liquid coat the tiny throbbing member and slide over her pink lips.

She moaned and tugged at her restraints.

"The oil will make your body even more sensitive. You should get a tight, tingling feeling. The special herbs will bring a focus to certain parts."

"I'm so hot." Her head tossed back and forth against the pillow. "Everything feels so strange. I'm floating, but my body is on fire. God, what are you doing to me?"

"I'm going to pleasure you." He settled over her, intending to enjoy every inch of her body before he took her again. His mouth settled over one breast, and his tongue slowly licked at the strawberry pink tips which gleamed wetly with oil. Her breasts swelled against him, but he kept the pace slow and easy, knowing she would be wild by the time he thrust inside her. His teeth scraped against her nipple, then he took the whole tip in his mouth and sucked hard. She tugged at her restraints as he palmed her other breast, then moved his mouth to its twin to continue the torment. He licked and sucked for long, long minutes, until her engorged nipples were so sensitive, even the slight rush of his breath against her made her cry out. Still, he continued his love play, while his thumb made lazy circles around the creamy mounds of flesh, his tongue flicked at the tips with the lightest of caresses.

She became a creature of basic, primal needs. Low, animal noises rose from her throat. Every part of her flesh burned to the touch. Her cleft felt tight and tingly, and she became frantic under his hands, her only thought of him and his rock hard penis taking her, possessing her . . .

He feasted on every inch of her. Nipped at her belly button. Ran his tongue along the path of her pubic hair.

Hailey cried out as he pushed her knees up so she was open to his mouth. He blew gently on the red curls, parting them so her throbbing wet lips were exposed. The hot warmth of his breath against her vulva, the tingling heat of the oil, the tight constraints of the rope rubbing against her wrists, all became a whirl of exploding sensations until she felt herself pushed toward the edge. Her head tossed back and forth on the pillow. Then a sob rose to her lips as she let go.

He chuckled with satisfaction, then lowered his head once again. This time his tongue separated the fold of her sex and found the throbbing knob. He licked at it, then let his tongue slide in and out of her in tiny little motions. "You're so beautiful," he said against her. "Like a flower opening to the sun. What do you want me to do to you? Tell me."

Hailey gasped as the second orgasm threatened to explode. Every muscle clenched. He gave a low chuckle. "Perhaps this is what you want to ask me for." He wrapped his lips around her and sucked. Another cry spilled from her lips. "Or perhaps this?" His tongue plunged in and out of her channel. Hailey let out a scream and exploded around him.

He drank greedily, loving her taste. Then with one swift movement he brought himself up and over and thrust into the swollen heat of her sex.

He took her hard, driving his penis deep, until it was buried to the hilt in her wet, clinging flesh. He slid easily in and out, the stinging oil making every movement more intense, the rubbing motions of his hardness against her clitoris throwing her into another orgasm. He let himself go and they both came together.

He collapsed on top of her. She reveled in his heavy weight. Her spread legs cradled him, their juices sticky and warm over her body. He untied the ropes, and she buried her hands in the crisp ebony strands of his hair.

Something within her rose in fierce waves of protective need as she held him to her. A connection had been formed that went beyond the physical. He had reached a part of her that she had kept locked up for so many years.

Her surrender did not make her feel weak. Her Phantom made her feel the strength of her sexuality, had helped her reclaim what she had feared, and revel in her freedom. And throughout their encounter, even though she was the one who was supposed to give everything, she never felt alone. Emotions warred within her, and she started to wonder what her feelings for him were. Could they be more than just about sex?

Could her feelings have something to do with love?

The bell rang.

He lifted his head. Their gazes locked. A question burned between them, unanswered, unspoken. He rose from the bed and watched her get dressed, then slipped on his cloak. Seconds slipped by but he made no other move toward her.

Hailey turned from him and ducked her head. Her voice was husky when she finally managed to speak.

"Good night, Phantom."

"Good night."

She opened the door and left, wondering what the next night would bring.

❧

The heavy four poster bed was quite comfortable, but her mind was focused on another bedroom, one with satin sheets and a masked Phantom.

Hailey tossed and turned, her thoughts troubled. Where had the idea of love come from anyway, she wondered. Logically, she understood her body had finally been freed from bondage, and she was a little vulnerable. She had confessed something in her past that no one had ever known, not even Michael. Perhaps, almost like a therapist, she had developed feelings for the man who helped her. She knew those years of controlling her sexuality were over. She could now be a full woman who embraced her physical desires, and not be shamed by them. Ciro Demitris had taught her that. She would always be grateful.

The phone rang.

She jumped and grabbed at the receiver. "Hello?"

"Hailey?"

She smiled when she heard Michael's voice. "I'm fine."

A sigh of relief echoed in her ear. "Good. I was a little worried. He didn't eat you for breakfast then?"

"No. It's been—wonderful. Everything I wished for."

"I take it you finally met the man."

"He's not what you think. He may have a lot of money, but he's lonely. I feel like we connected."

"Did you kiss him?"

She hesitated. Odd, she should feel almost guilty by telling her best friend. "Yes."

A pause. "Your knees buckled?"

Hailey laughed. "Yeah, they crumbled right beneath me. But I'm scared of unmasking the final night. What if he sees I'm just this ordinary woman beneath all the makeup and costume?"

"What if he does?"

She sighed. "I guess you're right. I've come too far to stop now. How are things on the home front?"

"The Bulls lost."

"See, you should have come with me," she teased.

"And cramp your style? Nah, someone has to get their full eight hours sleep."

"Then why are you up at 6:00am on a Saturday?" she asked.

He made a gruff noise over the phone. "I wanted to make sure you were still intact."

His voice in the dark was oddly comforting, and she thought once again how lucky she was to have a friend who cared so much about her. "Thank you, Michael."

"For what?"

"For always being there. For putting up with my moods and making me laugh. For being my best friend."

"Man, are you in a mushy mood tonight," he grumbled. "I only called to say good night."

Hailey laughed. "My romantic hero. You always run away when I get emotional."

"Yeah, yeah. How are the overnight accommodations?"

"Beautiful. He blocked a whole bunch of inns on the island for his guests. I'm staying at this little bed and breakfast with a huge four poster bed. I thought I'd need a ladder to climb up."

"Just don't break a leg getting down." He paused. "Hailey, did anything else happen between you two tonight?"

An array of erotic images flashed before her. Images of the Phantom thrusting inside her, his tongue deep inside her mouth, his arms pinning her against the bed. She shuddered with the memory and opened her mouth to tell her friend everything.

Then realized she couldn't.

Michael would never understand the dark, secret part of her who longed to be a sexual being. He supported her and kept her safe. He was sweet and kind. After his heart had been broken by his ex-wife, he had closed a part off. Hailey knew they had connected so well because she had done the same thing. Now, she wanted to be free.

But he was still trapped.

No, Michael was better off not knowing the truth. Hailey took a deep breath and lied. "Nothing else happened."

Silence hummed over the line. When Michael spoke his voice was tight with emotion. "I'm sorry I couldn't make you feel like that. Good night, Hailey."

"Good night."

She gently replaced the receiver and stared out into the darkness. A strange ache lay heavily around her heart and she wasn't sure why. Something in her friend's voice made her miss him. Almost as if he was as lonely in the darkness as she, and wanted to feel a connection. His last words were so odd. How could he possibly know how she felt about Ciro Demitris?

Thoughts of Michael whirled with images of her Phantom, until she closed her eyes to avoid the tangle of feelings and fell into a deep sleep.

Michael stared at the phone and fell back on the pillows. Hands clasped behind his head, he thought of her voice and what she had shared with him tonight.

For the first time, there was no barrier between them. Clothes had fallen away; skin touched against skin, but even more powerful was her gift of self. He understood now all the moments she distanced herself from him, afraid of the past, afraid of wanting something that could fly out of control. He needed to use these last nights to burn himself into her so deeply she could never run away again.

The masquerade had been successful so far. He always stayed behind as the guests left, waiting in the same bedroom where he had first spotted her in the garden. He had paid for his own private ferry to pick him up at the mansion a half hour past dawn, so she would never suspect he wasn't Ciro Demitris. Every last detail had been arranged, yet he still feared the final unmasking. He was the one who had set her free, but was she ready to accept the terms of a real relationship, or would she be driven to experience everything she had missed out on? Would she turn away from him to embark on affairs? He had set up his plan in order to claim his lady. Yet, he now realized by setting her free, he might lose her forever.

Chapter Three

He watched her walk in the room, her step halfway hesitant as she closed the door behind her. Tonight she wore an ebony dress that tied around the neck in a halter style, then plunged low in the front and left her back bare. Her mask was held together by vibrant feathers, making her blue eyes even more mysterious.

As she stopped before him, he didn't speak. Just looked at her. The sheer beauty of her presence made his heart pound faster. He'd dreamed of her last night. Their conversation haunted him, along with his troubled thoughts, and his weakness for her suddenly made him angry.

All those evenings they spent together, talking long after the sun set about their lives. She called him his friend, but never told him about her past. She believed him to be safe, but when he made the slightest move to deepen the relationship, she backed away. Yet here she was before him, thinking he was a stranger. With Ciro Demitris she revealed everything—underneath her clothes and into her soul in a way she never let him in.

He had slipped into the role of the tycoon with an ease that surprised him. When he donned the cloak and mask, he decided to let his own secret fantasies take hold. He became dominant and demanding with his pleasure. He knew Hailey wanted intrigue and fantasy, and he intended to give it to her. What he didn't realize was the emotions he used to be the Phantom were quite real. He was lonely and isolated. He longed for sexual freedom and a woman to fly in his arms. Everything he spoke to her as Demitris was the truth.

And that scared the hell out of him.

He didn't want to play the game anymore. He wanted to tell her the truth, and watch her reaction when he revealed himself to her. He wanted to hear his own name echo through the air instead of the false Phantom.

Jealousy bit through him. His eyes narrowed with a cruelty he no longer wanted to hide. "I'm not in the mood for elaborate games tonight. You've begun to bore me. I won't be requiring your service."

She flinched at his tone, knowing something had changed. She hesitated and watched him for a sign of his feelings, but he only walked to the dresser to take a cigarette and light it.

Hailey tightened her arms around her breasts in a protective gesture and watched him from under heavy lidded eyes.

The moment she had seen him, her body quickened, but her mind was now unsure. Tonight, he wore his cruelty like his cloak, but still Hailey remembered the first minute their gazes met. Anticipation had gleamed within his mossy brown depths. Along with a tendril of fear. The emotion was easy to recognize; she felt the same mixture.

He smoked his cigarette with leisure, refusing to turn and look at her. His shoulders remained stiff and unyielding. Hailey turned to go, half relieved at her dismissal, but paused with her hand on the knob. Her Phantom was not invulnerable to the game. Somehow, feelings had begun to develop, and Hailey refused to cower before them. She had made her bargain. Truth at all costs.

She moved toward him. Reached out and laid one hand over his upper arm. The muscles jumped beneath her touch, and he spun around in a whirl of black, his mouth turned down in a sneer. "Why are you still here? I told you, I don't desire you tonight."

"Then I will wait until you do."

"What are you doing? I'm the one who makes the rules of this game. You must obey me."

Hailey lifted her chin high in the air. "I will. Because we made a bargain, Phantom. We're supposed to tell the truth to each other, but you retreat from our pact. You're acting like a coward."

He grabbed her and lifted her up hard against him. His warm breath struck her lips. "You dare to call me a coward? Perhaps, you don't want to hear your own truth. That I don't desire you any longer. That you now bore me, and I crave another woman."

Her hands clenched around the folds of his cloak as she hung on. Hailey prayed her bluff would work. "Then I call you a liar. And if you must prove something to yourself, I will wait while you take another woman, and join you after. Because I made a promise. I want to be with you tonight, no matter what the cost."

He cursed under his breath. "Damn you!"

His mouth stamped over hers. With one quick thrust, his tongue parted her lips and conquered her with dominant, hard strokes, exploring every damp, hidden crevice, claiming her for his own.

She gave it all back to him. Her fingernails dug into his shoulders as she wrapped her legs around his waist and hung on. He thrust his fingers into the heavy weight of her hair to hold her head still, as he took more of her, his tongue battling with hers. His taste and the male scent of him swamped her senses. He nipped at her lower lip, then drew it deep into his mouth to suck her hard. When he finally pulled away, she struggled for breath.

Slowly, he allowed her to slide back down his body until her feet once again touched the floor.

"Phantom?"

He closed his eyes in defeat. Then took her gently in his arms. "I'm sorry, Hailey." She glanced up at him. Disgust carved out his features. "I wanted to hurt you."

"Why?" He remained silent. She pulled away and looked into his face. Then ran her fingers over the sculpted curve of his lower lip, his chiseled jawline, his cheekbone. "You didn't hurt me. I hear your voice and I become aroused. I close my eyes and all I can imagine are your hands on me. I want you all the time. But tonight you seem so angry at me."

"I was angry at myself."

"But you're not going to tell me why."

"I've never wanted a woman as much as I want you. I've never enjoyed a woman's company as I do yours. I hate when you leave at the night's end, and I wish I could sleep with you and awake to your smile. That's why I'm angry."

Hailey felt her heart lighten. A husky laugh escaped her lips, and she reached up to kiss him. Her lips moved over his and savored the taste of smoke, the sting of cognac, and the arousal of male hunger. Her tongue slipped inward, touching the tip of his tongue in a teasing caress, then drank deeply of him. When she finally raised her head, she couldn't hide her delight.

"Let me give you some advice. When a woman hears words like that from her lover, she becomes overjoyed. To know I've made an impression on you, especially after such a long line of women, gives me great pleasure." She paused. "I feel the same way about you."

"We shouldn't complicate matters." His hand cupped her jaw. "We've made a bargain. But there are no guarantees for a future unless we decide to unmask. Are you ready for the fantasy to end?"

The light died within her eyes, but she forced a smile. "I intend to enjoy those last nights with you. You make me happy."

Her simple words made him stare at her in astonishment. Her honesty humbled him. She constantly challenged him. And tomorrow night, she would know the truth, and reject him. He may never see her again after the fantasy ended.

He pushed the disturbing thought aside and cradled her in his arms. "How does one argue with a woman? Especially when she's so direct?"

"Why, have you met many who aren't?"

"Yes. I've met women who lied and betrayed me. Women who see what they want to see."

She heard his slightly bitter tone and tried to ease him out of his mood. Her hand traveled down his chest, over his muscled abdomen, and stroked the hard ridge between his legs. With one quick movement, her fingers grasped his jutted member. She squeezed carefully, felt the pulsing strength, and heard his quick indrawn breath. "Darling, I'm not lying to you. What I see before me is exactly what I want."

He laughed. "And I want to give it to you. Over and over in as many different ways as I can. But I'm confessing more of my secrets. It's time to get back to our bargain."

Within moments, he had undressed them both and laid her on the bed. She climbed on top of him, her fingers exploring his penis with gentle, curious strokes. He lay back and enjoyed her ministrations.

She smiled as she worked her palms up and down his ridged length and watched him grow longer. "A few more minutes and I'll be able to make any bargain I want."

"You're probably right. I better get my information fast."

"What do you want to know?"

"Name one guilty pleasure you never told anyone about."

She groaned and covered her face with her hands. Then peeked through her fingers. "I love art. I suck at painting and I can't draw a thing. I even tried to become an art investor but even my taste seemed awful. So I bought a coloring book and a huge box of Crayola crayons. When I'm stressed I color."

He drew back in surprise. "I never knew you did that."

She laughed. "Of course not, you don't know me."

Her remark seemed to throw him off guard and she caught an almost guilty expression. Then he seemed to recover and forged on. "One thing you hate."

"The New York Yankees."

His lip twitched in the need to smile. "Isn't that the team that wins the most World Series in baseball?"

She made a face. "I like the Mets. The Yankees are too perfect and I'd rather root for the underdog."

"You admit this to people?"

"Not really. I wore my Mets t-shirt once and got heckled. Almost got in a fight so now I just keep it safely in my closet."

"Sexual fantasy?"

In one swift motion she straddled him. She arched her back, her breasts thrust forward, crowned by rosy nipples. She still held him within her hand, her fingers teasing the tip of his rock-hard sex, eliciting drops of moisture. Red fiery waves fell down around her shoulders, and she gave a low laugh, her eyes full of secrets and passion and mystery.

"My sexual fantasy, Phantom?" She smiled slowly. Her tongue slid over her ripe bottom lip as if she imagined how he would taste. His breath hissed through his teeth as desire ripped through him. "This is my fantasy. What I'm about to do right now. I want to take you in my mouth and make you scream my name. I want you inside me, so hard and fast that you forget every other woman you've been with. Since I promised I'd do anything you want, I'm begging for permission." Her voice dropped to a husky purr. "Will you let me pleasure you?"

He swore and clawed for control. His member throbbed against the soft skin of her fingers as she continued teasing him, running her thumb over the turgid flesh. She had become his own personal sex slave, and now he was at her mercy. The excitement built as he gave her his answer. "I think I can allow it."

"Good. Now shut up."

Her breasts pressed against his chest as she lowered her head, and her tongue delicately licked at his flat male nipples. They hardened into little points, and then she used her teeth to gently pull. His low moan urged her on as she moved downward.

Michael groaned as her taut-tipped nipples caused a delicious friction against his skin, and he suddenly knew what it was like to be helpless under a woman's power. This was no longer his innocent, guarded Hailey. This was a sexual witch who used her nails and teeth and tongue to explore every inch of his body, as if crazy for the scent and taste of him. Her hands cupped his hips as she settled over his hard length, and then knelt between his legs.

She looked up once from her position. Gave a smug, half smile. Then lowered her head.

Her warm breath struck him first, and she opened her lips to take him in the slick, satin depths of her mouth. She teased him mercilessly, never taking in his fullness. Her tongue swirled around the tip, gathering the drops of moisture that spilled, then moved up and down the ridged underside as if he was a sweet lollipop she had discovered and decided to suck slowly.

Just as if he was about to go mad and force her to take him completely, her hands cupped his balls and her lips opened wide to plunge him to the back of her throat.

He cursed.

The pleasure was too intense. Her tongue swirled around him as her mouth held him tightly, moving in and out with a steady pace that tested his control. Her name spilled from his lips in a chant, and her suction grew even harder, luring him over the edge. She made hungry sounds in the back of her throat, as if she couldn't get enough of him, and his pulsing, pounding member throbbed within her wet mouth, the pressure building to a screaming point until he exploded in a sharp burst. She took it all. Her hair formed a silken curtain that swung back and forth over his thighs. Her tongue licked every last drop, until he swelled again and damned her to eternity.

He reached for her, but she avoided his movement. His head pounded with desperation and want.

"Tell me what you want."

He cursed, recognizing his own little game had been switched on him. His voice came out in a raspy groan. "Take me now."

She laughed low and a mischievous gleam lit her eyes. "Beg me."

With one swift movement, he lifted her up and plunged into her hot, slippery wetness. She gasped.

"I'm begging you," he said.

Then he began to move.

She took him to the hilt, her legs wide to accommodate every throbbing inch of him. She cried out and arched upward.

She rode him in a wild frenzy. Her hair streamed down her back, her heavy breasts lifted up and down as she took everything he could give her. Her body clenched around him each time he drove inward, then clung madly in a rush of dampness as he withdrew.

He felt her climb towards the ultimate release and decided to tease. As he thrust into her, he kept his sex away from the throbbing nubbin that would give her what she needed. His hands pulled and rubbed at her nipples, rolling the tips in his fingers until she begged him in low, frantic tones of arousal.

"Please, help me."

"How bad do you want it?" Again he plunged deep, keeping her inches away from the edge. He loved the way she looked as she took him in her body, loved the way she gave him everything she had and demanded he keep up with her.

She rode him faster and her hips shimmied against his engorged member. "I need you." She panted, her blue eyes dazed with passion. "I need you."

The words reached out like a fist and tore into his gut. He knew this woman had changed him in some way, had opened him up, and he wondered if he'd ever be the same. With that last thought, he reached up and slipped his thumb over the hard nubbin covered by her fiery curls, then rubbed.

He drove inside of her. Again. And again.

Hailey screamed. He felt her drench him, and he came again with her, emptying himself with a shout. She collapsed over his body like a rag doll, her hair spilling over his chest, her breathing rough and uneven.

"Damn, woman," he finally managed. "Any time you have another sexual fantasy, I'll be glad to help you out."

She laughed. "Donating your body to charity, huh?"

"It's a tough job but someone has to do it."

"I don't think I'll be able to walk tomorrow," she said.

He frowned. "Are you sore?"

"My thighs are still trembling."

He caressed her with soothing strokes. "As soon as I can get up, I'll run us a bath. That will take the aches away."

"I'm not complaining."

"It's for my own selfish pleasure. I want to show you the amazing things you can do underwater."

"I'll need a cane tomorrow."

He didn't answer. The realization of the end of their affair dangled before him with haunting urgency. Almost as if she knew his thoughts, she interlaced his fingers with her own and studied their hands. Fingers touching, pale skin against ivory. A man and a woman. Entwined.

"I don't want this to be over," she whispered.

Hope bloomed within, but he fought the emotion back. He refused to wonder what the last night would bring. The only thing in his power was to give her as much of himself as possible, and hope it was enough.

"I'll run the bath." He got up from the bed and disappeared into the bathroom. Hailey lay back on the pillows. His departure after her confession reminded her this was a game. A game for sex, a game for freedom. But to bring this masquerade into the real world may never work. She needed to face that fact. She was falling in love with him, but he could view her as a novelty which could pass. How could she be sure of his true feelings? At least, if she chose to walk away, she would have the memories to take with her instead of heartache.

She got up from the bed and followed him into the bathroom. The scents of jasmine and lavender rose to her nostrils. The mirrors steamed deliciously and wrapped them both in a world unto their own making. She quietly shut the door behind her and stood before him, naked.

He looked up. Caught his breath. She was beautiful. Her body peaked to attention just from his look, and he knew she was already aroused.

He reached his hand out. With a smile, she took it, and they stepped into the tub. The sharp sting of the hot water made her gasp. He positioned her so she lay over him, her buttocks pressed between his spread legs, her back against his chest. She sighed in deep contentment as he took the soap and rubbed it between his hands.

Slowly, he began soaping her shoulders, digging his thumbs into the sore muscles. A moan rose from her lips. His hands were slippery with bubbles as he worked on the tendons in her neck and moved downward—the line of her spine, her upper arms, and slid around to cup her breasts. He played with the soft mounds, cupping bubbles and allowing them to float through the air, grazing the tips of her breasts like a wet, dainty kiss. He washed every part of her, lingered on every curve with a tenderness that made tears sting against her lids. Her eyes closed with dreamy pleasure as she gave him her body, the gift he had asked for.

And he knew her body hadn't been the only gift. She had given her heart. To Ciro Demitris.

Long, supple fingers slid around her hips and lingered over the full curve of her buttocks. Her cheeks tightened in anticipation as she felt him gently explore the cleft, parting her pubic hair and softly touch her. Hailey floated in the water. Her muscles melted like warm, sticky honey, helpless under his spell.

"Phantom, what are you doing to me?" she asked in wonder, her eyes still shut as she drank in every sensation. The bubbles teased her taut-tipped breasts and sloshed over her quickening muscles. Her cleft felt swollen, and the warm water mixed with her own juices until her thighs floated open and her sex was exposed to his gaze.

"God, you're stunning," he muttered. His fingers clenched into the full cheeks. "I just want to look at you." He drew her knees up so she lay open to him. "I want to take you again. I can't get enough of you, Hailey."

"And I want you again and again," she whispered. "I want you to take me every way possible. I want to belong to you completely."

"You already do." The words slipped out before he could stop them, but he knew they were true. "Don't you?"

"Yes."

She arched her back. Her pubic hair was wet and allowed her pulsing inner lips and vulva to be exposed to his hot gaze.

"I have to taste you. Get on your knees and hold on to the edge of the tub."

She moved. Her fingers gripped the cold, white marble as she knelt. Her flesh quivered as the cool air rushed over her. She felt his hard hands part her legs and urge her forward so her buttocks rose in the air, awaiting his next move.

Her skin was rosy and dripping. She felt his gaze on the curve of her buttocks, the hot pink of her cleft. He leaned over her and blew gently, and she jerked back in response, a half moan caught on her lips.

He lowered his head, and his teeth bit into her firm cheeks, testing her. He moved inward, squeezing, cupping, while his tongue snaked out to take quick, sharp licks. She wiggled helplessly against him but he only laughed and drew out the anticipation. The tip of his tongue slid into her cleft and licked with slow strokes. Her swollen flesh became sensitive to every stroke, and then he flicked his tongue against her over and over with hard, quick motions. Hailey cried out, but he still held back. His fingers pushed the firm globes of her flesh apart so he tasted all of her. His hot tongue teased her clitoris again, and again, until . . .

She exploded against his lips, and then he pushed himself up and plunged into her.

Heat.

Fullness.

Possession.

The convulsions seized her body and ripped through her. She felt caught in the wind of a cyclone, helpless to do anything but ride out the wild wave of pleasure until she calmed.

Then he started to move.

She took every inch of him up her warm channel of flesh. She felt tight and hot as he pushed even deeper, and she met him all the way, her body arched like a bow, quickening in response to his fierce thrusts. Water slapped over the tub in gentle waves. Bubbles floated through the air. And then her last orgasm took hold like a savage fist that scooped her up and hurtled her toward the stars.

This time when he held her, she didn't allow herself to think of tomorrow. She laid her head on his damp, muscled chest, spent for now, and wrapped her arms around him. His heart pounded in a steady rhythm against her ear.

The clock ticked. She roused herself enough to speak, still greedy to learn everything she could about the man in her arms. "What were you like as a boy, Phantom?"

"More secrets?"

Hailey smiled against him as she heard the teasing note in his voice. "I want to know a little bit about you. As a man, you certainly know how to give a woman pleasure. Tell me about the boy."

The memories flickered past his vision in a series of taunting images. He waited for the usual wall to keep the emotions separate. Instead, he felt the dull ache of pain, and realized he wanted to share with her. Hailey already knew about his failed marriage. What he never shared was his upbringing, and what made him who he was today. He was so like her. He kept that part of his past buried deep where no light could ever stream in. She waited patiently, secure in his arms. And for the first time, Michael decided to tell her everything.

"I grew up very poor," he said. "My father ran out on my mother when I was seven. He found a local girl with no baggage, and they took off. That was the last time I heard from him. I was almost glad to see him go. Even at seven, I remember him yelling at my mother, hitting me occasionally. Telling me I was useless."

She kept her voice low and soothing, even though her heart squeezed in pain. "What did your mother do to support you?"

"Waitressed. Cleaned up after people in hotels. Anything to keep food on the table. I helped as much as I could, but it was years before I could earn any decent money."

She felt the coldness within him envelop the man who had shared the last three nights with her, the man who had laughed and teased and held her close. She held him tighter as if her body warmth could ward off the chill. "What did you like as a boy?"

"Things I could fix. Things I could control. Math, science, cars, computers."

"What business did you decide to embark on?

"Computers. One of my mother's boyfriends was decent to her, and loved to fool around on a laptop. He taught me a few things and something clicked."

"What?"

"I could finally control something. A computer has no emotions, and does what it's told. I decided I would learn everything." He shifted in the water and his hand played with the wet strands of her hair. "Eventually, I found a job at a computer firm and worked my way up. Just like you, I took my opportunity and made the most of it."

"Do you ever think about your father?"

"No."

She picked up her head and gazed into his eyes. The gleaming white mask covered half of his face, but the burning light in his eyes confirmed he was a liar. Hailey stroked his hard cheek, traced the full line of his lower lip, then cradled his jaw. Tenderness bloomed within her.

"I was invited to the senior prom when I was eighteen," she said. "I had never been asked to a dance before, so I was beyond excitement. I spent hours looking through magazines for a dress, talking to my friends about which party we'd attend. When I told my parents I was invited, they refused to let me go." She paused, wrestling with the memories. "They informed me most teenagers lose their virginity during prom. I was better than that. I would not barter my body for a chance at a solid, successful future. So, I called my date and told him I got sick. I watched out my window as the limos pulled out of the driveways with kids dressed in gowns and tuxedos. And I hated them. I wished I could just be a normal teenager and kiss a boy for the first time on the night of prom. I was so tired of trying to be good, of trying to follow my parents' rules. I actually had a rebellion that night and screamed. Told them how much I hated them and their stupid restrictions. I went to sleep that night and wished they were dead." She took a deep breath and angled her head so he could see her face. "Years later they died. I was finally free. So I turned my back on the past and vowed to never think about them again. I wanted to build a new life for myself."

"So, you won."

"Ask me, Phantom. Ask me if I think about them anymore."

"Do you?"

"Every day."

Understanding took hold and blossomed. The chill eased, and Hailey lowered her mouth to his and kissed him. Her lips eased over his as gently as the first hint of a spring breeze strokes a flower petal. Her tongue slipped inside to give and share and receive. He tasted of male hunger. He tasted of her essence. And she knew in that moment she loved him.

Hailey broke off the kiss as the realization shook her. Their gazes locked, and then the ringing of the bell in the distance cut through the air, and the moment was gone.

She eased away from him. God, she didn't want to leave.

He allowed her to slip out of his arms. God, he didn't want her to leave.

"Phantom?"

"Yes?"

"Besides computers, what did you really love when you were little? What made you happy?"

He studied her face. Damned if she didn't know how to reach into a man's chest and rip his heart out. With that simple question, instead of focusing on the rage and pain of his childhood, he remembered something he thought he'd forgotten. A smile played about his lips as the memory took hold. "Roses." He shook his head, almost embarrassed. "We had this neighbor who used to garden. She had fruits, vegetables, herbs. And flowers, incredible rose bushes in red and pink and yellow. She was nice to me. When my mother was entertaining her boyfriends, she would invite me to her house and fix me peanut butter and banana sandwiches, and I would stare out at the roses."

His vision blurred as vivid colors and fragrances danced before him. When his gaze re-focused, he realized she had given him a precious gift.

His one good memory.

She smiled, then leaned over to kiss him good-bye.

"Until tomorrow," she whispered.

Then she rose from the tub and shut the door behind her.

Michael sat in the cooled water for a long time after she had gone and thought about her smile.

Thought about tomorrow, when he unmasked.

Chapter Four

He watched her walk up the twisting pathway. Her dark cloak welcomed her into the shadows, and hid her fiery red hair as she made her way into the house. The music and laughter were deafening; the sexual orgies and encounters flooded through the rooms as they approached their final encounter.

He paced the room with long, graceful strides. His black robe flowed behind him. He still wore the mask, would wear it until the final hour of the clock, and then she would know his identity. Would she draw back with shock and disgust? Would she throw away the moments they experienced these past nights because he was flesh and blood, and not her millionaire fantasy? Did she want to continue this relationship? Did she have feelings for him—the real him—her best friend Michael?

He cursed violently. One last night to touch and taste her sweet body. To kiss her lips and claim her for his own. One last time until the truth was revealed and she made her decision.

The door opened. Her scent beckoned him, a musky, vanilla fragrance that swirled around his senses and got him hard immediately. She stepped in and closed the door behind her.

Then loosened her cloak and let it fall to the floor in soft, velvet folds.

He sucked in his breath.

She was naked. Her glorious red hair tumbled down her back and shoulders, playing peek-a-boo with rosy pink nipples. Her breasts were full and creamy white. Her long legs framed an inviting center of curls that hid her sex. Beneath the musky scent of her cologne he caught the undertones of female arousal.

She wore no mask.

His gaze greedily took in every familiar feature. The graceful curve of her jaw and cheek, the arching red brows, the red lips. Her Caribbean blue eyes flickered warily but she stood before him in all her glory, daring him to turn away.

He closed the distance between them. Thrusting his fingers within the fire of her hair, he lifted her face up and gazed deeply into her eyes.

"You're beautiful."

Then his mouth took hers

It was a kiss of raw hunger and demand, a need to possess and be possessed, a vow to give pleasure and to take. Her lips opened under his, her tongue tangling, thrusting as they drank from one another as if they had discovered a cool drink of water in the hot desert sun.

Her hands slipped around her shoulders as his lips closed around her tongue and sucked, drawing her very essence into him. His teeth sunk into her ripe lower lip, taking love bites, and he trailed kisses across her cheek, exploring every feature that had been hidden by the mask.

When he lifted his head, her eyes burned as if with fever. Her nails dug fiercely into his shoulders.

"Take me, Phantom. Take me now. I belong to you."

He lifted her up and they tumbled to the bed. There was no teasing, no love play as she ripped off his robe and ran her hands over his long, lean body, loving the feel of his hair-roughened skin contrasting deliciously with her silken limbs.

They were ravenous for each other, hands and tongues and lips tangled together. He cupped her buttocks and sucked on her nipples as she reached down and took his throbbing erection between her fingers and squeezed, reveling in his masculine power, desperate to have him inside of her. She wrapped her legs around his hips and they rolled over in the cool, satin sheets. She climbed on top of him and impaled herself on his rock-hard flesh with one smooth thrust.

He groaned.

She gasped.

She arched back so he buried himself to the hilt in her tight, clingy heat. He sat up on the bed and wrapped his arms around her so they were face to face, flesh buried within flesh, gazes locked. Her nipples pressed into his chest. His lips hungrily took hers and plunged into the honeyed cave of her mouth as deeply as his penis was inside of her. He rocked his hips. Once. Again.

She cried out as convulsions shook her body. He lifted her up and over him and guided her hips up and down, pumping furiously inside of her as he rode the wild wave of hot pleasure to the edge. The orgasms overtook her, and still he pounded his penis into her body while her inner muscles clenched around him in a silken, wet fist.

He shouted her name as he exploded in a hot rush, and she fell over him. Her teeth savagely sunk into his shoulder as she held him to her.

Hailey slid down from the pinnacle with his member still buried inside of her. Her flesh pulsed and quivered in tiny vibrations and she turned her head to press kisses over his mouth, enjoying his ragged warm breaths against her mouth. Her fingers gentled and stroked back his silky, black hair, then lingered over the gleaming smoothness of his mask which still hid him from her full view.

"I can't get enough of you," she whispered, then nipped at his bottom lip. "Would you like to know another one of my fantasies?"

His mouth curved upward in a smile, a deep chuckle rumbled in his chest. "If it's anything like the last one, they'll be carrying me out on a stretcher."

She licked at his jaw and tasted clean soap and the salty tang of male sweat. His rough stubble prickled against her tongue.

"Never. You're my new superhero. No Viagra ever needed. Hours of pleasure guaranteed, until the woman begs for mercy."

"What is this superhero called?"

"Studman."

He laughed. "Batman. Superman. Spiderman. Now Studman."

"Exactly. Still want to hear my fantasy?"

"Go ahead."

"I lock you in a room and take away your clothes. You're at my command every hour of the day, completely at my mercy, and you'll do anything I ask. The only way to escape is to please me, so you work very hard at it."

"Hmmm. Sounds like what we're doing now except I'm the one who has to obey."

"Exactly."

"Hailey?"

"Yes?"

"That's my sexual fantasy, too."

She laughed with him, snuggling into his arms, her fingers playing with the swirling dark hairs on his chest. "There's one other part in my fantasy I forgot to mention."

"You have whips and chains."

"No, but I may have to add that one in later."

"What is it?"

"You have no mask."

He grew silent. The sounds of the party drifted up the stairwell and reminded them of the short hours left. "Once I remove my mask, the game is over. I want a little more time with you."

She blinked back sudden tears, and concentrated on the moment, wanting to pull every second of pleasure from the man beneath her.

"Then take it, Phantom. Take me over and over until the bell rings."

His eyes blazed with promise. "I intend to."

He rained kisses over her face, naked from the removal of her mask. She shook slightly and knew no other man had ever taken her body and soul like her Phantom.

"Give me a little more on our last night together, Hailey," he said.

She tossed him a wicked smile. "I thought I already did."

He chuckled. "I mean truth. Tell me what you want from your life. Tell me what you still fear."

This time, when she spoke she had no mask to hide herself. This time, she didn't need one. She spoke to the man she loved, and refused to hide anything. Hailey wanted to tell him the only thing she wanted was him, but he seemed to ask the question with the assumption this was their final meeting.

"I want to build something that lasts," she said softly. "Don't all people want the same thing? Someone to remember them. If I can't do it with children or the love of my life, I'll pick friendship. I'll pick rewarding work that makes a difference."

He waited a while before answering. "If you had a chance to have this love of your life, would you be strong enough to reach out for him?"

"Yes." She spoke the truth. Ciro Demitris had given her that gift.

"And your fear?"

"You already erased my fears, Phantom. The only thing left to be afraid of is being without you."

He turned from her then, as if he couldn't bear the emotion of looking into her face. Hailey took the time to ask her own questions. "And you? What do you fear?"

His voice came from a distant place. "I fear the truth," he said. With one quick movement, he rolled over and pinned her to the mattress. "But you're here now. Mine for the next few hours. That's all I need."

Then his mouth took hers.

The evening slid by with slow strokes of the clock, as they roused one another to make love through the night. He took her places she had never been before. She showed him a tenderness and emotions he had never felt before. The bed became their escape from the world beyond, as the full moon shimmered in the sky and the sounds of the party rose and fell through the rooms. And when the bell finally chimed at dawn, when the music and laughter and screams grew to a crescendo, he sat up in bed and looked at her naked body.

"It's time, Hailey."

His eyes were filled with resolve, and another emotion she couldn't put a name to. A glint, a glimmer, something she needed to hold onto but was too afraid to demand from him. Did he love her? Would he walk away without a second thought? Was she just another woman involved in his masquerade, a rousing distraction to never be thought of again?

He watched her as she sat up. The sheet fell to reveal her creamy breasts. Emotions shuddered through him. He knew he loved her, knew they had formed a connection over these past nights, but did she love him in the same way? Had this been a pleasant distraction and a way to get what she wanted? Would she walk away without a second thought?

The questions whirled through his mind in a dizzying rush.

He reached up and with one savage motion, ripped his mask off.

Hailey sucked in her breath as she stared at the man before her. The man she knew. The man who had played a game and betrayed her trust.

Michael Rivers.

She watched in shocked silence as he dipped his head and popped out the contact lenses. Then he reached up and rubbed his fingers through his hair. The strands fell over his face as they had so many times in the past. The diamond in his left ear winked like a beacon signaling his deceit. His brown eyes gazed into hers with a steadiness that prevented her from turning away. And suddenly, his voice and scent and touch made sense, and she gasped as the pain shook through her body.

"Why?" she moaned. "Michael, why would you do this to me?"

He flinched at the accusation. His voice was low and urgent. "Hailey, listen to me. If you decide you never want to see me again, I can accept the consequences. But this was my only chance, a chance of a lifetime, and I'll never regret taking it."

Her eyes widened at his words, and she bit down on her lower lip to stop from crying out. She forced herself to remain on the bed and listen. Even if it was for the last time.

"When we first met, I only wanted your friendship. I was still recovering from my wife, from the breakup of my marriage, but you filled a part of me I've never really known before. I felt comfortable and accepted with another woman for the first time. But as our friendship developed, I fell in love with you. Every part. I loved seeing you in baggy sweat pants and no make-up. I loved watching the ballgames and taking you out to dinner. I even love all those habits of yours no one is supposed to know about. You sing opera when you clean, and panic if you don't brush your teeth four times a day, and insist on walking in the back door instead of the front because you're superstitious."

"Michael—"

He put up a hand and forged on. "I watched you every day with an ache in my gut because I knew you wouldn't give me a chance. I listened to you complain about your looks when all I wanted to do was yank you in my arms and prove how beautiful I thought you were. And I wanted more, Hailey, so much more. I wanted to give you pleasure until you screamed my name. I wanted to explore every deep fantasy you ever had and some of my own. But whenever I made a move, you backed away."

He took a deep breath and continued. "When you told me about the masquerade party and Demitris, I knew I could lose you. So I took advantage of the opportunity of a lifetime. Finally, you would see me as a man, not your best friend. I wanted to be both. I needed you to see all of me, because I already loved all of you."

"Michael—" she tried to say more but he was at the edge of desperation, knowing everything was over with the next tick of the clock.

"I want to marry you. Have babies. Work together, play together, I want it all. I want to take you to bed every night and make sure your knees buckle every time I kiss you. Everything I said this weekend was the truth. I only hid my face. My heart's been open to you."

Her body trembled helplessly from the onslaught of words and emotions. She drew in a ragged breath, trying to make sense of what he had told her. This was Michael, her best friend and confidante. But he was also Ciro Demitris, a phantom figure who kissed her breathlessly and set her body on fire.

Hailey closed her eyes. A rush of images whizzed before her. The comfort in his presence. The way he made her laugh. The burning edge in his eyes when he looked at her. The facts were all there, had always been there, but she had refused to face them.

A blinding flash of realization shook her to the core. This was what she had been afraid of. She had chased after a strange man this weekend and convinced herself she had been lacking excitement and adventure. In reality, Michael had always been the one she ran from. The man she could share her life with. She stubbornly built a wall around the possibility there could be more between them, afraid of the truth.

This was the man she loved.

Hailey opened her eyes. Her best friend stood a few inches away, his familiar features twisted with an agony that tore at her heart. Tears spilled over her lids as the knowledge sunk in. He had always loved her. Loved her enough to take the risk of losing her completely by setting up the entire charade. Loved her enough to wait until he thought she was ready.

With a low mutter, he closed the distance between them and took her into his arms.

His mouth took hers and claimed her for his own. Her arms came up to receive as she gave it all back. When he finally lifted his head, he smiled.

"You forgive me for not allowing you to meet your rich tycoon?"

She laughed in delight and threw her arms around him. "Who needs a tycoon? He probably has no idea how to do his own laundry."

Dark brown eyes gleamed with intensity. "This wasn't just a weekend fling, Hailey. All the things I did to you, with you, I intend to continue. And I have a long list of fantasies."

She laid back on the bed, naked, and slowly parted her legs, then smiled. "How long?"

"Oh, enough to last the next twenty years."

"Maybe we should get started."

"Maybe we should."

He leaned over her and pressed his body to hers. Put both hands on the inside of her thighs to open her wide to his gaze. Then deliberately thrust into her wet heat, while he watched her face gain the dreamy expression he had enjoyed the last few nights.

"Michael."

She watched his eyes darken with pleasure as his name echoed through the air. And Hailey gave herself completely over to the man she loved.

About the Author:

I've always wanted to be a writer, and I knew my calling was romance from the time I was thirteen years old. My life took on an edge of excitement I never experienced before, and as I grew older, I learned valuable lessons from those feisty heroines and alpha male heroes.

I live in upstate New York, in the beautiful Hudson Valley. I have a deep love for the mountains, chocolate, Frank Sinatra, and a good book. My first novel, Heart of Steel, was the beginning of a long and satisfying journey through the world of romance. I loved writing Masquerade, and look forward to many more stories with Red Sage Publishing.

I share my life with my wonderful husband and our two canine children, Bella and Lester. They've all suffered through late nights with me as I work. I look forward to hearing from all of my readers, so please check out my website: www.jenniferprobst.com.

Ancient Pleasures

by Jess Michaels

To My Reader:

A Victorian woman searching for the truth, an American tomb raider looking for treasure, and a tomb with a sensual curse. The Egyptians never had pleasure this potent . . .

Chapter One

Egypt, 1897

Isabella Winslow fingered the artifact in her bag and smiled at her Egyptian maid. "This is it, Anya. This is the place."

Anya shoved a lock of coal black hair from her shoulder and looked nervously around the barren desert. She'd made it no secret that she didn't want to leave the safety of Cairo for the wilds of the sand dunes and the unknown adventures of tomb raiding. Or that it was inappropriate for two unmarried ladies to be in the unescorted company of their handsome Egyptian guide.

"Yes, ma'am. This does seem to be the place described on your late husband's map, but are you sure we have to go inside Merytsat's tomb?"

Anya glanced at their guide out of the corner of her narrowed eyes. He was standing a few feet away from them at the top of the stone steps that lead to the round tomb door. His arms were folded in waiting, his long silky hair tied back from his face to reveal a black tribal tattoo that curled around the back of his neck. His brown eyes were always focused, though. Mostly on Isabella's maid.

Anya wrung her hands as her eyes darted away from his pointed stare. "Surai has told me stories about the curses placed on these ancient burial grounds. And I've heard the tales about English archeologists who haven't made it home after their adventures in dark places."

Isabella laughed at the superstitious drivel. "Surai only tells those stories to make you sit closer to him by the fire." Though the maid tried to deny it, Isabella had seen the spark between her two servants. It was one she chose not to discourage. She had too many other things on her mind. "If we don't go inside, we'll never finish Hiram's work. Or find out exactly what drove him to the way he behaved after he returned from the dig in this . . ." She looked around at the two worn, rock statues that guarded the tomb entrance, two half naked women who brandished sharpened spears and wore fox headpieces. "This strange place."

Anya's eyes narrowed. "I don't think you need to sneak away from polite society and come searching tombs to find out why a man would stray from his wife. Or die in bed with two Egyptian whores."

Isabella forced her thoughts away from the ugly facts. Facts she'd tried to soften with all her might since that horrible night so many months before, but to no avail.

"That's enough, Anya," she snapped. She turned away from her servant and switched from English to Egyptian to address their male companion. "Surai, open the tomb door and lead the way inside."

He nodded and descended the steps into a shallow, sandy pit where a thick door awaited. The sand storms had long ago turned the identifying hieroglyphics to mere scratches, but the outline of the door was still clear. He crouched to his haunches to run tanned fingers around the edge in order find the best place to pry open the door.

They'd been lucky Hiram had visited here first. He'd not only mapped their journey to the tomb, but his team had done much of the excavation of the site. Still, she knew the door had been resealed when Hiram departed and she expected they might have to stand in the blazing sun and swirling sands for a while before their guide managed to pry it open. But to Isabella's surprise, the covering opened with ease, as if the gods wanted her to come there, to find the answers she'd sought since she'd been widowed.

"Madam," Surai whispered in his native tongue. "The door is already open."

"This is not a good idea, mistress," Anya said as she clasped Isabella's arm with both trembling hands. "There is something foul about the tomb being open. Anyone and anything could await us inside."

Isabella shared her maid's fear, but shook off her feelings. This wasn't the time to have the vapors. She needed to go inside. Something called her to enter. And it was something she refused to deny.

"Light the lanterns," she ordered as she pulled away from Anya.

She spoke with far more bravado than she felt. “If you two are afraid, then I shall lead the way.”

Surai opened his mouth as if to protest but Isabella gave him the icy expression her mother had always utilized with servants in London and he grew quiet. After a few moments of shuffling, he handed her a glowing torch and let her take the first few steps into the tomb of Merytsat.

The air was hot and dry, dusty from millennia of being shut up. As far as she knew, only her husband had entered this place with his men since it had been sealed thousands of years before. The idea gave Isabella a shiver. The last man who had entered here was now dead.

With slow steps, she made her way inside. The low glow of the torch allowed her to see the intricate carvings on the walls. Prayers for the dead.

She had gone into the dim tomb about a hundred yards when a sound made her stop in her tracks. Had that been a laugh? And not just any laugh, but the sultry laugh of a woman? No. She had to be imagining things. No one should be in this place but her and her servants. No one else even knew it existed.

When only silence met her waiting ears, Isabella took another step. The dim corridor before her split in two directions and she hesitated as she lifted the light to peer down each one. Which way to go? Which way had Hiram gone?

“Who the hell are you?”

With a start, Isabella pivoted and found herself looking down the short barrel of a pistol. It was aimed at her by the most handsome man she’d ever seen. He had tousled brown hair and stubble that indicated he hadn’t shaved for at least two days. His eyes glittered in the torchlight, reflecting back an intense blue fire that almost had her turning away. Only she found she couldn’t. She was too drawn in, despite the threat he posed.

Swallowing, she managed to find her voice. “Who the hell am I?” she asked. “I think a better question is who the hell are you?”

“I’m the guy who’s laying claim to this place, lady,” he said in a decidedly American drawl. He inched the gun away from her face, though he didn’t holster it as he shot a side-glance toward Surai.

“Laying claim?” she repeated as shock and anger wiped away some of the sharp desire she'd felt when she first met this stranger's gaze. "You have no right, sir. My husband found this tomb and it is rightfully his to harvest its findings for the British Museum."

The man motioned his head toward Surai, who had taken up a battle stance in front of Anya. He looked every inch the ancient warrior. "That your husband?"

She blinked. "No. My husband is—well, he's dead."

The blue eyes widened and then the man had the audacity to laugh. And not a chuckle, either, but a low belly laugh that seemed to fill and shake the narrow corridor in which they stood.

"And just what is funny about that, sir?" she asked with as much dignity as she could muster when her cheeks were flaming with a blush.

"If your husband is dead, then he has no claim to anything in this world." The man's intense gaze lingered on her for a long moment. "Anything at all."

The knot that had closed Isabella's throat when she'd first seen this rude stranger now filled it again. She knew a man's desire when she saw it, and it was clear in every part of the unknown outsider before her. Worse was that her nipples hardened in answer to his pointed stare and her thighs clenched.

Obviously she'd been too long without a man's touch if she was considering this . . . this lout to be an object of lust.

"You still haven't told me your name," she said coolly.

He grinned as another man appeared from the narrow corridor behind him. Now the odds were worse for her party, though she strangely felt no fear. She wasn't sure why, but she knew without a doubt that these men wouldn't hurt her or her servants.

"Jake Turner at your service, my British lady." He jerked his head toward his friend. In the lamplight she could see he had blonde hair and coal gray eyes. Eyes that were focused not on her, but behind her at Anya and Surai. "And this is my partner in crime, Rafe Christian."

"Very nice." She thinned her lips to a frown. "Now, Mr. Turner, Mr. Christian, I'm going to have to ask you again to leave. This tomb is under the jurisdiction of the British Museum. Marauders are not allowed."

Turner gave his partner a look before he let out another low laugh.

This one raked over her senses and made her ever more aware of her reacting body. What was wrong with her? It wasn't like she'd never seen a handsome man before. Or heard a deep, throaty chuckle like his. But her body was behaving like a sex-starved wanton. She hadn't been so wet in . . . well . . . ever.

"Are *you* a representative of the British Museum now?" he asked. He leaned closer and the heat of his breath warmed her skin. "Because I'd like to see your papers."

She opened her mouth in outrage, but he held up a hand to silence her. "I'm sorry, lady, but this tomb is free to the public now. And my friend and I have our own plans for it. You and your crew are certainly welcome to whatever spoils it is you're looking for. I'm sure there's more than enough booty to go around."

He turned to walk away, but she caught his arm. Instantly heat and electricity shot between them. With a gasp, she yanked her hand away and he reeled back a few steps as if he'd felt the same reaction.

She struggled for equilibrium. "You mean to raid the tomb?"

"That's what treasure hunters do," he said, though his eyes moved over her again. "We ravage and pillage."

She shut her eyes as an image of this man ravaging her entered her mind. His broad shoulders gleaming in the pale lamplight as he entered her inch by inch. Though she shook the fantasy away, she couldn't pretend that a telltale tingle hadn't begun between her heated thighs.

"You know." He stepped closer. "You never told me *your* name."

She stiffened at the reduced proximity between them. He was invading her personal space, trying to intimidate her with his presence. It was working, too, though she'd be damned if she'd allow him to know it.

She straightened her spine and used her most proper and refined tone. "My name is Isabella Winslow. My husband was the late archeologist—"

"Hiram Winslow."

She jerked back in surprise. Her husband's death had been chronicled in the newspapers, but she was still stunned that a man like this would know Hiram's name.

Jake's eyes narrowed. "I'd heard of the circumstances of his death. I am sorry, Mrs. Winslow. But that doesn't change the fact that I don't accept your claim to this tomb. As far as I'm concerned we have equal right to the spoils here. So why don't we just try to stay out of each other's way."

"Mr. Turner!" she cried in outrage.

"Mistress," Anya snapped from behind her. "The walls!"

Isabella turned around. She'd been so caught up in arguing with the handsome tomb raider she hadn't noticed that the corridor was shaking.

"Oh my God!" she cried out as she stumbled back. She came in hard contact with Jake Turner's solid chest.

Clasping her arm, he began to drag her through the dim hallways away from the entrance. She pulled back against him, but he refused to let her go as he ran. "The tomb isn't stable. We must get closer to the center!"

"But the door!" she screamed as dust and years of cobwebs clouded her eyes and blocked her throat.

"It's the most unstable place of all!" he insisted just as a loud, ugly crash echoed through the passageways around them. Throwing all his weight on top of her, Jake hurtled Isabella to the floor and covered her with his body as a hail of stones and dirt settled around and on top of them.

Followed by a dark and sinister silence.

Isabella Winslow was yielding and warm beneath Jake's hard body. Though rationally he knew that was the last thought he should have been having, he couldn't help that he was a virile man and the supple body pinned beneath his own made his cock throb with powerful need.

But virile or not, the dust was settling in the total darkness and he had to get up to investigate how much damage had been done to the structure. And ascertain if anyone in either party had been hurt by flying debris.

As he shifted his weight in preparation to rise off Isabella, she let out a low moan. The sound was rich and throaty and made his blood run even hotter than it had been.

"You all right?" he asked quietly as he reluctantly shifted off of her and got to his knees at her side. He wished he could see her, but without the torch lights and the sliver of daylight from outside of the tomb door, he could only tell her location by touch and sense.

Still, he was sure if he could see her that her wide, brown eyes would be glazed with fear.

"I'm fine except for being crushed by you," she said, though her voice trembled and lacked the heat of her sarcastic quip.

"Well, better me than the walls," he answered as he pawed around on the ground for the torch he'd been holding when the tomb collapsed around them. He smelled the sharp tang of kerosene on the torch's rag nearby and finally managed to grasp the end. Using his cigarette lighter, he set it to flame again and held it up to look at her in the wavering circle of light.

She'd risen to her knees beside him, mere inches separating them. With a gasp, she skirted away, but not before he saw the fear he had predicted in her stare. Along with a surprising amount of desire. Isabella Winslow wanted him.

With a triumphant smile, he stood and dragged her up by her elbows. Immediately, she snatched her arms away and stumbled back a few steps. He frowned as he looked around through the dust. Everyone seemed to be getting to their feet. "Was anyone hurt?"

One by one Isabella's two servants and Rafe all answered in the negative. Mopping dirt from his face on his shirtsleeve, Jake surveyed the damage done in the tomb. In the dim glow of the torch, he couldn't see much of anything, but the walls around them seemed to have remained solid, despite all the dust and rubble that now littered the floor at their feet. Still, the deafening rumbling they'd heard indicted far worse should have befallen them.

What had set off the avalanche of debris? He'd been arguing loudly with Isabella, yes, but that shouldn't have been enough to make the very walls shake. Jake had raided plenty of tombs that were far older and in worse shape than this one. None had ever threatened to bury him with the long-dead mummies and their priceless treasures.

"Well, don't just stand there," Isabella said as she crossed her arms. The action forced Jake's gaze to her breasts. Even under the loose fitting man's shirt she wore, it was obvious they were round and perfect.

They'd probably overflow his hands when he cupped them. He wondered what color her nipples were.

He shook his head. What the hell? Where had those thoughts come from? And why did the corridor seem to be growing ever hotter and closer.

"Come on," he whispered in a voice made harsh by desire. "We need to go back to the entrance. If the tomb isn't stable, we should go outside. At least until we can get a crew to reinforce the walls."

Her brown eyes grew wide. "Go? No, I have to stay. I must find out—" She broke off the sentence with a suddenly panicked stare. "I just can't leave, that's all."

"Whatever it is you need to find here, it isn't worth your life," Jake barked out. "Now, come on."

When she shook her head in protest, Jake reached out to grasp her arm. Heat whooshed through him and set him off balance. She seemed to feel it too, for she pulled away from him with a squeal of protest.

"Surai!" she cried.

Jake turned to ready himself for battle against the large and menacing Egyptian guide, but was surprised to see that the two of them were now alone in the corridor.

"Rafe?" he called into the misty dark. "Where the hell are you?"

He waited for a response, but only his own voice answered him as it bounced along the walls in the maze of the tomb's many twisting corridors. It rang back at him, distorted from ricocheting off countless doors and around corners.

"What did your man do to my guide and maid?" Isabella asked with all the haughty attitude of a British aristocrat. It set Jake's teeth on edge.

"Look, lady, I have no idea where any of our friends are. But if they're smart, they aren't arguing in the corridor. They're heading toward the entryway and safety." With a growl, he pulled her closer and caught a whiff of the rich spicy scent of her hair and skin. It dizzied his mind. "Come on, your highness, let's go."

Her protests died on her lips as she stared up into his eyes. But then she shook away his hand and said, "Fine. But don't think that just because I'm going with you means I agree with you."

He rolled his eyes and used the flickering light from his own torch to find another for Isabella. With a curse, he brushed it free of dirt and lit it. Dim, sickly light finally emanated and Jake shoved the torch into her hand as he motioned for her to follow him.

"Stay close," he ordered. "We don't know what kind of debris may be in the path now and the torches have very weak light."

She muttered a sarcastic response, but did as he'd ordered and slipped up behind him. Her body heat warmed him through his shirt and he could have sworn he felt the brush of those full, lush breasts pressed against the plane of his back. With a shiver, he headed toward the entrance. Once they were out of the tomb, he hoped these strange desires would go with them. He didn't think he'd ever been so full of a need for a woman in his life. Especially a woman like this.

"It's so quiet," Isabella whispered. "Why can't we hear the others?"

Jake shook his head. That was what he wondered, too. If their friends were anywhere close by, they would have heard their echoing voices and footfalls.

"Maybe they've already gone into the desert and are waiting for us," he offered though he didn't believe it himself. Still, there was no use getting her even more upset than she already was.

"Anya wouldn't leave me alone," she answered quietly.

Jake was silent. Neither would Rafe. The two of them had been friends for over five years. They'd raided tombs and avoided authorities and enemies alike. Rafe had never left him before.

"What if they were hurt in the accident?" she muttered with a tiny catch in her voice.

Jake stopped in his spot and turned back to her. The tough woman she'd tried to portray since he'd first leveled his pistol in her face was gone, replaced by a fragile beauty. He set the torch in a sconce on the wall and drew her against his chest.

She stiffened at first, but within moments she relaxed in his arms. Her chest flattened against his, her legs molded to his own. Every tantalizing inch of her splayed across him like out of some erotic dream. But this wasn't a dream. It felt too good.

He struggled for words. "They each said they weren't hurt," he reminded her as his erection inched harder and longer. There was no way she couldn't feel him pressed against her thigh, yet she didn't pull away. "They just roamed off."

She looked up at him with cloudy, unfocused eyes. Her tongue came out pink and wet to slide across dusty rose lips. With a groan, Jake pulled her closer and slammed his mouth down on hers.

He half expected her to pull back and give him the slap of his life. Instead, she wound her arms around his back and returned his kiss with an equal intensity. He drove his tongue between her lips and she sucked it. His cock twitched. He was going to have this woman. One way or another he was going to enter her heat.

In a few long steps, he crushed her back against the nearest wall and pushed her legs apart with his thighs. All the while he continued to plunder her mouth, bruising her with his out of control need. Yet she whimpered in desire, not a request for him to stop. Already her nails raked along his back and he felt her hard nipples through several layers of fabric.

"Yes," she moaned as he grasped a handful of her skirt and thin silky underskirt. He yanked them up in jerky movements. She arched against him until her pelvis ground against his cock and he nearly spent himself there and then. But just as she pried a hand between them and found the top button of his trousers, a sound pierced the echoing silence around them. A sound that brought them both up short.

A woman's moan.

For a brief moment, Jake thought it must have been a trick of the corridor that had sent Isabella's cries of encouragement back to them on the hot, dry air, but then the moan came again, this time even louder.

"Is that Anya?" Isabella whispered as she shoved back against Jake's chest. "Is she hurt?"

Jake cocked an eyebrow at her. That was not the sound of an injured woman. It was the sound of a woman climaxing. The sound of a woman being well pleasured. Isabella's cheeks darkened as she met his gaze. She knew it as well as he did.

"We need to . . . go," she choked out as she turned away from his scrutiny with a red face. "We need to find our friends and get out of this place."

His erection jolted in protest, but Jake managed to nod. "This way," he muttered as he grasped the torch from the wall.

The outer door to the tomb was only a few hundred feet away, but with the moans and cries echoing around them in the oppressive darkness, it seemed to take an age to reach it. The sounds taunted him, reminding him that he could have been plunging inside Isabella's willing body right now if they hadn't been interrupted.

They rounded the last corner, but instead of being greeted by the filtered sunlight of the desert streaming in through the doorway, they were met by ominous darkness. The cavern door was shut, blocked by a pile of debris.

"Damn it!" Jake cried as he hurried toward the entrance. He thrust his torch in Isabella's direction and she took it wordlessly, then watched as he dug at the rocks and dust. Despite his best efforts, he was only able to free a few smaller rocks.

"We're trapped," she said behind him in a strange, low voice that made him turn. Her face had paled two shades and her eyes glazed with tears she was fighting to control.

He straightened up and tried to look optimistic. "For now. But you know that many of these tombs had more than one entrance. If we can't find another way out, I'm sure Rafe, Surai and I can dig our way out of the main corridor."

"But we can't find the others," Isabella whispered.

He reached out to her and was surprised when she took his hand without argument. "Well, we will. Come on, let's go back the way we came and see if we can work our way out of this maze."

Chapter Two

Isabella fought the urge to grasp the back of Jake's dusty linen shirt. Touching this man wouldn't help anything, especially considering how their last innocent contact had lead to that animalistic display up against the corridor wall. Her body tingled with just the memory of the way his erection had pressed against the junction of her thighs, encouraging the wetness that still lingered inside her.

She swallowed hard. Her fear and desperation had led to that moment of surrender, nothing more. She wouldn't let it happen again. And she wouldn't show a scoundrel like Jake Turner that she was afraid either.

She peered over his shoulder. Their two torches cast a sickly light up the ever twisting corridor ahead, revealing the beautiful carvings on the tomb walls. Isabella wanted to stop to chronicle them in her little notebook, but they had to find their friends before she did anything of the kind.

They rounded a corner, but this time instead of the never-ending passage, an open doorway came into view at the end of their circle of light.

Her heart leapt. "Is that a chamber up ahead?"

Jake lifted his torch higher and squinted into the dimness. "I think you're right." He half turned to face her. "Do we dare try it?"

Now that she was looking up into those amazing blue eyes, Isabella temporarily forgot her capacity to speak. Swallowing hard past sudden desire, she nodded.

"A-Anything is better than roaming around in the dark," she managed to whisper.

His breath rasped heavy in the echoing chamber, bouncing off the walls and making her ears and body tingle with the knowledge that looking at her made him want her. Made them both forget the fear associated with being trapped.

With a shiver, he turned away and began walking again. They passed through the chamber door and her fear returned, laced with a strange, dizzy sensation. One that wasn't entirely unpleasant.

"Let me raise the light in here a bit," Jake muttered as he crossed to a few torches on the walls. He lit them with his own and the chamber blazed forth in firelight.

Enough light that the hieroglyphics on the walls were clear. Tombs often contained sayings or stories of the departed's life written on the walls. But these weren't the usual symbols for words. These pictures were of men and women engaging in sex acts.

Isabella gasped as she took a step forward to put her torch in an empty sconce. She instinctively reached out to brush her fingertips along the long jut of an animated penis as it plowed into the waiting mouth of a woman.

"What is this place?" Jake muttered under his breath as he stared both at her and the walls.

"You're raiding this tomb, but you don't even know whom it houses?" she asked with purposeful superiority in her tone.

Still, she couldn't seem to take her eyes from the pictures drawn with paint thousands of years before. This one depicted a woman enjoying two handsome men. One suckled her breasts as he buried himself deep within her womb, the other pressed into her bottom. No detail was left undone, including the tell tale droplet of moisture that trickled down the woman's inner thigh. Though the position was foreign to Isabella, it excited her. She actually had to will her hands from straying up to stroke her own breasts.

"If you know so much," Jake said in a strange, choked voice from behind her. "Then why don't you fill me in on the details. All I know about this tomb is that it was rumored to hold riches."

Isabella continued to stroll along the wall's parameter, pausing to look up at the detail of a man gliding his pointed, red tongue along the nether lips of a woman in the heights of ecstasy. The wet heat between her own thighs increased and she had to labor her breathing to speak.

"This is the burial place of Merytsat. She is unique in that she was only a pharaoh's mistress, yet she was buried with the wealth and glory of a queen," she whispered as she found herself looking up at a picture of the beautiful Egyptian herself.

Merytsat was straddling the prone form of a well-endowed lover, riding his cock with fervor. Isabella could have sworn if she lowered her lids a fraction, she could almost feel the animal heat of that man between her own legs. Could almost hear Merytsat's moans of pleasure and power as she rode him to orgasm and took his hot seed deep inside her.

"Why?" Jake asked. His rough voice cut through the air and the timbre of it made Isabella shiver. He wanted her. And it excited her to turn him on with her every word.

"She was a very accomplished mistress. One who learned the art of sex with a zeal that put all other concubines to shame. Some say she had powers only making love could awaken, but I've never believed that." She leaned closer to the wall. "Still . . ." She reached out a trembling finger and stroked it along Merytsat's slit. "Looking at these hieroglyphics, you can almost feel her power. Her passion."

"Isabella," Jake murmured.

She turned to face him and found she'd unbuttoned the first three buttons of the shirt she had taken from her husband's dresser before departing Cairo. Her hands were inside the warm heat of her thin chemise and she was stroking her own breasts, teasing the nipples with her fingers and kneading the sensitive flesh.

Propriety dictated she be embarrassed by this stunning slip. That she apologize and cover herself decently. But somehow she felt no shame. Instead, a stir of the power Merytsat herself must have possessed began in Isabella's very center. In place of shame, she felt elation. Freedom.

And the need to have this man touch her. To make him groan as the men in these pictures around her had their mouths open in moans of pleasure. The pleasure she would bring.

Jake continued to stare at her and she was finally so bold as to meet his gaze full-on. "Would you like to watch me touch myself?" she asked softly. Her voice wasn't her own. Her hands weren't her own. And this moment was just one out of time. There were no consequences. Only sensation.

He shut his eyes for a brief moment, but she didn't need words to know the answer to the question. The hard outline of his jutting member was already clear through his trousers.

"Oh, yes," he finally breathed as his lids came open.

With a boldness she'd never known she possessed, she slipped the remainder of her buttons open and tossed her shirt aside. Then she slipped the slender chemise straps off her shoulders and bared her breasts to him. He mumbled something unintelligible under his breath, then gasped when she cupped her herself again.

"Then watch," she urged as she stroked her thumbs across her nipples. Her nerves sang as she fondled her skin with soft palms.

Normally her ministrations were limited to a few shy caresses in a bath or in the darkness of her lonely bed. A woman of her station was told over and over that sex was dirty. Isabella had touched herself, but it was always fleeting and had brought her shame. But now, to bring herself pleasure in front of a stranger, in the blinding light of a chamber filled with ancient erotic art, was exhilarating.

She unfastened her skirt and removed it, along with the remainder of her underclothes and boots. She stood before him naked, without even her long hair down around her shoulders as protection from his eyes.

"Isabella," he breathed as he reached for her.

"Not yet," she protested while she skirted his reach. Then she snaked her hand to the blonde curls between her legs and slid a finger along her wet slit. The slippery heat intensified with the touch, dampening her fingers and sending a flash of powerful pleasure through her. With another long sweep of her finger, she brushed the hardness of her clit and couldn't hold back a moan.

Without breaking eye contact with Jake, she lifted her finger to her mouth and licked it, tasting her own juices before she returned to touching herself.

He let out a low moan and moved toward her. "I want to taste you. I want to taste your desire."

Her knees almost buckled as he dropped down before her and placed a rough hand on the inside of each her naked thighs. Slowly, he backed her legs open until she stood splayed before him. With a grin, he leaned up and took a deep whiff of her woman's scent before he slipped his tongue across her.

"It's been so long," she murmured as she gripped a fistful of his hair.

"Then I'll make the wait worthwhile," he promised as he pulled her down to her knees to face him. He leaned down to kiss her and she tasted her own earthy flavor on his lips just as she'd tasted it on her finger.

With a groan, he laid her back on her discarded clothes. She bent her knees and spread her legs further, offering her feminine secrets to him without hesitation. He took them with equal determination, stroking his tongue first across her outer lips, just teasing her pulsing body with light nips and long strokes.

She rose to meet each flick of his hot tongue, writhing with the need for more of him than just his mouth, but wanting the moment to never end. Hiram had certainly never loved her like this. It was exquisite.

Jake finally delved his tongue deep inside her, plunging it in and out in a slow, languid rhythm that mimicked the one she knew he'd set with his cock later.

His cock. The hard, hot one she'd felt pressed against her earlier. The long length she'd seen jutting against his confining trousers.

"I want to see you," she whispered.

His head came up in surprise, but then he shook it. "Not yet. I want to lick every drop of need from your body before I create even more in you."

She shivered as he nuzzled his nose back against her. "No, I don't want you to put yourself inside me yet. I want to taste you as you're tasting me. I want to suck you."

She had no idea where that request had come from, but the desire was overwhelming. Blue eyes met hers with a heat that was burning hot and full of dangerous promise. He stood and shucked his shirt and trousers, revealing his nakedness to her. Her eyes widened. This man had both length and girth. He was far bigger than Hiram had been, and looked like he would fill her to the brim when he finally did enter her.

He looked delicious.

"Lay on your back," she ordered as she crawled to her knees.

He followed her command, laying across their discarded clothes in the soft sand. With a purr of satisfaction, Isabella straddled his mouth, then bent to take just the head of his magnificent erection between her lips. Jake let out one low groan before he went back to work on her pussy with renewed vigor. She mimicked his every action. When he sucked her clit, she sucked the head of his penis. When he ran his tongue down her slit all the way to the tightness of her bottom, she ran her mouth up and down the long, turgid length of his cock. When he drilled his tongue inside her, she filled her mouth with his length.

The pressure and pleasure was building, and by the way he twitched against her tongue and moaned into her body, it wasn't just nearing culmination for her. He was going to come, and she was going to drink every drop of his essence even as he lapped up the last bit of hers.

With a shift of her hips, she began to grind in slow circles against his unyielding mouth. Her clit rubbed just right against him, causing a delicious friction that would allow her a release she knew would go on for ages. She also increased the speed of her mouth, alternately sucking him and taking him down as deep as he would go.

Finally, in a release so powerful it actually made her scream against his cock, Isabella came. Her hips jerked wildly, only prevented from injuring Jake by the fingers he dug into her skin to keep her in place as he continued to lap at her mercilessly.

Just as she exploded, he joined her, pumping hot into her mouth and down her throat. Like he had, she continued her torture until he was spent and softened a fraction in her mouth.

Isabella blinked as she lay exhausted on his sweat-slick stomach. Slowly, reality set in. What had just happened? She and Hiram had been married for nearly three years. In that time, she'd never even considered the possibility of taking his member into her mouth. Of sucking him dry.

She shivered as a fresh, insistent wave of desire washed over her. What was driving her to do these things with a man who was nothing more than a stranger? A tomb-raiding, overbearing, American stranger.

Briefly she flashed to an image of Hiram. When he'd returned from Merytsat's tomb, he had behaved differently, too. He'd demanded things from her in their bedroom that he'd never wanted before. When she hadn't been able to provide him with those desires, it had driven him away. Driven him to his death.

And now she was experiencing the same powerful longings.

Her hands began to tremble with that association. With a start, she rolled off Jake's body and yanked her shirt from beneath his muscular backside. She was *not* going to end up like Hiram had. She wasn't going to let herself be driven by her suddenly awakened sexual desires.

Jake sat up on his elbows to watch her dress with unhidden interest and the flash of what she knew was desire. She ignored it, and her body's unwanted, wet response.

"From the look on your face, I'd never have guessed you got as much enjoyment from that as I did." His grin was wicked and intoxicating. She almost wanted to return the smile, even though she was terrified. "As unexpected as it was."

She turned her back on him to avoid the distraction he posed. Shoving her arms through her sleeves, she whispered, "Well, unexpected or not, I hope you don't think it will change anything." She struggled to button her shirt with clumsy fingers. When she'd managed to cover herself decently, she finally dared to face him. "And I hope you don't expect me to give into your charms again, Mr. Turner."

The amusement on his face was gone. "It's a bit late to call me Mr. Turner, isn't it?" he asked in a dry voice. "And it wasn't as if I held you down and forced myself on you. If I recall, you started this little encounter. And you were the one straddling me, riding me to your pleasure."

She blushed, hating that he was saying exactly what she knew to be true. She *had* started this. And she wanted more. Looking down at this man, with his tousled dark hair, his stubbly cheeks that she'd felt brush against her most private areas and his broad, utterly naked body, she wanted nothing more than to fall back into his arms. But this time his mouth wouldn't be enough. She wanted that strong thrust of cock she'd held in her lips. She wanted it inside her, rocking against her.

With a shiver, she looked away. Even when she was dressed, he was still far too dangerous a draw.

"I'm not like this," she muttered. "I am not the kind of woman who throws herself at a man. Especially one like you."

He laughed long and hard at her insult as he rose to his feet and pulled on his trousers. "Yes, that's probably true. Perhaps it's this place."

"What do you mean?" she asked as she allowed herself a glance over her shoulder. He was already buttoning his dusty, wrinkled shirt, covering up the body that had given her so much pleasure. And could give her so much more if she only asked.

And how she wanted to ask. She wanted to beg for more. Shaking her head, she steeled herself. She had to fight these strange desires no matter how hard it was.

He shrugged. "There have been many tales of explorers and tomb raiders who've encountered much more than history or treasures in Egyptian tombs. Some say these places held curses, as well. Warnings to invaders to take at their own peril. Maybe this place has a curse, too. One that involves the sexual skill of the woman who was buried here."

She pursed her lips. "I believe in science, Mr. Turner." Even if science couldn't explain what she'd seen her own husband do. Or how her aching body was betraying her at that very moment.

"Jake," he interrupted. "If you're going to let me give you the most intimate of kisses, Isabella, I'm going to have to insist you call me Jake."

Her breath hitched as he took a step closer. She could smell his skin from the short distance. A tantalizing mixture of sweat and man . . . and now sex. The new addition only made her all the more aware of the power he could hold sway over her.

"I assure you Mr.—" She sighed when he arched an eyebrow. "Jake, that what happened between us a moment ago will never happen again. And it had nothing to do with a curse or an enchantment or any other superstition."

"Then why?" He reached out a hand to brush across her face with gentle pressure. The challenge to her resolve was nearly overpowering. "Or are you admitting that you simply wanted me and against every regulation you would usually follow, you gave in to those desires?"

Her teeth sank into her lip as she contemplated a good answer for that question. If she admitted she'd given in to her desires of her own volition, that would be opening up the door to saying she still wanted more of this man's touch. Something that completely went against her every fiber. Even though it was true. She wanted what they'd shared again and even more, despite everything that told her not to touch him.

But saying their joining was possibly caused by something in the tomb went against her scientific instincts. And also took away from the sweet moments she'd found in Jake's arms.

"I—" she began, but then she stopped. In the distance, she heard a low, feminine moan. "Did you hear that?"

He looked around with a nod. "Yes. The same moan we heard earlier in the corridor."

"Perhaps it's a trick of the tomb," she whispered.

She shut her eyes as the sound came again, this time louder. It sounded like Anya. But not like she was in pain. It sounded like a woman being pleasured. Like the moans she, herself, had uttered while Jake suckled and teased her to orgasm. Her pussy clenched in response and her nipples puckered.

"Perhaps," he said quietly.

"I have to look for my friend." She shook her head to cast away whatever spell came over her when this man was so near. "I need to find Anya and then we can begin our work while you and the other men start digging us out of the tomb."

As she turned to leave the chamber, Jake's hand snaked out and caught her arm. He spun her back around to face him. His body heat hit her like a wall, then surrounded her in an embrace.

"Now wait just a damn minute, Isabella. There's no way in hell I'm going to dig you out of this tomb while you go sifting through the chambers looking for the secrets of a dead concubine. It's utterly ridiculous that you're willing to risk your life for some historical relic."

She yanked on her arm, but he wouldn't set her free. His touch burned, clouding her mind and awakening her senses. "I'm not looking for *her* secrets, I'm looking for my husband's!" she snapped without thinking.

Immediately he released her and she stumbled back, covering her mouth with a trembling hand. What had she done? Why had she revealed the truth to this man?

He stared at her with a hooded gaze. "What the hell are you talking about?"

"Nothing," she mumbled as she cast her eyes down to the dirty floor. "I didn't mean anything."

He frowned. "I'm not stupid. Just what are you doing here really?

And don't tell me finishing your late husband's work because I didn't buy that the first time you said it. There are plenty other archeologists at the British Museum who could take on that task. And you certainly didn't come equipped with the right tools for a dig." His fingers curled around her shoulders, this time gently. "Tell me the truth, Isabella. Maybe I could help you."

She gazed up into eyes so blue she was reminded of the ocean on a clear day. She could almost believe in him. Almost.

"And why would you want to help me?" she whispered.

His head dipped lower, moving ever closer to her lips. "I have no idea."

Just as their mouths met, the moan cut through the room as if the owner of the voice were right outside the door. Isabella jolted back.

"Anya," she said as she skittered away from Jake's grip. "I must find Anya."

Gathering her skirt into one hand and a torch in the other, she hurried from the room. Away from the man who drew her in such powerful and puzzling ways.

The moans told her which way to turn, which way to go. She followed them blindly until she stood outside another chamber. She could only pray Anya was inside. Once she found her friend, she knew she could fight the undeniable attraction that drew her to Jake Turner. If only she really wanted to fight it.

Taking a deep breath, she stepped inside.

"An—" she began, but then stopped dead at what she saw.

Her friend was there, and so were Surai and Jake's friend Rafe. But they were engaged in an activity that guaranteed they cared very little about who came into the room.

Anya was leaning back against a pillar, Surai kissing her deeply, while Rafe slipped the last of her under things from her smooth, round hips.

Chapter Three

Why the hell was he chasing this woman?

Jake ducked under a low beam and skidded around a corner as he continued his search to find the wily Isabella Winslow. She didn't mean a thing to him. She'd been a hindrance to his plans for the tomb, then nothing more than a fellow prisoner. Now she was something more. A sensual partner in a game he had no idea how to win.

He paused at a crossroad in the winding tomb and licked his lips. God, he could still taste her there. Heady and warm like her thighs had been as they clenched and she screamed out release. He still throbbed from his own orgasm, the one she'd brought with a skillful mouth. But he wanted more. He wanted to plunge into the warmth of her body, to feel her womb contract around him as he plundered her.

He wanted to fuck her until she shuddered beneath him and came as hard as she'd come when he sucked her clit.

He shook his head to make those images go away. This wasn't like him. He'd known plenty of women, had more than his fair share of their warm and willing bodies over his years of world travel. None had ever distracted him so completely.

This was an emergency, for God's sake, not some party. Here he was, trapped in a tomb, his friend and partner missing, and all he could think about was bending Isabella Winslow over the nearest pillar and making her scream his name.

Ridiculous.

And completely exciting. He adjusted in the hopes his throbbing cock would settle down.

"Jake."

He came to a complete stop and looked around. The dim corridor was empty as far as he could see in every direction. Only the hieroglyphics kept him company, yet he knew he'd heard his name.

"Jake."

There it was again, echoing around him in the darkness. It sounded like Isabella's voice far in the distance. Soft and low like a whisper in a bedroom.

"Isabella?" he called out, only to have his words bounce back off the tomb walls to his ears. She didn't respond. Jake hurried down the corridor in the direction of the voice and came to a stop again when he heard the moan that had been taunting them since the cave-in.

A woman being well-pleasured he had told himself, right before he and Isabella had lost all control and pleasured each other. Were the two things connected? Isabella claimed to believe in science, not superstition like curses, but even she'd admitted she didn't normally allow a man she hardly knew to bring her to shattering orgasm on the floor of a tomb.

Jake believed in science, too. But he also believed in his instincts. They were telling him there was something more going on in Merytsat's tomb than met the eye.

"Jake."

Isabella's voice was more urgent now, filled with a need that tingled through him to harden him even farther. He rounded a corner through the empty door of a new chamber and came to a sudden halt. The three people he and Isabella had been searching for stood against the back wall. They weren't hurt as feared. In fact, Anya, Surai and Rafe looked anything but injured. All three were naked and it was obvious they'd begun the process of making love.

Anya's dark hair had fallen over her exotic face, but by the way her hips ground against Rafe's lips, Jake had no doubt she was enjoying every moment of what was happening to her. Meanwhile, Surai, the huge guard who'd given Jake pause when he'd first encountered Isabella's party, was standing behind Anya, massaging her breasts as he sucked along her slender neck.

Jake couldn't move or say a word, even though he knew he should either stop the threesome and insist they all exit the tomb, or leave to allow them their privacy. Instead, he stayed, fixed in that spot and unable to look away until a soft whimper grabbed his attention.

Isabella.

He turned and saw her leaning one hand against the nearest pillar. Like she had been in the room filled with erotic images, she was staring at the threesome with wide, glazed eyes. Shocked, yes, as any good Victorian woman would have convinced herself she should be, but there was something more. She was aroused. It was clear by the way she licked her lips as Rafe dragged his tongue away from Anya's glistening slit and glided it up the long length of her body.

And when Surai urged Anya to her knees and slowly, gently parted her legs to enter her from behind, Isabella's hips lifted along with her friend's. Jake moved closer, but Isabella didn't seem to notice. He positioned himself so he could watch both the threesome in the corner and her reaction to her voyeuristic pursuits.

Surai thrust into Anya with long, smooth strokes, ones she met with little gasps and moans. Then the maid looked up at Rafe with a smile and wrapped her hand around the hard shaft of his erection. Slowly, she glided her tongue around the head, only stopping from time to time to moan out her encouragement to Surai as he pumped into her with a slow, lazy rhythm.

Finally, Anya took Rafe's cock entirely into her mouth and matched Surai's pace as she sucked him. Jake's friend tangled his fingers into her dark hair, gently urging her to suck faster or harder with just the flick of his wrist. She followed his silent orders with the expertise of a woman who took two men at once all the time, but Jake knew that couldn't be true. This had to be new to Anya, as it was to Rafe and probably Surai. Yet, like what had happened to Jake and Isabella in the chamber a short time before, they seemed to be swept away, their inner desires and pleasures awakened by something in the tomb. Nothing seemed shocking to any of them, and none seemed uncomfortable with their decadent acts.

Jake shivered as Surai grasped the long, silky coils of Anya's hair and eased her up into a standing position. He continued to thrust into her even as he backed up to sit down on a huge fragment of a shattered pillar.

He found himself moving, too, edging ever closer until he stood just behind Isabella. She was getting more and more excited as she watched Anya lift off of Surai's cock and position herself differently.

The guard spread the soft cheeks of her rear end, bending to tongue her there for a brief moment before he spread her wider and eased his cock into the tight, little hole. Anya writhed, gripping Surai's arms as he nudged further and further inside her, stretching her gently and allowing her plenty of time to get used to this new invasion.

Reaching around, Jake found the buttons of Isabella's shirt and slowly slipped them open. He eased his hands beneath her silky chemise. She gasped in surprise, but didn't pull away. Instead she leaned back, pressing her body against his and grinding her backside against his throbbing erection until he could have exploded at that very moment.

As he massaged her breasts, flicking the hard beads of her nipples to elicit a little gasp of pleasure from her, he watched the threesome in the corner. Now Surai had completed his entry into Anya. He reached around to spread her legs, opening her like a flower to Rafe's eyes. As Surai pumped against her, Rafe dropped to his knees and began to lick Anya's clit. Even across the room, Jake could hear the sucking sound as he rolled it with his tongue and let it slip in and out of his mouth.

Anya wailed, thrusting back against Surai as she tangled her fingers in Rafe's thick, blond hair. Just as she was about to orgasm, Rafe stood up. Bracing himself against her legs, he eased inside her until she was sandwiched between the two men. Anya didn't seem to mind. In fact, her wail became a scream as she thrashed out an orgasm that had both men gripping at her as they thrust in time.

As the grunts and moans from the other group bounced off the walls behind them, Isabella turned her head and sucked Jake's lower lip. Her mouth was hot on his skin, burning him, making him mad with desire. Desire he chose not to fight anymore. With a groan, he shoved her skirt up around her waist. As he fumbled with the fly of his own trousers, he slipped his opposite finger between her lips. Isabella sucked the digit obediently, rolling her tongue around him as if his forefinger were his cock. Every time she sucked, his penis twitched, longing to fill her anywhere, everywhere.

He withdrew his finger from her mouth and rubbed his hands over her behind, reveling in her soft skin before he slowly parted the globes and ran his damp finger along the cleft of her rear end. She gasped, but didn't pull away as he slowly eased the finger inside her. He pumped in and out, slowing when she moaned louder and increasing the rate when she strained against him.

"Please," she whispered and he could almost hear the tears in her voice. "Please just take me. Take me."

She didn't have to ask twice. Gripping her hips, he guided his throbbing erection to her wet entrance. He felt her humid heat against his tip before he drove up into her. She enveloped him like they were made to fit together, and was as hot and tight as he'd envisioned since the first moment he'd seen her wandering the corridors of the darkened tomb.

"Yes, yes, yes," she moaned as she braced herself against the pillar.

He withdrew until he nearly left her body, then surged forward again. She practically purred as she writhed against the stone, digging her fingers against the sandy rock, her breath coming in little pants and moans.

He plunged into her again and again, loving the way she arched and screamed with each thrust. Loving that she didn't give a damn that her cries were surely being heard by the copulating group across the room. Shc was his, and for the moment there was no one else.

Finally, with an ear-shattering cry, she came. Her pussy gripped him, milking him with wet heat as she convulsed around him. It was too much to take, even for the most controlled of men and he pumped hot into her, filling her with everything he was. Then he sagged against her to lean on the pillar with a satisfied groan.

"Mmm."

Even though Jake was pinning her against the hard pillar, Isabella felt nothing but satiated pleasure. He wasn't rock hard anymore, but he was still buried deep, filling her entirely and leaving her with a sense of . . . completion.

It had been a long time since she'd had a man inside her, and she'd certainly never experienced such bliss from her husband. Hiram had stayed in the safe territory of the missionary position. Not unpleasant, but never explosive, never addictive.

Her eyes fluttered open at that thought. What was she doing? Back in the chamber with the erotic art, she'd convinced herself that fear had driven her to such wild abandon with Jake. She'd sworn privately and even to him that she wouldn't allow it to happen again, yet here she was with his cock buried inside her. With her body twitching around him with the remainders of her pleasure.

Twice she had surrendered to needs she'd never even known she had. She could no longer pretend that surrender didn't mean something more than just fear. She'd abandoned all her standards, thrown away her inhibitions. In the outside world, coming upon her friend having a threesome with two men would have shocked and even horrified her. Here, it had made her an animal of lust. Out of control.

The thought was terrifying.

Jake nuzzled her neck and her body lurched back to the ultra-sensitive state he always inspired.

"Am I hurting you?" he murmured against her skin.

No, he wasn't hurting her yet, but it was obvious how easily he could do just that. Whatever was driving her to find sexual release at every turn was also driving her to Jake Turner. And not just because he was the nearest man available. While watching Anya with her men, Isabella had wanted to feel a man inside her. But not just any man.

The only person she'd wanted was Jake.

"Isabella?" he repeated.

"No, you aren't hurting me." She shook her head and the stubble on his chin rasped across her neck to set off an explosion in her nerves. She had to find a way to fight these urges, and the only way she knew was to escape the tomb.

She peered around the pillar to the rest of the large, open room. She fully expected to see Anya and the two men. It would be difficult to behave normally around her friend after what she'd witnessed, but to get out of here alive and with her sanity intact, she was willing to pretend she hadn't watched those erotic things. Hadn't been able to move until Jake touched her.

But the room was empty except for a few broken pillars and ceremonial tables. There was no sign of Anya, Surai or Rafe. Nothing but the heady scent of sex that now filled the air.

She jerked away from Jake, separating their bodies in an instant that left her empty before she shoved that emotion away.

"Anya is gone!" she cried as she motioned across the room.

Jake blinked, seemingly still lost in the haze of desire and whatever else kept driving them together. When her words finally registered, he lurched. "Gone?"

He yanked up his trousers and buttoned just the first few buttons. Coming around the pillar, he stared at the place where the threesome had been having sex.

"How is this possible?" Isabella wailed as desperation and frustration loomed up in her, threatening to overtake her with as much force as her lust had. "If we could see them . . . see them . . ."

"Fucking like animals?" he offered mildly.

She turned on him, shocked by his harsh language, and even more shocked by the images it conjured. Did everything the man said and did have to make her pant for him?

"Yes. They must have been able to see us, too. Why would they leave?"

Jake stared at her without answering and she slowly became aware of the fact that her skirt was still hiked up around her thighs and her shirtwaist was open. With an exasperated sigh, she yanked the fabric close to her chest.

"Is that all you can think about?" she snapped with more anger than she felt.

He arched an eyebrow. "You don't have to pretend like it isn't all *you* can think about, too. I haven't exactly been raping you, you know." He stepped closer and ran his hands over the fists she clutched around her shirt. "In fact, you've been most willing."

She swallowed, unable to combat the truth. She had been willing. In fact, standing so close to him and looking up into his eyes, she knew if he pushed her hands aside to touch her, she'd spread herself open for him again. There was something addictive about their joining. Something . . . magical.

"Why is this happening?" she whispered, unable to keep up the façade of bravery she'd shown him until that very moment. "We've been stuck in this tomb for hours, yet until we came upon them making love, we haven't seen or heard anything from our friends. And every time we spend more than five minutes in one spot together, we can't keep from tearing each other's clothes off." Her eyes stung with tears as she thought about Hiram and his behavior in Cairo. "Are we going crazy? Is this some kind of madness?"

For the first time since she'd met him, Jake's face softened. He didn't look like a man who wanted to ravish her, he looked like he wanted to take care of her. It made her heart lurch with sudden emotion and she wasn't sure which option was more dangerous.

"It isn't madness," he reassured her. "But I don't know what it is. You say you don't believe in magic or curses, but this isn't normal behavior for either of us." He smiled and her blood heated. "Not that I'm complaining."

"I don't know what I believe anymore," she admitted with a sigh as she leaned back on a pillar.

He wrinkled his brow. "Do you mean you're beginning to agree with me that something unnatural is happening in this tomb?"

Her bottom lip quivered uncontrollably as she lifted her gaze to his. She had to put a great deal of trust in this man, and trust was a gift she'd been punished for giving in the past. Still, staring up into the Mediterranean blue of his eyes, she felt . . . safe.

"Yes. There's no other explanation for why we can't find our friends or another door even though I've studied the plans for this tomb in detail." She sighed and tried to regain her composure. She failed and the tears flowed freely. "There's no reason why Anya would disappear with your friend and Surai, then show back up only to be indulging herself with both men."

Jake nodded. "So this isn't her standard behavior?"

"No." She sighed. "Anya has had feelings for Surai for months and never acted on them even though I know she's had ample opportunities. Is your friend Rafe the kind of man who would . . ." Blood heated her cheeks. "Do that?"

A small smile turned up one corner of Jake's mouth. "No. At least not under these circumstances."

She let her gaze drop to the dusty floor. Even the scientific use of deduction was leading her to a supernatural answer, no matter how she tried to pretend it wasn't possible. She ran a hand over her hair absently. "Besides, I know Anya wouldn't leave me once we'd found each other again. No matter what."

Jake reached out and brushed a tear from her cheek. Slowly, he raised his damp finger to his lips and licked the tear away. "And what about you and me?"

She shivered because his gaze had transformed from the kind and comforting one to one of desire. A desire she felt growing in herself, despite their predicament.

"I don't know what is drawing us together in this explosive way," she said on a sigh. "I can tell you I did find you handsome and was drawn to you, even when you leveled your gun in my face. But until the entrance to the tomb caved in, I was able to control that attraction."

"Are you sorry you can't anymore?" he asked softly as he slipped an arm around her waist to pull her closer. His breath heated her face, heated her blood. Made her want.

"I don't know," she whispered as her tears subsided. What he was asking her was so dangerous to her heart, but she felt as drawn to tell him to the truth as she did to take his body into hers. "Being with you has been . . . amazing. I'm not sure why this is happening, but I don't think I'd want to take it back."

He rewarded her honesty by dipping his head for a kiss. "You're not alone," he murmured as he probed his tongue between her lips. She arched against him. "I've never been this out of control with any woman before. I like it."

She shook her head, but was unable to break away from his kiss. How could being out of control, being unable to direct the longings of their bodies, be a good thing?

Finally, Jake managed to pull away. His face was flushed with need and his eyes sparkled. She nearly went down on her knees with the power of her disappointment, even though she knew keeping her distance, denying whatever was driving them together, was the only way she could hope to overcome this power and find a way out of the tomb.

"Isabella." His voice shook. "You told me in the cavern before you ran away that you weren't looking for Merytsat's secrets, you were looking for your husband's."

She nodded weakly, still reeling from her body's powerful drive to feel him. "Yes. I came here to find out what happened to him and why."

"Tell me more." Jake reluctantly moved away to one of the few broken pillars that littered the chamber and sat down on the stone. "Perhaps it can help us figure out what's happening to us."

She sighed. It was so humiliating to talk about Hiram and his death. But Jake was right. Her mortification was a small price to pay for her escape and her life. She stared at the handsome man she hadn't known just a day before. Though he was little more than a stranger, she knew he wouldn't judge her on Hiram's indiscretions. He wouldn't mock her.

With that thought relieving her, she began to tell her tale. "Hiram and I were married a few years ago. We had a good marriage, even though we had little in common but our love for the Egyptian culture and history. I was more than happy to relocate from London to Cairo. And although I wasn't allowed to join him on his digs, I enjoyed the tales he told me and the artifacts I was allowed to research after his return."

Jake nodded, but she thought she saw a flash of jealousy darken his eyes to nearly midnight. Then it was gone and she wondered if she'd imagined it. She must have. This man hardly knew her, surely he couldn't be jealous of her dead husband. Her eyes strayed down to his lap. Even if he was, he certainly didn't have anything to fret about. He was far superior to Hiram in so many ways.

"Something must have changed," he said quietly.

She shrugged and looked at the room around them. "Hiram came to this tomb. That's when everything changed. He was supposed to be away from Cairo for just two weeks. That stretched to a month with no word on his whereabouts. I was worried enough that I contacted the officials for the British Museum in Cairo. After reviewing the facts, they sent out a search party. Before they'd been gone for three days, they all returned to the city together. Apparently they met my husband and his crew along the road. Hiram scolded me for being such a worrying wife." She shivered. "But he was different right away."

"How?" Jake leaned forward with his elbows draped over his knees.

"He'd always taken his findings immediately to the Museum field offices in the past. We would do our examinations there and properly catalog the relics. This time, he illegally smuggled artifacts into our home. He was secretive and distracted. He went out at all times of night without explanation. And in our bed—"

She swallowed as Jake's eyes widened. Was this something she really wanted to share?

"Go on." His voice was choked.

"H-Hiram had always been a courteous lover to me," she stammered with a fierce blush. "He treated sex like a business that had to be done and the sooner, the better. But when he returned, he was different. He was rough with me. Not hurting me, but like an animal. Like he hardly saw me at all."

Jake didn't say anything, but the look of rage on his face was plain. The idea of Hiram taking her like that obviously bothered him.

"He told me I was unsatisfactory in bed." Her voice caught on the embarrassment she still felt. "And his passions for me faded, which I admit, was not an entirely bad thing since he was growing more and more aggressive. He began to find his pleasure elsewhere, and made no effort to hide it."

"He publicly cuckolded you?"

She hesitated a long, awful moment before she managed one short nod. "I caught him being pleasured by a parlor maid in my own bedchamber. When he saw me standing there, too shocked to say a word, all he did was tell me to shut the door."

Jake murmured a curse beneath his breath.

"Later, at a party at the Ambassador's mansion, he snuck off with the ambassador's wife. I went searching for him with some of the museum staff and we found him tied to a bed, with her riding him. Word of that indiscretion went all the way back to London and he nearly lost his job. I was utterly humiliated, yet nothing I said or did impressed upon him the seriousness of the situation. He was risking both our marriage and his career with his out of control behavior."

"And apparently, his life," Jake muttered, though his eyes never left hers.

She shivered. "Yes, apparently."

She drew in a shaky breath and readied herself to continue with the last and most humiliating part of her story. "The night he died, he told me I should find a less demanding lover to fulfill my small needs because he no longer intended to waste his pleasure on a woman too cold to enjoy it fully. He left our house and went to buy two Egyptian whores. He died in their arms before morning. The doctor said something about his heart giving way, though he'd never had any troubles with his health before."

Jake flinched. "Your husband was an idiot not to see what a passionate creature you are. The fact that you weren't enough for him speaks volumes about his lack of taste."

She couldn't help a smile at his defense. It warmed her heart after so many embarrassing months alone. "I appreciate that."

"So what made you decide his personality changes had to do with this tomb?" he asked. "I mean, a woman like you, one who's dedicated to scientific explanation, would surely explore other options before organizing an expedition and heading out for a dangerous trek across the desert to a place like this."

"Yes." Her heart lightened as she winked. "You never know what kind of scoundrels might be waiting for you in abandoned tombs."

He laughed and the rich, deep sound touched some part of her. It made her tingle with sexual energy, but there was something more. In all the years of her marriage, Hiram had never listened to her with the kind of focused attention Jake used. He'd never watched her every move, hung on her every word. Laughed at her jokes.

"So what did make you come?" he asked, neatly interrupting her troubling thoughts.

"When the circumstances of his death came to light in public, the officials at the museum came to raid the house. They found all kinds of items from this tomb. His name was pulled through the dirt in our professional circles. He was called a robber and—" She paused apologetically. "And a tomb raider. When I began to clean up the mess from their search, I found Hiram's diary. It detailed his trip to Merytsat's tomb. And I also found something else. An artifact he'd hidden so well that the museum hadn't found it. He talked about it endlessly in entry after entry in his book. He said he was drawn to it, obsessed with it. So I took the artifact and came here, hoping to find out more."

She sighed as she finished her story.

Jake rose from the shattered pillar. "You have the artifact with you now?"

She nodded and grabbed her bag. Reaching in, she wrapped her hand around the piece and felt its power throb through her, just as she had every time she touched it.

"Yes." With a sigh, she pulled the item from her bag and held it out to him.

He gasped as he stared at it. A stone phallus, perfectly carved to mimic a man's fully erect member.

Chapter Four

Jake had visited many foreign lands on his archeological digs. He'd seen sex toys of all kinds both in person and in pictures. Still, the sight of Isabella holding the stone dildo took his breath away.

What made the piece special were the delicate carvings etched with painstaking detail on every side of the stone shaft. Engravings of Merytsat, whore of a pharaoh, bringing herself pleasure. It was evident she had been as talented at that as she'd been rumored to be with the men of her time.

Reaching out, he ran his hand along it and was greeted by a rush of erotic energy. Had it come from the sexual power that snapped between Isabella and him, or the toy itself? He wasn't sure. He did know he was beginning to feel that low ache in his belly. The one that told him he was going to lose control and need Isabella again.

Her eyes gleamed as she looked up at him. Her wants were clear there. Hot desires, the kind her husband had been unable to spark in her.

That thought gave him more pleasure than was healthy.

"You believe finding this artifact was what made your husband so out of control?" he asked, his voice rough as he tried to rein in his body.

She nodded slowly. "A bit like us, don't you think?"

He continued to stare at the dildo, wondering if it could possibly be true. Could something such as this make a man mad with desire? So out of control that he would kill himself with sex?

She blushed. "I-I know it looks like a . . . a . . ."

"A cock," he supplied, watching the flush of her skin darken in the dim glow of the torches. "Fully erect and ready to service a woman in heat."

He knew that was unnecessary, but watching Isabella's nipples tighten beneath her shirt was worth the crude words.

"Yes." She smiled, the look a little feline and full of lusty power. "If you're wondering, you stack up nicely against it."

He grinned despite the shot of almost painful pleasure that worked through him all the way to the twitching head of his cock. "Thanks."

She shook her head, trying to clear it. Jake knew it wasn't going to be that easy. Once they started down this road of lust, it didn't seem like it was possible to go back. One thing would eventually lead to another and they'd be joined, experiencing the power of each other's touch.

He ached just thinking about it.

She let him hold the phallus as she turned her back to look around the large, open room. "I've been studying ancient artifacts for years, even before my marriage, but I've never seen anything like it. Perhaps that's why it draws me."

He nodded, though she couldn't see him. Sure. That was why the hard thrust of a stone cock enthralled her. The novelty. Still, if that made her feel better, he wasn't going to debate the point.

He examined the sex toy carefully. "I've read about the sexual customs of the Egyptians, but I admit, I've never seen anything like this, either."

She turned, but avoided his eyes. "What—" She licked her lips. "What do you think it was used for?"

Jake reeled back. This woman who had straddled his eager tongue while she sucked him to oblivion . . . the same woman who had watched a threesome and allowed him to fuck her until he was nearly comatose . . . she didn't understand what a woman in any time would do with an object such as this?

He was more than happy to show her.

Taking a step forward, he invaded her personal space. "You can't guess?"

She drew in a harsh breath, but shook her head slowly.

Jake dropped to his knees on the sandy floor, taking his time so he could watch every inch of her. She made a soft sound of pleasure in the back of her throat and it nearly unmanned him. Using the stone phallus, he stroked along her leg, still wrapped in the heavy cotton of her long skirt. With his other hand, he inched the fabric up and up, revealing her soft, pale skin to the firelight.

"Jake," she breathed and dropped her head back as she gripped his shoulders with both hands for support.

He leaned forward and blew a hot burst of air through her skirt, right at the apex of her thighs. Her knees buckled and he caught her with one hand to ease her to a sitting position on one of the broken pillars behind her.

"Relax," he said softly as he pushed her skirt all the way up. She splayed out before him, spread wide for his greedy eyes. He could have done anything his heart desired and the power of that increased his passion tenfold.

Gliding the stone artifact up her inner thigh, he measured his breathing. He wanted to be careful, slow and let her get all the pleasure she deserved, especially after she'd been forced to admit her darkest and most embarrassing secrets. He knew her candidness about Hiram had cost her.

He pushed her outer lips apart to reveal her sex. It gleamed in the light, wet with a combination of the juices he'd spent in her earlier and the ones made by her own desire when he touched her.

"This is what the ancient Egyptians used to do with these," he whispered. "What modern women still do in the privacy of their bedchambers and for the pleasure of their men."

With that, he stroked the stone phallus across her slit. She responded by lifting her hips with a sharp cry.

"Cold?" he asked as he watched her slick skin darken with increased desire.

"A little," she gasped. "But good, so good."

"You could tease yourself with this like I just did," he said as he breathed in her womanly scent. "Or if you get it wet, you could put it inside you like you would a man's cock. Either way, you could pleasure yourself with it. But judging from what you told me about her, I'd wager Merytsat pleasured both herself *and* her lovers with it."

"How?" she asked breathlessly, keeping her head dipped back as he stroked her.

"By letting them watch while she did this."

"They watched?" Her voice wavered and he was surprised that her skin had flushed even deeper. Apparently he had touched on one of Isabella's own hidden fantasies.

With a nod, he stroked her again. His excitement ratcheted up each time he fondled her. "Or by letting them please her with it as I'm doing to you now."

"It arouses you to do this to me?" she panted as her fingers curled around the edge of the pillar, clutching for a hold as she fought to keep her orgasm at bay for as long as possible.

"More than I could tell you," he answered, just inching the head of the phallus inside her. When he pulled it back out, it was dark with wetness. "She might have also let him use it on her while he was inside her. Kind of like making love to two men while remaining true to one."

She shivered and he knew she was thinking of what they'd witnessed between Surai, Rafe and Anya earlier. Her body contracted around the sex toy, trembling wildly as she danced on the edge of her explosion.

"Jake."

He looked up into her face to find her staring down at him. Her eyes shone as she glided her hand down to cup his cheek. The gentle gesture, so kind and loving when he knew she was feeling the burning heat of an orgasm, threw him off guard. His own reaction shocked him all the more.

Even in the midst of his lust-addled responses, her touch brought something even stronger to the forefront of his mind. A burst of tender emotion he'd never felt for a woman before, for anyone before. It was so powerful that he rocked back away from her, withdrawing the dildo and pulling away from her caress.

"Jake?" she repeated, her hand still outstretched as her expression changed to one of confusion. "Is everything all right?"

His fist contracted around the stone phallus and his heart raced. Was this some new trick of the tomb? These feelings, these wants that had nothing to do with sex? If they were, then why didn't they feel like a manipulation? Why did they feel so real?

"Jake?" Isabella's voice was filled with real concern and her eyes sparkled with more than just lust.

"Nothing," he stammered as he leaned back toward her.

With a relieved smile, she reached to cup his cheek again, but he dodged her. Instead, he took her hand and guided it to her breast, encouraging her to touch herself while he finished what he'd begun.

He pressed the dildo back against her clit and she let out a soft cry, one that made his cock ache and his heart swell with those strange emotions again. The complications he didn't need and hadn't wanted until that very moment.

Jake shut his eyes. This was only desire. Nothing more. He would give Isabella release. He would make her scream out his name, but he couldn't give her a piece of his life or his heart.

With that intent, he ground the head of the stone phallus against her clit. She clutched at her breasts with a keening cry then shuddered uncontrollably as she came. Jake watched her face as she moved through ultimate pleasure into relaxed satiation. She was so beautiful, so pure despite all the carnal pleasures they'd shared since being trapped together.

She let out a long sigh of satisfaction, then gave him a sensual smile. "Why don't you come down here?" she whispered on a short breath. "I want to feel you inside me."

How he wanted that, too, but his feelings were too raw, too close to the surface. He was afraid if he let her take him into her arms, he would do or say something stupid. Something he couldn't take back. Something that could only hurt them both once they'd escaped the tomb and the curse was lifted.

"No," he muttered as he pushed to his feet and shoved the damp sex toy into her hand.

She took it with a jump of surprise and slowly rose, smoothing her skirts down as she did so.

"What's wrong?"

"We-we don't have time for this," he muttered. Even as he said it, he knew it sounded like a cold lie. After all, he had been the one who'd stalled them when their friends had disappeared. But he could think of no other excuse when his body was still pounding hot and his mind was running scared. "We should look for the others. Come on."

With that, he grabbed a torch off the wall and motioned to the corridor. Even though he didn't look behind him, he felt her follow him. He also felt confusion and hurt emanating from her, but he couldn't bring himself to comfort her. If he did, he knew he wouldn't be able to escape the strong feelings that had begun in his heart. A place no woman had ever touched.

Isabella fought tears as she stumbled along the dark corridor behind Jake. She could only just see him in the circle of light from his torch and he seemed in no mood to wait for her. He didn't want to talk, either. When she tried, his response had been mere grunts.

What had happened to change his attitude? They'd been so close to making love. Her body still throbbed with the incessant need to have him inside her. Yet his face had twisted with . . . what was it? Horror? Fear? Disgust?

He'd pulled away, leaving her empty in more ways than one. She hated herself for it. Hated herself for coming to need this man in such a short period of time. She'd depended on a man before and he'd let her down. Hiram had promised to be there for her, but in the end he'd tossed her aside like so much refuse. A man like Jake could be no different. In fact, he had to be worse. He was a scoundrel. A tomb raider. A seducer of women.

She looked up the corridor at his broad back. It was so much easier to think of his unappealing qualities when she wasn't looking into his eyes. Now if only she could believe her condemnations in her heart.

With a sigh, she hurried forward to keep up with his long strides. She'd almost reached him when a noise echoed in the corridor around her.

The moan again. That rich, feminine moan that seemed to come from nowhere and everywhere all at once. The one that had her dripping wet in an instant, longing to be touched. To be filled to the hilt by a man. And not just any man. By Jake.

"Did you hear that?" she called out in the darkness.

His sigh echoed back toward her. "Hear what?"

"The moan." She stopped in the pathway and closed her eyes. It came in the distance again. "There it was."

"I didn't hear it," he insisted as he glanced over his shoulder at her. Just as quickly, he looked away and her heart stung with rejection. "Come on, maybe we should try this path."

She ignored him as she continued to listen intently. An undeniable urge to follow the sounds of passion persisted, even if Jake didn't want to listen. She shut her eyes and moved away from him. She found her way by hearing, sensing along the corridors with only her touch and ears to guide her.

The moans seemed to increase in intensity as she moved forward, pulling her toward something, making her body quiver with the anticipation of what that something might be.

This was madness. She knew it even as she followed the phantom groan. It was enough to make her believe Jake was right. This place was cursed. Haunted by the ghost of a concubine who had risen to the status of goddess.

Then, as quickly as they had begun, the sounds of pleasure faded away to nothing.

Her eyes fluttered open and she realized she'd entered another chamber in the tomb. It was large and open, lit by torches that couldn't have burned for so many hundreds of generations, but still glowed nonetheless. In the center of the room was a raised platform that held a large, square pool of water.

Moving closer, she climbed the first few steps of the platform. What she saw made her gasp and she stumbled over a missed step. The pool still held water, even after so many years beneath the dry sands. Even more outrageous was that the water was perfectly clean, as if the pool had been filled that very hour.

She looked down into the crystal waters at the cool marble that shone up from the depths. After so many hours of being trapped in the dusty tomb her muscles ached for a soak and her body screamed out to be washed.

"This is crazy," she murmured, but she found her hands moving up to her loosen bun as if by their own volition. One by one, she found the pearl pins that held her locks in place and her blonde hair fell in a fragrant wave around her face. Her scalp tingled as the air hit it, releasing the heat that had been pressed against her skin all day long.

"Isabella!" Jake's voice echoed just outside the chamber door.

She wanted to answer him, but the draw of the pool was a much stronger one. She *had* to climb into the water. She needed it more than she needed her next breath.

She unbuttoned her shirtwaist next and shimmied out of her skirt. Her mind emptied as she dipped a toe into the waters. They were cool on her sore feet and parched skin and she released a hiss of pleasure as she let her entire leg dip over the marble edge. When the juncture of her thighs hit the water, she nearly collapsed. It felt like the cool touch of a man's lips on her hot and throbbing body, but then the sensation was gone, snatched away as Jake had snatched away his body earlier.

"Isabella."

It was Jake's voice again, but this time he was inside the chamber. With effort, she turned her face toward the door and saw him as if she were looking through a fog. He stared at her, his mouth open just a fraction, but he no longer called her name. It was as if he, too, was controlled by the powerful forces in the chamber and could only watch her.

She lounged back against the smooth marble, enjoying the feel of her hot skin cooling in the lukewarm waters. She let her head dip under the surface, slicking her hair back as she emerged for a gulp of air.

Isabella began to smooth her hands over her skin. Even without soap, she was able to wipe some of the sandy grime from her body. She smoothed over her arms, her face, and finally her fingers brushed over her breasts.

Her nipples hardened to the touch, throbbing until she couldn't resist another swipe over them. The water allowed for no friction, just the glide of skin on skin. And the little beads seemed even more sensitive than usual, puckered from being suckled and rubbed so many times by a man's hands.

Leaning back against the marble, Isabella shut her eyes and simply caressed her own skin, imagining a lover's hands drifting over her, lazily arousing her in preparation for lovemaking.

She pictured her imaginary lover's body, hard from years of work, sculpted by muscle and strong, yet gentle. Then she pictured his face. Jake's image danced into her mind.

At the same time, she heard him take a sharp breath from the chamber door. When she looked at him, he had gripped his hands into fists at his sides. The jut of his cock was perfectly outlined on the front of his fitted beige trousers and his eyes were focused on her. Watching intently as she glided her hands over her breasts and tugged at her nipples.

She started at the look of desire on his face, sending a splash of water over the edge of the tub to slap against her bag. With a curse, she leaned over the marble edge and snatched it up. She reached inside to insure nothing important had gotten soaked and her hand found the stone dildo.

When her fingers clutched at the stone, that same thrill rushed through her. A thrill of desire, of sensual power. Of need. She let the bag fall and pulled the phallus into the tub with her.

She wondered what it would feel like to plunge this into her body. Jake had only teased her, refusing to enter her with it or with his own cock. It had left her aching and curious. And not just about the feel of the toy. When he'd told her about what women did to pleasure themselves and their men with objects such as this, it had given her a burst of sexual curiosity. Especially the idea of a man watching his woman pleasure herself with the stone phallus.

With a smoldering glance for Jake, she let the sex toy dip under the water. When she rubbed the unyielding stone against her stomach, her body crackled with awareness and need. She rasped it against her nipples and couldn't hold back the sigh that escaped her lips.

Across the room, Jake groaned. A surge of power moved through her. She was torturing him just as he'd tortured her earlier. He wanted her, but couldn't have her. And while she brought herself pleasure, she would also be bringing him to a fever pitch of desire.

She spread her legs wide and teased the head of the phallus along her inner thigh and up across her opening. Her sigh turned to a moan as she brushed along her clitoris. It swelled beneath the touch, hardened to exquisite sensitivity. She knew just a few strokes would bring her to completion, so she only teased herself with it. She rubbed the phallas along her outer lips, spreading herself with its head. When her fingertips brushed her slit, she was slick with desire.

Her hand seemed to move of its own volition now, swiping up and down, rolling along her clit just enough that she cried out with ecstasy, then backing away before she could find release.

Knowing Jake was in the room, panting out breaths in time with her, only made her desire more potent. Her need to come all the more intense. When she was writhing, sending bath water sloshing over the edge of the pool with a smooth rhythm, she plunged the stone cock into her body. She exploded around it, wailing and thrusting wildly as her orgasm consumed her, overtook her, so strong that it nearly made her lose consciousness.

She released the sex toy with a sigh as she slumped against the side of the pool, but didn't withdraw it from her body. She liked the way its unyielding hardness felt inside her.

Shutting her eyes, she let herself relax for a moment. She blocked out her worries about Anya and the others. Forgot her obsession with the truth about Hiram. And most of all, pushed away thoughts of Jake Turner and the fact that the pleasure he had brought her with his body far eclipsed anything she'd ever given herself.

Jake's body hummed with need. It coursed through every nerve, every fiber of his being, at once insanely erotic and intensely painful. He'd never wanted a woman more, but something in the room, something in the air kept him from taking her. He was forced to watch, motionless, as she pleasured herself with the ancient sex toy.

God, how he wanted to touch her. To fill her. But those other emotions, the ones that had sent him reeling, were still present. If anything, watching as she arched up in the pool of water just out of his reach only made those emotions stronger. He wanted to be inside her, but not just for his own pleasure. He wanted to give. To be the one that made her writhe like that, and the one who set her free from the fever of passion. After she shivered in release, he wanted to be the one who held her.

His mind spun. He'd pushed her away because of those deeper desires, but now it was as if the tomb was calling him back, forcing him to see what he would lose if he didn't face his emotions.

Isabella cried out as she came, thrashing water over the floor around the elevated pool before she slumped back against the marble.

Jake's cock throbbed in time with her gasps, pressing against his trouser front, but still he couldn't find the ability to move, neither to walk away nor give in to what his heart and body wanted most and join her.

Her eyes fluttered open. Unlike earlier, when she hadn't seemed to truly see him, they were clear now. Filled with questions, as well as needs.

She sat up straighter and locked gazes with him. Her voice was husky, sultry, when she asked, "Like what you see, Mr. Turner?"

The sound of her voice shattered the spell that had restrained him. He took one step toward her as her gaze moved over every inch of him with clear intent. She wanted him as much as he wanted to be inside of her.

But her expression also reflected another emotion. The same emotion he'd seen and felt when she had caressed his face before. It told him she could curl into his life forever, if only he'd ask.

Even more stunning was that he could see himself asking for just that. He had a brief, but clear image of comforting her, learning about her life the way he'd learned the needs of her body.

"Are you going to just look?" she asked, then slowly rose from the water like a goddess.

The dark blonde strands of her hair curled around her wet breasts, framing the pale skin and making the pink circles of her nipples even more pronounced and beautiful in the torchlight. Water droplets rolled down her skin, cresting over the hills of her curves and dipping into valleys that Jake longed to taste. He wanted to lick her dry, then caress her until she was sopping wet again.

She smiled as if she'd read his mind, then snaked her hands down between her legs. He watched wide-eyed as she eased the stone sex toy out of her body and set it on the edge of the marble tub. "Or perhaps you want to join me?"

He realized he now had a choice. He could run again. If he did, he had no doubt Isabella would fight the influence of the tomb as hard as he had, to keep her heart from being broken.

Or he could go to her. He could take everything she offered, from her lush body to her fragile heart.

But he had to choose now.

He didn't say a word, just shucked off his boots and clothes as fast as he could. He stepped into the water and for a moment was distracted by how good the cool sensation was against his overheated skin.

"That's right," she whispered, moving over to his side. She placed a hand on each shoulder and gently shoved him to a sitting position. "Relax. I'll wash you off."

She straddled his body and he reached for her, eager to enter her, to claim her. But she pushed him back.

"We're trapped," she said with a wry smile. "We've got all the time in the world. Let's enjoy it."

He bit back a moan as her hands began to slide down his body. She moved slowly, almost reverently, rubbing over his arms, his sides. She shifted closer until he could feel the entrance to her body rubbing against the head of his erection, but she didn't take him inside as she continued to touch him. He couldn't remember when a woman had spent so much time focused on his pleasure and his pleasure alone.

She glided her palms down the muscles of his chest, tangling her fingers in the soft hair before she flicked a thumb across his nipple.

His penis twitched against her in reaction. For a brief moment, she shut her eyes on a moan, then smiled. "You like that, do you?"

"I do." He lifted his hips until he brushed her slit again. "And I like that, too."

"So do I," she groaned. "But I'm not finished yet."

Her hands continued to move, spending time caressing his nipples, then moving down his stomach. She paused when she brushed against the scar that traversed his side.

"What is this from?"

He opened his eyes and gazed up at the ceiling high above. If he was truly surrendering to the effects of the tomb, to the effects of Isabella, he would have to give her some of his past. To his surprise, the reality of that wasn't as terrifying as he'd thought it would be.

"A dispute over rights to a tomb. Two years ago." He smiled. "You should have seen the other guy."

"How long have you been raiding tombs?" she asked as she adjusted her position and began to stroke her fingers along his legs. He stiffened when her hand closed briefly around the length of his cock.

"Five years," he said with effort.

"And do you enjoy your 'work'?" she asked, rubbing her wetness against him once more.

He locked gazes with her. "Some days more than others."

"What do you do with the antiquities you find and steal from the tombs?" she asked softly as she let the head of his cock enter her. He longed to surge all the way inside, but held back. She flexed her inner muscles around him, squeezing him rhythmically until she elicited an unbidden groan.

"What do you do with what you take?" she repeated.

"I sell some to museums or private collectors," he ground out as she let him slip into her another few, precious centimeters. "And some I donate."

She paused. "You donate?"

"Yes." He tilted his hips and she slid onto him even further.

Her gasp was a reward, as was the way she latched her legs around his waist.

"Why?" she asked, though her voice trembled.

"Why what?" He struggled to maintain his thoughts now that she had taken him into her almost to the hilt. Only a few more inches and he would be home.

"Why do you donate the things you find?" she asked. "I thought tomb raiders were motivated by the money they could make."

He shrugged as he glided his hands around to cup her rear end. The motion slid her forward and he filled her completely. A long groan issued from some deep, primal place inside him.

"Some treasures were meant to be shared," he whispered as he dipped his head to lap her nipple. She arched back and ground against him, whimpering in need.

Her reaction threw him over an edge and he responded by thrusting into her. The water allowed him leverage and a range of motion he didn't normally have. He stood up to wade into the deeper waters. He pushed her hips away, then yanked them back, using her to thrust as he pressed his mouth to hers.

She told him the rhythm she wanted by plunging her tongue into his mouth. She thrust slowly, pushing her tongue between his lips in soft time. But as her excitement grew, her mouth's movements grew quicker, more erratic. Jake kept up, taking her fast and hard as the water sloshed around them.

He loved every whimper, every moan she breathed against his skin.

Loved that he was giving everything he had to bring her pleasure. The fact that he wanted to give her more no longer terrified him.

He cupped her chin with one hand and tilted her face until she looked into his eyes. Searching, he slowed his rhythm, gentled his pace. Her eyes clouded with tears, but he knew they weren't tears of pain. He had reached her in that most emotional place, the center of her heart.

With a smile, he slid a hand between their wet bodies and found the hard nub of her clitoris. With a sweep of his finger and thumb, he drove her over the edge. Her legs latched around his waist like a vice and her spine straightened, lifting her up and against him as she cried out her pleasure and her release.

He tried to hold back, wanting more than anything to maintain control. To keep tormenting her until she came again and again, but the look of pure pleasure and the joyful tears that cascaded down her cheeks did him in. He dug his fingers into her backside and poured himself into her.

As they'd stood, locked together for what seemed like a blissful eternity, she looked down into his eyes. When he grinned at her, she gave him a wicked smile that stirred his blood, then she slithered down his body until her feet touched the bottom of the marble pool. Leaning up, she gave him a gentle kiss.

"That was amazing," she whispered as her arms came around his waist and she rested her head against his chest.

Jake looked down at her, so comfortable leaning against him, and slowly let his arms come around her waist. It was amazing. And so was this woman.

Chapter Five

Isabella rested her head on Jake's shoulder as the water in the pool lapped against their bodies with a gentle rhythm. She dragged her fingernails down his arm and loved the way the muscles bunched beneath her hand and his body tensed with pleasure.

"Do you think we'll ever get out of here?" she asked softly. "Or are we trapped forever?"

Jake drew back so he could see her face. When he looked at her, she knew he saw her fear. Fear she wouldn't have shared with just anyone.

He caressed her back, and she leaned into him, gathering strength from his warm touch.

"I'll get you out of here, Isabella. You and your friends. I promise you that," he whispered, but the power of his statement was in his words, not the level of his voice.

She knew it was a promise he might not be able to keep, but hearing him say those words helped her nonetheless. Until Jake gave up entirely, she would keep looking for a way out, too.

"You know, if I had to be trapped in a tomb that might be cursed, I'm glad I was trapped with you."

He smiled. "Me too."

He captured her cheeks between his hands. His gaze was so intense, so full of emotion that it brought tears to her eyes.

When he finally leaned down to kiss her, the reaction was even more powerful. The kiss was deep, but not possessive, not filled with the overpowering lust that had always accompanied his touch in the past. No, this was comfort, this was . . .

Love?

What did she know about love? She'd never felt that kind of powerful emotion for anyone or had it returned, even in the best of her days with Hiram.

Yet there it was, swelling in her heart, filling her with equal measures of joy and terror. Perhaps she had imagined it in Jake's kiss, but she didn't imagine it in her own soul. Somehow lust wasn't all she felt when she looked at this man. She felt love.

"You okay?" he asked as he slipped a damp lock of hair behind her ear.

For a moment, Isabella struggled for words. This wasn't the time for confessions of such complicated feelings. Not while they were trapped. Not while the powers in the tomb held such sway over both of them. For all she knew, the new emotions were just part of the game Merytsat was playing with them.

Only they felt so real.

"I'm fine," she whispered as she leaned up for another kiss. "I'm fine."

With reluctance, Jake ended the kiss, though he kept her pressed flush against him in the water. "So, now do you believe this place is cursed?"

She shrugged. It seemed crazy to talk like this, but she couldn't lie either. Not to him.

"There are things happening here that can't be explained by science. Like the woman's moan that keeps guiding us to each room. Or this pool, which should be dry or filled with rancid liquid. Instead, it's clean and filled with water that could have been pulled from a spring today. Even after we've made love in it, bathed in it, it's still fresh."

He nodded. "When you wandered away a while ago, I thought I heard your voice, but it couldn't have been you. And when I came into this room, I couldn't do anything but watch while you pleasured yourself in the pool. It was as if something was forcing me to stay in place."

"It was the same for me," she sighed as she drew small circles on his back with her fingertips. "I wanted to look at you, to call to you, but some force drove me to Merytsat's artifact and made me play out my fantasies around it. And my fantasies about you watching me."

His smile was hot and filled with desire as his hand slipped beneath the water to caress her thigh for an all-too-brief moment.

"So, what kind of curse could it be?" he asked in a voice thick with the same passion she felt when he touched her. She admired him for continuing to focus on the problem at hand. From her own experience, she knew how difficult that was. "You're the expert between the two of us. What kind of curses do tombs like this one hold?"

She shrugged. "That's the trouble. There's not another place like this that anyone knows of. Normally, these elaborate burials were left to royalty, but Merytsat wasn't a queen. She was a common girl who raised herself up in society by using her body. She gave pleasure and demanded it in return. She brought one of the most powerful Pharaohs to his knees . . . literally if you believe some of the writings about her."

He pondered that for a moment. "The curses that are detailed and warned of for a member of the royal family are meant to protect the riches they buried with them. The gold and jewels were what was important to those people. That's what they wanted waiting for them when they reached their final destination after death."

She nodded, amazed by his grasp of Egyptian history. "Yes. That's what folklore tells us."

"So what if Merytsat's curse protected what *she* held dear?" He cocked an eyebrow toward her and motioned his head toward the stone dildo Isabella had rested on the tub's edge.

"Her sex toy?" she asked with an incredulous laugh.

"Not the toy itself. What it represents. Her sexual power. Her hunger. Her life force."

Isabella rose out of the water in surprise. Jake's hypothesis made perfect sense. If there were such a thing as a curse, the woman who was buried in this place wouldn't have cared about her riches. She'd care about the things that could bring her power.

And those were the exact things Hiram had taken with him when he'd removed the artifacts buried with Merytsat.

"You know, you're much more than just a pretty face," she teased as she climbed out of the water and grabbed for her shirtwaist. "You are very smart."

He grinned. "Well, I was educated, you know. I went to university."

She stopped dressing. "You did? What did you study?"

"Archeology," he said without a hint of teasing to his voice or his face.

"What?"

He gave her a sad, fleeting smile. "In Boston. My parents wanted me to pursue medicine, but history and archeology enthralled me."

"You have a degree, but you raid tombs?" she asked with a shake of her head. "Isn't there a more official post you could take with a university or museum?"

His face tensed. "I went to university, but I don't have a degree."

She buttoned her shirtwaist before she sat down on the edge of the pool. She'd never seen Jake's emotions so clear on his face before. Anger, betrayal, but mostly hurt. Whatever had happened to keep him from completing his education was still a raw spot. And it inspired a need to comfort in her.

"What happened?" she asked.

His mouth thinned and his hands gripped into fists as they rested on the marble. "In my last year, I wrote a paper about my theories on the building of the pyramids. I proposed a field expedition to study my theory which was to be overseen by my mentor, Dr. Phillip Grasier, but conducted by me. Grasier read over my work and told me flat out that my ideas were incorrect and if I turned in the proposal I'd be laughed out of the university. I disagreed, but I appreciated his attempts to protect me."

The blood drained from Isabella's face. "But Phillip Grasier . . ."

"Did an extensive field study of the building of the pyramids five years ago, putting forth some new theories about how they were built." Jake's voice was harsh and tight, as if he were forcing the words past his lips. "When I found out he had put forth a proposal to the committee and what that proposal contained, I confronted him. He'd been my friend and mentor for four years and I couldn't believe he would really steal my ideas, my work from me. But Grasier not only told me I wasn't welcome on his expedition, he put me on academic probation. When I protested, he had me kicked out of school and put such a stain on my record that I wasn't allowed to finish my degree anywhere else."

"Oh, Jake," she whispered as she covered his hand with her own. He was still naked, powerful like the statues of gods she'd seen so many times. Yet he was a man. And there was more to him than she'd let herself believe. Much, much more.

"Is that why you became a tomb raider?" she asked, wiping a line of water from his cheek.

He nodded. "No one would let me work anywhere legitimately, but I didn't want a man like Grasier to take away what I'd dreamed of for so long. I wouldn't let him."

She blinked back sudden tears as she looked down into the face of this man who had been such a distraction and a savior to her since they'd met. She had judged him for the job he did, the job that so went against her academic sensibilities. But all along he'd only been trying to find a way to do the thing they both loved. The thing neither was allowed to do because of society. Her for being a woman, him for his lack of credentials. For the greedy robbery of a man he had revered and trusted.

"You and I are more alike than I ever thought possible," she whispered before she leaned down to brush a kiss along his jaw line. "And I believe that if any two people can figure out what's going on in this tomb, it's you and me."

"Are you saying you want to be partners with a dirty American grave robber?" he asked with a teasing smile, but in his eyes she saw the real need to hear her answer.

"More than anything."

She kissed him, pulling away only when the spark of lust between them began to grow again. As much as she wanted to sink back down into the water and worship his body, she knew their time was running short. They still had no idea where their friends were or what they were going through. They needed to find a way out.

"The key is finding Merytsat's burial chamber," Isabella said, breathless as she went back to dressing, fingers fumbling with the task. "If there was a curse put on this tomb, that's where we'll find the details of it. And maybe be able to figure out how to break it."

He grinned, a crooked smile that made him look younger and less harsh. A smile that touched her in those deep places in her heart she'd believed had gone cold.

"Where my lady leads, I shall follow."

He rose out of the tub in one smooth motion. Droplets of water cruised down his naked body and she had to force herself to look away as he dressed. It was far too tempting to push him back into the water and have her wicked way with him again.

As he buttoned the last button on his shirt, he smiled at her. "Or actually, I'll lead since I have the gun. But you get the point."

She laughed as he pulled a torch from the wall and followed him from the chamber and into the darkness of the hallways once again.

"How long have we been walking?"

Jake scrubbed a hand over his face. "Time is hard to judge here, but I'd guess about an hour."

Silence came from behind him and he didn't even have to look at Isabella. He knew he'd see the fear in her eyes and it was fear he couldn't ease. He'd promised to get her out of the tomb, but he didn't really know if that was possible.

"Should we stop to—"

She froze.

"Stop to what?" He finally turned to face her, hoping she meant stop to give into passion one more time. It was what he'd been aching to do for most of the last twenty minutes.

"Shhh." She held up a hand. "Do you hear it?"

He strained, hoping to hear Surai, Anya and Rafe. They needed all the people they could get to figure this riddle out, even if it meant interrupting their sex play. He went rock hard just thinking about it and willed himself to concentrate.

"There."

In the distance the low, needful moan floated through the corridors and sent a jolt straight to his cock. With a shiver of pure desire, he nodded. "I heard it. I think it came from this direction."

He motioned down one pathway and they followed it at a near run. When they'd gone a few steps, he felt Isabella move closer. Then her soft hand slipped into his. The shock of emotion that accompanied such a simple gesture surprised him. Just one touch from her and he was filled with desire, tenderness, but mostly pride. Her touch meant she trusted him to get her home. It meant she depended on him to keep her safe. Having her put that much faith in him was astounding and humbling.

He stopped and turned to her. The pride faded into the background, replaced by the lust that flared between them whenever they stopped for more than a moment.

Her eyes were soft in the torchlight. With the woman's moans echoing around them, Jake's desire filled him. He could tell Isabella was reacting similarly. Her chest lifted and fell on short breaths and her body swayed in his direction. He wanted her. Against the wall, on the floor, it didn't matter. He just wanted to be inside her.

He shook his head. "I think we're heading the right way."

"Yes. I want . . . well, I want to feel you inside of me. That seems to happen when she's trying to lead us somewhere." Isabella blushed.

"God, don't tell me what you want, sweetheart or we're not going to get very far," he groaned.

She nodded. "Just keep moving. Think about ugly things while we walk and maybe we can stave this off long enough to find what we're looking for. Then we can make love."

"Isabella!" His eyes grew wide with shock. He'd never expected her to say those words. Or expected it to be such a source of excitement for him.

"Okay, sorry," she stammered. "Ugly things. The sooty air of London."

"You think *soot* is going to tame my hard-on?" he asked as he dragged her down the hall. "All I think about is dirty and dirty makes me want to lay you down in the sand right here, right now—"

She made a strangled sound at the back of her throat. "Uh, war. War is ugly. You can't make something sexual out of war."

He sighed. Yes, he could. "There's a war raging inside of me right now. I'm fighting the urge to unsheathe my . . . saber."

"That's reaching a bit, isn't it?" she asked, but her voice was barely more than a squeak.

"Yeah, but you've got the image in your head, don't you?" He winked even though his erection was actually throbbing.

"Yes. The image in my head is of you and me—"

He let go of her hand to cover his ears. "Don't tell me. We're almost there and if you say one word I'm not going to be able to stop myself from ripping your clothes off and taking you."

"Wait," she said and the desire in her voice had faded a bit. "Wait, look at this doorway."

He shook away the image of Isabella stretched out naked and ready on one of the preparation tables in the chambers around them and stared where she was motioning wildly. It was a stone door, one of the first sealed chambers they'd found in their search. It had a painting on it, done in the same style as the erotic hieroglyphics in the first room where they'd made love. This one was a picture of a woman holding a dildo above her head. She wielded it like a sword.

"Merytsat's burial chamber," Jake breathed. He glanced at Isabella. She seemed mesmerized by the strong image, unable to do anything but stare up at the picture on the door. "Stand out of my way. I'll see if I can get it open."

She backed against the wall behind them. Jake was able to block her presence out for a moment while he dug into his bag and drew out a short stick. He slid it into the space around the door and pushed, hoping the leverage would assist him in getting it open. The door didn't budge.

"Can I help?" Isabella asked from behind him.

He shrugged. The extra weight couldn't hurt. "Just be careful."

She stepped into the circle of his arms, positioning herself in front of him. Her hands found a spot in the places where he didn't hold the wedge.

"Uh," he mumbled, suddenly finding concentration much more difficult with Isabella's scent filling his nostrils and her body heat permeating his clothing. "One, two, three . . ."

Before they even began to push against the door, it made a creaking noise and then rolled open. Without the wedge bearing their weight, Isabella and Jake fell backward into a pile. Isabella landed on top of him on her back, her legs splayed open. He couldn't help but imagining making love to her in this position.

Apparently, she thought of the same thing, for she pressed her backside against him with a little moan. He grabbed for her hips, pulling her up even more firmly against him. For a few moments, they lay that way, grinding against each other in slow circles that had him dancing on the edge of madness.

He was ready to hike up her skirt and just take what they both so obviously wanted when the throaty sound of a female laugh taunted them from the chamber they'd just opened. Both froze, then Isabella scrambled to her feet.

"Do-do you think she's . . . in . . . there?" she stammered and began to shiver.

Jake got up, ignoring the throbbing pain in his groin, and put an arm around her. "This isn't a ghost story," he reassured her softly. "We're going to be fine."

She nodded, but he could tell she was still scared. Hell, he was scared, even though he'd never admit it to anyone. They were about to go into the deepest chamber in the tomb. The chamber where Merytsat's body was buried. Where her presence would surely be the strongest.

They moved forward in tandem, with Isabella clinging to his arm. Inside, the chamber was dark.

"L-light the torches," she whispered.

He had to gently remove her fingers from their death grip on his shirt to do just that. When light softly filled the room and Jake's eyes had adjusted, he looked around. The space was enormous, as all burial chambers were. It was also filled with riches, things that the Ancient Egyptians believed Merytsat would want in her next life. Jewels and gold, tablets and exotic oils.

The sarcophagus sat in the middle of the room on a slightly elevated platform. Isabella moved toward it as if she were in a trance and gasped when she reached it.

"What is it?" Jake asked as he moved to her side, but he became immediately aware.

Egyptian sarcophagi almost always had the likeness of the person mummified within carved into the wood. This was no different. Merytsat stared up at them, her beautiful Egyptian face done up with colorful paints and beautiful carvings. But it was her body that was different. Instead of being memorialized in her finest gown, the artist who had done the concubine's coffin had carved her entirely naked. Only a few jewels adorned her body, including a dangling diamond that accentuated a swollen, aroused clitoris.

Isabella ran her hands down the carving. "She was beautiful. So exotic. So sensual."

Jake swallowed hard. What was sensual was watching her caress the carven image of a naked woman. He was distracted from their task by the lengthening of his penis. If he didn't have Isabella soon . . .

"Jake, look!"

He pushed back his desire and stared in the direction she pointed. A large statue sat a few feet away. It matched the hieroglyph that had guarded the door. A statue of Merytsat, her hands above her head, but the dildo that had been in her hand on the seal was missing.

Jake and Isabella stared at each other.

"The artifact," she breathed. "Hiram took it from the burial chamber. From the statue."

"Perhaps she wants it back," Jake offered as he examined the statue's face. Like the sarcophagus carving, it was done in exquisite detail. Merytsat had been extraordinarily beautiful, with a fierce warrior's face and a fine body.

"Perhaps." Isabella dug the stone sex toy from her bag and stepped forward. She looked up at the motionless, stone face. "Is that why you've trapped us here? Is that why Hiram died? Because he took this from you?"

She stood before the statue and lifted up on her tiptoes, but she couldn't quite reach Merytsat's empty hands.

"Want a boost?" Jake asked.

She nodded silently, stepping onto the hand he offered. She had perfect balance when he lifted her, and he had a great view up her skirt as she leaned up and slipped the stone phallus back into the hands of its rightful owner.

The moment the artifact was firmly attached, there was a huge crash in the distance. Once he'd lowered Isabella back to the floor, Jake spun on his heel to face the door. Had the tomb collapsed even further? Or had Merytsat shown them a way out?

"Look at this."

Isabella seemed oblivious to the noise that had rocked the tomb. She was on her knees on the dusty floor, wiping sand away from the foot of the statue with a little brush she'd produced from her bag.

"What is it?"

She smiled up at him, looking every bit the excited explorer. "It's the curse. It's Merytsat's curse." Taking a deep breath, she translated the words to English. " 'Take my secrets, but not my power. Use them for love or . . .' " She faltered.

Jake frowned. "Use them for love or what?"

Her face was pale when she lifted it to his. " 'Use them for love or suffer the consequences.' "

Chapter Six

A heavy silence hung in the air between them and for the first time, it wasn't because of desire. Isabella wondered what Jake could be thinking. Probably that the curse had killed one man in her life and he could be next.

But instead of turning away from the danger she posed to him, he took a few steps in her direction. Covering her hand with his, he gave her a squeeze.

"Your husband tried to steal Merytsat's power. Then he used that power in the wrong way. He could have come home and brought you enormous pleasure. He could have built your love with it. Instead, he grew greedy with lust. And it killed him."

She nodded slowly. "But do you think that returning the artifact will break whatever spell we've been under since we were trapped?"

Even as she asked the question, she wondered . . . did she really want that? If the spell was broken, that would be the end for them, wouldn't it? No more passionate encounters where their desires raged out of control. No more ravenous matings where caution was thrown to the wind. And if they escaped the tomb and returned to Cairo . . . no more Jake. The tomb raider certainly wouldn't want a permanent place in her staid life.

He let go of her hand, but continued to search her face intently. "Sure. It should, shouldn't it?"

By the wavering question in his tone, she knew he was asking her about more than her take on the tomb's curse. He was asking what she wanted. An answer she wasn't sure she had. But she knew she didn't want to let go of whatever had driven them together. She had to take a chance.

"Then why hasn't it?" she stammered with heat flooding her cheeks. "At least not for me."

Jake's eyes widened. "What do you mean?"

"I-I—" she struggled for words. How could she explain that she'd fallen in love with him? How could she tell him the feelings she had were real? There was no way he would believe her.

"Are you saying you still want to be with me?" he asked softly when she didn't answer him.

She squeezed her eyes shut to ward off the tears that pricked her. With a little shiver, she nodded. "Yes, I still want you. And it's more than just wanting you. I have—I have powerful feelings for you."

She heard him draw in a sharp breath. Drawing one of her own, she forced her chin up to meet his gaze. She had to be strong. And honest. If he turned her away, at least she could live the rest of her life knowing she'd given herself the best chance possible at love.

"But perhaps those feelings are just a trick of the tomb, too. After all, how can a person fall in love in such a short time?" she whispered, then held her breath for his reaction.

Unlike when he'd confessed his professor's betrayal, Jake's emotions were cloaked. All he did was search her eyes with a gaze so piercing she was sure he saw everything she'd ever felt and done from the time she was a girl.

"You think your feelings and desires are still a trick of the tomb, even though we've returned Merytsat's stolen artifact?" he asked in an even, unemotional tone.

She shrugged. "Perhaps."

"Let me ask you something. Do you want me right now?"

With her body trembling, she looked him up and down. Her breath hitched at just the sight of him in his rumpled clothing, wet dark hair, startling eyes and the body that had pleasured her in so many ways. "Oh God, yes."

He smiled and the expression relaxed her a little. "But do you have to have me?"

"I-I don't understand," she stammered.

"I mean, under the curse you couldn't stop yourself from making love with me. Even when you knew you shouldn't, you had to. Do you feel that way now?"

She considered the answer, then shook her head. “No. I feel the same way I did when I first saw you. I want you, but I can fight it. The difference is now I don’t want to fight it. I just want you.”

“So the curse no longer forces your body to follow its every desire,” he said.

“No. It doesn’t.”

He took a step closer and reached out to cup her cheek. Isabella let out her breath in a low hiss as pleasure spread from his fingertips throughout her body. Pleasure and powerful emotion. How would she go on if he didn’t return her love?

“Then doesn’t it make sense that if the tomb no longer controls your desire that it no longer controls your heart? If your desire is real, doesn’t that mean that your love is real, too?” His face swayed ever closer to her own, but he didn’t kiss her.

Her bottom lip quivered as she nodded. “Yes.”

“Because my love for you is real.” With his opposite hand, he caught her waist and pulled her closer until she molded against his body.

Her knees shook as his words sank in. “You love me?” she whispered as tears began to fall down her cheeks. “Did you tell me that you love me?”

“I love you,” he repeated slowly as he finally let his lips touch hers.

For a moment the kiss was gentle, filled with the love they both felt and the joy that rushed through Isabella as she realized her feelings were not only real, but returned. Then the passion and desire began to build, only this time, those drives weren’t overpowering. For the first time, she knew she could pull back if she chose. Only she didn’t want to pull back. She wanted to give this man her body, her heart, her everything. Forever.

He pulled away reluctantly. “We should find the others,” he whispered in a harsh, desire-filled tone.

With a small smile, she shook her head. “No,” she murmured as she took his hands and led him back through Merytsat’s burial chamber toward the preparation table behind the sarcophagus and statues. “I don’t want to find the others just yet. I want you. Without a curse. Without fear. Just you and me. As if it’s our first time.”

She backed up until her rear end pressed against the table, then released his hands to hoist herself up on the ancient stone surface. The table was the perfect height. She wrapped her legs around his waist and felt the heat of his erection against her core.

"The first time?" he repeated.

"Yes. Because it's like the first time for us." Slowly, she began to unbutton his shirt. "The first time where making love is just between you and me. The first time *she*—" Isabella motioned her head toward Merytsat's statue. "Has nothing to do with it."

Slipping her hands against the warmth of Jake's chest, Isabella let out a little sigh. Touching him was like coming home again, a home she never wanted to leave. And she wanted more. She wanted it all.

Whatever resistance he'd had melted away as he leaned into her and clutched her closer. She shoved the shirt off his shoulders and let it fall into the sand at his feet as he plundered her mouth with kisses that stunned and awakened her at the same time.

He pulled her to the edge of the table as he stroked his tongue into her mouth and began to inch her skirt up her leg with little slides. With every bit of skin he revealed, he caressed her with rough hands. By the time he had hitched her skirt up to her thighs, she was writhing with anticipation and need.

But before he touched her in the place that ached for him the most, he stopped and instead went to work on her shirt buttons. He met her eyes as he popped them open one by one, revealing more and more to him. It wasn't until he had her shirt entirely open that he actually looked down and took in the sight of her naked body.

"My God," he mumbled, almost more to himself than to her. "You are so beautiful."

She blushed like it was the first compliment a man had ever paid her. "It's the torchlight."

He shook his head as he bent to swirl the tip of his tongue around one taut nipple. "Torchlight." He sucked the little bead between his lips and suckled until she arched up with a cry. "Daylight." He switched his attention to her other breast while he kneaded the first with firm strokes of his palm. "Gas light. It doesn't matter. You would captivate me no matter where we were."

He glanced up when he made the last statement and Isabella drew in a sharp breath. In his eyes she saw his love, as stark and pure as her own.

With a wobbly smile, she bent her head and took his lips as his hips collided with hers. Her moan was lost in his mouth as he released her breasts and instead let his fingers travel down her body between her legs. She broke the kiss as his hand cupped her sex, then he slid a finger inside.

"Yes," she hissed as her head dropped back against her shoulders.

He placed a hand against her belly and urged her to lie down as he continued to glide first one, then two fingers in and out of her in a gentle rhythm that soon had her bucking her hips in time. She actually felt her orgasm coming, building in some deep place inside her. It rose up and billowed as he added a thumb to her clit.

"Please, I want to feel you inside me when I come," she whispered as she braced herself back on her elbows to look up into his face.

He shucked his pants down in one smooth motion and before she could ask again, plunged his cock deep inside her. Immediately, she spasmed out an orgasm so intense it bordered on the thin line between pleasure and pain.

It was made even more powerful by the way he caught her hands and pulled her to a sitting position. He wrapped her arms around his neck so they were face to face, eye to eye. As he thrust into her with deep, long strokes, he never broke eye contact. Never stopped holding her. Even when she stiffened in release a second time. Even when his own face contorted into a mask of ultimate pleasure. He held her gaze steadily until the last of his essence had filled her, until her last tremor of pleasure had passed and then he kissed her, deep and gentle.

"I love you," he whispered against her lips.

She smiled. "And I love you."

"Mistress!" Anya's voice echoed in the hallway.

Isabella pressed another kiss against Jake's throat before she allowed him to pull away from her and begin dressing again.

In another time, she might have pushed him away like they were children being caught by a schoolmarm, but now she didn't care if her maid found her in such a compromising position. Not after all she'd seen, all she'd done and all she'd come to feel.

"Mistress!" her friend called again and this time her voice was much closer.

Isabella buttoned the last of her shirt and grinned as Jake put his warm hands around her waist and set her on the ground from her perch on the preparation table. As she smoothed her skirt one last time, she called out, "In here, Anya!"

In a burst of fluttering hands, dark hair and colorful gown, Anya flew into the room. She hardly looked at Jake as she hurtled herself into Isabella's arms and gave her a hug so tight that Isabella almost couldn't breathe.

"I'm so glad I found you!" her friend panted. "After everything that . . ." She blushed. "Happened."

Isabella smiled. "I don't think we have to talk about that. What happened in this tomb was meant to be." Jake's agreeing smile warmed her. "I regret nothing I saw or did or felt."

Her servant's face softened with relief. "Mistress," she said. "Light. We see light. We've found a way out of the tomb."

"Go then and tell Surai and Rafe that we're on our way," Isabella ordered as she slipped her hand into Jake's. Anya looked from her to him and her face slowly widened into a bright smile.

"Yes, I'll do that." Her friend scurried from the room.

Jake wrapped an arm around Isabella's waist as they headed for the chamber door and the corridor that led out of the tomb.

"I'm almost sorry to leave," she said as they took the last few steps out into the cool evening air of the desert.

He looked over his shoulder at the tomb, then back at her. "Well, we'll do things differently than Hiram did. We'll use what we saw and did here for love, so we'll always carry a bit of Merytsat's treasure inside us." She looked up at him with unhidden love and he returned that love freely. "Come on, Isabella. Let me take you home."

About the Author:

Jess Michaels' dreams of becoming a writer began in grade school. The voices in her head started muttering then and have muttered ever since, even when she tried to ignore them. Eventually, her husband encouraged her to listen to those characters that kept harassing her in her sleep and she has been writing ever since. You can find her at http://www.jessmichaels.com.

Ancient Pleasures *is for Johanna, who made me send it. For my parents who instilled a deep love of the written word in me. And for Michael, who always believed . . . even when I didn't.*

Manhunt

by Kimberly Dean

To My Reader:

Those of you who read my story *Wanted* in ***Secrets Volume 9*** must be thinking that I've got fugitives on the brain. Well, you're right. When I finished *Wanted,* questions kept running through my head. What if I turned everything around? What if this time, instead of a bad girl/good boy combination, it was the opposite? What if instead of one hunter, the whole world was after him? And what if nobody—absolutely nobody—was running? The answer to all my questions was *Manhunt.* I hope you enjoy it.

Chapter One

It was freezing! Taryn felt the bite in the air the moment she stepped out of the shower. Teeth clattering, she reached for her towel.

"The furnace." She sighed. With the fall air turning from crisp to bitter, she'd meant to turn it on, but with so many other, more important, things on her mind she'd forgotten. She was tending to do that a lot these days—forgetting things, letting things slide, not caring . . . Briskly, she rubbed the terrycloth over her skin, trying to generate some warmth. She felt cold from the inside out. Unfortunately, she knew that had little to do with the lack of heat in her house.

Betrayal could be bitter, too.

Water dripped from her hair, and she shuddered as it ran down her spine. She couldn't remember a worse day in her career. She'd told the Diazes that it wasn't necessary for them to show up at the arraignment, but they'd insisted. They'd wanted to look their son's accused killer in the face as he entered his plea. The entire family had sat in the front row, faces full of pain and fists clenched. Poor little Benny had looked like he could be sick all over his new tennis shoes at any moment.

She'd known how he felt.

Not guilty.

The words were still bouncing around in her head. They sounded right. They rang strong and true. It was what she'd wanted to believe, what she'd been desperate to believe when the accusations had first been made. Not guilty had been the only option . . .

Until the evidence had convinced her otherwise.

Not guilty. Now the words turned her stomach. She rubbed the towel almost viciously over her dripping hair. She hated drug dealers. Hated their cockiness, their power, their sliminess. They were among the vilest creatures she faced—especially those that targeted kids.

But this one . . . This one had been a coworker. And a friend.

Or so she'd thought.

Her shoulders slumped. She needed to forget about all that and accept that it was going to be a long, difficult trial. The only way she'd ever get through it was to distance herself emotionally. If she was going to be firm, decisive, and dispassionate, she had to pull back. Way back.

And she would, but tonight . . . Tonight she had to allow herself a little slack.

Dejectedly, she wrapped the towel around her body and opened the bathroom door. First thing, she was going to turn on that heat. Then she was going to curl up on the couch with a weepy romance novel and a glass of wine.

Maybe a bottle.

A cold whoosh of air hit her skin, and she shivered anew. It was like the Arctic. She stepped into the hallway, but stopped before she'd taken two steps.

The hallway was dark.

She knew she'd left the light on.

Her muscles tensed, but before she could move, an arm circled her waist. A scream leapt into her throat, but a hard hand covered her mouth. Her heart nearly exploded when she was pulled roughly against a big body hidden in the shadows.

"Hello, A.D.A. Swanson."

Fear swamped Taryn's system when she heard the low voice. It couldn't be. *It couldn't be!* She *knew* that voice.

Darkness magnified the danger. With a muffled cry, she began to fight. She clawed at her assailant's face and kicked out, aiming for anything she could hit. She heard a sudden expulsion of breath and felt a second's worth of success until the man hauled her closer. Hard hands circled her wrists and twisted her arms behind her. The position arched her back and flattened her breasts against the man's chest. Her fear took on an edge. He was all around her. His arms encircled her, his belly rubbed against hers, and his legs . . . They'd gotten tangled with hers during the short struggle.

The forced intimacy was almost sexual.

Unbidden, her nipples started to stiffen, and Taryn's conscience screamed at her. He was evil. Malevolent. Heartless. She knew the truth now.

She tried to squirm away, but his whipcord arms held her immobile. The ease with which he held her alarmed her. If he could subdue her this easily, he could do anything he wanted to her. Anything. His breath brushed her neck, and she flinched.

"You smell good," he growled against her ear. "Let's see how you look."

A whimper escaped her lips. This couldn't be happening!

He pushed her towards the bathroom. Moist air hit her back, and she trembled. *What was he doing here?* Her feet touched the linoleum floor, and she slipped when he unexpectedly let her go. He caught her before she could fall and, for the first time, she looked up into his eyes.

Michael Tucker.

Her heart began to pound double time. He wasn't supposed to be here. He was supposed to be in a holding cell!

She jerked when he reached out and touched her hair. She backed away quickly, but he followed and trapped her against the wall. He hovered over her, big and ruthless. Taryn shrank from him. They'd always been equals before. No more. Helplessly, she watched as he wound a blonde strand of her hair around his finger.

"I see why you always wear it up at work," he said. "You look like a sex kitten with it down."

She swallowed hard. He was trying to rattle her. She needed to concentrate and keep her senses about her. It was her only chance of coming out of this situation unharmed.

Or at least alive.

"What are you doing here, Tucker?"

One dark eyebrow rose. "Why am I not behind bars?"

She nodded slowly.

He stroked the soft tips of her hair against her chin. He watched the movement with an intense expression on his face. He seemed to be considering his own question as he moved the caress up to her lips. "I had a little problem with that plan, but nobody seemed to want to hear my side."

Goosebumps rose on Taryn's skin as he brushed her hair down to the pulse in her neck. The light caress was at sharp odds with the harshness in his voice. His touch might be gentle, but his temper was barely tamped.

"You had your day in court."

"Yeah, one of many to come, I'm sure." His dark gaze locked with hers. "You know what, Swanny? I'm still pissed about that."

Her stomach knotted. She'd never been afraid of Tucker before, but then again, she'd never seen this side of him. There was something about the tone of his voice and the bleakness in his eyes. He was angry—not just with the trial, but with her. "I'm an Assistant D.A.," she said cautiously. "I'm just doing my job."

"Just doing your job?" he repeated. His teasing caress stopped, and his hand fisted in her hair. "I expected a hell of a lot more than that out of you."

"More? I . . . I don't understand. I have to prosecute the case. What more do you want out of me?"

"A little thing called trust, Taryn," he said in a low voice. "Out of everyone, I expected *you* to have more faith in me."

The accusation hung in mid-air. Taryn stared in disbelief at the man she thought she'd known, the man she'd thought she'd *liked.* She couldn't believe he was turning this on her, trying to make her feel bad—and that it was working. He abruptly turned her loose, but she hugged the wall for support. Uneasily, she waited as he paced the tiny room.

He was wet, disheveled, and dirty. A day's growth of stubble covered his chin, and dark circles underlined his eyes. A too-small trench coat strained to span the breadth of his shoulders, but the dull gray material managed to cover most of the bright orange jumpsuit he wore. She didn't know where he'd gotten the coat, but it had obviously managed to hide him from detection. Her gaze dropped to his feet. His boots were wet. He'd shoved the pant legs of the jumpsuit into them to try to hide more of the jail uniform, but they, too, were wet and muddy.

"You've escaped."

His lips twitched. "You always were quick."

Taryn desperately tried to make sense of her predicament. The county lock-up was on the other side of the city. How had he managed to get all the way here, and why had he made this his destination? What did he have in mind? Revenge?

Oh, God.

She hadn't really known him at all, had she?

Her gaze flew to the bathroom door. If she ran, could he catch her?

Yes.

Tears burned in her eyes, but she fought to stay calm. He was bigger, stronger, and faster than she was. The only area where she matched him was brainpower. She couldn't allow herself to fall apart, couldn't let her emotions cripple her. She might not be in control of the situation, but she could keep control of herself.

She focused. Information was power. She needed to approach this situation like she approached a case. Logically. Straightforward. Observant for any loopholes.

She desperately needed to find a loophole.

"Why are you here?" she asked.

"To talk to you. Alone. Just the two of us."

She watched as he raked a hand through his thick, dark hair, rumpling it even further. He looked around the room, and she got the vague impression that he didn't know what his next move should be, that he was acting on instinct now—a hunted animal trying to avoid its pursuers.

It made him all the more dangerous.

"What are you doing?" she squeaked when he suddenly moved.

He looked up from his crouched position. "I'm grungy, stinky, and cold to the bone. I'm going to take a shower and see if I can get my head on straight."

A shower? He'd come all this way for a shower? Her focused mind started sliding down the slippery path towards panic.

Calm down, she told herself. If he got into the shower, she might have a chance to escape. A slim chance, but a chance nonetheless.

A rare smile crossed his lips. He pulled off a boot and dropped it onto the floor with a thud. "Here's some advice, Swanny. Never play poker. That angel face of yours gives away every single thought that runs through your mind."

He tugged off the other boot and began to peel off wet socks. "You're not going to bolt for the door when my back is turned. Know why? Because you're going to be in that shower with me. I'm not letting your sweet tush out of my sight."

Frozen, Taryn watched as the trench coat hit the floor. He reached for the zipper of the jumpsuit and any thought she might have had fled her mind as it slid downward. The bright orange material parted. With unwilling fascination, she watched as he shrugged it off his shoulders.

His chest was enough to make her mouth water. Muscles and sinew wove their way under smooth skin. She remembered his strength when he'd grabbed her, and her knees went a little weak. "Please, don't do this," she said softly. "If you leave now, I swear I won't tell anybody you were here."

"The moment I hit that door, you'd be on the phone."

She shook her head. "No, I wouldn't do that."

He stopped in the act of pushing the jumpsuit over his hips. The expression on his face was cold as he looked at her. "And why am I supposed to believe you'd be that generous? Because you like me?"

Her throat tightened. She'd like to think they'd been friends, but they both knew their relationship was more complicated than that. The stolen glances, the brushes of skin, the pounding heartbeats . . . She'd tried to keep things strictly professional between them, but something hot and wild had always lurked just below the surface. It had boiled over once . . . She pushed the heated memory from her mind. "I used to," she said quietly.

"Yeah? Well, I used to like you, too."

She looked at him closely, looking for any sign of the old Tucker—the whip-smart detective, the good-humored friend, the audacious flirt. She looked at the hard lines of his face and saw none of those people. All she saw was a big, angry man. A big, angry, *naked* man.

"Oh," she gasped.

Without a shred of modesty, he'd pushed the jumpsuit over his hips and taken the white briefs he wore beneath with it. He was naked and, suddenly, she realized that a towel was the only thing standing between them. Their forced proximity had abruptly become starker and more intimate.

Her gaze dropped to between his legs. Good Lord, he was hung like a racehorse. She couldn't look away as his penis swung heavily between his muscled thighs. It twitched, and something inside of her tightened in response.

"Keep staring, and you'll have to do something about it," he said in a low tone.

Shocked to the core, Taryn tore her gaze away. The mere thought of doing that big erection made her pussy clench and her nipples stiffen. The inappropriateness of her reactions horrified her. How could she be attracted to him when she knew what he'd done? What he was?

He reached past her to turn on the shower, and she bumped up against the wall. Hastily, she crossed her arms across her chest and tried in vain to concentrate on anything else in the room but him.

That was nearly impossible. He took up all the space.

"Get in the shower."

Her gaze snapped back to his. "No!"

He whipped back the shower curtain. "In. Now."

His tone brooked no argument, and she was once again reminded that he held all the power. She had to choose her battles, and this wasn't one she would win. She bit her lip, but stepped over the edge of the tub. She took the spot at the end, as far away from the shower head as she could get, but the confined space made her claustrophobic. The room closed in on her. Threatened and self-conscious, she clutched her towel to her chest like a security blanket.

Tucker had been imposing before, but naked? Forget about it.

He stepped in beside her. His gaze was hot, but she couldn't return it. Instead, she centered her stare on the middle of his broad chest. That wasn't such a great idea, either. Steam started to rise around them, and the effect was unnerving. Heavy moisture enveloped them, enhancing the intimate nature of their close quarters.

Taryn shifted nervously. Knowing that Tucker was an accused killer didn't reduce his sex appeal. She'd wanted him when they'd both been fully clothed, working across the table from each other. This? This was just unfair.

He reached for the soap and began to work up a lather. She watched as trails of water sluiced over his tight form. The uninhibited way he washed made it clear that he wasn't trying to entice her. He'd had a tough day. Lord knew what he'd gone through during the escape and the trek to her house. He was tired and dirty.

Oh, so very dirty . . .

His dark gaze connected with hers, and she realized that he *knew.* Appalled, she looked blankly at the shower curtain.

He grunted, but turned away to reach for the shampoo. He ran his hand through his wet hair, and white bubbles dripped down his neck. Mesmerized, she watched as they slid downwards. Her rational side kicked her out of her reverie. What was she doing ogling him? This was her chance! His back was turned, and his eyes were closed.

In a flash, she was out of the tub and lunging for the door. Her hand closed over the doorknob and gave it a quick twist.

It was as far as she got.

She yelped when Tucker caught her from behind. He jerked her back against him so firmly, her feet left the ground. She gave another cry and reached for the iron band circling her stomach, but his voice in her ear stopped her struggles.

"You just proved to me that I can't trust you, baby. Don't expect to get a chance like that again."

His body was hot and slick against her back. They were pressed together so tightly, she could feel his heart pounding. Skin to skin. The sensation made her toes curl.

Her eyes flew open. "My towel!"

The terrycloth had slipped during her brief sprint and was down to her waist. Frantically, she wrapped her forearm across her chest and reached for it. Without its protection, her vulnerability threatened to incapacitate her.

"Damn it, Tucker. Let me go!"

She was panting now. The towel was trapped beneath his arm and wouldn't budge. Whatever sense of calmness she'd achieved vaporized like the steam clouding the room. She couldn't stay logical and controlled when she was stripped bare. Not when he was touching her!

He lowered her feet to the ground, and she tried to scramble away.

"Not so fast." His strong arm kept her locked to his damp side. Bending down, he reached into the pocket of the trench coat.

Her eyes widened when he came up with a set of handcuffs. "What do you think you're going to do with those?"

"I'm going to try to take a shower in peace."

"Tucker?"

"Relax."

Relax? She was trapped in her own bathroom, naked as a jaybird, with a fugitive of the justice system. She couldn't relax! She was scared. Flat-out, pure terrified. Some of that panic slipped into her voice. "Please don't hurt me."

The words stopped him cold. He turned her in his arms, but she couldn't meet his gaze. The silence soon became deafening.

His voice was gruff when he finally spoke. "I'm not going to hurt you, Taryn. I just need a shower."

He gently pushed her backwards. One handcuff slid over her wrist, and she heard the ominous click. His hand settled on the forearm covering her breasts. She resisted, but he was insistent. She bit her lower lip as he lifted her arms above her head. The handcuffs went over the shower curtain rod before he locked them.

A low moan left Taryn's lips. The position left her mercilessly exposed. Her breasts jutted forward, their tips puckered into stiff little peaks. It was worse than it had been before when he'd caught her. Then, he'd been behind her. Now he was looking at her, studying her. She'd never felt so defenseless in her life. Or so submissive. She pressed her thighs tightly together and tried desperately to ignore the tingling between them.

"Taryn, look at me."

The calm tone was familiar. It was the Tucker she knew, the Tucker she'd trusted—justifiably or not. Hesitantly, she opened her eyes. She was surprised when his gaze settled on her face, not her body. Some of the tenseness left her muscles, but nothing could relax the wariness in her nerves.

He planted a hand on the wall beside her head and leaned in, crowding her. "Listen. I'm tired, I'm sore in places I didn't know I had, and I'm in a nasty mood. Yes, I'm a little peeved at you. What innocent man wouldn't be?"

Her shocked gaze collided with his even as her gut tightened. How dare he lie to her again? Especially like this.

"Don't give me that look. You heard me—*innocent.* I didn't sell those drugs to Justin Diaz any more than you . . . Well, any more than you slept with Marty Sheuster."

"What?" she gasped. The incongruity of his accusation threw her. "Marty? I never—"

"Exactly."

"But, but . . . Why would you say something like that?" she sputtered.

"To get my point across." He reached up and ran his wet finger over her cheek. "And to see how you'd react. I knew that scuzball was lying."

That one, slight touch sent a shiver through Taryn and effectively brought her back to her senses. What was she doing listening to him talk trash about one of her coworkers? He was an accused drug dealer. He'd lived a double life without anyone knowing. And he'd just taken her captive! Still, she couldn't help but ask. "Marty told you that we'd . . . slept together?"

"He was a little more descriptive than that. I wanted to rip his fucking head off."

She swallowed hard and tried to concentrate. She was in a bad situation; the last thing she needed to do was worry about Marty Sheuster. Still, she knew the A.D.A. well enough to know what he was capable of. The creep. They had a casual relationship, at best. She'd never even considered anything more. To hear that he'd spread rumors about her after she'd fought so hard to keep her reputation spotless angered her. "How did you know he was lying?"

One of Tucker's eyebrows lifted. Slowly, his hand moved from her face. His callused fingers trailed down her neck and stopped against her thundering pulse. He timed it, and a small smile touched his hard lips. His hand slid lower, and Taryn's breath came more quickly. His touch was confident and all too comfortable. She shouldn't be excited by it. She shouldn't enjoy it. She shouldn't . . .

"Ahhh." His fingers had settled over her naked breast.

"He said your nipples were brown." He leaned closer so he could whisper in her ear. "He was wrong. They're a light, pretty pink."

He trailed his thumbnail over the sensitive tip, and it popped up like a jack-in-the-box. Arousal unfurled in Taryn's stomach, and she tried to roll away. The handcuffs didn't let her get far. She couldn't escape. He could touch her as he wished. "Tucker," she groaned.

He cupped her breast, taking its weight, and she saw a flutter in the pulse at his temple.

"I'd never hurt you, Swanny," he said quietly. "I might be pissed and tired, but that's something I couldn't ever do."

Her hands formed fists as she fought the sensations that spiraled in her belly. His words lingered in her ear, and his touch burned. It felt so sinfully delicious. Her head dropped back against the bathroom wall. What was wrong with her? Why was she letting him get to her? She was smarter than this. She knew better than to trust him.

But she did trust him. At least when it came to her safety. He wouldn't hurt her physically; she knew that deep down inside. But emotionally? Emotionally, she was in jeopardy. "I know," she whispered.

His eyes flared. Slowly, his other hand trailed down her waist to cup her buttocks. She whimpered lightly when his fingers dipped into the crevice between them and squeezed.

"This thing between us—it feels good, doesn't it, baby?"

She squirmed against the intimate contact, ashamed to be wanting more. He loomed over her, so close that the air from his words brushed against her lips. She pressed them together to stop their sudden tingling. Her mind refused to let her be attracted to this man, but her body didn't seem to be listening.

"We could have been doing this for the past two years if you weren't so stubborn."

She flinched when he pinched her nipple. The sharp pain made her breast swell even more, and she rolled her head against the wall. The move stretched her arms tightly overhead, but it felt good. His touch felt so good.

His big, rough hands were sure and bold. They set off sparks everywhere they touched. And they touched everywhere. Her shoulders, her breasts, her quivering belly, the crease of her upper thighs . . .

Her mouth went dry as he traced the crease inward, approaching the part of her that craved his intimate strokes the most.

Suddenly, his touch was gone.

Her eyes flew open, and she saw him take a step back.

"Don't go anywhere," he said with a hard smile on his lips.

She watched in disbelief as he turned his back on her. A frustrated cry left her lips when he went back to his shower and pulled the curtain closed between them.

"Tucker! Don't you leave me here!" Angrily, she pulled at the handcuffs that held her in place. They refused to budge. Her body ached with wanting, and she realized that he'd brought her to that point on purpose. She'd been afraid he'd hurt her, but this form of revenge was even more cunning.

He'd made her want him.

A child killer.

"Arrrg!" she growled. She pulled harder against the handcuffs, but all that got her was the harsh sound of metal against metal. Her breasts jiggled as she fought the restraints, and the sensation angered her. All he'd had to do was touch her, and she'd forgotten her fear and her distrust. "That was low, Michael! Do you hear me? Low!"

Tucker hung his head under the spray of water. He listened to Taryn's struggles behind him, but for the moment, he just let the liquid heat soak his aching muscles. Why argue with her when she was right? He was fighting dirty. Why the hell not? Playing by the rules had gotten him nowhere.

The handcuffs scraped loudly against the metal shower curtain rod. "Damn you, Michael. I'm going to send you to prison so fast, your head's going to spin," she yelled.

"Not if I have anything to say about it," he muttered under his breath.

They were going to do things his way now. He'd come here for one reason and one reason only—to clear his name. And he had a definite, if unusual, plan on how to get her to help him do that.

He knew he could have just run. When the opportunity had presented itself, he could have hit the road and disappeared. He knew the system well enough; he could avoid it if he wanted. That wouldn't have solved anything, though. He'd be looking over his shoulder for the rest of his life, and he'd have to stomach the fact that everyone thought he was guilty of causing a kid's death.

Everyone. Including Taryn.

Of all the things he'd had to endure since the charges had been brought against him, her betrayal had hurt the most.

She was at least going to listen to him, by God.

The sound of her fighting the handcuffs roused him enough to glance over his shoulder. The silhouette of her body played against the opaque plastic of the shower curtain like an x-rated black and white movie.

"Perfect," he breathed. She was perfect. Her breasts swayed as she struggled with the handcuffs, and his gaze zeroed in on the voluptuous globes. They were full and firm, with nipples that practically begged for the rasp of his tongue.

His cock sprang to attention, but he couldn't move. He stood frozen as his gaze slid down the outline of her form. Her ass didn't rank far behind her tits when it came to rating points. The curves had fit his hand perfectly. It had been all he could do not to spread her legs open wide and thrust up into her.

He was about two milliseconds from pulling back the curtain and doing just that now.

But she was afraid he'd hurt her.

He wiped the water from his face and leaned back against the shower wall. "Damn."

That put a definite kink in his plans.

He wasn't here to scare her. It had just been a bitch of a day. He'd walked for miles through mud and muck. He was cold, hungry, and tired. She'd been a major player in getting him into this predicament, and he was hardly a saint. Knowing that she was the one leading the trial against him pissed him off royally.

Still, that gave him no right to scare her physically.

And it wouldn't help him get what he wanted.

"Stick to the plan," he muttered. Irritated with himself, he reached for the bar of soap and began to lather up again. His muscles protested when he reached to wash his back, and he knew that he'd be sore in the morning. Still, a night in bed with Taryn Swanson could do a lot towards curing his aches and pains.

He couldn't stop himself from glancing at her again.

The thought of crawling under the covers with her had his cock standing at full mast. Erotic thoughts pulled hard on him, and he clenched his teeth. Before he lost his senses, he shut off the water. He refused to jack off when she was only three feet away.

He threw aside the shower curtain, and she jumped. Her eyes

rounded when she saw his stiff cock, and she renewed her struggles against the handcuffs.

"Just hold on," he said. "I'll only be a few more minutes."

"Get me out of these things," she demanded.

He ignored her and reached for a towel. She looked even better without the shower curtain between them. He rubbed the towel over his chest, but choked back a groan as he lowered it to his swollen cock.

He tossed the terrycloth aside. First things first. He needed to do something about his appearance. Half the state's law enforcement community was probably out there looking for him. He reached for the razor he'd seen in the shower. "Is this blade sharp?"

"Why?"

"I want to shave, that's why."

"I hope you cut your throat."

He lifted an eyebrow. "And then who would let you out of those things?"

She gave a growl of frustration. "The refills are in the medicine cabinet."

He found the new blades, but scowled when he saw the scented shaving cream in a lavender can. Great. That was all he needed—to smell like pretty flowers when the boys in blue finally caught up with him and carted him away. He made do with what she had and started scraping the growth of dark beard off his face. It felt good to finally stop the itching. The whiskers had been bothering him all day. Finally, he turned to the mustache he'd grown for his last case. The Ramirez case.

Damn, he hoped that wouldn't fall through the cracks without him.

He watched Taryn out of the corner of his eye as he worked. She stood quietly, but the glare she was throwing at him nearly seared his skin. And that body . . . It was frying his brain.

He decided to work slower.

Getting rid of the mustache helped, but it wasn't enough. He rubbed his chin as he looked at his reflection in the mirror. "I don't suppose you have any hair coloring around here."

She sniffed haughtily.

He looked pointedly at the tangle of hair between her legs. "No peroxide there."

She shifted uncomfortably, and he saw her glance again at his cock. It still stood at attention. Her look quickly darted away.

Good. He wanted her aware of him. Not scared. Aware.

She didn't have any aftershave. He picked up a bottle of lotion and glanced at the label. Good enough. "Has the media caught wind of my escape yet?" he asked as he squirted some into his palm.

The question brought her head up. "It was plastered on every network."

He clucked his tongue in disapproval. He'd always loved her spunkiness. "What did I tell you about that face, Counselor? If I had been on the news, you wouldn't have been so surprised to see me."

She glared at him. "Fine. I didn't see anything. Yet."

"That's good. It gives me more time." He smoothed the lotion onto his face and wiped away the white streaks.

"Time for what?"

He might as well tell her flat out. It would give her some time to get used to the idea. He watched her carefully as he turned and leaned back against the sink. "Time to screw you until you'll listen to me."

Her restless movements stopped, and her eyes went wide as a doe's. She stared at him for a heartbeat—and then ten.

"Don't you dare lay a finger on me, Tucker."

He knew that tone. He'd heard it often enough in court. Too bad the pulse fluttering at the base of her neck gave her away.

He looked her straight in those startled eyes. "I'll lay my fingers, my hands, my mouth, and my cock on you. Whatever it takes to break down that barrier you've erected against me."

She swallowed hard, and tension reverberated around the room.

"Don't take it personally," she said, her voice hardly above a whisper. "I hate all drug pushers. You should know that by now."

Enough. He'd heard enough of that crap to last him a lifetime. "And you should know that I'm innocent, damn it! We've worked side by side for too long. You know me better than this, Taryn."

"Stop it! Just stop with the lies." The handcuffs screeched against the curtain rod as she started struggling again. "I've been through the evidence. I've gone over it a hundred times."

Lies? He was the only one who'd been telling the truth. He was the victim of a frame-up, and he was sick of seeing that look in her eyes—

the one she usually saved for drug runners, murderers, and pimps. He didn't deserve to be lumped in with that crowd.

"I've never lied to you, Taryn. No matter what else happens, before I leave here, you'll be convinced of that fact."

Her chin lifted, and her mouth took on a stubborn set. "Why? Because you're going to force me to have sex with you?"

"I won't have to force you," he said in a low voice. "We both know that."

Her cheeks turned pink. Her mouth worked for a moment, but she didn't have a comeback. She knew just as well as he what had happened the one and only time he'd touched her. The stain in her cheeks spread down to her chest, and her thighs clamped together. Almost desperately, she looked at the handcuffs overhead.

Tucker reached up to rub a kink in his neck. "I didn't have to use force to get that search warrant."

Her eyes flashed fire. "Don't."

He shrugged. "Sex got me what I wanted then. I figure, hell, why mess with success?"

Her hands fisted above her head, but he didn't go into the specifics. He didn't have to. They both knew well enough what had happened.

He'd been knee deep in the Rodriguez case when her buddy, Marty, had stalled on getting him the search warrant he'd needed. It had gone against protocol to bring in another ADA, but Tucker had had it with the idiot. They'd never bring the kingpin down at the rate Sheuster had been moving, so he'd called Taryn down to the station.

She hadn't been pleased about stepping on someone else's turf, but he'd pulled her into an interrogation room to explain. That had been the idea anyway—to talk to her.

Instead, he'd practically jumped her.

The warrant had soon been his. She would have been, too, if Sheuster hadn't been in the next room.

Sheuster wasn't here to stop them now.

Tucker watched Taryn's reactions closely. He'd been blunt about his intentions. Expediency was the name of the game now. People were coming for him. He needed her on his side, both for her brains and her power within the judicial system.

There was more, though. Most of all, he needed to regain her trust.

He'd never have peace of mind if he didn't right things with her. He'd seen how she'd steeled her heart and her mind against him when he'd entered his plea. There was only one avenue left for him to take, and he wasn't above using it.

They'd been attracted to each other from the first day they'd met. He had to get her close to him. They'd start physically. The rest would follow.

He let out a long breath. Her eyes were still wide, but fear was no longer part of the equation. He saw uneasiness, though. That could be soothed . . . *with time.* It was one luxury he didn't have.

He had a good head start, though, and he was hiding in the best place possible—right under the authorities' noses. A familiar image of Taryn in a big, soft bed flitted into his weary mind and the decision was made.

He took a step towards her. "Let's go to bed, Swanny. It's been one hell of a long day."

Chapter Two

Taryn's head whirled. Bed. The word brought up muddled visions of sex. Heat. Betrayal. Deception. Justin!

No. She couldn't do this. She couldn't let it happen.

She watched as Tucker bent down to search the pockets of his trench coat. Her resolve strengthened when he emerged with a key. "I thought you escaped," she said. "How convenient for you to have the keys to your own set of handcuffs."

It had been impossible to avoid the controversy that surrounded the Tucker drug case. The media played up the sensationalism in every newscast. It was the hot topic in diners, barbershops, and churches everywhere. Even inside the police department, there were two distinct factions. There were those who believed that Detective Michael Tucker had gotten pulled under by the temptations associated with vice work. The people closest to him, though, couldn't even stomach the notion. It was possible that he'd found a sympathetic guard.

His eyes narrowed. "Don't even think it. Everybody did his job. We had an accident during my transport, and I managed to get loose. Unlike most people in that situation, I didn't just run. I knew I had to have the key, so I made sure I got it."

He lifted the key to her handcuffs, and Taryn's nerve endings went on the alert. He stood so close, her nipples brushed against his chest. Softness against hardness. Coolness against heat. Light, pretty pink against fading tanned flesh. Her concentration began to waver. "They'll find you," she blurted. "They'll use dogs to track your scent. They're probably outside right now."

He released the handcuffs from one wrist, and the freedom disconcerted her. She couldn't decide whether to rub the soreness or cover her body from his sight. With him this close, shielding herself seemed to be the most prudent choice—especially since her body was reacting like a lit firecracker. She wrapped one arm about her chest and, handcuffs jingling, used the other to cover the curls at her groin.

She jumped when he touched her.

"I know how things work, Swanny. Why do you think I was so wet and grungy?"

He didn't try to move her hands to expose her. Instead, he lightly circled her wrists and applied soft pressure to the joints. The flow of fresh blood made her fingers tingle, but it was impossible to determine if the circulation or he was the source of new heat.

His unexpected display of tenderness confused her. With his hands placed as they were, his knuckles came into unavoidable contact with her breast and belly. The twin points of contact zinged with electricity, but he didn't push the intimacy to the next level. It left her on edge, comforted by his touch, yet poised for something more.

"I ran through more than a few creeks on my way here," he said, his voice a little gruff. "I even boarded a bus when I found some spare change in that coat. There's no way a dog could track me."

Taryn bit her lower lip. Her hopes of a quick rescue were fading fast. Nobody would think that Tucker would come here. The idea was just too far fetched.

Maybe her neighbors . . . No, they wouldn't be any help. Her house sat too far back from the road, and she had a large plot of land. Even if she did scream, the seventy-year-old Parsons wouldn't hear her. Nervously, she began clutching at straws. "My roommate will be back any time now."

He actually chuckled. He moved his hands away from her wrists and began massaging the stiff muscles at the base of her neck. "Nice try. You don't have a roommate."

He turned her by the shoulders and directed her to the door. She jumped in surprise when he gave her bare bottom a quick pat. "To the bedroom."

Taryn's mind went blank. He wanted to go to bed.

She just couldn't think of a way to stop him. The idea of slipping under the sheets with him turned her hot and cold at once. Her body wanted to, but her mind rebelled. He was using her. She had to remember that.

His arm wrapped around her waist to steady her. The touch was gentle, but it felt unbearably hot against her skin. With a jolt, she realized that she wasn't scared so much as hypersensitive. It was a mind game now. He'd said he wouldn't hurt her, and she believed him. Still, he'd been blatant about his intentions. He'd come here to have sex with her.

And he'd already proven to her how readily her body gave in, no matter what her heart and her head told it to do.

He knew her weakness; she had to find his.

Tucker guided Taryn into the bedroom. The bathroom light spilled in from the doorway. When he saw the queen-sized bed, he knew he'd rebounded straight from hell into heaven. "Oh, yeah," he murmured.

He let out a shuddering breath. He'd been running on adrenaline for too long. He was at the end of his rope—mentally, physically, and emotionally. All he'd been able to think about as he'd slopped through ice-cold creeks and shuffled through dank alleyways was *this*—being with her. Taking comfort from her.

He gently pulled her back against him until they touched, skin against skin. Intense pleasure uncoiled inside his chest. Her skin was like raw silk. He spread his hand across her midriff and luxuriated in the feel of her. The sensation was doubly powerful where her soft backside cradled his erection, and he couldn't help but nudge his cock against her more firmly. A sensual haze began to overtake him, and he buried his face in her sweet-smelling hair.

"Taryn," he whispered.

Suddenly, the weight of the world settled on his shoulders. This wasn't how he'd wanted things to be between them. He'd wanted her to be with him willingly.

Of course, that had been before his world had turned upside down. And inside out. He'd always thought he'd have time to coax her into his bed. He'd thought things would evolve between them naturally.

There was nothing natural about this. Somehow everything had sprung out of control. How the hell had things come to this? A few weeks ago, he'd been a cop, and she'd been his sexy ADA. Now, he was an accused murderer on the run, and she was his hostage.

Fuckin' A.

He gave her a gentle squeeze. "Come on, baby. It's cold in here."

Her feet didn't move. "I won't do this with you."

The stiffness had reentered her body. Tucker sighed. Damn it, he shouldn't have told her. All it had done was lift her defenses against him, and he really didn't have the energy to chip away at them. Not tonight. He brushed a kiss against her proud shoulder. For a hard-nosed attorney, her thoughts were pretty easy to read.

"Just get under the covers, Swanny. I swear we won't do anything you don't want to do."

"But I don't want to do anything with you," she said tightly. "I don't want to get in that bed with you."

Her gaze was focused hard across the room, not on the bed, but on the picture above it. His own stubbornness took hold. Like it or not, she was getting into that bed with him.

For one thing, he had to keep an eye on her. He had her at a disadvantage physically, but she was wickedly smart. If she saw another opportunity for escape, she'd take it. Keeping her plastered to his side limited those opportunities.

It also provided him with other, more obvious, benefits. If they slept together—just slept side by side—she'd get used to the weight of his body, the feel of his hands on her skin, the brush of his breath at the back of her neck . . .

Just picturing it made him rock hard.

"All right," he said smoothly. Before she could react, he opened one hand possessively across her breast. The other slid down her stomach as he spread her legs with his knee. "We'll get busy right here."

As expected, she bolted before he'd barely touched her.

But it wasn't soon enough. She'd been hot.

And slick.

He almost groaned out loud when she flew across the room and hopped into bed. She tore at the covers and pulled them up to her chin. Light from the doorway slashed across the bed, illuminating her nervousness.

Anticipation made Tucker's fists clench. His cock had been too hard for too long. There were things he wanted to do with her—and to her. Intimate things. Shocking things. This might be the one and only time they had a chance to be together.

Slowly, he crossed the room. He'd promised her that he wouldn't force her, and he'd hold true to that. It was just that combining a sexual seduction with a mental one was going to be tricky. He needed to find just the right approach, because in the end, he needed her help. She was the only person who could get him out of this godforsaken mess.

She was the only one who could save him.

Taryn watched Tucker as he came towards her. How many times had she fantasized about this? About him? Her rules about dating coworkers had kept them apart, but abstinence hadn't stopped her from daydreaming. Her fingernails curled into the soft comforter. Her simple dreams paled in comparison to the reality of him.

Light from the doorway silhouetted his shape. He was masculinity in its purest form. Tall, dark, and built. His muscles were sleek and powerful. His chest was wide, his hips were narrow, and his legs were long. The very heart of him was no exception; he was thick, hard, and ready.

For her.

It was enough to make a woman beg.

But she couldn't, and it made her want to scream. Why did it have to be this way? Why couldn't he be innocent like he claimed? She wanted to believe him—even now. Even after she'd pored over the evidence, the statements, and the rest of the case file looking for something to clear him. She'd been desperate to find even the tiniest detail that would cast the light of doubt on his guilt. In her obsession, she'd nearly gone blind.

But she'd come up empty-handed.

She shook her head. This wasn't how she'd wanted it to be—with them at odds, time running out, and the cold of winter slicing through the room. She pulled the covers around her more tightly as shivers wracked her body. Her mind raced. The drugs. The dead teenager. She had to resist him. She had to.

He came at her like a silent predator. Before she could react, he'd tugged her security blanket out of her hands and uncovered her. A combination of fear and excitement froze her in place. She watched breathlessly as he crawled onto the bed with her. Their gazes locked; his dark eyes were fathomless.

"Stop fighting it, baby," he whispered. He planted a hand on each side of her head, trapping her. Watching her reactions, he stretched out full-length on top of her and gradually lowered his weight. "Stop fighting us."

Taryn clutched his shoulders as he came down upon her, unable to make up her mind whether to push him away or pull him closer. She could feel his strength, his textures, and his desire as his body pressed her deep into the mattress.

Pleasure hummed through her. He was better than any blanket she'd ever owned.

"See?" he said, his nose brushing against hers. "See how good it is?"

Her resistance drained. Her hands came up hesitantly, and she heard the handcuff on her right wrist jingle. She hadn't had a chance to touch him before. He'd kept her restrained. Now, her fingers itched.

She spread her palms wide on his back. He felt so solid. So warm. She caressed the plateau of muscles and warm flesh and was delighted by the groan that rang in her ear.

"Don't stop," he whispered as his head came down.

His mouth pressed against hers, open and hungry. She moaned as her eyelids fluttered shut. Their lips sealed together. Textures and tastes filled her senses. Her grip on him tightened. The kiss was firm, coaxing, and determined. Desire smoldered deep in her belly as she met his tongue.

Why would she want to stop this?

Because of the drugs! Because of the dead teenager!

Her hands stiffened on his lower back.

What was wrong with her? *Was she insane?* She couldn't take Michael Tucker as her lover.

She tore her mouth away from his and gasped for air. "No," she said harshly.

He pulled his head back and looked at her in confusion. "What?"

Anxiety rolled in Taryn's stomach. What she wanted and what was right were two different things. She swallowed hard and looked into his face. "I'm saying 'no'."

The quiet words rang throughout the room. Tucker's body became rigid on top of hers, and the tension seemed to make him even heavier. Anger and frustration flared in his eyes.

"You're already charged with possession of drugs with intent to distribute, providing drugs to a minor, and third degree murder," she said painstakingly. It was getting harder to talk with each word. "The list is only getting longer. You're holding me hostage. Do you really want to add—"

"Don't say it," he snarled.

With a harsh curse, he leveraged himself off of her and rolled onto his back. He covered his eyes with a forearm as his hands clenched into fists. The friction in the room heated as his harsh breaths echoed.

Taryn didn't dare move. She didn't dare speak. They both knew what her one little 'no' meant. He had to stop or he'd be charged with rape.

She felt miserable.

She'd done the right thing, she knew. Kissing him and touching him had felt incredible—but she would have regretted it in the morning. He wasn't the Michael Tucker she'd lusted after for the past two years. That man was a facade, but thank God he still had enough decency in him to stop him when she asked.

The tense seconds turned into tense minutes. The light that slashed across the bed didn't help. It glared in Taryn's eyes, refusing to let her hide. The rays lit Tucker's chest as it went up and down in strictly controlled breaths. His body was like a primed spring. She was afraid to set him off.

But he'd rolled right on top of the covers, and she was cold.

She curled into a ball to try to retain her body heat. She looked into the clock as the minutes clicked off one-by-one. When her teeth started to rattle, she couldn't stand it anymore.

"The heat," she said. Her soft words boomed in the darkness. "I was heading to turn it on when you . . . grabbed me. Do you . . . Would you mind if I went to adjust the thermostat?"

"Yeah. I'd mind."

His flat refusal made her look at him. His face was like granite. She couldn't read him at all.

He let out a long breath and sat up. "Give me your wrist. I'll go take care of it. I have to fix your window anyway."

Her wrist. He meant to handcuff her. She tucked her hand under her body. Not again. "What's wrong with my window?"

He ran a hand through his hair and actually looked embarrassed. "You have deadbolts on the doors. I had to break in."

Dread crawled down Taryn's spine. Intellectually, she'd known that he'd found a way into her house. Hearing how he'd done it was another thing entirely. Her guilt fizzled away. "One more for the list," she said bitterly.

He threw her an angry look, and suddenly they were right back to where they'd been when he'd first snatched her in the hallway. "I'll pay for repairs when this is all straightened out. Hell, I'll even come over and replace it myself."

"That will be a trick, considering how you'll be in prison."

"Give me your wrist."

She rolled onto the hand with the clunky bracelet. "No."

"Damn it, Swanny." He ran a hand over his face. "I've got to do something about that window before it attracts attention, but I can't trust you to stay put. This isn't easy on me, either, but I've got to look out for number one."

"You're not going to lock me up again. I won't let you."

One of his eyebrows rose at the challenge. When he moved, it was like a big cat pouncing on its prey. Taryn let out a screech and tried to pull away. His hands groped her as they wrestled for control.

She was quickly subdued.

"You know you're only making this more fun for me," he said. There wasn't even a glimmer of a smile on his face. He lifted her arm and locked the bracelet around one of the rods in the headboard.

Taryn grumbled at the sound of the click.

Shaking his head, Tucker ran a finger across her cheek. "You're the most obstinate woman I know, but you still look like one of my favorite teenage wet dreams."

She lunged at him, and the blankets fell to her waist. "If you don't go fix that window, the pipes in this house are going to freeze."

His chest rose and fell slowly as he stared at her nakedness.

"And your nipples will be hard enough to cut glass," he said in a voice like sandpaper. He reached out to test one with his index finger. "Oh yeah, wet dream material. Hard core."

"Get out!"

"Right. The window," he said as he stood. He was completely oblivious to his own nudity as he turned on his heel and displayed a tight backside. He plucked up the key to her restraints as he headed back into the light. "And I'll turn on the heat. What are you? A miser?"

Taryn slouched back against the pillow as he left the room. Damn the man! Not only were her nipples taut, her breasts felt heavy and engorged. She quickly pulled the sheet over herself, but gasped when a jolt shot straight down to her core. Even the touch of cotton was too much.

Double damn him! All it took was a word or a look from him, and she was aroused. But a touch? A touch made her delirious. She flopped onto her stomach to try to ease her discomfort.

She couldn't believe what she'd almost allowed him to do. It shouldn't have taken her so long to stop him. Where was her brain? More to the point, where was her backbone? He'd broken into her home. He'd taken her hostage and bound her to her own bed. How could her body betray her like this?

The hard press of the mattress against her breasts gave her some relief. Groaning, she dropped her head onto the pillow and tried to think. *What was she going to do?*

She knew that there had to be people out there looking for him, even if there hadn't been anything on the news. Her head snapped up. The Diazes! They were going to be panic-stricken when they heard about Tucker's escape. She thought again about little Benny. She had to do something.

Her gaze settled on the nightstand on the opposite side of the bed. The phone. The answer to her problems was staring her right in the face! Flinging her arm wide, she reached out for the receiver. The muscles in her shoulder pulled tight as she stretched across the bed.

"Taryn, where's your broom?"

The sudden question made her start, and she accidentally knocked a book off the nightstand. It fell to the floor with a thud, and she cringed. She quickly looked over her shoulder to the doorway. Had he heard?

"It's in the laundry room beside the dryer," she called loudly.

Her ears craned to hear his movements. For once, the squeak of the floor in the laundry room was welcome. She relaxed, and her concentration returned to her task. The phone was so close, yet so far. She stretched out and wiggled her fingers. They brushed against the corner, but she couldn't get a solid grip.

It was right there!

"Got any cardboard?"

She slumped against the pillows, but her mind raced. This might be the only chance she got. She needed to call for help—because for as much as she'd resisted him tonight, she knew she couldn't last much longer.

Right or wrong, she wanted him.

An idea occurred to her, and she rolled onto her back. Squirming around, she repositioned herself so her legs were pointed towards the phone.

"Taryn?" His voice was closer. "Cardboard?"

He couldn't come in here now!

"There might be some under the sink," she yelled.

She didn't wait to see if he followed her directions. She had to give it one more try. Her legs were longer than her arms. It took three attempts, but she finally managed to grasp the receiver between her toes. Gingerly, she pulled her knees to her chest.

A harsh gasp escaped her when she lost her grip. The phone and her hope nearly toppled onto the floor, before her quick reflexes saved her from disaster. She clamped the phone between her feet and paused to get her pulse under control.

She knew she didn't have much time. Contorting her body, she dropped the phone onto the bed where she could reach it. With one hand, she dialed 911 and lifted the receiver to her ear.

Silence greeted her.

Anxiety settled like a rock in the pit of her stomach.

"Flexible, aren't you?" The deep voice came from the doorway.

Her head snapped towards the sound. Tucker was standing with his arms propped overhead against the doorframe. The casual pose was at odds with the steel in his voice. He seemed totally unconcerned with his nudity, but she couldn't ignore it. Her gaze was drawn to his body like a magnet to steel. He was still blatantly aroused, but his good humor had vanished. The dangerous combination sent a sizzle down her spine.

"What did you do to the phones?" she asked, going on the offensive.

"I took the cords."

She looked at the wall jack and a discomforting thought made her pause. "How long have you been in my house?"

He hit the hallway light, and the room plunged into darkness. "Long enough to hear what a fumble fingers you are."

The back of Taryn's neck tingled when she heard him push himself away from the door. She'd dropped the soap in the shower—twice. She'd been thinking of him locked in that jail cell with nothing but a hard cot, a sink, and a toilet for company. But he hadn't been in a cell. He'd been here. How long had he stood in that hallway listening to her? How long had she had an intruder in her house while she'd been naked, vulnerable, and unaware?

She heard him moving across the room, and her heart began to thud in her chest. Her eyes adjusted to the moonlight that filtered through the crack between the curtains and she found him standing over her. He took the phone away from her and set it back in its cradle.

"Time's up, baby. Enough with the fake-outs and excuses. I'm tired."

His gaze ran over her intimately. His hot hand settled against her waist and lightly backtracked up her body. The light touch brushed against the side of her breast, tickled her armpit, and caressed the tender inside of her elbow. "Let's make you more comfortable," he said in a low voice.

Taryn lay still as he reached for her handcuffs. His behavior made her edgy. She'd angered him more than once tonight; she felt justified to be scared.

With the sound of a click, she was free. Hesitantly, she lifted her wrist to him. The handcuffs jingled, and the sound reached the four corners of the room.

There was a silent battle of wills as they stared at each other. She held her ground, but was somewhat surprised when he reached for the metal bracelets. Relief started to flow through her, but it faltered when he slipped the handcuff around his own wrist. "No!" she cried.

"Yes," he said firmly. He climbed over her and put the key on the far nightstand. Then he settled down as guard, pulled the blankets up, and adjusted his pillow. "I've had enough of your tricks, so I'm not even going to give you the opportunity to try to sneak out of this bed while I'm asleep. It's not going to happen. Deal with it."

She pulled hard on the handcuffs, but she was chained solidly to him. "Tucker, I'm tired of this. It isn't funny anymore."

"You're complaining to the wrong person, Counselor." He stopped her sharp tugs by grabbing her wrist and pressing it against the mattress. "I've spent a hell of a lot more time in cuffs than you have. Believe me, your experience has been a lot more pleasurable than mine."

She quieted when she heard the flare of temper in his voice. Stiffly, she lay down on her back. It was unsettling to stretch out beside him, especially with his anger still heating the room. He was a big man, and there wasn't much she could do to avoid touching him. Even the sound of his breathing seemed to press on her.

The darkness magnified her trepidation. She'd been warned about the dangers she could face in her line of work. Angry defendants seeking retribution were rare, but she'd always known it was a possibility. What was it that she'd been told to do to protect herself?

She couldn't remember.

Tucker sighed. "Come here."

With a tug, he pulled her across the sheets until her back was flush against his chest. Taryn tried to calm her thundering heart. His body cocooned hers, and the heat he exuded nearly made her faint. She waited anxiously in the darkness.

"Go to sleep, Swanny. You said 'no', and I heard you. Relax."

Relax? Her nerves were stretched like a tightrope.

Tucker didn't seem to have the same problem. She was amazed when, all too soon, the arm around her waist went slack and heavy. The handcuff loosened as his hand covered hers on her belly. She glanced over her shoulder, but his breathing was deep and steady.

He'd fallen asleep.

She waited, but the more time passed, the more she realized that he was dead to the world. Gradually, her wariness eased. She'd been on pins and needles ever since she'd stepped into that darkened hallway. Knowing he was asleep, she finally allowed her guard to drop.

This was better. With him sleeping, she didn't need to use all her energy battling wits with him. Now was the time to think. She had to find a way to escape. A way to call for help. A way to incapacitate him.

It was hard to plot out a strategy, though, with his body pressed so close to hers. She stretched luxuriously. She liked the feel of his big hand spread across her bare stomach even if the handcuff felt cold. She loved how his muscled chest rubbed against her back with every breath he took. And the intimate tangle of their legs . . . Nothing had ever felt so deliciously sinful.

The more she tried to think, the less the ideas came to her. Her body became heavy. The tightness in her neck loosened, and her head sunk into the pillow. Finally, her eyelids drifted shut.

Behind her, Tucker finally relaxed. Playing dead was damn near impossible with a hot babe in his arms. He lifted his head and looked down at her. The lines of worry on her forehead had smoothed. He brushed a kiss across her temple and settled back down behind her. As much as it rankled him, she'd outwitted him tonight. He had to give her credit for that.

But there was always tomorrow, and he was a persistent type of guy. Tomorrow, he wasn't going to give her so much time to think. Tomorrow, she wouldn't be saying 'no'.

Chapter Three

Taryn awoke hours later as the pre-dawn light was beginning to erase the blackness of the night sky. Consciousness pulled at her, tugging her out of the depths of sleep, but she fought the urge to wake up. Her sleep had been too heavy, too satiating. She hadn't slept this well since Tucker had been arrested.

Tucker!

She nearly moaned out loud as she came fully awake. He wasn't in custody anymore; his big body was spooned against hers, warming her like a furnace. They were in her house. They were in her bed.

She'd spent the night in his arms.

She closed her eyes tightly as failure overwhelmed her. What had happened to her plan to escape? She was supposed to have plotted a strategy. Instead, she'd *cuddled.*

The bed suddenly shifted, and her pulse skipped a beat. Was he awake? His feet stretched outward, and his hand flexed on her stomach. She let herself go limp. She wasn't ready to start the battle again, not before she had a plan.

A jingling sound drifted softly through the morning air, but was quickly muffled. The key! Instinct told her to remain still.

She kept her breaths deep and low as Tucker leaned over her. His nearness made her want to tense, but when he lifted her wrist, she let him take its weight. The lock on the handcuffs clicked, and hope sprang forth in her chest.

He watched her closely; she could feel his concentration focused on her like a laser beam. With a murmur, she rolled away and pressed her face into the pillow.

Seconds stretched into an eternity before his hand ran gently down her side. She nearly cursed aloud when her traitorous body arched into the touch, but the bed shifted as he slid out from under the covers. He left the room silently, but she didn't allow herself to move until she heard the bathroom door close.

Then she kicked into high gear.

He hadn't chained her to the bed. She was free!

She had to move *now,* and she had to move fast. Flinging back the covers, she shot out of bed.

She'd made it three steps before she realized she had to be quieter. Tucker hadn't gone deaf. He was only a room away. Any unusual noise and he'd pounce.

To make matters even worse, she had to pass through the hallway by the bathroom door in order to get out of the house. Sweat broke out on her forehead, but she knew she didn't have time to worry about such things. If she thought too long, her chance would be gone.

So would her courage.

Her robe lie in a heap by the bed. She swooped it up and slid it over her shoulders.

She scurried by the bathroom on tiptoes. She didn't know how he didn't hear her. Her heart was pounding like a big bass drum. Luck was with her, though, and she made it to the living room without catching his attention.

Her immediate choice for a getaway was the back door. The front door was too far, and she needed to get outside as soon as possible. Once there, she could run. She could hide.

She flew to the kitchen. Her fingers shook as she unlocked the dead bolt. Flinging open the heavy wooden door, she reached for the screen.

A big hand came crashing down on hers as she gripped the latch.

"Going somewhere, Counselor?"

The growl in her ear made Taryn wince. If Tucker had been mad before, he was doubly ticked off now. Her fingers gripped the latch tighter. He pried her hand away and set the lock.

His body heat buffeted her as he stood behind her. Defeated and a little scared, she dropped her head against the glass window. Its chill nearly gave her a headache, and she reflexively backed away from the cold.

It was the wrong move to make. She collided solidly against him, and his steel-like arms wrapped around her.

"You shouldn't have done that, baby," he whispered into her ear. "Didn't you learn yesterday that when you run from me, there are consequences?"

A low moan slipped from Taryn's suddenly constricted throat. She didn't need to be told what the consequence would be this time. His hands were already working on the tie of her robe. She reached to stop him, but her efforts had little effect. He was too strong—too intent on his purposes.

His wildness sent a secret thrill through her.

The robe was pulled open, and she sucked in a gasp as the cold seeped through the screen door and onto her skin. She squirmed against him, trying to find relief, but instead, he pressed her forward.

She cried out when her nipples touched the frost-covered window.

"I'm tired of your teasing, baby—and I'm not talking about just last night. You've been teasing me for years with that stupid rule about not dating coworkers, with those sexy little suits, with your perfume . . . Do you know how many times you've gotten me all hot and bothered and then run away?"

"Tucker!" she gasped. The cold nipped at her, shocking her. "Please!"

"I've had it with your little 'look but don't touch' game. I've learned what happens when I touch, and I like it." He pulled the robe down her arms, and it pooled at their feet. He stepped forward and pressed her more fully against the glass. "Your running days are over, Swanny."

Taryn was in turmoil. Her belly and thigh muscles constricted from the cold, but the heat of her skin was enough to make the frost melt. Soon droplets of water were running down her legs. The icy sensation was as sharp as her anxiety—and as acute as her growing desire.

"Tucker, it's too cold," she begged.

"Don't worry. I'll warm you up."

Instead of backing away, he squeezed his hands between her body and the glass. His rough palms covered her breasts, and the resulting heat shocked her. He fondled her tender flesh, creating such a fervor she could hardly stand it.

The contrast was just too much. The door was a big sheet of ice, but her backside was bathed in heat. His chest rubbed against her shoulders and back, but it was her bottom that was on fire. He thrust himself suggestively in the cleavage of her buttocks, and the friction sent her need skyrocketing.

"It's too cold. Too hot." She couldn't think. "I can't take this."

"You can, and you will."

She shuddered. He wasn't talking about the cold.

"Do you know how pissed I was at you yesterday in that courtroom when you were strutting around in your little blue suit?"

He nipped at her earlobe and excitement shot through her veins.

"You think those outfits make you look professional, but I'll let you in on a secret. They get me hot. I always wonder what you're wearing underneath them."

He pinned her with the weight of his body as his hands roamed. To her breasts. Around her waist. Along her thighs. He spread his fingers across her stomach and stroked downwards until they tangled in her blonde curls. Her lungs shuddered as yearning poured through her.

"You were intent on putting me in prison, but all I could think about was the slit going up the back of your skirt."

"Tucker," she panted. Sensation was about to overwhelm her.

"You should have believed in me, baby. You owed me at least that much."

He slid one foot inside hers and bumped her leg outwards, widening her stance to give him better access. Taryn's muscles quivered as she waited for him. Finally, his hand covered her mound. His devious fingers snaked along the grooves of her pussy, making her legs go weak. She groaned from both the ecstasy and the torment. He was intentionally avoiding the tiny bud that would give her the most pleasure.

"We're going to deal with this little problem first." He gently squeezed his fingers together, and a jolt of energy made her jump. "Then we'll talk about the other."

Taryn rolled her forehead against the door, and water trickled down her face. The collision of hot and cold air had fogged over the glass everywhere except the places where she touched. Anybody looking in from the outside would have a clear view of her naked, undulating body. The thought only heightened her arousal.

"Are you ready for me, baby?" he whispered.

Ready? She was about to come unglued. He parted her lower lips and pushed two thick fingers up into her.

"Ahh," she cried out. Her need sharpened to a razor's edge.

"Christ, you're tight."

The strain in his voice nearly matched hers. His fingers plunged deep, hard, and fast. Little sounds left Taryn's throat. Her hips begged to move, but she couldn't. He had her trapped. Soon, more than condensation was running down her legs.

Tremors started radiating out from her belly. She spread her palms wide on the smooth surface of the glass and braced herself. Suddenly, Tucker spread her legs even wider apart. He bent his knees and positioned his throbbing cock. She was given no time to prepare before he surged straight up into her.

She cried out sharply, and he cursed.

It was almost too much to take—the shock, the amazingly full penetration. He pulled back and her pussy burned with friction. Before she could gather herself, he was pushing inexorably upwards, stretching her wider. He found a rhythm and was soon pounding into her with long, deep thrusts.

Taryn felt herself spiraling out of control. Oh, God, she'd needed this. She'd needed him.

She whimpered when he stopped and adjusted her stance so her body pressed flush against the pane of glass. The chill was almost welcome against her overheated flesh. Almost. One of his hands slid around to the front of her mound. His fingers opened her so her clit was subjected to the cold glass, and the concentrated sensation pushed her over the edge.

"Michael!" she cried.

He began stroking into her again; each hard thrust lifted her right up on her tiptoes.

The tension inside her sprang loose with a vengeance. Pleasure pumped through her body, and she let out a scream as the orgasm shook her.

Tucker rode Taryn hard as she climaxed. It had taken everything inside him to wait until she went first, but now, it was his turn. And he wanted more. Hell, he hadn't even kissed her yet.

"I can't get at you good enough," he growled.

Abruptly, he pulled out of her. She gasped at the loss, and a tight smile pulled at his lips. He turned her and lifted her in his arms. Unable to bear being apart from her for another moment, he plunged back into her.

"Better?" he snarled. His civility was quickly coming to an end.

"Uh," she whimpered. "So full."

Her back arched, and he took advantage of the access to her breast. He pulled her nipple into his mouth and sucked. Her skin was cold—like a big, delicious ice cream cone. He was more than happy to have a taste.

Her legs tightened around his waist, and he was lost. The way her muscles gripped him made the top of his head nearly come clean off. He worried that he might be too much for her from this angle, with thrusts this hard.

"More, Tucker. I need more."

The words sifted through the mists in his head and scattered his remaining coherent thoughts. With both hands, he grabbed her ass and rammed into her. It didn't take long before he was spurting like a volcano.

Weak with the aftershock, he sagged against the door with her securely in his arms. His body was mush; his brain was a complete blank. He felt her fingers run through his hair, and his knees nearly buckled.

Holy hell. He'd dreamt of screwing her for two years. Two long, frustrating years. He could have chosen better circumstances, but *damn,* even with the threat of capture hanging over his head, coming here had been worth the risk.

But did she feel the same way?

The thought caught him from out of the blue, and a zap of wariness shot down his spine.

Ah, shit. There wasn't much hope of that. She'd been running from him before he'd caught her and literally screwed her to the wall. He couldn't have planned a less romantic scenario.

The world began to right itself on its axis as they stood in silence. Cool water dribbled down his hand, and he plucked Taryn away from the glass door. In a vain effort to warm her, he ran his palm up and down her spine.

She didn't respond. She was already withdrawing from him mentally; he could feel it. Her body began to stiffen, but he wouldn't allow it. He *couldn't* allow it—not after what had just happened.

He kissed her, coaxing her back into the moment. She went still at the touch of his lips, and he took it as a sign of encouragement. She felt so soft. So vulnerable. He wove his fingers into her hair, nearly desperate to bring back the closeness he'd felt only moments ago. Keeping it slow, he deepened the kiss. When his tongue touched hers, though, she trembled and pushed at his shoulders.

"You don't play fair, Tucker."

He was breathing hard. "Fair doesn't always win. I play for keeps."

She looked at him as if seeing him for the first time. "And you don't care who gets in your way, do you?"

The accusation stung, and he nearly lashed back before spotting the anguish that swirled in the depths of her blue eyes. "You've got it wrong. All wrong. I'm not a drug dealer," he said emphatically. He wanted to shake the truth into her, but instead he rubbed the base of her spine in soothing circles. She was looking at him so guardedly, it made him anxious. "You know me, baby. I'm a cop. I drink bad coffee, I type with two fingers, and I catch the bad guys."

"But you—"

He stopped her with a finger to her lips. "I didn't do anything wrong other than to trust the system to clear me. I swear it, Taryn. I didn't come here to scare you or to hurt you. I came here for your help."

A shuttered look settled onto her face. "Put me down, Michael."

Frustration made him want to put his fist through the door, but he'd learned she was serious when she called him that. Carefully, he uncoupled their bodies. Her face turned red with embarrassment, and he hated that. He tried to make her look at him. "Taryn, I didn't give those drugs to Justin."

She wrapped her arms about her body and stared at a point somewhere over his shoulder. "Please let me go. I'm cold, and I need to clean up."

He wasn't going to let her do this. "No."

Her indignant gaze snapped to his. "No?"

He saw the shiver that ran across her skin, and a feeling of protectiveness hit him hard. "Shower? Yes. Let you go? Absolutely not."

Before she could protest, he leaned down and swept her up in his arms. She let out a sound of outrage, but he didn't care. She wanted to be stubborn? She'd just come up against the king of bull-headedness. "You've proven to me that I can't let you out of my sight. Until I've convinced you that I'm innocent, it isn't going to happen again."

He bumped the back door closed with his hip. "Lock that."

Amazingly, she complied. He carried her to the bathroom, her body stiff in his arms. It was a disappointing change. Only moments ago, she'd been warm and pliant. Aggravation made him clench his teeth together so tightly his jaw hurt.

What was it going to take for him to change her mind? He was innocent, damn it. Why couldn't she see that? Why didn't she just *know*?

Taryn stepped as far away from Tucker as she could when he stood her on her own two feet. A huge ball of fire mixed with regret and humiliation had settled somewhere just under her lungs. How could she have let that happen?

She'd just had mind-blowing sex with a drug dealer. A murderer. He might not have pulled a trigger or thrust a knife, but he'd killed that poor boy just the same. By supplying Justin Diaz with those drugs, Tucker had caused his overdose.

And she'd just let him touch her as he saw fit. She'd taken pleasure from his hands, his mouth, his . . . She lifted a hand to cover her face.

"Don't look like that," he growled. "You got off on it as much as I did."

"Are you taking the first shower, or am I?" She refused to talk about what had just happened. She was too ashamed of herself.

His lips thinned. "We're showering together."

"But . . ."

"I told you that I'm not going to let you out of my sight."

"Fine." Whipping back the shower curtain, Taryn stepped inside. She turned on the water, but flinched when it smacked against her. The heat was heavenly, but her body was still overly sensitized. Especially her breasts. When the water pellets sprayed against her nipples, it was all she could do not to whimper.

"Here," he said with a sigh. He stepped in behind her and settled his hands on her waist. "Body heat is better."

She resisted, but he turned her around. She batted at his shoulders in a late display of defiance, but he wrapped his arms around her. A soft "shhh" and a kiss to her temple made her go quiet. She stood in his embrace with her head hung low.

"Taryn, you know me," he said calmly. "I've never supplied drugs to minors—or to adults, for that matter. My job was to get the drugs off the streets. You saw me do it. You *helped* me do it."

The irony wasn't new to her. She'd spent many sleepless nights thinking about how and why he could have turned. "It was always a losing battle, though. We both saw how much money the pushers were making on the streets. The temptation obviously became too strong. You crossed the line."

His voice took on an edge. "No, I didn't."

She lifted her head. "Then prove it."

"Counselor, our justice system works on the presumption of *innocence.*"

Her shoulders slumped in disappointment. She knew how the system worked better than anybody. She also knew how much evidence there was against him. All she'd been asking for was a bone—just one little bit of info she'd missed that would refute the charges against him.

Yet he couldn't give it to her.

"I'm warm," she said dejectedly. "Please, let me go."

His hands tightened on her, but after a moment, he let them drop. Turning around, Taryn reached for the soap. Her throat was tight as she fought back tears. When it came to the case, she didn't believe him. She'd seen the evidence. She'd been over it forwards, backwards, inside and out. She'd approached it from every angle, trying to find a flaw. There wasn't one.

She swallowed past the lump in her throat. She'd always thought so much of him. He was bright, funny, determined, and the best damn cop she'd ever seen. How could he have tossed all that by the wayside for dirty money?

The need to be clean was suddenly overwhelming. She kneaded the bar of soap between her hands and scrubbed her legs, her face, her chest . . . She halted abruptly when she realized that Tucker was watching her every move. "Stop it!" she hissed as she wrapped her arms around herself.

"Damn it, Taryn. Why are you so ready to believe the worst about me?"

"I'm not! Or I wasn't—until I saw the proof."

She gave him her back. The proof—it made her feel even filthier. She didn't want to touch herself in front of him, but the stickiness on her thighs reminded her what she'd done with him. Steeling her nerve, she reached for her sex. Her senses were still on overload down there, and she bit her lip to keep from groaning.

He grabbed her by the shoulders and spun her around. "Forget the so-called 'proof'. Evidence can be planted. I was framed."

She gaped at him. Hastily, she pulled her hand away from her crotch and slammed the bar of soap into its tray.

"Framed? I don't see how." She stepped around him and reached for a towel. "Your fingerprints were found all over the pack of heroin in Justin's pocket."

"I didn't give it to him."

"They were also covering most of the stash discovered in your gym bag at the Y."

"Anybody could have put that there."

"It was in your locker."

"The Y isn't known for its high security measures, Swanny. Besides, do you know how much heroin, cocaine, marijuana, and other crap I've handled in my career? How many bits of evidence I've seized? Shit, look how much stuff we found during the Rodriguez case."

He hit the faucet handle and stepped out of the shower after her. "Hell, that doesn't even have to be the explanation. My fingerprints were on the plastic baggies, not the drugs themselves. I've been known to pack a few lunches in my day."

Taryn wrapped the heavy weight towel around herself and relished the protection it provided. The war between her body and her mind was disconcerting. She tried to retreat to her role as prosecutor. "Fifty-thousand dollars was found in your house. Explain that one away, Detective."

That seemed to humble him. He stopped rubbing his towel across his chest, and the expression he gave her was pained. “I can’t.”

She felt her last flicker of hope die.

“You knew Justin Diaz,” she said.

“Sure I did. He played on the basketball team I coach at the Y. He was a good kid.”

“He was also a kid who’d had drug problems in the past. Most of the kids on that team have had similar problems. That kind of makes them good targets, good buyers, doesn’t it?”

She didn’t expect him to react so swiftly. His hand whipped out and caught her by the nape of her neck. His eyes shot sparks as he glared at her. “I’ve never put a kid in danger in my life. I coached that team to keep the kids off the streets. I can’t believe you would accuse me of something like that.”

“I can’t believe you would do something like that,” she shot back.

The look on his face changed.

“Then don’t believe it,” he growled. “Believe in *me,* Taryn.”

Oh, God. Why was he making this so hard? She braced her hands against his chest.

“Stop it! Just stop,” she said, losing her tenuous grip on her control. “You’re trying to spin things. You’re trying to twist everything around in my head so I have doubts.”

He caught her chin. “As in ‘beyond a shadow’? You bet your sweet ass, I am.”

She was at a loss for words.

He took a deep breath and softly brushed his thumb over her trembling lips. “Think about it, Swanny. How would you feel if you sent an innocent man to jail? What if that man was me?”

Emotion clogged her throat. She didn’t want to hear things like that. She knew her actions affected people’s lives every day. That was why she was so careful. That was why she double and triple checked everything. She couldn’t afford to make mistakes—especially mistakes like that. They would destroy her.

He saw her hesitation.

“Come on, baby,” he said coaxingly. “Work with me, if for nothing but your own peace of mind. What have you got to lose?”

Chapter Four

Taryn tried to steel herself, but she couldn't stand to see him this way. Lying or not, he could be anywhere right now, running for his freedom, but he'd chosen to come to her. He'd covered miles just to talk to her.

And the possibility that he was telling the truth? Frankly, it terrified her. Putting away an innocent was one of her most secret, darkest fears.

But he knew that.

They'd talked about it many times before, on long nights, during confusing cases . . .

She rubbed her aching forehead. Her head was spinning out of control. He'd set her off-balance on purpose, but if there were even the slightest possibility, no matter how remote . . . "All right, I'll listen. I just don't see how you're going to change my mind. I've been over the evidence a million times, looking for something that would clear you."

An unidentifiable emotion flashed in his eyes. "You looked?"

She sighed. "I looked."

He kissed her again hard and quick—just enough to muddle her senses.

"Then let's talk," he said.

She pushed him away and clenched the towel to her chest. "I want to get dressed first."

He looked down at himself. He'd wrapped a towel around his waist, but the clothes that he'd worn the night before were lying in a heap on the floor. "That might not be such a bad idea. We need to think, and that's hard for me to do when you're naked. Hell, it's hard enough when you're twenty feet away and fully dressed."

Taryn felt herself begin to weaken, but she stiffened her backbone.

She refused to let him sweet-talk her. She'd listen to his side of the story, but she was good at her job. In all the years she'd been a prosecutor, she'd never come across a criminal who didn't claim to be innocent. Just because she wanted Tucker to be didn't mean that he was. "My dad left a sweat suit behind last time my parents visited. You can wear that."

As they dressed, she desperately tried to pull on her professional cloak. If she was going to listen to his side of the story, she needed to detach herself. She tried to put on one of her work outfits, but he tossed a pair of jeans and a T-shirt at her. An attempt to put her hair up was firmly vetoed, too.

"You're not going to hide behind your armor," he said as he followed her into the kitchen. "I won't let you."

She scowled when she saw the broken window, but opened a cupboard, pulled down a box of cereal, and grabbed a bowl. When she turned, he was blocking her way.

"I said I would listen to you," she said. "What more do you want?"

His arms bracketed her as he braced himself on the counter. He leaned down to her level, and his gaze seemed to pierce into her soul. "I want all of you—ADA Swanson, the soft woman who slept in my arms last night, and the fireball who just nearly burned off my cock. You've spent so much time trying to prove yourself as a lawyer, baby, I think you've forgotten that there are more sides to you."

She pushed the box of corn flakes against his chest. "Do you want to talk about the case or not?"

He gave her a hard look, but backed off. "Yes, I do."

She took her breakfast to the table. She turned to get the milk, but he was already standing there with the gallon out of the refrigerator and a bowl of his own. Veering in a different direction, she opened a drawer and returned with two spoons. Stiffly, she sat. "So talk."

He glanced at the small TV on the kitchen counter. "I think I'll check up on the posse first."

He clicked on the television and soon found a morning news program. By the time he got his bowl of cereal prepared, the news anchor was talking about his case.

"Authorities are still searching for Michael Tucker, the former police detective charged with drug running," the blond Ken doll reported. "Yesterday, Tucker escaped when the police vehicle transporting him from his arraignment hearing was involved in a two-car collision at the intersection of Highway 16 and Maple Road. Armed guards in charge of watching Tucker were injured in the accident, but have subsequently been treated and released from a local hospital. Due to their injuries, neither guard witnessed Tucker's escape. The driver of the car, who is believed to have run a stop sign, remains in critical condition and has not regained consciousness."

The camera changed angles, and the anchor cocked his head accordingly. "At this time, Tucker's whereabouts are unknown. He is not believed to be armed, but should be considered dangerous. If you have any information, you are encouraged to call the authorities at 555-4000."

Tucker shot her a look. "Don't even think about it."

Taryn dipped her spoon into her cornflakes. "Why would I? My phones don't even work."

The jab must have landed, because he scowled. "I'm sorry about that, babe. I know I must be acting like a crazy man, but you're my only hope."

"So you take me hostage." Milk sloshed over the side of her bowl. "That's always a good way to win over people."

"Swanny," he said shortly. "I'm the subject of a statewide hunt. They're coming after me, and I've got two choices—run or clear my name. I'd prefer to do the latter, but for that, I need your help. Unfortunately, you don't seem to be in a very helpful mood."

"Can you blame me?" She gave up on her breakfast, and her spoon came clattering down.

"Hey, I'm sorry, but I've got my reasons."

"Your reasons. Remind me again what they are."

He gave a short bark of laughter and ran a hand through his hair. "You got me into this mess. You're going to get me out."

She glared at him. How dare he turn this whole thing around on her! She slapped her hands on the table, stood from her chair, and advanced on him. "*I* got you into this mess? Sorry, but that doesn't compute, Detective. I've got file upon file of information that shows that *you* did just fine getting *yourself* into this bit of trouble."

Tucker caught Taryn's finger as it poked him in the chest, and his senses went on the alert. The tingle in the back of his neck had saved his butt too many times to count. He wasn't about to ignore his instincts now. "Where are those files?"

She hesitated, and her face went intentionally blank. "At the office."

The tingling intensified. "Liar," he said smoothly.

Her jaw dropped, and she jerked her hand back. "I'm the liar?"

"I warned you about that angel face." He reached out and caught her chin. He ran his thumb across her lower lip, and it quivered. "I know when you're bluffing, babe. Go get the damn files."

She pulled back so she was out of his reach, and her anger shimmered like a halo around her. "Fine," she ground out.

She spun around and headed out of the kitchen. He was right on her heels. He could hardly believe she had the files here. He'd wanted to get his hands on this information. If he could just go through it, he might find something that the investigators had missed. At this point, he would be grateful for anything, *anything* to go on.

The office was actually a small, second bedroom that had been converted into a workspace. With the desk, computer gear, and file cabinets, there wasn't a lot of empty room. He immediately headed to the desk. There, sitting right on the desktop were at least a dozen files marked with his name.

"Wow." For a moment, he was taken aback. He thumbed through the stack and shot her a quick look. "This is a lot. Do you have everything here?"

She shrugged and glared at him. "Maybe."

"But why would you keep it here? Why not at the office?"

"What else am I supposed to do in my spare time?" she snapped.

Tucker felt a surprising surge of satisfaction. So the ADA did have doubts. It made him more optimistic than he'd been in a long time.

In a swift move, he grabbed her and pulled her hard against him. "I can think of quite a few ways to pass the time," he murmured as his head dropped.

He caught her mouth in a steamy kiss. She resisted at first, but soon her body melted against his. He brushed his lips across her cheek and nipped her earlobe. "Go through them with me," he said.

"I can't," she said in a strained voice.

"Why not?"

"I've been over everything so many times, I've practically got it memorized. I can't look at it again."

He was beginning to understand. It wasn't that she didn't want to help him; it was that she couldn't find a way. The files were so dog-eared, she must have spent hours going through them. From her perspective, though, everything pointed to him being guilty.

"That's okay," he said. He gave her a comforting squeeze. "Help me carry them out to the living room, and I'll look at them."

"What's wrong with here?"

"The room's too small," he growled. "If we stay in here ten more seconds, I'm going to be banging you like a bull."

It took nine seconds for her to help him move things to the floor of the living room. Tucker didn't know whether to be amused or offended. The files were too tempting, though, and he dropped to the floor to read them. Taryn sat well across the room from him with her back leaning against the couch. It was just as well, he supposed. Any closer and he wouldn't have been able to concentrate.

He was soon immersed in the reports. After about twenty minutes, though, he felt a flare of annoyance. His head snapped up, and he glared at her. "You questioned my *mother*?"

Her cheeks flushed, and she toyed with the weave of the carpet. "I was looking for a second set of keys to your house. If somebody planted the money, they had to have gotten in somehow. There were no signs of tampering with the locks. I thought she might have had access."

"You thought my *mother* was involved? Swanny!"

"No, I didn't think your mother was involved," she snapped. "I was looking for keys. Somebody might have taken her set without her knowing."

"Oh, Mom would know." A smile pulled at Tucker's lips. "Did she give you a hard time?"

"She was . . . protective."

His smile turned into a full-out laugh. "That's a nice way of putting it. I know how she can get."

"She hates me," Taryn said quietly.

He winked at her. "She'll change her mind when you help clear me."

She shrugged uneasily and glanced around the room. "Mind if I open the shades? I'm getting claustrophobic sitting around in the dark."

"The light's good enough," he said. He looked back down at the file in his hand. His mind was already focusing on its contents. "Leave them closed."

"Fine," she sighed. She leaned her head back against the couch and closed her eyes.

Tucker dove into the files. Many of the pages were worn and crinkled, but he still felt he had a chance of finding something useful. After all, he had a unique perspective on this case. He should be able to see things his former coworkers hadn't. Reading through the notes was strange, though. These tidbits of info were all about *him*. It was almost like he was having an out of body experience, but he shrugged off the feeling. It needed to be done.

Half an hour later, he roused Taryn from her short nap. "Was this bag in my gym locker checked for prints other than my own?"

Groggily, she opened her eyes. "Hmm? Yes, the bag was analyzed."

"What about the locker, especially this area around the door latch?"

"What? Where?" She rubbed her eyes and leaned closer.

She gasped when he pulled her onto his lap. "This will work better if we go through them together," he explained.

Over time, the two of them had developed an uncanny method of communication when it came to casework. They played off each other's thoughts and often came up with answers that neither of them would have concluded alone. He'd never needed that calculating mind of hers more.

He quickly arranged them so that his back was against the couch and she was leaning against his chest. Her butt fit snugly between his outstretched legs. His cock automatically reacted to the contact, but he ignored the ache for the time being. Patiently, he held the picture in front of her. "How much of the locker was dusted?"

She sat stiffly in his arms. No doubt, his erection was as distracting to her as it was to him. "The whole thing," she said.

"The whole thing?" He looked at her sharply. "The floor? The roof?"

"Everything. Including the lock."

He felt a surge of irritation. "I told you before, that lock wasn't mine."

"Then why did it have your fingerprints on it?"

"Hell, I'd just come out of the shower. My clothes were in there. How was I supposed to know what was going on? I saw the lock and looked at the locker number. It didn't compute. It was stupid, I know, but I touched the damn thing."

She squirmed, so he adjusted her into a more relaxed position.

He grabbed another file. "It says here that you found metal shavings on the floor. That proves that somebody used a bolt cutter."

"The police unit did that. And before you say anything, they had a valid search warrant."

"Provided by that son-of-a-bitch Sheuster." Tucker ran a hand through his hair. "So compare the shavings. If they don't match the lock you have, I've got proof."

"The shavings aren't conclusive. I've already checked with a metallurgist. The same type of steel is used in both the brand of lock we found and the one you claim to have used."

"All right," he said, his chin brushing against her hair. "All right."

They weren't getting very far, but it was clear that she had tried to find holes in the case. That, at least, made him feel a little better. Wrapping his arms around her again, he lifted the stack of pictures so they could both see them. "Let's look through the rest of these."

He flipped to the next picture, which was a shot of the tank of his toilet. The lid had been removed, and a plastic bag of money was stuffed inside. "Somebody's been watching too many bad movies. At least you haven't broadcast it on the news that I hide my valuables in the toilet."

"I still can."

"I'm serious," he said as he rubbed his chin against her temple. As angry as he'd been with her, he had to admit that she'd behaved professionally. She'd even showed small signs of compassion. "You did me a big favor by not fighting the judge's ruling to bar cameras from the courtroom. I appreciate that."

"If I'd known you'd come to my house and hold me hostage, I might have acted differently."

"I don't think so." He brushed his lips against her hair and turned to the next shot in the stack.

Taryn felt Tucker's muscles freeze when he realized what he'd uncovered. It was a picture of Justin Diaz's body as it had been found in an empty alleyway downtown. The boy lay on his back with his empty eyes staring blindly at the sky. He wore workout clothes that were still sweaty, and his hand was draped limply over a basketball. She'd checked. The last time he'd been seen alive and well was earlier that evening at practice.

Tucker quickly put the picture aside and turned it facedown. The next one was nearly as upsetting. It was a picture of him with the teenager. Tucker was spinning a basketball on his finger, and Justin had his arm slung around his coach's shoulders.

Taryn struggled to find something to say. "It looks like you two were very close."

"We were." His voice was raspy with emotion.

Instinctively, she covered his hand on her stomach. She didn't know why, but she felt compelled to comfort him. Her brain told her that he'd killed this kid. It was probably unintentional, but still, he'd given Justin the drugs. Her brain knew all that, but her heart hated seeing him this distressed.

She rubbed her palm against the back of his hand. "I know you didn't mean to hurt him."

"I didn't hurt him, Counselor." He threw out the title like it was garbage, but sighed and settled his chin against her shoulder. "I was trying to help him off the streets. I know how the Diazes presented themselves in court yesterday, but his home life sucked. I was trying to show him there was a better way."

"Drugs are enticing to kids that age. If they can help them escape, they want them badly."

"You think I don't know that? I was trying to get him away from that crap. I would never have given him more."

She linked her fingers through his. She could feel his pain, and she did believe him. He might not have given the drugs directly to Justin, but somehow the kid had gotten his hands on them. "Did he know the combination to your locker?"

"Are you kidding me?" He turned his head to look at her. "I'm not stupid. Those were good kids I coached, but they're street kids. If I wanted to keep my wallet, I didn't give them the temptation."

She returned his look, and their noses almost brushed. "Then give me something, Tucker. Explain to me how this happened. I'm out of ideas."

Lines wrinkled his forehead, and his jaw hardened as he glanced at the files strewn across the floor. "What about the money?" he said. He reached for the photograph of his bathroom. "I never touched that."

She blinked. He was usually sharper than that. It proved how desperately he was grabbing at straws. "The money was found in a plastic bag inside your toilet tank. Water and fingerprints don't mix."

He grimaced and the photo fluttered to the ground. Tiredly, he reached up to rub the back of his neck.

"Who could have framed you, Tucker?" she asked quietly. "Who had the knowledge, the opportunity, and the motive?"

"Hell, I don't know." He rubbed his hand against her stomach and sighed. "But I like hearing you ask the question." He softly nuzzled her earlobe. "This is much better. I don't like fighting with you, Taryn."

They'd gotten nowhere. He'd done nothing to prove her wrong, but he was getting harder and harder to resist. "I don't like it, either," she admitted.

"Do you know how much I've enjoyed working with you over the past two years?" His tongue rimmed her earlobe, and the little hairs on the nape of her neck perked up. "I liked seeing your eyes light up as you put a case together."

Taryn felt goose bumps pop up on her skin. His lips and the hand on her belly were creating havoc with her system. "I like puzzles," she said, "and you always brought me all the right pieces."

"I wish I had them for you now."

So did she.

He tugged her white T-shirt out of the waistband of her jeans so he had access to her skin. He settled his palm on her abdomen and electricity shot through her nerve endings.

"Tucker," she groaned. Not again. She'd never be able to resist him.

His voice dropped to a whisper. "You made me wait a long time, Swanny."

She squirmed, but stopped when she realized she was only rubbing herself against his erection. "It wasn't appropriate for us to become involved."

"Why not?" he asked. He leaned over her shoulder so he could see her face. "You never told me why."

She bit her lip. She didn't like talking about that, but she didn't see what it could hurt now. And anything that would ease his anger towards her would be a bonus. "I dated another ADA at my last job. It ended . . . poorly."

"You got dumped?"

"I dumped him, but that wasn't the problem. After we broke up, everyone looked on me as the ex-girlfriend, not an ADA in my own right. I had seniority, but cases that should have come to me started going to him. I didn't get a pay raise that year. It finally got so bad, I had to leave. I transferred here and swore that I'd never let my personal life and work life cross again."

"Weren't you ever tempted? I tried my damnedest."

"Of course, I was t-tempted." Her voice hitched when he placed an open-mouthed kiss on the side of her neck.

"Temptation doesn't even begin to cover the feelings I had for you," he said. "Your perfume, your body . . . Hell, I could get a hard-on just by hearing your voice on the phone."

His hand slid up her stomach and began toying with the front clasp of her bra. Taryn knew she should push his hands away, but instead, her fingers sank into the muscles of his thighs.

He grunted with approval. "Did you ever cream your panties when we were talking on the telephone?"

Lust hit her hard. She moaned when her bra clasp let loose, and his hand slid under one of the cups.

"Did you?"

"Yes," she groaned.

His other hand slid under her T-shirt, and he cupped her possessively. "That still doesn't explain why you went out with Sheuster," he growled. "Why him, but not me?"

"I never went out with Marty." She hissed when his fingers pinched her nipples in rebuke. "I didn't. We might have had a working lunch or two, but it was all platonic."

"Not from the way he described it. The picture he painted was of the two of you humping like rabbits."

"I never . . . Tucker!" He'd pushed her breasts together and was simultaneously assaulting her nipples with his thumbnails.

"Mind if we get rid of this bra?"

His teeth nipped at her earlobe, and Taryn couldn't voice a protest. She didn't want to; desire had her wound too tight. She started to pull up her T-shirt.

"No, no. Leave that on. I like the way the material pulls tight over your tits."

She squeezed her thighs together. He could make her wet with only words, but she didn't stand a chance when he touched her and talked dirty at the same time.

With his help, she managed to shrug out of the bra. He pulled it through the arm sleeve of her shirt and tossed it to the side. He then settled his hands on the waistband of her jeans. With slow, intentional movements, he undid the button and slid down the zipper. Together, they watched as his hand glided under her panties to her moist sex.

"You needed this as much as I did."

"God, I've never been this horny before," she groaned.

"You've been screwing the wrong guys."

Unable to stop herself, Taryn lifted her hips to give him better access. He penetrated her with two fingers. As he ground the base of his palm against her pubic bone, he let out a soft laugh. "You need a slippery when wet sign, baby."

She was beyond conversation. She arched her neck back against Tucker's shoulder and pushed her mound hard against his hand. His fingers were scissoring inside of her, stretching her, preparing her for more.

His other hand was practically mauling her breasts, but she loved it. Her hips lifted completely off the ground. Soon, she was moaning in delight and panting with exertion. She wanted more. She needed . . .

The doorbell rang.

They both froze. Taryn dropped to the floor and stared at the door in confusion. She was horrified when the bell began ringing non-stop and insistent pounding began.

Thank God he hadn't let her open the drapes!

"Who do you think it is?" she asked hoarsely.

"Nobody good, that's for sure," he said. He pulled his wet hand out of her panties and hurriedly zipped up her jeans. "You'd better go see who it is before they send for back-up."

She was disconcerted when he helped her to her feet and pushed her toward the door. Her head snapped toward him when she comprehended what he'd said. "You think it's the cops?"

"Probably," he said as he disappeared from the room.

The doorbell was still buzzing, and the knocking had intensified. Dazedly, Taryn headed towards it. With every step, she could feel the moisture that had collected in the crotch of her jeans. They'd be sopping wet within a few minutes. The seam of the denim was rubbing against her clit, keeping her arousal right on the edge.

There was nothing she could do about it now, though. Taking a deep breath, she pushed her disheveled hair over her shoulder and opened the door. A uniformed officer stood on her doorstep.

She went still.

It was the police. She hadn't thought about what that would mean.

This was it—her rescue.

But for Tucker, it was the end of the road.

Indecision jammed her thought processes.

"Ma'am?" the man said.

She looked at him blankly. "Officer," she said, the word awkward on her lips.

Tell him!

No, don't. You'll regret it for the rest of your life.

"Can I help you with something?" she asked.

She needed time to think; time to make a decision.

For a moment, the officer didn't respond. He simply stood there gaping at her with wide eyes. It was only then that Taryn realized that she hadn't put her bra back on. The T-shirt was close fitting, and her nipples were distended. A cold breeze swept into the house, and they promptly perked up higher.

Her face flared. The cop was getting quite the show, but he was distracted. She needed to use that to her advantage.

She needed to consider her options.

Steeling herself not to cover her exposure, she repeated her question. "Is something the matter, Officer?"

He licked his lips, but couldn't seem to tear his gaze away from her breasts. The attention only focused her awareness of her nipples. They itched under his concentration, and she felt the stickiness on her thighs. "Officer?" she said, her voice strained.

"Um, yes, ma'am. We're on the lookout for Michael Tucker. You haven't by chance seen him, have you?"

Seen him? She'd seen him, touched him, kissed him, screwed him . . .

Tell the cop he's in the next room . . .

The place he went when he let you answer the door.

Her fingers tightened on the doorjamb. Tucker had put his fate securely in her hands.

Would a guilty man do that?

A cunning guilty man might.

Stop it! Just stop it!

Circular thinking was getting her nowhere, but it all came down to one thing.

She couldn't turn him over. Not now. Not until she'd fully explored his side of the story. He seemed honestly intent on proving his innocence. She had to see that through, for better or for worse. He wouldn't hurt her; she knew that with every fiber of her being. She needed to play this out until the end.

At least then she'd know for certain whether or not he'd killed that poor kid.

And whether this attraction growing between them was real or a twisted, cruel ploy.

"No, sir, I haven't." Guilt hit her square in the chest, and she gripped the doorjamb tighter. "Why would you think he'd be here?"

"You're the one prosecuting the case, ma'am. He might have revenge on his mind."

She shifted her weight, and the officer's gaze followed the swaying motion of her breasts. By now, her nipples were two pink tent posts under the material, and he'd given up all pretense of not looking at them. "If I know Detective Tucker, he's in another state by now," she said.

"We haven't been able to pinpoint his whereabouts yet, ma'am." The officer pushed his hat back on his head and finally met her gaze. The lust in his eyes was unmistakable. "You should be careful. ADA Sheuster was concerned when he couldn't reach you by phone."

The policeman looked over her shoulder. Taryn realized that her files were still spread out all over the floor. And her bra! It was draped over the hassock in front of her chair! She took a quick sidestep to block his view. "I'm working on a new case. I unplugged my phone so I wouldn't be disturbed. I must have fallen asleep."

Playing the part, she ran her hand through her mussed hair. "Your knocking woke me up."

With her arm lifted the way it was, she was practically pushing her tits in the man's face. It didn't escape his notice. "Must have been quite the dream, ma'am."

Her face flamed, and she dropped her arm. She tugged at her T-shirt in embarrassment, but that only pulled the material tighter. The officer practically began drooling.

"You can tell ADA Sheuster that I'm fine," she said. "If there's nothing else, I really should get back to work."

The officer hooked his thumbs in his gun belt, but didn't move from her doorstep. Desire hardened his features, and Taryn felt an inappropriate shiver of response run down her spine. There was something about a man in uniform.

His voice went low. "Do you need any help with that work? Ma'am?"

The respectful term touched her like a caress, and Taryn flinched. Enough. She'd let things go too far as it was.

"Good-bye Officer . . ." She looked closely at his badge. "Denton."

She finally crossed her arms over her chest. The free show was over. "Good luck with your search."

He got the message. The glint in his eyes dimmed, but he took a step back and tipped his hat. "The best with your case, ADA Swanson."

He turned and walked down her steps, but moved gingerly. Taryn shut and locked the door behind him. Groaning, she leaned her forehead against it. She couldn't believe the extremes she was going to—all for Tucker, a man she didn't even know if she could trust.

"Swanny?"

She slowly turned around and leveled a look on him.

So help him, she'd better not regret this.

"I just broke my code of ethics for you."

His face was solemn. "You couldn't give me up."

Tucker took a step towards her. "You believe me."

Her hand whipped up, and she pointed at him to ward him off. "No, I don't. I don't know what to believe anymore, and you've twisted my thoughts into knots. I'm just giving myself time to straighten everything out."

He kept coming. "You *want* to believe me."

"That's beside the point."

"No, it's not." He walked right up to her and settled his hands at her waist. In a flash, he whipped down the zipper on her jeans. "To me, that's pretty much all I've got."

Taryn gasped in dismay. Her jeans hadn't even been buttoned! Heavens, she'd been parading in front of that dazed police officer with her breasts standing at attention and her jeans halfway undone. She batted at Tucker's hands. "Don't touch me," she snapped. "I swear I'll call him back here and have him arrest your ass."

"Who? Denton? He'd be too busy looking at yours."

"Damn it, Tucker!" She shoved at his shoulders, but he didn't budge. "I just crossed the line for you, and all you can think about is sex?"

"All I can think about is you." He pulled her into a hard kiss. "You're listening to me, and you're protecting me. You can't blame me for being excited about that."

She tried to slither away, but he slid his hands right under her panties and cupped her bottom. The intimate touch was shocking, and she had to fight the inclination to shimmy against it. "Well, I'm not excited," she said stubbornly.

"Liar. You don't want to send me back to that holding cell anymore than I want to go. What we both want is me right here, screwing the daylights out of you."

With a flick of his wrists, everything she was wearing below the waist dropped to her knees. Her clothes didn't stay there long, because he set his foot in the crotch of her panties and pushed down. He lifted her out of the pile and kicked it away. He took three steps and dropped her on the couch. "Stop denying it."

Chapter Five

"I can't believe you! You cocky bastard! I lied for you. I put my reputation on the line and, now, you expect me to put out?"

Taryn had never been more furious in her life. She tried to kick Tucker, but he just caught and held her legs. With a tug, he brought her hips to the very edge of the cushions. He tore off his borrowed sweats. When he dropped to his knees between her legs, her anger turned to acute self-consciousness.

She was still wearing the T-shirt, but it only came to her waist. Everything below was left exposed, and he wasn't being shy about looking. She could practically feel the heat of his laser-like stare. He'd spread her legs wide, and the position left the most private part of her defenseless. Unable to bear his intense examination, she covered herself with her hands.

"No, baby. Let me look at you." He gently gripped her wrists and moved her hands aside. He held them against the couch and renewed his inspection. "You're gorgeous."

Taryn squirmed on the cushions. "Manhandling me isn't going to change my mind," she hissed. "I'm still mad at you."

He gently held her in place. "I'm getting that fact loud and clear. If you'll just lie back and relax, I'll try to help you out of that grumpy mood."

For some reason, she felt more vulnerable half-clothed with him than she'd felt totally naked. Looking down, she saw her nipples rubbing against the white material of her T-shirt. If possible, they'd grown even redder and stiffer. Below, Tucker kneeled in the vee of her legs. He was only inches from the tangle of curls at its apex.

It was too much.

"Please, Tucker," she said. "This is making me uncomfortable."

His gaze shot up to her face. He read whatever emotion was in her eyes and gave her a soft smile. "We can't have that."

Reaching over, he grabbed a pillow from its place against the arm of the sofa. He tucked it in the hollow space between the curve of her spine and the couch cushions. She had to admit it eased some of her physical discomfort. Still . . . "That's not what I meant," she whispered.

"I know," he said in a low tone that rippled over her skin. He pushed himself up from his kneeling position and hovered over her. "You just put yourself in the line of fire for me, baby. Let me show you how grateful I am."

He kissed her softly before backing away. "Trust me, Taryn."

His gaze connected with hers and a shimmer of excitement shot through her system. He was waiting for her approval, and an emotion she didn't want to define gripped her. "All right," she said slowly.

She'd thought he'd smile again. He didn't.

Instead, his expression turned intense. His weight came down on her, and his open-mouthed kiss was hot, hard, and very personal. He kissed her forever, until her anger, her discomfort, and her uneasiness all vanished.

Taryn found herself clutching him as his lips left hers, but he wasn't through. He ran soft kisses across her closed eyelids, her cheekbones, and the point of her chin. His gentleness was driving her mad. She turned her head to give him access to the side of her neck. His tongue on her pulse made her wriggle, but this time she wasn't trying to get away.

His hot mouth dropped lower, and she gasped when his teeth closed on her nipple. Need spilled through her veins. "Tucker!"

"That cop wanted to do this. He couldn't take his eyes off your tits."

"You were watching us?" she gasped.

His tongue ran across her aching flesh, leaving a big wet spot on the T-shirt. "I saw the whole thing. Including your reaction. You liked having him watch you."

"I did not!" The words ended with a moan when he drew her breast, T-shirt and all, into his sucking mouth.

"Oh, yeah?" His hand suddenly pressed hard between her legs. He dipped a finger inside her and tested her wetness. "Evidence is evidence, baby. You liked teasing that poor bastard. Admit it."

His touch made her all the more aware of how vulnerable she was. She bit her lip as he explored her, and the muscles at the small of her back clenched. She looked at his slick finger when he held it in front of her, and shivers coursed across her skin.

He was grinning at her again.

"Well . . . maybe I did," she confessed. Strutting around in front of the helpless policeman had made her feel naughty. But not as naughty as this. "It was all your fault though. You got me all worked up and then just left me there."

"If you remember our situation, babe, there was a cop at our door. I'm on the run from the law. Is any of this ringing a bell?"

"Excuses, excuses." Her eyes widened. Had she said that out loud?

He closed his teeth softly across her nipple. "I promise to finish the job this time," he said.

She gave in. Why fight it when she wanted it so much?

She trailed her fingers through his dark hair. "You'd better get back to work."

He smiled deviously. "Yes, ma'am," he drawled in a dead-on imitation of the police officer.

Taryn's belly clenched. If he'd been looking for an aphrodisiac, he'd just found one. She'd never been one for games, but combine Tucker and that leering cop, and *ohhhh*!

He dropped his head to her other breast, and she felt her pleasure mounting. The wet material abraded her nipples and made her want more. "Harder," she groaned. "Oh, please. Harder."

Tucker pulled back and looked at his handiwork. The front of Taryn's top was one big wet spot. She was breathing roughly, and her breasts shuddered with every breath she took. Her nipples were in plain view, and he liked the effect. "We're going to have to take you down to Flashers next Tuesday night, baby. You've got that wet T-shirt contest in the bag."

"Michael," she panted. Her impatience was beginning to show.

He loved it when she called him that. She only seemed to use it as a last resort whenever she was really mad or really horny. The really mad part could be fun, but the really horny part was better. Way better.

Using his thumbs and forefingers, he reached out and clamped down on her wet nipples. She nearly came off the couch.

He calmed her with a path of kisses down her stomach.

His own breaths were getting short. She did things for him . . . incredible things. He couldn't remember ever getting so hard so fast—not even when he'd been a sex-starved teenager.

Then again, at sixteen, he hadn't had a blonde bombshell laid out like a sacrifice before him.

He dipped his tongue into her belly button and felt her quiver. He could hardly believe that he was with her. Just when his life had been jerked out from under his feet, things between them had clicked.

Wasn't that just his luck? He'd finally gotten the girl, but he was most likely headed to prison for the next twenty-five years of his life.

He kicked the thought out of his head. Nothing was going to spoil this.

Nothing.

He determinedly ran his hands down her hips. Giving in to an impulse, he slid them under her buttocks and squeezed the round globes. Her low moan told him how much she liked the attention.

"I'm going to have to search you, ma'am," he drawled. He'd seen how sharply she'd responded to his imitation of Officer Denton, and he wasn't above using it to his advantage. If she got off on it, so did he.

His fingers nudged into the crevice of her ass, and her butt cheeks clenched. "But Officer, what did I do?" she said on a high note.

She was into it.

Looking down, Tucker saw the prize. Her legs were spread, and she offered no resistance. "You've been a very bad girl, Ms. Swanson."

He raked his hands from her buttocks down to the back of her thighs. Her breath caught when he lifted her and draped her legs over his shoulders. The position put her right into his face. He gave her one, long lick.

She gave a strangled cry, and he deliberately went in for more. Using his tongue, he sought out every crevice, every curve, and every sensitive nerve ending. She was thrashing on the couch by the time he found her opening. He pushed his tongue inside her as far as it would go, and she arched like a bow.

"Don't resist, ma'am," he said, his mouth moving against her.

"Officer," she panted. "It's too personal."

"Let me do my job."

Simulating the sex act, he thrust his tongue in and out of her. She gave a high-pitched whimper, and he increased his pace. He felt the flutters begin, and he quickly changed tactics. He slid his mouth upwards until the bud of her clit popped inside. He gave the epicenter of nerve endings one hard suck, and she came undone.

"Ah, Michael!"

Her orgasm was hard and violent. She shuddered in his arms, but he continued working her with his mouth until the last palpitations drifted away. Only when she lay limp against the pillow did he give her a reprieve.

But not for long. His dick was as hard as the nightstick he'd carried as a beat cop. All he could think of was getting it inside of her and doing a different kind of beating.

"I'm nearly finished, ma'am," he said through heavy breaths. "But I'm afraid I'm going to have to do a more thorough body cavity search."

Her heavy-lidded eyes opened. "But, Officer, is it really necessary?"

"Oh yes, ma'am, it's *absolutely* necessary."

His control was unraveling at a frightening pace. He couldn't wait for her to catch up. His fingers dug into her hips as he lowered her to him. He let gravity help, and she slid right off the couch and onto his waiting cock.

"Oh!" she cried. Her sleepy eyes popped open, and her hands clutched at his shoulders. "Tucker?"

"You can do it, baby," he growled. "You're flexible enough."

She was nearly bent in two. Her legs had slid down the front of his chest and were now pointed straight up in the air, with her ankles somewhere around his ears. Wedged between his body and the couch, she had nowhere to move.

But he could move. He drew his hips back, slowly pulling himself out of her. At the very end of the stroke, he reversed directions and filled her again.

Her eyes glazed over, and her neck arched back. "Ah! You feel twice as big."

"Good, huh?"

"I . . . I don't know."

He did. The expression on her face was primal. Her hair was wild around her shoulders, and hunger burned in her eyes. What they were doing was beyond good, so much so it was almost frightening.

He gave another experimental stroke. "Too much, ma'am?"

He'd hit her trigger.

"No," she said slowly. Her breaths started pumping faster as her excitement returned. "I can . . . I can handle it, Officer."

"All right, ma'am. Take a deep breath and relax. Let me work, and it will all be over soon."

Tucker gave another thrust that made his head spin. She was so hot and wet. And tight. She gripped him like a vice. Carefully, he increased the speed of his thrusts to see how she would take it.

She took it well.

Suddenly, his gnawing arousal couldn't be held back any longer. The need for her overwhelmed him, and he began to buck against her. If anything, his cock seemed to grow bigger inside her tight passage.

She made a mewling noise and her toes went en-pointe. Her inability to move seemed to thrill her, because she was already making little sounds at the back of her throat.

He was beginning to love those little sounds.

"Michael," she whined in desperation.

His control snapped, and he slammed into her. Her mouth opened in a soundless cry, but he kept plunging. He shagged her until sweat was running down his back, and stars shimmered behind his eyelids. Finally, *finally* he felt his balls draw up tight.

With a roar, he exploded. She gripped his shoulders hard, and collapsing, he pulled her down to the floor with him. Her damp skin clung to his, and her hair spread across his shoulder. He wrapped his arms around her to keep her close.

"Holy hell, Swanny," he said when he could catch his breath. "You're going to be the death of me."

"I was only trying to cooperate, Officer," she said shakily.

Lifting an eyelid took supreme effort, but he managed to give her a look. "That guy's starting to piss me off."

"Why?"

"He makes you hot."

She glanced away shyly. "No, Michael. You make me hot."

Tucker lifted his head sharply. "Say that again."

Her cheeks turned pink. "I didn't mean . . . You also make me angry, frustrated, and—"

He caught her chin and made her look at him. "Come on," he prompted.

She sighed and looked at the ceiling. "You make me feel a lot of things, and it's all jumbled up inside my head. You've been charged with murder, and you've taken me hostage. Yet when a policeman shows up at my door, I cover for you. I'm not myself. I'm not thinking straight."

"So don't think. Go with your gut."

She ran a hand over her eyes. "I can't trust myself."

"Why not?"

Finally, she looked at him. "Because I want to believe you, but for *me.* I can't tell anymore if I'm being selfish, if you deserve it, or if it's because of . . . you know . . . the sex."

"Ah, baby," he sighed. "It's all of the above."

"How can I be sure?"

Her mistrust cut deeper than Tucker expected, but he pushed the hurt aside. He had to remember that Taryn Swanson was the whole package: beauty, personality, and brains. They'd already confronted the physical. Now, he had to appeal to her logic. "If you thought I was a cold-blooded killer, you would've rushed into Officer Denton's arms, half-naked or not."

She opened her mouth to say something, but he covered her lips with his finger.

"If you didn't have doubts about the case, you wouldn't have dog-eared copies of the files lying around your home. You wouldn't be having chats with metallurgists, for God's sake. Your gut is screaming at you, Taryn. Your brain just isn't letting you listen."

"It would be easier if there was a hole in the evidence."

"You're picking at details, Swanny. It shouldn't be that difficult for you to have faith in me. You *know* I wouldn't do what I'm accused of doing. You wouldn't let me touch you, kiss you, or screw the daylights out of you if you weren't sure."

A sharp pang of uncertainty suddenly caught him. "Would you?"

Time stood still as they hesitantly looked at each other, and panic flared up inside Tucker's chest. He'd never even considered that she might be screwing him because she was scared or biding her time. Or even worse, manipulating him.

The tension slipped from her face. "No," she whispered.

He went still.

"I couldn't be with you if I thought you were a murderer." Her body relaxed against his. She shook her head as she stared at him incredulously. "It doesn't make any sense. I've got nothing to back it up, but I don't think you did it."

"Swanny." He dropped his forehead against hers. Relief made him lightheaded. "God, it's good to hear you say that."

"Don't make me regret it," she warned.

"You won't," he promised.

He pressed his lips to hers and all the emotion that had built inside him over the past few days poured into the kiss. The anxiousness, the tension, the frustration, the anger—and the fear. This was why he'd come here. He'd needed her faith in him.

He'd needed her.

He tucked his head into the crook of her neck and breathed deeply. Her body felt warm and comfortable pressed against his, and he savored their closeness. All of it. He hadn't realized how much he'd had invested in his plan, but thank God it had worked. Knowing that she was in his corner made him feel stronger. Together, they could fight this.

Her fingers tightened in his hair. "We have to do something to fix things," she said anxiously, "and we can't get sidetracked again. The police have already been at my door."

He wasn't ready to let the rest of the world back in. "Let's just stay like this for a little while longer."

"No, Tucker," she said gently. "We need to make plans. Let me up."

She cupped his cheek, and the one, little touch turned him to putty in her hands. He gritted his teeth. "Ah, hell."

He slowly disconnected their bodies, rolled onto his back, and rubbed his eyes with the balls of his hands. It was damn hard to fall back into the role of Detective Michael Tucker, Super Cop, when she'd just given him everything he wanted.

Well, nearly everything.

"What's our next step?" he asked tiredly. "I thought the files would help, but nothing popped out at me."

"Get dressed," she said. "We need to think."

"Right." He ran a hand over her tangled hair. "Can't do that naked."

She reached over him and grabbed the remote. He looked at her in bemusement as she clicked on the TV and began intently flipping through channels. With a sigh, he sat up and stuffed his legs into his borrowed sweatpants. His head came up, though, when she hit a news report.

"Michael Tucker, accused drug dealer, remains on the run today," the reporter said. "Authorities have narrowed their search to the Wurthington Heights area. A man matching the escapee's description was seen getting off a bus at the corner of Wilmington and Neiman Avenue. Residents in the Heights area are encouraged to be on the lookout for a man matching this description."

"How far behind are they?" she asked as she gathered up her clothes.

"A ways."

"That's good, at least," she said. She headed for the bedroom to change.

Tucker watched her backside until she was out of view and then reined himself in. *Think, man. Think.*

He made himself mentally review his movements as a picture of his scruffy face filled the TV screen. After getting off that bus in the residential area of the Heights, he'd followed the creek bed down to the business district. He'd caught another bus there. So far, the police hadn't made that connection.

He picked the remote up off the floor and tossed it onto the end table with a clatter. Damn, but it pissed him off that his own friends and coworkers were hunting him down like a dog.

His picture was replaced by video of the Diaz family walking up the steps of the courtroom to his arraignment, and the anchor's voice spoke over the clip. "Tucker is at the center of a controversial murder case that has brought to light cracks in the city's law enforcement system. Sources say that—"

"Wait a minute!" Tucker blocked out the Ken doll's words as he watched the video behind the man's head.

Something wasn't right.

He dove for the remote and frantically searched the menu buttons. He jabbed the instant record button and prayed there was a tape in the VCR.

"What is it?" Taryn said as she poked her head out. Her eyebrows went up when she saw what he was doing. "My soaps!"

He waved her off and focused on Justin's younger brother, Benny. He couldn't have seen what he'd thought he'd seen.

But he had.

"Oh, shit," he breathed.

"What?" she asked. She pulled her robe on as she hurried back to the living room to look at the screen.

The news reporter had gone on to the next story. Tucker squinted at the remote and pressed stop. He rewound the tape and hit play. "How do you slow this down?" he asked.

She took a step closer and peered into his hand. She poked a button and the film slowed down to a frame-by-frame advance. "There. What is it?"

"Look at what's on Benny's feet."

Her eyes narrowed. She watched intently as the boy climbed the steps, but just shrugged. "They look like new tennis shoes."

"Exactly," Tucker said in a hard voice. "Those are Mercury Wings. They cost about two hundred and fifty dollars."

She looked at him in confusion. "I don't understand. Is that supposed to mean something to me?"

Tucker's gut turned, but he went back to the stack of photos he'd left next to the couch. A few had been crumpled by their sexual acrobatics, but he found the one at the bottom of the pile—the one he'd turned over so he wouldn't have to look at it.

He flipped it over and tried to be impartial, but he couldn't. This wasn't just evidence. He'd known the poor kid in the photograph. He'd known his quiet intensity, his dry sense of humor, and his quick move to the basket. Tucker swallowed hard. "Look at the body. Look at the shoes."

Taryn nibbled at her fingernails as she examined the photo. The teenager lay on his back with his feet pointing limply at the sky. "Is that duct tape?"

Tucker couldn't look at the picture anymore so he passed it to her. "The Diazes didn't have enough money to buy Justin a decent pair of cross trainers, and he was the basketball player in the family. Why the hell is Benny walking around with a shiny pair of Mercury Wings?"

Taryn's face was blank for a good ten seconds. When she finally put the pieces together, her breath hitched and her eyebrows rose to almost her hairline. "But he's only twelve!"

"Remember that case a year ago? The kid was ten."

"Oh, God." She raked her hand through her mussed hair and turned swiftly back to the television. The video was still running in slow motion. "Oh, God! I've been worried about him. He's gaunt and every time we start talking about the case, he looks like he's going to be sick."

She stared at the TV for a long time, and Tucker could practically hear the gears grinding inside her head. His were already spinning at high speed. Had Benny been around the evening that Justin had died? Was he strong enough to use bolt cutters?

Taryn's gaze suddenly turned to meet his. "He's been on your side the entire time. He kept saying 'Coach couldn't have done it.' I thought he was in denial, because he liked you."

Tucker wanted to punch his fist through a wall. Instead, he clasped his fingers at the back of his neck and started circling the room. "He was always hanging out around practice. He wanted to play. I told him when he was fourteen, he could try out."

Taryn slowly sank down onto the chair. Her gaze kept flicking between the television screen and the picture in her hand. "Why would he plant the drugs in your locker?"

Tucker let his hands drop. "Panic?"

She shook her head. "There's got to be more to it. He wouldn't have been calm enough or sophisticated enough to plant the evidence. Your fingerprints were on everything."

Tucker jerked when the answer came to him. "He's got to have a supplier. And if the guy knew I was a vice detective, it would be one helluva way to get me off his back."

Taryn's eyes widened. Abruptly, she pushed herself to her feet. "This is it," she declared.

He looked at her sharply. Raw determination had settled onto her features. She walked straight across the room towards him and laid a hand on his chest.

"This is the break we've been looking for," she said.

His pulse leapt, and he stared at her hard. He trapped her hand against his heart. "We?"

"Yes, *we*."

Her eyes went soft as she looked up at him. Still, he was surprised as hell when she went up on tiptoe and covered his lips in a long, sexy kiss. Tucker's heart tumbled over itself. It was the first time that she'd kissed him, and the implications sent his mind reeling. He couldn't even try to stop her when she pulled back and looked at him solemnly.

"I'm sorry I've been such an idiot," she said.

He watched mutely as she disappeared into the bedroom. After a few minutes, he heard the bathroom door open and close. Water was running before he was functioning enough to sit down and stop the tape, which was now showing a muscle-bound bartender kissing the socks off a sultry brunette.

Oh, man. Was he in deep.

Absently, he began searching for another newscast, but he couldn't think straight. He didn't want to get his hopes up too high. A new pair of tennis shoes could mean nothing. But that kiss . . . That had felt like it meant something.

The door to the bathroom opened, and he glanced up from the television broadcast. Taryn stood in the doorway, dressed to the nines in one of her high-powered business suits.

She might as well have slammed a sledgehammer into his brain.

"What the hell do you think you're doing?" he barked.

She wasn't intimidated. Calmly, she took a stance he'd seen her perfect in the courtroom.

"I'm going to my office."

Chapter Six

Taryn forced herself to stand her ground when Tucker came out of his seat like a warrior springing into battle. It took him only three steps to cross the room.

"What did you say?" he asked in a low voice.

She brushed a speck of lint off her dark jacket. "I'm going to my office. Somebody needs to talk to Benny. There's obviously only one of us who can do that."

"Think again, baby. You're not going anywhere."

Her eyes narrowed at the tone of his voice. "Why? Are you afraid of losing your hostage?"

"Damn it, Swanny!" He took a step closer. "You know better than that."

Did she? She clicked her tongue against the back of her teeth. He'd sure expected a lot out of her. Now that the tables were turned, though, things weren't as easy. "You don't trust me," she said pointblank.

She sucked in a hard breath when his hands whipped out and closed about her waist. He jerked her to him, and his nose nearly brushed against hers as he stared into her eyes. "I don't want you to get caught in the middle of this," he bit out.

The intimidation tactics only made her more stubborn, and she met his stormy gaze in challenge. "You came here for that exact reason."

A muscle worked in his jaw. "That was then. This is now."

"So what's changed?"

Butterflies swirled in her stomach. She refused to let them show. There was something important going on here, and she had to hear his answer.

"Everything," he finally said in a raw voice. "It's too dangerous. I didn't realize the scope of the frame-up, but if this guy will use kids, he'll do anything. If you somehow got hurt, I wouldn't be able to take it."

He cared. The tortured look in his dark eyes showed that it wasn't all lust for him either. Emotion clogged Taryn's chest, but it only strengthened her resolve. With an unsteady hand, she cupped his cheek. "I'll be fine, Tucker. I'm the ADA trying your case. It would look suspicious if I didn't go out there and make some kind of statement."

The muscle in his jaw only ticked faster. "At least let somebody else question Benny."

"Will your captain and your partner do?" She ran her thumb along his lower lip and smiled to lighten his mood. "Joe's been a royal pain in the butt ever since the charges were first brought against you. He'll jump at the chance to look at another suspect."

Tucker shook his head. "It's going to draw attention to you. You've got to look like you're taking part in the manhunt."

"I will. I plan on inviting the Diazes down under the guise of updating them on the progress of the search. I promise that nobody else will know what we're really doing."

He stared at her hard. "I don't like it."

"Trust me, Michael," she said softly. He'd asked her to put her faith in him. It was time to give a little in return.

She could see the war within him, but he didn't answer with words. Instead, his arms wrapped around her like bands of steel. He pulled her close and buried his face in her hair. She wrapped her arms around him and clung.

"I believe you, and I want to fix my mistake," she said in a choked voice. "I don't want you in prison. I want you right here, screwing the daylights out of me."

That got a rough laugh out of him. He gave her a hard squeeze and reluctantly let her go. Running a hand through his rumpled hair, he shot her an amazingly shy look. "That's what I want, too."

He was vulnerable. The realization threw her. She'd seen his tough side when he was working, his caring side when he was coaching, and his passionate side when. . . . Well, that was obvious. But vulnerability? To her? It was disconcerting, and it sent her protective instincts surging. Suddenly, she wanted to lock him in her bedroom and barricade her home against anyone who tried to invade its sanctity.

"Then let's do something to make that happen," she said. "And fast. I'm sure the media will be knocking on my door next."

Purposefully, she reined in her emotions and headed to the kitchen. There was work to be done. She couldn't let her feelings overwhelm her, not when he needed her help so badly. She'd done a lot of thinking alone in the shower, and she had a plan. A good plan.

She could lock him in her bedroom later.

"I'm going to give you the keys to the Vallingers' car. They're snowbirds that live in the yellow house next door. They went to Florida last week and asked me to look after their things."

She picked up her purse and jumped when she sensed him right behind her. He moved so quietly, she didn't think she'd ever get used to it.

"You can use their Taurus if you need it," she continued. "I don't want you trapped here with no escape route."

He lifted an eyebrow, but took the keys she offered.

"Nobody will report you. That should give you some valuable lead-time."

He gave her a calculating look, but still didn't answer. His silence was beginning to make her uneasy. She'd thought he was through fighting her on this.

"I've thought of someplace you can go," she said stubbornly. "My parents have a cabin on Indian Horse Lake. Nobody's using it this late in the season."

She grabbed a pad and pencil out of her purse and leaned down to write the address. Her breath caught, though, when he suddenly grabbed the hem of her tailored skirt and pushed it up to her waist. "Tucker!" she gasped.

She quickly looked back over her shoulder, but he was already staring at what he'd uncovered.

"That's what you've been hiding," he said. His hand spread wide on her backside and rubbed in a slow circle. "Niiiice."

A delicious feeling of naughtiness caught Taryn unexpectedly. On impulse, she'd worn her good black lingerie. It was a sexy combination that she rarely wore. She'd just been thinking ahead to how they could celebrate when she returned with good news. She shivered when he ran his finger along the elastic band of her garter belt to the lace atop her stockings.

"So I take it you've got this all figured out," he said in a low voice.

His touch was decadent, but she'd warned him they couldn't get sidetracked again. She cleared her throat and looked at him from her bent-over position. "I got you into this mess. I'm getting you out."

To her surprise, his jaw went tight. "Listen, Taryn. When I said that, I was a little hot under the collar. I didn't really mean it."

She quivered as he slid his finger under the elastic and ran his knuckle over her buttocks. "Sure you did, but that's okay. I'd be a little put out if you did the same to me."

He shifted his weight uncomfortably, and his attention focused on her thong. "You just did what you thought was right. There were a lot of things that had to come together for this to happen. Somebody went to a lot of trouble to frame me."

The pad of his finger traced the triangle of material to the point where it disappeared into the cleavage of her buttocks, and Taryn fought desperately to clear her fogging brain. "And I was just a pawn?"

Tucker shrugged.

He hooked his forefinger under the triangle of material and gave a tug. Her thong popped out of its hiding place and the thin line of black silk rode atop the crevice of her buttocks.

She let out a soft cry, and her back arched. *Sidetracking*. They were sidetracking. "We're going to get the person responsible for this. I swear."

"Swanny?"

With his thumb, he pushed the thong back home. It slid in with a distinctive pop.

"What?" she groaned.

He jerked the material back out. "Do you always wear risqué panties underneath your starched suits?"

The soft question pushed her right past naughty. She felt absolutely wicked when he slowly tugged the thin line of material upwards again. Her head dropped to the table. Sidetracking be damned. Good God, she hadn't realized she was so sensitive back there. The action was so erotic, her toes were curling inside the cramped confines of her pumps. "No," she whispered.

"This is all for me?"

He could now flick the material in and out of the tight space using his thumb alone. Her butt cheeks clenched tight, and she couldn't relax them. With every move of that clever thumb, the thong brushed against the tightly pursed rose of her anus. The slight, rhythmic brush of silk was driving her crazy. "Yessssss."

"Then this is for you," he growled.

Unexpectedly, he changed the action of his hand. Instead of pulling the thong out from between her buttocks, he pulled the material straight up towards her waist. The silk rasped in her sensitive crack, directly over the bud that was causing her so much distress. The crotch pulled tight over her sex and her wetness flooded the cotton-lined panel.

"Michael," she said on a tight note.

"Oh, yeah," he growled. He reached around and anchored her with his palm against her pubic bone. The position left his fingers free to clench her underwear from the front.

Taryn's anticipation sharpened. "Please."

"Hold on, babe. I'm getting there."

Her entire body went rigid when he began to saw her panties forwards and backwards. The friction lit up every erogenous zone between her legs. Her clit, her pussy lips, and her anus burned with fire.

A high-pitched cry erupted from her lips. "Mi-chael!"

His front hand ground harder against her, and he increased the speed of the sawing motion.

It was too much.

The fire was going to eat her alive.

Taryn tried to shift her hips away, but he held her down. The rubbing became faster and hotter. Still, she couldn't reach her peak. It was right there—just out of reach. She was hovering below it, aroused beyond belief, but she couldn't quite get there.

She gave a cry of despair and lifted her hips higher. Suddenly, the hot motion of the material stopped. She nearly started crying at the loss, but her back bowed when she felt his hot hand take its place.

With his front hand still tightly cupping her mound, his back one burrowed into the crack of her ass.

He touched her anus with the pad of his thumb, and she came.

She screamed, and her body shook from head to toe. Through it all, he held her tightly. He held her as she reached the precipice, and he held her as she came back to earth. He even held her as she lay like a puddle of protoplasm on the kitchen table.

"Oh, God," she gasped. She had to wait several seconds until her lungs functioned properly. "What did you just do to me?"

His voice was raspy in her ear. "That was hot."

"But you didn't even . . ."

"I know—and it was still fucking hot."

She pushed herself up onto her elbows. "Damn you, Tuck. Now I've got to take another shower."

He chuckled and dropped a kiss onto her temple. "You are such a fussbudget. Do you know you've spent half the time I've been here in the shower?"

"That's because you keep making me . . ."

"Cream?"

"Shut up."

He nipped her earlobe softly. "Stay where you are. I'll clean you up."

"You'll what?" Her palms dropped flat onto the table and she nearly pushed herself all the way to a standing position before he pressed her back down. His fingers began working on the clasps of her garter belt. They were undone with an efficiency that made her eyebrows lift, and her mushy muscles tensed again.

"Relax."

That was hard to do when he hooked his thumbs under her panties and pulled them down her legs.

"Step out of them."

She stared straight down at the tabletop as she followed his orders. To her amazement, he simply reattached her garter belt to her stockings.

"Don't move."

She stayed put as he left for the bathroom, but unsureness gripped her when she heard water running. He was busting through all her sexual hang-ups like a wrecking ball. There was just no stopping him.

And she didn't want to.

He returned, and she felt self-conscious when a warm washcloth settled between her legs. It began moving, and the intimacy alarmed her. She must have made some sound, because he quieted her with a soft "shhh" before continuing.

She flinched when his nimble fingers caught sensitive areas, but he calmly repeated the procedure until she began to crave his attentive touch. She went right up onto her toes, though, when he used his finger to push the washcloth deep into her.

"Got to get you clean," he said silkily.

His finger was twice as thick with the washcloth wrapped around it. The shocking fullness made Taryn clench the edge of the table until her knuckles turned white. Her hunger returned, sharp and voracious. He refused to feed it. He worked slowly and meticulously until he was satisfied he was done. He finished by wiping the stickiness off her thighs and, just as carefully, dried her.

"There you go," he said as he pulled her skirt back down over her hips.

She didn't know what to say. "Thank you" seemed so inappropriate. "More please," sounded downright greedy. "Well," she said.

She turned around and smoothed the skirt over her hips. She felt the lines of her garter belt and struggled to get herself under control. She was overwhelmed by his easy familiarity with her body—and her eager responses. It was going to take some time to get used to it all.

And time was something they held in very short supply.

"Yes, *'well',*" he mocked.

"Stop it," she said. Embarrassed, she settled her hands on his chest and pushed him away. "What am I supposed to say after something like that?"

He didn't stop laughing as he caught her by the waist and pulled her close. "Did you enjoy it?"

She felt herself flush. "Yes."

His grin stretched wider, and he dropped a kiss onto her forehead. "That's all I need to know."

She pushed him away again. She was onto him. "You're trying to stall me, but I'm still heading out that door."

"I expected as much." He finally backed away to lean against the kitchen counter. He crossed his arms over his chest and gave her a serious look. "You need to be careful."

"I will," she promised. Still feeling extremely self-conscious, she sought out the mirror on the refrigerator. She was stunned to see that her make-up and hair were still intact.

"Lawyer look still in place?" he asked cockily.

She caught his intimate look in the reflection of the tiny magnetic mirror and hesitated. There was something about the sparkle in his eyes. . . .

Her suit! He'd told her that they made him horny, but she hadn't dreamed . . . How long had he been fantasizing about doing that to her? A year? Two?

Her pussy clenched, and his cleaning job turned out to be a waste of time.

She turned to head to her bedroom, but he moved in that smooth, lightning quick way of his and caught her about the waist. "Don't," he said softly.

"But I'm not wearing—"

"I know."

"You want me to go to work this way?"

"Yes."

"But why?"

"That way, I'll know you're thinking about me."

Hours later, Taryn was pacing around her office like a tiger. Thinking about him? She was obsessed with wanting to get back to him! With each step she took, she was clearly reminded that under her conservative business suit, she was stripped bare.

She stopped pacing and pressed her thighs together to try to stop the ache. If something didn't break loose soon, she was going to have to go to the ladies room and take care of matters herself.

She glared at the clock for the hundredth time. The delays and holdups were driving her stark, raving mad!

She'd wanted to meet as soon as possible, but nobody was conforming to her schedule. Captain Holcomb was busy in a meeting. She didn't doubt that the main topic of discussion was the manhunt for Tucker. Joe Payne had headed out of town for the weekend, most likely to avoid the search for his partner, but she'd managed to catch him by cell phone. He was headed back, but it would take at least another forty-five minutes. And the Diazes. Justin's mother had sounded drunk when she'd answered the call, and his father hadn't been in much better shape. She'd finally convinced them to come down for a talk, but they'd groggily muttered that they needed to find Benny first.

They didn't know where he was.

Taryn's hands closed into fists as she turned to pace in the opposite direction. *They didn't know where he was!*

She let out a long breath. It was possible the boy had just gone out to shoot hoops or hang with his friends. Her fingernails pressed more sharply into her palms. It was also possible he'd heard about Tucker's breakout and had freaked.

She felt panic rising in her chest. Benny was their one link. He was their best hope in clearing Tucker's name. If he ran away, she didn't know what she'd do.

One step at a time, she told herself.

She forced herself to unclench her fists, but the clip-clop staccato of her heels echoed off the office walls. She needed to calm down. She was getting too far ahead of herself. She didn't know that Benny was gone. Heck, she didn't even know if he had a reason to run.

She swiveled around, but teetered unsteadily when she saw a familiar form in the hallway. Marty Sheuster was walking past her office with a cell phone plastered against his ear. She quickly ducked. He was the last person on earth she wanted to see right now.

The ADA walked by, but his footsteps stopped abruptly. He leaned back and looked through her open door. "Taryn?"

"Damn!" she hissed under her breath.

He clipped his cell phone onto his belt and strutted across her office. "Hey, beautiful. What are you doing here?"

She impatiently brushed back a tendril of hair that had fallen out of her French twist. She could barely look at the man after hearing all the lies he'd told about her. Just picturing the two of them together made her sick. He was at least two inches shorter than her, but twice as big around. His hairline was receding and those teeth . . . Ugh.

"Unless you've been living under a rock, you must have heard that Michael Tucker has escaped," she said. "I came in to find out what's being done."

Sheuster sidled up to her desk and propped a hip against it. "If you're nervous with him out there, I'd be happy to keep you company."

"I'm not scared, Marty. I'm mad." *At you,* she nearly added. You lying pig.

"No, really," he said in that sugar sweet way of his. "You shouldn't be alone. Why don't you come stay with me until things settle down?"

She took a deep breath and tried not to let her revulsion show. "Thank you for your concern, but I feel secure in the privacy of my own home."

"Are you sure?" He leaned towards her, and she fought not to shrink back. "The policeman I sent out to your house said you looked disheveled when he dropped by earlier today. Quite disheveled, I might add."

"He woke me up."

"I'm sorry. Were you in bed?" With the last insinuating word, he reached out and covered her hand.

"Marty!" She snatched her hand back, and fought for composure. She couldn't let him draw her into an argument. She had more important things to do. "Listen, I don't mean to be rude, but I really need to work right now."

"It's nothing to be embarrassed about." He threw her a wink. "I understand."

"The officer caught me at a bad time," she said flatly. "Let's just leave it at that."

He smiled, and her skin crawled.

"All right, but my invitation still stands." He absently picked up her favorite pen and began rolling it between his fingers. "I've got plenty of room and a nice, big, king-sized bed. I think we'd both sleep better if you were under my protection."

She snatched the pen away from him and threw it into the trash. No amount of disinfectant would ever make it clean enough for her to use again.

"We could invite Officer Denton to guard you, too, if that would make you feel safer." Sheuster's voice dropped to a conspiratorial tone. "I don't suppose you're into that sort of thing?"

Warning alarms sounded in Taryn's head. Officer Denton . . . Marty couldn't know. She and Tucker had been locked inside her house. How could he have picked up . . . ? No, he didn't know. He was just taking a stab in the dark.

"Are you here for a reason, Marty?" she asked, ice dripping from her voice. "Other than to sexually harass me, that is?"

Sensing he'd pushed her too far, Sheuster stood up and stuffed his hands into his pockets. "Same as you. I came down here to get the scoop on Tucker."

"What do you care? It's not your case."

"No, but my Rodriguez case is crumbling because of that crooked cop's association with it. All the evidence is tainted now."

Taryn's stomach soured. "You think Rodriguez could walk?"

"There's no 'could' about it. He *will* walk."

"Oh, God." She hadn't even considered that. She reached up to rub her shoulder. Could things get any worse?

Marty watched her for a moment. Finally, he cocked his head and looked at her through slitted eyes. "So where do you think the bastard is?"

She stopped massaging the kink at the top of her shoulder blade. "Who? Tucker? How would I know?"

He shrugged. "I got the impression you two were tight."

The fax machine started to whir, and she gratefully turned towards the distraction. She walked over to look at the message, but found another interview request from a local news station. "I worked with the detective on quite a few cases," she said as she tossed the fax into the recycling bin, "but that all stopped when he was arrested for drug dealing."

"I wasn't talking about work, sweet cakes."

The hair on the back of Taryn's neck stood on end. "I don't know what you're implying, Marty," she said coolly, "but I don't date people from work. You know that probably better than anybody."

He shrugged. "Semantics."

She hesitated. She didn't like the look in his eye. "What are you talking about?"

"You might not 'date' them per se, but you are open to other . . . *propositions.* Say when a vice detective wants a search warrant. I could see you letting him stick his tongue halfway down your throat when you're in an empty interrogation room and you think nobody's watching."

She stopped breathing.

"Or allowing his hands to slither up under your skirt."

She felt like she was going to be sick.

"Or humping your hungry cunt against his leg."

She reached for the table to steady herself.

"Oh, wait a minute. I *did* see all that. You did realize the big mirror in that room was a two-way window, didn't you, sweet cakes?"

The implications sent Taryn's mind spinning. Marty had seen her and Tucker together! If he'd told anyone about their relationship, she would be suspect. For all she knew, he could already have attained a search warrant for her house.

Tucker was in danger. The police could be on their way. He'd be caught unaware.

And he'd think that she'd turned on him!

"I . . . I've got to get ready for a meeting," she said clumsily.

Marty stepped closer and whispered into her ear. "I've got some propositions of my own. Why don't we head down to the janitor's closet and I'll show you?"

His hand settled intimately on her backside. Revulsion rocked Taryn. Gut instinct sent her hand flying towards the man's ugly face, and she slapped him hard.

The sharp sound pierced the air like a thunderclap.

Air heaved in her lungs as she stepped back and watched him rub his jaw. She was stunned by her actions, but she refused to be sorry for them. The man had spread vicious rumors about her. He'd made filthy insinuations. She wouldn't let him paw her.

Unbelievably, he smiled. "You're a fiery one. I like that."

"Don't you ever come near me again," she hissed.

The slimy snake. His touch had been nauseating. Had he felt that she wasn't wearing any panties? The possibility made her nearly retch.

Her gaze dropped unwillingly to the front of his pants. The bulge behind his zipper gave her the answer.

She straightened her shoulders. She couldn't show any signs of weakness before this pervert. "And if you ever question my commitment to my job, I will turn you in for sexual harassment."

Out of the corner of her eye, Taryn saw Captain Holcomb striding down the hallway. She'd never been more grateful to see anyone in her life. "Captain," she called. "Could you wait just one minute?"

She picked up her things with as much grace as she could muster. "Get out of my office, Marty."

"Touched a chord, did I?" he chuckled.

"Get out or I'll have the Captain make you get out."

"Fine, fine. Don't get your panties in a bunch."

His phone rang again as she swept up her purse. She maneuvered around him as he whipped the cell phone out of its holder like a gunslinger.

"Hit me," he said cockily.

She'd hit him, all right.

"Captain," she said efficiently as she stepped into the hallway. "Thank you for coming. Let's go to the conference room. I've got something I want you to take a look at."

It was all Taryn could do not to run to her car when the meeting with the Diazes ended. It took supreme self-control, but she kept her pace to a quick walk as she headed down the hallway. She made sure to say good-bye to everyone she saw as she left the building and headed to her car. She let herself inside and locked the doors, but she couldn't tamp down the impulse to rev the engine.

She'd gotten it! She'd gotten what they needed!

Her fingers tightened around the steering wheel, but she reined herself in. She put the car in gear and drove sedately out of the parking lot. Okay, she'd gotten half of what they needed. There was just one more link that needed to be made.

Once things fell into place, though, Tucker wouldn't be the subject of a statewide manhunt. She couldn't wait to give him the good news.

After the hell that he'd been through, he was going to have a hard time believing the tale she had to tell.

Benny Diaz had cracked like the Grand Canyon.

The weekend traffic was light, but she passed three patrol cars on the way home. They reminded her that the danger wasn't gone yet, and she eased up on the gas. The trip seemed to take forever and when she finally turned onto her street, she didn't even bother to pull her car into the driveway. Instead, she parked in front and bolted to the house. She took the front steps two at a time and unlocked the door. "Tucker?" she called as she stepped inside.

She dropped her briefcase onto the table by the couch and bumped the door shut with her hip. As an afterthought, she turned and locked the deadbolt. "Michael? You're not going to believe this."

She kicked off a shoe. "You were right. Benny's in this up to his neck."

The house was silent.

Eerily silent.

"Tucker?"

Her heart began a slow, dull throbbing. She slipped out of her other pump and, in stockinged feet, slowly walked to the bedroom. "Tucker?" she called again.

He wasn't there.

In a rush, she checked the second bedroom, the bathroom, the kitchen, and even the basement. She was frantic by the time she thought about the Vallingers' car. Unmindful of what would happen to her hosiery, she ran down the back steps and across the yard. She yanked open the side door to her neighbors' garage.

The car was gone.

So was Tucker.

Chapter Seven

He'd left.

Taryn's knees buckled, and she grabbed the doorframe for support. Had something happened? Had Marty sent Officer Denton back? Had reporters spooked Tucker into leaving? She'd told him to take the car if he needed it.

Another possibility sprang to mind, and pain rippled through her.

Please God. Don't let him have run because he hadn't trusted her.

She clapped a hand over her mouth and choked back a sob. It was too strong a possibility to ignore. The house sat undisturbed, and reporters tended to hang around like vultures when they sensed a story.

If Tucker had left, it had been on his own volition.

And that meant one thing . . . He'd thought she was going to turn him in.

The hurt she felt was devastating, but she should have seen this coming. He hadn't wanted to let her go. He'd tried everything except strong-arming her to make her stay. Even when he'd finally relented, he hadn't been supportive.

Carefully, she closed the garage door. She turned and walked stiff-legged back to the house. Unshed tears made it swim in her vision, but she grabbed the metal railing and pulled herself up the steps.

Now she knew how he'd felt when she hadn't had faith in him.

The screen door slammed behind her, and she winced. The sound had such finality to it. She closed the wooden door more quietly and made it as far as a kitchen chair before she collapsed.

She'd made such a mess of things. This was all her fault. If only she'd listened to him before . . .

She took an unsteady breath, but she just couldn't find it in herself to be angry with him. His life was on the line. He had to be very careful about whom he trusted, and she'd been quick to believe the worst of him.

But things had changed. She'd thought that they'd made a connection. The sad thing was that if the situation were reversed, she would have trusted him to help her. She'd already trusted him with her body and her very life. A single tear trailed down her cheek, and she dropped her face into her hands.

She'd trusted him with her heart.

She closed her eyes and tried to think past the pain. Where could he have gone? Would he have headed to her parents' cabin? Maybe—if he'd been flushed from her house. There was no way she could know for certain. He'd never answer if she called.

She let out a shaky breath. She had to believe he was okay. Whether he trusted her or not was inconsequential, because she knew the truth. She had to help him. The only way she could do that now was to follow through on what she'd started.

She needed to stop this manhunt.

She leaned her elbows onto the table and let out a hysterical laugh. And how was she supposed to pull off that miracle?

A creak sounded from the back door. "Hey." Tucker eased into the house. His eyebrows drew together when he looked at her face. "What's wrong?"

Taryn stared at him in astonishment, but then nearly flew out of her chair. She launched herself at him, and he stumbled back a step as he caught her. The look of concern on his face grew stronger. Carefully, he wiped the dampness off her cheek.

"What happened? Did your talk with the Diazes go that badly?"

"Where were you?"

His eyebrows shot up when she grabbed him by the lapels of his jean jacket. She pushed him down into the chair she'd just vacated and surveyed him from head to toe. "Did you go out? Where did you get those clothes? Did you go shopping? *Are you crazy?*"

"Whoa! Ease up on the interrogation bit, babe."

"The car was gone!"

"Well, yeah. I moved it around to the alley in case I need to make a quick break for it. Driveways are easily blocked."

Taryn raked a hand through her hair and pulled loose the last pins that were holding her French twist in place. She couldn't believe he was sitting in front of her. She'd thought he'd left her. "I looked for you," she said. "Why weren't you here? You were supposed to be here."

"Settle down. I thought it would be safer to hide out at the Vallingers', and I borrowed some of the old guy's clothes. Your dad's red sweat suit made me stand out like a sore thumb."

Her adrenaline was rushing through her veins too fast to be stopped. Everything he said made sense, but she wasn't thinking with her head. "Why didn't you come back when I got home?"

His eyes narrowed. "I had to make sure you weren't followed first."

And there it was. He'd been watching her, testing her. He'd done everything he could to prepare for a fast getaway in case she failed.

His mistrust cut like a knife to the chest. She folded her arms to try to contain the pain. "Don't you mean you were watching to make sure I didn't bring a S.W.A.T. team with me?"

He went dangerously still. "What?"

"You hid because you didn't trust me to come back on my own," she said flatly. "You thought I'd turn you over to the authorities."

He moved fast. This time, it was he who grabbed her by the lapels. He pulled her forward until she was straddling him on the chair, and his nose bumped against hers as he glared into her eyes. "I thought no such thing."

"No?" she said challengingly.

"No," he growled. He yanked her to him and planted a hard, chastising kiss on her lips. "You're the only one I let myself count on, Swanny."

She watched him like a hawk. "Really?"

"Really."

With that one word, all of Taryn's hurt and fear seeped out of her like a pricked balloon. Weakly, she dropped onto his lap and wrapped her arms around his neck. Just minutes ago, she'd thought she'd never see him again. She couldn't remember ever being so scared—including when she'd stepped out of her bathroom and been grabbed by a dark stranger. "I was so afraid somebody had found you," she said.

He smoothed her hair away from her face. "I'm trying my best to make sure that doesn't happen. Or to at least hold it off for as long as I can."

"It might not be that much longer," she said. Her hysteria was subsiding, but her need for him was growing. She craved to touch him, make sure he was all right. Shifting in his lap, she settled more firmly against him. She sank her fingers into his hair and held him still for another hot kiss.

He pulled back. "Why do you say that? What happened?"

Her patience had reached its end. She'd been tied up in knots for hours and hours—and she'd been naked under her skirt ever since she'd left him. She'd never gone so long without panties, and it made her feel sexy and reckless. She reached down between them for the tab of his jeans.

"Taryn," he said. He grabbed for her hand. "Tell me."

"You were right about Benny's tennis shoes," she said fiercely. Her concentration was on his zipper. It was difficult to work her hands between their tightly pressed bodies, but she managed. She undid the button and slid down the zipper, but she didn't have time for the niceties. She wrapped her fingers in his belt loops and yanked down on the denim. "Lift," she demanded.

He raised his hips but caught her face with both hands and made her look at him. "You're killing me here, babe."

Within seconds, she had his jeans and underwear down to his knees. For all his concern about the case, his body wasn't able to ignore her. His erection already stood like a flagpole. With hurried hands, Taryn pulled up her skirt. Her blonde curls brushed against the tip of his penis as she hovered over it, and he let out a curse.

"Benny has been dealing to make a fast buck," she said. "Justin got the drugs from him."

"He what? Damn it, Swanny. Justin overdosed on . . . *Christ*!"

She'd begun to slowly lower herself onto his erection. The broad tip pressed at her, and she felt her body stretch to accommodate him. She grabbed the chair behind his shoulders and braced herself. Every nerve ending inside her tingled. Using her body weight, she began to impale herself onto him.

"Wait," he gasped. "Talk first."

"I want you inside me." She was so wet and needy.

He gripped her waist. "No. It's too fast."

"It's not fast enough!" He'd started this hunger when he'd sent her out into the world bare. He had to finish it.

"Taryn!" His hand dropped between her legs, and his fingers found her bud. He began to pluck at it insistently. "Give me a minute."

She grabbed his wrist. "I can't," she moaned. "Deeper. Get in deeper."

"I don't . . . Ah, shit!"

She'd dropped another inch onto him, and pleasure seared them both. Taryn swayed in his lap. She was uncomfortable, but *Oh, God!* She wouldn't do anything to change this. He'd never felt this thick before.

"Baby, you're swollen," he hissed. "We've gone at each other too hard today."

"Touch me!"

He swore under his breath, but pushed off her suit jacket. The only thing she wore underneath it was the black bra that matched her thong. He yanked a strap off her shoulder and hungrily dropped his mouth to her breast. All of her concentration had been on the connection below her waist. To feel the tug of his mouth on her nipple nearly caused sensory overload.

"Michael!" With a cry, she let her muscles relax. Gravity pulled her solidly down until she was filled to the brim. She closed her eyes, and her head dropped back.

Tucker clenched her ass as if he was never going to let her move. She didn't know if she could. His fiery rod was standing straight up inside her—stretching her, inflaming her. If she moved, she might combust.

She moved.

Determinedly, she began to pump herself up and down on his erection. Her ripped stockings made her feet slippery on the kitchen floor, but she found what traction she could. Her thigh muscles burned as she lifted, sank, retreated, and surged forward. Gripping the chair hard, she ground herself onto him, needing him.

"Swanny!" he said desperately.

In unison, he pinched the bundle of nerve endings between her legs and bit down softly on her nipple. Taryn shuddered and felt the moisture gather inside of her. Her juices slathered his cock, and her thrusts became smoother.

"I'm not going to last," he warned.

"I don't want you to," she said on a hard breath.

Her excitement was out of control. Rising up, she let herself slam down onto him. She found a hard, fast rhythm, and the muscles in his jaw clenched.

He gave her a frantic look. Then his hand was between her legs again. He pressed firmly against her clit. With a yell, he spurted into her.

Taryn squeezed her eyes tight as her own orgasm gripped her. She rode him for as long as she could before she collapsed against him. His arms came up around her, and he held her tightly.

"Are you all right?" he asked between heavy breaths.

"Mm."

"You could have given me a little more warning."

She sagged against his shoulder. "I couldn't help it," she whispered. "You scared me."

He groaned and ran a hand down her spine. He slid it under her hitched up skirt and caressed her buttocks. "So fear does it for you, huh? I can't wait until Halloween."

The hand on her backside stilled, and she glanced up at him. "Don't even think it," she said firmly. "You'll be here."

He took a deep breath. "Tell me about Benny. And no more fooling around until you do."

Taryn's excitement came back in a rush and her head came up so sharply, she nearly clipped his chin. "He's been dealing on the streets for almost six months. You were right about the family. His mother hadn't even noticed that her youngest son was throwing around wads of cash. His father did, but instead of asking questions, he just borrowed from him."

Tucker's gaze was steady on hers. "Did Benny admit giving the heroin to Justin?"

"Yes. He was there when his brother started convulsing." She shook her head. "It only took Joe two questions about the Mercury Wings before the entire story gushed out of the kid. I couldn't help but feel sorry for him. He killed his own brother. The guilt has been eating him alive."

"Did he plant the stuff on me?"

"No. He swore he had nothing to do with that, and I believe him. He's sick about how everything got turned on you. He never expected that to happen, but he didn't know how to help you without admitting what he'd done."

Tucker's face remained detached. "Who's his supplier?"

She grimaced. "That's where the problem lies. The guy's slick. He networks by phone. He hooks up with kids through other pushers. Once they start working for him, he keeps in contact by voice only. If Benny were low on product, he'd call a number and schedule a drop-off. He never even saw the guy."

The impassive look on Tucker's face slipped. "So I'm still not in the clear."

"Not yet," she said quietly. "The stash inside your gym locker was the same grade as that found in Justin's system during the autopsy."

His head dropped back, and he stared at the ceiling. "When am I going to catch a break?"

"Easy," she said. She rubbed the tight muscles at the back of his neck. "Let me finish."

His dark eyes narrowed.

"The night that Justin collapsed, Benny panicked. He didn't know what to do, so he called his supplier. The man said he would 'take care of it'."

"He didn't mean Justin."

"He meant the situation. We're dealing with a professional."

Tucker's hands bit into her hips. "We're dealing with a heartless psychopath. A kid was dying in an alleyway, and all the guy thought about was pinning the rap on me."

"Listen." She caught his face with both hands. "We have the phone number."

He looked at her blankly. "You're kidding."

Goose bumps popped up on Taryn's skin. They were so close to clearing him, she could practically taste it. "The guy told Benny to destroy it, but the kid's been carrying it around in his back pocket. Joe checked it. It's a secure cell phone, one of those kinds that you buy with minutes on it and then throw away."

Tucker sat up a little straighter. "But they could get the phone company to pull up the calls made to and from the number."

"Exactly. Joe's already on it. He's hoping he can cross reference the information and figure out who Benny's contact is."

"Has anybody thought about just dialing the number and seeing who answers?"

"Your captain's putting together a trace right now."

"Fuck the trace."

Taryn gasped when Tucker lifted her off of him. Their bodies disconnected, and she felt gapingly empty. Her legs wobbled when he set her on her feet. She smoothed her skirt over her hips as he stood and zipped up.

"Give me the number, Counselor."

She didn't like the reckless look on his face. "I don't have it."

"Bullshit. I know you. Give me the damn number."

She understood his impatience; she felt it with every cell of her being. Still, there was a right way and a wrong way to handle this. She didn't want him to lose his freedom because they couldn't contain themselves.

"We can't jeopardize the investigation," she said firmly. Her head snapped up when she remembered something. "Besides, my phones are dead. You can't call from here."

By way of answer, he strode into the living room and picked up her phone. Turning it over, he slid off the bottom panel. Her eyes rounded when she saw he'd just wrapped up the cords inside.

"Hide in plain sight," he said. "That's my motto."

He held out his hand. She glared at it.

"The number, baby."

"Oh, all right!" she snapped. She stomped over to her briefcase. "The guy's probably ditched it already anyway."

"These aren't brain surgeons we're dealing with," Tucker muttered. He looked at her notes and punched the numbers she'd written down. "Whatever's between me and this guy is personal. I might be able to recognize him."

She gave it one last shot. "Wait! My name will show up on Caller ID."

His lips curled up in a smile that held no humor. "Nice try, but you've got an unlisted number. It doesn't come through. I know. You've called me from home before."

"Fine," Taryn muttered.

She went to stand next to him. If he was going to do this, she was going to help. She had nearly as much experience with the lowlifes in the city as he did. He tilted the receiver and leaned down so she could press her ear against it.

They both tensed when they heard ringing on the other end of the line. Taryn tried to quiet her breathing. It was all she could hear, and she knew she'd only get one chance at this. She wiped her damp palms on her skirt and bit her lip. The phone rang three times before it connected.

"Hit me."

Her breathing stopped, and she looked, wide-eyed, at Tucker.

"Hello? Is anybody there?"

Her heart lodged in her throat. She knew that voice. Tucker's eyebrows drew together, but she wrenched the phone out of his hands. It would arouse suspicion if they hung up, and she didn't want to leave any sort of forewarning. Not if she was right about the person on the other end of the call. "Is this A-n-A Dry Cleaning?" she asked in a breathy voice.

"Wrong number, sweetheart."

"Sorry," she said before disconnecting.

"Was that—"

The telephone bell jingled when she slammed down the phone. "Marty!"

"Sheuster? Why, that son-of-a-bitch!"

The pressure built inside Tucker's head until he thought it would explode. He couldn't believe it! That fat little slime ball had set him up! He jammed his hand into his pocket and pulled out the keys to the Vallingers' car.

Taryn saw the keys in his hand, and her blue eyes turned flinty. "Don't even think about leaving now."

The tension was so strong, electrical sparks nearly flew across the room.

Tucker took a step towards the door. Marty Sheuster. The bastard was playing God with kids' lives, and he'd tried to frame him for murder. The guy was going to pay.

Taryn stepped into his path and pointed a threatening finger at him. "Don't."

His muscles strained towards the door. "I can make him talk."

"So can I!"

A tight band wrapped around Tucker's chest. God, this was exactly what he hadn't wanted to happen. His sweet Taryn was planted smack dab in the middle of all this. That slimy Sheuster had cost them both.

"We need to reason this out," she said.

He dragged a hand through his hair. He didn't want to reason it out. He wanted to take a more proactive approach—like pounding the truth out of the doughboy. It would be much more satisfying.

She stomped over and waved a hand in his face.

"Work with me," she snapped. "Marty. He has access to the drugs in evidence lock-up. Has any of that come up missing?"

Tucker planted his hands on his hips. "No. At least not up to the time I left."

"But he had access to things such as the plastic bags with your fingerprints on them. And your keys! They booked you on the basis of what was found in your gym locker. He could have gotten into your personal effects."

"And with the keys to my house, he could have planted the money before the forensics unit got permission to search it." Tucker let out a curse. She was right. They did need to go through it step-by-step. He couldn't afford to miss anything. Not now.

"Why you, though?" she continued. She began to nibble on her fingernails out of nervous habit. "Why would he try to frame you? Were you onto him?"

Oh, that one hurt. Tucker hadn't seen this thing coming at all, and it killed him that Sheuster had been working the streets right under his nose. "I didn't have a clue," he admitted. "I don't know why he chose me, other than out of spite. I can't think of anything else that might have been in it for him."

A funny look crossed her face. "What about me?" she asked hesitantly.

The question was like a kick in the gut. Suddenly, Sheuster's raunchy talk about her seemed even more lurid. Tucker had never tried to hide his attraction to the pretty ADA. If Marty had seen him as a competitor . . . "But you weren't mine to take. Not then."

"He saw us," she said quietly.

"What do you mean?"

"He saw us in the interrogation room."

Tucker took a step back. That had been private. The idea of that creep watching them . . . watching *her* . . .

He was going to kill him.

The keys bit into his palm as he made a move to the back door. Taryn stopped him by grabbing his arm and throwing herself fearlessly between him and the exit.

"Could he be working for somebody?" she asked.

Tucker stopped in his tracks. Red-hot anger filled his brain, but she'd just tapped something in the recesses of his mind . . . Something he was missing . . . A connection of some sort.

He tried to pull in his wandering thoughts. Sheuster a patsy? It made more sense. The idiot wasn't smart enough to plan something as elaborate as this. Somebody was pulling his strings, but who? Who could have that much against a vice detective?

The answer lit up his brain like fireworks on the Fourth of July.

He rubbed a tired hand across his forehead. Why hadn't he thought of this before? "Who would have the most to gain by getting me off the streets?" he said wearily.

"I . . . I don't know."

"Think about it, Swanny. We're talking about drugs and money."

Her face paled. "Oh, my God. He's working for Rodriguez!"

Tucker nodded slowly. The rage building inside his chest was nearing its boiling point. "It explains why Sheuster was dragging his feet on that case. He did everything he could to get in my way."

"The search warrant," she hissed.

He gritted his teeth. "Marty's the operation's inside guy, and I got too close. Rodriguez wanted me off the streets, but coming after me directly would have caused too many problems."

"Killing you would have resulted in an investigation."

"Framing me and sending me to prison would be easier and more gratifying. I don't know if they planned what happened to Justin, but the opportunity certainly fell into their lap."

She pressed a hand to her temple, and he could see the gears turning in her brain. "Marty was just saying today that his case was falling apart due to your involvement."

It was all coming together. Sheuster and Rodriguez had turned his life upside down, and there'd been nothing he could do to stop it. He rubbed a hand over his burning stomach. "They got two birds with one stone. I'm locked up and Rodriguez gets turned loose."

"Damn him!" Taryn swore.

Tucker spun away. Thoughts were screaming through his brain, and his heart was pumping like a steam engine. Fury colored everything, but hope and excitement tinged the edges.

Freedom was at his fingertips. He'd never thought he'd get this close again.

"It's all speculation," he said with a tinge of desperation. He knew with everything inside him that they were on the right track, but they didn't have hardcore proof. "We still don't have enough on them."

"But we'll get it," she said determinedly. She picked up the phone again, but her fingers shook as she dialed. "All we have to do is put Joe on it."

He hadn't expected her to call his partner. Uneasiness rocked his already unsettled stomach, and he grabbed for the phone. "No! You'll have to tell him what we did, and it could be considered interfering with the investigation. I don't want you to get in trouble."

"I'm not interfering. It's *my* case." She spun away. "Hello, Joe? This is ADA Swanson. I know who has that cell phone."

Tucker reached around her and made another grab, but she scooted away.

"How?" she said. "Well, you're not going to be happy with me, but I dialed the number. I recognized the voice on the other end."

He backed her up against the wall, but she straight-armed him like a NFL receiver.

"It's Sheuster, Joe. Go get him."

Tucker suddenly heard his partner's voice booming over the line.

Taryn grimaced and held the phone away from her ear until the tirade ended.

"Yes. ADA Marty Sheuster," she said, bringing the phone closer with care. "Bring him in for questioning and check the cell phone he has on him. The number should match the one Benny gave us."

Tucker planted his hands on the wall on either side of her and hung his head. There was nothing he could do to stop her when she got like this. He knew from experience. He just hoped to God they hadn't made a mistake and jumped the gun. They should have let the department trace the call first. Joe or somebody else probably would have recognized Sheuster's voice.

Taryn hung up and lowered the phone to her side. There was empathy in her eyes when she looked at him. "It will be okay," she said softly.

"They're going to find a way to slip through the cracks." He knew how the system worked. So did Sheuster and Rodriguez.

She dropped the phone. It fell noisily onto the floor as she wrapped her arms about his neck. Her hair was wild, and her breasts hung heavily in the little black bra. "We'll make it stick," she said in a tone that brooked no argument. "Joe will drag Marty down to the station and go one-on-one with him. He doesn't stand a chance. You know that better than anyone. Payne will be all over him. Marty will give it up."

Hope flickered again. She could be right. He'd take his partner over Sheuster any day. "How long do you think it will be before he tracks him down?"

"Marty was at the office when I left. He's either still there or at home. It shouldn't take long."

"Damn." Needing to hold onto something, he slid his hands down her back and cupped her bottom. "I don't think I can take any more waiting," he admitted.

"No?" She sidled up closer. "Would you like me to distract you?"

He didn't know if it would work, but he wasn't going to turn her away. He jerked her up to him, and she wrapped her legs around his waist like a vice. Flinging her hair over one shoulder, she leaned down and began kissing the side of his neck. His toes curled when her tongue flicked against his pulse.

It would work.

He started for the bedroom, but his steps slowed. He didn't know how all of this was going to work out, and the boys in blue were still out there looking for him. A lot of things could go wrong. "Swanny," he said hesitantly. "I just need to tell you . . . in case something happens . . . I never should have come here and put you in danger. I'm sorry for intimidating you. Manhandling you. I just didn't know what else to do or where to go. You were my only hope."

"It's all right," she whispered into his ear. "I understand."

"No, it's not all right. I should have found another way."

"I'm glad you came to me. I wouldn't have wanted it any differently." She pulled back slowly. "I love you, Michael."

He jolted so hard, he nearly dropped her. She met his stunned gaze shyly, but then glanced away.

"I love you," she whispered again.

He hadn't realized it, but that was what he'd needed to hear all along. He tightened his arms around her and buried his face into the crook of her neck. "Ah, baby, I'm head over heels about you, too. I'm so crazy about you, I can't think straight."

"So don't think," she said, repeating the words he'd told her. "Go with your gut."

All of a sudden, Tucker knew everything was going to be okay. *Everything.* With a sigh of relief and a refreshed sense of purpose, he headed to the bedroom. He felt an unexpected need to celebrate.

The phone rang just before midnight. Taryn dove for it over Tucker's prone body and had it to her ear before the second ring. "Hello?"

"ADA? This is Joe Payne."

"Yes?" she said breathlessly.

"The captain's called off the manhunt for Tucker. Sheuster confessed."

Epilogue

Eight months later. . . .

Tucker sucked in air and tried not to let his weight crush Taryn. She was bent over a desk in the custodian's room at the courthouse with her legs spread wide. He'd just taken her from behind, and the aftermath of the orgasm had left him powerless. They were both breathing as if they'd just completed a marathon.

"Now that's the way to celebrate," he said into her ear.

"I'll say." She fought hard for oxygen, and he could still see the pulse pounding in her throat. "Do you think anybody heard us?"

He nuzzled the soft hair at her temple. "I don't give a rip if they did. We deserved this. It took us eight months of hard work to put that bastard away."

She reached up and cupped the side of his face, coaxing him into a slow kiss. "We got him, didn't we?"

Her grin was contagious.

"Alejandro Rodriguez isn't going to be dealing drugs to anybody for a long, long time."

"Do you think they could put him in a cell with Marty?" Her eyes sparkled with mischief. "I think they'd make a cute couple."

Tucker let out a laugh. He gave her another hard kiss and slipped his hand under her belly. He was already hard inside her again. He gave a soft push, and she groaned. With a smile, he stood upright. Another smooth, deep stroke made him clench his teeth.

"Not as cute as us, baby," he growled. "Not as cute as us."

About the Author:

Kimberly Dean also writes for Black Lace Books out of the U.K. When not slaving over a keyboard, she enjoys reading, sports, movies, and loud rock-n-roll.

Wake Me

by Angela Knight

To My Reader:

To me, there's nothing as much fun as taking a standard plot and turning it sideways and inside out. Fairy tales are perfect for that. *Wake Me* is my take on *Sleeping Beauty*—only in this one, the guy is the one asleep. And I can assure you, Walt Disney will not be making a movie out of this version any time soon . . .

Chapter One

Chloe Hart eyed the newspaper with all the enthusiasm of a woman surveying a dentist's chair before a root canal. "Don't be a wuss, Chlo'," she muttered to herself, and picked the paper up.

Gripping it like a club, she marched back into the house to the kitchen table, where a bracing cup of coffee and a Danish waited to fortify her for the coming ordeal. She tossed the paper on the table, plopped down in her chair and picked up the mug. An incautious sip scalded the tip of her tongue.

At Chloe's lisped obscenity, Rhett Butler looked up from his Tender Vittles with an inquiring "Meow?"

"Ignore me, Rhett," she managed around her boiled tongue tip as she unfolded the newspaper with a series of grim snaps. "Just having a bad morning."

Happy to comply, the muscular black tom settled back down over his bowl. Like his namesake, he frankly didn't give a damn. But as she'd told her dog-loving buddy, Amanda Rice, there was something to be said for blunt feline honesty.

Chloe paged past a murder, a house fire, and a really spectacular pileup on I-26 to reach the account of her personal Waterloo. She found it on page four in section C.

The bride smiled her familiar grin from a dozen yards of tulle and seed pearls, clutching a bouquet of white roses that cascaded to her silk-covered knees. Chloe could almost hear her mother sniff that a woman with three kids had no business in that much white. From a professional standpoint, she herself thought the composition was a little off; the tilt of the bride's veiled head and the position of her flowers didn't quite lead the eye in the proper flow.

"That's what you get for using a cheap photographer, you backstabbing bitch," she muttered at the photo. "Then again, if I'd shot you, I wouldn't have used a camera."

Without bothering to read the description of the wedding—she wasn't that big a masochist, thank you—she closed the newspaper and looked at Rhett. "As God is my witness," she drawled in her best mock-Scarlett O'Hara growl, "I'll never be a sucker again."

Knuckles rattled the storm door. Chloe looked up in surprise. Amanda wouldn't bother to knock, and she wasn't expecting anybody else. "If that's Debbie and Chris, stopping by to beg for forgiveness on the way to the honeymoon," she told the cat as she got up to answer it, "you have my permission to attack."

Rhett yawned and twisted around to lick his furry backside.

She looked back at him. "Or you can do that. Does express the general sentiment pretty well."

Chloe opened the door to find a man in a familiar brown uniform, a huge box tucked awkwardly under one arm. "Delivery," he said, and juggled his electronic clipboard into her hands.

She took it and signed her name in the window, eying the package. "Wonder who that's from?"

He shrugged, supremely indifferent. "Looks like a picture to me."

It did have the right dimensions—four feet across and more than a yard wide, but only three or four inches thick. Curiosity piqued, Chloe accepted the heavy parcel and hauled it inside as the delivery truck roared off. Putting it down on the kitchen table, she went in search of a pair of scissors to attack the packing tape. "If it's a portrait of the bride and groom," she told Rhett as she dug through the kitchen drawer, "your litter box is gonna get filled with little bits of photo paper."

Ripping off a strip of the heavy brown cardboard, Chloe lifted her brows at the intriguing sight of bare, tanned chest and a tight male nipple. "I take it back, Rhett," she murmured. "Somehow I don't think this is going in the litter box."

Ten minutes later, the box lay ruthlessly demolished on the floor, and the oil painting it had contained stood propped on the kitchen table.

Chloe stared reverently.

The knight sprawled in sleep across a tumble of rich sable fur, one hand resting on the jeweled hilt of a sword. It looked as if he'd stripped and fallen asleep after a battle.

He was a big, blond Viking of a man, his hair cropped short, a neat beard framing his lush sinner's mouth. His starkly handsome face looked as though it had been carved by God's own chisel, but if so, He'd been in a hurry. There was something a bit crude and brutal in the angles of the knight's cheekbones and big, square chin. Luckily, those features were balanced out by a regal Roman nose and thick blond brows. The whole effect was intensely masculine—and just a little intimidating.

So was the rest of him. He had the build of a man who'd spent his entire life swinging a blade in an era when losing could cost you your life. He'd cut it close a time or two; his brawny body was slashed here and there with scars that reminded Chloe of a tiger's stripes.

"Really big hands, too," she purred under her breath, eying his long fingers and broad palms. Unfortunately, one of the pelts lay across his hips in a pool of sable, preventing her from determining if the interesting bits lived up to those hands. Chloe sighed, wishing the artist had been less coy.

Coy or not, though, he'd had a firm grasp of history. Artists too often painted knights in the full Germanic plate mail that was only worn in the sixteenth century, when knighthood was actually breathing its last. But the conical helm by the warrior's elbow looked thirteenth century, as did the chain mail coat that lay on the floor, its hammered links gleaming with a muted shimmer.

Emphasizing all that barbaric splendor, the knight's sword glittered with rubies and gold, engraved with intricate symbols she couldn't quite make out. Similar runes were worked into the heavy gold frame.

Chloe stepped close and bent to examine the ancient designs. But the longer she stared, the more they made her think of witches dancing in the firelight, chanting ancient spells. She felt the hair rise on the nape of her neck.

And instantly felt a little silly. *Don't be ridiculous, Chloe,* she told herself, impatient. *There's no such thing as magic.*

Chloe was still staring at the painting in awed fascination fifteen minutes later when Amanda walked in, a fencing bag looped over her shoulder.

"Ready to get your ass kicked?" her friend asked, pushing the kitchen door open with her usual blithe disregard for the custom of knocking.

"As if," Chloe retorted absently before nodding at her gift. "Was this your idea of a distraction? Because it's doing one heck of a job."

"Whoa." Amanda joined her at the table to gape. "Where did you get that? And do they have any more?"

Momentarily distracted, Chloe glanced at her friend. Amanda was dressed in her usual Saturday morning workout togs—a red T-shirt and sweat pants with a pair of white Nikes. She wore her blond hair scraped back into a curling pony tail that emphasized the clean contours of her pleasantly angular face.

They'd met in the fencing class Chris Jennings taught at the local Y, back when they'd all attended the same college. Since Chloe, Amanda and Debbie Mayes had been the only females in the class, the three women had started practicing together. Before long, they'd fallen into such an easy, close friendship, everybody called them the Three Musketeers.

Chris, for his part, quickly took up the role of their seductive young D'Artagnan. He'd set his sights on Chloe, and it hadn't taken him long to get her. She'd moved in with him a year later, about the time Amanda fell head over heels for a budding young housing contractor named Richard Rice.

Debbie, for her part, wed her high-school sweetheart, who morphed into an abusive son of a bitch even before she gave birth to their three kids. She divorced him a year ago, but he already owed her twenty thousand in child support.

Debbie's solution to being flat broke was to seduce Chris. When Chloe finally caught them at it, Debbie had whined, "But I need him more than you do!" True, but hardly the point.

Amanda had come down firmly on Chloe's side in the resulting ugly brawl. Which was a good thing, considering that by then, she and Chloe had been business partners in H&R Graphics for three years.

Their unswerving friendship was the reason Chloe had been so sure the painting was a gift from Amanda. Only . . . "You mean you didn't send it?"

Amanda was gazing at the knight's naked glory with glazed eyes.

"Chlo', I love you like a sister, but if I'd found *him* anywhere, I wouldn't have given him away."

Chloe snorted. "Yeah, right. Richard would just love coming home to find a naked man hanging over the couch."

Ignoring that entirely likely prediction of her husband's reaction, Amanda asked, "So where'd it come from?" She took a step back and cocked her head to one side, the better to ogle.

"Delivery guy just brought it. You ever heard of a company called Evanesce?"

"Nope. I think there's a rock band with that name, though."

Chloe shot her a dry look. "Somehow I doubt it's them."

They contemplated the painting in reverent silence a moment before Amanda suggested, "Maybe your mom and dad—?"

"Yeah, right. Can you imagine Emily Hart sending her unmarried daughter a picture of a nekkid man? I don't think so."

"It's not a nekkid man. It's art. With a capital A."

She was right. Now that the bass throb of Chloe's libido had subsided to a thrum, she realized the painting did look like the work of some Renaissance Old Master. There was obvious skill in the composition, in the warm golden glow of candlelight falling on bare skin, in the juxtaposition of colors, even in the angle of the brush strokes.

Not exactly Elvis on black velvet.

Yet at the same time, there was a carnal sensuality to the painting that was starkly modern. Classical painters had dared that level of eroticism only when painting martyrs.

"Damn," Amanda said. "Wouldn't you love to kiss *him* awake?"

"Yep." Chloe shot her a wicked grin. "But failing that, I'm gonna hang him on the wall. And I know just where."

Her friend rolled her eyes. "Honey, I'd bet money he's already hung."

Five minutes later, the two women manhandled the heavy painting as they tried to catch the wall hook in Chloe's bedroom. Finally the hook snagged the wire strung taut across the painting's back, and they settled it into place.

Chloe nodded in satisfaction as she surveyed the new addition. It fit right in with her heavy walnut furniture, while the colors complimented the warm gold of her drapes and carpet. "Much better."

Amanda gave her a look. "Certainly more so than asshole's photo, anyway."

"Hey, I thought that was one of my better pieces."

"Yeah, you almost made the skinny little bastard look sexy."

The artistic nude she'd shot of Chris had hung in that spot for the past five years. Chloe had taken it down six months ago—in order to sling it at him like a Frisbee as he rolled off Debbie. One corner had caught him right in the nuts. The memory of his howl still made her grin.

Reading her mind as usual, Amanda laughed. "I would have paid money to see you nail that particular target."

"Just as well you didn't. It wasn't one of my finer moments." She squared her shoulders. "Let's go fence. Suddenly I'm in the mood to kick some ass."

"Dream on."

"Don't you think it's time you started dating again?" Amanda asked, holding her foil in an efficient guard that protected her right side.

"No." Chloe bounced on the balls of her feet, letting the point of her practice weapon dip in hopes of luring her friend into an attack.

It was a beautiful spring day. The new-cut grass felt thick and fragrant under her Nike-shod feet, and there was just enough breeze to keep her from sweating too much in her thick protective fencing jacket.

Chloe and Amanda had been getting together to fence every Saturday since they'd discovered the sport. Days like this were the reason why.

"No?" Amanda glared at her through the thick black mesh of her fencing mask. "Do you want to give that bastard the satisfaction of knowing he hurt you?"

"The only male I want in my life right now is Rhett." Chloe launched herself into a blurring lunge, pushing off with her left foot, her long body uncoiling like a spring as she feinted toward her friend's shoulder. Amanda retreated smoothly, angling her blade to parry the attack. Chloe dropped the point of her foil beneath it and popped her in the ribs. "At least I expect him to tomcat around."

Amanda held up one finger, acknowledging the hit. "You need to get back on the horse, Chlo'. You're never gonna find a guy like Richard if you don't."

"There are no more guys like Richard. Face it, kid, you hit the jackpot in the hubbie lotto."

Amanda sprang at her, and she scrambled into a retreat, parrying, the two blades scraping. "Well, yeah. But Richard knows this gorgeous carpenter . . ."

"Forget it." Chloe's lunge was so hard and fast, her blade bent as the buttoned tip dug into Amanda's chest. "I'm not going on another blind date."

"Touché, dammit! Would you quit aiming for the tits?"

"I'm not aiming for the tits. And anyway, you're wearing breast protectors." The metal cups were tucked into pockets sewn in the lining of their jackets.

"I don't understand why you won't go out."

"He said I'm a sex addict, okay?" Suddenly unable to tolerate another second of the conversation, Chloe stopped dead and tore off her mask, the better to glare. "I'm *not* a sex addict."

"Who said that? Dickless?" Amanda dropped her own point.

Chloe threw down her mask and tugged off the fencing glove that covered her right hand. "He said that's why he started doing Debbie. He said she's *normal.*"

Her friend curled a lip in a sneer. "Only Chris would complain about having a woman who wants sex. Let me guess—he's impotent."

"Not with her." She jerked down the zipper on the side of her jacket, letting it hang open. A cooling breeze instantly swirled in to reach her sweat-damp T-shirt. "I told him once I wanted him to tie me up. He said I was a pervert."

"And he's a congenital liar with the morals of a mink." Amanda tore her own mask off and slung it across the yard. "Asshole."

Now that she'd brought it up, the story came pouring out of her in a bitter flood. "I just thought we could try it. You know how I love those old historicals—you know, the ones where the hero ties the heroine up and seduces her? The idea struck me as hot, and God knows our love life sucked. I thought maybe he'd get into it, and we'd both have a nice little climax for once. Instead he just got all pissed and offended and said I was disgusting."

Amanda snorted. "Probably because you were the only one who wasn't getting any."

"Yeah, it's occurred to me to wonder if he was doing Debbie by then. But still . . ."

"You're not a pervert, Clo'. It was an excuse."

Needing to move, to do something, anything, Chloe walked across the yard and picked up Amanda's mask. "Doesn't look like you dented it," she said, examining the thick black wire mesh. "You really need to watch that kind of thing. Screw up your mask, and somebody'll drive a point through it in competition. I did that to a guy once. Scared the crap out of me."

Amanda stomped over to take the mask out of her hands. "Quit trying to change the subject. I can't believe you swallowed Chris's bullshit."

She smiled slightly. "Well, he always gave such good bullshit. I just got in the habit."

"Let me set you up with . . ."

"Not now." Chloe took a deep breath. "Look, you're right. I need to start dating again, but I'm not ready yet. I just . . . don't feel like trusting anybody right now. Later. Later I'll be ready."

Much, much later.

Chloe lay sleeping in her big bed, a shaft of moonlight falling pale and bright across her face.

She was the first thing Radolf saw when he stepped from the painting.

He walked soundlessly to the foot of the bed, then strode through the thick oak footboard and the mattresses beyond them like a man strolling through mist.

Pausing at her pillow, he stood looking down at her clean profile. Thin red brows arched over her closed eyes, matching the cap of auburn curls that framed her face. He wished her hair was longer. He loved wrapping his fist in long, silken strands while he rode a woman hard.

As if sensing his attention, she turned over on her back, a faint frown gathering between those soft brows. Contemplating her oval face, Radolf decided he liked its sweet, subtle elegance. Her lips were particularly pleasing, seductively full and pink.

He wanted to watch her suck him. It had been a very long time since a woman had pleasured him with her mouth.

"At least this one is passably pretty," Radolf murmured. Chloe didn't even stir, of course; his voice made no sound. Holding out a hand, he ran it the length of her sheet-covered body. "Decent breasts."

"Did I not tell you that you would like her?" Belisarda said, striking a pose in a patch of moonlight. Radolf did not look around, though her dark, seductive beauty was enough to steal a man's breath. He had known her too long to be fooled. Besides, he no longer breathed. At least, not in this form.

"Look at her," the demon witch continued, her voice a suggestive purr. Her great, oval eyes flickered with crimson reflections as her mouth curled into a smile. It had taken Radolf years to notice how thin Belisarda's lips really were. "All lush promise, just waiting for your touch. Surely she will love you."

He shot her a shimmering glare. "The last one loved me."

"Not enough." The witch pushed off with one bare foot, drifting toward him wrapped in her glittering diaphanous robes. "None of them loved you enough to come for you. None has even attempted to give you the kiss of freedom, no matter how you seduced and tempted."

Radolf curled his lips back from his teeth. "I know how that grieves you, witch. You feed from what I make them feel."

"Well, of course." Even as he'd spin his dreams, she'd float above the girl's sleeping body, drinking the mortal's pleasure to sustain her own magical life. "It would be a sin to let such glorious effort go to waste." Belisarda extended pale, slender fingers toward his naked shoulder. He flinched away, and her eyes chilled. "Since you fail at all else."

He looked down at Chloe. "Not with her. This one will love me."

The glare he threw Belisarda shimmered with hate. "By God, I'll see to it. And then I'll be free of you."

Radolf turned and bent over the girl buried under a mound of covers. Lifting a big, translucent hand, he touched her forehead and sank into her with a last soft, low growl for his enemy. "This one will break the spell."

The witch's smile was small and catlike. "I do hope so, my lord Radolf," she whispered as he vanished into his prey. "I do indeed."

"The conqueror comes!"

Chloe jolted and looked around. She stood in the great hall of a medieval castle. All around her, people in the garb of thirteenth century knights and ladies milled under the vaulting stone ceiling, faces pale and eyes wide.

"Whoa," she muttered. "What the heck is going on?"

"See where thy willfulness has brought us!" Gnarled hands clamped around her forearm, spinning her around. A tiny, bird-like woman in blue wool glared up at her, faded periwinkle eyes accusing. "He has taken the castle," the woman continued, "and his anger is terrible to behold!"

Chloe blinked. "Who?"

"Lord Radolf of Varik, of course. Who do you think? Now, heed thy old nurse, milady. I know you are but a maid . . ."

"A virgin? Me?" She snorted. "What medieval mushrooms have you been smoking?"

". . . But 'tis as I told you. Lord Radolf hungers for you. You must curb your willfulness, set yourself to please him, or 'twill go badly for us all!"

"Who the hell is Lord Radolf?"

"As if you don't know!" The old woman threw up both hands. "The King's Champion. The man you swore you'd not marry, king's command or no."

Damn, this sounded just like one of her favorite romances. *Dreaming,* Chloe realized suddenly. *I'm dreaming.*

Of course. The portrait had triggered something in her fertile little subconscious, and it had spit out a scenario from one of those used bookstore historicals she loved so much.

Though, she thought, gazing down at the woman's liver spots, she'd never had a dream quite this *real.*

"My lord Radolf!" someone called in ringing tones.

The old lady shot a hunted glance over her shoulder before turning back to her. "Heed me well, girl!" She shook an arthritic finger under Chloe's befuddled nose. "None of your sharp tongue! Make him happy, or . . ."

"Wait a minute," Chloe interrupted in growing outrage. "Let me get this straight. You expect me to play hide the broadsword with this guy so he'll make things easier on everybody else? Forget that. No way am I . . ."

The man from the painting walked through the castle's great doors, his chain mail ringing with every long stride. He looked even more stunningly gorgeous in person.

As Chloe gaped, he headed straight for her. His eyes burned hot and hungry, green as emeralds in sunlight, and his smile was raw, distilled sex.

Aimed right at her.

Chloe licked suddenly dry lips and squeaked, "On the other hand, what's a little self-sacrifice between friends?"

When Radolf of Varik finally stopped to loom over her, her knees went weak. Damn, he was big. His green gaze flicked down to her cleavage in blatant anticipation, then up to her face again. Something in his expression put her in mind of Rhett stalking a particularly fat chipmunk. "Well met, milady."

She gave him a dazed blink. "Right back atch . . ."

He snatched her off her feet before she could even get the rest of the sentence out of her mouth.

The kiss was not even remotely foreplay. It was a sex act all by itself, conducted with lips and tongue and teeth as Radolf's big hands cupped her head and turned it here and there for his leisurely conquest. He bit, he licked, he suckled. He claimed every last millimeter of her mouth.

And while he was at it, he made all kinds of feral promises about what he'd do to the rest of her, without ever saying a word beyond soft male growls. He made her feel more thoroughly plundered in five minutes than Chris had managed in six years. By the time he finally put her back down again, she was swaying.

It took her a full thirty seconds to realize she was also trussed like a turkey on a cooking show.

Chloe blinked down at herself in astonishment. Her wrists were tied behind her back and lashed tightly against her body with multiple turns of rope that circled her torso just under her bust. The pose thrust out her breasts, making the hard peaks of her nipples doubly obvious under the thin blue silk of her kirtle. "How the heck did you do that?" she demanded, too surprised for anger.

Radolf gave her a lazy grin. "Magic."

Glancing wildly around, she realized they were no longer in the great hall. Somehow he'd transported her to a medieval bed chamber, complete with massive oak bed and roaring fire. A thick pile of furs lay beneath her bare feet, as if just waiting for all kinds of illicit activities. But how had . . .

Oh, yeah, Chloe remembered again. *This is a dream.*

Damned if it felt like one, though. She'd certainly never gotten a kiss that hot in any dream before.

Glancing up at him, she drew in a startled breath. Radolf's armor had disappeared since the last time she'd looked, leaving him gloriously nude, his big body tanned and muscular and dusted in golden hair. Half hypnotized, she scanned down all that mouth-watering male anatomy. . . .

Yep. His cock definitely lived up to the promise of his big, sinewy hands. He was darn near as thick as her wrist, smooth and massive and uncircumcised, with heavy balls already tight with lust.

"Now, this is more like it," Chloe said, unable to drag her eyes away from that luscious erection. "I usually dream about knife-wielding psychos with serious anger management issues. You are definitely an improvement."

"On that, we are in agreement," Radolf rumbled, doing a hungry scan of his own. " 'Ere this, Belisarda has given me naught but mincing virgins who expect me to compose sonnets to their eyelashes, or bitter wives who wish to punish me for their straying husbands' sins." He curled his upper lip. "I've spent more time on my knees than a scullery maid."

Not quite sure what to make of that, Chloe ventured, "You don't strike me as the kind of guy to crawl well."

"Indeed, milady," he purred, curling big hands in either shoulder of her kirtle, "I am not."

"Hey . . . !" Chloe began.

Too late. He did it anyway, shredding the fabric of the thin gown like tissue paper, leaving her breasts bare and quivering.

"You know, the whole bodice-ripping thing is *so* politically incorrect," she told him, her heart pounding as a smile of dark anticipation spread over his face.

Radolf cupped one breast in a big, callused hand. "At the moment," he said, lowering his head, "I am not remotely interested in politics."

His mouth closed over her, surrounding the tight flesh in such heat and hunger that she gasped. "Now that you mention . . . AH! . . . it, neither am I." The gasp became a whimper as his teeth gently raked the little peak. Damn, but he was good at that.

Finally Radolf drew back to give her that predator's smile again. "Perhaps I'll go to my knees for you after all."

Then he did just that—the better to attack her nipples with his wickedly skilled mouth. While she was reeling from that luscious assault, he slid one big hand under the remains of her skirt. His palm felt deliciously warm against her thighs as he sent it questing upward.

Her arms bound helplessly behind her, Chloe could do nothing but stand there and moan. "This is really kinky," she managed at last, as his pointed tongue swirled around one hard peak.

"Oh, aye." He sucked her nipple into his mouth, bit gently. "Sinful, too."

She eased her legs apart. "A good feminist would never let a guy treat her this way."

"Absolutely not." One long finger traced the creaming opening between the swollen lips of her sex.

"I think you're missing the point."

"No." Radolf strummed his thumb over her clit. "I know exactly where your point is."

Chloe caught her breath. "Ohhhh, yeah. Yes, you certainly do."

He licked her nipples slowly, carefully, like a starving man forcing himself to take his time with some luscious dessert. As if that wasn't enough to drive her insane all by itself, one thick finger parted her labia, then gently screwed its way deep. She closed her eyes and moaned.

Radolf lifted his head to watch her as he added a second finger. “Wet and responsive,” he said, his voice a rasping murmur. “And so deliciously snug. I can’t wait to sink into you. I’ll ride you hard, sweet one. Ride you like none of your bloodless lovers ever has.”

For a long, delicious moment, there was no sound but her breathy sighs as the knight tormented her, twisting his fingers, scissoring them apart, then pushing in right up to the knuckles. Pleasure swirled and danced up her spine with every magical caress until she writhed, mindless and teetering on the brink.

“Now,” he breathed, and abruptly thrust inside her, simultaneously circling his thumb over her clit. “Fly for me.”

She convulsed, crying out in maddened joy as the heat rose in a sweet, burning flood.

His breath caught, then released in a growl. “Yes, that’s it—tighten. Let me feel you pulse. . . .”

The climax surged on and on, lifting her into a keening arch, arms bound, helpless in the face of the searing pleasure. She lost her balance, but even as she started to fall backward, he caught her and lowered her gently.

Dazed and panting, Chloe watched Radolf rise to his feet. She could feel sweat rolling down her back as her thigh muscles trembled deliciously.

Towering over her, he threaded those big fingers into her curls, his expression fierce. “Open your mouth.”

She looked at his massive cock inches from her lips. With a shudder of arousal, she leaned over and took the thick, round head of his cock into her mouth.

“Yes!” he groaned, the powerful muscles of his abdomen lacing as Chloe engulfed as much of his shaft as she could. “Jesu, it’s been so long . . .”

She’d never found giving a blow job all that hot, but there was something about the feeling of Radolf’s big body trembling against hers that was unspeakably erotic.

Listening to his gasps, Chloe drew away to swirl her tongue over the flushed, nubby head of his cock. He shuddered.

She smiled.

Slowly, carefully, she licked along the shaft and each of its snaking veins. When she swooped in again to suck, his rasping groan sent a sense of sensual power rolling over her.

He might be six inches taller, and she might be trussed so tightly she could barely wiggle her fingers, but at that moment he was all hers.

Suddenly he arched his back, his hand fisting involuntarily in her curls as he pulsed against her tongue. "Ah, sweet Christ!" he gasped. "Yes!"

Smiling around his thick shaft, she swallowed.

When she drew away from him at last, she found him staring down at her, his gaze curiously desperate for a man who'd just come in a woman's mouth. "Wake me." Both big hands cupped the sides of her face, stroked just beneath her cheekbones. "Wake me. Wake me, and I'll show you such pleasure every night."

A slight, puzzled frown still curved Chloe's mouth as she slid gently into a deeper sleep. Radolf echoed it as he rose from her. Though he had not had a physical body in a very long time, he felt shaken. "That," he murmured soundlessly, "did not go at all as I planned."

Chapter Two

Radolf stood in Belisarda's palace in the realm of Evanesce, gazing down at his own helplessly sleeping body. "Wake, curse you," he muttered, but of course, his enchanted self did not so much as stir. He lay as he had for the past eight hundred years in this magical prison of his, his mail and his sword around him, unaging and eternal.

And asleep.

Only his spirit was free. Free to enter the dreams of women and try to seduce them into lifting the spell that held him. He could read their thoughts, their secret dreams. He could become any fantasy lover they wished, speak the language they spoke, create any world they wanted. Sorcerer, seducer and slave in one desperate man.

Yes, his spirit was free, if you could call it freedom. If you could call whoring for a demonic witch "freedom."

He, the greatest knight in Christendom. The man his brothers in the Order of Varik had called The Champion of God. How appalled they'd be to see him now, a failure and a slave, vows broken, plying his dick in woman after woman. Pursuing the lying hope his enemy dangled in front of him because it was all he had left.

He was surely damned.

"You arrogant dog."

On the bed, his body twitched, reacting to the terror pouring through him at the rage in the witch's voice. Radolf wheeled to defend himself, knowing it would do him no good.

Belisarda strode toward him, her face twisted and malevolent, her eyes burning with a cold glow. She was flesh here in her kingdom of Evanesce. Flesh as he was not.

And she had power.

Automatically, he tried to knock her hand away as it flashed toward his heart, but her arm punched right through his ghostly fingers. And kept going, plunging deep into his chest to wrap around the core of his soul.

He tried to brace himself, but it did him no good. Waves of black energy poured from the witch's deceptively slender fingers. Energy that tore into his spirit like a cat sharpening its claws on silk.

Radolf believed this must be what it was like to be drawn and quartered—gutted alive and ripped apart by horses whipped in opposite directions. He doubted such a death could be any worse.

"Scream for me," Belisarda sneered.

He clenched his insubstantial teeth. She'd broken him, aye, but he was not so bent beneath her boot that he'd give her a casual victory.

He did not scream.

He would not scream.

Radolf fought to cling to that last bit of dignity in the ruins of his miserable existence. He knew he could outlast her. She would grow tired or bored or drained if he could only hold on a little longer. If he could only lock his psychic shriek between his teeth another second, oh dear sweet Jesu . . .

Belisarda tore her hand from him and watched him swirl in glowing wisps, unable to maintain even the illusion of a physical form. "I am displeased with you."

Radolf wanted to use the phrase he'd just learned from Chloe's mind: *No shit.* It was probably fortunate he was not yet capable of speech.

"She could have taken more pleasure from her own right hand than that pitiful climax you gave her," the witch raged. "And then you dared—dared!—order her to suck you, as if you were master rather than crawling slave!"

When she started to reach for him again, Radolf somehow managed to re-form. "A master . . . is what she wants," he told her in the silent communication that was all he was capable of. "At least in . . . bedroom fantasy. She wants no man to crawl to her."

"She's a twenty-first century woman who's been tricked and cheated, fool! Of course she wants you to crawl."

"No." He felt himself growing more cohesive in his certainty. "I've seduced enough women to know my quarry. She does not want protection, but she does want a lover strong enough to give it. Even if all she needs protection from is the lover himself." He hesitated, thinking of the pain he'd sensed in her. "Mayhap especially then."

"Huh." Belisarda curled her lip. "Well, if it's strength she wants, you'd better play lord and master to the hilt." Whirling, she strode away down the dark stone corridor, the heavy gown she wore now whipping around her long legs.

Just before she vanished around a corner, she paused and glowered over her shoulder at him. "Because if she ever discovers what a weakling you are, she'll not waste her time with you."

"You're thinking about that dream again," Amanda said, dropping into the chair beside Chloe.

Startled out of her haze, she hastily clicked her mouse. "Nope. Sorting through candids."

Dammit, she needed to finish weeding out the clunkers from the wedding she'd shot this morning. If she didn't get the digital shots uploaded to the lab in time, the photos wouldn't be back by the time the clients returned from their honeymoon. *Wake up, Chloe.*

"You know, when you're sorting, I hear busy little click-clicky sounds," Amanda drawled. "Since I haven't heard a click in ten minutes, I can only conclude you're thinking about that dream. Again."

Chloe felt heat flood her cheekbones. She and Amanda had been partners in H&R Graphics for the past three years. They'd set up shop in an office in this converted warehouse, with her friend contributing the business know-how and Chloe handling the photography and graphics creation. She rarely felt as if she wasn't pulling her weight. She did now.

Sighing, Chloe rubbed her temples. "I don't know what's wrong with me."

Amanda hooked an arm over her shoulder. "You had a rough weekend, sweetheart. It's not really surprising your mind's wandering."

"It's just . . ." She stopped.

"What?"

"I've never had a dream like the one last night. Ever. It was so . . . detailed."

Amanda smirked. Chloe had already entertained her with a play-by-play. "You mean, beyond giving the blow job to Sir Lottalance?"

She grinned reluctantly. "Beyond that. I never . . . Look, I almost always dream in color, but I never dream in smells. Or tastes."

Her friend pursed her lips, considering. "You know, I don't think I have either." She slanted Chloe a look. "What kind of tastes are we talking about here?"

"*That* taste. And . . . him. I could smell him. He smelled . . . exotic. Like leather and spices and iron."

"You know, they didn't bathe a whole lot back then. . . ."

Chloe grinned. "Well, no, but evidently this dream wasn't going for that much accuracy. Or else he'd just bathed. Anyway, he smelled really good." She sighed, her eyes falling half shut in pleasure at the memory. "And his hands. He had these calluses, like you'd expect from a guy that swings a broadsword all day. They were just a little bit rough on my skin."

Amanda gave a salacious shiver. "Damn, girl. You keep this up, and I'm going to have to go home and attack Richard. My dreams are never that good."

Chloe frowned, drumming her fingers on the mouse pad. "That's what I'm saying—mine aren't either. I mean, I dream a lot. Weird stuff that doesn't make much sense, based on what little I can remember about it the next day. But I can remember this, down to the last little detail. And other than the time he transported me into another room with a kiss, it all made sense."

Amanda lifted a brow. "Did it ever occur to you that maybe this is just your body's way of telling you it's time to get laid?"

Chloe glowered. "If you're about to offer to fix me up with that friend of Richard's again, forget it."

"Well, it is pretty obvious that you could seriously use some, babe. Why else are you dreaming yourself into a medieval porno movie?"

"Maybe because somebody sent me a really hot painting that totally caught my imagination?"

"Which reminds me," Amanda said. "Just who did send you that painting, anyway? Have you figured that out?"

She frowned and pushed the mouse around, watching the cursor skitter across the screen. "No. I've been wracking my brain, but I haven't got a clue. I made half a dozen phone calls, but all my female friends plead ignorance."

"And somehow, this just isn't the kind of thing a guy would send," Amanda agreed.

"Yep. Heck, I even asked Mom and Dad. Neither of them knew anything about it either. I'm planning to call the shipping company on Monday."

"Maybe somebody was just trying to cheer you up."

Chloe clicked on an out-of-focus shot of the bride's face and deleted it. "Except I've got a feeling this was a damned expensive gift. Too expensive, maybe."

Amanda frowned. "What do you mean?"

"Well, that frame." Frowning, she scanned absently through the rest of the images, deleting those that didn't meet her standards. "I took a look at the frame this morning. It's not just gilded wood, it's actual metal. And it looks like real gold."

"Oh, Chlo', it can't be." Amanda sat back in her chair. "That frame's got to weigh thirty pounds. If it was gold, it'd be worth . . ."

"Thousands. Or even more, if the painting's as old as it looks. And another thing, I was looking at the designs engraved into the frame. They look like runes."

Amanda digested that for a long moment. "Okay, now you're beginning to freak me out."

"Yeah, well, I'm freaking me out too."

"Maybe you ought to get rid of it," Amanda suggested.

Chloe's blue eyes narrowed. "Oh, no. Oh, hell no. What if it really is gold? What if it's as old and valuable as it looks?"

"And what if it's freakin' cursed, Chlo'? What if it's hot?"

"You mean, what if some international art thief shipped a stolen painting to me just for giggles?"

"You got a better explanation?" Amanda nibbled on her manicured thumbnail, visibly worried. "People don't just send strangers fantastic pieces of art in solid gold frames for no reason. There's a catch, Chlo'. We may not know what it is yet, but there's got to be a catch."

Chloe lay in her bed, staring at the muted golden glow of the painting's frame as a shaft of moonlight fell across it.

Would she dream of him again tonight?

Did she want to?

Well, yeah. Which meant that she probably would. But with her luck, Radolf would morph into Ted Bundy, and she'd spend the whole damn night running from him. Her dreams were never that happy. Certainly not for long.

But wouldn't it be nice if tonight's was an exception?

Out in the hall, she heard her big grandfather clock chime in long, rolling bongs.

Midnight.

Who was she trying to kid? As wound up as she was, she'd never get to sleep to *have* the dream. She'd toss and turn all night, staring at that stupid picture, unable to sleep a . . .

A rich female voice said, "This grows tiresome."

Hey, wha . . . ?

It was her last conscious thought until morning.

The floor pitched, almost tossing her completely off her feet. Chloe flailed a hand, grabbed something taut and prickly, and steadied herself. Shooting a look at what she held, she realized it was a taut hemp rope, more cable than anything else. Something boomed overhead, and she glanced up to see enormous sheets billowing overhead.

No, not sheets. Sails.

She was on a boat.

And not a sailboat either, Chloe realized, squinting up at the blinding blue sky that framed an intricate web of rigging, spars and flapping canvas. This was a tall ship, a . . .

BOOM!

Somebody bellowed a curse. Steel clashed on steel.

Chloe jolted, staring wildly around. Now men surrounded her in surging, thrashing knots of combat, hacking at one another with cutlasses or trying to bash each other's brains out with belaying pins. Blood was everywhere, rolling across the wooden deck, pooling around the corpses until men slipped and cursed in it.

Across the pitching deck of the ship, another massive warship bucked alongside. A flag flapped from its mast. The wind dragged the black fabric straight out to reveal a grinning skull, a rose between its teeth.

"Well," Chloe muttered, "I always did have a thing for pirate romances." She glanced down and wasn't even remotely surprised to see all the cleavage revealed by her tight laced bodice.

But as she contemplated the miles of blue silk hugging her body, she spotted something else. "Now that's convenient."

Just past one slippered foot, a rapier lay abandoned on the deck.

Chloe picked it up, smiling in appreciation at the way its cleanly balanced weight rode her hand. Giving the crowded deck a scan, she muttered, "So where is Captain Hardcock, anyway? Isn't it time he . . ."

High overhead, a powerful male figure stepped off one of the pirate ship's spars.

"Cue sex god," Chloe muttered, "swooping stage left."

She watched Radolf swing toward her, one big hand wrapped around a length of rope, the other holding a sword. At just the right instant, he let go of the line and dropped ten feet to land lightly on the deck. His grin lit his tanned face with a broad slash of white. "Ho, wench!" he called.

Chloe grinned back, ridiculously happy to see him. "You do realize you just violated half a dozen laws of physics?"

"Oh, aye," he said, swaggering toward her. "I just don't care."

Tonight Radolf wore a flowing white shirt open to the waist and a pair of black pants so tight she could tell he dressed to the left. A rapier swung from the leather baldric that draped his impressive chest, and a pair of black leather boots sheathed his muscled legs to the thigh. Though his blond hair had been cropped short in the previous dream, now it tumbled to his shoulders. Only the goatee framing his rakish grin was the same.

With a sigh of pleasure, Chloe admired his lazy, long-legged stride as he approached. His path was oddly free of inconvenient corpses. Looking around, she realized everybody else had disappeared from the ship, taking the blood and assorted body parts with them.

She and the pirate were alone.

A little quiver of lust snaked up her spine. Ignoring it, she said, "I'm beginning to think you've got a thing for dramatic entrances."

"No, milady. You do."

Chloe thought about it. "Now that you mention it, yeah." Bracing the point of her rapier on the deck, she let her eyes skim down to contemplate those skin-tight trousers. Judging from the bulge, she wasn't the only one who approved of the scenery. "So what's on the menu for tonight?"

"Actually," Radolf drawled, "I thought I'd bend my pretty captive over a cannon and see how many times I can make her beg for mercy before she starts begging for more."

He did that pirate grin extremely well.

Her heart started pounding. "Tacky, Radolf. Very tacky."

"Very." His green eyes crinkled at the corners. "And yet it made you cream."

"Did not," she lied.

"It certainly did." One big hand dropped to his sword. He drew it with a slither of steel.

She licked her lips and tightened her grip on her own rapier. "Now, what are you going to do with that?"

"Not much." The ends of his mustache twitched up like Rhett's whiskers. "Just find out how many laces I'll have to cut before your breasts spill out of that bodice." His point flicked toward her.

"Nuh-uh." Her rapier snapped up into an automatic parry, knocking his aside. "Not gonna be that easy, Captain Radolf of the good ship *Raging Hardon*."

He straightened, breaking into a delighted grin. "Oh, surely you jest."

Chloe awkwardly gathered a mile or so of skirt in her left hand and fell into guard. "What, you think I watched all those Errol Flynn flicks in film class because I liked his dimples?"

He lifted a golden brow as he surveyed her. "The concept of your fighting me at all is ludicrous, but it's particularly laughable given those skirts."

"Hey, I'll have you know I was state fencing champ . . ." She broke off as his feral grin broadened.

When Chloe glanced down, her gown had disappeared. In its place was a white corset that pushed her breasts up and together until they strained to spill free. A tiny pair of thoroughly modern thong panties made very little pretense at modesty, while a white garter belt held up delicate lace stockings. A pair of stiletto heels rounded off the whole Victoria's Secret effect.

She glowered. "This is not even remotely period."

His grin widened. "I know."

"And if I try to fence in these heels, I'm going to break both ankles."

"Actually, you won't, but I suppose they do push credibility rather far."

The shoes instantly became delicate dancing slippers. Not mollified in the least, Chloe demanded, "I thought you were a medieval knight. How do you know so much about modern lingerie, anyway? Or seventeenth century piracy, for that matter? Or, hell, twenty-first century grammar?"

Radolf shrugged broad shoulders. "Actually, I know very little about any of that. You, however, know a great deal, and since you're the one having the dream, that's enough." He began stalking her, moving as lightly as a panther over the swaying deck. "The question is, what do you know about using that sword?"

"That's a . . ." Very good question. It suddenly occurred to Chloe that neither of their weapons were buttoned fencing foils. If one of them actually hit the other, the phrase "agony of defeat" could have real meaning.

She scuttled back from his advance, wondering what the hell to do now.

"Probably lose," he told her, as if reading her mind.

Then he launched into a long, slow, lazy lunge.

He was so big, Chloe had plenty of time to see him coming. Retreating hastily, she flicked her blade for the parry, but his weapon did an intricate dance around hers and kept right on coming. Panicking—this was going to hurt—she tried for the parry again, missed and . . .

Pop. Chloe cringed as she looked down, half expecting blood.

The top lace of her corset was neatly cut. "Hey!"

Radolf straightened as he regarded her cleavage like a connoisseur. He let his rapier dip, but the weapon between his brawny thighs strained at full attention. "As I said," he purred, "the concept of fighting you is ludicrous, but I find myself willing to indulge your fantasies." He grinned wickedly. "Whatever they may be."

Chloe had a redhead's temper, and now it flared into full, glorious roar. This wasn't the first time she'd encountered blatant sexism in the men she fenced, but somehow—God knew why—she'd expected better of Radolf. "I," she growled, "am going to kick your arrogant ass."

"Actually, you're going to get stripped naked and bent over a cannon while I impale your tight, creamy little . . ."

With a snarl, she went after him with teeth bared.

Chloe often fenced with men. She was feared on the tournament circuit, because though most of her opponents were bigger and stronger, she made up for her weaknesses with skill. Too, she excelled at the kind of strategic play that turned fencing into highly physical chess.

None of which did her a bit of good against Radolf.

Nobody that big should be that fast. He parried her most nimble attacks with flicks of his blade that looked deceptively gentle. At least until he connected and damn near tore the rapier from her hand.

Radolf's offense was even more murderous. Trying to block his attacks was like trying to parry a 747. It should have taken him about five minutes to turn Chloe into sushi. Luckily, all he was interested in cutting were the strings on her corset. It wasn't long until the garment gaped wide enough to reveal the areolas of her nipples. And worse, encumber her arms.

"Hell with it," she growled, and started jerking at the corset with her left hand, trying to pull it off and maintain her guard at the same time.

But though the three remaining laces did nothing to hold the corset closed, they were snarled tight. She couldn't seem to get them untied, especially with one eye on her opponent. Frustrated, she looked down. . . .

A rapier point danced in, flicked. All three laces popped, and the corset slid down around her hips.

Chloe shot Radolf a glare. Spreading his free hand, he attempted a guileless smile that wasn't even remotely convincing. "I was simply trying to help."

"Yeah, you're a real gentleman." As she jerked the garment off and threw it aside, his green eyes lit at the sight of her bare, bouncing breasts.

Enough's enough, she thought with a snarl, and launched right into an attack.

Radolf was so busy admiring the sweat gleaming on Chloe's chest that he missed the parry. He had to scramble back out of range of her lunge.

"Ha!" she crowed, throwing herself into another combination. Pressing ruthlessly, her blade beating against his, she managed to back him into one of the twelve-pounder cannons that stood on the deck.

Radolf leaped away from her assault, landing on top of the big gun as lightly as Rhett jumping on the kitchen counter. "Not fair," he told her. "I was distracted by those hard little nipples."

"I'll show you distracted," Chloe growled. "I'll distract you with a sucking chest wound." She slashed her sword in a ruthless cut right for his muscled calves.

He bounced over her stroke to hit the deck on the opposite side of the cannon. "That doesn't sound at all pleasant."

"Oh, it won't be." She thrust at the muscled V exposed by his open shirt.

A big brown hand flashed out and locked around her sword wrist. One hard jerk dragged her halfway across the gun.

"Now, look at that." Radolf tossed his own rapier aside and casually plucked her weapon from her hand. "Half naked and draped across a cannon." His grin was pure lupine threat. "Whatever will I do with you now?"

I'm screwed now. Literally, Chloe thought in dismay, staring into his wickedly hungry gaze. Rallying, she managed a glare. "Forget it," she growled, fighting to jerk out of his hold. "I wouldn't have you if you were the last romance hero in publishing."

"Of course not," Radolf said, cupping the back of her head to lean in for a quick kiss. He pulled back just before her teeth could snap down on his lower lip. While she glowered, he gave her another one of those Red-Riding-Hood-eating grins. "Assuming I gave you a choice."

Realization dawned. "Dammit, you've done it to me again, haven't you?"

He grinned. "Oh, aye."

Sure enough, her wrists were tied together behind her back, while her wide-spread ankles had been tethered to rings set to the deck.

"Have I mentioned," Radolf purred, tracing a big finger along the naked contours of one hard nipple, "how much I adore your breasts?"

Both the nipples in question tingled and hardened. Chloe licked her lips. "Cut that out."

He smiled slowly. "No."

Callused fingers stroked and teased until curls of pleasure swirled through her breasts. "I don't want this," she managed.

"Liar."

"Rapist."

He dropped to one knee. "I'll make you a bargain, my sweet one. If you still want me to stop in five minutes, I'll stop."

He tilted his blond head so that one of her hard little peaks pouted just above his lips. Then, ever so slowly, he licked. Chloe gasped at the silken pleasure that cascaded through her body with the first pass of his clever tongue.

And knew she wouldn't be telling him to stop.

Chapter Three

Radolf had a great mouth.

And he knew how to use it too. He swirled just the tip of his tongue over and around Chloe's breasts in tiny little circles that made her jerk against her bonds.

"Sweet," he whispered. Green eyes flashed up to meet hers roguishly. "And so helpless."

His sinner's lips opened just a bit wider so he could rake his teeth over a tight, pouting point. One big hand came up to cup the other breast. His callused thumb rasped over its peak.

She squirmed.

"Your little pussy is next," Radolf told her, his voice a velvety male purr. "I'm going to lick and suck . . ." He paused to demonstrate. "And bite . . ." A quick nip made her gasp. "Do you know why?"

"You want to drive me crazy?"

He smiled slowly. "Yes. And I need you very, very wet. Because my cock is thick and hard, and you're so exquisitely tight." He squeezed both breasts with those big hands of his, gently milking pleasure from her flesh. "It's going to take a long time to work my entire shaft in up to the balls."

She swallowed and managed, "Oh, now you're just bragging."

"No." He gave her an exquisitely slow, careful bite. "I'm not."

Remembering what it had been like to suck him the night before, Chloe knew he was right. Imagining her slow impalement on that big shaft, she shivered.

God, this was going to be good.

Radolf's long fingers ceased their seductive stroking. "Unless you tell me no, of course." Blond lashes veiled knowing green eyes. "I wouldn't want to force you."

She snorted. "Except on days ending in Y."

He widened both green eyes, as if trying for an innocence he missed by a mile. "You malign me, milady." Gently he twisted her nipples, sending twin streams of pleasure streaking right for her sex. "Do you think me such a barbarian I'd rape some poor lass, simply because she was foolish enough to think she could best me in combat?"

"After you'd stripped her naked and tied her over a cannon? Gee, let me think—Yes."

"I'm wounded, lady. Truly I am." The laughter rumbling in Radolf's seductive voice made heat well deep inside her. "I'm the very soul of chivalry."

She snorted. "In the words of the Big Bad Wolf, '*What* Three Little Pigs?' You'd be more convincing without the bacon on your breath."

"Oh, sweet, nobody could ever mistake you for a pig of any sort." He flicked an auburn curl with one big finger. "Now, Red Riding Hood . . ."

"As long as you don't try to dress up as my grandma. The concept of you in drag . . ." She gave a mock shudder.

Radolf lifted a blond brow. "Oh, you have nothing to fear on that score." A sly smile quirked his mustache. "Though now that you mention it, I am interested in your basket of goodies."

When he rose to his feet, she got a crotch level view of his own goodies. "My, Grandma," she muttered, *sotto voce*. "You're hung like a Clydesdale."

His laugh as he walked around behind her was wicked enough to make her quiver in her bonds.

She quivered even harder when he caught the fragile waistband of her lace thong and ripped it off her body. "Now," he purred, "that's better."

"Yeah," she managed. "I'd say so."

A big finger stroked down the crack of her bare backside to find her sex. His fingertips traced between the swollen lips. "Ah," Radolf rumbled, "a creamy little tart. My favorite dish."

Chloe tried to crane her head around to see what he was doing, but the cannon blocked her view.

Which didn't keep her from feeling every glorious sensation. Like the tickle of his beard against her ass. Or the hot, masculine tongue that licked the length of her, catching her clit and the opening of her vagina in one pass.

As she gasped and squirmed, he did it again. And again, back and forth, slowly, in long, teasing laps.

In minutes, he had her on the edge of shameless begging. She wanted him to circle his tongue around her clit the way he had her nipples, but he was too intent on driving her out of her mind. Every stroke of that clever tongue sent pleasure sizzling up her spine. She could feel her body tightening, on the verge of a hard, pulsing climax. If only he'd circle her clit just once. . . .

"Radolf," Chloe gasped at last, unable to stand any more. "Please!"

"Please what?" he drawled.

She felt no shame at all. "Let me come!"

Another deliciously torturous lick. "Do you deserve to come?"

"God, yes!"

"But you've been wicked." One big finger explored her. Entered slowly. "You drew a weapon on me. And you lost." Slid out again. His thumb brushed her clit, just enough to make pleasure jolt through her, but not enough to trigger that pulsing climax. "I won. So now . . ." Another mind-blowing entry. ". . . I get to punish you."

"Radolf!" It was a whimper.

"You're so tight and swollen and wet, Chloe." She heard the jangle of a belt, the rustle of clothing. "I think you're ready for your punishment."

She closed her eyes as hot lust roared through her. "Be my guest."

"Sweet, do you really think I need permission?" Radolf laughed as the head of his massive cock brushed her creamy flesh. While she caught her breath in an agony of erotic anticipation, he began to work his way inside.

He was much, much bigger than Chris.

Then he stopped and pulled out. "No, on second thought, you're not ready yet."

"Radolf!"

"I can't do it too soon, sweet." He stroked the big head between the lips of her sex, teasing her opening but carefully avoiding her clit. "I'd hate to take you before you're completely ready."

"You know how ready I am!" Frustrated, Chloe rolled her hips, trying to capture the taunting shaft.

A big hand landed lightly on her ass in a gentle swat. "None of that, sweet. You lost, remember?"

"Take me already, you big jerk!"

He slid inside a bare inch. "Now, is that any way to talk to your lord and master?"

Her inner feminist rebelled, but her inner hedonist promptly strangled it into submission. Chloe didn't care what delusions he cherished, as long as he gave her more of that magnificent cock.

Radolf obliged her, slowly feeding her a little more of the broad shaft. And then still more. Damn, he made Chris feel like a toothpick by comparison. Slick, sliding heat, stretching and filling her. More. And more.

And more.

She could feel her climax gathering power, like a tidal wave roaring toward shore.

"Aye," he gritted, when he was seated to the balls. "Oh, aye. You're ready. . . ."

And then he began to thrust. He started slowly, gently rocking against her, teasing her with delicious little strokes down in her hot depths. His big hands rested on her ass with blatant possession. As he lengthened his thrusts, she felt him lean back and part her, as though to watch his cock delving between her lips.

"I love the way you grip me, sweet," he said softly. "Wet and snug." He drove in a deep stroke and groaned in pleasure. "And good. Sweet Jesu, you're good."

"You're not—AH!—so bad yourself," she gasped.

He started riding harder, faster. She could feel her climax building, gathering, the tidal wave whipped higher by his masculine storm.

Radolf was lunging hard now, his hips slapping her ass. He reached beneath her with one hand, found her clit. Stroked.

Chloe screamed as the white hot explosion rolled over her, ecstasy jolting through her entire nervous system like a lightning blast. "Radolf! Oh, God!"

"Aye!" He jammed to his full length and froze, coming, his roar blending with her cry.

It went on and on, blazing, creamy spasms of it jarring her body. Until finally, she collapsed, only dimly aware of the cool metal of the cannon under her and the heat of Radolf's hands.

He was softening inside her when at last he spoke, his voice hoarse. "Wake me."

A furry weight thumped onto Chloe's chest, jolting her ruthlessly awake. Green, glowing eyes stared into hers. Her heart gave a startled slam.

"Mrroooow?"

Her head fell back on the pillow in relief. "Jesus, Rhett, you scared the stuffings out of me!"

The cat turned to stare into a darkened corner beside the bed, ears folding flat to his head. He hissed—the long, distinctively vicious get-the-hell-away hiss he normally reserved for the neighbor's Great Dane.

Gooseflesh popped up along Chloe's skin in a cold wave. She flailed out with one hand, found the bedside lamp. Designed to turn on at a touch, it instantly blazed light into the room.

Chloe's wide eyes searched the corner Rhett stared into with such malevolent feline hostility. It was empty. She relaxed.

"There's nothing there, Rhett." She looked at the cat.

He was still staring at the corner, ears flattened, lips pulled back from his fangs. He hissed like something out of a horror movie.

"Oh, hell, Rhett, don't do this to me!" Chloe scooped the cat into the curve of one arm and threw back the covers with her free hand. "I just had a really good dream, and you're breaking the mood. Big time."

Rolling to her feet, she gave the corner another wary look. Still empty. She looked down at Rhett.

The cat seemed to be watching something move across the room.

Toward the painting.

And was the knight lying in a different position than he had the last time she looked?

"Okay, this is just toooo creepy." Chloe trotted toward the door, eying the painting warily. "Let's go watch CNN."

Probably for the rest of the night.

In Evanesce, Radolf lay sated on the pile of furs next to his sleeping body.

"Thrice-cursed cat," Belisarda snarled. "I was not finished."

"I was," he said lazily.

She hissed at him, sounding remarkably like Chloe's tom.

After watching an entire CNN headline cycle and drinking a mug of cocoa, the cat incident began to seem like a bad dream. Chloe went back to bed, hoping for another delicious encounter with Radolf.

She didn't get one.

But when she fell asleep Monday night, he returned as an Arab sheik with an English mother and a taste for redheaded Scottish travelers. On Tuesday, he became an adopted Apache warrior who captured a pretty settler.

On Wednesday, she played Confederate spy to his ruthless Union major. He was a Viking warrior on Thursday, making off with a lovely Celtic lass. On Friday, he became an English lord who won the virtue of a wastrel's daughter in a card game.

And each and every night, he taught Chloe more about pleasure than any flesh and blood man ever had.

She saw the attack coming in plenty of time to parry. Chloe dropped her blade . . . but not in time. Her opponent's weapon struck home between her ribs.

"Touché, dammit." Sighing in disgust, she dragged off her fencing mask and wiped her sweating face with the back of her wrist.

"Which makes it five-oh, my favor." Amanda frowned as she took off her own mask. "I have never beaten you five-oh in my life. What's wrong?"

Chloe reeled over to the porch and collapsed on the top step. A muscle was jerking spasmodically in her thigh. She rubbed it absently. "Just tired, that's all. Haven't been sleeping well."

"You look like shit."

Chloe looked up at her friend and lifted a brow. "Thank you."

"You've got dark circles under your eyes, and you're paler than even a redhead has any business being." Amanda walked over to crouch on the grass in front of her, concern in her eyes. "And you were fencing at half speed. You anemic or something?"

"Maybe." Sighing, she leaned back to brace her elbows on the edge of the porch. "I don't know. I've felt rough for the past couple of days now. Guess I'm coming down with something."

"Better see a doctor."

"I will."

As if relieved, Amanda smiled and changed the subject. "So," she said, in a teasing voice, "had any more dreams about Sir Lottalance?"

"Not since the last one." Chloe told herself it wasn't really a lie. She couldn't help it if Amanda drew the wrong conclusion about which one the last one had been.

Her friend grinned impishly. "Too bad. After that Union major/spy thing, I was looking forward to finding out what romance novel you'd dreamed yourself into this time. I was kinda hoping for a western."

"Yeah," Chloe said. "That does sound like fun."

That night, she leaned against the kitchen counter, watching a frozen dinner turn lazy circles in her microwave. It dinged at last, and she pulled the plate out, hissing at its heat.

Peeling the plastic off, Chloe watched steam roll up without much interest. She dug her fork in with a grimace and scooped up a bite of Thai chicken. This particular dinner was one of her favorites, but tonight it tasted like sawdust. She forced herself to eat it anyway.

She'd lost seven pounds since Saturday. Seven pounds she'd always wanted to lose, true, but not by being unable to eat.

Too bad last night's dream didn't count. Radolf had fed her a deliciously exotic meal of roast pheasant before ravishing her on his endless dining table. It had tasted a lot more real than the Thai she was choking down now.

"Bllrtt?" Rhett reared onto his haunches and threw himself against her calf in a butting rub designed to get her attention. As if unconvinced he had it, he leaped up onto the counter.

"Hey." She shoved his furry muzzle away from her plate. "You already had two cans of cat food, not to mention my lunch. Keep this up, and you'll be too fat to terrorize the neighbor's dog."

"Mmrr." He rolled over on his back, presenting his fluffy black belly.

Too wise to fall for that trap, Chloe scratched him under one ear instead. If she'd tried for the tummy, he'd have gone after her hand with all four sets of claws. "What is it with you guys?" she asked as he started purring like a Jag after a tune up. "You beg for love, and then you go all Ginsu when a girl tries to give it to you. It's no wonder I prefer dream men."

Talking about Radolf reminded her she'd lied to Amanda. Chloe frowned guiltily as she gave the cat's ears another scratch. She'd always been able to tell her friend anything, and yet somehow this particular secret had grown too delicate to share.

"He's not even real," she grumbled to Rhett as the cat nosed her plate. "And yet, he is. Or this little voice in my head insists he is, anyway. How weird is that?"

"Blrtttt?" The animal looked up at her, green eyes intent.

"You think I'm nuts, don't you? You're probably right." Chloe sighed. "It's just—Chris never made me feel the way Radolf does." Absently, she poked at her dinner. "And I'm not just talking about the fantastic orgasms, either. In the entire six years of our relationship, Chris never once gave me the look Radolf gives me every damn night. As if I mean something to him. As if he needs me."

"Nrrrrr?"

She tossed down her fork and raked both hands through her hair as she turned to pace. " 'Wake me.' What the heck does that mean? Radolf says that at the end of every dream. But how do you wake a dream?"

She stopped in the middle of the kitchen, head down, both hands laced behind her neck. "But it doesn't feel like a dream. That's the problem. His touch, his kiss, his body—it all feels so real."

Taking a deep breath, Chloe admitted, "And every morning, I hate waking up even more."

The moment she slept, Radolf stepped from the painting, eager to be with her again. He was only vaguely aware of Belisarda floating after him, as insubstantial in this plane as he was.

All day, he had waited impatiently for Chloe to sleep again. He had come to crave her company in a way he'd never craved any of the other women he'd known over the centuries.

Chloe was different.

Beautiful, yes, sensual, yes. But she was just as intelligent as she was lovely, and her wit was a match for both. Which was ironic, really, since he'd never considered either a prerequisite in a lover.

Just one more of his assumptions Chloe had turned on its head. Before, he'd had more frustration than pleasure with the women whose dreams he inhabited. Yet he enjoyed being with Chloe for its own sake. Something about her made even his eternal captivity bearable. He. . . .

Something was wrong with her.

Radolf stopped dead in the mattress, staring into her sleeping face. She lay huddled beneath a pile of blankets as if cold, though he could tell the night was pleasant. Illuminated by a pool of silver moonlight, her face looked thin, drawn, and there were shadows under her eyes.

"What's wrong with her?" he demanded, glancing at Belisarda. "She looks ill."

The witch's eyes widened in startled interest. Then her expression smoothed. "She's well. The moon casts strange shadows, 'tis all."

Radolf studied his lover's face anxiously. "Nay, I think not. Could it be something we've done? I have . . . visited her longer than the others."

Belisarda nodded. "Most of your past lovers would have blocked you out by now." She shrugged. "They seem to sense . . . something. But she is unusually obsessed with you."

"Yes. Obsessed. She's not getting enough sleep," he decided, turning reluctantly back toward the painting. "Best let her rest tonight."

As he strode past, Belisarda gaped at him in dismay. "But she's so close! This very night, she might break the spell." The witch hurried after him. "And then the two of you can sleep all you wish."

"No," Radolf said shortly. "I want to be free, but not enough to risk her."

The witch stopped in her tracks. "You've fallen for her!" Her burble of malicious laughter dragged him to a stop. "Radolf of Varik has finally fallen in love!"

A wave of ice rolled over Radolf's skin. He knew he didn't dare let Belisarda know how much Chloe had come to mean to him. "Don't be ridiculous," he snapped. "She's just another girl, no different from the others."

"Aye, Black Lord? Then why are you so willing to spend the night alone?"

He shrugged, fighting to keep his expression cool and unconcerned. "It may be some time yet before I convince her to free me. If she sickens, I could loose this chance."

The witch studied him, her eyes shimmering with that hellfire glow he'd come to fear. Then, slowly, she smiled. "The child is fine. Look." She gestured, and a cool, glowing orb appeared over Chloe's sleeping face, illuminating her features.

The shadows he'd thought he'd seen were gone. She was as beautiful and healthy as ever.

"You see?" Belisarda purred. "It's as I said. It was but a trick of the light. Go to her."

Sweet Christ, he wanted to. And yet . . . "I know you feed from the heat of her passion. Have you taken too much?"

The demon witch flicked long fingers in dismissal. "What I take, she'll not miss."

He frowned, his instincts clamoring.

"Unless your lover's heart fears to take even so small a chance as this," Belisarda said, her voice soft with mock sympathy.

Radolf shot the witch a glare and strode back toward Chloe. "Fine. Mayhap tonight she'll break the spell, and you and I will be quits."

"Oh, milord," Belisarda said as he sank into Chloe, "I look forward to the day."

"Not as much as I," he growled, and disappeared into his lover's dream.

Chloe smelled woodsmoke, leather, and horse.

She frowned, suddenly, uncomfortably aware that she was lying on something coarse and prickly spread out over something hard and lumpy. Like a wool blanket on sandy ground.

If this was one of those dreams, it wasn't getting off to a very enticing . . .

A loud CLICK interrupted her train of thought. Her frown deepened as she struggled sleepily to place the noise. It sounded like . . .

A revolver being cocked.

Her eyes popped open.

Radolf stood over her, straddling her body, in a pair of Levi's that did amazing things for his long, muscular legs. A white shirt hugged his powerful chest, unbuttoned halfway down his washboard belly. Over the shirt, he wore a leather vest, a silver sheriff's star glittering against the rough, dark hide.

The gun in his hand was pointed right between her eyes.

"What a purty little thing you are," he drawled. " 'Specially for a murderin' outlaw."

Chapter Four

Chloe stifled a snicker. "Did you actually say, 'purty'?"

He swooped into a crouch, almost sitting on her chest, the Colt an inch from her nose. "Yeah," he snarled. "And I cocked this here *gun,* too."

This was going to be fun. She banished her grin and batted her lashes. "Oh, please don't shoot me, mister!"

His eyes narrowed to deadly green slits. "You got a lot of gall beggin' for mercy, lady, after the way you stabbed that poor son of a bitch you were married to."

If she knew this particular kind of plot, the dearly departed had probably been trying to kill her at the time. If this was a novel, he'd turn up alive in chapter nineteen, just in time for his comeuppance. "It was self defense!"

"Tell it to the judge, lady." Radolf was really getting into this.

Probably because he intended to get into her.

Which sounded like a pretty good idea to Chloe. She widened her eyes, hoping she looked seductively helpless rather than goofy. "Please, Sheriff—I'll never get a fair trial! His daddy bought off the judge." They always did.

"Too bad," Radolf said, cold and implacable. "You're goin' back."

Chloe laid an artistically trembling hand on his bent knee. "I'll do *anything*!" God, what cheesy dialog. Good thing she wasn't a romance novelist.

He stood, six feet plus of luscious male slowly unfolding. Chloe hoped she wasn't visibly drooling.

He aimed the Colt between her breasts and sneered, "Now you're bein' insulting. You think you can seduce me dressed in those dusty boy's clothes?"

Now, there was a cue if ever she heard one. Chloe bit her lip and toyed with the top button of her cambric shirt. "I could . . . take them off."

Radolf didn't move a muscle, but heat leaped in his gaze. She unbuttoned the button, then, slowly, the next.

Green eyes narrowed, burning hotter in his expressionless face.

Her heart began to pound. She slid the next button free, then paused to pull the edges of her shirt open a little more, revealing a V of cleavage. Daring a glance up at him through the screen of her lashes, she saw his poker face had not softened one bit.

But the erection straining his jeans would have made a stallion weep with jealousy.

She opened another button.

"Faster, sweetheart," he growled, gesturing with the Colt. "I'm gettin' bored." Apparently he wasn't in the mood to magically strip her naked this time.

Chloe opened her eyes wide and then gently bit her lip. His gaze flicked to her mouth. She could have sworn that massive erection got bigger.

She unbuttoned another button.

By the time all the buttons were free, she was as wet as he was hard. She let her hands fall away, leaving her shirt open only enough to expose an inch-wide strip of bare flesh.

"That's not good enough," he growled. "Take it off."

She lifted her chin in mock defiance. "Make me."

His grin was every kinky fantasy she'd ever had. "Oh, it'll be my pleasure."

Radolf went to one knee, the other straddling her, as oiled-silk smooth as a cat. Deliberately, he touched her breastbone with the muzzle of the Colt. The metal felt cool against her heated skin.

"Now, wait a minute." Chloe caught her breath. "I don't think . . ."

"You don't need to." Slowly, he dragged the barrel of the gun over the swell of one breast, pushing her shirt aside until he raked the Colt right over her nipple. The little nub instantly drew into a hard, pointed peak. She whimpered.

He reversed his stroke, pushing back the other side of her shirt, baring the full swell of the other breast, again teasing her nipple with the gun.

"You've got real pretty breasts," he said, his voice hoarse and raw with need.

Then he raised the Colt until its muzzle pointed at the sky. "Play with 'em."

"Radolf . . ."

"Now."

Sweet Lord, this was getting hotter than the time he'd banged her over the cannon. Feigning reluctance, her heart pounding, Chloe reached for one breast and cupped it shyly.

"Squeeze it," Radolf ordered. "Offer it to me."

Licking her lips, she shifted her grip on the soft, full mound, kneading gently. The peak popped out at him, hard and insolent.

He looked at it, his eyes darkening into shadowed emerald. "That's a sweet little nipple. Nice and pink and tight." He contemplated it a long, burning moment. "Flick it with your thumb," he ordered finally. Bracing the elbow of his gun hand on one knee, he rested the other hand on his thigh, drawing her attention to the horse-choking bulge behind the tough denim. "Get it good and hard."

From the looks of it, it's already good and hard, Chloe thought, but obediently stroked her thumb over the little peak. The curl of pleasure made her gasp.

He smiled at her, slow and feral. "You like this, don't you? You like gettin' me hot. You like gettin' *you* hot." Gesturing with the Colt, he purred, "So let's get you hotter. Twist that nipple."

She hesitated.

He leveled the gun at her again. "That wasn't a request."

Biting her lip, Chloe obeyed, intensely conscious of his glittering gaze. "You really are a very bad man, aren't you?"

"Yeah, well, at least I'm not a killer." His beard twitched around his wicked grin. "Well, not lately. Both hands, sweetheart. Tug 'em for me."

Her heart was pounding a heavy metal drum solo as she tugged and twisted the swollen pink peaks under his gun.

As she milked both of the hard points, he reached back with a big hand and cupped her sex through the fabric of her jeans. She caught her breath, freezing like a rabbit. He pressed two fingers against the seam that lay between her thighs, rasping the coarse, thick fabric over slick, delicate flesh.

"Radolf!" she gasped, squirming.

"Keep milkin' those pretty tits, girl." He stroked, pressed, never taking those glittering green eyes off her. "You know," he said, lifting his hand away, "maybe what you need is something harder."

Chloe almost sobbed in gratitude. "Yes. Oh, yes. I want you so . . ." She broke off in alarm as he reached back with the gun and ran the muzzle along the seam of her jeans. "Radolf!"

"You know," he said, ignoring her yelp, "you're wearin' too many clothes. Take off these britches."

"Now, look . . ."

Like a rattler striking, he whipped the gun around. Chloe knew perfectly well the weapon wasn't real, any more than he was, but her blood chilled in her veins. "You'd rather hang?" he snapped.

"No." Her voice actually shook.

"Didn't think so." He stood, unfolding to his full, menacing height, and took a step back. "I want you naked, Chloe."

Something about the silken note in his voice sent heat pumping in to replace her fear. She licked her lips and decided to throw in the obligatory protest. "I'm not . . . like that."

"Yeah." He gave her a cynical Clint Eastwood smile. "You are." He gestured with the Colt. "Take 'em off." When she started to sit up, he growled, "No. Laying down. I want a good look."

This felt way too real. So why was she creaming inside her Levi's? Swallowing, she reached for her fly.

As she fumbled the buttons open, Radolf settled on the ground to watch, crossing those booted feet and propping up on one elbow. His biceps strained the sleeves. He put the gun down, but she knew just how fast it could be back in his hand.

"Strip 'em off," he ordered, his voice rough and dark.

Time for another obligatory virginal protest. "Radolf . . ."

"If I have to do it for you, I'm gonna paddle that little ass once I get it bare."

Her heart leaped in her chest. For a moment she was tempted to goad him into doing just that—but decided she'd much rather get that horse-choking erection where it would do her the most good.

Slowly, spinning it out, Chloe wiggled free of the jeans, knowing every little squirm made her breasts bounce.

Radolf really, *really* liked the view. She only wished he was naked, so she could see the source of that intimidating bulge without his jeans in the way.

When she finally lay on the bedroll in nothing but her open shirt, Radolf looked at her for a long, long time while she grew steadily wetter. "Damn, you really are a redhead, aren't you? Touch yourself. Deep." He lowered his lids, his mocking smile a white slash within the blond frame of his beard. "I want to make sure you're good and ready when I start working my cock in past those pretty copper curls."

Oh, she was ready. God, was she ready. But masturbating in front of him felt so damn kinky . . .

Still, she knew better than to refuse, so she reached shyly between her thighs and ran her fingers over the slick, swollen flesh.

"I want a better view," he rasped. "Spread 'em."

With an inward shudder of arousal, Chloe raised her knees and opened her thighs.

"Yeah, you're wet," he said, and started unbuttoning his Levi's. "Finger yourself."

She eyed his cock as his tanned fingers worked to free it from his fly. "Wouldn't you rather . . . ?"

"Not yet. Do it."

She slipped a middle finger inside the tight entrance as he liberated his massive shaft. Radolf purred approval and told her to add another finger as he lazily began to stroke himself.

Arousal flowed through Chloe's veins like heated honey as she watched him caress his own hard shaft while rumbling erotic orders at her.

Shuddering in pleasure, she stroked her clit and pumped her fingers in and out of her swollen flesh. He watched her like a cougar picking its moment to pounce, naked lust in his eyes, triumph in his smile. All the while, one big hand pumped lazily at his big, straining cock. The other held his gun trained on her in silent threat.

She didn't think she'd ever done anything so kinky in her life. She could feel her climax simmering, just about to boil over . . . "God, Radolf, I'm coming . . ."

"On your feet!"

The rough bark froze her fingers. "But . . ."

He pointed the Colt right between her eyes. The long fingers of the other hand were still wrapped around his thick rod. "You come when I say you can come. On your feet!"

"Go to . . ."

"Finish that sentence, and you're goin' over my knee. And you won't like what I'll do to that pretty little ass when you get there." He bared his teeth. "On . . . your . . . feet."

Glaring at him, she stood.

Radolf gestured with the gun. "Turn around and bend over. I want a good look at that luscious butt." Brazenly, he cupped his heavy balls with his free hand and watched her like a wolf.

Another squirt of heat shot through Chloe at the stark eroticism of his pose. Which still didn't mean she liked what he was doing to her. Reluctantly, she turned around, set her feet apart, and bent.

"Finger your pussy," he growled.

Chloe threw him a simmering glare over her shoulder. His cock looked about a yard long. She imagined what it would feel like as he drove it hard into her.

"Aren't you going to do anything with that?" she demanded.

"Not yet. Now I want you to . . ."

She straightened and spun on him, furious. "And you can kiss my pink, puckered . . . !"

"Finish that sentence and you'll get that spanking—among other things. Now turn back around and bend over."

"Creep!" Snarling in frustration, she whirled—and spotted two saddled horses that stood at the edge of the campfire's light.

Chloe didn't think twice. She didn't think about being naked, or wonder where the hell she was going to go. She just sprang for the nearest horse, shoved a bare foot into the stirrup, boosted herself into the saddle, and banged both heels into the mare's silken white sides. The big animal leaped under her and tore off into the night.

Behind her, Radolf roared in fury.

She grinned and leaned over the horse's whipping mane. He'd catch her, of course. And when he did . . .

Well, he wouldn't be in the mood to tease.

The night wind whipped into her face, carrying the smell of sagebrush and sand. *Damn,* Chloe thought, for what had to be the hundredth time that week, *this all seems so real.*

Hearing hoofbeats drumming behind her, she grinned at the full moon floating high in the night sky. She couldn't wait for him to catch her.

Radolf plunged after her on the big black stallion, enjoying the hot wind in his face. None of this was real, of course; he'd created it in her dreaming mind out of her own fantasies, aided by details he'd picked up over the centuries from other women's thoughts. Yet illusion or not, it seemed as real to him as it did to her.

Though her pale, luscious ass bobbing in that saddle looked more like something out of his own dreams than hers.

His stallion ran hard, its long strides gaining rapidly on the little mare's lead. Radolf licked his lips in anticipation, his heart pounding. Tonight might be the night she freed him, but even if it wasn't, he'd soon know the lush pleasure of Chloe's glorious body. And for now, that was enough.

It had to be.

One minute she was tearing through the night with the rolling thunder of hoofbeats in her ears.

The next, a hard male body slammed into hers, knocking her right off her horse.

Chloe had time to think, *This is going to hurt,* just before she tumbled onto a thick feather mattress and cool satin sheets. "Oof!" she gasped.

They both should have somersaulted right off the bed, as fast as they were going, but once again, the laws of physics gave them a break. They bounced just once and fell back into the slick, cool sheets, safe but shaken.

Winded, Chloe didn't even bother to struggle as Radolf settled on top of her and caught her wrists in both big hands. She was too busy surveying the brass bed that had somehow materialized in the middle of the Texas plains. "Well now, this is convenient."

"Definitely more so than breaking your neck," he agreed, lowering his head to sample one of her nipples.

"Got me there."

"I certainly do." He grinned sidelong at her and gave the hard peak an erotic rake with his teeth.

Chloe caught her breath and wiggled under him. He tightened his grip on her wrists, silently warning her she wasn't going anywhere. "So, Sheriff Radolf," she purred, "what are you planning to do with li'l ole me?"

He lifted his head, heat and humor in his gaze. He'd evidently decided to drop the big, bad sheriff act. "Ride you until you beg me to stop."

Chloe grinned. "That's what I thought."

"Clever wench." Returning his attention to her breasts, he settled down to suck one with a wicked skill and devoted attention that soon had her gasping.

Craving the feeling of his strong, naked body under her hands—his clothes had vanished—she tried to pull her wrists free. "I want to touch you."

"Not yet." He transferred both wrists to the grip of one hand as his gaze flashed up to meet hers. "You're my captive, sweet. I'm the one who does the touching."

Gently, ravenously, he moved over her, stopping here and there to nip and nibble and suckle, stroke and squeeze. In no time at all, he had her writhing mindlessly in the sheets, begging for his cock.

"No," he whispered the fourth time she pleaded with him. Then he lowered his head between her spread thighs to circle her clit. Almost bringing her to climax. Almost.

She could feel it shivering there, like a huge soap bubble filled with magical fireworks, just waiting for one tiny thrust.

Desperate for release, she ground against him. "Please, Radolf! God, you're driving me insane!"

"Only because I want company," he murmured, sliding one big finger slowly into her core. "I'm mad for you."

"Radolf!" Chloe cried, rolling her hips desperately.

He laughed softly and sat up, moving into the eager cradle of her thighs. "I can't resist you when you beg."

She caught her breath as he aimed his thick cock for her silken opening and slid inside in one long, hard thrust.

"Ahhhh, Christ," he whispered when he was in to the balls, his tone oddly reverent. "You're so sweet."

Chloe tossed her head on the pillow in pleasure as he settled over her in a delicious blanket of muscular strength. "God, your cock—!" There were no words for the glory as the hot satin shaft drew out of her, then thrust back inside in a searing lunge.

Lost, half-blind, she stared up at his face, silvered in moonlight. The muscles in his powerful shoulders worked as he braced himself, stroking slowly, his eyes half closed with the delight of being so deep within her.

Realizing he'd finally released her hands, Chloe wrapped both arms around his brawny torso and held on as his thrusts jarred her body. The glittering bubble of her climax swelled impossibly, trembling on the verge of breaking.

Mindless, she ground her pelvis against him, her breath sobbing in her throat as she stared up into his lost green eyes.

Radolf shuddered at the feeling of her silken calves riding his working ass as her nails dug into his back. He'd learned to make it real for his partners, but it had never been so real to him.

Then he felt her slick, tight walls pulse around him, and she threw her head back as she came, writhing against him.

He'd never in all his centuries seen anything as beautiful as Chloe's face, transported in hot joy.

As he stared into her eyes, he felt his own climax roll up his spine in a ferocious wave. Throwing back his head, Radolf bellowed his pleasure at the moon.

They lay together when it was over, tangled in the satin sheets like ordinary lovers.

Radolf lay still, listening to her heart as it slowed its desperate beat. She felt impossibly soft and precious in his arms.

He'd seduced so many women so many times over the past eight hundred years that he'd long since lost count. Yet none of them had ever touched him the way Chloe had. None had ever surprised him, aroused him, reached him the way she had.

Would she be the one to finally set him free? Would she believe him?

Would she pass the test?

If, pray God, she did, he'd stay with her. If she'd let him. If she loved him in truth as much as she seemed to in these delicious dreams. As much as he . . . He cut off the thought, unwilling to admit it to himself.

Feeling too much for her was dangerous. And not just because of what Belisarda might do to them both.

He tightened his grip on her narrow waist at the thought. "Wench, you've destroyed me." He'd intended the words as a joke, but they sounded all too fervent.

Chloe smiled at his words, looking up at the moon as she traced designs over his forearm with her nails. She could feel tendon and muscle ridged beneath his smooth skin. Golden hair dusted his flesh like threads of silk under her fingertips. "This isn't a dream." The words popped out of her mouth, without any conscious premeditation at all. They still rang with truth. "Somehow it's real." She turned her head to gaze into his face in wonder. "You're real."

His smile was a little sad. "You're only half right, I'm afraid." He swept a hand in a gesture at the brass bed sitting in the middle of the desert under a breathtaking night sky. "All this is a dream. But aye, I'm real."

It was impossible. Ridiculous.

Yet Chloe didn't doubt him. She knew he existed, felt the truth of it on some level that went beyond reason and logic.

Somewhere all the way down in her soul.

"How are you here, Radolf? How did you get inside my mind?"

He looked away, staring around across the darkened landscape. A muscle worked in his jaw. "Magic."

Chloe nodded. What other explanation was there? "Are you some kind of . . ." She searched for a word. "Wizard?"

He flashed her a cool look. She realized she'd somehow offended him. "I'm a knight. I belonged to the order of the Knights of Varik."

She digested that. "That sounds . . . medieval. Like one of the Holy Orders, like the Templars."

"Very like, but we were an order even more secret. Some called us heretics, which is why the Church eventually wiped my brothers out. Ironic, that, for we were formed to defend her." He shrugged. "But we used magic, and most churchmen believed the source of all magic is the Devil."

Chloe looked at him. "Just how old are you, Radolf?"

"I was born in the Year of Our Lord, 1232."

She found she wasn't at all surprised. "So you're immortal."

"No." A muscle worked in his jaw. "Bespelled."

And from the sound of it, it wasn't a spell he enjoyed. "By whom?"

"Belisarda. A . . . I know not what she is. I call her witch, but I do not believe she's human. Demon, perhaps, or Sidhe. Or succubus, most like." He shrugged. His speech had slipped back into its medieval cadences again, as though that was most natural for him.

Chloe rolled on her side so she could drape an arm across his waist and prop her chin on his chest. "So how did you get on her bad side?"

"I was sent to kill her."

"That would do it."

He smiled slightly. "Indeed. At the time, it was possible for her to live in corporal form on Earth. Your science, your beliefs, have made that impossible today."

"A lot of people believe in magic," Chloe objected. "I'm not one of them, but still . . ."

"It's more than that. There are beams in the air . . ." He paused, frustrated.

She lifted her head, interested. "You mean radio waves? Electrical fields, that kind of thing?"

"Aye, those. They block Belisarda, disrupt her magic. 'Tis like breathing acid to her." He shrugged. "But when I was sent for her these eight centuries past, she could come and go as she pleased. And she pleased to live in a castle in England and feast on wayward young knights."

"She *ate* them?"

"Not the meat of them. But their pain, their pleasure. And eventually, when she slew them, their souls."

Chloe curled her lip. "Eeeww."

"Exactly. My order had been formed to fight such creatures. When we heard rumors of what she did, I was sent to investigate, since sometimes such tales were born of nothing more than malice."

"Wait a minute." She frowned, outraged on his behalf. "They sent you to fight her *alone*?"

Radolf shrugged his brawny shoulders against the silk pillow. "I had battled such creatures before and won. My sword was bespelled, worked with runes that made it possible for me to slay them. So I was confident." His expression turned bleak. "Too confident."

He fell silent so long she finally felt driven to prod him. "What happened?"

"I had been taught to shield my mind from magical invaders, so Belisarda could not read my thoughts—she would certainly have slain me if she had. She was wary of me on that account, so I set out to win her trust, the better to learn if the accusations were true." His green gaze turned brooding. "There were many knights around her who seemed bewitched, right enough, but she was beautiful, so that alone was no evidence of dark power."

Feeling a little prick of jealousy, Chloe asked, "How beautiful?"

"Enough that I grew to love her a little, until I learned of the evil in her." He stared up at the sky, his expression going grim. "I tarried with her longer than I should have, trying to decide if she was the demon the rumors said. Enough that she grew confident in me, and slipped back to her old ways."

"What happened?"

"One of her young knights grew jealous and challenged me. Fool that I was, I drew my sword, prepared to fight him—but she struck him down with a bolt of magic. I could only watch in horror as she moved to stand over him and drink down his soul. I could see it pouring from him in glowing streamers."

Chloe winced. "That must have been an ugly surprise."

His nod was short and grim. "Very. I knew I'd been duped. Here was no lovely innocent, but the very demon we'd been told. I lifted the blade I held, spitting curses on her. She turned, raging, and with the life force she'd stolen from that lad, she struck me down."

Chloe lifted her head and stared at him in horror. "Oh, God. You're a ghost!"

He stroked her cheek soothingly with a big, warm hand. "Nay, milady. I but sleep. I have slept for all the centuries since."

" 'Wake me,' " she whispered in a burst of realization. "That's what you meant! But if you're asleep, how are you here? And why didn't she kill you when she had the chance?"

"As to that, I know not. But I believe Belisarda was frightened by how close I came to killing her. She decided she no longer wished to stay on mortal Earth to run such risks. Instead she returned to her own realm, somewhere in a world beyond this, taking my sleeping body with her."

Chloe frowned. "Why? I mean, why keep you?"

His expression grew even more grim. "I was provisions."

A sense of chill horror grew in her belly. "What do you mean?"

"Belisarda prefers to devour souls, but she can subsist well enough on the emotions mortals feel. Passion. Pleasure. But what she enjoys most is suffering."

The chill deepened. "But if you were asleep . . ."

"Only my body sleeps. My spirit walks like the ghost you named me, aware and feeling. So she used her powers to torture me for two hundred years until I agreed to be her whore."

Her horror took on a cast of sick understanding. Unable to lie against him any longer, Chloe sat up, staring down at him. "You go into women's dreams, and you seduce them. And Belisarda feeds on the pleasure they feel." Anger began to simmer in her blood. "The pleasure *I've* felt!"

"Aye, but . . ."

She ignored him, rolling the bed to pace. "That's why I've felt so damn weak. That's why I can't eat. You *fed* me to her, you bastard!"

Radolf stared at her. "You've been unable to eat? I thought you looked drawn. Damn the witch! She told me she did no harm!"

Chloe wheeled on him, shaking with hurt outrage. "You *used* me. Just like Chris! Get out!"

"No!" In an eye blink, he was in front of her, gripping her shoulders in both big hands. "It's not like that. Chloe, I love you. Yes, I need you to come into the painting, to give me the kiss that will wake me. But that does not change what I . . ."

"What are you, Sleeping Beauty?" She sneered at him, so angry and sick she wanted to throw up. "Find some other sucker, Radolf."

Anger ignited in his eyes. "I used the other women, aye. As they used me to live their secret dreams. But you are not like them. You *are* my dream, Chloe!" His voice dropped, going warm and deep. "You are my love."

She wanted to believe him so badly, she clenched her fists and seriously considered punching him in his beautiful, lying face. "What kind of idiot do you think I am? Get out of my head, Radolf. And don't come back."

His eyes widened as he realized she meant it. For an instant, raw desolation filled his face.

Then it was gone, and he drew himself to his full height. "It will be as you say. In forty-eight hours, the painting will disappear, and me with it. If you change your mind ere then, touch the heart and come to me. If not . . ." Bitterness darkened his eyes. "I will still love you the rest of my days, whether I will it or not. Now, wake you."

With a gasp, Chloe sat up. Staring wildly around, she realized she lay in her own bed.

A patch of darkness lay on the pillow next to her. Her heart gave a violent thump, and she rolled onto the floor with a yelp.

Then she realized the black shape was Rhett. The cat was staring at the painting, his green eyes unblinking.

Chloe's chill deepened. Licking her dry lips, she walked toward the moonlit canvas.

Before, Radolf's painted face had worn an expression of sleeping serenity. Now there was sadness in the line of his mouth, grief in the set of his thick brows.

She braced a hand against the wall beside the painting and bowed her head. "Radolf," she whispered, her voice choked. "What have you done to me?"

Her shoulders shook as she began to cry.

Chapter Five

Chloe sat staring numbly at the computer screen with eyes gritty from lack of sleep. She'd spent all day Sunday pacing the floor in front of the painting, trying to convince herself the events of the night before had been nothing more than a dream.

Her heart insisted differently.

She finally dropped off around four in the morning, but even then, Radolf had kept his promise to stay out of her dreams.

Now it was Monday. The painting would disappear at midnight.

And Chloe had no doubt at all it would disappear. Illogical or not, she believed what Radolf had told her in the dream. He really was a thirteenth century knight under a mystical spell cast by some kind of succubus, or witch, or whatever Belisarda was.

Suddenly a hand clamped over the back of her chair and spun her around. Chloe yelped.

And met Amanda's hot glare. "Dammit," her friend growled, "why are you letting them do this to you? They're not worth it!"

But he is, her heart whispered. *He is*. "Amanda . . ."

"For God's sake, it's been six months since you caught them in the sack! I thought you were over this!"

Chloe blinked. "This has nothing to do with Chris and Debbie. I'm not in love with him anymore." Thoughtfully, she added, "I'm not sure I ever really was." She'd felt hurt and humiliated when she'd realized what was going on between her lover and her friend, but she hadn't felt anything like the kind of desolation Radolf's betrayal had caused.

"What?" Glowering, Amanda fell into the chair next to hers. "So what the hell is going on?" Her blue eyes widened in sudden fear. "Did you get a bad report from the doctor?"

Chloe shook her head. "I haven't even been to the doctor. No, this is about something else. Somebody else."

"Gotta be a man," Amanda decided. "Nothing else would depress you this bad. So who is this guy, and why don't I know about him?"

Chloe glanced away helplessly, knowing her friend would never believe the truth. "It's . . . somebody I just met. I've only known him a week."

"You've gotten this flipped in a week? Must be a hell of a guy."

For once she could reply honestly. "He's like nobody I've ever met. He really puts Chris in perspective, you know? He's so damn hot, and he does things to me that . . ."

Amanda's jaw dropped. Then, thoughtfully, she closed it. "It's not just infatuation, is it?" she said slowly. "You're really in love with this guy! You've known him a week, and you've still fallen for him like a ton of bricks. So what's the problem?"

"He's . . . leaving tonight."

"So stop him. Or go with him. Or something."

Chloe sighed and rubbed her aching temples. "It's complicated, 'Manda."

"He's married."

"No, nothing like that. But I found out there've been . . . others."

Storm clouds gathered in Amanda's loyal eyes. "He's fooling around on you already? Hell, you're well rid of the creep."

"No. The others were from before he met me."

"Oh, God, he's HIV positive!"

"Of course not. That's not even a possibility. He's just . . . had a lot of women."

"So we're restricting ourselves to virgins now?" She snorted. "Girlfriend, unless you're only going to date fourteen-year-old boys—and I think there's a law against that—every guy on the planet is going to have some kind of romantic past."

Unable to sit still any longer, Chloe rose to pace. "But he says he loves me, Amanda! How do I know he's not just using me? It was bad enough when Chris did it. I don't think I could survive if I found out this man was just playing me for what he could get."

Amanda stood and caught her shoulders, halting her nervous strides. "Listen to me, sweetheart. You can't go through the rest of your life wearing body armor. For one thing, Kevlar and Victoria's Secret do not match."

Chloe slumped, thinking of Radolf and Belisarda, of demons and enchanted knights. So much could go wrong. "I just don't want to get hurt again."

"Baby, that's the thing about the Lover Lotto. You gotta play to win."

Chloe stood staring at the painting.

From the hall outside her room, the grandfather clock began a series of sonorous bongs, one after another as it chimed eleven.

You're running out of time, she thought. *Make up your mind, dammit.*

Her heart was pounding violently, even as her gritty eyes burned. She could almost feel Radolf's lips on her skin, his hands on her breasts, his thick cock surging into her sex. She could almost hear his whisper: *I will still love you the rest of my days, whether I will it or not.*

"You have to play to win," Chloe whispered.

She straightened her shoulders. Her heart began to pound even harder. "All right. Look out, Bitch Witch, here I come."

Chloe reached for Radolf's sleeping face—and touched canvas. Frowning, she ran her fingertips over the painting, but it remained stubbornly solid. "Dammit, I thought he said I was supposed to come through the painting. How do I get in?"

There had to be a way. And she'd better figure out what it was, because midnight was growing closer by the second.

Radolf stood on the other side of the painting, watching Chloe's beloved face as she frowned in concentration. "She's going to do it," he whispered, hardly daring to believe. "She forgave me. She's coming for me!"

"It does look like it," Belisarda whispered in his ear.

Something about the dark pleasure in the she-demon's voice made his heart clutch. He glared at her over his shoulder. "Will you go back on your word to free me, then?"

Belisarda gave him a chilling, catlike smile. "I would not dream of it, Lord Radolf. The moment her sweet lips touch yours, you'll be free." The smile widened into a cold, triumphant grin. "And I'll have my revenge."

Radolf's stomach sank as he spun to face her. This was it. The trap he'd always suspected was hidden somewhere within the rotten heart of her offer. "What treachery do you plan, bitch?"

Her eyes glittered with malicious pleasure. "You never asked what would happen to the girl, Radolf."

Sweet Jesu, it was worse than he thought. "No. Belisarda, I've whored for you. I've endured your torture and screamed for your pleasure for eight endless centuries. Surely that's enough revenge to sate even a devil's appetite!"

"It's not." Her inhumanly beautiful face twisted with hate. "Not for what you did to me."

"I did nothing!" Radolf roared. "You stopped me before I could strike!"

Her hand flashed out, drove into his ghostly chest and closed around the core of his soul. "You made me love you, cur! You made me ache for your touch. I, who was worshiped as a goddess, blinded by a mortal's pretty lies!"

Agony tore at him as her fingers tightened. He ached to spit defiance into her face, but in his pain he couldn't speak.

Belisarda raged on. "I should have slain you then, knowing what you were, but no. I kept you by me these eight hundred years, thinking that perhaps, one day, you would come to love me as I deserve. Instead you give your heart to one of those puling whores who feed me with their lust!"

Now outrage gave him strength. "You tormented me without cease! How could you imagine I'd ever care for you, you black hell bitch?"

"I am a goddess!" she shrieked in his face. "But if you won't give me what I deserve, I'll take what pleasure I can. When that slut's lips touch yours, you'll return to her world to live out your mortal life, just as I've sworn. But she will take your place in sleep!"

"No!" he bellowed.

"Yes! And she will suffer such torment as to make your time with me seem a pretty spring day. I will whore her, my lord Radolf, whore her as I have you, to every twisted thing whose polluted male mind I can force her into. They'll rape her in their dreams as she curses your memory. While you live out your mortal days, tortured by the thought of her torment."

His fury drained away, stolen by sick horror. "No. Belisarda, don't." He knew he begged, but for once, he didn't care. If the demon wanted him to crawl, he'd crawl. Anything to save Chloe. "I will serve you however you want, but don't do this to her! Keep me and I will . . ."

A malicious cat smile curled her mouth. "No."

And she was gone, leaving him to float in thin, sick wisps, cold with despair.

"Touch the heart," Chloe murmured, suddenly remembering what Radolf had said the moment before he'd disappeared. "He said 'touch the heart.' What heart?"

She scanned the painting desperately, conscious of the minutes ticking past.

Then she saw it. There, at the bottom of the painting, in the very center of the frame. A tiny heart shape. Her heart gave a nervous thump.

Chloe hesitated a moment, saying a silent prayer. Then, carefully, she reached out and pressed her fingers against the inlay.

Nothing happened.

She frowned, then reached to touch the surface of the canvas again. Her hand sank into the painting as if sliding into water. "That's it!" A broad grin spread over her face. "That's it! Oh, Radolf, I did it! I'm coming!"

Except . . . Chloe hesitated, remembering his description of Belisarda's powers. She really didn't like the idea of just popping into the painting. No way was the witch going to let her simply kiss Radolf and waltz off with him.

It couldn't be that easy.

But—what kind of weapon could Chloe use against somebody with that kind of power . . . ?

An idea popped into her head. She smiled in savage pleasure. "Oh, yeah!" But would it work?

There was only one way to find out.

Chloe spun away from the painting and ran to the night table beside her bed. Finding what she was looking for, she stuffed it into a pocket of her jeans and hurried back to the painting.

To her relief, when she touched the canvas, she found it was still liquid.

"Question is," Chloe muttered, taking a step back, "how am I supposed to get in there?" She threw a quick glance at her bedside clock.

11:45 p.m.

"Screw it," she muttered.

And, taking a running step forward, Chloe leaped up and threw herself through the canvas in a long, flat dive.

Fire danced over her skin, lifting every hair on her body. She heard wild laughter and sobbing screams as a flare of cold blue light blinded her.

Then she hit cold stone hard enough to jar her teeth. Tucking into a ball, she rolled with a fencer's agility across the marble floor, tumbling to absorb the momentum of her fall.

When Chloe bounced to her feet again and glanced around, she immediately recognized her surroundings. The gleaming stone walls were splashed with the same golden light she'd seen in the painting.

On the bed before her lay Radolf, lying asleep in all his glorious blond nudity, his hand on his sword, his armor around him, a sable pelt spread across his bare hips.

"Real," Chloe whispered in wonder. "Oh, he is *real.*"

As a giddy grin broke over her face, she stepped toward him. She'd never wanted to kiss a man so badly in her life.

Stop.

Radolf's voice, faint, ghostly. It made the hair rise on the back of her neck. Chloe turned, heart pounding.

He stood behind her, a glowing, insubstantial presence. *It's a trap,* he said, though she didn't hear his voice with her ears. *Belisarda has lied to me all these years. If you kiss me, you'll wake me—and you'll take my place in this hell.*

Chloe nodded, not at all surprised. "Yeah, I figured it was something like that. But if I kiss you, you will wake, right?"

Aye, but 'tis not worth it, Chloe. The expression on his ghostly face was grim and urgent. *"You'll be imprisoned here as I have been, hers to torture for centuries. You must go back. The painting will vanish in minutes, and you'll be trapped.*

"And leave you here? I don't think so." She reached into her pocket and pulled out her weapon. He watched, uncomprehending, as she prepared it with a flick of her thumb. "That magic sword still work?"

Aye, but she'll give me no chance to use it. His eyes blazed with urgency. *Chloe, you must leave. Now. I have no wish to be free if it means you'll sleep an eternity in torture!*

"Yeah, well, I guess you'll just have to wake me, then." She held up her secret weapon and tapped it with her thumb. "When the time comes, press this button."

Chloe, for the sake of all the saints . . .

She turned away and crouched to tucked the object in the left hand of his sleeping body. Her heart was pounding a wild adrenalin beat, but she felt no fear as she looked down into his familiar, roughly handsome face.

"I love you," Chloe whispered, and pressed her lips to his.

Radolf's eyes flew open for the first time in eight centuries to meet her gaze in horror.

Then her lovely blue eyes rolled back in her head, and she dropped in a heap beside the bed.

"Chloe!" he roared, flinging himself from the bed. "No!"

"Yesssss!" Belisarda purred, appearing beside him as he dropped to one knee. "Time to leave, my lord. I want to be alone with your pretty lover." The demon witch lifted her hands to cast her spell. He knew he'd never be able to stop her in time.

Then he felt the small, cool object in his left hand.

He didn't even take the time to feel hope. Desperately, Radolf lifted Chloe's weapon, pointed it at the witch, and hit the button his lover had pointed out.

The one marked SEND.

Belisarda staggered as the cell phone sent out its pulse of radio waves, dialing the number to Chloe's house in a series of cheerful beeps, just as she'd set it to do.

"Bastard!" the witch shrieked as the phone's radiation ripped into her magical body. "I'll tear out your cursed heart while she . . ."

"You'd do nothing but die, bitch." Radolf snatched up his sword and drove it hard into her chest. She staggered, but reached for her power, obviously determined to destroy him even as she died.

Not this time, Belisarda, he thought, and flung all his mental strength into the spell he'd memorized eight centuries before. Even as the witch's clawed, glowing hands reached for him, Radolf drove the burst of magic down the blade and into her black heart.

She shrieked in agony as a wave of pure white light rolled up her torso from the enchanted blade. For an instant, he saw the twisted, demonic thing that was her true nature.

A soundless explosion flung him back. He hit the ground hard and rolled to his feet, turning his eyes toward the spot where the witch had stood.

She was gone, the blade with her.

But before he could feel any sense of relief, Radolf heard the first rolling bong of Chloe's grandfather clock.

The painting! The gate was about to close!

He scooped Chloe's unconscious form into his arms. Whispering a silent prayer, Radolf turned and raced for the painting that, on this side, showed a view of her empty bedroom.

BONG!

He threw himself in a flat dive into the frame, Chloe clutched against his chest. The two of them surged through the gold framed opening . . .

BONG!

Something snagged his left foot just before they hit the carpeted floor of Chloe's bedroom. Canvas tore. Radolf twisted, taking the brunt of the impact, as they tumbled together.

BONG!

They fetched up against the bed. Heart pounding, he looked back at the painting.

BONG!

Now the canvas showed only the empty castle chamber, though there was a torn place in the center. He remembered the sensation of something catching on his foot and winced. It had been too cursed close.

BONG! The last chime.

Tiny shimmering flames raced across the canvas. The painting vanished with a sullen hiss.

"Thank God," Radolf whispered, then looked down into Chloe's face. He caught his breath.

She still slept.

Oh, sweet Christ, what if Belisarda's death meant the spell could no longer be broken? "No," he whispered. "Sweet one, wake. Please wake . . ."

Taking her chin in his hand, he tilted her face upward and pressed his lips to hers.

Radolf gave the kiss everything he had, lips and tongue and teeth as he plastered her slim body desperately against his own.

Until . . .

"Mmmmm," she purred into his mouth, "promise me you'll always wake me up this way."

Hope expanding in his chest, Radolf lifted his head to gaze down into her face. She smiled up at him sleepily. He grinned back, suddenly drunk with pure happiness. "Oh, aye! Every single morning!"

"I knew you'd save me," Chloe murmured, turning her face sleepily against his throat.

"No, lass." He closed his eyes in relief. "You're the one who saved me."

"Witch dead?"

"Oh, aye."

"Good." She settled against him with a sigh. " 'Cause I've been up for two days straight, and I really need some sleep."

Carefully, he got to his feet, holding her cradled in his arms. "You go ahead, sweet. I've had all the sleep I need."

A soft snore was her only answer.

He smiled and crawled in the bed with her, wanting only to hold her for the rest of the night.

Chloe awoke to a warm male mouth moving over hers, coaxing, suckling. The hot, liquid stroke of a tongue, the gentle nip of teeth on her lower lip. She opened her eyes and lifted her head.

Radolf looked down at her as the morning sunlight ignited his blond hair into a golden blaze. Stretching in his arms, Chloe smiled sleepily up at him. "Mmm. Tell me this isn't a dream."

He cupped her bare breast, thumbed her nipple until it tightened, pouting pink. "No, sweet, this is definitely real."

"Good." She slipped both arms around his torso, feeling solid muscle and bone working under her hands. " 'Cause if it's not, I never want to wake up."

The arm around her waist tightened. "Never say that, sweet. It came too close to coming true."

"Well, it didn't." Chloe threaded one hand through his hair, enjoying the silken slide of the strands against her fingers. "We beat the bitch."

"Aye," he breathed, his eyes closing in relief. "Oh, aye, that we did."

She frowned slightly. "I only wish I'd seen it. What happened?"

He lowered his head to her breast. "Your gambit with the cell phone worked. It disrupted her magic long enough for me to kill her." Radolf's gaze flicked up to meet Chloe's. "And no, I don't want to talk about the details. I have other pastimes in mind."

As satin masculine lips closed over her nipple, Chloe arched into the mattress and lost all interest in anything else.

Finally, finally, she could touch him, kiss him, however she wanted.

As his teeth raked the taunt peak of her breast, she indulged herself, stroking her hands over the fine, hard muscle of his broad shoulders, exploring tendon and bone that lay under his smooth, tanned flesh.

It was so hard to believe. This amazing man—this literal knight in shining armor—had fought for her. Had been willing to sacrifice himself for her.

And she'd almost lost him.

So when he started to nibble and lick his way down her torso, obviously intent on even more erotic kisses, Chloe stopped him. "No," she whispered. "I want to pleasure you, too."

He gave her a hot sidelong look as he traced her navel with his tongue. "This does pleasure me, sweet."

She knew her own grin was equally wicked. "But we can make it even better."

So with a little coaxing, Radolf rolled over on his back, allowing her to straddle his face as she bent over him to pay loving attention to his bobbing cock.

"Well," Chloe purred, as she ran her tongue down the violently hard shaft, "I'm glad to see my dreams didn't exaggerate."

He gave a mock growl and closed his mouth over her clit in retaliation, sending pleasure shooting up her spine like a Roman Candle.

Humming in delight, she licked the tight plum head, enjoying the salty taste of his pleasure almost as much as the delicately erotic sensations his tongue created.

Radolf reached down and caught the tip of one breast, squeezing and rolling the little peak as he circled her clit with his tongue. She shivered at the heated honey pleasure and nibbled the head of his cock.

He growled and slipped one big finger into the slick opening of her sex. Stroking in and out, he caught one of her labia between his teeth and gave it a gently maddening tug.

"You're not a nice man," Chloe moaned.

"Oh, I'm a very nice man," Radolf rumbled, and proved it when he added a second finger to the next deep stroke.

In gratitude, she angled his cock upward and engulfed it in one long swoop that had him gasping against her sex. He felt lusciously smooth and tight against her lips as she suckled him.

She'd never tasted anything as erotic as Radolf's hot, taut shaft. The smell of him made her feel dizzy with a breathless combination of joy and lust. Moaning—half from the sensual pleasure of taking him, half from what he was doing to her with his own talented tongue—she swallowed around his massive shaft.

The feeling of her mouth on him made Radolf moan against her sweetly astringent pussy. Her sweet, full breast filled his palm with silk as he squeezed each of her tight little nipples in turn.

Radolf had never felt like this in his life. Despite the hundreds of women he'd seduced, he'd never known the delicious sense of having found the other half of himself. He wanted to tell Chloe how he felt, but he had no words for the sheer dimensions of the thing. He, the erotic sorcerer of so many female dreams, felt as overwhelmed as a virgin.

So he said nothing, instead trying to show her with his body even as she drove him mad with her hot, silken mouth.

"That's enough!" Chloe gasped at last, pulling suddenly away from him.

Radolf growled a protest, but before he could snatch her back, she took his cock in one cool, small hand, and guided it to the opening of her sex.

Then she sank down over him, impaling herself one glorious inch at a time.

"God!" Chloe moaned at the sweet, burning heat of taking him to the very heart. "Radolf, you feel so good!"

"Oh, aye, sweet," he groaned, as her silken little ass settled across his hips. He clenched his teeth desperately, fearing that he'd lose control and spill in her before she even made her first thrust.

Somehow he held on as she rose again, wet and slick and tight around his aching cock. Then, slowly, she began to move up and down, bare breasts quivering, her little hands braced on his chest.

He'd never seen anything as beautiful as her face, blue eyes wide and dazed, full mouth open as she panted.

Joy swelled in him, as hot and savage as the pleasure of her slow strokes. Finally, after so many centuries, he was free. Free to love the exquisite woman who'd freed him.

Suddenly he found the words for what he felt. "I love you!" he gasped.

"Yes!" she cried out, arching her back, grinding down hard. "Oh, God, Radolf, I love you too!"

It was that glorious admission that shot him over the edge. He came, roaring her name.

As Radolf arched hard under her, driving to his full length, Chloe felt her own climax fountain up through her body in a burning electric surge. She threw back her head and screamed out her ecstasy.

They ground together, writhing, for endless, exquisite moments before she collapsed, panting and spent, across his powerful chest.

It took her two tries to manage speech. "I do love you."

"And it's a lucky man I am." She felt his strong arms wrap around her sweating ribs. "For I'd hate to love like this alone."

Epilogue

One Year Later

Chloe watched as the two masked, white-garbed figures faced each other across the fencing strip. Each held a fencing saber in a gloved hand as four judges watched, two on either side of the strip.

The state championship rode on this particular bout, and she knew neither man was in any mood to lose.

Suddenly, with a blood-chilling roar, the taller of the two sprang forward. His opponent parried and scuttled aside from his charge.

The big man shot past, twisted, and slashed backward with his saber, catching the other squarely across the buttocks. The thinner man yowled as all four judges threw up a hand, indicating they'd seen the hit.

"Yes!" Chloe, Amanda and Richard howled in joyful chorus from the gym bleachers, applauding wildly.

Radolf pulled off his fencing mask, tucked it under one arm, and stepped toward the man he'd beaten so thoroughly, offering his hand in the traditional fencer's gesture.

Chris Jennings ripped off his own mask and shot the bigger man's hand a fulminating glare before limping off the strip. Debbie hurried out to meet him, stepping back when he snarled.

Chloe stifled a snicker. The thin, flexible sabers, unlike the stiffer fencing foil, were designed to be used in cutting strokes, like cavalry swords. Though too dull to break the skin, a saber blade could whip viciously in the hands of a fencer as skilled and strong as Radolf.

She didn't envy Chris his bruises. Especially since Radolf had caught him twice across the ass and once over the hips, along with a couple of good solid blows to the mask that had probably rung his chimes.

"That was mean," Chloe told her husband as he pulled open his jacket flap and collapsed on the bleachers beside her.

"Don't listen to the little hypocrite," Amanda said. "She loved every minute of it."

"So did I," added Amanda's husband, Richard, slapping Radolf on the shoulder. "That bastard has needed an ass-beating for years. Good to see him finally get one."

Radolf grinned and wiped his sweating face with the back of his hand. "Well, my loving wife wouldn't let me jump him in an alley, so it was the best I could do."

"Civilized people," Chloe told him firmly, "do not jump their wives' ex-boyfriends in alleys."

"Don't bet on it," Richard drawled. Amanda smacked him on the arm, and he ducked, smirking. "I mean, *of course* we'd never do anything like that. Really."

"Hardly ever," Radolf agreed, deadpan.

The two men had become fast friends over the past year as Radolf struggled to adjust to life in the twenty-first century. He wasn't completely ignorant, having picked up a great deal from the minds of the women he'd pleasured, but he still had broad gaps in his knowledge.

There'd also been his complete lack of identification, but he and Chloe had managed to solve that problem with Richard's help. Apparently not all the skilled brick masons and carpenters the contractor used were legal aliens; among his contacts was someone who knew how to produce the needed documentation.

Neither Chloe or Radolf was inclined to look a gift horse in the mouth.

After that, the former Dark Lord enrolled in an adult ed program while she taught him to drive. Meanwhile, he'd gone to work for Richard, whose thriving business had almost grown too big to manage alone.

Though Radolf started out doing grunt work, he proved to have a real talent for carpentry, as well as an eye for construction. Add to that his natural leadership skills and taste for hard work, and Richard quickly decided he was an obvious choice for foreman.

The two men now split the job of overseeing Richard's various residential building projects. They were seriously discussing a partnership, since they'd be able to build twice as many houses as Richard could alone.

Still, sometimes Chloe wondered if Richard suspected the truth—that Radolf was far more than he seemed. But if he did, he never asked.

"Hey, Chloe Varik!" one of the judges called, dragging her back to the present. "You're up!"

Grabbing her foil, she jumped to her feet, then caught her husband's bearded face and swooped down for a kiss. He gave back in kind, putting so much tongue and enthusiasm into it, somebody started applauding.

When they finally came up for air, Radolf grinned at her. "What was that for?"

"My happily ever after," Chloe said, and sauntered off to meet her next opponent—who just happened to be Debbie.

Radolf watched her go, a hot glitter in his eyes. "No," he murmured, "Thank *you*."

About the Author:

Angela Knight's first book was written in pencil and illustrated in crayon; she was nine years old at the time. But her mother was enthralled, and Angela was hooked.

In the years that followed, Angela managed to figure out a way to make a living—more or less—at what she loved best: writing. After a short career as a comic book writer, she became a newspaper reporter for the Spartanburg Herald Journal, among other newspapers. She covered everything from school board meetings to murders. Several of her stories won South Carolina Press Association awards under her real name, Julie Woodcock.

Along the way, she found herself playing Lois Lane to her detective husband's Superman. He'd go off to solve murders, and she'd sneak around after him trying to find out what was going on. The only time things got really uncomfortable was the day she watched him hunt pipe bombs, an experience she never wants to repeat.

But her first writing love has always been romance. She read The Wolf and The Dove *at 15, at least until her mother caught her at it.*

In 1996, she discovered the small press publisher Red Sage, and realized her dream of romance publication in the company's ***Secrets 2*** *anthology. Since then, her work has appeared in four Secrets anthologies. She's tremendously grateful to publisher Alexandria Kendall for the opportunity to make her dreams come true.*

Angela enjoys hearing from readers. You may email her at angelanight2002@bellsouth.net. *Check out her website at* www.angelasknights.com.

Dominique Sinclair

Jess Michaels

Leigh Wyndfield

Saskia Walker

Volume 12

Secrets

Satisfy your desire for more.

Secrets

Volume 12

Good Girl Gone Bad

by Dominique Sinclair

To My Reader:

When a man comes along who makes you want, makes you crave . . . When a man comes along who is everything you secretly desire, everything you secretly need . . . When a man comes along, go. Willingly, wantonly. Let there be no regret. Let there be seduction. Let there be love.

Chapter One

"One shot, Reagan," Paxton Anderson, the senior editor of *Glimmer Magazine,* said looking over the top of her black rimmed glasses with her piercing green eyes. "Blow it and you're filing paperwork for the rest of your days here. I need a continuous piece, fifteen hundred word per segment, four issues."

Reagan scrawled notes on a flip notepad fast as she could, trying to stamp down the elation building inside her like a helium balloon. An unfortunate Aspen skiing trip had ended with the broken right arm and leg of the writer originally assigned to the piece, leaving no one but Reagan available to turn out the continuous article on relationships for the independent woman.

"First installment on my desk by Friday; we're chasing a deadline. Questions? Good. Get to work." Paxton swiveled her chair and yanked out a file drawer.

Reagan closed her notepad. "Thank you, Ms. Anderson, you won't regret assigning me—"

"Are you still here?"

"No, ma'am, I'm-a-going. Gone. Thank you." She back stepped to the door and reached blindly for the handle. "I'm so grateful for your belief in me—"

"Shut the door behind you."

Reagan nodded, stepped into the hallway and softly closed the door. Then jumped up and down, barely concealing a delightful scream. She had spent a year working for *Glimmer* as a staff writer. But her duties rarely went beyond refilling coffee cups and line editing other writers' pieces. Oh, she had submitted idea after idea of her own, hoping to have an article published and her by-line shinning back at her like a beacon to a full time writing career. All had been rejected.

Now she could visualize herself answering fan mail. Offers would come flooding in from magazines across the country to steal her away from *Glimmer* with the promise of more money, more exposure, more fame. Ah, she was on her way to being the new, savvy, voice of today's women. All her hard work had finally paid off.

A little niggling douse of guilt tried to interject that she shouldn't be so happy at the expense of another's trip down a mountain head over heels, but darn it! She deserved this opportunity, no matter how it came about.

She fairly skipped back to her cubical. She even ignored a few requests for coffee refills, saying, "Sorry, deadline to meet."

She sat at her desk, deadheaded a dried flower from the African violet her mother gave her, then pulled out a fresh pad and sharp pencil and scrawled across the center RELATIONSHIP-INDEPENDENT-WOMAN and circled it. She tapped her pencil on the pad, biting her lower lip, waiting for brainstorm release.

Nothing came.

Nadda. Zip. Blank.

The little niggling of doubt began filtering through her happiness like a gray mist.

She opened her drawer, pulled out the file containing her already rejected article ideas and scanned through them, hoping to find something worthy of re-working into a masterpiece.

The gray mist turned to a big, black rain cloud. She wrote about topics like skin care and choosing a reliable nanny—topics she felt were of interest to the modern woman—topics Paxton said over and over *Glimmer's* readers weren't interested in.

Maybe Reagan was trying too hard, maybe she just needed to relax and allow ideas to freely come. Maybe she should just admit she wasn't the type of writer *Glimmer* was looking for—

An arm wrapped around her shoulder. "Um, um, um, sweet thing. Heard you got an assignment. Whadda say we hit the town tonight, paint it purple?"

Reagan sniffed and glanced up at Michaelo. Today he wore a zebra stripped satin shirt unbuttoned to the naval, tight leather pants and four inch boots. She tried to smile, but her bottom lip trembled.

He knelt down at eye level with her, swiped a tendril of hair behind her ear. "Oh, pooh, something has my Reggie upset. Tell Michaelo about it."

She shoved the file back in the drawer, not caring she didn't return it to its alphabetical position. "I'm never going to be a writer! Why did I ever think I could do this? Everyone was right, I should just find myself a nice husband and have babies."

"Whoa. What's happening here? Five minutes ago you looked like you could fly as you sailed past me in the hallway. Now you've got tears in your eyes."

"Paxton wants me to do the article on relationships for the independent woman. In three days!" She buried her hands in her palms.

Michaelo rubbed her back. "Now, now. It can't be that bad."

"Yes, it can! I've just been fooling myself. I can't do this. I know nothing about men, or relationships, or being independent. I still take my laundry to my mother's every Sunday for heaven's sake!"

He spun her chair, tilted her chin to look at him. "You're forgetting one thing, Reggie."

"Yeah? What's that?"

"You're a writer. Research is what you do best. Okay, so you are a bit of a *Little House on the Prairie* type of girl, but you can learn about women that go *va-va-voom.*"

"How?"

"I'll take you out on the town. We'll go to all my hotspots; you can interview some *real* women."

Reagan couldn't help but laugh through the hiccups of despair. "Are you trying to get me fired, Michaelo?"

"Just wanted to see you smile. All you have to do, *suga,* is what you do best. Observe. Research. Read." He reached under her desk, pulled out her purse and tucked it under her arm. "Michaelo says, go!"

Reagan smiled and stood. "Thank you, Michaelo."

"Hey, what are friends for? Oh, would you mind if I borrow that strawberry gloss again? Got a lunch date."

"Top drawer. See you later."

Michaelo waved goodbye with the end of his scarf.

Reagan browsed the bookstore for over an hour and compiled a stack of research materials including a *Cosmo* magazine, some of the new Chic Lit books that were all the rage and a guide to being an assertive woman. Nothing sparked a topic. She was no closer to an article than before.

She glanced around the bookstore in one last hope at inspiration. A man sat at one of the tables, cup of coffee and newspaper in hand. Maybe that's what she needed to do. Get a latte—double the whip cream and chocolate sprinkles—sit and take a deep breath, let the ideas come freely, naturally.

The man lowered the paper.

Reagan tripped over her feet.

She darted into an aisle, books crushed to her chest. She blew out a long, slow breath. *Calm down, Reagan, act natural.* She peeked around the corner and sighed. She hadn't seen him since this past summer, when for two glorious weeks she had taken her three year old niece for swim lessons at the city pool. Fourteen marvelous days when Reagan handed Josie over to his outstretched, muscular, tanned arms and wished it were she he took by the waist and gently lowered into the water.

Every day while Josie splashed in the pool under his careful supervision, Reagan had waited on an empty bench in various *please-please-please* notice me positions. Draping her arm over the back of the bench and crossing her legs, one sandaled foot swinging. Sideways, knees bent and head tipped back to glory in the sun. Elbows on knees, her forearms pushing what little breasts she had together, feet vee'd outward.

Two torturous weeks and Reagan finally resigned herself to the fact she wasn't the type of woman who attracted tanned, buff summer boys. Never had been, never would be.

What would she have done with a man like him anyway?

What would they have had in common?

What would her mother say if she were to bring a man like that to a family dinner?

Only, the man sitting across the bookstore seemed completely different than the golden boy of summer past. The blonde highlights had faded, leaving his hair dark. His once smooth face with chiseled features now had a day's growth of beard. He wore reading glasses, of all things, and a beige cable knit sweater taut over muscles. He was dark and sexy and edgy and dangerous and handsome. And, *oh my* . . .

Who was she kidding, anyway? She couldn't even muster the courage to say hello. The "good girl next door, meant to marry, have kids, bake cookies," everything her mother wanted in a daughter summed up Reagan to a tee. Well, almost. She could never be as perfect as her mother wished.

She glanced down at her pile of books. No use continuing to fool herself. *Glimmer* had been her dream job, but dreams had to come to an end. Paxton would simply have to hire out a freelancer, and she'd be fired.

Reagan set down her pile of books on the lip of the shelf, then happened to scan a title on a bookspine: *Time Tested Secrets of Seducing Mr. Right.* And the next: *365 Nights of Passion.* And *The Karma Sutra. The Joy of Sex. Make Love to Your Man. Learn to Pleasure Yourself.*

Good heavens. Reagan took a small step back. She heard of books like these, but good girls like her never would dare . . .

She glanced over her shoulder left and then right, then slid out a book titled *Learn to be a Bad Girl and Get the Man You Want.*

She opened the book to a full color picture and quickly slammed it shut. She swallowed thickly. Women did that? With another glance around, she slowly opened the book again.

Before long Reagan had a book tucked under her arm, a *must buy* pile of three on the floor, and her nose in another. According to the books, even *she* possessed the potential to be a sexual vixen, to attract the man of her dreams and become the type of woman men fantasized about.

She stepped back and leaned against the bookshelf behind her, the book crushed against her chest. She closed her eyes, allowing the pleasure of fantasy, of imagining herself a brazen woman she'd never be in true life. A woman Luke would respond to, want, need.

If she were that woman, Reagan would tousle her hair, lick her lips and saunter toward him, slide onto the table and put one leg on either side of his chair. Her skirt would be short and tight instead of the ankle length floral she wore now, and it would hike up to her panty line—no she would be wearing no panties at all. She would slip the top button of her blouse while her eyes smoldered her desire.

"Reagan," he would growl as he took off his reading glasses.

She would run her hands through his hair while he gazed at her with dark, hungry eyes. His hands would slide up her calves, around to her knees and gently open her legs further—

Reagan swallowed, didn't dare allow herself to continue on with the fantasy. Already her breasts ached in the confines of her sensible bra. Her sex pulsed in her lightweight control top undies. How quickly her brief fantasy aroused her, how quickly she succumbed to her licentious desires.

Reagan bit her bottom lip and nearly whimpered. What she wouldn't do for the brazenness to walk over to his table and act out her fantasy. She peeked around the shelf one more time.

He was gone.

"Excuse me."

Reagan moved her foot to slide the pile of books out of the way with her sensible flat sandal. "Sorry," she said, glancing over her shoulder.

Oh. My. God.

She swallowed hard and slowly turned around, hiding the manual on multiple orgasms behind her back. "Luke."

Luke studied her a moment. "Josie's aunt, right?"

Heat swarmed like hungry butterflies from her head to her toes. She felt faint, lightheaded. He remembered her. *Wow.* "Um, yeah. Reagan. My name. It's Reagan."

He leaned his hip against the shelf, nodded at the book behind her back, cocking an eyebrow. "Find anything good to read?"

She glanced down to the couple posed seductively on the scarlet red cover of the top book by her feet. *Oh god, oh god, oh god.* She shrugged as she slid the stack further out of the way. She could absolutely die. "Oh, you know, just browsing."

Luke smiled, stepped forward, reaching around and taking hold of the book. His hard body pressed against her breasts; his mouth hovered just above her. "Let's take a look."

Reagan clutched the book as Luke tugged. His hot breath caressed her nape. Dizzy from the masculine scent of him and the seductiveness of his rich, deep voice, she involuntarily loosen her fingers.

He slid the book from her hand. "Interesting."

She closed her eyes in nothing short of complete embarrassment, then peeked one eye open to assess the damage as he flipped through the pages. He paused to study an illustration; she could only imagine what he thought of her.

"It's, ah—for work." She grabbed for the book. "May I have it back now?"

Luke swung it above her head, a smile tugging at the corner of his mouth. "Work, huh?" He lowered the book and held it in one hand, seemingly taunting her to try for it again.

Of all her imagined fantasies about Luke, being caught reading about sex had never come into her thoughts. "I . . . it's . . ."

If she were going to be an honest to goodness writer, she needed to act like one. She raised her chin a notch and looked him squarely in the eye. "Research," she said.

He set the book down, braced his hand on the top shelf above Reagan's head and leaned closer. "What exactly is it you want to learn from these books, Reagan?"

Little vibrations hummed through her body from the way he said her name, deep, rich chords, almost a whisper. She dropped her chin and glanced away. "I—I don't know, exactly."

He captured her chin with two fingers, lifting her gaze to meet his for several long moments that held Reagan's breath. "Tell me."

"I . . ." She moistened her bottom lip, craving for him to lean down and kiss her.

He lowered his gaze to her damp lips as he lightly traced his fingers from her chin down her throat to cover her wildly beating pulse. "Don't you know what's in those books, Reagan?"

Luke's words swirled over her mouth in a moist caress. Reagan breathed the faint taste of coffee and sugar. How she wanted his firm mouth to press against hers, to kiss her, to ravish her. Slowly she shook her head, biting her lower lip.

His fingers left her pulse; his hand moved down over the ruffle of her blouse and skimmed across the fabric to the swell of her breast, cupping it so softly Reagan nearly cried out. She contained herself, knowing someone would come to investigate if she made a noise. For now, their corner of the bookstore was empty.

"Look at me."

She sucked in a breath and slowly returned her gaze, fearing she would find him amused. Instead he rewarded her with a look of satisfaction, and his hand pressing harder against her breast, lifting upward and squeezing her nipple between his thumb and forefinger.

Reagan fought against a twinge of pain and unexpected pleasure, tensed against the warmth radiating between her legs.

"Do you want to know what's in those books, Reagan?"

She never knew her body could feel like this, tight and aching, yearning and alive. If those books could teach her how to have this again and again . . .

"Yes, Luke. I want to know." She barely recognized her tone. She sounded ragged, out of breath. *Seductive.*

Luke lowered his mouth and suckled her bottom lip, nipping it before moving to her throat. The stubble of his beard scraped against her skin, sensitizing her flesh. Reagan dropped her head back, fingers digging into the wood shelf behind her for support.

"Do you want me to show you what's in those books?"

"Y-yes."

He trailed his tongue up her neck and kissed behind her ear, turning her body molten gold, ready for his molding. His hand left her breast and teased down her stomach, the lightest of touch and yet her body shivered.

"I'll need you to be a very good girl." His erection, taut against his jeans, pressed against her hip. "Do everything I say." He bunched the fabric of her skirt, pulling it slowly up her thigh. "I need you to say yes, Reagan. Tell me you'll obey."

Reagan arched as he reached up her skirt and palmed her heated juncture. Her head thrashed to the side. She adjusted the width of her legs, opening wantonly for his touch. "Yes. Anything."

Luke slid a finger beneath her damp panties, parted her swollen folds and pressed against her nubbin. Nothing had ever felt so good as being touched by Luke. A flood of pure pleasure washed through her, weakening her knees. Her body slid down the bookshelf.

He edged her bottom onto his thigh, supporting her as he slowly began to stroke the engorged pleasure point as he kissed her.

Heat built with each stroke, her breasts swelled and ached. The back of her throat went dry. She both wanted to end the orgiastic sensations and stay suspended in the intensity of it, die of the pleasure.

"Tell me again." He sought her channel, the pad of his finger pressing just at the opening and she knew the fulfillment she needed wouldn't come until she offered complete abandonment.

"Anything, anything you ask. Just please—"

He thrust his finger deep inside her, his thumb pressing against her nubbin. She cried out against his shoulder, biting as her internal muscles tightened around him, drawing him further in as she climaxed.

When she finally relaxed against him, he said, "I'm sure you will." Luke slid his finger from her, rounding his hand to her bottom. "We'll start soon."

Reagan's legs still trembled an hour later when she returned to work. She sat at her desk, dropped her head back in her chair. *What did she just allow to happen?* She placed her hand over the flutters in her stomach and went over every touch, every kiss and tried to hate herself for her licentious behavior, only she found her body responding to the memory. Even now with the sounds of phones ringing, faxes humming, copy machines spitting out paper, her body felt damp, dewed with wanting, anticipation.

"Soon . . ." she heard Luke echo.

Good heavens, in one encounter she'd went from being a good girl to very, very bad. And yet she knew if Luke wanted her again, she wouldn't hesitate. Bad had been very, *very* good.

Reagan leaned forward in her chair, turned to a fresh page in her notepad, and scrawled in bold letters: *Good Girl Gone Bad* and circled it. She tapped her bottom lip with the pencil several times then began filling the page with associated words to what she'd just experienced and knew, thanks to Luke, she had the topic for her article.

Chapter Two

Good Girl Gone Bad, segment one, hit Paxton's desk first thing Friday morning, and Reagan spent the day with damp palms and her heart beating like a hummingbird waiting for her summons. It finally came at four o'clock. Feeling like she could throw up at any moment, she left her cubicle and walked toward the lion's den. She knocked on Paxton's door.

"Enter."

Reagan drew in a deep breath and placed her hand on the door handle. A hand wrapped around her stomach. She nearly jumped out of her skin. "Don't worry, baby doll, you're gonna rock," Michaelo said, his baby soft face buried just behind her ear.

Reagan turned around. "What if she hates it?"

"Honey, I got hot reading it. When you're through with him, I'll take him."

She shook her head, eyes wide. "It-I-uh—it wasn't me!"

Michaelo sucked in his cheeks, which if she wasn't mistaken had a sheen of glitter today, and struck a pose. "Uh-huh, and I'm wearing men's underwear. Your secret's safe with me."

"But-but-but—"

He reached around her and opened the door. "TTFN."

Reagan swiped her palms on the back of her skirt and stepped into Paxton's office. She took one glance at Paxton, perched behind the large desk, glasses on, shaking her head as she read over her pages, and Reagan wanted to run.

"You wanted to see me?" Her voice sounded barely louder than a mouse.

"Sit."

Reagan moved to the padded leather chair and perched on the edge, a sinking feeling in her stomach. There was no need to get comfortable. She folded her hands in her lap, unfolded them, folded them again while Paxton flipped page after page.

"*Good Girl Gone Bad.* Did I not make it clear the article was on relationships for the independent woman?" Paxton didn't bother to look up.

"I-uh . . ."

"How many articles have you submitted to me in the past year?"

"Over fifty?"

Paxton set the pages down, leaned back in her chair and took off her glasses. "And how many did I accept?"

Reagan felt herself shrinking into the chair. "Er, none."

"None. So why did you think submitting a piece off-topic would be acceptable?"

"Well . . ."

Paxton leaned forward, peering down her long, straight hawk-like nose. "Let me make one thing clear. I don't like my chain yanked. When I ask for something, I get it. You newbie writers think you can come in here and run the show. That's my job. I say what goes into print, nobody else. Do I make myself clear?"

Tears brimmed in Reagan's eyes. She nodded and stood. "Yes. I'm sorry to waste your time."

"Did I excuse you?"

Reagan shook her head.

"Sit."

She complied like a scolded puppy. There was no need for a tortured rejection, a simple "No thanks" would have sufficed. Clearly Paxton had a point to hammer home.

She picked up the article. "Is this piece fiction?"

"No-no-no. Of course not. It's the, um, actual experience of the, er, subject. Names have been changed, as noted." As well as the city and their physical descriptions.

"And you can follow this up with three more segments?"

Reagan's mouth dropped open. She gulped. This wasn't a rejection. *Oh my god, oh my god, ohmygod!* She nodded her head repeatedly.

Paxton lifted the cover page and read aloud again, "*Good Girl Gone*

Bad. All I can say, Reagan, is good goddamn work. It's sexy. It's sensual. It's every woman's fantasy. Congratulations."

Congratulations. Reagan could have cried. Any doubts over writing about her experience with Luke floated away. She leapt to her feet, reached her hand over the desk to shake Paxton's hand. "Thank you, Ms. Anderson. Thank you so much."

Paxton simply raised a brow. "Make sure the other pieces are as good. You could be looking at a regular column. And bonuses."

Oh. My. God. *Her own column? Bonuses?* "They will be, I promise. Thank you, thank you, thank you," she kept repeating until she was out the door. She jumped up and down in the hallway and squealed, then rushed to find Michaelo.

She found him by the water cooler and flung her arms around him. "I did it! I did it! Paxton's accepted the article. She might give me a column! I get bonuses!"

Michaelo swung her around, then set her on her feet. "Hot damn, you're on your way, Reggie. Feel good?"

She dropped her head back and closed her eyes. "Awesome. It feels totally awesome." Now that she experienced being a bad girl, she could turn out three more articles. No problem.

Reagan's elation climbed to a higher level when she listened to the message on her home phone. She'd tried not to dwell on the fact she hadn't heard from Luke since their first encounter, instead she'd focused on writing the article. But in the back of her mind a little voice niggled constantly, saying she'd never see him again. She wasn't good enough, or bad enough, or whatever it took enough to hold a man's interest.

"Tomorrow. Six o'clock. I'll pick you up," Luke's smooth voice said on the recording.

The little voice of doubt was finally silent.

Reagan danced in a circle. "I did it, I did it, I did it!" Excitement and anxiety and a thousand more emotions flowed through her. She had energy to burn.

Knowing the next twenty-four hours would pass with excruciating slowness if she didn't do something to occupy her mind, she suddenly beamed. There was work to be done. Grabbing her purse and keys, she headed for the bookstore way across town to pick up the titles she'd left behind at the other store, where she'd never dare enter again for fear an employee had seen her and Luke.

Paxton would be impressed when she turned in the next segment of *Good Girl Gone Bad* early and in the process, she'd have a jump-start on Luke's next *lesson*.

Six hours later, Reagan sat at her kitchen table and slashed her pen across the words she'd written, ripped the sheet out of her pad, waded it and tossed it into the growing pile on the floor. The books only made her crave Luke, and she'd found no direction for the second article.

Slapping down the pen, she bowed her head into her palms. Three more articles, *hah*. She couldn't write one. Dumping the books in the trash, she went to bed, only to sleep fitfully. She tossed and turned, considering and dismissing topic ideas. Slipped in and out of sleep, dreaming briefly of Luke touching her, kissing her. Of standing on top of a table in the bookstore reading her article word for word for everyone to hear. Of Paxton sitting behind her desk, eyes growing huge behind her glasses, her mouth moving but no words coming out.

Reagan woke feeling as if she barely slept. She laid in bed staring at the ceiling, mourning the loss of her column and bonus, possibly her entire career. If not for Luke she would never have wrote the article Paxton loved so much.

She smiled. *If not for Luke.*

If not for Luke indeed.

He was picking her up tonight for the next lesson. If Luke delivered anything even close to what he showed her in the bookstore, Reagan would have all the inspiration she needed for the next segment. Just a different kind of research, something she'd never find in a book or on a website.

It's not like Luke would never know. She'd used a pseudonym and changed their names and physical descriptions. He'd never read a women's magazine. She'd already featured their first encounter. One more couldn't hurt.

Besides, she may be a good girl, but she wasn't naïve. Luke wouldn't show up with a bunch of daisies and a box of chocolates and take her on a real date. No, he'd take what he wanted from her while giving her one heck of a lesson.

And during the process, she'd do some research for her next article. Mutually beneficial for everyone.

Research never promised to be so fun.

At six o'clock the doorbell rang. Reagan's heart thudded to her stomach. She took in a deep breath and counted to ten. She crossed the room slowly, smoothed her sweater, and opened the door. Luke leaned against the doorjamb. A tailored black suit molded his broad shoulders, a white dress shirt setting off his golden tan. He still had the shadow of beard giving him a dangerous, sexy edge. A tug pulled at the corner of his mouth as his gaze lingered over her body.

She closed her eyes and inhaled the scent of him, a combination of earthy spice and clean soap as he stepped inside. She shut the door and leaned against the wall for support. "I, um, didn't know how to dress." She waved a slightly trembling hand to her typical ankle length skirt and sweater set. "You didn't say where we were going."

Luke lifted a shopping bag. "Brought what you need."

She eyed the package, a little *humm* of pleasure vibrating through her. Imagine, him taking the time to pick something out for her, his hands selecting it. She took a hesitant step forward, then stopped, her earlier thoughts of this not being a proper date coming to mind. "Thank you, but really, you shouldn't have."

He set the bag on the floor by her floral print sofa, turned and leaned against the back. "Take off your clothes."

Reagan gulped. He couldn't be serious. "Here?" *Now*? Her two-bedroom house sat on a quiet street with hedges obscuring the view inside if someone should pass by. *Still!* She never even walked around in her bathrobe without closing the curtains.

"Yes." He stuffed his hands in his pockets and crossed his long, powerful legs at the ankles. "If you want to learn, Reagan, you must obey."

The table lamps were shinning bright. There were no shadows to conceal her body from him, no way to hide the heat flaming her cheeks. The one and only lover she had, a boyfriend she dated all four years of college, use to call her a prude when she'd insist he turn off the lights before she would dash nude from the bathroom and jump under the covers.

"Could I dim the lights, maybe light a candle?"

Luke shook his head.

Reagan wished she'd thought to create a romantic atmosphere before he showed up. Light a few candles, turn off the lights. Now it was too late. She'd agreed to do anything he asked. She needed this experience for her next article. No, she needed to experience this for herself . . . Her trembling fingers went to the top pearl button of her soft gray sweater and slipped it through. She gazed downward as she worked on the next, gathering courage to see this through.

"Look at me, Reagan." His tone was soft, yet commanding.

She bit the inside of her bottom lip and slowly lifted her gaze, only she focused on the Monet print hanging on the wall just beyond his shoulder.

"You have beautiful eyes. Has anyone ever told you that before?"

She looked at him then, into the warmth of his gaze, and shook her head. "No," she whispered, nearing the last button.

"That's a shame. You're a very pretty woman."

She lowered her lashes, savoring his seductive tone as she slid her arms out of the sweater, folded it and held it against her stomach.

"But you don't believe that, do you?"

"I think, I mean, I know I'm attractive, but I'm not—I'm not sexy." Nothing felt sexy about standing in her white cotton bra and plain skirt.

Luke moved toward her, his sensual eyes moving languidly the length of her body. He took the sweater from her and tossed it aside. Reagan's mouth parted. She could hardly breathe.

He walked behind her, barely touched her shoulder. "Sexy isn't something you're born with." The warmth of his words swirled her shoulder. A shudder coursed through her, her nipples budded. He skimmed a finger down her spine. "Sexy is something you feel when you're confident, know what you want and aren't afraid to get it." He unfastened her bra.

Reagan crossed her arms to hold it in place, unsure what to do, what to say. She wasn't confident. Always second guessed herself and changed her mind about what she wanted from one moment to the next. Except for this. She wanted Luke and all he promised to teach her.

He lifted her hair and kissed her nape. "You need to trust yourself, Reagan. Stop denying what you want, who you want to be."

Reagan leaned against the hard planes of his body. Her body slowly caught fire as his mouth traveled to just behind her ear to the spot she'd dabbed on perfume. Heavens, she could scarcely breath. She wanted Luke to take her, end the madness of his slow caress. She closed her eyes and let go of the bra.

"Tell me what you want." The deep cords of his voice vibrated through her, deliciously awakening more craving.

"I don't know. I—"

"Let go and trust yourself. Your body knows what it wants, listen to it."

She turned her head to nuzzle her lips under his jaw. "I want you to touch me."

He braided his fingers in hers and lifted her hand to her breast, pressed her palm to her nipple, squeezing his hand over hers. She rolled her head into the hallow of his shoulder, her back arching.

He kissed her shoulder lightly. "Your body was made for touch."

Sensations swirled and danced in a sultry rhythm as she rotated her bottom against Luke. He hardened against her. "Make love to me."

He lifted his mouth to her ear, nipping her lobe. "You're nowhere ready for that. You wanted to know what's in those books. You're going to learn, slowly, one torturous step at a time."

One step at a time? Reagan could barely handle Luke's touch. Luke's kiss. How could she survive this drawn out game?

He pressed his erection against her. A moan rumbled deep in his chest, the pads of his fingers dug deeper into her breast. "And it has nothing to do with love. Finish undressing." He swatted her bottom as he moved away.

Reagan watched him return to the sofa, her bottom stinging, and knew she wouldn't deny him anything. Luke was her teacher of carnal delights; she would accept all he offered and ask nothing more. She stepped out of her shoes, slid down her skirt and panties and looked to look him for guidance.

"Turn around."

She obeyed, watching over her shoulder as Luke's gaze languidly roamed her body. When she faced him again, it took every bit of strength to stand with her head high and not attempt to cover her body or shy away.

He took a pair of strappy black high-heeled sandals out of the bag and walked over to her. He knelt on one knee, whispering a hand down the side of her breast, her ribcage, smoothing over her hip and down her leg. Goosebumps prickled in his wake, delicious shivers radiating through her.

"You have a beautiful body, Reagan. You have soft curves and contours that don't belong hidden." He lifted her foot and slid on the shoe.

Reagan placed her hand on his shoulder for balance as he buckled the strap at the ankle. He moved to the other foot, pausing to kiss the inside of her knee. Liquid honey flowed from the spot, heating as it spread.

A good three inches taller, Reagan adjusted to both the height and the womanly power wearing high heels and nothing else gave her. Her breasts lifted upward, her calves were taut. Luke stood, took her hand, and led her toward the sofa.

She caught her reflection in the gilded mirror over the fireplace, and for a moment barely recognized herself. Her cinnamon hair was tousled, her green eyes wild. Luke sat her down and eased her backward. He took her sandaled foot and set it on the coffee table, her knee bent high, then repeated the process with the other.

She gazed at him questioningly as he moved away and discarded his jacket. She dared not move, though her legs were spread open, her pelvis tilted. Revealed. Bare. Aroused.

He walked behind the couch and ran his hands over her shoulders, squeezed gently. "Touch your breasts, Reagan."

Her first instinct to his command was to refuse, but as his hands massaged, she closed her eyes and leaned her head back against the cushion. "Trust yourself, Reagan. Become one with your body's pleasure."

She cupped her breasts, lifting slightly. Her toes curled. "You've got perfect breasts, just the right size," he said and Reagan opened her eyes to watch his hands slide over her shoulders to the tips of her breasts. He squeezed both nipples, keeping the pressure just shy of pain.

Reagan cried out as her womb contracted in one fierce spasm, and her womanly juncture pulsed, readying for his touch. Silver heat moistened her depths, and tracers of light flashed around her vision. Her body arched for him, silently begging, wanting the complete fullness of him now.

Luke leaned down, his breath hot against her lobe. "Tell me, are you so easily aroused by every man who touches you?" He pinched her nipples harder.

Yet her body responded. Her sexual response heightened to a new level. "No. No man has aroused me the way just looking at you does."

He released and gently soothed her nipples with the lightest touch, then took her right hand and guided it downward. "I want you to come for me." He ran his tongue down the length of her neck, kissed her collarbone.

Reagan was too lost in the sensation of his mouth and his hand on her nipple to realize where he was taking her other hand until her fingers touched the soft, dewy hair on her mound.

"Open your legs wider. Touch yourself for me."

"I've never," Reagan began, but found herself obeying his command. She could deny him nothing. Her body wouldn't allow her.

She spread her thighs further apart and dropped her knees outward as she slid her hand around the curve of her womanly juncture, parting her folds with her middle finger. She pressed against the throbbing nubbin; her breath hitched as another spasm shot through her center.

Luke's breath became shallow, hot against her temple as he pressed her breasts flat, the pads of his fingers digging in. "Come for me, Reagan. Come for me," he whispered, his breath ragged.

Reagan entered her sheath, surprised to discover how wet and hot her channel had become. She withdrew and caressed her nubbin with the moisture of her sex, at first slowly, in little circles and then with more pressure, dipping into her well to slicken her touch. Her body began to tighten from head to toe. Heat filtered through her like a sauna. The air thick and fragrant with her desire.

"Luke," she cried as his hands began to work her nipples in rhythm with her own touch.

"Let yourself go, Reagan." He pinched her nipples again, harder.

Her hips began to rotate, her hand moved quicker, fiercer until the breath stole from her lungs. Her muscles bunched and shivered. Suddenly a white-hot paroxysm of iridescent glow exploded from her core, blinding her of all but sheer, glorious sensations ebbing and flowing.

She slid her finger deep into the flow of molten release and gripped her thighs together. She arched her back, thrashed her head to the side and sought Luke's mouth, bit his lower lip, her cries drowning in his throat. Knocking over a bowl of potpourri, she gulped in the scent of lavender and held herself tight, climax pulsing.

When her body began to relax, and her ragged breathing calmed, Luke released her breasts and kissed her tenderly, suckling as if to soothe her scattered senses, bring calm to the storm that tossed her body with undeniable pleasure.

"Good girl," he said, against her mouth and stood.

Sated, exhausted, Reagan slid her hand from between her legs and realized her knees trembled. She never knew how erotic it could be to have a man watch her, guide her through such tortuous pleasure. It was beyond the realm of anything she ever experienced or fantasized.

The muscles flexed across Luke's broad back, stretching his white shirt as he took something black out of the shopping bag. Reagan's body stirred again, little pulses of begging want. She wanted Luke inside her, to feel the power of her pleasure while touching him, kissing him.

Luke returned to her, pulled her to her feet and raised her arms, her tender breasts thrust high. Floating on an orgiastic cloud, Reagan dropped her head as he bound her wrists with one of his large hands and lowered his hot mouth to her nipple and breathed.

A moan slipped from her swollen mouth as he soothed an aching nipple with his tongue, moistening and laving away the pain he deliciously inflicted. He then moved to heal the other nipple and then kissed his way down her stomach, releasing her hands as his tongue glided through her damp, curly hair.

She dropped her arms and gripped his shoulders when he parted her swollen folds with his tongue. She gazed down through half-mast lids as he suckled her nubbin. "Luke," she breathed, knees wobbling.

He stood and kissed her with the flavor of her passion and raised her arms again. He draped a silky black dress over her body, smoothing it out over her hips, her bottom, and then turned her around to zip it. “We’re late.” He nipped her shoulder with soft teeth.

Reagan leaned against his frame, reached around and held his hips. “Hmm, late?”

He groaned and pressed hard against her, his mouth nuzzling behind her ear. “Go put your hair up, but don’t touch your makeup. You have that just-fucked-look that drives men crazy.”

She bit her bottom lip, turned around and linked her arms around his neck, pressing her sensitized body to his hard planes and gazed into his dark eyes. “Does it drive you crazy?”

“More than you could ever know.” He nudged her nose with his. “Now hurry up.”

“Just let me find my underclothes.”

“You’ll go how you are.”

Chapter Three

A college professor? Reagan tucked a wayward strand of hair behind her ear and smiled at the stodgy old man who just revealed Luke's occupation, hoping her surprise didn't show.

"How did you two meet?" he asked, puffing on a sweet-scented cigar and swirling a tumbler of cognac.

"Um, I—we," she glanced across the dark, smoke filled room where Luke stood with a group of men, his hands in his pockets. "Actually, my niece took swim lessons from Luke this past summer."

The man next to her let out a deep, belly filled laugh. "Luke still doing that, huh? Son of a bitch, he's got more stamina than I ever had. I look forward to quiet, peaceful summer breaks, and he goes out and works with youth groups. One summer it was some big brother program, another year he coached a basketball team for gangsters."

Reagan sipped her wine, trying to absorb this new, unexpected twist on who she thought Luke to be. Instead of some golden summer boy who lived for girls in bikinis, he was a college professor, saint for troubled kids, preschool swim instructor extraordinaire and teacher of seduction and sexual discovery. And the main topic of her article in *Glimmer Magazine,* circulation nation wide. Reagan inwardly groaned. What had she done? If anyone discovered it was Luke she had written about—she gulped down another swig of wine—his job and obvious stellar standing in the community were in jeopardy.

She glanced over to him again and found him watching her. Instantly she forgot about the article. His dark gaze languidly traveled her body. Heat flamed her cheeks knowing he was seeing her as she'd been earlier, naked and lusty for him, and how she was now, bare underneath the silk, her womanly body still slick and fragrant.

"It was nice meeting you, Reagan," the man said with a nod and stepped away.

"Ah, you, too." She bit her bottom lip, wondering what to do now that she'd been left alone.

There were plenty of women at the party, mingling or talking in groups. Reagan normally had no problem meeting new people, or simply blending in a crowd if she didn't feel like socializing. Tonight was different.

For the first time in her life, she stood out from the crowd. In the little black dress, high heels, hair swept off her nape carelessly, lips swollen and red, Reagan looked like a vixen. Since the moment she'd walked into the party on Luke's arm, the women had eyed her as if she were the enemy, as if she intended to steal their husbands and corrupt their morals. God, what would Mother think?

Luke made her this way with his words, his touch, the way he guided her to a culmination of passions never before explored. Just thinking about it stirred a longing in her to be alone with Luke again. Her body was ready for him.

She loved the way he transformed her. She didn't recognize herself when she was with him, and yet somehow she seemed to be the person she always craved inwardly to be.

Reagan touched her wine glass to her chest to cool her heating body and swept her gaze upward beneath her lashes to watch Luke again. He looked at her, a tug playing the corner of his mouth. She melted into a moment where Luke seduced her with nothing more than his gaze and silent desires.

Everyone in the room faded out, leaving only Reagan exposed and raw under Luke's visual seduction. Her breath turned shallow, tingles of heat spread through her. She moistened her bottom lip. She wanted Luke to come to her, touch her. He raised an eyebrow, turned back to the group of his colleagues and excused himself.

Reagan waited a moment, then followed him through a set of double doors leading to a terrace. She slipped into the crisp early autumn air tinged with the taste of salt and sea. A breeze whisked off the ocean and pressed the silk fabric of her dress against her body and lifted loose strands of hair to dance in ribbons. She smiled at Luke, who was standing with his hands on the balustrade, staring out to the black vastness of the Puget Sound. The midnight blue sky melded with the ocean in the distance, the lights from ships and the stars almost mirroring each other as they passed silently in the night.

She wrapped her arms around him, attempting to steal his warmth. "What are you thinking about?" she asked, running her hands over the hard muscles rippling his stomach beneath his crisp white shirt.

"You." His voice, smooth and deep, drifted on the billows of fog rolling in off the ocean like dunes of cotton.

"Hmmm. Me, huh?" She snuggled further against him, her nipples budding, chills coursing her arms and legs. She braved a hand under the waistband of his trousers.

His body stiffened, shoulders to toes. "Don't."

Reagan smiled, stroked the length of him, feeling him swell and lengthen in her palm. "Why not?" Knowing she could make him respond made her feel a touch of the power he possessed over her. Knowing his colleagues were just inside while she touched him made her feel naughty. Wicked. Sinful. "Afraid someone will find us out here like this?" She gripped him low at the shaft and squeezed softly.

He sucked in a breath and let out a long growl. "Damn it, Reagan." He took her hand and withdrew it, turned around and glowered down at her, his eyes onyx in the darkness. His jaw tensed.

He didn't scare her. She straddled his leg, pressing her heated juncture against the hard muscle of his thigh and rode him with little glides, her hand cupping his balls over his slacks. "I want you, Luke."

He crushed his mouth to hers in a searing kiss, hauling her off her feet and backing her until she rammed against a trellis climbing the weather beaten stone wall. His teeth sank into the pulse at her throat as she tore at the button of his slacks. He freed his erection and hiked her skirt, slid two fingers deep into her.

"Are you sure, Reagan?" he asked against her mouth, delving his tongue deep into the hallows. His thumb worked her nubbin, fingers pressing deeper into her.

Reagan clenched her fingers around the rungs of the trellis as she fought against an orgasm. She thrashed her head to the side. "Yes, Luke. Now." If she didn't have him inside her, now, she would surely die.

Withdrawing his hand, Luke wrapped her legs around his waist and gripped the trellis on either side of her head. He rammed inside her until his full length was buried deep to her core, stretching her walls. Instantly an orgasm shattered. Luke held taut as red petals from a crushed Clematis fell onto her shoulder.

When the pulses eased and her body relaxed, Luke withdrew and entered into her again and again with excruciating slowness. Each thrust was so intense, her body cried out in pain and pleasure. She feared she could take no more. She couldn't breathe. Couldn't not.

Reagan abandoned the trellis to dig her nails in Luke's back, wanting him deeper inside her, wanting to be closer still. The scent of the crushed Clematis petals, the scent of her passion swirled as she cried out against his shoulder, begging him to stop . . . to never stop. In answer to her plea, he began to thrust harder, deeper. She hurt, she wanted. Her knees trembled as they locked tighter around his waist.

He covered her mouth with his, and in one final thrust, his hot semen filled her in union with another climax of her own, raking her with a searing and delicious release. She sobbed his name, then went limp in his arms.

Despite her protests, Luke carried Reagan from his Jaguar, into the parking garage elevator and to his First Avenue penthouse, where he gently sat her on a chair in his bedroom. He removed her shoes, then gently pulled her dress over her head.

"I'm sorry for embarrassing you," she whispered.

He shushed her apology with the tip of his finger to her swollen mouth, followed by his mouth.

She didn't know what had overcome her. One moment she was in the throws of orgiastic pleasure, the next she was being carried out of the party in Luke's arms, his colleagues watching with wide-eyed expressions, the wives gasping.

Luke left Reagan naked, slipped through a door and moments later she heard water turn on. She didn't regret for one moment giving her body to Luke. After tonight, she would never be the same. She had experienced the rawest element of man and woman, found pleasure she hadn't known could exist.

Luke returned to her, swept her hair back and kissed her forehead before scooping her into his arms and carrying her into the hunter green bathroom. The lights were off and he'd lit vanilla scented candles peppered on the counters and edge of a Jacuzzi tub. He lowered her into the pool of warm, circling water, soaking the sleeves of his shirt.

"Are you okay?" he asked, tone deep and soft and caring.

Reagan nodded, the water soothing. "Yes, thank you. I'm sorry—"

He pressed his finger to her lips again. "Shh." Lowered his head and kissed her softly as if she were made of delicate glass. "Rest now." He stood, dried off his hands and left her alone.

She closed her eyes, dipped back her head to drench her hair. How could any man be so tender and yet so fiercely passionate? Never did she believe a man like him existed. Never did she believe a man like Luke would want her. Never in her wildest dreams did she believe she could experience such passion.

Whatever he was willing to give, to show her, to teach her, she would accept and ask for no more. He'd already given her more than a good girl like her could hope for, and she'd die remembering every vivid detail of their time together.

Luke returned sometime later with a big, white fluffy towel, offered his hand to help her from the tub then dried her, taking care to soak up every droplet of water shoulder to toe, then wrapped the towel around her middle, tucking the end above her breast.

He swiped a wet locket of hair behind her ear, cupped his hands on each side of her head and gazed deep into her eyes. "Better?"

She nodded and parted her lips for his kiss. His tongue glided under the tender lining of her upper lip. Then he softly nipped her bottom lobe before taking her hand and leading her through the bedroom and into the living room, where a fire burned in the black stoned hearth, and soft music played in the background.

He knelt on an ivory bearskin rug by the fire, smoothed his hands up her calves, under her towel to cup her bottom. Reagan gazed down at him, the fire casting hues of burnt sienna across his handsome face. He bunched the towel in his hands and tugged until it fell away. Taking her hands, he lowered her to kneel before him.

Without breaking the magnetic gaze he held her in, she reached for the button of his shirt, worked it through the tiny hole, moved to the next and the next, her gaze finally dropping to the sight of his chest. She reached the last button, smoothed her hands under the flaps, rounded his shoulders and shed the shirt. Lightly she traced her fingers back up his arms, ran her palms over his pecks, pressing her right hand to feel the beat of his heart.

"Thank you," she whispered.

He cupped her cheek, pulled his thumb across her mouth. "For what?"

She glanced away, suddenly feeling shy. "For showing me what it can be like."

"I've only just begun."

The words reached in and soothed away Reagan's worry that he'd taken what he wanted and would be done with her now. "What more is there?"

He lowered his hand to cup the underside of her breasts and lifted them for his mouth to softly take one dusty peak after the other. Reagan shivered and melted, and heated and quaked.

"You'll have to wait and see," he said and guided her to lie on her stomach.

The fur soft beneath her, the fire warm on her naked flesh, she closed her eyes as Luke spread out on his side beside her and smoothed his strong hands over her back. "I didn't mean to hurt you," he said, lowering his mouth to the back of her shoulder, circling his tongue.

"Hmmm, I wouldn't have changed a thing." She burrowed deeper into the fur, snuggling in like a cozy kitten.

"It's not like me to lose control like that."

"I enjoyed knowing you wanted me so much." No one had ever lost control like that with her. Because of her.

His hand slid over the arch of her bottom, between her legs to the heat of her juncture and pressed against her nubbin. "I want you still." He moved behind her to kneel between her legs, held her hips and pulled her upward and back.

"Take me." She held herself on her forearms, tilting her pelvis by instinct for him. Thick and hard, he entered her, slowly, pushing to the honeyed core of her, the pads of his fingers digging into her hips, thumbs rotating. His legs trembled as he rotated his pelvis against her, eased out and delved deep inside her again. He moaned her name, then a rumbling curse as he began to pump, ramming the sweet insides of her with delicious thrusts.

Reagan woke Sunday morning and found herself lying on the couch between Luke's legs, her head on his chest, a throw blanket tangled around her hips. A slice of morning hazed through the window, brushing Luke's sleeping face with a touch of sunshine. She smiled up at him, brushed a soft kiss to the underside of his jaw and slipped her fingers through the soft hair on his chest, over the sculpts of his pecs to play with a dark nipple. She'd never woke to a day feeling more alive, more wanted, more satisfied.

She only wished the enchanting discoveries Luke gifted upon her were equally poetic for him. Oh, she knew he desired her, lost his control for her, but she wouldn't be foolish enough to believe she'd been the only one. Trying not to think about the other women before, the other women he'd shown such pleasure to, she closed her eyes and simply felt him breathe beneath her.

His hand came up and tangled in her hair. "Morning," he rumbled, pressing his lips to her crown.

A glow spread through her as his hand slid down her neck to tightened around her back, possessing her, claiming her, if only for the moment. "Luke?"

"Hmm?"

"I just want to let you know," she began, knowing she needed to be the first to say the words, for she couldn't bear to hear them from him, "I understand how this works. I don't expect anything of you because of last night."

He opened his eyes, angled his head to look at her. "Then maybe I should let you know you're the first woman I've allowed to stay."

Her heart gave a little lurch, then she realized although he'd allowed her to stay, but he hadn't taken her to his bed. "Why me?"

"Because you're sweet and sexy and beautiful. At my touch, you abandon your innocence and you give me your complete trust without question. You feel with every part of your body and mind." He positioned her atop of him, her knees sinking into the cushions at his sides, and he guided her down the hard length of him. His eyes closed on a sharp intake of breath. “Because I don’t know if I can ever get enough of you.”

After a morning, afternoon and evening of sex in varying degrees, hot and wild, slow and excruciating, Reagan wondered if Luke would get enough of her.

Heaven help her, she hoped not.

Chapter Four

Reagan wore her dark Marilyn Monroe style sunglasses to work Monday morning, afraid if anyone looked into her eyes they'd see the sinful secrets she kept. She went straight to her cubicle, forgoing coffee in the break room, and sat down at her desk. Her chin and cheeks were chapped from Luke's beard stubble despite the cream she'd laved on. Actually, her entire body was tender and sore, delightfully so. Every inch of her was branded with the memory of her time with Luke.

She took off her glasses and spotted the weekly addition of *Glimmer,* all shiny and new, sitting on her desk, the side bar in bold pink letters: *Good Girl Gone Bad.*

"Oh my god," she breathed, staring at the cover. During the weekend, beneath Luke's hands, his kiss, his body, she had forgotten the magazine hit the newsstands Sunday morning. She ran her finger over the words, then quickly flipped to the article.

Wow. The article looked even more fabulous than she could ever have imagined. And the picture. *Double wow.* Paxton had used a full color photo of a woman in the throes of passion, sex book in hand as she leaned against a bookshelf, and a man, cover model gorgeous, with his hand up her skirt.

Heavens, is that how she had looked?

Reagan traced the bold letters across the top, *Good Girl Gone Bad* and italicized underneath, *The true story of a woman's journey to discovering her wild side.*

How very true the title was. Luke had opened a door for Reagan, invited her to step inside a realm she never dreamed existed. Though she'd stood scared and unsure, it was Luke who had guided her across the threshold, took her hand and led her on her journey.

His words returned to her, *"I don't know if I can ever get enough of you."* Reagan couldn't suppress the delightful spread of tingles coursing her skin.

Reagan read the article three times, elation climbing inside her almost as delicious as her time with Luke. She couldn't believe she'd accomplished her goal. She'd published an article. And it was just the first rung on her ladder to success.

Ready to climb, she fished out a clean tablet and began to outline the next segment, writing until her hand cramped and the smell of heavy perfume brought her out of her licentious world. She glanced up to see Michaelo standing at the cubicle entrance. He wore a black net shirt she knew to be his "lucky" one.

"Hot date tonight?" she asked with a smile, feeling enough joy to share with the world.

He cocked out his hip, planted a hand on it and tapped his foot. "Would you mind checking your email? The Internet guy is saying you went way over your quota for the week just this morning alone. The servers keep shutting down."

"What?" Reagan reached for her mouse and clicked open her email. Sure enough, her inbox was flooded, with more email popping up every second. "Oh. My. God. Michaelo, look at this!"

He grinned and knelt beside her. He took control of the mouse, opened an email at random and read the letter:

"Dear Ms. Smith," Michaelo looked at her, rolled his eyes. "Not very original."

"Yeah, yeah, just read." She closed her eyes and braced herself for the words.

He cleared his throat.

"Dear Ms. Smith, I just wanted to say thank you for writing Good Girl Gone Bad. I've always fantasized about doing something naughty in a public place. Your writing truly made me feel as if I were Roxanne in the bookstore with Logan, I could barely breathe as I read and reread. Thank you for sharing this experience with me. I'll remember it forever. P.S. Hurry with the next installment, pleeeeeasssse."

Reagan opened her eyes and plucked a tissue out of the Kleenex box. "I'm going to cry. I've dreamed of this day forever. It seems almost too good to be true!"

Michaelo opened another email.

"Dear Ms. Smith,

"I'm writing to let you know that your article in Glimmer magazine has saved my marriage. My husband and I have been together for fourteen years and over the past few years the spontaneity and passion has fizzled from our relationship.

"No more! After reading your article, I took my husband to the bookstore and we reenacted the scene in Good Girl Gone Bad. It was the most amazing sex we've ever had, and we can't wait to read about Roxanne and Logan's next encounter (I should have my DH bailed out of jail by then—he got so carried away in the bookstore, he screamed out my name when he climaxed and knocked over the shelf, which toppled several others like dominos. He didn't have time to pull up his pants before the manager came running over—but believe you me, it was well worth it!)."

Reagan and Michaelo stared at each other for a long moment, then burst out in laughter. "Oh. My. God." She clamped a hand over her mouth. "Someone got arrested because of my article!"

"Don't worry, toots, sounds like it was the most exciting day for them in a really long time. Bet he'll ask to keep the handcuffs as souvenirs."

They went through dozens more emails, printing off the ones Reagan wanted to keep. She'd start a memory book—she had all the supplies from her sister's scrap booking party last spring.

"Oh, no!" Reagan grabbed her purse and jumped from her chair. "I forgot I was suppose to meet my sister and mom for dinner."

Reagan rushed into the Italian restaurant twenty minutes late. She spotted her mother and sister at their usual table by the window overlooking Elliot Bay. She slung her purse strap up her shoulder, took in a deep breath and crossed the restaurant, ready for the guilt trip.

"Sorry I'm late," she said, forever apologizing to her mother while her perfect sister with her perfect hair, makeup and clothes sat perfectly straight and had undoubtedly arrived ten minutes early.

"I took the liberty of ordering for you," Mother said, lifting a glass of ice tea, three ice cubes, a lemon wedge and sprig of peppermint—as always.

Reagan's sister rubbed her slightly protruding belly. "I really wish you'd be considerate, Reagan. Mother is very busy this evening. Even in my delicate condition I was able to make it on time."

Reagan snapped open her red linen napkin and draped it over her lap. Oh, how much she wanted to tell her do-all-good sister she was late because she wrote her first article and was reading fan mail. That she had a deadline to meet and really shouldn't be taking this dinner break at all.

Instead, Reagan reached for patience. "Since Mother ordered for me, I don't see that I've really caused much of a delay, now have I?"

"That's not the point—"

"Girls," Mother said in the tone that reprimanded more than words or threats ever could.

Reagan and Catherine put on fake little smiles and let a would-be argument go. *Again.* Sometimes Reagan wished they could just pull out the claws and tell each other exactly how they felt, instead of walking on eggshells and pretending to be the best of friends.

Since they had been little girls, it'd always been that way. Blonde and blue eyed like Mother, Catherine was the princess of the house who lived up to all Mother's expectations of the perfect daughter. Prima ballerina, honor roll, social graces matching the Queen of Britain. Catherine had married a wonderful husband, lived in a lovely house and had a beautiful daughter with another grandchild on the way.

While Reagan, with her father's features, had buried her nose in novels from the age of six, achieved average grades in high school, went to college and wanted a career before family. Mother never asked how Reagan's work was going. Instead she would inquire if Reagan had met a nice young man who wanted to settle down, followed by a *"And just why not? You'll be too old to get a decent husband if you wait much longer."*

Reagan sighed.

"Something wrong, dear?" Mother asked.

"No, work has just been busy."

"That's nice. Have you met any nice young men lately? You know

Mrs. Bollox from the garden club mentioned her son is coming home from *Harvard* for Thanksgiving break. How about we throw a nice little dinner party and you two can . . ."

Mother droned on. Reagan remembered being in the back of the car on the way to private school. Every day, Mother would deliver one of her *"Now remember, you're a good girl. Boys only want one thing,"* lectures despite the fact there were no boys to give *it* to at the all girl school.

These days Mother had a radar three counties wide for single, eligible, suitable men in the hope her daughter would do the respectable thing: marry, have kids, and join the garden club.

Reagan was tired of apologizing for wanting a different path than her mother and sister, and decided from that moment on, she wouldn't.

The waiter came to the table and laid a single stemmed red rose in front of Reagan. "From the gentleman at the bar."

Surprised, Reagan looked across the room and saw Luke. Dressed in a pair of worn denims, loafers and a soft button up navy blue shirt, he was leaning against the bar, talking to another man. Her heart skipped a few beats as she picked up the rose and inhaled the sweet fragrance. Luke turned to look at her, meeting her gaze, holding it in a long, slow seduction of secret pleasures they shared. Warmth spread deep and low in her stomach, her breath turned shallow.

"Yummy," Catherine said, shocking Reagan. She didn't think her sister had a raging hormone in her entire body.

"Who is *that*?" Mother asked.

"A friend." Reagan stood. "I'll be right back."

"*Humph.* Looks like trouble to me," Mother said with her notorious air of superiority.

Reagan stared down her mother. "It's what he looks like to me that matters."

The waiter appeared with their order and set down a plate of spinach lasagna at Reagan's place setting.

"This isn't what I want. Take it away. Bring me the biggest piece of chocolate cake you have, two scoops of vanilla ice cream—make that French vanilla, and a cup of coffee, please. I've had a long day."

The waiter nodded and backed away, looking at Reagan as if she were completely insane.

No, not crazy, she thought. *Liberated.* She wove through the tables, leaving her mother and Catherine in their wide-eyed, speechless state, and headed to the bar.

She took the hand Luke held out for her, grateful to have something to clutch. Never had she stood up to dear old mum. "Fancy meeting you here," she said, forcing the tremor from her voice.

He pulled her against the length of his hard body. "Do you remember Reagan, from the party?" he asked the man next to him.

"Dean Nelson's house. How could I forget," the man said with a wink.

Oh, heavens, no. *The Dean's house?* She gulped and offered her hand. Bad enough when she thought she was at a party with Luke's colleagues, but she'd—they'd ruined the Dean's Clematis vine! "N-Nice to see you again. I, um, er, apologize for my untimely exit. Something just overcame me."

"No apologies needed. I better get back to my table. We'll talk soon, Luke, about that after school program. The kids in this community need more people like you believing in them. And give your dad a hello for me. Nice seeing you again, Reagan."

She nodded, but before she could give her licentious actions any more thought, Luke nuzzled his lips to her neck just behind her ear and slid his hands around her waist. "Having a good time?" he asked, breath damp and moist against her neck.

"No, terrible." She turned into his arms and linked her arms around his neck. "That's my mother and sister. I'd do anything to get out of here."

Luke slid his hand over the arch of her bottom and fisted her skirt, hiking it up to mid-thigh and pulled her taut against him. The soft flannel of his shirt rubbed through her satin blouse, his denim through her skirt, sensitizing her still raw flesh. "Anything?"

Reagan dropped her head back as his mouth moved to nibble the column of her throat. Any thought of her disapproving mother and sister disappeared as he adorned her with his affections. "Hmm, yes. Anything."

He cupped the back of her head and pulled her mouth to his. He swept his tongue between her lips and fully claimed. Her fingers nipped his shoulder blades. The world beyond her sensations ceased to exist. Reagan melted into the golden delight of Luke's kiss, the texture of his body pressing against hers, the strength in which he held her.

He ended the kiss with a nip at the corner of her mouth, then he rested his forehead to hers. "Go back to your table now before I take you right here."

Reagan nodded and stepped away. She would have opened for him then and there if he'd chosen to take her. Nothing else mattered when his hands and mouth were upon her body. She returned to the table and sat before her piece of chocolate cake with melting ice cream.

She lifted a spoon and scraped off a mound of frosting, licked, and moaned. "Now, where were we? Catherine said you had a busy day, Mother. Garden Club tonight, is it?"

Her mother seemed to have lost her ability to speak. She poured herself a glass of house wine from the decanter on the table, her manicured hand trembling slightly as she gulped the entire glass down. Then she proceeded to do something Reagan had never heard her do her entire life.

She belched.

Reagan turned to her sister. "Josie still enjoying preschool? I hung the watercolor she did for me on my office wall. She really has talent, don't you think?" Her sister didn't seem to hear; she was too busy stealing glances at Luke and trying not to be obvious about it. Reagan snapped her fingers in front of Catherine's face. "Hello? Josie? Preschool?"

"Oh, yeah. Um, she's doing great. Misses you. If I didn't say so before, I really appreciated your help with her this summer. The morning sickness was so terrible."

For the first time Reagan truly felt Catherine's thank you was heart felt. "You're welcome."

Catherine glanced at Luke again. "Wow. He's gorgeous. Did you really, you know?"

"Yes." She smiled. "Yes, I did. And I enjoyed every moment of it." Reagan shoveled a big slice of cake into her mouth, swiped a bit of chocolate from her bottom lip.

Mother poured another glass of wine.

Chapter Five

Reagan turned the next segment of *Good Girl Gone Bad* in before deadline and spent the rest of the week answering fan mail. Dreams achieved were so much better than she ever could have imagined.

But the fact she hadn't heard from Luke weighed heavily on her mood.

She contemplated calling him, sending him a little note, maybe stopping by his house. Only, she didn't want to seem like one of those needy women who expected the stars and moon just because the sex was out of this world.

It proved to be more difficult during the weekend. Without the distractions of the office to occupy her thoughts, she remembered over and over the way Luke had made her feel when he touched her, as if she were the center of his every focus and desire.

Like a spinster, she spent the entire weekend alone.

Back to work Monday morning, Reagan sat at her desk staring at the week's edition of *Glimmer* that held her second article. On a sigh, she planted her chin on steepled fingers. None of the excitement she'd felt just a week ago bubbled inside her. The second article made her feel a fool, an imposter. Luke said he could never get enough of her. *Hah.* That lasted all of two encounters.

Now she faced another deadline. She pushed the magazine aside and flipped to a fresh page in her note pad. Tapping the pencil against her chin, she knew her readers expected another interlude. Fine, she'd write fiction for the next segment. Besides, she couldn't rely on writing about sex with Luke for her entire career.

Michaelo said research was what she did best. Leaning back in the chair, Reagan sighed and closed her eyes. She'd definitely done some very good research with Luke. Problem was, she didn't want to end her discoveries. She knew there was so much more he could teach her. She ached for Luke's touch, physically and emotionally. Craved him like she never knew possible.

Unable to concentrate, Reagan packed up her brand new briefcase, the first purchase after receiving her bonus for *Good Girl Gone Bad,* and headed home early. She just didn't have fiction in her today.

Paxton stopped her in front of the elevators. "That column is looking like a very good possibility, Reagan."

Reagan tried to smile, failed, and simply nodded. She didn't deserve the column. She was a fraud. If anyone deserved the column, Luke did.

The elevator door dinged open and Reagan stepped inside, murmuring a soft "Thank You" to Paxton.

Curled up on the sofa, where she'd been all afternoon, Reagan let the phone ring four times before turning down the TV volume and lifting the receiver. "Michaelo, I've told you twice already, I don't want to come out and play." The last thing she wanted to do was celebrate something she was in the midst of failing.

"Michaelo, huh? Should I be jealous?"

Reagan sat up, clutching the phone to her ear. "Luke?"

"Disappointed?"

"No." Her heart skipped a beat, another. "I—I just didn't know if I'd hear from you again."

"Been out of town."

All that worrying, believing he was through with her. "I've missed you."

"Bring me there," he said, his voice low and seductive. "Tell me what you're wearing right now."

Reagan stretched out her legs and glanced down at her fuzzy pink slippers, gray sweats and white t-shirt. Maybe fiction wasn't so bad. "Umm, a sexy little red thing?" Okay, so she needed a little polishing in the impromptu department.

"Hmm, sounds nice. If I recall, there's a mirror hanging over your fireplace."

"Uh-huh."

"Go to the mirror, Reagan."

Nibbling her bottom lip a moment, she stood, stepped before her reflection. "Okay, I'm there."

"Every detail, Reagan. Tell me what you see."

She would deny him nothing, but one glance at her hair pulled back in a low pony tail, strands sticking out here and there, at her smeared makeup, and she knew further creative thinking would be required.

"Tell me how beautiful you are."

The words made her delve a little deeper, past the lingering doubts where she still believed herself to be the family's ugly duckling, to the place where she felt beautiful, the secret place of pleasures and orgiastic discoveries.

Closing her eyes, she imagined herself as she wanted to be, returned to that first night Luke came for her. She imagined him standing before her, his dark gaze lingering a caress over her body.

She pulled the band from her ponytail and lifted her hair off her shoulders. "My hair is swept up, just as you like it. There are little wisps falling down, tickling my nape with butterfly kisses."

"You have a beautiful neck, Reagan. A smooth column of softness."

She smiled, encouraged to play his game. "I've dabbed perfume behind my ears."

"I can smell it. The scent is warm and fragrant, intoxicating. Where else did you dab your perfume?"

Dropping her hair, she ran the tips of her fingers down her neck, over the front of her t-shirt, between her breasts. "Well, the negligee is cut low and there's, ah, lace edging it, white, no, black lace." She breathed in deeply, her tone dropping to a whisper. "The perfume is there, beneath a little satin rose."

"Hmmm, I can smell you, Reagan. The light mist of perfume mixing with the sweet smell of your skin, and the heat of your valley. Are you wet, Reagan?"

The begging pulse began to throb between her legs, echoing a hunger for his touch. How easily he commanded her body into want. "Oh, yes. I wish you were here."

"Tell me how the silk feels between your legs, Reagan."

She slid her hand down her belly, over her drab gray sweats to slip between her legs. Only in her fantasy, her touch didn't find cotton. She found molten heat simmering beneath silk and lace. Inhaling a deep breath, a shudder rippled through her, and she nearly dropped the phone. "It's like warm oil, slippery and smooth. Hot. I'm ready for you."

"Hmmm, not just yet," he said, his voice seemingly coming from within her dream world rather than over the line. "Sometimes the greatest pleasures come after anticipation. Tell me, Reagan, have you been wanting me?"

She glided her hand between her legs in a slow stroke. "Like I've never wanted before," she whispered, breath catching in her throat. "No matter how hard I try, I can't stop thinking of you."

"Why should you want to stop thinking of me?" Humor rode the current of his smooth, rich tones.

"Because I can't bear the thought of not being with you."

"And if I tell you I don't think I could ever get enough of you, would that satisfy you?"

Only if he told her every day for a million years. "Y-yes."

"Good. Because I want you, Reagan. I want to be inside you. Will you take me there, Reagan?"

"Yes," she breathed, untying the draw string of her sweats and slipping her hand beneath her panties, easing a finger within her swollen sex, adjusting the width of her legs to grant his wish. Her sheath begging to be filled.

"Take me there, now."

She plunged deep inside her core at his command, pressing the pad of her middle finger upward, the palm of her hand pressing hard against her nubbin. "Luke . . ." She sobbed his name as her sheath clenched. An orgasm exploded from her core, sucking her breath away, filling her closed eyes with tracers of light. The phone dropped to the ground as her hand fisted her hair, pulling it free of the ponytail.

Her entire body shuddered, and her eyes clamped tighter. She bit her bottom lip. Her nipples pinched into nail heads, and she imagined herself leaning back into Luke, his hard frame supporting her liquefying body. She lolled her head to the side as she imagined his kiss, warm and moist on her neck.

"Again," his voice said, the word swirling her earlobe like a mist off the warm ocean.

She opened her eyes to see hands lifting her breasts, her nipples pinched between thumbs and forefingers. Suspended in a realm of fantasy pleasure and reality, she glanced in the mirror to see Luke standing behind her, his mouth working kisses over her shoulder.

"How . . ." she began to ask, words dying off as a shiver slid down her spine.

"Again. Now," he demanded with a growl, releasing her breasts to push her sweat pants to the floor.

She braced a hand on the fireplace mantel and slowly withdrew her finger from deep within her core, then slid it back into her fiery sheath. "I thought you were out of town," she said, hips rotating to the rhythm of her stroke.

"I was. Now I'm back and ready to have you, Reagan. Would you like that?"

She nodded, heat and pressure building deep within her upon the aftershocks of her first release.

"Tell me." He took her hips in his hands and tilted her pelvis back. She heard the sound of his zipper as he opened his pants, his gaze on hers in the mirror.

She withdrew her hand to find her nubbin with her slick finger and played upon it with little circles and varying degrees of pressure, teasing herself as she said, "Yes. Now. Please, Luke."

"With pleasure," he said, easing his erection between her legs and pressing upward into her. Another orgasm shattered through her, her body milking him with the ebb and flow of her release. He growled, his member jutting inside her, hands clenching her hips as he held taut, waiting for her climax to ease before he pulled out and thrust inside her again and again until she screamed his name.

The next orgasm, which came upon his, was so forceful, so extreme, so powerful, she could only bow her head on her arm and sob.

Reagan's fear Luke was done with her completely disappeared over the next several days. He constantly surprised her—with intimate dinners, cruises on his yacht under the moonlight, the movies with a huge bucket of buttery popcorn, a salsa dance lesson. Intense, funny, charming, and handsome, Luke made each and every moment special and memorable.

And he stole every opportunity to continue the "lessons." Positions, places, and experiences even her research books didn't cover, and no doubt a few new moves invented along the way. The only place Luke hadn't taken her was his bed.

With all the unending adventures, nothing could have surprised Reagan more than when Luke pulled her through the heavy metal doors of the gymnasium located in a part of Seattle where she'd never go alone, even in the daylight, and onto a basketball court where at least thirty kids were hanging out.

Some were in street clothes standing in small groups back in the shadows, smoking cigarettes. Another group at the far end of the court played booming music from a portable CD player and were doing a combination of old break dance moves and new dance steps. A few girls sat on the stands, leaning back, elbows on the bench behind them, sipping soda from mini-mart cups and popping chewing gum.

The largest group of kids was dressed in worn sneakers and tattered gym clothes, shooting hoops on the scuffed gym floor, the boundary marks long wore off. At Luke and Reagan's arrival, the ball suddenly stopped bouncing.

"*Whazzup* Mister N?" a kid holding the ball under his arm asked with a jerk of his chin.

"Not much, Julio. Get that application in?"

"Last Tuesday, just like you said."

"Who's the *be-atch*?" another player asked from the back.

Julio turned and thrust the ball at the other player's chest, knocking him back several steps. "Don't you be *dissin'* Mister N's girl."

"Yeah," one of the girls from the bleachers called out, elbowing the girl beside her. "Any fool can see Mister A's got himself a classy ass bitch."

Reagan took a step back. Luke squeezed her hand. "They're just testing you," he said, voice low.

"Yo, ever shoot hoops before?" Julio asked, catching the ball on a return throw.

Luke wouldn't have brought her here if it wasn't safe. He was sharing a part of his life with her, the part that mentored trouble teens, the part that cared about his community. She realized she was not just being tested by the kids, but by Luke as well.

She released Luke's hand, took off her jacket and tossed it to the sideline, then clapped her hands for the ball. Julio tossed it to Reagan. She caught it, began to dribble, passing the ball between her legs.

"Just in case you're wondering," she said, maneuvering around a player who tried to block her. She picked up speed, jumped into the air and shot from behind the three-point line. The ball swooshed through the net as she landed with the grace of a ballerina. "White girls *can* jump."

The girls in the back stood and did a cheer.

"She's *aye-right,*" Julio said, slapping Luke on the shoulder.

Later, sitting in a booth next to Luke in a all-night diner, hair limp, clothes damp from sweating through four games of hoops and one disastrous lesson in street dancing, Reagan felt exhausted. And deliriously alive.

"Where'd you learn to play like that?" Luke asked, putting an arm around her shoulder and kissing the top of her head.

She snuggled into him, reveling in the simple pleasure of being near him. "My basketball team went to state all four years I played. I wasn't the tallest on the team, but I had a lot of heart, according to my coach. Thanks for taking me with you tonight. I had a lot of fun. "

"Any time. It was good for them. They don't welcome outsiders easily."

"Them against the world?"

"Something like that, yeah."

She looked into Luke's eyes and realized being with those kids meant more to him than simply adding to a list of good deeds. "Why do you do it? What makes you care when so many don't?"

He tucked a strand of hair behind her ear, glanced over her shoulder. "Someone has to."

She leaned her head on his shoulder, his arm tightened around her, and she knew without a doubt that she loved him.

Chapter Six

"Hmm, mmm, um." Michaelo held the spread of *Good Girl Gone Bad,* segment three open in front of his fiery orange satin shirt and sauntered back and forth in Reagan's cubicle. "Girl has definitely gone bad." He played his hand over the photograph of a woman kneeling before a naked Greek God type man. "Any idea who this model is? I'd love to look him up."

Reagan laughed and pulled the magazine out of his hands. "You're incorrigible. Did you really think it was as good as the first two articles?"

He fanned his face with his hand. "It's H-O-T-T, suga. You're one lucky woman."

"It's not me." And this time, Reagan told the truth. The third segment was indeed fiction. She had what it took to write a unique, sexy, interesting piece using her own skills and imagination. Thanks to Luke's lessons and her research skills.

"Uh-huh." He snagged the magazine back, opened to the article, glanced it over and back at Reagan. "Right."

"Don't you have work to do?"

"Who can work with men like this loose in the city? Tell me, is the real thing as hot?"

She tossed him an *I'll never tell* look. The phone rang and she shooed Michaelo out of her workspace.

"Oops, sorry," Michaelo said to someone outside her cubicle before he waltzed away with an imaginary partner.

Reagan shook her head and picked up the phone. "Yes. Uh-huh." *Wow.* "Well, I'm so very pleased that you enjoyed *Good Girl Gone Bad,* but I'm afraid I'm declining all public appearances." She held up *a one moment please* finger to the person giving a little rap on her cubicle wall. "Yes, well, I appreciate that, but since the subject matter is a little provocative, I feel it's in the best interest of—" She looked up as the knocker stepped inside her cubicle. The phone dropped from her hand. "Mother!"

Her mother picked up the open magazine from Reagan's desk with her thumb and forefinger in the fashion of a stinky diaper and dropped it into the trash. "This is what I put you through college for, to write trash?"

Reagan looked from the garbage and up into the face of severe disapproval. "Wh-what are you doing here?"

She pulled a hanky from her designer bag and dabbed her eyes. "I came to prove that my daughter would never shame our good family's name."

Remembering the phone, Reagan picked it off the floor and hung it up, hoping the caller hadn't heard what her mother had said.

"How could you do this to me?"

Reagan bit the inside of her cheek for a moment, but she simply could not stand to watch her mother play *poor me* once again. "Do what, Mother? Write a successful article? Gee, that's so terrible, isn't it?" She turned to her computer and began clicking on random keys.

Mother stuffed the hanky back in her purse and closed the clasp with a snap. "It is when it's nothing but smut, and the entire garden club knows it's *my* daughter who wrote it."

Her fingers halted, she whirled around. "What?" No one outside of the office knew she penned the articles, and Paxton had promised her identity would be held in the strictest confidentiality. Her emails were sent to a special folder listed in her pen name and her calls directed to a second extension.

Her mother extracted the hanky again. "Now, because of you, I won't be able to show my beautiful African Violets at the festival. Oh, Regan, how could you?"

Regan stood, squared her mother by the shoulders, not caring one iota about her mother's violets. "Stop being so melodramatic. Tell me what's going on."

Mother placed the back of her hand to her forehead and swooned.

"Dammit." She lowered her mother into the desk chair. Mother put her elbows on the desk, head bowed in her hands and let out an inhumane wail loud enough to cause heads to peep up over the cubicles throughout the office.

Reagan glared at her co-workers, sending them back down into their chairs. "Who knows I wrote the article, Mother?" she asked in a harsh whisper.

The older woman's shoulders shook with barely contained sobs. "The garden club met this morning. Oh! It was so terrible!"

Patience slipped another notch. "What happened at the meeting?"

Her mother lifted her head and took in a deep breath. "Pansy Wilcox brought the past three copies of *Glimmer* to the meeting, ranting and raving about some silly article she claimed would . . . would . . ." She dabbed at her eyes, soaking up dry tears. "Well, never mind what she said, it's simply too inappropriate to repeat. Imagine, a refined woman like Pansy Wilcox reading that smut."

Reagan let the smut comment slide; she expected no less from her prudish mother. "Then what happened?" she asked, gritting her teeth.

"Everyone passed around the magazines, laughing and giggling like naughty schoolgirls. What a fool I felt sitting there, knowing my daughter worked for the company responsible for publishing that trash!"

Reagan's shoulders sagged in relief. "So no one knows I wrote the articles?"

Her mother began to sob, yet again, mascara running down her face in black furrows. "Oh, they know all right! Everyone knows! The garden club met today at Mrs. Nelson's house. Do you have any idea how long we've waited for an invite to her home? Imagine her surprise to find the very incident that ruined her prized Ernest Markham Clematis vine, trained and pruned for five years to climb just perfectly up the trellis, right there in the magazine!"

Reagan closed her eyes a long moment, the name repeating her in her head, over and over. Mrs. Nelson. The Dean Nelson. She gulped. *Luke Nelson.* "Oh, god." She braced a sudden headache with the palm of her hand. Not only did she and Luke have sex at the Dean's house, but it was his parents' house as well!

Oh god, oh god, ohgodgodgod.

Regan counted to ten. "Okay, so she knows what happened to her Clematis. How does she know *who* did it and that *I* wrote the article?"

Her mother lifted her head and raised her finely plucked brows. "Because, my dear, Pansy suggested that since my daughter worked for *Glimmer,* I should ask you to investigate the Clematis killing, and then Mary Bollox—she's the one who grows those amazing orchids in her green house—she picked that very moment to remember that I had told her my daughter was dating a college professor and couldn't meet her son over Thanksgiving. Oh!" Mother plucked five tissues from the Kleenex box. "The connection was made. I denied it, of course, and came here to prove your innocence, only to be slapped in the face by, by that *filth.*" She waved her hand toward the magazine in the trash. "How could you do this?"

"That's exactly what I'd like to know," Paxton said from behind Reagan. "My office, now."

Reagan heard a loud pop of her dream cloud bursting into a zillion pieces as she followed Paxton toward the end of her career.

Reagan lay with her head on Michaelo's lap as he smoothed her hair off her tear dampened cheeks. He'd shown up at her door an hour after she was fired with two half melted large DQ Banana Splits, doubled toppings.

"Thank you for being here," she said, tears finally spent.

"Anytime, *suga.* Chin up, now. It's time to start focusing on the positives instead of the negatives."

"And what would those be? My mother thinks I'm a slut and a Clematis killer. I've been fired. The man I love won't take my calls." Apparently Mrs. Nelson wasted no time in informing her son of the articles.

"Your mother will get over it, just as soon as those biddies find something better to gossip about. You have offers from other magazines, you won't be out of work long."

"The offers have been rescinded."

"As for the man," Michaelo continued, a thoughtful expression on his light shimmer-powdered face, "you're just going to have to prove to him that you're truly sorry."

"I can't prove anything to him when he won't even speak to me!"

Michaelo patted her head like a lost puppy. "If he loves you, he'll give you a chance once he's done being angry."

Her heart frowned. "That's just it, Michaelo. He's never said he loves me."

A long pause. "Then we may have a problem."

"I liked it better when you were pointing out the positives," she said, reaching for a spoon of melted ice cream, dripping it across the coffee table, carpet and Michaelo's leg to her mouth.

"Now, now. I said we may have a problem. Didn't say we can't find a way to fix it. But the first thing you need to do, Reggie, is pull yourself together, get your cute little heiny off this couch and do what you do best."

She sniffed. "Observe, research and read?"

Michaelo pushed her up and held her rag doll body by the shoulders. "No, that was the old Reagan. The new Reagan goes *va-va-vaoom.* You gotta get your motor going again, baby. Ask yourself what you want, answer it honestly and then lead foot that pedal and go after it. Now, I've gotta jet, unless you need me to stay."

She shook her head. "I'm going to miss working with you."

"Anytime you need me, just stick your head out the window and call. I'll be there." He kissed her cheek, leaving a smudge of pink lipstick. "TTFN."

Reagan watched him go, then took her sorry self to bed. She just didn't have any *va-va-varoom* in her. Maybe a good night's sleep would make her feel better.

❧

Reagan didn't sleep; instead she tossed and turned, thinking about Luke, the experiences he had shared with her. She thought about her job, about Paxton's threat that if Luke sued the magazine for being written about without permission Reagan would be blackballed in the writing community from Seattle to New York—Paxton promised to see to it personally.

Not that it'd matter much now. Word of her lack of journalistic integrity probably had already made rounds.

Just before daybreak, Reagan dragged herself from bed and went to stand before the mirror over the fireplace. She closed her eyes, asked herself what she truly wanted and answered herself honestly, as Michaelo told her to do.

When she opened her eyes, she looked in the mirror and saw herself as that woman, despite the puffy eyes and tousled hair.

She saw herself as Reagan Malone, independent woman, creative writer, beautiful and strong.

For a long time she stood there, in the daylight playing through the open windows, realizing even if Luke never forgave her for betraying his trust, she would forever be thankful to him for showing her she was the woman she wanted to be all along. She just had to stop hiding, had to be brave enough to say *"This is what I want. This is what I deserve. This is who I am."*

She had to believe in herself, in her inner beauty, strength and talent. She'd made two terrible mistakes; she'd betrayed the trust of the man she loved and the trust Paxton placed upon her.

The old Reagan would have gone back to her bed and stayed there crying, believing herself a failure.

The new Reagan was going to take this lesson and learn from it, make things right, no matter what it took.

Finding her briefcase, she took out her notebook, sat down and began to write the fourth installment of *Good Girl Gone Bad.*

Chapter Seven

Reagan returned home after yet another day using the public Internet service at the library to send her résumé and clips to the magazines who'd previously contacted her with fabulous job offers.

She had yet to hear from a single one.

With the journalist equivalent of the plague, no one wanted Reagan anywhere near their office. She was a potential liability. She couldn't be trusted.

The old Reagan would have given up. The new Reagan was going to keep trying, fight like hell to keep her head above water and prove she deserved another chance.

She plunked down her briefcase and took the day's mail to the kitchen table, tossing aside the junk mail and the bills she wouldn't be able to pay for much longer. All that was left were two manila envelopes.

She opened the first and pulled out this week's edition of *Glimmer,* thinking the writer who had tumbled down the mountain sent it to twist the knife in Reagan's lost career.

She didn't need a visual reminder that she was no longer an employed writer, *thank you very much.* Ready to toss the magazine in the trash, a small headline near the bottom of the glossy cover caught her attention.

Conclusion:

Good Girl Gone Bad

Which Prevails? Pg. 52

Heart stammering, Reagan flipped to the page, ignoring the sheet of paper that fell from the magazine. She sat staring at the magazine for a long time, unable to believe Paxton actually had printed the fourth installment.

Reagan hadn't thought the last article would see the light of day since she wrote it after her termination. She simply wanted to prove she could fulfill a commitment, that she had learned from her mistakes.

And Reagan had written the article for herself. She needed to write about her discoveries, her growth, her lessons, her failures. Neither good girl nor the bad prevailed. Rather a combination of both emerged, strengths and weaknesses from both, to create a new Reagan. Wiser, stronger, confident.

She just wished Luke hadn't been hurt in the process. She owed him so much.

Picking up the sheet of paper that had fallen out of the magazine, she read:

"Reagan,

"I'm not forgiving your actions, but I cannot deny the readers' response to your work. I would like to discuss freelancing, within certain guidelines.

"Paxton."

Oh. My. God.

Setting the letter and magazine aside, Reagan tore open the second envelope, expecting a freelance contract. She pulled out a sheet of paper, scanned it and gasped.

The paper slipped from her hand. She shoved her chair back and jumped to her feet. Staring down at the paper, she slowly stepped away until she backed into the counter. Keywords and phrases from the letter popped through her mind like ugly red graffiti.

Ten o'clock tonight.

Expose.

Luke.

Be there.

Reagan swallowed thickly. The cryptic message was clear. Luke would be publicly exposed as the subject of her articles unless she met with an unknown person at ten o'clock tonight to discuss terms of keeping quiet.

She was being blackmailed.

Dear God. What had she done? What was she going to do?

She didn't have enough money to pay off a blackmailer.

Terror struck again and again, like lightning rods from the sky. She reached for the phone, then let her trembling hand drop. If she reported this to the police, she'd have to reveal Luke's identity and someone would surely leak it to the press.

"Okay," she said aloud. "No one knows the truth except Paxton, Michaelo and Mother." *And* the entire gardening club.

Reagan dropped her head on her palms and groaned. *Keep calm. Think this through.* Who among the list of suspects would dare stoop to blackmail?

Paxton, Michaelo and Mother were immediately off the list. Paxton had offered Reagan freelance work. Michaelo was her best friend. Mother—she'd already suffered enough embarrassment—she wouldn't dare do anything to add to the shame she believed Reagan bestowed upon the family.

Which left the members of the garden club.

Reagan straightened her spine. She wasn't shy, timid Reagan Malone anymore. She could handle any one of those self-righteous, flower pruning, black-mailing women.

Following the blackmail letter's instructions, Reagan drove into the parking garage at exactly ten o'clock. Her gaze swept the dark, empty space; her hands gripped the steering wheel. Whichever garden club member was behind this would regret messing with the new, improved Reagan Malone.

Oh, she fully intended to protect Luke's identity. She had already embarrassed him personally with his family. Publicly she could cost him a whole lot more, possibly even his job. She'd take the Fifth to the end, would never admit Luke was her subject.

Reagan also fully intended to teach whatever green thumb, greedy woman behind this a couple of lessons.

One, blackmail was against the law.

Two, Reagan Malone would never back down again, would never again shy away from confrontation.

Three . . . well, she'd think of a third lesson when the time came.

Reagan reached into her purse and took out her cell phone, dialed her home number, then set it on the center console. Per the blackmailer's instructions, she rolled down her car window and waited.

She had made a mistake writing about Luke without his consent or knowledge. But it was *her* mistake. She refused to allow Luke to pay for it more than he already had. So she'd go along with this game and make sure the woman behind the scheme never tried anything like it again.

"Close your eyes," a muffled voice said from somewhere in the dark parking garage. "And don't try anything stupid."

Reagan drew in a deep breath. "I'm sorry, I couldn't quite hear what you said." She reached for her cell phone and pressed send. She'd set her answering machine to pick up automatically and extended the record time. "Would you repeat that?"

"Close your eyes," the voice said, clearer and louder this time, "and don't try anything stupid."

She closed her eyes. "Now what?"

The sound of high heels clicked toward her. A moment later something soft landed on her lap. "Tie that over your eyes. No peeking."

Reagan slid the fabric through her fingers. It felt like a Pashmina scarf. She tied the scarf around her head, smelling the perfume lingering on the buttery soft fabric.

"Step out of the car."

"Tell me what you want first." Reagan needed to get as much incriminating conversation recorded as possible. Then all she'd have to do is threaten to go to the police and that'd be the end of it. "Tell me the terms of your blackmail request."

"Don't make me ask twice."

Whoever it was even did a great job of making her voice sound deep, almost like a man. Reagan blindly reached for the door handle and stepped out. She knew exactly how many steps away from the car she could take and still have a clear recording. She had practiced several times before coming, altering her voice to different levels. More than three steps, the recording became inaudible.

"Turn around and put your hands behind your back."

Reagan hesitated.

"Don't make this hard. I won't hurt you if you cooperate."

She turned around, hands in the small of her back. "Please, just tell me what you want. Tell me your terms."

A hand, a very large hand, suddenly grabbed both of Reagan's, squeezing them together and wrapped what felt like slim rope around her wrists. "Okay, you're taking this a bit far," Reagan said, trying to jerk her hands free, only to find them already bound.

Panic struck. The voice, the large hands. This was no woman. Reagan screamed. Another scarf was suddenly in the bite of her mouth, muffling her cry for help. The blackmailer tied a knot behind her head, securing the gag.

"Relax, and everything will be just fine." The back door opened, he folded Reagan inside. "Understand?"

She nodded. The door slammed shut, and a moment later the engine started and the car backed up. Inhaling a deep breath through her nose in an attempt at finding calm, she got a deeper smell of the perfume of the scarf.

She knew the scent.

Matter of fact, she knew who wore the scent *and* who owned a Pashmina scarf.

Anger and betrayal burned hot as Reagan sat blindfolded and bound in the back of her car as Michaelo drove to heaven knew where. Why was Michaelo doing this to her? They were best friends. She trusted him, relied on him. He knew how she felt about Luke.

Which was exactly why Michaelo was doing this, Reagan realized. Michaelo knew she'd do anything to protect Luke from being exposed. She just never thought Michaelo could be this cruel to turn her pain into profit. He'd always been so sweet and friendly and caring.

Which were probably exactly the same things Luke had thought about her. Reagan herself didn't think she'd be the type to betray a friend's trust for money and fame. She hadn't meant for it all to get so out of control. She'd just been so, so *inspired.* Luke had shown her a whole other world, possibilities and experiences she'd never dared believe possible. It didn't matter that she knew she was wrong, or that she'd learned her lesson. Luke had every right to hate her.

Michaelo's betrayal, Reagan realized, hot tears soaking the Pashmina, must be some kind of cosmic payment for realizing too late her mistakes.

The car finally stopped, and a minute later, Michaelo opened her door and took her by the elbow. He moved her forward, across what felt like pavement beneath her shoes, into what must have been an elevator by the ding of the doors and the lift, then out into a hallway by the feel of carpet. Each time she struggled to free herself, Michaelo held tighter. He knocked on a door, and whispered, "Sorry I had to do this, toots."

Do what? Reagan wondered a frantic moment before hearing the door swoosh open. "What the—" a man's voice said, then broke off.

Michaelo pushed her aside. She heard him speak in low tones that she couldn't understand, then he moved her forward and closed the door behind her. Again she was taken by the elbow, but she could tell by the grip it was someone else. Furious with Michaelo or not, she wanted him to stay with her.

"I'm going to take the gag off," a voice said, again muffled, but different, confirming a change in abductor. "First, promise not to scream. Understand?"

Reagan nodded, praying if she cooperated, this nightmare would end. It was just about money, she assured herself. Once she agreed to pay for silence, she'd be free. And Michaelo was going to be in big, big trouble.

As the gag came off, Reagan sucked in a deep breath. "What do you want?" she asked in a hoarse whisper.

"That's a very good question. Why don't we start with you telling me what you want."

"I . . . I," she cleared her throat, determined to be brave and strong, "I'll pay any price. I don't have much, but I'll make payments." A lump lodged in her throat. Luke was worth all the money in the world. "Whatever it takes."

"Takes to?"

Reagan stood erect, her heart hammering. "To keep Luke's name from being released. He doesn't deserve to be publicly humiliated."

"So let me get this straight. You're here to pay for silence."

"Yes."

"How much money did you bring with you?"

"None, I thought we'd discuss your, er, fee."

"Hmm. And why should you care if his name is released? You didn't care when you wrote your articles."

Reagan turned away, fresh tears hot beneath the blindfold. "Yes, I did care! I just thought—I didn't think—no one was suppose to know. I told you, he-he doesn't deserve this, and I-I love him. I'll do anything to protect him. I made a terrible mistake."

"Yes, you did. He had a right to know about the articles. But you made your biggest mistake by coming here."

Reagan swallowed, hard. "What are going to do to me?"

"Oh, I can think of plenty of things. You're blindfolded. Tied up." He ran his hand along her jaw. "But first, promise me you'll never do anything as stupid as this again," he said, no longer altering his voice.

Reagan recognized it instantly. Her knees went weak. Her heart skipped a beat. Oh. My. God. "Luke?"

Chapter Eight

Luke's fingers threaded into her hair above the blindfold. He drew her closer. "Yes, Reagan, it's me."

Reagan leaned her head into his palm. "What . . . how . . . why?"

"I was as surprised as you to open my door and find you blindfolded, gagged *and* bound."

"I don't understand what's going on."

"I think I do. Your friend, Michaelo, came to see me the other day, wanted to know why I wouldn't return your calls. Why I wouldn't give you a chance to explain what happened."

"*Oh, no.* I didn't send him, I promise. He's just—" Just her best friend in the entire world. "Would you please take this blindfold off?" She needed to see Luke, gage his mood. Make him understand just how sorry she was, for everything.

"Hmm." Luke slipped his fingers through her hair, twined his finger around the end of a lock. "Not just yet." His voice sounded deep, low. Sensual.

Heaven, how she missed his voice. His touch.

"It's not everyday I get a visit from someone as . . . unique as Michaelo. So I let him speak, heard what he had to say. And then I explained how I had thought I could trust you. How I thought you trusted me."

"You can—I did. I'm sorry—"

He pressed his finger to her mouth. "*Shh.* Michaelo demanded I give you a chance to prove your trust. I wasn't sure I even wanted to see you."

So Michaelo had planned the whole blackmail scheme to prove to Luke she could be trusted. Reagan should be furious with her best friend, but knew he thought he was helping. "I-I'll go," she whispered. "If you want me to."

"The thing is, Reagan, when I opened my door and saw you standing there, I realized I never stopped needing to see you. Since the day in the bookstore, I've needed to see you. Be near you." The heat of his body closed in on her, his words soft and warm over her ear. He slid his arms around her and stroked her back, then took her bottom in his hand and squeezed, angling her hips to press against him. "Be *inside* you. Do you know why?"

Reagan bit her bottom lip and shook her head.

Luke slid his other hand beneath her blouse, tickled up her side, skimmed over her breasts and stopped over the beat of her heart. Sensation tingled in the wake of his touch. Her nipples budded, warmth stirred to swirls of heat. It was so hard for her to think when Luke touched her, so difficult to breathe.

"You react with such emotion. Give all of yourself to the moment. You feel, and you experience." He moved soft kisses along her jaw, worked his way to her mouth, one hand capturing the back of her head, over the knot of the blindfold.

"Only with you," she whispered. "You taught me, showed me . . . I never felt before the way you make me feel."

"Neither have I, Reagan. Which is why I wouldn't have stayed away much longer." His words were moist and warm against her mouth. "You drive me crazy when I'm near you, drive me insane when we're apart. I need to be near you, feel you. But damn you, if you ever do something like this again—what if the blackmail letter had been real?"

His words played in her heart and mind. *He wouldn't have stayed away much longer.* "I knew I was safe. I thought it was someone from the garden club."

"But it wasn't." Luke eased away and walked her across the room.

Reagan heard a door open, and he moved her inside. Completely disoriented in her blindness, she didn't know which room he had taken her into until he sat her down and eased her backward onto something soft. Her heart sang as she realized it was his bed he laid her on.

"Promise me you won't ever again do something as stupid as running off to meet with a blackmailer alone." The mattress bowed beneath the weight of him kneeling over her thighs.

She shook her head. "No, I won't promise you that. I made a mistake. I had to make it as right as possible."

He slipped his hand beneath her skirt, moved upward beneath the edge of her panties and skimmed his thumb between her legs, over her lobes, dipping into the heat of her valley to press deliciously against her nubbin.

Heat rushed from the tips of her breasts to coil low and deep from the pleasure of his touch. Her hips began to rock ever so slowly against his touch; warmth and dampness seeped deep inside her. Sprays of sensation radiated everywhere, lighting her darkness beneath the blindfold.

The bed shifted as Luke leaned down, his hand bracing beside her head. Soft and moist, he laved the tip of her breast through her blouse and the cotton fabric of her bra, suckled her already hard nipple. He buried his thumb deeper, pressure against building pressure. Her back arched and her head fell to the side, a moan escaping from her throat.

Releasing the tension of his thumb, he slid his finger into her core, ever so slowly. Reagan tucked her bottom lip under her front teeth and whimpered, her hips lifting to coax him further, needing to feel him deep inside her. "Fuck me, Luke," she breathed, needing his fullness, the length of him inside her.

"Not this time, Reagan." His mouth trailed down between her breasts, over her stomach. He tickled the hallow of her hip with his tongue. "This time I'm going to make love to you."

His words were amazing. Make love. Dreams and hopes coalesced into a moment so incredibly sweet, she wanted it to never end. Moving lower, he slid down her panties, kissed the inside of her thigh. Perhaps she was dreaming all of this. If so, Reagan never wanted to wake up.

Luke drew his tongue to the center of her, where heat and pressure and tiny throbs begged for more. Pressing open her legs with his hands on the inside of her thighs, he tortured her nubbin with the lightly rough tip of his tongue. "But not until you make that promise."

"Luke, please." Breath shallow and breaking on tiny gasps, Reagan tried to fight the intensity of her pleasure. She tried to focus, to form coherent thoughts. She couldn't take anymore of his sweet torture, couldn't not. She loved him, loved him, loved him. But she would protect him, would show him she could be trusted. "No, I—oh . . ."

He eased his finger from within her, stroked back inside, pushing further, gliding along her upper wall while drawing his tongue down her wet slit, up again to suckle her nubbin. Her fragrance bloomed the air, sweet and pungent. Such slow, sweet, beguiling pleasure. Pleasure orchestrated by a master, bringing each melody of her body together to sing a licentious song. Feelings and emotions blended on the chords of crashing need.

He plunged two fingers deep inside her, held taut, her tender walls pulsing against his touch. "Promise me, Reagan."

Her hips jerked off the bed, so helpless as he held her dangling from a thread just shy of climax. "I want . . . I need you to know you can trust me," she managed, gulping in drinks of air, sprays of light playing behind the blindfold. She bore her hips against his hand, circling, pushing, needing.

"You've already proven your trust by coming here tonight. Your trust was proven the first time you allowed me to touch you."

It was difficult to think when all she wanted was him, inside her. "But I-I wrote about you in my articles. I've shamed you in front of your family."

He moved, his knees between her open legs, pressing her open further, slipping his fingers from within her. "Reagan, nothing I've done with you shames me." The weight of his body shifted to one side, and she sensed him reaching for something. Moments later what felt like little petals fluttered down over her belly.

She inhaled the scent of flowers as he slid his erection deep into her core ever so slowly. Her begging body took him fully. "If the whole world finds out how much I enjoy making love to you," he said, pressing even deeper inside her. "Then let them know." He pulled his hips back, then reentered her, building her desire again with slow strokes. He reached to untie the blindfold and slipped it away.

She blinked open her eyes and focused on Luke's handsome face above her. "Let them know I love you," he said, his eyes darkening as he stared deep into her eyes.

"I love you, too," she whispered, the words catching on her soul. "I promise, I won't ever do anything to betray your trust again." With him she climbed to a plateau where love and trust heightened their passion.

As they came together in an orgasm more powerful than any before, her words of love flowed again and again with their release.

Afterward, lying in a tangle on Luke's bed, a place he had never brought a lover before, Reagan, finally free of the binds tying her hands, picked up a rich red Clematis petal dewed with the union of their bodies. "Oh, no. Please don't tell me this is what I think it is."

Luke plucked up another petal from Mrs. Nelson's prized Ernest Markham Clematis vine and ran it across her cheek. "Ah-uh. I've kept a bunch beside my bed to remind me of you. You wouldn't believe how hard it is to get those out of her house undetected."

Luke had stolen flowers from his mother. For her. Reagan smiled and snuggled up closer to him. "You really shouldn't have."

"Hey, it'll give our mothers something else to gossip about. And maybe something for you to write about next."

She nuzzled her nose to the underside of his chin, drew her tongue along his jaw. "Hmmm, I doubt I'll be lacking topics for a very long time."

Luke cupped the back of her head, lifted her mouth to his. "At least the next seventy years or so."

Reagan smiled against his kiss. "Hmmm, that's a lot of research."

"You know what they say, 'Do what you love.' "

"Can I quote you on that, Mr. Nelson?"

"Absolutely, Mrs. Nelson."

Reagan's heart stilled, her breath caught in her throat. She searched Luke's gaze, disbelieving the implication of his words. "Did you . . . Are you . . . ?"

"Asking you to marry me?" Luke kissed her once again, softly, tenderly, deeply. "Yes, Reagan. That's exactly what I'm asking."

She cupped his beautiful face in her palm. A tear slid down her cheek. "I love you. Yes . . . yes . . . yes . . . I'll marry you."

About the Author:

Dominique Sinclair, who also writes romantic suspense and contemporary romance as Jewel Stone, lives in beautiful Washington State. When not writing, Dominique spends her time doing lots of research—which can be quite exciting when researching erotic fiction!

Good Girl Gone Bad *is Dominique's second erotic romance piece, a genre which she has discovered addictive. You can read her first novella,* Private Eyes, *in **Secrets, Volume 10.***

To learn more about Dominique and her sensual, seductive, sinful world of erotic romance visit www.dominiquesinclair.com.

Aphrodite's Passion

by Jess Michaels

To My Reader:

When I read about the ancient cults who worshipped the goddess Aphrodite, I knew immediately that there was an erotic, romantic story there. I hope you enjoy Gavin and Selena's journey through passion, duty and ultimately, love.

For Michael, who is everything I ever wanted, and everything I never knew I needed.

Chapter One

London, Summer 1885

Rain trickled down the windows, and the muggy warmth made the dark sitting room stifling. Gavin Fletcher shifted on the hard, cushionless chair as he looked at the group of people staring at him. It was as if he'd been sent before a firing squad.

"I still don't understand why you require my assistance, Miss Kelsey," he said as he took a sip of tepid tea. It took all his willpower not to wince at its lack of flavor or heat. The drink was as bland as his surroundings, as pale and insipid as the woman who glared at him from her ramrod straight position on the settee.

"My father is dead because he saved your life, Major Fletcher." Amelia Kelsey frowned, thinning the light skin around her flat, pursed lips, her expression more sullen than it had been a moment before. "Isn't that true?"

Gavin flexed his left arm instinctively. A shadow of pain shot through both the damaged bone and his heart with her words, and the raw memories they evoked. Memories of a day in India. The day when he'd nearly been killed but for the intervention of his superior officer, Colonel David Kelsey. Fletcher had lived, but Kelsey had been gravely injured. Watching the man slowly bleed to death in the oppressive heat and filth of the field hospital had been agony itself.

"Major?"

This time it was Amelia Kelsey's younger sister, Adelaide, who snapped out his rank. She could have been her sister's twin with her flat blonde hair, watery blue eyes and pinched, pale face.

"Yes, your assessment is correct." As guilt clawed his heart, Gavin let his gaze slip to the shiny hardwood floor. It reflected the dim light of the lamps and a shadowy image of Gavin's own face. "Your father saved my life during a skirmish with Indian radicals. In the process, his own life was taken. My apologies to all of you. I wish to offer my most sincere condolences for your loss."

He forced his stare back up to the family. The two sisters wiped their eyes with matching black handkerchiefs, while their younger brother, Arthur simply appeared bored.

"Then you are beholden to him." Amelia set her handkerchief down and smiled for the first time since his arrival. To his surprise, it was even more unattractive than her scowl. "Beholden to *us.*"

He drew in a sharp breath as he nodded with reluctance. "Yes. That is true."

"If you wish to repay your debt, you can help us."

Gavin's eyes narrowed as he looked from one Kelsey offspring to the next. That feeling of the room closing in on him began again, more acutely than before. "How can I be of assistance?"

"Our stepmother is missing." Amelia spat the words out with as much care as a viper for the comfort of its prey. "Her parents believe she's been taken by white slave traders, thanks to that ridiculous article in the *Pall Mall Gazette* last week."

"I'm afraid I've only been in the country for a few days," Gavin said as apologetically as he could muster. He was beginning to despise this family with their cold, cruel stares and dark, dank parlor. He hadn't liked their father much either, but the man had saved his life. Only that unalterable fact kept him from storming out and never looking back.

"I thought as much." Arthur stepped forward with a folded copy of the paper.

Gavin scanned the story the young man pointed to. It was sensationalist drivel about the dangers of letting young women out on their own. It told of kidnappings and the systematic deflowering of virgins by lecherous foreigners who then forced them into the horrors of prostitution.

"And you believe your stepmother was taken by one of these ringleaders?" Gavin asked quietly, just managing to keep the disbelief from his voice. Even if the rumors of white slavery were true, it was unlikely a widow in her late twenties would be taken.

"No." Amelia snatched the paper from his fingertips and tossed it behind her on the floor in a show of violence that surprised Gavin. "I don't think that. Her minister father and mother think that. *I* believe she left on her own. I believe she's been overtaken by some kind of sexual hysteria and is off to make a spectacle of us all."

Gavin rubbed his temples. He had been polite, but his patience was coming to a swift end. "Why don't you tell me the entire story, Miss Kelsey? And then explain what you want from me."

"Our father's wife," Amelia began, acid dripping from each and every syllable, "is the same age as I am. She was far too young for him and she only married him for his wealth and the purse he left for her in his last will and testament. Our father was miserable every moment he shared with her and couldn't wait to escape and do his duty in India."

Gavin arched an eyebrow but remained silent. The Widow Kelsey must have been unpleasant if a man would rather 'escape' to the horrors of war than stay with her in safety and comfort. Not that he was entirely convinced this shrew's version of the story was correct. "Go on."

This time Adelaide Kelsey spoke, continuing where her sister left off as if they had rehearsed the telling of this little tale. "After our dear father left the country, our stepmother went wild. She consorted publicly with questionable people and stayed out until indecent hours of the night. When we confronted her with our questions about her behavior, she treated us abominably and refused to answer."

Again, Gavin held his tongue. He could only imagine what kind of inquisition Mrs. Kelsey must have endured with these three. His dealings with them were trying enough, and it was clear the two women, at least, held their stepmother in very low regard.

"Do you know where she went?"

Amelia shook her head with a scowl. "No, though I have my suspicions. After my father died, our stepmother hardly mourned a few weeks before she returned to her lifestyle as if he meant nothing to her. Her attitude toward us grew more and more outrageous. Finally, we felt we had no choice but to have her committed. Unfortunately, she got wind of our plans before we could . . . could . . ." She paused with a malicious smile that turned Gavin's blood cold, even in the muggy heat of the parlor. "*Help* her. She disappeared nearly a fortnight ago, and we've had no word of her whereabouts since."

Leaning back in the uncomfortable chair, Gavin flexed his fingers across his thigh. A shot of pain burst through his arm, one he forced himself to ignore. Somehow he doubted the prudence of showing weakness in this snake's nest.

"I am sorry to hear your family lost your stepmother so soon after your father's untimely death," he said. "But again, I'm at a loss as to what this has to do with me."

Arthur Kelsey sighed with theatric exasperation. "Since you are beholden to my father and our family, my sisters feel *you* should undertake the task of finding our stepmother and bringing her home." He frowned at the two women. "You see, they cannot rest until they insure our poor stepmother is 'treated' for her illness."

Gavin snapped his gaze toward the two young women who were nodding in unison. They couldn't be serious! He had only just returned home. "You want me to track your stepmother down and drag her back to London so you can institutionalize her?"

"She needs treatment," Amelia said firmly.

"Yes," Adelaide chimed in with a cruel smile. "She needs our help whether she desires it or not."

Gavin got to his feet and paced to the window. He watched the rain for a long moment as he considered his options. Though he did feel beholden to the Kelsey family for their sacrifice, the idea of tracking down some wayward widow, one who might be legitimately insane, didn't appeal to him. After months of being away, he had looked forward to spending time at home. To seeing his ailing mother. To meeting the nieces and nephews who had been born while he toiled away in service to the Queen's Army.

He certainly hadn't planned for a journey to find a strange woman.

He allowed himself a glance over his shoulder at the siblings. They were gathered in a semi-circle, staring at him like vultures aching to peck at rotting meat. He shuddered. If he refused their request, he had no doubt they would plague him until they felt some satisfaction that he had repaid his 'debt'. He didn't relish the idea of being summoned here more than this one time, yet his honor demanded he fulfill his obligation.

"Do you have any idea where your stepmother might have gone?" he asked softly.

Amelia Kelsey made no attempt to hide her triumphant grin. "Her closest friend and confidante was a woman named Isadora Glasier. She was married to an officer stationed in Greece, and after his death, she stayed on that heathen island far longer than was proper. We believe she and Mrs. Glasier returned to Greece or possibly the nearby island of Cyprus."

Gavin wrinkled his brow. "Why?"

Adelaide turned to the table behind her and opened a small box. From it, she withdrew the charred remains of a leather bound book.

"This is our stepmother's diary. She tried to burn it before she left the house, but one of our parlor maids rescued it. Though much is destroyed, what remains details her sick obsessions. In it, she often mentions Cyprus, as well as some kind of twisted group Mrs. Glasier introduced her to." She held out the diary as if it were a poisonous snake that could turn on her at any moment.

Gavin took the delicate book carefully. "And how will I know what your stepmother looks like if I do manage to discover where she's gone?"

Arthur dug into his pocket and produced two items. "This is a miniature my father had done of his wife before he left for India. And she had this photograph taken for her mother and father. They live in the country and rarely saw her after her marriage."

Gavin reached out to take the items and was surprised when the young man clenched them for a moment before he relinquished control. Gavin searched Arthur Kelsey's unlined face for a moment before he refocused his attention on the two items.

When he turned the photograph over, he could hardly contain his gasp. Mrs. Kelsey was far and away the most exquisite woman he'd ever seen. She had a heavy silken mass of dark hair with little wisps that spun around her cheeks and a curvaceous, voluptuous body that called out to be touched. Worshiped.

Though she was posed in the stiff posture required for the long photography sessions, her face and eyes were alive with personality and a dash of sensuality that reached beyond the picture and stirred desires in him that had been dormant since his injury.

"What is her name?" he choked out as he continued to stare at the photograph.

"Selena." Arthur Kelsey answered, his voice as strained as Gavin's had been. "Her name is Selena."

Gavin looked up and found himself locking gazes with the young man. A dangerous desire glittered in Kelsey's pale blue eyes, as dangerous as the need that suddenly burned within Gavin himself for this woman he had never even met.

"I shall do my best to find her and bring her back," he said quietly. "But you aren't giving me much information to work with."

"You will make do." Amelia folded her thin arms across her chest as she glared from Gavin to her brother and back again. "I can tell you some heathen goddess named Aphrodite is mentioned several times in the disgusting pages of that journal. Perhaps that is a clue you can investigate."

Gavin forced himself to put Selena Kelsey's grainy photo into his pocket. Even though the image was no longer in sight, he could still see it in his mind. Feel it in his pocket as much as if it were Selena's own hand there, teasing him. He struggled to keep the evidence of his sudden desire at bay, at least until he got out of this house and into the privacy of his rented rooms.

"Yes," he choked out. "I'll work as quickly as possible to uncover her whereabouts. I will inform you before I leave the country to begin my search." He edged toward the door. "If there is nothing else, I shall take my leave."

Amelia looked at him through narrowed eyes. "That is all. Our butler will show you to the door." Gavin held back a sigh of relief as he made for the foyer, but hadn't quite left the room when the young woman stopped him with the sound of her shrill voice. "Major Fletcher?"

"Yes?" He turned back with a false smile.

"Selena may be beautiful, but I wouldn't recommend falling under her spell." The young woman arched an accusatory eyebrow. "Our stepmother is not well, and if you aren't careful, she could drive *you* mad, too. Good day."

Gavin gave the family a last nod before he left the room. He burst out into the rain and raised an arm to hail a hackney. Once he was safely out of view from the public street, he sank back against the worn seat, then adjusted his trousers around the raging erection that had sprung up the moment he'd looked at the image of Selena Kelsey. Like a thief gazing hungrily at a hoard of treasure, he brought out her picture again and stared at the sultry woman with a shiver of need.

Perhaps his savior's widow *was* sick. Perhaps she was driven by hysterical needs and did require the institutionalization the Kelsey family seemed so anxious to impose. Gavin didn't know enough about her to answer those questions yet. What he did know was that Selena was utterly desirable, and that she was destined to haunt his dreams until the moment he found her.

Cyprus, two months later.

Selena Kelsey shuddered to think what London would be like at present. Cool and rainy, with the ever-present haze of coal smoke more oppressive than ever. She looked out her window with a deep sigh and a wide, if wavering, smile. Although fall was coming, the island of Cyprus remained bright and warm. Sunlight sparkled off the brilliant blue ocean waters in the distance, while a warm breeze stirred the sand and tropical foliage. It was paradise.

She shivered as she thought of the city she had left behind months before. Emotions swamped her with their intensity. The loneliness of her empty marriage. The anger and fear her stepchildren had inspired in her. The disappointment in her family for putting her in such a situation. The guilty relief when David Kelsey's death had been reported to her. And the horror when she realized that just because her husband was gone, didn't mean she was free. In fact, without his small protection, her life was in even more danger than before.

She shoved those awful memories aside. Drawing in a few breaths, she focused on slowing her racing heart and pounding blood. She had escaped the torment London meant to her. And as she had since she and Isadora arrived on the island a few weeks before, she gave a silent prayer of thanks for her newfound freedom.

Turning away from her window, she sighed. She was grateful, yes. But she was also lost. Confused. Afraid, though for different reasons than she had been in London. But despite her gratitude, she feared she didn't belong in Cyprus any more than she belonged in the repressive society of England. The free sexuality practiced by her friends in the hidden temple along the sandy beaches titillated Selena. She'd watched the sensual rituals and passionate matings of her friends with interest and desire. Still, she hadn't participated, even after Isadora's continued prodding. She hadn't yet chosen a partner to share in her awakening passion.

But her passion *was* awakening. Feelings she had been afraid to let loose in England were alive in Cyprus. Both her inhibitions and her shame were fading like the island flowers that wilted with the coming of fall.

Was it enough for her, though? While her fellow temple dwellers seemed content in their decadent lifestyle, often Selena was . . . lonely. Even more so than she'd been in her terrible marriage.

With a frown, she gazed in the mirror of her dressing table. Her dark hair was unbound and hung down to her waist. When she brushed it back over her shoulder, she could clearly see the dusty rose outline of her nipples through her thin sleeping sheath. Lower down, the shadow of her pubis pressed against the fabric. She watched in the mirror as her hands glided down her body. She flicked a thumb over one hard nipple, sucking in a breath as pleasure spiked through her blood.

Months ago, bringing herself pleasure had been a secret kept to dark nights in her lonely bed. A shame she tried to deny herself. But now, she was free to experience pleasure without recrimination or charges of hysteria. And she was far more aware of her body's wants and needs.

She concentrated on her breasts, tugging at the nipples with enough force to leave them tingling with sensation. She let her hands drift lower, never taking her eyes off her reflection as she pressed her chemise against her suddenly hot skin. Her fingers drifted over the hollow of her belly button, then finally found the soft folds of her pussy.

She blushed when she thought of that word. Isadora had insisted she learn all the terms for her body, from the bawdy to the medical. Her friend had even given her piles of books with explicit pictures and shocking words so she could learn about herself, learn about passion.

The boat trip to Cyprus had been educational to say the least, between reading the erotic books Isadora had given her, and watching her friend act out those stories from behind the thin sheet that separated their cabin.

That thought enflamed Selena even more. There had been so many nights when she had been a voyeur, watching Isadora act out what Selena was still ashamed to imagine. Images flashed through her mind as she lightly played her fingers along her own slit. With a deep breath, she let the images assault her senses.

There had been a night when Isadora had invited the most handsome of the ship's mates to their shared quarters. With a chiseled body, strong jaw and wild blond hair, the man had been a source of much giggling and coarse talk between the two women. But Selena never expected to awaken to his low, sensual voice just feet away from her bed.

She had peered between the separating sheet just in time to see Isadora drop to her knees. Her friend was already naked and yanked the man's trousers down to his ankles as she slithered to the floor to gaze up at him with an expression filled with promise and desire.

While Selena held back her unbidden moans of shock and wanton curiosity, Isadora had grasped the thick base of the man's fine cock and glided her fist from the root to the throbbing, red tip. He'd dipped his head back with a groan even as he thrust his hands into Isadora's hair and pulled her toward him.

Selena's fingers worked along her slit as she recalled the way Isadora laughed before she wrapped her lips around the round head of his erection and swiftly took the entire, massive length of him deep within her throat. Selena had seen pictures of the act before, but to see it happen, just feet away from her, had aroused her to a fever pitch. She'd been unable to keep from fingering herself, just as she was doing now, as she remembered the wet sucks of Isadora's mouth, and the way the veins in the man's neck lifted up as he strained in pleasure with every thrust.

Finally, he had grabbed Isadora's shoulders and yanked her to her feet. Before Selena could react, he had flipped her friend onto her stomach on the bed and speared his impressive member deep into her body. He thrust into her so hard Selena had feared he would hurt Isadora, but when her friend lifted her face, it was clear the screams that escaped her lips were cries of ecstasy, not agony.

Selena grew wetter with each hot memory. She pressed the fabric of her nightclothes up against herself and began to stroke in a firm, smooth motion. She let her eyes flutter shut as she pictured doing the same thing she had observed her friend doing all those hot nights ago. She imagined the hard thrust of a lover's cock, jutting proudly toward her as she looked up from her bent-kneed position on a soft bed.

Only her fantasy lover's face was blank.

Frustrated, Selena opened her eyes. She was on the brink of orgasm, but couldn't seem to take herself over the edge. She was too distracted, too filled with doubts about her place in the Cult of Aphrodite. Certainly, the Greek goddess of sensuality wouldn't approve of her standoffish ways.

She refocused her attention on the mirror, determined to take herself over the edge. And gasped. His image reflected in the mirror, a man stood in her doorway. Not some male member of their group, not a man she had ever seen before. A stranger.

For a moment, she was frozen by his sudden presence. She didn't turn, but took a long look at him in the mirror. He was tall, with dark hair and bright blue eyes that stood out even from across the room. Dressed in the garments of a middle class man from London, he should have seemed drab, but he wasn't. Even in a plain, brown suit and slightly crooked cravat, he had a presence about him. If she had passed him on a busy street, she wouldn't have been able to keep herself from staring. She certainly couldn't stop now, when he stood in her doorway, watching her pleasure herself.

He was handsome, perhaps only a few years older than she was. But despite his apparent youth, he had a wisdom and knowledge in his eyes that told Selena he'd seen more of the world than most of the men in her acquaintance.

He also had a hefty dose of lust glittering in the blue depths of his stare. Along with an obvious erection that strained against the front of his wrinkled brown trousers.

The part of her still repressed by societal expectations told her to stop what she was doing. It warned her to cover herself decently and call for the guards this man had somehow bypassed.

But a larger, and now much louder part urged her to continue. Because seeing this man watch her, seeing his reaction to her act of self-pleasure, had taken her even closer to the brink of orgasm. Her wayward thoughts were now entirely focused on the sensual, on this man watching her. If she touched herself again while this man looked on, she would reach completion.

Their eyes locked a second time in the mirror, but he remained silent. Hands trembling, she allowed herself a long, calming breath before she let her fingers move. The stranger's lips parted as he realized she wasn't going to stop masturbating simply because he had invaded her sanctuary.

Instead of focusing on the memory of Isadora and her conquests, Selena concentrated on the stranger who watched her. She imagined his large hands on her skin, touching her as she touched herself. When his tongue darted out to wet his lips, she couldn't help but groan as she pictured that same tongue dragging against her. Her fingers moved at a faster, more purposeful speed against her clit as she imagined him spreading her legs while he revealed the hard thrust of his cock.

Her pleasure spiked, peaked and she found herself wailing out an orgasm that buckled her knees. She tipped forward as she spasmed, gripping at the ornate metal mirror frame with one hand as she bucked the other against her clit, over and over. Her hot, harsh breaths left a circle of steam on the glass as her body quivered one last time. Finally, she found some equilibrium and was able to balance on her shaky legs.

Each movement seemed to take an eternity as she turned to face the intruder who had driven her over the edge of pleasure with just his presence. Her heart slammed against her ribcage with trepidation and excitement. She had absolutely no idea what would happen once she looked at the man without the protection of a mirrored image, but she wasn't afraid. She wanted this stranger to touch her. She wanted him to take her, stroke inside her. To be the first man who brought her to orgasm with his cock or tongue or fingers.

She shivered at the thought. She looked up and let her gaze meet his. A thin sheen of sweat had broken out on his upper lip and his eyes were wide with desire.

"Selena," he whispered as he crossed the room toward her in long, purposeful steps that left little doubt to his intention once he reached her.

She started. How did he know her name? She'd never met him before, of that she was more than certain. Judging from his attire, he wasn't a new member of the cult Isadora had sent to her as a gift. Yet her name fell from his lips as if it were an answer to his every prayer.

He was only feet away now and each purposeful step made her sex clench. But before he could reach out to touch her, before she could give in to him or even ask how he knew her name, the door behind him flew open to slam against the packed mud wall of her hut.

Her intruder seemed to be in too much of a passionate fog to recognize what was happening. He didn't turn at the opening of the door, but continued to walk toward her with the same undeniable gleam in his blue eyes.

Two guards burst into the room behind him, brandishing sharp spears and yelling first in Greek and then accented English as they rushed forward to grasp the man's arms. Only then did he snap out of his haze. He winced in pain as the two men shoved him to the ground, and one of the guards pressed a spear into his back until his suit jacket creased.

"Stop!" Selena cried as she hurried toward them. An uncontrollable desire to protect this unknown man swelled within her, even though the guards had only come to protect her. Still, she ached to see him pinned to the ground, his face twisted in apparent agony as he tried to break free from the iron grip of the Greek guards.

"He is an intruder," one of the guards barked as they jerked her struggling stranger to his feet and dragged him toward the door. "And he must face the counsel."

Chapter Two

"What is your name?" The sharp, female voice spoke to him on what was barely more than a hiss.

Gavin winced as a spear pressed against his back, the blade slicing through his shirt, etching a warning on his skin.

"Take the damn spear out of my flesh and we can discuss this situation like civilized human beings," he snapped before he bit his tongue.

He couldn't afford to lose control of his emotions again. In Selena's room, he'd been so wrapped up in lust that he'd lost all sense of time, his surroundings, even approaching danger. Where had his passion gotten him? Caught before he could talk to Selena alone. And now he was paying the price.

His female captor laughed. Gritting through the pain, he forced his eyes up to look at her. Her stunning red hair was piled on her head, patterned after the ancient Greek style. Her chiton was also traditional, except for the round, firm breast it bared.

The woman seemed anything but embarrassed by her partial nudity. Even in a room filled with nearly two dozen men and women, all of whom stared openly, she didn't blush or move to cover herself. In fact, she appeared to thrive on the attention as she thrust out her breasts with a proud air.

From her accent and the descriptions Gavin had read in Selena's diary, he guessed this was Isadora Glasier.

"You want to talk to us about civility?" Isadora's laughter faded as a flash of sudden anger glittered in her dark eyes. "*You* who invaded our sanctuary? *You* who violated the purity of the temple of Aphrodite?"

Gavin stiffened. Selena had written often in her journal about Aphrodite, the Greek goddess of sex and sensuality. And about how Isadora had slowly tutored her in the ways of the goddess through books and voyeuristic adventures. The stories Selena recounted in the surviving pages of her journal were erotic and passionate. They had awakened Gavin's lust more than once as he read them during his long boat trip to Cyprus.

And now this woman who had dragged Selena away from London, was mentioning the goddess again.

"A sanctuary? A temple?" he repeated with a shake of his head. "What the hell is this place?"

For the first time, he let his attention shift from his guards and the woman who lead them and looked around. From the exterior, the building looked like an ordinary hut, but inside, it was patterned after one of the famous shrines of Greece where ancient people had worshipped gods like Zeus, Poseidon and Aphrodite.

The center of the room held a large, square pit. It had been sunk deep enough that an average man could stand upright and his head wouldn't clear the crevice's marble walls. The pit was surrounded by a marble railing. The other members of the cult clustered around, looking down on the 'trial' with interest, disdain and even hatred.

A throne sat on an elevated platform facing the railing. Above it were a series of elaborate paintings, done in an ancient style. But instead of detailing offerings to the gods or great battles, these depicted various sex acts. And the marble pillars supporting the high ceiling had been carved with lewd intent as well. A naked man with a thrusting cock, his head dipped back as he stroked the firm flesh. A woman being pleasured by two kneeling men.

Isadora used the toe of her sandal to turn his face toward hers. "My questions first, intruder. And yours later if I feel you deserve to know more. What is your name?"

He jerked away from her with a scowl. "Gavin Fletcher."

She smiled in triumph. "And what are you doing violating our temple, Mr. Fletcher? You were certainly not invited into our sanctum by any of our members."

He shook his head. There was no use lying about the purpose for his journey to Cyprus. If Isadora's lackeys searched his bags, they would find Selena's picture and diary. "No, I was not invited. I came looking for someone."

"For whom?" The woman's voice grew sharp and wary.

"For Selena Kelsey."

"What?"

This time, it wasn't Isadora Glasier who answered, but Selena herself. Although he'd only heard her voice once, it was burned in his memory like his own. He watched her push her way forward through the crowd. She struggled to the short staircase that lead to the pit and stumbled down into the area where he was being questioned.

Just as when he saw her the first time, his heart skittered to life. For two months Selena had been nothing more than an image in a photograph, one he had looked at over and over until he'd memorized everything about her, from the quirk of her eyebrow to the slight parting of her lips. She became his obsession, his torment, his desire as he sailed to Cyprus and an uncertain future.

He'd tried to convince himself that she could never live up to his fantasies once he encountered her in reality. He was right.

She far surpassed his fantasies. Her voice was more beautiful. Her scent more alluring. Her eyes more vibrant.

Now those same green eyes that had held him captive while she pleasured herself were dark with surprise and fear as she stared down at him.

"You came here for me?" she asked softly, and the sound of her words cut through him with a blast of need.

The room faded until he was barely aware of the hostile crowd of people, of the sharp press of the spear against his spine, of Isadora's pointed stare. For a moment, all that existed was Selena.

She, too, was dressed in a chiton like Isadora's. Her left breast was exposed, and he took a long, hungry look at the perfect globe of flesh. Her nipple darkened and hardened under his stare, and her lips parted in surprise. As he had in her bedroom, he wondered what her skin would taste like . . . what she would feel like when she arched beneath him and whispered his name in pleasure.

"Answer the question."

The sharp ache of his injured arm dragged Gavin from the fantasy when one of the guards twisted it behind his back. He tried to control the pain, to discipline his mind not to register the sharp burst that seemed to rush through every fiber of his body, but he couldn't help but cry out.

"Stop, don't hurt him." Selena rushed forward to push the guards away. Leaning down, she placed a soft hand on his painful arm. It was like a balm and the throbbing subsided a fraction. "Let him answer, for pity's sake."

She sank down beside him and looked into his face. She was so close, her body heat burned at him. And he could smell her, too. A tantalizing mix of the sharp, spicy flowers he'd discovered while looking for the temple and a womanly scent that belonged only to her. The remnants of her pleasure.

Despite the danger and unknown elements of his situation, his cock stiffened.

"Then speak," Isadora commanded, though she was staring at Selena, not him. "The lady has given you a reprieve from measures that would force your answers."

Gavin cleared his throat and kept his attention focused on Selena. "Mrs. Kelsey—"

She turned her face as if she'd been slapped, and her hand abruptly left his arm. "Selena. I have no other name in this place but Selena."

He hesitated at the pain and fear that flashed in her eyes, but went on. "Selena, I was sent here by your stepchildren. They were worried about your welfare."

She rocked back on her heels with a gasp.

"My stepchildren?"

"They wish for you to return to London." He grimaced as he thought of why the Kelseys wanted that.

"They hired you to take me back to London?" she whispered.

The absolute horror in her voice cut through him and hurt as much as his injured arm. "Yes."

For a moment, she appeared to struggle with her emotions, but then her jaw set and the glitter of fear faded from her even stare. "How much did they pay you? I shall double it if you simply go away and never tell them you found me. Tell them I'm dead, for all I care."

He reeled back. Despite his dislike of the Kelsey family, the idea of lying to them, of telling them this woman was dead when she wasn't, of breaking her parents' hearts, was utterly distasteful. And he had a duty he held to her late husband.

"They didn't pay me." He sighed. "I owe them a debt, and this is my method of repayment."

She pursed her lips in frustration. "Then tell me the amount of the debt and I'll give you that and more so you'll no longer be beholden to them."

He shook his head slowly. He wasn't sure how she would react to the truth, but he had to tell her regardless. "The debt is a life. Your late husband's life. I am the reason he's dead."

An audible gasp went through the curious crowd, but Selena didn't seem to notice it. Her eyes widened impossibly as she scrambled to her feet and backed away from him.

"*You* are why he is dead?" she repeated slowly as her hand came up to cover the mouth he had longed to kiss for months.

Gavin moved to rise but the guards stepped forward, brandishing their spears to keep him in place. "He died saving my life in India."

The color that had darkened her face slowly bled away until she was as pale as her chiton. "My God, that means you're . . . you're . . ."

"Didn't you tell me your husband died saving an officer in his regiment?" Isadora's harsh stare suddenly focused on Gavin with a sinister gleam.

"Yes," Selena whispered. Her hands trembled and her eyes sparkled with unshed tears. "Major—"

"Major Gavin Fletcher," he finished.

Isadora flinched back. "If you are an officer in the Queen's Army, we have no choice. I hate to do this to such an amazing specimen of a man." She snapped her fingers. "Guards! Kill him!"

As the two men advanced on his helpless position, spears pointed at him with deadly intent, Selena screamed.

"No!"

Isadora hauled Selena across the temple floor into one of the alcoves facing the sea. In the large open chamber, it was the only place that gave them some small measure of privacy. Selena flinched as her friend's fingers sunk into her shoulders and she gave her a hard shake.

"What are you thinking? This man is in the Army, perhaps stationed in Greece. If he knows the truth about our temple and we release him, the grounds will be swarming with officers in a matter of hours. Everyone here will be arrested. The men may be let go within a few days, but the women will be returned to abusive husbands and repressed lifestyles or even institutionalized for hysteria. We cannot risk setting him free."

Selena sank her teeth into her lower lip as she stole a glance over Isadora's shoulder toward Gavin Fletcher. He was still down on his knees, the guards holding him. Seeing such a strong man in that compromised position made her heart ache.

Everything her friend said was true, but it made no difference.

"I cannot be responsible for his death, Isadora. I can't live with that hanging over my head." She shrugged apologetically.

"Are you mad?" Isadora's voice went up a level before she controlled herself. "He came to Cyprus with the express duty of hauling you home to the fate your stepchildren have laid out for you. An institution, Selena! How can you feel any responsibility? What you do is to protect yourself and your friends. If anyone has his blood on their hands, it's the triplets."

Selena stifled a smile. Isadora always called her stepchildren the triplets because of their similar names and the drab coloring and ugly attitudes that made them all so distasteful.

"Yes, Adelaide, Amelia and Arthur do hold a lion's share for forcing this man to come here," she said slowly, again looking at the Major. Even crouched on the ground with menacing guards threatening to kill him, he looked every inch in command. Every part of him seemed calm, as if he was assessing his situation and waiting to see what would happen next before he reacted. He was the epitome of control.

Except in her chamber when she'd pleasured herself before him. His mind had definitely not been leading his actions in those moments. Despite herself, she took great pride in that fact.

"Then you understand we must be rid of him."

"No." Selena shook her head. "Major Fletcher is here under false pretences. I can only imagine the horrible lies my stepchildren told him and threats they held over his head. I won't see him dead because of them. Not when they wanted me dead or worse. I will not sacrifice his life for my freedom."

Isadora sighed heavily. "Then what do you suggest? For the sake of the temple, I cannot allow him to leave."

Selena stepped around her friend, affording herself a long, appraising glance at the man whose life was in her hands. He was even more handsome than she believed during the passionate moments in her bedchamber. His body was hard and lean, muscled from his years in the military. And his face had a sense of wisdom to it. An intelligence and experience that drew Selena in.

But those weren't the only reasons why she was drawn to him. Just his mere presence had triggered her most powerful orgasm to date. And when he'd told her he was responsible for her husband's death, she had wanted nothing more than to give herself to him as a reward for ending the life of a man who had tormented her for years. She was in debt to him, much as he believed he was in debt to her stepchildren. Because of Gavin, she was free from her husband's cruelty. She had to save his life.

"Let me keep him."

Isadora's mouth fell open. "Did I hear you correctly?"

Selena drew an unsteady breath. She was shocked to hear the words, herself. "I know you have been frustrated with me since my arrival. I haven't chosen my first man since we landed on the island. I've been living on the fringes of the group, watching, but never participating."

Her friend shrugged one shoulder. "You will choose a man when you find the one who suits you. Until you let go of all your inhibitions, I know you'll find it difficult to be with someone you aren't comfortable with."

Selena motioned toward Gavin. "What if this man is the one?"

Isadora shook her head in disbelief. "You truly want to choose *this* man for the ceremonies we perform here? For your pleasure, both in private and in the public forum? This man who wants to spirit you back to a life you loathed?"

Selena shrugged as Gavin lifted his gaze in her direction. The vivid blue of his eyes froze her in place as he gave her body a slow, sensuous sweep. Every nerve crackled with awareness as her body prepared itself for his touch. For him to take while she shivered around him.

"When he caught me in my bedroom, I was pleasuring myself in the mirror," she said softly. "But he wasn't horrified as many repressed society gentlemen would have been if they'd encountered such a scene. In fact, seeing me do that excited him."

"There are many men here who would be happy to watch you do the same," Isadora argued.

She shook her head. "But he is the first man *I* want to give myself to." She looked her friend in the eye. "I want him. My body aches for his touch. I may not be as experienced in the pleasures of the body as you are, but I know he wanted me in my room. If I touched him, he wouldn't resist. In fact, I think he would have me trembling in a moment."

Isadora looked at Gavin with an appraising tilt of her head. "He is magnificent, I must admit that. So strong and handsome. But with something more there than just his looks."

Selena refused to look at the distracting Major. She had to convince Isadora to allow Gavin to live. "Our studies of Aphrodite tell us the goddess was able to control a man with her sensuality. If what we teach here is true, I ought to be able to do the same. If I can put him under my spell, I can make him do whatever I wish. I can insure he'll never speak of this place or my presence here."

Her friend nodded. "Making a man like that bend to your will won't be easy." She smiled. "But trying would be most entertaining."

Without another word, Isadora slipped from the alcove and returned to the main temple floor. She mounted the platform and seated herself on the throne.

"Selena has chosen her first mate. This is a great honor, for this man will be her tutor as she enters the world of Aphrodite. As her sensuality awakens, he will benefit from her desires." She looked over her shoulder at Selena with a sly wink. "Selena?"

Her hands trembling, Selena took a few steps forward. She remembered watching other women choose their mates and tried to follow the ritual as well as she could. With a flick of her wrist, she unhooked the mother-of-pearl clip that held her thin chiton over her covered breast. The cotton swished down until she was naked from her waist up. Gavin's eyes widened impossibly, but he didn't move.

Fighting the urge to cover her nudity, Selena stepped closer and closer to the man who had intruded into her home and her sanctuary.

She drew in a whiff of his scent, manly and clean even in the oppressive heat of the hall. Reaching out, she pressed her palm against his chest. His heart throbbed against her hand, wild with desire he didn't visibly show.

When he reached for her, the guards grabbed his arms and held him steady, forcing him to remain passive as was the way of the ritual. Here women had the power to choose, at least the first time.

She glided her hands up his chest, burned by his heat even through his white shirt. His taut muscles contracted with every stroke. She cupped his cheeks and lowered her trembling mouth to his. Just as she was about to take his kiss, he tipped his head up and claimed her mouth. His tongue speared between her lips, lapping at her like a thirsty man who could only be satisfied by her touch.

She wrapped her arms around his neck. God, how she wished his arms were free to hold her. Still, as she leaned her full weight against him, the thrust of his erection pressed into her belly, letting her know just how much he wanted her.

Her womb contracted with the feel of it, and her heart fluttered. With difficulty, she pulled back and whispered the words in Greek.

"You are mine until I choose to set you free."

To her surprise, he seemed to understand. His eyes darkened with desire. In a rough voice, he answered her in English. "Then take me."

Chapter Three

Gavin locked gazes with Selena. Her eyes were the darkest green he'd seen in all his travels, and impossibly wide with thrilling desire. Never before had a woman looked at him like that.

Genteel women hid their feelings in English society. They weren't allowed to be any one extreme or another. But Selena . . . Selena was different in more ways than one. She wanted him, needed him and wasn't afraid to show her desire or the myriad of other emotions that played across her face.

With her honesty, something remarkable happened. His regrets no longer tormented him as they had since David Kelsey's life bled away. Even the sting of physical pain in his injured arm faded into the background. And his sense of duty? His obligation to Kelsey's family?

All those thoughts disappeared as her bare breasts brushed the rough fabric of his shirt and her warm body molded to his. Everything in his heart, his body and his mind focused on her. He wanted her, despite being surrounded by strangers who would have him dead to protect themselves.

Strangely, having their gazes on him only inflamed his need all the more. With a shrug of his shoulders, he yanked away from the guards and freed his hands. They trembled for a brief moment before he finally did what he'd been aching to do since that afternoon in the Kelsey sitting room.

He touched Selena. She shut her eyes with a tiny sigh as he glided his fingertips up her exposed arms. Her skin was so impossibly soft, so supple. The reality of Selena Kelsey was far more than any fantasy. If he didn't have her soon, he feared he would explode with pent up emotions and unsatisfied need.

As his control wavered, he gripped her upper arms tighter. The rougher touch seemed to break the spell she was under. With a soft gasp, she pulled back, eyes glazed.

"Oh, my." Isadora's taunting voice shook him from his distraction. "I never would have guessed it, but this looks like it will work out well." She stepped closer and ran a finger down the line of Gavin's shirt buttons. "Very, very well."

Selena stepped away. Her gaze shifted to her friend and some of the strong emotion faded. "Y-yes."

The other woman gestured for Gavin to approach her. She leaned close until her mouth was just a fraction of an inch from Gavin's ear. "When Selena has tired of you, come to me. Seeing you touch her like that has made me want you next."

When she leaned back, it was with a feline smile Gavin refused to return. Did she really think he would come to her bed when she had given the order to have him killed?

Isadora didn't seem offended by his scowl. "Take your Major back to your rooms, Selena. You can explain . . ." Her wicked smile was once again directed toward Gavin. "*Everything* to him. Prepare him for his first ritual tonight."

Gavin shivered at the unknown nature of her order. Ritual? Selena's journal had explained many things, but most had to do with her own burgeoning desires, not the true nature of Aphrodite's cult.

His mind spun with questions now that he was to be a participant in the group's activities. He gazed around at the crowd, their garb fashioned after ancient times. Somehow he doubted the twenty or so people who stared like he was some caged lion would explain anything to him. In fact, most continued to glare with unabashed anger, even hatred that he had intruded into their secret society. He would wait to ask his questions when he was alone with Selena.

The thought sent a fresh wave of desire and lust through him. Alone. Able to do anything he desired. He was afraid what he wanted right now was nothing more than a heated, quick coupling.

She turned to him with a smile that was surprisingly shy for a woman who was half-naked and had already passionately kissed him in front of a large group of people. She reached for him and took his hand. Sparks of desire arced from their intertwined fingers and had his cock at full attention.

"Come, Major Fletcher. I'll answer your questions when we return to my room." She glanced back over her shoulder at him with a bold look. "All your questions."

Selena paced across her chamber, lighting a few lamps and straightening her bedclothes as she went. Why was she so nervous?

Stopping, she peered over her shoulder to look at Gavin. He stood by her door, appearing much as he had when he caught her pleasuring herself. A wash of desire worked through her with the memory. *He* was why she was nervous.

He was a stranger. Sent to take her back to a life she loathed. And yet, she ached for his touch. Her desire for him went deeper than mere physical attraction, yet she couldn't explain it. Not to herself. And certainly not to him.

Now she was alone with him. She'd chosen him to be the first man she would take to her bed since her husband. This dangerous man who brought out needs she hadn't realized she had, even as she allowed her sexuality to be awakened by the teachings of the temple.

She sighed. The temple. There was no doubt this man had questions about the temple, the cult and what they did here. How could she tell him enough to soothe his fears about what would happen to him without telling him so much that he could destroy the group?

When she paced passed the mirror, she caught Gavin watching her. Her cheeks heated with embarrassment. Oh, what if she did this all wrong? What if she hurt her friends? Or worse, what if she disappointed him, proving she wasn't really a sensual being at all? Proving she belonged in the straight-laced society she hated and fled from.

"Now that you have me here," he said softly when it became more and more apparent she couldn't find words to speak. "What will you do?"

She struggled with an answer for a moment before her eyes fell on the large metal tub in the middle of her room. It had been filled, probably on Isadora's orders. Steam rose from the water.

"You must be tired from your long journey. A bath has been drawn for you. First you will wash, then we'll discuss our options." She was surprised how cool and strong her voice sounded when nerves caused her whole body to tremble.

"Very well." Still he didn't move away from the door and continued to watch her with caution. "I'll bathe if that's what you want, but why don't we talk while I do so?"

She nodded once. "Fine. Undress."

He looked around the room, then at her. "In front of you?"

She was pleased that his eyes widened. Obviously, he was as unnerved by the situation as she was. Probably even more so since he didn't understand where he was and his life had already been threatened.

She paused at that thought. No matter what Isadora wanted, Selena wasn't going to allow him to be killed.

She managed a smile. "Do you have something to hide, Major?"

Now it was his mouth that quirked up with arrogance. He reached up to the collar of his shirt and slid each button free. "Absolutely not. The only one in this room who has secrets is you."

She pursed her lips. How dare he take that taunting tone when she had saved his life not half an hour before? She opened her mouth to retort when he freed his shirt from his trouser waist and pulled it over his head. Then all words, all coherent thoughts disappeared.

Gavin Fletcher had felt good beneath her hands when she touched him. He had looked good in his fitted clothing. But it was nothing compared to the way he looked naked. His shoulders were broad and his arms rippled with muscles. The only marring element was a long scar jutting down his left arm. His chest was magnificently muscled with a peppering of dark chest hair that tapered into a V and disappeared into the waistband of his trousers.

She shivered as she pictured rubbing her breasts against that chest. Having those muscular arms hold her. Those strong, skilled hands touch her in every aching place. It was a body made for pleasure.

Hers and hers alone.

"Oh," she whispered as she tried to make herself stop staring. She was giving him power by making her needs so obvious, yet she couldn't control herself.

"I take that as a compliment," he said softly, though his voice had taken a husky timbre that resonated through her blood stream and vibrated through every sensitive part of her body.

He came further into the room and sat down on one of the simple, soft armchairs beside a window. He never broke eye contact with her as he lifted his foot to rest on his knee and began to unlace his boots.

Selena found herself gliding across the floor toward him. She sank down on her knees at his feet and whispered, "Let me help you."

He watched as she glided her fingers up the soft leather boot and finished the work he'd started. When her fingertips brushed his bare calf beneath his trousers, he shut his eyes with a moan.

"I'm glad you weren't my valet in the field," he murmured. "I would have died from distraction."

She smiled as she worked each boot from his feet. She ran her fingers to his knee and sighed. "You said I was keeping secrets." His eyes came open to meet hers, and she nearly tumbled backward at the piercing blue fire that captured her stare. "I suppose I am. And I cannot promise you I won't continue to keep secrets. But I will tell you everything I can in order to keep you safe while you're here."

"Can you really do that?" He pushed off the chair and began to unbutton his pants. Finally, he shoved his trousers and drawers around his ankles and stepped free. He was gloriously naked, not a foot in front of her.

She suddenly couldn't find enough breath to speak, let alone coherent words to answer his question. She was too mesmerized by every line of his strong body. His upper body she'd already worshipped, but his legs were no less developed. He was lean and hard. And the hardest part of all was the cock that now thrust toward her.

He was much bigger than her late husband had been. She found herself wanting to touch.

To suck.

To take deep inside her sheath, ride him until she screamed his name.

On trembling knees, she shoved to her feet and motioned to the tub. "Why don't you get into your bath, Major?"

To her surprise, he stepped toward her instead of away. Their bodies brushed just a fraction, but the tiny touch sent off explosions of lust inside her. She shuddered uncontrollably.

"Gavin," he corrected softly. "I have a feeling it's far too late for formalities, Selena."

She swallowed hard as she motioned toward the tub a second time. "Yes."

His smile warmed her heart before he followed her order and climbed into the painted metal tub. When his body hit the hot, clean water, he hissed out a sound of pleasure that rocked her body. She wanted to force that same sound from his lips when she touched him, pleasured him. Settling back and resting his arms against the tub edge, he looked at her evenly.

"So tell me."

She shook her head, trying to clear her thoughts. She was reeling from the sensual assault he was unleashing on her with his body, his deep voice, his male scent. She was supposed to be seducing him, taking *his* power away through sex, not the other way around.

"About what?"

He arched an eyebrow. That was a foolish thing to say. It was obvious what he meant. He wanted to know about the temple. About her plans to keep him safe from Isadora and her minions.

Crossing over to the tub, she sank down on her knees on the cushioned bench next to it and reached over to a silver tray which held soaps and perfumed oils. She took a bar of fragrant soap and rolled it in her hand nervously.

"I read your diary."

She gasped as the soap slipped through her fingers to hit the water with a splash. Gavin turned his face away from the splatter.

"That isn't possible," she whispered. Her voice trembled, no matter how she tried to control it. "I destroyed it."

"One of the Kelsey's maids rescued it from the fire. Your stepchildren gave it to me so I could find you." Gavin reached into the water and retrieved the missing soap. With a soft smile, he handed the wet bar back to her. "And it worked because I'm here."

She sighed. "Damn that Maude. I knew I couldn't trust her." So he knew at least part of her story. He'd read her deepest desires and about her most depraved adventures. Yet he was still here. And need was in his eyes, not judgment or censure. With care, she began to soap her hands. "If you've read the journal, than you need no explanation."

He shook his head, but he was staring at her soapy hands. His pointed, heated stare brought a new flush of desire through her. Every nerve ending seemed more focused, sensitive. Even the brush of wet soap on her fingers made her pussy clench and her nipples tingle. How did he do that with just a look?

"Yes, I do need an explanation," he rasped out. "The diary wasn't complete."

The room was growing hotter. She rolled the soap over her hands again and again. The want that crackled between them made it impossible for Selena to keep her well-practiced guard up.

"What do you know?"

"I know you felt little sadness when Colonel Kelsey died. That you already knew Isadora, but after his death she began to introduce you to a life somehow related to Aphrodite. You liked the things she—"

He cut off with a moan as Selena finally put the soap on the edge of the tub and let her fingers dance across his damp chest. She let out her own sigh of pleasure as skin touched skin. The wet slide of the soap suds left no friction, and her hands glided easily along his impossibly hot body. She wove her nails through the dusting of wiry hair and sucked in a breath at the way the rough curls rasped and bunched against her soapy palms.

She dipped lower, gliding each hand against his nipples. They hardened beneath her touch, just as her own were doing. Did his nipples tingle with maddening pleasure as much as hers?

Her fingers brushed lower, lower, moving toward the one part of him she wanted to touch most. But she only teased her hand below the water's surface, trailing her fingers against the muscles of his abdomen instead of grasping his fine cock in hand. There would be time for that later, and the anticipation was too enjoyable to cut it off so soon.

"Go on, Major." Her voice was now just as husky as his had been earlier. "Finish your story."

He swallowed as he shifted in the tub. Through the soapy water, she could see his cock. It was hard, thrusting toward her with uncontrolled need. A need her body echoed with a growing ache, an increasing wetness.

"You liked what Isadora exposed you to," he continued. He reached out as he spoke and pressed a wet hand against her covered breast. A ragged cry burst unbidden from her lips at the touch as the water made her chiton transparent. Her nipple was clearly outlined as if she were nude. "I read your stories about watching her. About watching others when they made love. Your descriptions and your reactions. They . . ."

He trailed off, rubbing his thumb against her wet breast in a slow rhythm that drove Selena mad with want. Her breasts tingled and sent an answering ache through her body to the slick nub of her clit. She squirmed in the hopes she could ease some of the pleasurable frustration, but could find no relief.

"They what?" she managed to whisper.

"They made me want you." He locked gazes with her and she was lost in blue. "Your diary and your picture drove me to find you, and not just because of my sense of duty to your late husband and his family."

She drew back in shock. "So you came all the way to Cyprus—?"

"Because I wanted you." His hand moved to her other breast, massaging gently and sending a burst of pleasure through Selena's body. Wetness slid down her thighs, and the ache was unbearable.

She wasn't going to deny herself any longer.

Pushing off the side of the tub, she leaned in to kiss him. He took what she offered greedily, winding his wet fingers into her hair. Its strands came down around their faces in a wave, rolling onto his soapy chest and into the water.

He caught her shoulders and pulled her even closer until her upper body molded to his. The water slapped against her skin. With a growl of frustration, she pulled away just long enough to climb into the tub and straddle his lap.

He kissed her, drawing her in deeper and deeper even as he shoved her sopping chemise up around her hips so that the thrust of his cock rubbed against her thigh. That touch of hard steel against her sensitive skin rocked her until she thought she would explode from touch alone.

He pulled back to cup her face, and the intensity in his eyes was almost too much to bear. "Later, later I'll kiss you all over. Later, we'll act out all those fantasies you wrote in your journal. But for now . . . now . . . I just want to be inside of you."

He said it almost apologetically, but she didn't want him to be sorry. She didn't need platitudes or preludes. All she wanted was to feel the iron thrust of him in the folds of her body. She wanted to grind down over him and ride him. She wanted everything.

Now.

"Yes, please, I want that, too," she groaned as she shifted over him to allow him better access to her dripping slit.

She expected him to slide his cock inside her with little pretense. In fact, she hoped he would. But when his fingers slid into her wet heat instead, she arched with unexpected pleasure.

No man had ever touched her like this. So intimate, so gentle and yet starting a fire that nothing but his cock would put out. She writhed, riding his hand as he slipped another finger inside. She was so close to coming, so close to losing control.

"It's been so long," she wailed as her head rolled back. "So long."

He nodded as he brushed his stubbly cheek against her breast. The friction was fantastic, and she rode his fingers even harder, coming ever closer to the brink.

He seemed to sense her crisis, for he withdrew his hand. She protested with a loud moan that echoed in the chamber. "Don't go," she murmured as she leaned down to kiss him.

"I'm not going anywhere," he promised as he positioned her above him.

No sooner were the words out of his mouth than he thrust up. Her body stretched to accommodate him as he filled her completely, molding with her body in every way possible. With just that one thrust, her body quivered on the edge of an amazing climax. He met her eyes and rocked out a second thrust that took her over that edge into blissful oblivion. A cry echoed around them, and she realized through a haze of explosive pleasure that it was her own.

She had experienced release by touching herself, but had never achieved orgasm through a man's touch. The difference was amazing. Her body trembled, the pleasure peaking up and down in long, powerful waves until she thought she would collapse in exhaustion. All the time, Gavin kept thrusting into her, holding her steady by her slippery hips.

The rhythm he set was far too good to just let him do all the work. She rode him, meeting his thrusts with equal passion, kissing him as deeply as he was delving into her body. Her soul.

Riding him brought her back to the trembling spasms of release so quickly that it shocked her. Gavin's face showed the strain as he tried to keep his own passion at bay. He was going to climax, just as she was. She wanted them to do it together.

"Kiss my breasts," she whispered, shocked she'd order him to do such a thing. Titillated to hear her voice say such sensual words.

He complied by taking her nipple between his lips and laving it with a rough tongue. The subsequent pleasure arced to every part of her body. It sharpened her awareness until finally she gripped his shoulders and rode out another powerful release.

"Now, Gavin," she cried out. "Now!"

Seeming to understand her order, he clenched her hips in an almost painful grip and let out a roar of pleasure as he pumped hot into her body, filled her with his essence.

With a groan, she sank forward to rest her head on his shoulder. They were both wet with sweat and bathwater, hot with exertion and long repressed desires.

She had never been so satisfied in all her life. How could she experience so much pleasure over and over again? It certainly explained why Isadora was devoted to her worship of Aphrodite. The exploration of sensual appetites was far more enjoyable than Selena had imagined, even in her most erotic dreams.

Without moving from her comfortable spot sprawled across his broad chest, she murmured, "I'm so glad you found me."

And it was true.

Chapter Four

Gavin swiped a damp lock of hair away from Selena's face as she rested her cheek against his chest. He wasn't sure how long they had been tangled together in the water. Time seemed slow and suspended, held still by his lazy, satiated state.

She didn't seem to be in any greater hurry to move than he was. When he touched her, she merely turned her face a fraction so she could smile up at him, then sighed as she snuggled back against his body.

He thought about what she'd said just after she exploded with her final orgasm.

She was so glad he found her.

It made no sense, but he mirrored that statement in his heart. Even though he knew so little about her, even though she was no more than a heated fantasy until a few hours before, he could no longer imagine his life before he knew her touch.

"Selena?"

She barely lifted her head with a sleepy, "Hmm?"

He sighed. Back to reality. One that could get him killed if he didn't regain some focus. "You never told me what this place is."

Her mouth thinned into a frown as she pushed away from his chest and sat up in the bathtub. Lukewarm water sloshed around them both, clinging to her sopping chemise as she dug around for the soap beneath their bodies. As she had been before they had made love, she went back to washing him as if nothing out of the ordinary had happened. As if his world hadn't been knocked out of its safe orbit by her touch.

"Aphrodite is the Greek goddess of sensuality and sex. I'm sure you gleaned that information from my journal," she explained as her hands glided over his skin in slick circles and sent shockwaves of awareness careening through his body.

He nodded, surprised that his need raged up again. It was as if he were a green boy of eighteen rather than a jaded man of thirty. Selena noticed his desire as well, for her eyes grew wide when her hand brushed the thickening thrust of his erection. Still, she continued her story.

"In ancient times, people worshipped her. They were called the Cult of Aphrodite, and they allowed themselves a free exploration of lust. Sensuality." She swallowed hard. "Love."

"Is that what this place is, then?" he managed to ask. What was left of his rational mind told him getting the answers that could save his life was more important than bedding Selena a second time. Still, his rational mind was fading behind the throbbing desires of his cock.

"Yes." She looked around the small room, and her eyes became distant with memory. "I met Isadora right before my husband left for India. I was both shocked by and drawn to her open personality. She has an uncommon zeal for life and for pleasure. One I envied."

Gavin looked at her sharply, surprised by this unexpected glimpse into Selena's past. It was like the pieces of the puzzle that made up this woman were coming together. She had been unhappy, not that he blamed her. He had met her stepchildren. But her unhappiness had been much deeper than simple regrets over marital choice.

"As she grew to know me better, Isadora told me more and more about her activities. Not just the scandalous tales of her bedroom escapades, but also about her beliefs. And the history of Aphrodite. But it was only after my husband died that I learned her real plans."

"And what were her real plans?" he whispered.

"To restart the cult. She wanted to bring women like me into her world. Women who were sensual. Women who wanted . . ."

She hesitated with a blush that made his entire body clench with need. How could a woman be so innocent and so sensual at the same time? Shifting, he let his erection rub against her leg. It was a sweet torture that nearly unmanned him.

"What did you want, Selena?" he asked without breaking eye contact.

Her eyes drifted shut with a quiet moan. "More. I wanted more."

Desire jolted through him like electricity, making him feel more alive than he had in months. He reached for her, but she avoided his touch and scrambled to her feet. In a stumbling motion, she got out of the tub. Her shift slopped water on the stone floor, but she hardly seemed to notice as she paced away to look back over her shoulder at him.

"Gavin, these men and women are serious about their lifestyle. They have taken vows which go beyond simple pleasure."

"What kind of vows?" he asked as he tried to rein in his disappointment at her departure.

"Vows to protect the temple." Her expression tightened. "At any cost. If the soldiers in Greece realize we have started a pagan temple here, they'll come for us. They'll destroy the temples. As for the people . . ." She broke off with a shiver, as if her words reflected her private fears. "The men will probably be only lightly punished. Society tends to forgive what they expect from what they call a man's uncontrollable desires. But the women . . ." Her face paled. "Women are not expected to be driven by passion. When they are, they are punished. It will be no different here. They will be returned to places from which there is no escape."

Gavin's mind slipped to Selena's stepchildren, of their plans to institutionalize her for what they claimed was for her own good. Except now that he had touched her, filled her, watched her face constrict with pleasure, he was sure hysteria didn't drive this woman. If that were true, how could she pull back when he touched her? Why would she be more driven to explain her actions than to make love to him again?

Protecting Selena wasn't what the Kelsey children truly wanted. Revenge for whatever wrong they believed she had done their father was more likely. And perhaps a chance to take her inheritance they had spoken of with such contempt.

He stood up, sloshing water over the edge of the tub as he reached for a towel on the table nearby. He wrapped it around his waist and crossed the room to be closer to her. Somehow he needed proximity, needed it as much as he needed to draw breath.

"I understand your fears," he said softly. "And I know you're desperate to protect your friends, but they have made it clear they'll kill me." He motioned his head toward the door. "Guards are just outside waiting for me to make the wrong move."

Her gaze dropped. "Yes, if they feel threatened by you, they will kill you. In their minds, it's the only way."

"Do you feel the same?"

"No, of course not!" Her gaze grew painfully distant for a second time as expressions flashed over her delicate features. "I was trapped once. I was dying inside. I would *never* be the cause of that to another person."

"Aren't I trapped now?" he asked softly. He reached out to run his finger down her cheekbone, dipped it beneath the curve of her chin. With gentle pressure, he tilted her face toward his. She shivered with the touch.

"I chose you." She looked into his eyes and raw need glittered in her stare. "Unless you do something to force their hand, these people will respect that choice and won't harm you."

He drew away in a flash of anger. He hated cages, even those that were infinitely pleasurable.

"And I am to do . . . what? Am I supposed to just resign myself to a life of serving your sexual needs? And when you've tired of me, am I to be passed to Isadora, as she asked?"

Selena's face froze into a mask of surprise and betrayal. "Isadora asked to have you?"

Gavin examined her closer. Was that jealousy? It was. And he liked it. Liked that her time on this island of freedom and passion hadn't taken away her natural desire to have one man and one man alone. That the man she wanted was him . . . at least for now.

"Yes. She told me to come to her when you finished with me," he admitted. Selena held his life in her hands. He couldn't be anything but honest with her, at least about this.

"I see," she said softly as she walked passed him back to the edge on the tub.

She slipped her hands beneath her soaking chiton's straps and shoved the entire contraption around her ankles. She snatched up a towel and began to blot droplets of moisture from her skin. The sight was so mesmerizing Gavin nearly didn't hear her when she spoke again.

"If you wish to stay here, wish to be with Isadora, I certainly won't stand in your way." She let out a soft sigh. "But if you would truly like to leave this island, return to England and your life there, I have a plan."

He murmured in agreement, but his attention remained focused on the soft towel. She brushed the fabric across her breasts and her nipples stood at full attention as she pushed the towel lower, lower. It brought him to mind of watching her pleasure herself. But now he knew what that body felt like, gripping him as she found her release.

"Gavin?" Her voice was husky.

"Yes?"

"Do you want to hear my plan?"

He struggled with an answer. Here he was facing questions about his life, his very survival, and yet all he could think about was the woman who stood staring at him. Her skin flushed as he drank in the sight of her gloriously naked body gleaming in the dying light of the afternoon sun.

"I do." He nodded as he swallowed past his dry throat. It was hard to breathe now, let alone speak. "But not right now. Come here."

Her eyes widened with understanding. His wants were clear, and she returned them. Her lids drooped as she slowly crossed the room in long, sure strides.

He didn't have to tell her what to do or what he desired. The moment she reached him, she wound her slender hands into his hair and kissed him. His knees nearly went out from under him with the force of his lust.

"The bed," she murmured against his lips.

He followed her order wordlessly, guiding her back across the room until he reached the bed. It was surrounded by a filmy canopy that he shoved back with growing impatience.

The coverlet was soft and pale, cool even though the room seemed impossibly hot. His bare knees brushed satin as he laid her back against the pillows. It was a bed meant for passion, and if he had his way, it would fulfill that purpose. He could only hope this time he would sweep her away with his lovemaking. In the tub he had been too needy, too quick and heated to act out the fantasies he'd composed in his head during the months of travel to Cyprus.

Now that he had slaked his desire, he was ready to do what he'd dreamed about. Ready to fulfill Selena's deepest desires. Ready to make her moan out his name.

"Lie back," he said softly as he settled his weight lightly against her. She was like heaven beneath him, soft and warm. She rose up to meet his body with a moan most of polite society would have called wanton.

It was like music to him.

"Gavin," she murmured, as she laced her fingers through his hair. "Oh, please."

He nodded. He knew what she wanted. She wanted his touch, his mouth, his body. She wanted to tremble beneath his thrusts, to cry out as she spasmed in delight and fulfillment.

He kissed her mouth for the briefest of moments. Just long enough to fill his senses with her flavor. Honeyed sweetness. He wondered if she tasted that way everywhere. There was nothing like a journey down her body to find out.

She gasped as he dragged his lips down the column of her throat, nipping her collarbone as he massaged his fingers into her hips. She arched in encouragement, sighing as his mouth closed over one taut nipple. Her breath came shorter as he suckled her. It was almost as if she would explode if he did so much as touch her.

The temptation was too much. Sliding his hand down, he urged her legs apart and brushed a thumb across her sex. She let out a wail that filled the room, then her cries grew louder when he repeated the action and at the same time, entered her with a finger. She bucked beneath him, quivering out a release that went on and on until she begged for mercy he refused to give. When she finally relaxed against the pillows, he withdrew his hand from her warm body with reluctance and returned to his odyssey of taste.

His lips moved over her belly. Pausing only to dip his tongue into her navel, he continued. Lower and lower, ever closer to her center, ever closer to heaven. She seemed to come out of her haze just as he pressed a kiss against her inner thigh.

"Gavin?" Her voice was tense, questioning.

In the entries of her diary, Selena had written about this act. She'd read about it in the erotic stories Isadora had shared, and even seen it while she watched Isadora play her sex games. The entries were filled with such curious longing that he doubted Selena's selfish husband had ever given her such pleasure. It thrilled him to know he would be the first man to taste her so intimately.

The first stroke of his tongue elicited a surprised gasp from her lips. He didn't pause to let her become acclimated to this new invasion, but tasted her again in a long sweep. This time she arched up, gripping at the sheets with both hands.

"Please," she wailed. "It's too much."

"There's never too much when it comes to pleasure," he whispered against her, then dragged his tongue across her wet slit another time.

Her legs drooped wider naturally, opening her to him like the petals of a flower. Within the folds he found the nub of her clit and concentrated his attention on it. He teased her with his fingers, stroking her with sure touches until the little bud swelled and darkened. Finally, he dipped his head and took it between his lips. When he sucked her gently, she exploded, writhing above him with a series of uncontrolled cries.

When she shuddered one final time, she propped herself up on her elbows to look down at him. Her eyes were wild, filed with desire and other emotions he dared not label.

"Come up here," she said softly. "I want to feel you inside me."

He nodded, his cock aching as he rose up on his knees. "Turn around."

She did as he'd asked, glancing back over her shoulder with wary interest.

"You described this in your journal," he said softly as he grasped her hips and rubbed his iron cock against her backside.

"Yes," she murmured. "I saw a picture in one of Isadora's books. Later, I saw it acted out. Both here and on the ship."

"Why did you want this?"

As he spoke, he positioned himself at her cleft, nudging back the wet, heated folds with the head of his erection.

She shivered and gripped the headboard with both hands. "It's so primal. Animal. Possessive. To drive into a woman from behind is to make her yours. Really yours, not like the romantic drivel in some books."

"Then you . . ." He drove hard inside her. "Are mine."

Her hands tightened on the headboard as she flexed around him. "Oh yes. I'm yours."

To accentuate that promise, she leaned forward and slammed herself back, setting a hard, rough pace for their sex that drove Gavin to the edge almost immediately. He closed his eyes as her body welcomed him in, massaging him to the brink with heat and wetness.

It took effort to exert control over his raging lust. He wasn't going to make this another quick coupling like in the bathtub where the sensations rose and fell in a flurry.

He slid his hands up her hips to cup her breasts. Rolling sensitive nipples between his fingers, he eased her up until she was upright on her knees. She could no longer move forward and back without separating their bodies. Instead, he ground inside her in slow, purposeful circles while one hand found its way back to her clit. He stroked her between his thumb and forefinger as her cries grew louder and more intense.

Leaning forward, he pressed a kiss against her damp neck. "Is it everything you hoped for? Fantasized about?"

She nodded with a moan. "You are more than any fantasy. You're better than all my dreams."

On the last syllable, her spine stiffened and her body clenched around him like a vice. She shattered and he joined her, filling her with his essence as he wondered if he could truly live up to the expectations of her dreams.

Especially when those dreams would keep him trapped on this island forever.

Chapter Five

Selena draped the thin chiton over her shoulder and adjusted her naked breast. When her thumb brushed her nipple, it swelled and hardened, made ultra sensitive by Gavin's touch. In fact, her whole body hummed with anticipation and a powerful desire that didn't seem to stay satiated for more than an hour at a time. She finally understood why Isadora was so driven to fulfill her baser needs.

"You're sure this is what I have to wear?"

She turned to watch Gavin struggle with his loincloth. He looked magnificent with his bare chest and long, naked legs. Like a god from an ancient fairytale, come to Earth to bring pleasure. And she was the one lucky enough to be the recipient of that gift. At least for a little while.

The only thing that marred the perfect image was the scar that ran down his arm. How had he gotten it? Despite their passionate joining, she didn't feel close enough to delve into something so private.

"That's the traditional garb for this ceremony," she said with an apologetic shrug.

He took a glance in the mirror. "I feel ridiculous. And if there's a breeze, this isn't going to keep me covered."

"Then I'll pray for strong winds." She laughed as she looked him up and down. Seeing him so exposed made her want to touch him. More than touch. She wanted to drop to her knees and take him into her mouth. It was only the time constraints that kept her from doing just that. With a shiver, she said, "I must say, I've never seen another man wear it better."

He smiled as he walked across the room and took her into his embrace. A feeling of warmth and safety surrounded her. She hadn't felt like that for so long she barely even remembered it.

The thought was so startling she had to force herself not to shrug away from him.

He seemed to sense her tension and looked down into her face with concern. "Selena, is anything wrong?"

She forced a smile. How could she explain that in the span of a few hours, she felt closer to him than she'd felt to anyone in her entire life? She barely knew him. And he had been sent to destroy her dreams and return her to a life of repression and torment.

"I'm just—" she stammered as she searched for a good explanation for her sudden shift in emotions. "I was just thinking about how dangerous your position here is."

Now it was his turn to stiffen as he released her and turned away. Yet when he looked back at her, it was with a wicked grin. "We were *distracted* before you could tell me about your grand plan to protect me. Would you care to share that with me now?"

She couldn't help but laugh at his teasing, even though she sensed the seriousness of his question. She held the key to his fate, and he knew as little about her as she knew about him.

"Of course," she began. But before she could finish, there was a loud rap at her door. "Yes?"

The two guards who had been standing watch for the past few hours entered the room. Both men sent menacing glares in Gavin's direction before they spoke to her in Greek.

"The ceremony is beginning. You and the prisoner have been ordered to come with us to the temple."

Selena frowned. "He's not a prisoner. He is my chosen mate, and you will treat him with respect." She folded her arms and met each of the men's eyes. "Is that clear?"

"Yes, Selena," one of the men answered, his voice dark and sullen like a petulant child. "Still, Isadora asks for your presence."

"Thank you." She turned to Gavin with a smile. "They've told me—"

"That it's time to go to the ceremony," he said softly. "I know."

She started. "You speak Greek?"

"Yes." He shrugged. "I was originally to be stationed in Greece, but ended up in India instead."

Blushing, she turned away. Earlier when she had spoken her words in Greek in the temple and he had replied, she believed it was the heat and power of the moment that had helped him understand what she meant. She'd never thought he spoke the ancient language. Somehow she felt exposed because she had defended him to the guards.

He reached out to take her arm as they followed the guards down the sandy path to the temple. "Thank you," he whispered.

Just the benign touch of his hand sent shivers up her spine. "You're welcome," she murmured as they reached the temple.

It was the same building where Gavin's 'trial' had been held earlier in the day. When they stepped inside to reveal the high pillared ceiling and deep pit, he stiffened.

"Don't worry," she whispered before she was forced to walk away and prepare for her part in the ritual. "It won't be like before, I promise you."

Before he could reply, the guards motioned him to move away to be with the other men of the group. There he would be prepared and given instructions on his part in the nightly ritual. She could only hope he would understand and comply with what he was to do.

A man like him would be used to being in control. He wouldn't like taking orders from his captors. The ritual might even seem like the perfect opportunity for escape, and if he tried that . . . well, she shuddered to think of the consequences. Her intervention wouldn't stop his execution this time.

"My, my," Isadora said as she approached Selena to ready her for her part in the night's events. "I would have captured you an officer long ago if I had known it would be like this."

"Like what?"

Selena glared at her friend. Knowing how Isadora had offered Gavin a place in her bed sparked a curious jealousy in Selena. One that had no place here. Freedom was the mantra of the Cult of Aphrodite. Possessiveness had no place.

But it didn't erase the fact that Selena didn't want her friend anywhere near the handsome Major. Not after what they had shared.

"You actually look satiated. In fact, I've never seen you so relaxed." Isadora folded her arms and gave Selena a feline smile. "Of course a man like that would be to any woman's liking. Is his body as magnificent as it appeared to be this afternoon?"

She gritted her teeth. "The Major is everything I wished him to be."

Isadora's eyebrow arched. "No details? Very well. Does your soldier know what to do tonight?"

"It is being explained to him at present."

"What about you? Do *you* understand?"

She frowned. "Of course. I've seen this ritual many times since my arrival. I have chosen Gavin, claimed him in my bed. Now it's his turn to choose me in a reflection of the rituals of old. If he doesn't want me, he may pick another. Then the ritual starts again."

A curious ache filled her at that thought. What if she hadn't pleased Gavin the way he had fulfilled her? What if he wanted to take Isadora's offer of a more experienced bedmate? After the horrors of war, a soldier could easily wish to sink into the pleasures of sex for a while. And then Selena would be alone again and Gavin . . .

Gavin would be in more danger than he comprehended.

All she could hope was that he would choose her. To save his own life and for the sake of her burgeoning desires.

❧

The shiny, metal mask constricted his nose and reduced his peripheral vision. Gavin hated it. He hated the idea he could be attacked at any moment, especially in this volatile place ruled by sex and emotion.

More than that, he hated what the mask represented. He had been told in the old days of the temple, a woman would prostitute herself to a stranger, allowing any man to choose her in the name of Aphrodite. The mask he wore now made him that stranger. It gave him the right to choose his bedmate. He could take Selena, confirm he wished to be her pick until her induction was over.

Or he could walk into the crowd and take any other woman. Including Isadora Glasier. He had no doubt the red head could destroy him if she wished, but she'd made it clear she wanted him in her bed, too. After a few weeks with her, he was sure he could find a way to make it off the island.

"Get out into the pit, you son of a bitch soldier."

The guard pushed him none too gently out of the hallway. Gavin stumbled into nearly the same place where he'd stood during his 'trial' that afternoon.

Was it only that afternoon? It seemed like a lifetime ago.

He gathered his composure and slowly walked into the center of the pit.

"The stranger approaches." Isadora's voice echoed in the darkened room. She sat high above the small crowd in her throne. He couldn't see her in the darkness, but he heard the sneer in her voice.

This evening only a few torches lit the room, and they all surrounded the spot where Selena stood waiting. She looked so beautiful bathed in torchlight. The fire danced off her tanned skin, reflected in her eyes. Yet she seemed nervous, fearful.

Unlike him, her life wasn't threatened in this strange place of sex and violence. Was she concerned about his safety? Or did she fear he wouldn't choose her as she had chosen him? That he would take his chances with another woman.

In that instant, he knew he wouldn't betray her. Not after everything they had shared. What they had experienced together was more than any other woman could offer him. And he was willing to risk personal safety for even just a few more of those stolen moments in Selena's arms.

"Choose from all the women here," Isadora said softly. "You may have the one who has picked you, or you may take any another to your bed. Aphrodite teaches us freedom is the only way."

He looked up at Isadora, seated in her throne of marble, above all others in the temple. Though the firelight was dim, he now caught the gleam in her eyes. To her, this was all some twisted game. The island. Sex. Him. Even Selena was a toy to her. One he was sure she would destroy if it suited her purpose.

He broke their stare to turn his attention to Selena. She avoided making eye contact when he tried to capture her gaze. She shifted nervously. Even when he started across the pit toward her, her body remained tense and ramrod straight.

Stopping in front of her, he briefly thought of the instructions he'd been given. He was supposed to remove her chiton, bare her body to the entire group, then stake his claim right then and there with the members of the temple looking on. His claim was to be taken with the mask on, keeping him a 'stranger' as in the old ways.

Normally, he would have gone along with the twisted ritual, if only to make his captors think he had surrendered. But he didn't want to share the wonders they experienced together in front of the others in the temple. He wouldn't treat Selena like a common whore.

He slipped his fingers into the folds of her robe but didn't pull it away from her shoulders. The rough pads of his fingertips brushed her skin, teasing over her covered breast until both her nipples puckered. Her eyes drifted shut with a soft whimper he was sure only he heard. He dipped his hand lower, teasing her stomach and then casually cupping her sex. She was already dripping wet, hot as a fire and ready for him. She arched closer with a louder moan, and his cock throbbed in response.

Just as she dipped her head back, he withdrew his hand so he was only playing with the edging of her robe. "I choose you," he whispered for her hearing alone.

Her shoulders sagged with relief, and the tension bled away from her face. "Now you're to remove my clothing and stake your claim," she prompted. It was clear her reminder had as much to do with growing desire as with the dictates of the ritual.

He shook his head, though he wanted to do as she asked as much as he wanted to take his next breath. Instead, he raised his voice and said, "I came across an ocean to find you, Selena. I chose you the moment I saw your photograph. After finally having the chance to touch you, my choice is no different. I choose you. However, I also choose not to share you. Not now, and not until you have tired of me."

Reaching back, he yanked the mask free and tossed it across the marble floor. It clattered against the stone in front of the watching crowd in their ancient garb.

A murmur of surprise worked its way around the waiting group. Selena's face, which had softened during his initial declaration, paled. Her gaze shot up above in Isadora's direction. Gavin refused to do the same, even though he wondered how the other woman was taking his speech. He was flouting her rules without regard to the consequences. It could work or it could backfire with terrible results.

To his surprise, Isadora's husky laugh came out of the darkness above. "Your soldier is bold, Selena. I expect he is no different in your bed. If he will not claim you for the crowd to enjoy, then let the nightly festivities commence for the rest of us."

Gavin gave a long exhale in relief. His gamble had paid off. He caught Selena's hand and drew her up close to him. She pressed against him and gave him a small smile.

"You didn't want to share me?" she whispered.

He shook his head. "Never."

He swept her into his arms and turned toward the door. Unfortunately, he didn't get two steps toward the staircase leading out of the pit when the guards blocked the exit, spears raised in readiness.

Selena shook her head. "Once the ritual starts, no one is allowed to enter or exit."

"The ritual?" he asked.

She laughed. "You haven't noticed?" She pointed over his shoulder.

Gavin turned and nearly dropped Selena. He had been so wrapped up in her that he hadn't notice the crowd. The dozen or so women in the group, including Isadora, had lined themselves up on one side of the pit. On the other, the same number of men watched and waited in a group. Slowly, each woman removed her chiton and stepped away. The men did the same with their loincloths.

Isadora cupped her own breasts, strumming her nipples as she looked at the now naked crowd. "I want you." She pointed to one of the men. "And you." Another stepped forward at her order.

The remaining crowd watched as the two approached their leader. As Isadora deeply kissed one, the other dropped to his knees, spread her legs and began to lick her slit. Her head dipped back as the second man went to work on her breasts.

"The rest of you," she panted, "may choose."

Immediately, the crowd of men and women came together. Without ceremony, one man bent a woman over a marble bench and thrust into her with a rough, hard rhythm, while at the same moment she took another man's cock deep into her throat.

Two women chose each other, laying head to foot as they licked each other with enthusiastic moans. Men and women lay in piles, hands stroking over skin, cocks plunging into mouths and pussies.

Moans and cries echoed around Gavin and Selena as the sharp scent of sex filled the warm air.

"*This* is a nightly ritual?"

Selena nodded. "I've watched this every night for weeks." Her voice grew husky. "Aphrodite teaches us to enjoy the passions of the flesh. Without guilt or shame."

Gavin looked down at her. Her eyes were slightly glazed as she watched the group stroke and lick each other to orgasm. "But you never participated?"

She shook her head. "I wasn't allowed into the larger group until I picked my first mate. So I only watched. And pleasured myself."

Gavin groaned at the image of Selena watching and giving herself pleasure in reaction to the shocking, decadent display. He had to have her, but he didn't want to take her as part of this festival of lust.

She gave him a wicked smile and darted her tongue out to swipe along his exposed collarbone. "If you want privacy while we wait, I suggest one of the alcoves that face the sea. They're somewhat separate, though we can still be seen if someone chooses to look."

She glided her hand between them and gently caught his already hard cock. She stroked him only once before he grabbed her hand and strode toward the alcoves in the back of the temple.

There were four in all. Stone entryways that lead to a small room. Each had a low bench below an open window that faced the sea. In the distance, the sun was setting, sending a rainbow of colors to dance off the temple walls and set off the crowd in erotic shadow.

Gavin chose the alcove farthest from the temple's center in the hopes it would give them some privacy from the moaning, gasping crowd outside. He set her down, putting his back to the others to block any potential view they might have of her.

Selena looked at him with dark eyes that told a tale of desire he couldn't ignore. Her gaze held an appealing combination of innocence and want, the same duo that had driven him across the continent to find her.

"What you did tonight, it was dangerous. You shouldn't have thwarted Isadora's instructions."

"Perhaps you're right." He crooked his finger. "Come here."

She swallowed hard, then took a long step toward him and pressed flush against him. Her naked breasts dragged across his bare chest, sending a shockwave of desire to harden his cock painfully.

"Perhaps I *should* have taken this scrap of fabric from your body." He slipped his fingers into her robe, but this time he yanked, and the flimsy contraption fluttered around her feet. "Perhaps I should have spread you open for the world to see and suckled you all over."

Her breath caught as he dipped his head to catch one pebble-hard nipple between his lips. He sucked, and she arched beneath him with a little cry that was almost lost in the sounds of the sexual frenzy going on in the room behind them.

"Gavin," she moaned as her fingers slanted through his hair and pushed his head lower.

He followed her order and glided his tongue down over her belly. He dropped to his knees and breathed in the heady fragrance of her woman's scent. Her legs trembled as he pushed them apart and licked one long stroke across her heated sex.

"Yes," she hissed out low. "I wanted you to. I wanted to feel you so much, I didn't care who watched."

He slid his tongue across her again as an answer. When her hips thrust forward, he sank his fingertips into her skin to hold her steady. He wanted to torture her before he let her come. He wanted her to beg him, to plead for release.

Focusing his attention on her clit, he rolled his tongue over her and suckled her, taking her just to the edge of release, but never letting her have it. Finally, her hands clenched into his hair and pulled his head away until he was forced to look at her.

"Please," she murmured. Her flushed face was taut with the strain of want. Need. It gave him a rush of power to know he'd taken her so far with such little effort. "Please."

When she released his hair, he immediately obliged her. He buried one finger inside her clenching, hot sheath while he suckled her clit one last time. In a burst of wailing cries, she trembled around him, bucking wildly as her body found ultimate pleasure.

When she went limp and leaned against him, he slowly stood up. The length of her body rubbed against his as he came to his feet. With the cries of passion filling the room behind him, the feel of her nearly unmanned him. Holding her against his chest, he looked down into her eyes.

"I choose you, Selena," he whispered. "By doing so, I put my life in your hands."

She nodded once before she glided her breasts across his bare chest in a tortuously slow motion. "I know. Your trust is a great gift. I treasure it and your life. I swear I won't let you down."

His breath caught in his throat, cutting off any ability to form words or even coherent thoughts. His entire focus was on Selena, on the way she touched him, on the way her gaze came up to capture his. Her smile was gentle and then crooked with a wicked gleam as she began to slide her way down his body as he had done to her not moments before.

She pushed aside the loincloth and captured his cock in one hand. If he had thought himself hard before, his body now went twice as rigid, filling her hand with his heat. She gave a little laugh, then leaned forward to blow a puff of warm air across the head of his erection.

His knees trembled as a wash of ecstasy rushed through his every nerve. Even though he'd made love to her just hours before, when she touched him now it was like the first time. The need raged out of control, and he was ready to explode with just the right touch.

Except she didn't touch. She sucked. The very moment she ended her initial torture, she took his cock between her lips and sucked.

He delved his hands into her hair and cried out softly.

"Mmmm." She leaned back to see his face. "I've wanted to do that for hours."

Before he could answer, she drew him deep into her mouth, rolling her tongue around him until he had to brace himself on the wall behind her to keep from collapsing with pleasure.

Her rhythm was constant and as intense as her stare. Forward and back, deeply in and then almost all the way out. His balls tightened, his limbs grew heavy as he fought to keep from exploding with pleasure.

"It's too much," he groaned.

She darted out her pink tongue to trace just the head of his erection. "You told me there wasn't such a thing."

He grasped her by her upper arms and yanked her to her feet for a long, hot kiss.

She murmured something against his mouth, but he didn't hear it. Instead, he pressed her naked back against the stone wall, stepped between her legs and drove into her in one smooth thrust. She wrapped her arms around his shoulders and clung to him like he was a lifeline. Her nails dug into his back as he took her fast and hard. Riding every thrust with an equal measure of passion, she reached the brink with lightning speed and thrashed around him, rocking out her pleasure. He had no choice but to join her, pumping hot before he thrust one last time and claimed her as he hadn't in the room behind them.

The cool sea breeze stirred across Selena's arms. Her eyes fluttered open, and she watched the curtains billow from her place on her bed. Her place in Gavin's warm arms. The sun was just beginning to rise in the distance, bathing the world in shades of warm purple and pink.

Hazy memories returned to her. Gavin taking her again and again in the alcove at the temple. Carrying her back to her quarters once the ritual was over, to continue there long into the hot night.

With a sigh, she snuggled closer to the man beside her and laced her fingers through his. His hands were so big, so strong. As a soldier, he had been capable of great destruction with those hands. He'd caused death. But here, sheltered from the world, he only brought pleasure. His hands were gentle tools of love and life.

"You're awake," he murmured against her hair. His breath warmed her neck, and the warmth spread through her body, filling her with a sense of peace unlike any she'd ever known.

"I am. Were you watching the sunrise?" she asked as she glanced over her shoulder at him.

"No, I was watching you." He kissed her neck. "You're more beautiful than a hundred sunrises."

She laughed as she looked back out across the sea. "The sunrises on our island might prove you wrong." They lay in companionable silence for a moment before she said, "Why were you really awake, Gavin? Because I know I wore you out last night."

"You did." He chuckled, but it ended on a sigh. "But I can't help but be restless here. I'm a prisoner no matter how pretty a cage you put me in."

She stroked her fingers back and forth against the back of his hand. "Yes, I am sorry for that."

"I don't blame you." He shifted slightly so he could wrap one arm around her hip. "But you must understand, I'm not used to having so little control over my own destiny. To being under constant threat without having tools to fight back. And I'm not accustomed to depending on someone else. Not for my life or my freedom."

Regrets chilled her. "It must be all the worse for you since we never talked about my plan to help you, as I promised you we would."

He shrugged. "I told you at the ceremony last night that I put my trust in you. I assume eventually we'll stop making love long enough for you to tell me how you plan to help me escape this place with my life and manhood intact."

She rolled on her back to look up into his face. No man had ever made her the focus of such attention before. His blue eyes pierced all the way into her soul. She feared that intensity yet was also enthralled by it. Gavin seemed not only to see her every thought and feeling, but want to explore them to their deepest level.

He wanted her secrets, her desires . . . he wanted everything.

She traced his lips with her tongue. "I want to tell you my plan. I want to put your mind at ease before you put my body at ease."

The eyes that had pinned her with such intensity now softened with gratitude. "Very well."

Continuing to examine every curve of his face, she said, "In one week's time, the members of Isadora's temple will begin a grand celebration. With the change in season from summer to fall, they'll hold a festival of decadence, a sensual feast to honor Aphrodite. The entire cult will be distracted. It will be the perfect time for a prisoner to make an escape. Especially with my help."

He was quiet for a time as he traced her cheekbone with the back of his hand. Finally, he whispered, "And what will I do for the next week?"

She reached up to cup the back of his head and drew his mouth down until it was a mere breath from her own. "Be careful. Be safe. Be mine."

His head jerked back as he locked eyes with her. Slowly, he threaded his fingers through her tangled hair. "I may have chosen you last night, but I am *yours,* Selena. I have been since the moment I saw your picture."

His mouth descended, and this time he didn't hesitate to kiss her. She was stunned by his declaration, even as she was swept away by the pressure of his lips. He belonged to her? The idea made her heart soar, even while her stomach dropped. She had vowed never to let a man into her heart, never be subjected to the demands of one person ever again. Yet Gavin was a temptation she couldn't seem to resist.

One she didn't *want* to resist.

She stroked her tongue against his, and the tug of desire grew from the tips of her breasts all the way to her clit. With just a touch, he made her want. With a kiss, he melted her. And when he entered her, she forgot all about the rest of the world, and her focus shifted to him and only him.

His fingers slid down the apex of her body with lazy intent, playing over her nipples, then settling between her legs to nudge at her clit. A moan escaped her lips as that familiar spike of pleasure wracked her body.

Pulling back, he looked down into her eyes. His hand stilled, trapping her between explosive pleasure and the pain of withdrawal. "Will you come with me when I leave?"

She struggled to respond, stunned by his question. How could she answer that?

Even though he had only been on the island for a short time, the idea of his departure stung. How could she lose him when they just found each other? Pain mushroomed in her heart at the thought of never seeing him again.

But she was still unsure about his motivation. Here on the island he was willing to let her do as she pleased, but if she went with him, would his sense of duty return?

Here she was an erotic distraction, but away from this place rules and regulations might make him regret his choice of a sensual woman. Then what?

Would he take her back to London and her stepchildren? Doom her to thc fate they had planned for her?

She wanted to trust him, but trust was something she gave reluctantly. She had paid a heavy price for it in the past. She didn't want to pay again.

His fingers twitched across her slit, erasing her thoughts and fears in a wave of pleasure. Before his mouth came down on hers, Selena caught a glimpse of Gavin's expression.

Disappointment hardened his features.

"Gavin—" She wanted to explain even if she didn't know the words to say.

He didn't allow her any further opportunity. His tongue delved between her lips as he rolled on top of her. His fingers continued to move inside of her with slick insistence until she arched up with a cry of release.

No sooner had she found completion then he pushed her legs open and pressed the head of his cock against her. Bracing one hand on either side of her head, he looked down at her. She rose up to kiss him, but he held back, keeping out of her reach as he slowly entered her just an inch.

She groaned, clenching him. This was punishment. He had given her pleasure, but now he was going to torture her to show her how unhappy he was that she couldn't answer his question.

"Gavin, I—"

"Shhh," he admonished and glided another inch inside. Her body stretched deliciously to accommodate his hard cock.

Her eyes fluttered shut with a soft sigh.

"Look at me," he said.

When she did as he ordered, he moved even further into her. With their eyes locked, the sensations became even more intense, more focused. Her world started to revolve around pleasure. If he didn't move all the way inside, she was sure she would disintegrate, cease to be entirely.

"Please." It was a whimper, but she didn't care.

He answered by sliding forward, but he was still a few inches from home. With a little cry, she lifted up and forced him even more. He gave a laugh, gripped her hips and ground a circle that made her explode. Her orgasm was so powerful, she forgot to breathe, forgot everything except that he was inside her and she was his, even if she hadn't told him.

She was his. And as he set a rhythm that would give her at least one more powerful release, she knew there would be a part of her that would be his for the rest of her life, whether she left the island with him or not.

Chapter Six

Gavin caught up with Selena in a few long steps and grabbed her hand. She smiled up at him as they walked down the beach in the warm late summer air. Sand slid between his toes, and the breeze stirred his hair across his forehead. For a moment he forgot his troubles completely. Cyprus was perfect.

Or it would have been if he hadn't been a prisoner.

"You look very serious for a man who continues to claim he looks silly in that loincloth," Selena teased gently before she lifted his hand to her lips and brushed a kiss across the knuckles. "Would you care to share the thoughts that trouble your mind?"

He frowned. The thoughts that kept him awake at night were so complicated, he could hardly understand them himself, let alone explain them to her.

He wanted to escape the dangerous prison of Aphrodite's temple, but when he thought of leaving the island without Selena, it pained him. In the days he had known her, she had become the most important person in his life. In the past, that kind of attachment to a woman would have driven him away. Now, the only thing that caused him real fear was the thought of losing her.

Still, each time he asked if she would escape with him when he left, she changed the subject. Or distracted him with pursuits more pleasurable than talking. That silent rejection stung him again and again.

She pursed her lips when he didn't answer. "Very well. You don't have to tell me if you don't want to. I understand why you wouldn't trust me. After all, I'm the reason you're trapped here."

Her eyes grew distant as she looked out over the crystal blue waters before them. As always, her stare held a bevy of turbulent emotions, and he doubted all of them were related to him.

"It isn't that I don't trust you, Selena," he reassured her as he came to a stop and gently turned her to face him. "I'm trusting you with my life."

Her face softened. "Yes. That's true."

"In fact, I wonder how much *you* trust me." He brushed a long strand of dark hair away from her stormy eyes. "After all, I know very little about you."

She gasped in disbelief. "Very little? Thanks to the prying of a lady's maid and my wicked stepchildren, you know my every desire, my every fantasy! You know each private thought I shared with my diary. I'm not complaining since you're adept at making those fantasies come true, but to say you don't know me . . ."

"Yes, I know what your body craves." He nodded. "But what about your soul?"

She stiffened and tried to pull away. "I don't know what you mean."

"Why did you turn to Isadora Glasier? What made you run from the Kelsey family with only a small portion of the fortune you'd inherited? Why didn't you tell your parents where you were going? Hell, I'd settle for why you married a bastard like David Kelsey in the first place."

With every question, Selena's face tightened and her body shifted until she held him at a full arm's length. He had no doubt if he hadn't been holding her hands, she would have run away down the beach to avoid his intrusive words. Over the time they'd spent together, he had learned Selena kept her secrets close to her heart. He doubted there was any person in the world who really knew her completely.

But damn if he didn't want to be that person who held the keys to her soul. Who knew her every wish, and even her every heartache.

"Why would you want to know those silly things?" She laughed, but it was a false, high-pitched sound. "After all, you and I could be doing things that are much more enjoyable."

To accentuate that statement, she stepped into his arms and tilted her face up for a kiss. Her lips were just inches from his, pink from the wind and copious kissing in the past few days. Her eyes glittered, reflecting the desire that grew in his own body.

But beneath her desire lay fear. And her fear kept him from taking what she offered, no matter how much he longed to plunge into her body.

Soon, but not yet.

"I want to talk to you, Selena," he whispered. "Let me know you a little. I swear I won't betray you as you've been betrayed before."

Her lip began to quiver, but this time she didn't pull away. She continued to stare into his eyes with an appraising expression that seemed to delve into his very soul. He was being tested, yet all he could do was wait and hope he would pass.

Finally, she relaxed in his arms with a long sigh. "I married David Kelsey because the time had come for me to marry. It is as simple and yet as complicated as that. I hadn't found another man who interested me, and my parents were becoming desperate to tie me to someone who could take care of me . . . and them, too, I suppose. David fit that description. He was wealthy, he was of a class slightly higher than theirs, and he had impeccable manners." Her face darkened. "Of course, during the negotiations for my hand, he never mentioned how he wished to deny me my right to have children, or that he often preferred the back of his hand to a meeting of the minds during a disagreement."

Gavin's fists bunched at his sides. "Kelsey struck you?"

It was amazing he could get the words out considering the tremendous rage that coursed through him.

She gave one matter-of-fact nod. "Not often, but occasionally. He was far too stupid to win an argument in a fair fashion. I learned very quickly to say what he wanted to hear and do whatever I desired the moment he wasn't looking. His children despised me, of course."

Gavin flexed his hands as he counted to ten in his head. For months, his part in David Kelsey's death had crushed down on him with growing weight, but now he wished he'd been the one to cut him down on the battlefield. To avenge the pain Kelsey had caused Selena, both to her body and her heart.

"Yes." He relaxed his clenched jaw. "That was very clear to me when they called me to their home. The girls, especially, have a strong dislike for you."

"I am the same age as David's eldest daughter." Selena paced down the beach. "I almost couldn't blame them. They hated that I'd come into their home, and their father expected them to treat me like a stepmother instead of an equal. But I would have taken a month trapped in a tiny room with Adelaide and Amelia over a few moments alone with Arthur."

Gavin cocked an eyebrow. "Why? Those two women are vipers. I would think the meek and mild Arthur Kelsey would be easy in comparison."

"Meek and mild?" She laughed, but the sound was bitter. "What would you say if I told you Arthur is the answer to all your other questions?"

He shrugged. "I don't understand what you mean."

She shook her head as she sank down on a log that had washed up on shore. Her shoulders trembled almost imperceptibly. "You asked me why I turned to Isadora, why I ran from London with so little money, and why I didn't inform my parents of my plans. I am telling you the answer to all those questions is Arthur Kelsey."

Gavin sat down next to Selena with a thunk. He had a sick feeling he knew where this story was going to go, especially when he remembered the possessive way Arthur had handled Selena's picture in London; the way the young man had said her name. Gavin saw the lingering disgust and fear in Selena's eyes when she spoke of her stepson.

"Tell me." He caught her trembling hand for what he hoped was a reassuring squeeze. "I want to know."

In the time he had known Selena, he had seen her expose herself to a crowd of strangers, make love to him where they could easily be caught, and do things that would have made prostitutes color. She had flushed with pleasure, her cheeks had turned pink from a compliment, but he had never seen her blush with embarrassment.

Until now.

"I have never told anyone these things before," she murmured, more to herself than to him. "Not even Isadora knows the whole truth. But you . . ." Her gaze flitted to him and softened. "I can tell you."

He nodded as a swell of pride and awe filled him. Her trust was the greatest gift she could give. "You can."

She took a deep, shaky breath. "It started a few weeks after I married David. Arthur caught me alone in my private library one afternoon. I was writing a letter home and didn't notice him standing there until he cleared his throat." She shook her head with the memory. "When I looked up, it was clear he was aroused by the sight of me. He didn't even attempt to conceal it or leave the room as a gentleman normally would in that awkward situation. In fact, he seemed proud of his desire."

Her eyes fluttered shut, and she struggled with her breathing for a moment before she continued. "I was shocked by the openly lustful way he stared. Since he wouldn't leave, I tried to escape without causing a scene. But-but he wouldn't let me. Arthur closed the door, blocked my escape. And then he—" She shivered though the breeze was warm. "He touched me."

Gavin shut his eyes. He could actually feel her fear, taste her pain as he pictured how shocked and horrified she must have been. It took every ounce of control for him not to slam his fist into the wood they sat on. "How did he touch you?"

"He pushed me up against the wall, groped my breast and made a lame attempt at kissing me." She shook her head in disgust. "I made enough noise that a servant interrupted and Arthur was forced to leave."

"What did you do?"

She shrugged. "I told my husband, of course. David was furious, not at Arthur, but at me. He accused me of doing something to cause his son to behave in such a fashion. Still, Arthur didn't approach me again, though at least three parlor maids quit without asking for references. I'm sure he took advantage of them. I settled into an uneasy peace in my own home. Until David went away to India."

"Without your husband in the house, Arthur felt free to pursue his interest in you," Gavin said softly as he watched the pain from those memories flicker across her face. He longed to take the hurt away, to erase the memories.

She nodded slowly. "Yes. He wouldn't leave me be. He trapped me in rooms; he followed me into closets. He groped me, tried to kiss me. A few times he went farther, but I was always able to fight him off. That was why I attempted to find interests outside of the house. Interests that would take me away in the evening when Arthur was home, before he went to the clubs or whoring with women who had no means to fight back. Before I could lock my door and keep him out."

"And that was what Isadora offered." He understood so much more now.

She sighed. "I met Isadora at a society meeting, but our association soon grew much closer. She told me she sensed I was a kindred spirit the moment she saw me. Isadora offered me friendship, and eventually a glimpse at freedom."

"I'm surprised you wanted anything to do with sensual experiences with a man like Arthur Kelsey molesting you at every turn."

She shook her head and finally looked at him without the glitter of shame in her eyes. "Just because Arthur wished to abuse me didn't mean I wasn't the same person. I had always been sensual, had appetites a woman wasn't supposed to feel. Before my marriage, I found guilty pleasure in touching myself in secret. I even looked forward to the lovemaking I expected to find in my husband's bed. But when my parents matched me with David, they took those dreams . . . and many others . . . away." Her voice was bitter. "Isadora told me I could get the promise of sexual fulfillment back. She allowed me to feel those desires without shame, without fear."

"And since you felt shame and fear at home, what she offered must have been even more attractive," he said softly.

Selena's face contracted in surprise. "Yes. I did crave the things Aphrodite represented. Freedom, power and a lack of fear. Isadora encouraged me, but never forced me to do anything. For the first time in a long time, I was in control, and I needed that feeling once we got the news of David's death."

She shivered again, and this time Gavin gave into his desire to comfort her. He was pleased when she allowed him to drape an arm around her shoulders. She even leaned against his chest with a little sigh.

"Arthur grew more persistent when his father died?" he prodded gently.

She nodded, and her hair tickled his bare chest to send a tingle of fresh desire through his body.

"Without the threat of his father's punishment hanging over his head, he grew bolder. One day he managed to catch me alone again. He told me I was now free to be his. That he expected me to give in finally to his demands. The bastard thought I had been resisting only because of my marriage vows. He tried to reassure me by telling me he would marry me if I came to his bed."

Gavin twisted his face in disgust. "But in the eyes of the law, you were his mother."

"Exactly right. I reminded him of that fact, but it didn't help. He flew into a terrible rage. He told me even if we couldn't be together legally, he would have me in his bed. He even wanted me to bear his children. And if I didn't . . ." She swallowed hard. "If I refused him, he revealed that he was aware of who I was consorting with and what I was doing when I went out at night. He said he would use his sisters' hatred of me and their desire to control their father's fortune to have me committed for hysteria. He said if I wouldn't be his whore, I would have no sexual pleasure with another man for as long as I lived."

Selena's face twisted, but she managed to continue. "I fled to Isadora that night, and she revealed her desire to return to Cyprus and introduce me to the temple she had begun here. To give me my sexual freedom and let me experience the pleasures I'd missed with my husband. I departed with her within the week."

Gavin drew in a deep breath, overwhelmed now that he had heard her troubling story from beginning to end. His emotions roiled inside him. Rage, pain, hatred . . . ugly emotions that made him want to return to London and give Arthur Kelsey his just rewards. But there was something more important, and it had nothing to do with vengeance.

"Selena." He tilted her face toward his. Despite her fragile appearance, she had such inner strength.

"It's an ugly story, isn't it?" She sighed. "I wouldn't blame you if you wanted to leave my bed."

How could she think he would blame *her* for all she had been through?

"You are the strongest woman I know. I admire you all the more for the strength and poise with which you handled your difficult circumstances, both with David and with Arthur Kelsey. Most women would have let their husband's cruelty and their stepson's sexual predation destroy their souls. But you not only kept your head, but found a way to escape." He dipped his chin for a gentle kiss. "If anything, I want you all the more."

She stared at him, stunned joy on her face. Then she pulled him down for a deeper, more passionate kiss. Her tongue speared between his lips, tangling with his in the mind-melting way only Selena seemed capable of. She filled his senses with her taste, her scent and the feel of her in his arms. She filled him with her, and he never wanted to be without her again.

"Selena," he whispered, his voice hoarse as she nibbled her way along the column of his throat. "What if someone sees us?"

She stood up and unhooked the clip that bound her chiton around her smooth shoulders. The gown fell around her feet with a swish, revealing every curve of her sensuous body in the warm sunlight.

She stepped forward with a swing of her hips that had Gavin's cock at full attention with painful speed. "The rest of the group is having luncheon on the hill behind the temple, and the bluff gives us protection." The tip of her tongue moistened her bottom lip. "I need you, Gavin. I don't want to wait. Please."

He pushed his loincloth aside to reveal his throbbing erection and opened his arms. With a smile, she straddled his lap, and her wet, warm pussy slid effortlessly over his cock. His eyes fluttered shut and for that moment he forgot about his anger, his feelings of being trapped, and simply enjoyed the gift she gave him. The gift of her body, and the gift of her past.

He knew all her dirty, humiliating secrets, but Gavin hadn't run away from her. In fact, as she straddled him, rubbing over his iron heat in slow sweeps, he seemed closer to her than ever.

With his head tilted back and stunning eyes shut, she drank in his every expression as she slowly eased herself down over his cock. She loved the way his mouth twitched as he struggled to suppress a groan of pleasure. The way his lips parted as he expelled one long, hot breath that stirred over her skin and had her nerves firing all at once.

Finally she took him all the way to the hilt and took a moment to enjoy the sensation of his body filling hers, stretching her, pressing her in all the right ways. They had been made to fit together, and she found herself wishing the moment could last for eternity.

Gavin's eyes fluttered open and he met her gaze with a warmth and an intensity, different than before. He tangled his fingers through hers, then pressed their intertwined hands against her hips. Slowly, he began to move inside her, using her hips as leverage to glide in and out, round and round, merciless as she reached a fever-pitch of need and pleasure. He never let her break away from his gaze, and he never let up, even when she cried out, even when she tried to break her hands away from his so she could guide the pace of their sex.

Finally, he mouthed one word, gave her the permission she yearned for. "Now."

The order was all her aching body needed. She came in a powerful explosion of pleasure. Her wails were lost within his mouth as he rose up to kiss her. He continued his slow torture of thrusts that ground his pelvis against the swollen, aching nub of her clitoris.

Her release went on and on until finally he matched her, stiffening on a last thrust. He filled her with his heat and the proof of her ultimate power over him.

As her throbbing heart slowly returned to normal, she examined his face. The angles and curves were relaxed, now that he had surrendered. Having such power over him wasn't as enjoyable as it should have been.

No, the emotion that lifted her heart and made her soul sing when she was with him went much deeper than mere sexual control and lust.

She was in love with him. With a man who had come to take away what she'd fought so hard to obtain. The man who would leave her side in just a few short days.

Of course, Gavin had asked her to accompany him, but could she do that? Could she leave this place where she had finally found acceptance and freedom? Depart with a man who might still follow his duty instead of his heart and return her to her hideous family.

She dismissed that thought. He wouldn't do that. Not after all they had shared, in the communion of both body and mind. But she didn't know if her love would be enough. The strains of society would still exist if she returned to England with him. Over time the tenderness between them would fade. The lust would lessen.

She couldn't bear losing him physically, but losing him emotionally would break her heart all the more. If Gavin eventually regretted bringing her home . . . tears stung her eyes with just the thought.

"Selena?" he murmured as he cupped the back of her neck and placed soft, melting kisses along her collarbone. "Did I hurt you?"

She shook her head even as her body reacted to his touch. "No, Gavin. You could never hurt me."

As he stirred inside her, and she braced herself for a second barrage of sensual warfare, she added silently, "I'll never let you."

Chapter Seven

Selena was distracted. Gavin wasn't fooled for a moment by her false smiles. And though their lovemaking had been as passionate as ever, she distanced herself from him whenever they weren't tangled in her bed.

Like now, when she insisted they come to the common area to eat with Isadora and the other followers of Aphrodite. Her need to be in a public place had more to do with hiding from him than it did with seeing her friends or keeping up some act for Isadora's benefit.

The heat of the other woman's stare burned into him, and he shifted slightly under it. Isadora Glasier made it no secret she wanted him, whether he was currently with her best friend or not. Her brazen desire upset Selena, as well. Her jaw had been set ever since they joined her friend, and she kept stealing glances from Gavin to Isadora.

Gavin could never be attracted to Isadora. She had already threatened his life and taken his freedom. He suspected she was far more dangerous than Selena wanted to admit. Control was clearly something the redhead wanted above all else, and not just in her bed.

"Selena, why don't you give me a moment with your Major?" Isadora asked with laughter thick in her voice. "You can go speak with Benedict and Reggie. Now that you are able to fully participate in the rituals of the temple, both have expressed an interest in you for the next cycle of the moon. I want you to determine if either of them strikes your fancy."

Selena was drinking when her friend began to speak and started to choke on her wine. When she was able to draw a breath again, she looked at Isadora in disbelief.

"You want me to be with Benedict or Reggie after this week?" she asked softly. Her gaze darted over to Gavin for a brief moment.

He clenched his teeth as he waited for Isadora's answer. The people on the island traded partners like most people traded gardening secrets, but he hadn't considered the prospect that Selena would turn her affections to another man. The idea of her sharing her lush body with another man had him seething, though he did his best to hide his emotions. They were far too dangerous to reveal in front of Isadora.

"Selena, you know better." Isadora clucked her tongue condescendingly. "This island is about choice. You may be with any man or woman you like. But the new moon will arrive just after the upcoming festival, and the cycle of passion will begin again. It's the perfect time for *all* of us to choose a new . . ." She trailed off and looked Gavin up and down. "Mate."

Selena's breath came short. "I see."

"Run along now. If you don't like either one of them, you don't have to choose them."

She waved Selena off like she was a child. With a frown, she did as she'd been told, leaving Gavin alone with Isadora. He was suddenly put to mind of the moments he'd spent in the Kelsey home before he departed for Cyprus. There he had been surrounded by snakes masquerading as ladies. When he looked at Isadora, he saw a dangerous python.

She slithered a bit closer and gave him what he assumed was meant to be a come-hither smile. "I certainly intend to choose a new mate once the festival is over."

He nodded slightly. "Since you make the rules in this place, I assume you make them to your own taste. Which means you like having a new partner in your bed each month. I'm surprised you haven't worked your way through your followers already."

Isadora looked at him evenly. "You don't like me. That's fine, Major. In fact, a good dose of hatred can make the passion all the higher. Because you see, I intend to pick you. You will be my mate for a month."

She leaned closer and trailed a painted fingernail across his lip. Just the right flick of her wrist would cut him. He had a feeling that for Isadora, the threat was as important as her touch. She was sending him a message.

"You told Selena that Aphrodite's Temple was all about choice." He stepped back from her and searched the small crowd until he found Selena.

He watched as she talked with the two men, as Isadora had instructed. They both ogled her mercilessly, leaving no doubt either one would take her gladly. Unfortunately, Gavin couldn't see her face. He had no idea if she liked their attentions or not.

"I'm sure Selena has explained some of the teachings of Aphrodite to you," Isadora replied as she took a sip of wine. "Or perhaps you've been too *busy* for study."

He turned his attention back to her with a glare. "She told me Aphrodite used her sensuality as a tool for power. That she believed in freedom in love, as well as equality when it came to the bedroom. A woman could choose who she bedded with as much right as a man. That's what you purport to teach here."

She nodded with an impressed smile. "It's good to know you've been listening."

"But just now you told me you would have me in your bed. That sounded like an order rather than a request. Don't I have the right to turn you down?"

Isadora's face twisted with anger. He had a suspicion none of her followers had ever dared refuse her advances.

Slowly, her rage faded to bored amusement. "Are you actually saying you wouldn't like to sample this body? That you wouldn't want to wash away the horrors of war and hardship with a month of pleasure between my legs?"

"A year with you wouldn't be enough time to wash away the horrors of a sprained ankle. You are cold, Isadora Glasier."

In an instant her earlier rage flashed back, more powerful than ever. She drew in a sharp, angry breath. "Is that right?"

"Yes. What you couldn't do for me in a year, Selena did in a moment. Why would I give her up?"

He snapped the question out and the moment he said it, he was struck by its truth. He didn't want to give up the healing balm of Selena's touch or the passionate release he found in her body. He didn't want to give up the emotions slowly binding them. He wanted her to come with him when he left the island, and not just for her own protection.

Most of all, he didn't want to lose her.

"You fool." Isadora laughed, and the sound chilled Gavin to his very bones. "You've fallen in love with her."

He refused to answer even though her accusation rushed through him like lightning. Love? It was something he had never sought. Something that had never touched him with another woman. But she was right. When he looked at Selena, the emotions that overwhelmed him went much further than desire. And much deeper than passion.

He loved her.

"Selena will *never* love you," she hissed as she moved in closer. "She told me long ago she will never let another man grow close enough to harm her. And she will always see you as the man her family hired to return her to hell."

"I would never harm her."

"Wouldn't you?" Isadora wound her fingers through his hair and pulled his face to hers. She thrust her tongue between his lips and kissed him hard. He yanked away to wipe his mouth on the back of his hand in disgust. "Try and convince her of that."

He heard the little gasp behind him. Without seeing her face, he was sure Selena had witnessed Isadora's false kiss, and it had hurt her. He rose to his feet and spun around. Selena's jaw was set in a rigid line and her normally full lips were a thin frown. By the time he looked into her eyes, Selena had hardened herself to him and to the woman she was foolish enough to call her friend.

"I think you're right, Isadora," she said softly, without even a waver to her voice. "Benedict and Reggie are both fine specimens. Either one would make a good choice for the next moon's cycle. I will have to review all my options fully before I choose."

Gavin wanted to strangle Isadora for forcing this ridiculous misunderstanding. If she thought she would get her way by pushing Selena aside, she was wrong. Even if she were the last woman on earth, he would want nothing to do with her cold touch.

"At any rate, I think I've had my fill for today. I'm going to return to my quarters to have a bath and change." She nodded dismissively in Gavin's direction but wouldn't meet his gaze. "I've no need for you at present, Major. Please feel free to stay as you seem to be having a fine time."

She turned on her heel and started toward the little huts in the distance. Gavin glared at Isadora over his shoulder before he strode after her.

"I always get what I want, Major." Isadora's laugh echoed behind him, taunting him. "Always."

"Not this time," he muttered as he hastened to catch up with Selena's long, angry stride. "For once, I plan to get what I want."

Selena sensed Gavin behind her, his presence growing ever closer even as she rushed to escape him and the pain he had caused her. She had just begun to let the walls around her heart down. She had trusted him enough to tell him her history with her husband and stepson. He had seemed to understand that, had pretended to feel her hurt.

But then he kissed Isadora.

The teachings of Aphrodite said freedom in lust was a virtue, but she couldn't help a pang of hatred toward the woman who had been her savior and friend. It was coupled with a stab of jealousy that stung her heart like salt in a wound. She didn't want Gavin to kiss anyone but her. She didn't want him to touch any woman but her. Not ever again.

Why had she fallen in love with him? It only complicated an already untenable situation.

"Stop running," he called out. "Please."

She froze and took an all-too-brief second to calm herself. When she turned, she hoped she wore a mask of disinterest.

"Oh, I didn't realize you were following me," she lied as she folded her arms in a protective shield around her heart. "You don't need to chase me. I told you I don't require your presence."

"Am I now a slave who can be so easily dismissed?" he asked as he strode up the path with wide, even steps. It was the gait of a man who was coming to claim what was his. Could it be that he was coming for her?

"You are whatever you want to be." She yawned. "I'm sure if you want to play slave and master games, Isadora will be happy to oblige. I'm not interested."

"You didn't like it when she kissed me," he said softly, and his eyes glittered with what looked like triumph.

"Don't be ridiculous." What was meant to come out as a strong denial was more like a squeak of derision. "That's what this place is all about. You can kiss whomever you like."

He reached out to wrap strong hands around her upper arms. With one yank, he pulled her flush against him, sliding one muscular thigh between her own and cradling her back until there wasn't even a breath between them. Then he lowered his mouth and claimed her lips. There was no mistaking the possessiveness of his touch. She became his the moment their breath mingled, the second their skin touched.

And she loved it. She loved feeling safe. Protected.

Even loved.

She started at that thought. Could this man love her? Had duty and honor and desire been eclipsed by some deeper, more tender feeling? One that could keep them together for a lifetime, no matter what they faced.

She pulled back, dizzy from emotion and lust. "What? . . . Why—"

"You said I could kiss whomever I wanted. I only want to kiss you." He searched her face, looking into her eyes, into her soul, seeing the deepest parts of her with only one glance.

"But . . ."

He covered her lips with two fingers. "I didn't come here to find freedom, Selena. I didn't come to bask in the sun or the heat of lust. I came here for you."

She stiffened at what his words forced her to remember. "To take me back to London."

"No." He smiled, and his mouth curved with tenderness. "To make you mine. From the moment I saw your picture, you were all I wanted. Duty to the Kelsey family became secondary, and now it no longer exists. My only duty is to make you happy. To make you feel safe. To wash away your torment and sorrow, as you have washed away my pains from the past with your touch, your kiss."

She touched his face as tears pricked her eyes. His confession was the sweetest thing she'd ever known. "You've already done that, Gavin. More than you'll ever know. I came looking for an escape from the repression and persecution in my life in London, looking for freedom here on the island. I searched for it in the teachings of a goddess. But I didn't find it until I touched you. I found my freedom with you. My salvation."

"Then come with me when I leave. It isn't safe for either of us here. Please."

She shook her head sadly. "What you think you desire now may not be what you want in a month or a year. I will *never* be a woman whom society accepts. I will always be too sensual, and I cannot bear to hide that part of myself as I once did. When we return to the 'real' world, you may regret taking me with you. It would break my heart if you grew to resent me over time."

His lips parted. "Do you think that would matter to me? I want *you* Selena. All aspects of you. The sensual. The innocent. The kind and compassionate woman. The lustful vixen. I don't give a damn what anyone else says about it."

He accentuated that vow with a hard, passionate kiss that set her world spinning. She clung to the hope he gave her with his statement.

She broke away. "Look into my eyes and tell me that is true."

He cupped her cheeks and locked gazes with her. "I will *never* regret taking you with me. Ever. Nothing will ever change the bond between us. I swear that to you on my life."

She stared at him and saw . . . truth. Her heart soared, and her eyes filled with tears. After arriving in Cyprus, she had thought of leaving a few times, but the idea of wandering the world alone had been terrifying. Now, knowing wherever she journeyed, Gavin would be at her side, was wonderful.

She no longer hesitated. "Yes. I will go with you."

His mouth came down on hers again, and she felt his joyful smile as he kissed her. Then his hands threaded into her hair and dragged down the loose binds that held it back from her face. Her hair fell in a perfumed cascade around them, shielding them from the sun and onlookers as it twined around them.

"Come back to my quarters with me," she said softly, pressing kisses along Gavin's sculpted jaw line. "I want to show you what you mean to me."

Later she would say it. Later she would tell him how much she loved him. But for now, she would follow Aphrodite's teachings and express her love physically. Not to gain power, as the goddess had. No, she would give her physical love to gain a future with this man. One where emotion and passion stretched outside the bedroom.

"Yes."

He pushed her back along the path until they were pressed flush against her hut's door. With a hot kiss, he turned the knob and they stumbled inside. Before the door was even closed, she ripped the loincloth from his hips, revealing his proudly jutting cock.

"Were you frightened the first day I came into your room?" he asked as he pulled the clips from her chiton and threw them across the room where they clattered against the ceramic floor.

"No." She pushed the chiton down around her ankles so she could step naked into his waiting arms. She hissed out in pleasure when her hot skin pressed against his. "When I saw you in my mirror, I thought you must be my fantasy come true. It gave me the most powerful orgasm of my life . . . until you actually touched me."

Though she was telling him intimate things most women of her class would shy away from, she didn't even blush. He had always accepted her sensual side without reproach. He was her safe place. She could tell him anything without fear of recrimination or loss of his affection.

"I want to touch you," he murmured as he guided her back toward the soft bed where they had pleased each other so often the past week.

"Yes, I want that, too. I want that more than anything."

Her breath came in short pants as he lowered her on her bed. It was like the first time making love to him, a moment filled with excitement and trepidation and pleasure. His hand came up to glide over her collarbone, cup her breast. She arched under the touch with a long sigh. This was what she wanted for the rest of her life.

His mouth came down to suckle her nipple, and all other thought was lost in a wash of sensation. Pleasure throbbed from where he sucked, pulling through her body all the way to the wet heat of her center.

"I want to prove to you that I will never regret choosing you," Gavin murmured between laps against her tingling nipples.

She smiled even as she arched up. "H-how?" she managed to murmur.

He pulled back slowly, looking down at her with such powerful feeling in his stare that tears of joy and wonder burned at her throat and eyes.

"I want you to see how beautiful you are when you make love to me. How there is no shame in your sensuality."

She stuggled up to lean on her elbows. "See it?"

Stepping away from the bed, he went to her full length mirror, the one she had been looking in when he first entered her life, and dragged the heavy metal frame across the floor to set it at the foot of the bed.

"Watch me make love to you." His eyes darkened as he crawled back up the bed to lie beside her.

She drew in a sharp breath as their eyes met.

"Watch how beautiful our joining is."

He motioned to the mirror at the bottom of the bed. She followed his movement and sucked in a harsh breath at the reflection in the mirror. Their bodies close together, his large and masculine and muscled, hers paler, smaller, softer. Yet as he wrapped his arms around her, they merged into one body, beautiful and erotic. Made for each other.

She watched, fascinated as his large, dark hand slipped down her stomach and between her legs to toy with her. He rolled his hands over her clit until she thought she would weep with pleasure, then abandoning the nub to move his fingers inside. One, then two, she watched as he stretched her, prepared her for the cock that rubbed against her thigh as she waited, breathless.

"Sit up," he murmured.

She obeyed, and he scooted around to sit behind her. She understood what he wanted to do. Moving into a crouched position she spread herself open and lowered her wet slit around his cock. From that position, she could see every thrust in the mirror, as could he. She was able to watch him move in and out of her, watch her own fingers play across her clit as she rode him closer and closer to heaven.

Which she did. With breath coming in ever-shorter bursts, she moved up and down, circling and thrusting over him, following the urgings of her aching body. Every movement brought her closer to completion, and seeing the look of bliss on his face in the mirror only urged her on. Still, she tried to hold back. Tried to prolong the release as long as she could to prolong his pleasure.

It was a battle she lost the moment he leaned forward, sank his teeth gently into her shoulder and reached around to strum a thumb over her clit.

She exploded, rocking back and forth with a cry of pleasure she couldn't have held back for all the gold in the world. She was amazed to see her expression of release and the tears of joy that finally trickled down her cheeks. The release went on and on, dancing on the edge of pleasure and pain until finally her body sagged, totally sated, against Gavin's sweaty chest. He came inside her with a groan as she quivered one last time around him, milking him dry.

"Amazing," she gasped when she could draw enough breath to speak. She stole another glance at the mirror and reveled in the sight of their intertwined bodies. Then she cast her eyes toward him. Their gazes met and she smiled. "*You* are amazing."

"Only when we're together," he whispered in the gathering darkness of her room.

"Then we'll be amazing together, forever," she said softly. "As soon as we get away from the temple."

"Tomorrow."

Chapter Eight

"I was able to retrieve your clothing from Isadora's private rooms," Selena said as she slipped back into her quarters where Gavin was preparing for their departure. "But if you are seen wearing your London garb, it will rouse suspicion, so you'll have to wait to change until we're safely away from the compound."

Gavin nodded and tried a joke to ease her tension. "Do *you* have anything else to wear?" He gestured to the chiton that left one breast exposed. "As much as the sailors on the ship will appreciate this stunning outfit, I'm not sure my arm can take too many fights to keep you all to myself.

She laughed, but there was no humor in the sound. Leaving here made her just as anxious as it did him. Perhaps even more since she had no idea what her future held. Only that she would be with him.

The knowledge that she was putting her life entirely in his hands was awe-inspiring. He couldn't let her down. Not now. Not ever.

"Isadora burned most of my clothing in a goddess ritual when we arrived on the island, but I managed to hide one regular gown from her minions." She looked around the hut that had been her lonely home. "I suppose I always knew I would leave this place. I never fit the mold Isadora created in her image."

In a few steps, Gavin gathered Selena into his arms. Her pulse pounded against his chest as she clung to him. He smoothed a hand over her hair and attempted to comfort her with the warmth and strength of his embrace. When she pulled back, it was with a shaky smile.

"I'm sorry I'm being so silly."

"No, you're not," he reassured her with a squeeze before he let her go. "Your life before you came to this island was horrible. Isadora and the people here were the first ones to give you a taste of the freedom you so craved. Now you're afraid to let that go for another life of uncertainty."

Dropping her gaze to the floor, she nodded. He cupped her chin and turned her face toward his with a gentle nudge.

"Selena, your life with me will be nothing like what you had with the Kelseys or your own family. I promise you that."

Her lower lip trembled, but she straightened her shoulders with a brave nod. "Of course, I trust you. You've put your faith in me to get you away from this place. I've put my faith in you for what happens after our escape."

He smiled. Her trust overwhelmed him and roused every protective instinct he'd ever experienced. And awoke a deeper love for her than he'd imagined was possible.

"There's no time to be afraid. I've always made decisions and never looked back. I won't look back from this one, either." She touched his face briefly, but stepped away. "I have a small part in tonight's ritual. Isadora cannot know I'll be gone long before I do my duty. I must go meet with her as planned weeks ago to keep her doubts to a minimum."

"Of course. You go and I'll complete the final arrangements. Is there anything you received here you wish to take with you when we leave? We can't take much, but I'll try to pack anything that's very important to you."

She turned in a slow circle, looking from wall to wall, trinket to trinket. A soft and loving expression crossed her face. "The only thing of value I found here was you. I want nothing more than that."

With that, she hurried out the door toward her meeting with Isadora. When the door shut behind her, Gavin sighed.

"You have me, my love. You have me forever."

Isadora's quarters were dark and sultry. The windows had been blackened so even when the sun was blazing, her bedroom had to be lit by the multitude of candles that surrounded the huge bed in the center of the room. Selena shivered when she entered, dreading this final encounter with Isadora.

"You're late."

Isadora's voice came from the darkest corner of the room, and Selena jumped before she turned to face her former friend. "I'm sorry. As you said yesterday, my choice of mates has been keeping me occupied. I lost track of the time."

Isadora strolled into the dim light with a cold smile, one that didn't quite reach her beautiful, dark eyes. "I'm glad you have enjoyed the Major. It's too bad you'll be giving him up soon."

Selena's heart leapt at the mere thought of losing Gavin, but she managed to maintain her composure. "I don't know, Isadora. I've been enjoying him so much I believe I might keep him. I was cheated by choosing him so late in the month. I think a full cycle of passion is required before I turn him loose for another to have."

Isadora didn't answer, but walked over to a large leather chair beside her bed. She sat down and crossed her legs, staring at Selena with an appraising glare.

"Indeed? You mean you would like to keep him even though you have your choice of any man in the Temple?"

Selena quivered under the coldness of her friend's voice. She'd never known Isadora to sound so threatening, yet her words were innocuous. Voices of warning sounded in her head, which she tried to push aside in an effort to remain calm.

"Or perhaps I'll change my mind and take another man or two. As you said, I have many choices," she stammered with a shrug.

Why did this situation suddenly feel so much like a trap?

Isadora surged to her feet and drew her hand back. Before Selena could dodge, her friend slapped her with enough force that Selena's head whipped around. Her cheek stung like fire as she gripped the back of the closest chair with one hand and cradled her face with the other.

"Why—"

"You ungrateful little wretch!" Isadora paced to the ornate fireplace across the room. "How could you betray me? Betray Aphrodite this way? After I freed you from the prison you lived in? After I taught you about passion?"

"I don't know what you mean!" Selena protested even though

everything was becoming perfectly clear. Isadora knew. Somehow she knew.

Her friend's eyes narrowed. "You dare to lie to me? I have ears everywhere, my little fool. You're planning to run away tonight. To smuggle Gavin Fletcher from the group and leave with him. Back to London, no doubt. Back to the society you hated not so long ago. Has his cock been so good that you cannot see what he wants to steal from you? Or are you just so frigid that any cock will turn your little brains to mush?"

Selena forced away her shock. Enough of this. She would not tolerate this abuse from Isadora. From anyone. "What I feel for Gavin has nothing to do with his skills in my bed. My decision to leave with him has everything to do with emotion. Real and pure emotion. Something you have always shied away from, Isadora. Even with your friends."

"Emotion?" Isadora laughed, but it was an ugly, empty sound. "Emotion is weakness. I learned that in my marriage very quickly. Sex is power, and power is everything. I tried to teach you that. I tried to show you the glory of Aphrodite."

"No, this place isn't about Aphrodite," Selena whispered as the truth became clear. "It's about *you.* You aren't teaching the people here to worship the goddess. You're teaching them to worship you. They aren't free. They're your slaves. And I won't be your slave anymore."

"You're ridiculous." Isadora's lip trembled even as she denied what Selena said. "Aphrodite is the center of our group. She is sex, sensuality, power—"

"Freedom." Selena finished emphatically. "If you read the legends about her, what she valued above all else was freedom. Freedom in love, whether that meant choosing ten partners to play with at once, or one to love for all time. I choose Gavin. And he chooses me."

Isadora let out a scream of rage as she slammed her hand down against her mantelpiece. Sensual trinkets, sex toys and velvet ropes scattered in all directions. She drew in a few long breaths and turned to face Selena. Isadora appeared strangely serene, considering her angry outburst.

"Freedom is one virtue I cannot give you now. You betrayed me. I can't trust you won't reveal all you know to forces who would destroy everything I've built." She smiled. "And your friend, the Major, must die. Then you can continue worshipping here as you did before, with a guard by your side at all times, of course. It's for the best."

Selena gasped in shock, but before she could protest, Isadora walked away. She went to the door where a guard stood ready for her orders.

"Bring Major Fletcher to me immediately. And prepare the altar. We're going to have a sacrifice tonight to start the festival."

Selena lurched forward in horror as she realized this time Isadora would grant Gavin no reprieve. "No!"

Gavin pulled against the guards, despite the throbbing pain in his injured arm. The two men had taken great pleasure in cruelly twisting his injured arm when they had bound him. If he was being hauled away like a prisoner again, it could only mean one thing. Selena's plan for escape had been discovered.

He didn't care so much about what these people did to him. He had endured pain and could endure it again. But what about Selena? Isadora would be mad with rage when she realized Selena had betrayed her. What had they done to her? His heart raced as a thousand sexual and physical tortures filled his mind.

No, he had to remain calm, clear headed. He couldn't let his fear for Selena overcome him. Control was his only remaining defense.

At one of the huts, the guards stopped and knocked.

Isadora's cold voice answered. "Come in."

It was as he feared. Isadora was behind this. The men pushed the door open and forced him inside. It took a moment for his eyes to adjust from the fading afternoon sunlight to the darkened sensuality of Isadora's chamber.

"Unbind his hands," she commanded. Isadora was sprawled across the bed in the center of the room, her naked body gleaming white against the darkness of the room. "And leave us."

The guards looked long and hard at her splayed legs and her exposed glistening sex, then one asked, "Are you sure, m'lady? He fought us the entire time."

"I'm sure. I only hope you didn't overly tire him," she murmured in a voice filled with sensual promise.

The guards untied his hands and shoved him inside, then they shut and locked the door behind him. He stumbled to keep from falling and winced when he caught himself on the closest chair. Pain shot up his arm.

"Hurt, Major?" she asked with a wicked smile. "Do you need any aid?"

"No." He straightened. He refused to show this woman any weakness, physical or otherwise. "I don't want anything you have to offer. Where is Selena?"

Her smile widened. "You'll know in due time. Meanwhile, why don't you sit with me on my bed? It's the most comfortable spot in the room."

He watched her slender hand slide back and forth across what looked to be Oriental silk sheets. Expensive, as were all the items in her chamber. Where had she found the money to finance this venture? Selena had mentioned Isadora's husband had been a soldier stationed in Greece. He couldn't have had much money. A widow's pension definitely didn't stretch this far.

"If I sit, will you tell me about Selena?" he asked as he folded his arms across his chest. Surreptitiously, he rubbed his injury. Slowly, the pain faded as his muscles relaxed.

She lazily stretched one arm towards him, arching her back and thrusting out her breasts. "I'll do or be anything you want if you come to my bed."

He did not want to play Isadora's game, but did as he'd been asked, believing it would be the quickest way to discover what had happened to Selena. Once he had taken a place by her side, she draped her arms around his shoulders and placed a kiss on his collarbone.

"Mmm, delicious. No wonder she wants to run away with you."

He controlled his reaction to her words. Isadora might not know all the details of their plan. There was no need to give her any information she didn't have already.

"What are you talking about? Who wants to run away with me?"

She laughed and began to rub her bare breasts against his back. If it had been Selena doing that same thing, he would have already been putty in her hands. Instead, he was only put more on guard.

"You are a silly boy. I have spies everywhere. You were overheard yesterday when you and Selena declared your undying devotion to each other on the pathway. You really ought to be more careful about where you speak, but I imagine you were—" She reached around to cup his cock through the thin fabric of his loincloth. "Swept away by passion."

Resisting the urge to jerk away from her touch, he asked. "If you thought we were going to escape yesterday, why didn't you take us then?"

"I needed time to prepare. As I told you when you first arrived here, I cannot let you leave this island alive. You know too much. If you told the wrong people, my entire society, everything I've built, would be destroyed."

She ran another series of kisses from one shoulder blade to the other. They seemed cold in comparison to the burning heat of Selena's touch, certainly they didn't inspire his lust or any other emotion rather than disgust.

"So you've brought me here to kill me?" he asked quietly. Desperation blossomed in his chest, but not for himself. He had fought in a war, seen death and caused it. He could hold his own if it came to a fight, even with a compromised arm. But Selena . . . she had never experienced those things. He ached to see her, to know she hadn't yet been harmed. If she was unhurt, they still had a chance.

"One of the two of you must die," Isadora's voice grew low and husky. "Either Selena for her insolence or you for your knowledge. I will offer you a trade."

He paused. "Trade?"

"Lay me back on this bed and show me what you did to Selena to make her melt at your feet," she whispered before she licked his neck. "Fuck me until I beg for mercy. If you do that, I'll let you live, and Selena will be the one to suffer for this outrage."

He looked over his shoulder at her. Isadora's eyes were glazed with a combination of passion and anger. Both were equally dangerous.

"Where is Selena?" he growled. "Tell me before I consider any offer you make."

Isadora's face twisted with indignation. "I have offered you my body, and you ask me about Selena?"

"Why did you really bring her to this island?" He shifted away from her touch. He could hardly bear her cold hands on his skin. "Was it really to free her as you've convinced her, or was there some more sinister motive? Perhaps that large inheritance which was the source of her stepchildren's hatred? Was that money she took with her part of what helped to fund this temple and the decadence you enjoy here?"

Isadora's smile returned. "You're a very intelligent man, Major Fletcher. Perhaps too intelligent for your own good. Part of why I chose Selena Kelsey as a disciple was because she would bring her funds with her, as was the reason I chose all the women here. Of course, the little fool only took a small portion of her inheritance when we left London. But it was enough to fund my project another half a year." She leaned forward until her sultry red mouth was only inches from his. "Now that I've answered your question, Major, what say we discuss the terms of my deal? I would like to tell you exactly what you'll do to me in this bed tonight.

"If you please me, as I know you will, I'll keep you alive for a few more weeks while you do my every sexual bidding. Perhaps we can make another arrangement during that time."

He rose to his feet with a shake of his head. "No. I won't touch you. I am in love with Selena, and I wouldn't betray her by dallying with a woman she once thought was her friend. Or any other woman, for that matter."

Isadora's face contorted in disbelief. "You're saying you won't make love to me, even to save your own life?"

"I wouldn't make love to you for any reason."

She scrambled off the bed and darted over to the darkest corner of the room. She pulled a candle from a sconce on the wall, and when the light flared, he saw a chair covered with a thick sheet. Isadora tore the sheet aside to reveal Selena. She was bound and had a gag in her mouth, but tears streamed down her face as she locked eyes with Gavin.

"And what about to save hers? If you don't make love to me, I will choose *her* for the sacrifice I make for your sins. What do you say about my offer now?"

Selena made a muffled no, and her eyes grew wide as she shook her head back and forth. Gavin stared at her helplessly. She had been tied cruelly; her hands were beginning to turn purple from the tightness of the velvet ties binding her wrists. Her hair was bound in the knot for her gag, pulling at the roots painfully. Still, all she focused on was him, telling him without words that she would rather die than watch him pleasure Isadora.

"She called you friend!" he burst out with horror. "How can you treat her this way?"

Isadora shrugged as she glanced at Selena. "She betrayed me. If I wish to remain in control of this group, I have no choice but to dole out swift punishment. I grow tired of these arguments. Choose, Major. Now."

He dropped his gaze to avoid witnessing Selena's pain at his words and answered, "Yes. If you set Selena free, let her leave Cyprus, I will stay here as your sex slave. I'll pleasure you in every way imaginable." He was careful to conceal any expression of emotion so Isadora wouldn't see his utter disgust.

Isadora's crow of triumph couldn't drown out Selena's muffled scream of torment. He couldn't stand that Selena had to witness his betrayal with Isadora. He could only hope she would understand that he had no choice. He had to agree to keep Selena safe from harm.

"I have a vast imagination," Isadora said as she sashayed closer. "First, I want you to take that wicked tongue of yours and lick me all over. I want you to make me writhe. And I want her—" She motioned over her shoulder toward Selena. "To watch."

"Come here," Gavin murmured as he pushed back his disgust. Isadora obeyed. She wrapped her arms around his shoulders and hooked one long leg around his thigh. The heat of her throbbed against his cock, but it did not stir him. Selena quietly sobbed in the corner.

With a growl, he crushed his mouth down on Isadora's. After a moment, he trailed his fingers up to stroke her silky hair, then stroked a line down her neck. When she finally relaxed into his embrace, he pressed his thumbs down into a special pressure point as hard as he could.

Isadora stiffened beneath his hand, then went limp in his arms. With little fanfare, he dropped her unconscious form into a heap on the floor and rushed to Selena's side. Her eyes were wide as he ripped her bindings loose and rubbed her hands to get the circulation back into them.

She pulled one hand free to yank the gag down from her mouth and winced when a few strands of long, tangled hair ripped free from her scalp.

"Is she—is she dead?" she whispered.

He shook his head. "No. It's a trick of hand-to-hand combat. She'll be unconscious for a while, enough time for us to escape if we can get past the guards."

He drew her into his arms and held her tenderly. "I was so afraid she had harmed you."

"I thought I would have to watch you make love to her. I don't believe I could have borne that."

He cupped her neck and eased his face closer to hers. "Hear me, Selena. I am in love with you. I want no one else but you."

A little squeal of pleasure made him smile. "I love you, Gavin. I love you with all my heart."

She leaned up to kiss him, pouring the passion of her heart into the touch. Unlike when Isadora had embraced him, Selena's kiss inspired love and passion that had him aching all over.

"I wish I could lay you back on that bed and show you how much I love you, make you scream with pleasure," he said softly. His words had her shivering, and a surge of triumph worked through his bloodstream. "But we have no time now. Later, once we escape the compound and get to a boat leaving Cyprus, I'll have the first captain I see marry us. I will make love to you all the way to our next destination. As my wife."

Selena froze. "You want me to be your wife?"

"Yes. I never want to be apart from you. If we're married, we can return to England any time we like. Your stepchildren will have no power over another man's wife."

She wrapped her arms around his neck and hugged him so tightly he almost couldn't breathe. "Yes, yes, yes. I will marry you, Gavin."

Outside, voices sounded, drawing near, breaking up their tender moment like ice water thrown on a fire.

She released him and immediately began to untie her ankle binds. "If we don't hurry, there won't be a wedding, but a funeral."

Her bravery, her inner strength was amazing. "We need a plan to get past the guards. He surveyed the room. The hut is small; there are no back doors. And Isadora appears to have blocked all the windows even if we could use one for our escape."

She looked up at him with a smile so devious and sensual, it nearly unmanned him. "I think we ought to use the same tactic that took Isadora to her knees." She unbound her chiton to reveal her perfect breasts, her shapely hips, the dusting of feathery hair between her thighs. His body lurched in reaction. "I'll offer the guards a little candy, and you give them their just reward."

Gavin looked from the unconscious Isadora to the woman he would make his wife with a smile. "Help me move her to the bed and get those ties from the chair."

Selena took a deep breath to calm her jangled nerves, then opened the door and leaned against the frame. She could only hope she looked seductive and not terrified.

"Hello, gentlemen," she said in a low, breathy voice she'd heard Isadora use from time to time with her lovers.

She'd captured their attention with her nudity, for the guards lowered their weapons and stared at her breasts, then lower. She fought not to squirm as she thrust her breasts out further for their leering eyes.

"Isadora has decided Gavin and I aren't enough to satisfy her urges. She was hoping you two might join us." With a wink, she motioned behind her toward the bed where Isadora was currently bound, legs spread seductively. In the darkened room, the guards would not be able to see that Isadora was unconscious. Or that the bed was prepared with restraints to bind the guards along with Isadora, once they had been dealt with.

"Isadora wants us to join you in her bed?" her target asked as his weapon hit the dirt with a clatter.

"Absolutely. Please, won't you come in?"

The two guards looked at each other, then scrambled for the door.

With a wince of disgust, Selena wrapped her arms around the man she'd chosen and let him kiss her as the second man headed for the bed. When she heard the sounds of a struggle behind her, she knew Gavin had struck and rubbed her breasts against her own guard to keep his attention away from the commotion behind them. He tasted like tobacco and onions as he pushed his fat tongue between her lips. As his hands roamed around to cup her bare backside, she slammed her knee up into his groin, rendering him helpless as he rolled on the ground in apparent agony.

She pivoted to face the second man, but Gavin had already taken care of him, as he was lying on the ground in a crumbled heap. He glared down at the man who had kissed her then grabbed a handful of his shirt and dragged him upright. Gavin drew his hand back and struck him a powerful blow. The man's eyes rolled back and he went limp. Gavin caught him beneath the armpits and dragged his motionless body across the floor toward the bed.

"Very well done, my love," she said.

He shrugged as he tied the man roughly. "I would have preferred killing him after the way he was touching you, but I held back."

She laughed as she helped him move the second guard. Once both men had been securely tied and gagged, Selena let out a sigh of relief and stepped into Gavin's arms. She clung to him.

"The first part of our escape is over," he said, stroking his hands over her hair in a soothing motion. "You did marvelously well."

Selena pulled back with a shaky smile. "I'm just glad to be done with it. Now we just have to gather our things and run."

He nodded. "In just a few more moments, we'll be free."

She shimmied into her shift and grabbed his hand. As they crept along the pathway, her heart throbbed. Even though music played and torch lights glowed in the temple on the hill in the distance, she and Gavin were far from safe.

"They've started the ceremony," she whispered, as they slipped inside her hut. Their bags were within reach, and he snatched the satchels up. She flung one over her shoulder.

"How long before they'll come searching for Isadora?" he asked as he took her hand a second time and led her away from the temple toward the harbor city of Pafos where they could board a ship.

She shrugged. "It's hard to say. Often Isadora arrives at the ceremonies late. She generally indulges in pleasures of the flesh before. She told me it primes her for the erotic stimulus to come."

At the time, Isadora's explanation had seemed titillating, but now, knowing how badly she'd been betrayed and used, it made Selena sick. How could she have considered Isadora a friend? How had she been so blind and stupid?

"Then we may have just enough time."

Gavin led her away, further and further from the temple, from the compound she had called home since her escape from London. From the life she thought she wanted. Now it turned out it was all a sham.

Just as the temple lights disappeared over a bluff, Selena stopped.

"Wait. Let me look one last time." She rose up on her tiptoes and looked down at the area. With a sigh, she shook her head.

"Are you sorry?" Gavin asked quietly.

"Sorry to be leaving?" She shook her head. "No. I thought I belonged here. I thought I was a sensual spirit, a slave of Aphrodite caught in a tangled web of a society that didn't understand my needs. That was what Isadora told me."

She looked at the distant compound again. "But really, she thought I was a silly prude who had money she wanted for herself. I wasn't a disciple of Aphrodite. I was only a repressed widow after all."

Gavin grasped her shoulders and turned her to face him. With him so close, she could see his features clearly. "You think just because Isadora Glasier used you for her own devices that you aren't truly everything you believed yourself to be? You *are* sensual, the most sensual, alluring woman I've ever met.

"But, you're right. You aren't a slave to Aphrodite. You aren't anyone's slave. If anything, I am *your* slave. And I'll happily do your bidding for the rest of my life."

She smiled as a little of her confidence returned. "I don't want a slave, Gavin. I want a husband. A partner. A lover." She leaned up to place a gentle kiss on his warm lips. "Forever."

"And you'll have that with me," he whispered before he draped an arm over her shoulder. "Come, we'll reach Pafos by morning and then we'll start our new life."

"Together," she murmured as they walked down the hill and away from Aphrodite's temple. "Forever."

About the Author:

Jess Michaels has been writing since she can remember and has always loved happily-ever-afters. Of course when she discovered romance, it was the perfect fit. She also appeared in ***Secrets, Volume 11*** *with* Ancient Pleasures *and writes for Avon as Jenna Petersen. You can find her at* http://www.jessmichaels.com.

White Heat

by Leigh Wyndfield

To My Reader:

On an ice planet in the middle of nowhere, two loners who never should have met find each other. One has decided to stop running. The other has just started . . .

Chapter One

"Let me guess. It's going to snow. Now *that's* something new and different."

Raine placed her feet into the indents she'd cut in the ice wall. Pulling herself up, she straddled the top and stared off to the east. The wall didn't provide protection, since the gate had long ago blown off in a storm, but it offered a great view of the surrounding plain.

"It's going to be a big one," she said, studying the building black clouds in the distance. "White Out, for sure."

She'd long ago gotten over the fact that she now talked to herself on a regular basis after being alone for two planet rotations.

Briefly, she debated if she was finally losing her mind. She didn't think so, but perhaps she'd be the last to know if she was.

"I need to get off this planet before I *do* lose it." If she hadn't already.

There was a reason she couldn't leave. "Oh yeah, a crazed psychopath will kill me in a very unpleasant way if he catches me." She rolled her eyes.

The threat lessened the longer she stayed on this ice block. Death didn't look so bad after all, when the years stretched on before her with only the occasional big storm to keep her interested.

"Of course, I *am* rich." She grimaced. Being rich meant exactly zilch when she couldn't spend any of it. Millions of balseems scattered in hidey-holes all over the galaxies and here she was on Sector 9, one of thirteen unlucky planets in the Danthium quadrant of Galaxy Grid 219. In other words, the middle of nowhere.

The wind picked up, whipping back her hood. She let it go, scanning the horizon without the interfering fabric. Winter here lasted three quarters of a rotation, so she might as well enjoy her bare skin touching the outside air one last time before it got so cold, it would freeze her flesh off if she ventured out.

If there was one place in the whole of Creation where Malachi Delmundo might not find her, it was right here.

And she knew he was trying, knew he would never give up until he held her beating heart in his hands after cutting it out with a blunt knife.

"Revenge," she whispered.

Three years ago, Malachi had killed her team, all six of them, and she still wasn't sure why. They'd been offered a contract to kill him, but they'd turned it down. As a rule, they didn't take contracts from cybergangs, since the money hadn't been worth the risk. So why had Malachi sent his assassins after them? Now she wished they'd taken the job on and blown the bastard away.

Only she had been left alive by sundown that day, a fluke that still left her with an angry ache of guilt every time she thought about her lost friends. Malachi's men had thought she was dead, too. They were wrong.

Her vengeance had been sweet. She'd hit him where it hurt him most—his wealth. She'd taken a little under half of it and led him on a long, merry chase across the galaxies. He'd burned through more of his remaining balseems trying to run her down.

But she couldn't keep that up forever, so she'd come here.

She watched the clouds swirl in the distance. "Yep, it's going to be one hell of a storm. Early, too."

Just what she needed. Extra time locked in her icehouse.

Grasping the top of the wall, she swung herself over, somersaulting and landing on her feet. But instead of taking her customary bow to her non-existent audience, she scrambled back up the wall again.

Out of the corner of her eye on her way down, she'd caught sight of a storm building to the west as well. Her heart pounded in her chest at the thought of two blizzards clashing right above her house.

Sitting on the wall, Raine scanned the black clouds.

"Gods," she whispered.

Then she blinked and looked again.

"Not clouds. Smoke."

The only thing on this chunk of ice besides a trading station was the notorious prison, Inter-world Council Penitentiary number 56900987, known to the people on Sector 9 as "Hell Frozen Over," or "HeFO" for short.

If it had been any other building on Sector 9, it wouldn't have burned because they were all made up of ice and rock. But HeFo was made of wood. After the first few prison breaks where the inmates managed to melt themselves out, the IWC had rebuilt the majority of the prison with imported lumber.

"And it's been drying out for weeks now, since we haven't had any snow." She whistled.

But one look at the coming storm made Raine jump down again, this time landing on her feet, then diving to execute a perfect roll.

No matter what she did, she had to keep in shape. Malachi would find her eventually. It was only a matter of time . . .

Walker staggered, forcing himself to move towards the relative safety of the rocks, across the slick, bare stretch of ground he'd traveled for hours. It never seemed as if he got closer.

The wind had picked up to a howl, and ice chips whipped through the air, ripping at the small patch of exposed skin on his face. Tears streamed, trying to clear the ice, which felt like grains of sand in his eyes.

His burned hands were more painful than anything he'd ever experienced. Every beat of his heart produced pain in his fingers as they throbbed with his pulse. He didn't have even a small amount of energy left to heal them.

He made his feet shuffle forward, just a few more steps. Come on, don't give up, he chided himself.

Merrium had laughed out loud when they sentenced him here. She knew he couldn't use his hidden power if he was unable to build the large amount of heat required. Being on a cold planet had cut off a piece of him as efficiently as if they'd chopped off one of his legs. Every second in HeFO had seemed like an eternity.

Or maybe she'd laughed because he was convicted of a crime he didn't commit. He couldn't provide himself with an alibi, and Merrium had known it. He'd spent the evening healing other Mixed

Breeds, people like himself who looked human enough but carried alien blood in their veins. It was an automatic death sentence if the Inter-world Council found out that he or others like him had dared to bring their alien-infected blood onto IWC planets. Breeds couldn't chance going for traditional medical help, so they came to him. He'd chosen HeFO over death for himself and his patients.

Walker glanced up to find the rocks had finally gotten closer. Just a little further and he'd be there.

Raine rolled onto her back and panted at the ceiling. She could now do a hundred push-ups without pausing. Her body was in the best shape it had ever been in her life.

"Maybe it's time to go back onto the offensive."

The wind outside moaned and howled. Everything inside her screamed for her to leave Sector 9. She hated it here.

A loud bang shuddered down the ice tunnel. She sat up with a start.

"If the front entrance has collapsed again . . ." She didn't finish. Because if it collapsed, she'd dig herself out. What other choice did she have?

Hurrying from her main room, she ran along the entrance hallway, finally dropping to her knees to crawl to the portal at the end. The hall was set up to provide only the smallest exit possible, to keep in most of the heat.

She opened the portal slowly, shouldering the weight of the snow on the other side. She had a backup gate at the top of the hallway if she couldn't reseal this one.

Instead of the snow she expected, the portal crashed wide and a body fell on top of hers.

Malachi's assassins had finally found her!

She fought like a wild thing, punching, kicking, bucking her body below his.

The man fought harder, pinning her with his much heavier weight, his arms holding hers to her side.

Wind gusted ice and snow into her house and life-giving heat escaped. She had to do something to get the door shut.

She brought her knee up to catch him in the balls.

He moved at the last instant, deflecting most of the hit. In the unguarded moment, she managed to roll him onto his back. He tried to flip her under him again by throwing all his weight and momentum to his side. Scrambling out of his reach, she launched herself at his body. He fell onto the icy hallway, smacking his forehead hard. She wrenched his arm in a tight twist behind him.

"Who are you?" she demanded. She needed to close the door. It would take a week to build up the heat in the house if she didn't act fast. "But better to be cold than dead."

"What?" he asked and she knew she'd spoken out loud.

"Who are you?" She jerked up on his arm to add emphasis.

He groaned. "My hand."

She leaned in to growl in his ear, sliding her knife out of her belt to press it against his throat with her free hand. "Who. Are. You."

"Walker," he gasped, his body shaking from the cold. "My hand."

His eyes shut and his body went slack. He'd passed out.

At first, Raine thought he was trying to trick her. But as his body slumped, her knife nicked his neck, and blood ran onto her floor. "Nope, guess he's not faking."

Standing, she dragged his heavy body backwards as fast as she could. Which wasn't as fast as she needed. He was huge and weighed as much as a freighter in his unconscious state.

She shut the portal after one last look outside. It was a White Out and a bad one. It would be days before the snows stopped. Then the whole planet would be covered in deep mounds of powder.

Crawling into the taller part of the tunnel, she stood and tried to catch her breath. Who in the hell was this man? He moaned and it spurred her into action. She needed to tie him up before he woke.

It took awhile, but she dragged him into the room by the shoulders of his jacket, then rolled him over. His clothing was minimal, only several thin layers of fabric, indicating he was one of the most ill-prepared assassins she'd ever encountered. Then she saw the IWC Penitentiary stamp on the jumper beneath his jacket.

"He's a prisoner," she breathed.

"What to do, what to do," she whispered, pondering. She couldn't bring herself to throw him outside.

A towel covered his face, with only a small slit in the material for him to see through. When she unwound it, the exposed flesh had the crackled appearance of snow frosting, an unpleasant and dangerous condition that could lead to death. It ran all over his skin, even where the cloth had covered it.

Something she was sure had died long ago uncurled inside her. She had to help him, for no other reason than he so desperately needed it.

She placed her hands over his cheeks. His breath hitched in pain. Even her cold fingers must feel too hot to him. His condition was more serious than she'd thought. She pulled off his boots to check for more snow frosting. No sign of that, but she wrapped his feet in Thermo-blankets just in case.

The inner lining stuck to his hands as she wrestled with his gloves. Had he gotten them wet? The first one came off and she gasped.

"Gods and Goddesses!"

His hand was black, covered in blisters and cuts.

She dragged off the other glove, then ran for her first aid kit.

"The fire. He's burned his hands."

She threw the case down and rummaged for burn cream. She knew she had it in here somewhere.

The tube wasn't as large as she wished. She spread the oily paste all over his hands. Then she slapped a bandage across the small cut on his neck. No one would say she had a great bedside manner. She had been part of an elite fighting squad before Malachi killed them all, not a healer.

"You're probably that serial murderer they caught on LackSui last year. After I go to sleep, you'll kill me and eat my eyeballs for breakfast." Even as she said it, she dismissed the idea, although she'd keep a close eye on him just in case.

From her bathroom, her only extravagance in this ice hell, she grabbed two towels and wrapped his hands in them. Then she dragged him to her bed, falling on her butt once in the process. She needed to warm him fast.

The heating system in an icehouse was such that the hot air didn't have one specific point of entry, which would cause melting. Rather, warm air circulated throughout the rooms from a series of ducts. Which meant the house was freezing since they'd had the portal open.

No way could she get him up onto her bed. Spreading a thermal tarp to prevent melting, she pulled her mattress to the floor and rolled the man onto it. He moaned when his weight came down on his hands.

"Oops, sorry," she said.

Then she piled every blanket over him that she had in the house and finished by stuffing his head into one of her bigger hats. She sat for a while, warming his cheeks with her bare hands.

For the first time, she looked at him. Before she'd jammed on the hat, she had seen that his hair had been shaved almost to his scalp in typical prison fashion. A dark blond, although it was hard to tell with it that short.

"His face isn't exactly handsome, is it?"

His mouth turned down as if he understood her words. She had to remember not to talk out loud. She didn't even realize she was doing it half the time.

Still, he was good-looking, in a rugged way. He had nice, strong features, and full, sensuous lips. A shadow of beard covered his face, making him seem mysterious.

She grinned at her musings and resisted the urge to peel one eye open to see what color they were.

Lowering her head, she placed her lips to his cheek to check the temperature. Cool but not ice cold. He was warming up fast. Faster than he should have. She realized the snow frosting had disappeared. She was sure she hadn't been mistaken, but there wasn't any sign of it now. Strange.

Suddenly, his head rolled and his lips caught hers, his arm curving around her neck to hold her down, his hand kept carefully aloft.

For a moment, she was shocked into stillness.

Her body, which hadn't felt the touch of another human for three years, exploded with fire. His lips feathered on her mouth, before his tongue slowly stroked across her lips. His arm tightened around her neck, as if he was afraid she would pull away.

But Raine didn't want to move. She had thought she'd been okay here. Annoyed maybe, but fine without companionship. With this stranger's kiss, she realized she wasn't fine. Her stomach tightened with a need so great, she didn't try to fight it.

Instead, she opened her mouth and let his tongue slip inside. Suckling lightly, his taste exploded into her mouth. Different from anything else she'd ever savored, like warm bread straight from the oven, something that brought to mind fields of grain blowing in a summer breeze.

The kiss wasn't demanding. Soft and gentle, it felt pleasant and right, as if she'd been sitting here on Sector 9 for two years just waiting for his lips to touch hers. And maybe she had, she thought, reveling in the burn of desire between her legs, making her body yearn for release.

Pulling slowly away, unsure if he'd let her go, she was careful not to jar his hands. Warm green eyes stared up from only a hand-length away. They were the color of green moss or Orchid leaves in the heart of a lush, tropical jungle.

For a brief moment, her mind showed her a picture of what they must look like heavy lidded with passion, intense before the moment of climax. Her stomach flip-flopped with desire.

Walker stared up at the woman and, with a certainty that shocked him, he understood exactly what she was.

Mate.

The word breathed through his mind, through all his reawakening senses, shaking him to the core. That he could have found the one person meant for him in all of Creation, here in this icy hell, boggled his mind. All this time, he'd thought his mixed blood had meant he wouldn't have the bonding of his father's people, that the generations of inter-mating with humans had taken this destiny from him.

But for the first time in many lunar cycles, his power stirred, even though his body temperature wasn't high enough to support it. The touch of her body had set him on fire and increased his heat level in the way his father had told him it would if he was ever lucky enough to find his mate. His blood pounded through his veins, his senses on overload with the smell of her body, the taste of her lips, and her dancing gray eyes.

He wanted to tear off her clothes, rip away his own, and press his naked body tight against hers. The warmth would be amazing. He could heal his hands and bring her to orgasm with his touch. The way she poured heat into him during their kiss, he knew he could do it.

He forced his body to remain still. His hat had fallen off and her fingers filtered through what was left of his hair. The scalp was a great conductor of heat, and hers flowed into him, building his reserves even more. The sensation filled him with a burning need only she could fulfill.

Right now, he was almost helpless, his body exhausted by the fire and the long walk in the storm. If she kept going and kissed him a few more times, he'd have enough energy stored to heal his hands.

"Kiss me again," he said, his voice rusty from lack of use.

He could tell she was reluctant, her hands stilling.

"Please." He'd spent his whole life never begging for anything, but at this moment, he'd do whatever it took for more of her touch.

Her mouth pulled into a frown, her brows lowering, then she shrugged and dipped her head.

Pleasure ran the length of his body and back again, tightening every muscle, making his cock rock hard as she slanted her lips and slipped her tongue inside his mouth. He wanted to grab her, roll her beneath his body, but instead, he kept his hands out to the side. He bent his fingers, the spike of pain reminding him to go slow with her.

He didn't know how he was going to do it, but he needed her to take off both of their clothes and press her body against his. As his mind cranked through possible scenarios, his lips enjoyed her kiss. He tried to think, even though her taste filled his mouth with warmth and pleasure exploded inside him.

Then a plan came into his mind, something he'd never considered before.

Chapter Two

Walker had spent his life concealing his power until he'd witnessed another Mixed Breed being beaten by the Council police. The man's tainted blood had been discovered when he went for medical help. In that moment, a weight of responsibility had come crashing down on his shoulders, because he knew he could provide the medical help his fellow outcasts needed.

Even though he'd used his talents to help others, he'd rarely made use of them to help himself, and he'd only once tried them during sex. Merrium had been appalled and had rejected his efforts, but even before that, he could tell his power didn't react to her. It didn't stir to life, tingling below the surface of his skin.

Not like it did now with the woman he kissed, the woman who ran her warm, magnificent hands through his hair, making his whole body throb.

He wanted to explore everything she was from the inside out, but he couldn't let her know about his skills. All Inter-world people were disgusted by Mixed Breeds. Still, he could push energy into her slowly, increase the burn between them so it felt like desire. Intense, wonderful, amazing desire.

For a moment, he struggled with his plan. His hands throbbed with every beat of his heart. If he used the energy to heal himself, he could cut his pain in half. But he would lose everything if she stopped kissing him.

Slowly, tentatively at first, he breathed power into her mouth, the act much like a mini-orgasm, relieving the growing pressure as a wave of pleasure sped through his body into hers.

He must have pushed too hard, because she jumped and pulled away. Gray eyes, the color of icy seas, stared down at him, blinking in surprise. "What was that?" she asked. "It felt like lightning racing through me. Did you feel it?"

He still had his arm around her neck but resisted the urge to drag her down. He'd seen how strong she was when he had tried to force his way into her house.

"Please," he whispered. If she was his mate, she would want him too. Badly. He could only hope the sharp bite of desire between them would overcome her resistance.

Her head cocked to the side. "It feels good, but this is probably one of your stupider ideas," she murmured.

"What?" he asked, shaking his head. He glanced around the room, but couldn't figure out who she spoke to.

"Oh," she said, a blush streaking across her face. Dropping her head, she kissed him quick, as if she tried to cover up for something.

He didn't understand and quite frankly, he could care less. This. This is what he wanted. Following the seam of her lips with his tongue, he asked for entry. She parted for him, and his tongue brushed hers. Energy poured from her body into his, making his skin break out into a sweat. How long had it been since he'd been this warm?

Unable to fight the desire to give her back some of the pleasure she gave him, he carefully returned some power to her. Just a flash of heat that would feel like a whisper of warmth filling her from the inside out.

She moaned and as she deepened the kiss, her fingers splayed across his cheeks, down his neck and buried in the top of his jumpsuit. Gods and Goddesses, if she would just strip his clothes and run her hands along his skin.

As if she could hear his thoughts, she bared the top of his chest and trailed her hands over the muscles that had built from months of hard labor in HeFo.

It felt so good. So good.

But not enough. No, he wanted more. Much more.

His energy level was high now. Hotter than he'd been in so long, he healed his hands with a thought, the flash of pain at the healing making him break the contact with her on a gasp.

She stared at him in wonder, her tongue darting out to lick over her lips in a slow, sexy glide.

"I'm Raine," she whispered.

"Walker," he said, forcing his gaze to meet her eyes instead of staring at her lips. He kicked away the blankets, too hot now to stand them.

Raine looked down the line of Walker's body and saw that she wasn't the only person totally, completely, one-hundred percent turned on. Oh no. She closed her eyes and grasped for her sanity. She didn't even know this man. He'd been in HeFO, a prison for murderers and thieves. She lowered his head to the ground, sliding her arm from beneath it.

"Raine." He allowed her to straighten, but she could tell he didn't want to. He gritted his teeth on whatever else he wanted to say.

She moved until she was sitting beside him instead of kneeling at his head. "You don't look cold anymore." Unable to resist the overwhelming urge to touch him, she rested one hand on his exposed upper chest and raised an eyebrow.

"I'm warmer than I've been in months," he murmured, his green eyes studying her intently.

Watching him for any sign that he might not want what she was about to do, she ran her hands down his bare skin.

She was sick and tired of being cold and alone on this heap of ice. If this stranger fell into her lap, she was going to make the most of it. He felt right to her, and her mind whispered that she could trust him. If something went wrong, he wasn't in any condition to hurt her. She didn't think he would do anything but bring her pleasure. And she wanted pleasure. She deserved it, dammit.

Didn't she?

A brief hesitation flitted through her and she studied his bright green eyes. He was in HeFO for a reason.

Her hands glided down to his crotch, and he groaned and closed his eyes against the feel of her brushing his rock hard erection.

"Oh yes," she might have whispered out loud. Or maybe she didn't. Who knew? Who cared? Not her. Not right now. A burn filled her body, driving her onward like nothing she'd ever felt before.

Leaning over him, she spread open his jumpsuit to study his body.

Smooth muscled perfection greeted her, the sheen of sweat catching her eye. He shouldn't be this hot, should he? Maybe he had a fever.

Then the thought was swept away as he shrugged the coat and jumpsuit off his shoulders, sitting up on his own and peeling the fabric off his body in one sweep. When he lay back, he was naked.

"Oh my," she thought or said. Who knew with this man lying before her?

Every inch of him was hard perfection. What his face lacked in handsomeness, his body far, far made up for in sheer flawlessness.

Somewhere in the back of her mind, she worried about the snow frosting. Where had it gone? She hadn't imagined it, had she? She'd never gotten the condition herself. Maybe the crackling hadn't been what she'd thought it was.

She blinked and the thoughts fell away as she gazed at his shoulders. Double the width of hers, they ran down into rippled abs, that moved into slim hips, that flared back out into well muscled thighs. The curve of his leg glided gracefully down into trim, solid calves.

His erection matched the rest of him—big and hard, the head pulsing and engorged, a drop of pre-come dotting the top.

She wanted to touch so very, very badly, so she did.

She dragged her hand along the bounty of his thigh, skirting his sex and stroked across his lightly haired chest. Circling a nipple, she watched in utter fascination as it hardened with her stroke.

"Raine," he said, his breath catching with her action.

As if she was in a dream, she slowly gazed up at him.

"Kiss me." He wasn't begging anymore and he wasn't asking. His voice was all command.

Her natural rebelliousness flared to life and she narrowed her eyes. Keeping eye contact, she lowered her head in degrees until she planted a chaste kiss on his nipple.

Even that simple action made him swallow. He'd liked it, she thought, and, still keeping her gaze locked to his, she ran her tongue in a circle around the hard bud, then sucked it into her mouth. The taste of his skin exploded into her mouth, spicy male and salt from the sheen of perspiration that covered his body.

He hissed in a breath, his sex jumping up to briefly touch her side where she rested across his body while she kissed him.

With a shaking hand still wrapped in the makeshift bandages she'd put on, he attempted to drag off her thermal sweater.

"No, you'll hurt your hands." She pulled out of reach. With one movement, she was out of the sweater, but immediately regretted it as the chilly air hit her breasts, tightening her nipples into painful peaks. "Oh! It's too cold."

"Come here," he growled, his gaze on her breasts. "Don't put it back on. I'll warm you."

She stretched out beside him, and he immediately rolled to cover her, supporting himself on his forearms. Their chests were pressed together and it felt so amazing, she moaned. Briefly, her mind questioned why she felt this way, how she'd never before felt so much desire that she didn't care about her safety, didn't care about anything but touching him. He was steaming hot now, able to keep them both warm in the freezing cold of the room.

"Strip off your pants," he said, nuzzling his face into her neck and biting lightly.

Now was T-minus Zero in the countdown. *Speak now or forever hold your peace, Raine.*

She felt him smile into her neck. "You talk to yourself, don't you?" he asked, and for the first time she could hear humor in his voice.

It irritated her. "Yes, dammit, I do." She pushed on him. "Back off, buster, or I can't get naked for you."

He blinked and the corners of his eyes crinkled as if he fought a smile.

She narrowed her eyes, and he frowned to stop the grin from spreading to his mouth. She could tell.

He distracted her by raising up so she could reach her belt. When her hands found the buckle, she brushed his erection and then neither of them was smiling.

"Gods, you feel like the sun on a tropical day. All lightness and wonder." His voice sounded pained.

She fumbled with the closure at her waist, then pushed down until her pants were caught at her boots. He rolled to one side to let her sit to undo the fasteners. The moment her clothes were free, he caught her and brought her beneath him, as if all he really wanted was to press his skin to hers. He sighed and it was a joyous sound.

Then his eyes opened and he kept her gaze as he worked his legs between hers. "Yes, Raine, speak now or forever hold your peace."

His voice was hoarse, but the head of his erection slid along the top of her thighs until it ran into the wetness she'd accumulated there. Then it raced down her clitoris to stop at the very edge of her opening.

For once, she was speechless. All she could do was pant and wait for this wondrous thing. Had she really been thinking about going after Malachi, who would surely kill her, when she could have *this*?

"So be it." He said the words as if he sealed her fate.

Before she could dwell on the significance, he eased his cock into her channel. Even though she was ready, she had gone a long time without someone in her bed. He stretched her to the limit, the strength of his cock expanding her so that all she could do was grasp onto the bulge in his biceps and experience the feel of him sliding into her body.

When the team had lived, she'd been lovers with Antilli, a small, wiry assassin. Gods, she had missed him after he'd died. They hadn't been in love, but he had been her friend and her confidant.

She hadn't been touched by a single other person since that day. She'd been too fragile at first, then too angry, then she'd ended up on this hunk of rock where she went months without seeing another living soul.

But Walker wasn't like Antilli in any way. Walker was all muscle and bulk. Huge.

He pulled back out and reached between them to glide his erection over her wetness. "You're tight. I don't want to hurt you," he said, his green eyes intense, his face tightened with desire.

He slowly thrust into her, this time sliding all the way in to the hilt. She hummed, feeling as if some piece of her soul was reborn, as if she had finally come home.

"Did that hurt?" he gasped, lowering his body fully onto hers.

"No."

He took a deep breath and let it out. "I'm not going to last long." Rocking forward, he seemed purposely to grind his body on her clitoris.

Raine bit her lip to stifle the scream that threatened to erupt at the intense storm building inside her.

He repeated the gesture, his whole body drenched in sweat, the light hair on his chest scraping over her already sensitized nipples. She fought to have him touch every part of her at once. All she could focus on was the feel of him filling her after being alone for so long.

"I need you to come, Raine." His voice sounded desperate, as if willpower alone kept him from climax, but she didn't open her eyes to look at his face. All she could do was experience the pleasure.

Then he kissed her and that strange, wonderful sensation breathed through her body, tightening her from the inside out. She came in a blaze of heat, the powerful release making her arch and grab his shoulders.

Walker ground himself into her and his body jumped with his own release, causing another ripple of pleasure to surge through her.

He collapsed, enveloping her body with his, his erection still connecting them in the most intimate of ways.

Chapter Three

"You're from the prison." Instead of wanting to push away from him, she kept her legs wrapped around his body to keep him close. She felt wonderful, dreamy, right.

He nodded. "The fire freed me."

His voice slid like warm honey down her spine. Everything about you is warm, she thought.

But he answered her with a nod, so she must have spoken out loud again. "I'm from the Gratermor Quadrant."

"The Outer Worlds?" She shook her head. That was on the edge of some very scary alien territory. No one lived there if they could help it.

He closed his eyes. "It's warm there." He blew out a breath. "Gods, I miss the heat."

"What were you in prison for?" She absently ran her fingers through his wheat-colored hair, wondering why she didn't move away from him. She should feel embarrassed at what had just happened between them, since she hadn't even spoken a dozen words to him before they'd jumped into bed. Or more accurately, *he* hadn't spoken that many words. She'd babbled enough for both of them without even meaning too.

But the human contact was more than she could resist. Just touching another person's skin felt like heaven. She hadn't realized how much she'd missed it.

Green eyes opened and turned hard. "Murder," he said.

She stilled, her hand on his cheek.

"I won't bother telling you I didn't do it. Why would you believe me?"

She searched his eyes. *Why indeed?*

"Yes, why indeed." His lips curled as if he was disgusted, but he didn't move away.

She tried to decide why she thought he was innocent. Or maybe not innocent, but not guilty. After all, she'd taken quite a few lives herself. Or the team had, but they couldn't have done it without her planning skills. Did it matter that the men they had killed were all killers themselves? The team had specialized in taking out the baddest of the bad—kidnappers, rapists and baby killers. But the fact that she had been the team's strategist and had contributed to the deaths of the targets her team had terminated made her a murderer too, didn't it? In the strictest form of the word?

She'd never really thought about it before. Since she was a child, she'd known that she was born to take down the bullies of the universes. It was her mission in life, the one thing burning in her soul.

"Raine the Avenger," she heard herself whisper self-mockingly.

He narrowed his eyes. "I'm not returning to HeFO. I'll kill myself first."

She raised her eyebrows. She believed him. It was there on his face. She knew what it felt like to die for something you believed in. Only she hadn't died. Her team had.

"I took the punishment of another. I had to, or reveal something much worse, and the bastard who framed me knew it."

She shifted to get more comfortable, and he hissed in a breath, the movement of her under him making him grow hard inside her once more. Desire shot through her body, her mind flashing back to the intense orgasm they'd just shared. Her channel tightened around his erection in a pleasure-filled pulse.

She fisted her hands and battled the need to have him again. Where had her normal control gone? What had happened to her constant diligence and threat assessment? She wouldn't let herself be distracted. "Why did they frame you?"

"Because they could. What burns me is that it was nothing personal. I took the fall because I was an easy mark." For a moment, he met her gaze, then he kissed her, hard and long. It wasn't sweet like the kisses he'd given her earlier. He kissed her as if he wouldn't let her go, as if he'd fight to the death before he'd let her free.

He left her gasping, distracted by the rising need inside her body, which is why at first she didn't comprehend what she was seeing when he leaned on one elbow and stripped the bandage off one hand, then the other.

"I have to run my hands over you," he growled. He withdrew from her and sat on his knees between her legs. His fingers wandered along her stomach, drawing her gaze with the feather-light, worshiping touch. She shivered as need spiked through her again. Her reaction to him wasn't normal. Too intense, too amazing, as if he held the key to her body's pleasure.

Finally, she took two big breaths and formed a coherent sentence. Kind of. "Your hands. Burned."

He stilled with a jerk as if she'd slapped him, looking at his hands as if he'd noticed them for the first time.

Slowly, without the hammering pleasure he gave to her senses, her mind clicked back into itself. She turned one of his hands in hers.

"Perfect. Not a scratch."

He let her move him as she would. She dropped that hand to study his other with an equally close inspection.

He was silent.

"Walker," she whispered, smoothing her fingers over the perfect skin of his palm. "What happened?"

Walker watched his woman—and she *was* his, she just didn't know it yet—stare at his hand. *Yeah Walker, what happened?*

He struggled to come up with the words to tell her. The truth might cause her to run screaming from him. She couldn't do that. She was his. They were fated to be together. If he lost her, he would spend the rest of his life without the soul-redeeming closeness of a mate. They would both have a piece of themselves that would be left half formed and aching, a constant reminder of what they'd lost.

"The snow frosting." Her fingers brushed his cheek, causing him to meet her gaze. "You had it all over your face. I know you did." Her soft hands flowed across his healed skin. "I thought at first I must have been mistaken, yet now I know I wasn't."

She shivered, and he resisted the urge to pull her into his warmth, knowing she wasn't cold but unnerved.

"Your hands should have taken months to heal." She choked on a strangled laugh and pulled away the bandage on his throat. "Even your neck." She pressed on his skin. "I nicked you with the knife, and now I can't even tell where I did it."

"Raine," he said, finding his voice in the face of what looked to be impending hysteria on her part. He had to calm her, make sure she didn't leave him during this crucial bonding stage. He had to stay with her long enough to cement the fragile link he could already feel woven between them. "Listen—"

"No." She shoved away but before she could stand, he launched himself forward, pinning her with his body.

She couldn't leave him. She couldn't reject him.

"Wait," he yelled, when she started to fight.

She paused long enough for him to say, "Listen, I—I can heal—" He stumbled on the explanation, opening his mouth and closing it several times.

She snorted. "Heal what?" She thrust against his chest. "What? What?" Each word grew progressively louder.

"You," he whispered, then hummed in irritation and said, "and me. I can heal anyone." He took a deep breath. Might as well tell all of it. "And I can do other things. With my hands."

She collapsed back and closed her eyes while she shook her head. "Of course he can, Raine. What do you expect? You can't think that a normal male with this hot of a body would waltz in your icehouse when you're living in the freaking middle of nowhere!" She smacked her palm on her forehead. "You freaking idiot!"

Walker cleared his throat, and her eyes flashed open. He didn't think she'd meant him to hear all that.

"So what *are* you?" she asked, anger clear in her snapping gray eyes.

He blew out a breath. Now was when she'd go ballistic. Merrium certainly had. And then she'd betrayed him. He was a Breed, an abomination, something that had to be destroyed. His heart clenched at the thought that Raine would betray him, too. That he'd lose his mate.

Gritting his teeth, he decided he wouldn't give her the chance. He would be at her side every moment of every day until she realized she had to be with him, that the Gods had intended it. It wasn't just that his power liked her, either. Everything about her was perfect and right. The way she looked, the way she'd fought him, the way she hadn't thrown him into the storm when she'd found out he was an escaped prisoner. Beauty and strength. Courage and compassion. It was a heady mix any man would want in his woman.

"Hello." She waved a hand before his face. "Are you in there?"

Holding her in place with the weight of his body, he said, "I'm a Mixed Breed. I have magic, passed from my father's line."

Her mouth dropped open, and her gaze rolled to the ceiling. Instead of fighting him as he'd thought she would, she laughed.

Big, breathy guffaws.

She wiped the tears from her eyes. Every time she got herself under control, she went into another bout of laughter.

It annoyed him.

"Something funny?" he ground out.

"Y-y-yes," she managed.

"Care to share?"

If she didn't feel so damn good naked beneath him, he'd strangle her.

She cleared another trail of tears with the back of her hands. "What are the chances," she said, suddenly sober, "that the first person I touch in three years is a Mixed Breed? I mean, the Inter-world Council's bounty has basically brought your kind to extinction and in you stroll, having escaped HeFO." She frowned. "No way HeFO knew you were Mixed. They would have killed you, not put you in prison."

"They didn't know." He tried not to let her see that her words hurt him. On the bright side, she hadn't tried to pull away. That counted for something. A lot of somethings, actually.

"You said earlier you were framed. Whoever did it knew what you were?"

"Yes." *Touch me,* his mind begged her. *Forgive me for being who I am. Want me for me.* But he kept his face blank.

"But your accent is from the Inner Worlds."

"I've lived most of my life within the IWC, most of it on Borrus itself."

"The Capital Planet," she breathed. "I'm impressed. You blend in well." She gazed at him critically, as if trying to see his tainted blood.

"My father was a third generation Mixed Breed. Only the magic of his line is left inside me. The rest has been bred out." He kept his voice flat. The magic and the ability to mate, he knew now.

"What did you do on Borrus?"

"Heal other Mixed Breeds."

Her eyes widened. "That's your job?"

"Yes."

"There are enough Breeds for you to spend all your time healing them?" Her tone held disbelief.

"Yes."

"Gods." She seemed impressed rather than outraged.

"What do you do?" he asked, turning the tables on her. It finally occurred to him that she shouldn't be here on this planet any more than he should.

"Me?"

"Either you or the other person you speak to all the time. Either of you is welcome to answer."

She frowned at him and tapped his shoulder with one finger. "For your information, I have lived here by myself for two whole planet rotations. There wasn't anyone else to talk to and it just seemed so . . ." she shrugged as if she searched for a word, "lonely not to hear voices, even if I only heard my own."

His heart twisted. Holy hell. At least he'd had human contact while in HeFo.

"I'm sorry."

Her eyes widened in surprise. "For what?"

"That you were lonely."

"It's not your fault. It's my own." An impish grin flashed across her face. "I am Raine the Avenger."

"You said that earlier, but I wasn't sure who you were talking to." For the first time in his life, Walker had hope. Hope that someone would accept him for what he was. She knew and she hadn't rejected him. "Who are you avenging?"

The question made the smile fade from her lips. "My team."

He waited for her to go on. Something about the sudden sadness in her eyes made him cautious, made him want to curl around her and hold her tight.

"They were killed three years ago, and I made the bastard who was responsible pay."

"Literally?"

"Oh yeah." Mischief returned to her eyes. "I stole half his net worth and then he had to spend more to chase me." Some of the spark went out of her eyes, and she sighed. "But then my luck began to run a little low, and I had to hide out. You have to admit, this is the last place anyone would look for me."

Something in her voice made him ask, "How bad did your luck run?"

"Move off me and I'll show you."

Walker released her reluctantly. Her body felt like heaven below his, firm muscles and womanly curves. He shifted so his body pressed against hers. He almost halted her when she rolled away from him onto her stomach, because he didn't want to lose the contact.

The sight of her back stopped him. He hissed in a breath.

She craned her neck over her shoulder trying to see her back. "I haven't looked at it in awhile. Is it that bad?"

"It must have hurt," was all he could say as he stared at the scar that ran from the top of her left shoulder, down her back, and across her right buttock. In some places, the brown streak was two fingers wide. Rage that someone had done this to his woman flashed through him, the thought of her pain hitting him like a physical blow to the stomach.

"Too bad you weren't around to heal me."

Stroking along the scar, he silently agreed, although if he was honest, he'd never healed a full human before. He didn't think it made a difference, but he couldn't be completely sure.

"You must have made this person pretty mad if he's still chasing you."

"Oh, Malachi is still pissed, I'm sure." She grinned over her shoulder.

Walker's heart stopped, then started again at double-time. "Malachi who?"

Raine gave him a funny look as she sat and gathered several blankets around her. "Delmundo, why?"

Walker couldn't speak for a long moment. It was too much of a coincidence to be true.

Chapter Four

Walker finally spoke. "Malachi Delmundo framed me for the murder."

"No way." She almost laughed, but the coincidence unnerved her enough to keep her sober.

"It's true. A woman I had thought was my friend told him about my Mixed Breed status and that I worked each night at the Breed hospital."

He'd told someone about the hospital, which meant he'd trusted them very much. A weird feeling curled through her as she realized this woman must have been his lover. "Breeds have their own hospital?"

Walker's mouth twisted with wry humor. "Of course we have a hospital."

"And it hasn't been discovered by the authorities?"

"Who would betray the only place they can go for medical treatment?"

Raine made sure she stayed silent as she thought about the fact there was always someone who would give you up, if the price was right. Someone had told Malachi where her team had been staying the night they'd all been killed.

"It was easy for him to plant evidence that I had been at the murder scene."

"Who did he murder?" she interrupted.

"As far as I can tell, he was just a citizen, although there must have been some reason Malachi wanted him dead." He pinched the bridge of his nose. "All I could say is that I was at home during the time the murder took place. I had no alibi that wouldn't end in my own death or put others in jeopardy."

Raine whistled. *Lord, that sucks.*

"That's an understatement. On this ice planet, I've not been able to generate enough heat to use my powers, essentially losing one of my senses. I lost part of who I am."

"But you healed your hands."

He wiggled his fingers, and a grin flashed across his face. "You helped my heat level immensely."

"Yeah, I guess sex will do that," she admitted, snuggling into the blankets.

He still sat without anything around him, totally naked, with his gorgeous body showing in all its perfection. Every one of those muscles curving in all the right places. She would love to run her hands over him again. Her palms itched with desire.

"Raine!" she said sharply, then silently lectured herself to stop gawking and stay on track.

When she met Walker's gaze, his eyebrows were arched in an unspoken question.

She shook her head. "So sex makes you hot enough to use your talent?"

"Not sex exactly." His hand tapped one muscled, fantastic thigh, drawing her attention. "It's hard to explain, but let's just say my power likes you."

"What in the hell does that mean?"

"Just touching you gives me energy." He knee-walked up the mattress and sat beside her. "Since I haven't touched you for a while, I'm starting to take on the room's temperature."

She slid a hand out of her warm cocoon and felt his shoulder. He wasn't hot anymore. "Wild. You want one of these blankets?" She made herself retract her hand, even though she longed to stroke him.

"I'd rather join you, if that's okay?"

She studied his face. His features were almost harsh, softened by his intense green eyes. He would look much better with some hair framing his face. Of course, the prison cut wouldn't make anyone look good. He waited, his expression blank, as if her decision to let him close didn't matter, but she thought it might.

The impact of what he'd shared hit her with a jolt. The last time he'd trusted someone with this information, he'd ended up in HeFO, but he'd told her anyway. He'd essentially trusted her with his life, since if she revealed who he was, he would be killed as soon as they could catch him. And she didn't think he was as savvy about running as she was. After all, she'd made a career of it.

Raine was humbled he had so much faith in her, although she wasn't sure she was worthy of it. Gods knew, her team had trusted her, too.

Walker sat silent, waiting for her answer.

"If you want to raise your heat levels, we should take a bath." She wasn't ready for this to end, she realized. Her heart skipped a beat, and she wondered why she felt this strongly about this man. Maybe she *had* gone insane.

He pulled back a bit, as if her answer wasn't what he was expecting. "You want to take a bath with me?" he asked, his tone carefully neutral.

She stood, suddenly excited to show off her bathroom. She'd never had anyone to brag to before. "Come on. Come on." She skipped across the freezing floor, knowing that very soon she'd be in luxury.

When she reached the portal, she turned to find out why he hadn't followed. Her abrupt stop had him catching her shoulders to keep him from running into her.

She started in surprise. "Whoa! I didn't think you were behind me."

He tightened his hold on her and grinned. "Where else would I be? I'm not giving up the offer of having a bath with a beautiful woman."

She disengaged herself and turned to fling open the portal.

He hummed in appreciation.

"It is amazing, isn't it?" She could hear the pride in her voice, but dammit, look at it!

Tile lined the room, while the floor was covered in rugs so her bare tootsies didn't have to step on the ice floor. She'd done the whole room in a sea foam green. It looked like heaven, if she did say so herself. Walking to the bathtub, a sunken monstrosity from the Gods raised on a special platform so the heat wouldn't melt her house down, she threw the levers to fill a space big enough for four.

She turned to give him a history of her struggles to bring greatness to an ice heap in the middle of nowhere and jumped because he was once again behind her.

His hand shot out to steady her before she pitched backwards into the tub.

"You are abnormally quiet when you move," she said, huffy because he kept surprising her.

"I don't mean to be." He peered around her. "This tub is the best thing I've seen in my lifetime, except for you."

Before she could stop herself, one of her hands fluttered to her chest. It was the second time in minutes he'd said nice things to her.

It made her feel downright girlie. It had been a long time since she'd been flattered.

He climbed the two steps of the platform and sat on the rim to dip his feet in. "Oh yeah. It's scorching hot in here."

She waited until the tub was half-filled before dropping her blankets, dashing up the stairs and sinking into the water with a sigh.

Pulling her knees to her chest, she said, "How do you like my Secret Palace of Pleasure?"

He sat beside her, unnecessarily close given the size of the tub. The water rose higher. "I love it."

"The only sad thing is that you can have just one bath a week. It takes that long for the water to warm up again." She hugged her knees. "Occasionally I'll push it by taking another at day four or five." She paused, a thought coming to her, "But you know, with your weight in the tub, I bet we'll use less water to fill it."

"I'm glad I am of some use."

She laughed. "You sound offended, but honestly, I could keep you around forever if I thought I would get two baths a week in this tub."

His eyes sparkled oddly, and she wondered what he was thinking, but all he said was, "This is nice." He groaned and leaned against the side. The water had reached chest level quickly.

Raine pushed off beside him to float to the levers and shut the water off. Yes, he was handy. It hadn't taken long at all to fill it.

Keeping her body below the water's surface, she asked the question she'd been thinking about for a while now. "So when are you going after Malachi?"

Walker watched his woman float in the huge tub and forced himself to stay still when he wanted to swoop down on her like a hawk on prey.

Gods, she was beautiful. Even her back with the streak of brown scar begged for his mouth upon it.

He made himself speak. She wasn't going to figure out how much she wanted him if he didn't talk to her. Heart, body, mind, he had to win them all or he'd spend his life mourning her loss. His gut twisted with wonder—how amazing to know who you were destined to be with for your whole life? To look at that person and know that if you were with them, you'd be happy forever. He couldn't make mistakes. The price of failure would be too high, for both of them.

"I hadn't planned on going after Delmundo."

She sat up with a splash. "What? Why not?"

He shrugged. "What good would it do?"

"He harmed you, took your freedom. Took your powers." She knelt beside him. "He deserves to pay."

Walker could care less. He wasn't wasting his time and energy on that cyber-scum.

She blinked, then shook her head, and frowned. "Well, that's okay." Settling across from him, she pulled up her legs to her chest and rested her chin on her knees. "I'll take care of him for you."

Now it was his turn to say, "What?"

"After this White Out, I'm leaving Sector 9 to go on the offensive again." She grinned, and it was bloodthirsty. "I plan to hit Malachi where it hurts. It's been so long that I'm sure he's relaxed his guard. He might even think I'm dead by now."

Walker's heart constricted at the thought of Delmundo capturing Raine. He was a sadistic bastard who had framed Walker for a murder just because he was a handy victim. The thought of Delmundo's hands on Raine made Walker shiver, even though he was sitting in steaming hot water.

"Raine," he said, searching for the right words. "Haven't you gotten your revenge?"

"I will never finish punishing him until he's paid six times over." She cupped some water in her palm and let it trickle from between her fingers. "I figure he's only paid three so far."

"He might catch you. I've seen his torture victims and they weren't pretty." He tried not to panic. She was smart as a whip. She had to be to have survived Malachi's wrath for three years. He might be able to talk some sense into her.

She lifted one shoulder in a shrug. "If he does, I guess that will be that, but at least I'll have earned a gold star for effort."

Walker wanted to shake some sense into her. Then he realized he now had a perfect reason to stay by her side. "Fine, if this is how you feel—"

"I do," she interrupted.

"Then I'll come with you. Three lunar cycles ago he was still on Borrus."

"I suppose you deserve to have revenge too." She studied him for a long moment before nodding once. "Then I guess we'll be going to the Capital in a few days, if the snow isn't so bad that we can't leave. It's early for this type of storm, so we shouldn't have more than fifteen feet. We should be able to make it to the trading station."

Walker pushed off the bottom of the tub and zoomed over to her. "I guess we will," he said, and sealed their bargain with a kiss.

Walker breathed just a small push of power into her mouth, and Raine rewarded him with a moan deep in her throat. The sound heightened his pleasure almost as much as pushing his heat into her did. Usually touching another person meant nothing to him, but touching Raine was so very different. Something inside her fed power back to him. Receiving her energy felt like a sensual stroke of her hand below his skin. It was addicting in the extreme.

He pushed her knees down, encouraging her to unfold, then straddled her legs. He kept his lips on hers, eating at her gently.

Fitting his lower body close to hers, he enjoyed the surge of heat between them at the skin-on-skin contact. When he was locked up in HeFO, he had spent his time there staring at the walls, convincing himself that he would never find a mate. After all, he was three generations away from the pureness of his father's people. Part of him would then argue that his father and grandfather and great grandfather had found mates who were human, so he might too. He'd grown up learning from his father all the wonders of having a woman who not only could increase his power, but who would be his match on spiritual, mental and physical levels.

Framing her head with his hands, he explored her mouth. She'd said the storm would last days, and he planned to spend that time with her in bed. Already he could feel her body responding to his touch. From that first kiss, the strong chemical attraction they had between them had exploded into something so amazing, it still had him shaking inside. She would become as addicted to the power he fed her as he would be to the response of his talent to her touch.

He had this time and the week long journey to Borrus to sway her heart and mind, to bind those two parts of her to him and turn her from the idiocy of revenge against an evil asshole like Malachi Delmundo. That path would only lead to death.

He had a bad feeling it would be easier to bind her heart than sway her from her plans of revenge.

Cupping her neck, he let heat build in his palm, then slid it down her skin. At the intense sensation he created, she threw her head back and arched her body, thrusting her breast towards him. Following the line of her chest, Walker brushed her nipples with the power he held, enjoying the deepening of color in her areolas. Heat rebounded from her, making him shudder.

"Oh, Gods," she groaned between clenched teeth. "That feels like lightning."

"Good?" He knew the answer. He could tell by the way her lower body squirmed closer to his.

"Yes. Oh Walker."

He circled her other breast and caught her free nipple between his teeth, scraping the puckered bud. A strong urge to taste her desire, lap it from her core, leapt inside him. Her skin tasted so very good, like sunlight in the middle of the storm.

"Dammit," she said, mindless, her hands gripping his shoulders, tightening when he stroked her with his power, his heat.

His pleasure was intense just from watching her face as she came close to orgasm. Her full lips opened on another moan, her beautiful face pulled into lines of passion.

He had known he could do this, knew from the minute she touched him he could bring her with his power. What he hadn't known was how amazing it would feel to give her pleasure.

Licking her nipple, he lowered his hand, trailing along her flat stomach to press against her sex. Increasing the pressure in slow increments, he added power bit by bit. It took all his concentration, like a surgeon performing a complex operation. He wanted this to be perfect, to draw it out to bring her maximum enjoyment. He increased the heat, while rotating the heel of his hand. Capturing her nipple between his lips, he pressed warmth there as well.

She surged upwards against him and came with a wordless cry.

Water crashed over the side of the tub. Walker widened her legs to drop his knee between them, then caught her hips and impaled himself to the hilt before the water could wash away the slickness of her desire. His control snapped with the tightness of her channel.

The unexpected assault caused her pleasure to peak again and his orgasm washed through him as he lost control at the feel of her body contracting around his shaft in strong pulses.

"Raine!"

He held her as tightly as he could without crushing her in his arms.

Chapter Five

Raine carefully eased away from Walker and moved out from under the covers. It was cold as icy hell in the room, especially after sleeping cuddled tight against his always-warm body.

Throwing on a pair of pants, shirt and sweater, she dropped into a chair to put on her socks and shoes. She needed to check the weather. It had been a few days since the storm blew up.

Her body was sore and had a well-loved, heavy feel to it. As if she'd over-indulged—which she had. He'd kept her busy.

Gods, he could bring her to orgasm just by touching her. It had been all she could do to leave the bed.

But leave she must.

It was time to stop playing with Malachi and finish it once and for all.

Tugging on her parka, she strode towards the far wall. The person who'd owned the icehouse before her had put an observation nest in the ice and rock above her. Most of the time, she could open the main portal, but if the wind and snow had been as severe as she'd thought, she'd need to be elevated to see how bad things were. They might even have to exit that way, although if the snow had fallen that deep, they wouldn't be able to ride the Snow-doo into town. It was way too cold to walk.

Raine put gloves on before grabbing the first of the loops that had been inserted into the wall. Her skin had stuck to a metal object her first winter here, forcing her to peel off layers of flesh to get free.

Climbing the ladder at a fast clip, she reached the ceiling and opened the trapdoor.

She'd made every mistake in the book when she'd first come here, and the worst one had been in this room. She had opened the observation portal and enough snow had flooded in to not only briefly bury her, but cover the trapdoor. It had taken her hours to dig out by hand.

It had been unpleasant, but more than that, she'd been shaken, the accident proving just how alone she really was here.

She had learned to be more careful after that.

Pulling herself into the room, she went to what was essentially a round cutout in the rock, covered in a durable, clear plastic. In the non-winter months, it provided a beautiful view of the plain below. In the winter, frost covered it to the point she could see nothing.

The room temperature hovered below freezing, but she didn't close the trapdoor. After the last episode, she couldn't shut herself inside.

She grabbed the latch and tried to lower it so she could take a quick peek outside. It didn't budge. She put more pressure on it.

Then some more.

It must be frozen in place. That hadn't happened before.

She leaned on it a little more.

Then she hummed in irritation and jumped up to land her whole weight on the latch.

For a moment, she hung suspended.

With a snap, the window released. Raine plunged to the floor, and she had a moment to think, 'Oh shit,' before snow flooded into the room, covering her.

A loud thump told her the trapdoor had slammed shut under the onslaught.

In a panic, Raine fought her way to the surface. She gasped for breath. "Calm down, calm down, calm down," she counseled herself.

It wouldn't do to lose her cool. This had happened before, and she'd been just fine. She needed to save her strength to dig herself out.

Stumbling to her feet, she waded to the window. During the White Out, the wind had packed a large amount of snow onto the deep-set ledge.

"Architectural design flaw," she griped, as she stared out at the bright snowscape. They'd gotten perhaps ten feet of snow, maybe a little more. The good thing was she could get to town. The Snow-doo could handle the depth easily.

Shutting the view-port, she threw the latch into place.

"Idiot."

She waded back to the trapdoor and heard him.

"Raine! Raine! Where in the hell are you?" Walker's voice filtered up through the floor.

The slamming trapdoor must have woken him.

"Walker!" she yelled at the top of her lungs.

Long pause. "Raine?" Walker's voice came from far away. "Where are you?"

The echoes made his last sentence almost unrecognizable.

"The ceiling," she screamed.

She pictured him wandering around the room, looking up.

"I see the ladder."

"Don't come up!" She didn't want him wasting his energy trying to open the trapdoor. The snow would be too heavy to move. "I'm snowed in."

"Are you okay?" Even through the floor, she could hear his worry.

"Yes!"

She started digging.

An hour later, she was still burrowing her way out.

It was slow work and she'd stripped off the parka because she'd begun to sweat.

She was so caught up on her task that she didn't notice that the snow on top of the trapdoor was melting.

"It must be the heat from the room below." She picked up speed.

The ring handle appeared, and she grabbed it and yanked hard. The trapdoor thumped but didn't open. She knelt again and worked at the snow around the edges for several minutes.

When she tried again, the trapdoor lifted, and the snow on top slid off all at once. She went flying backwards.

Picking herself up, she grabbed her parka and pitched it down. Then she climbed through the hole, caught the door handle and closed the observation room with a bang.

She was on the ground again in seconds, but tripped on Walker's prone body when she turned.

"Walker!" She knelt down beside him, brushing her parka away from where it landed half covering his body. "Gods."

He lay on his back, one of his legs at an odd angle.

Green eyes blinked open, and she knew what he'd done. He'd heated the door to melt the snow. It had cut her captivity by hours, but he must have run out of energy and fallen from the top of the ladder. She couldn't believe he'd risked himself like this for her.

Blinking back tears, her heart twisting at the amazing thing he'd done for her, she asked, "How badly are you hurt?" She knew what to do now and threw off her gloves. "Your leg is broken. Anything else?"

He shook his head, only a small motion, and took shallow breaths.

"I take it you can't speak. That's bad, then." Her growing panic and pinging emotions made her furious. "This is unacceptable, Walker. I would have dug myself out eventually. It wasn't worth you getting hurt." She cupped his cheeks with her bare hands and leaned down to press her lips to his.

She had a flash of worry that he might not be able to heal himself. Then she pushed it from her mind.

Picturing a raging fire, she exhaled into his mouth. She had no idea if it would work, but figured if he could heal snow frosting and his hands the first day she met him, he could heal whatever he'd done to himself here.

He made a small noise, and she pulled back. "This working?" she asked.

Slowly, he nodded his head once. His eyes were big, and he gasped for breath. "Str . . ."

She leaned down, trying to decipher what he said.

"Straighten . . ." He took a deeper breath.

Meeting his eyes, she shook her head. "Noooo. Not your leg."

She glanced down at it, fighting nausea.

"No way," she thought or said or whatever.

"Must," he whispered on an exhale.

Raine closed her eyes and waged an internal battle, making sure she kept silent. She didn't want to freaking straighten his leg. It would hurt him and besides that, the thought was just plain creepy.

Looking down at his face again, she met his begging eyes and growled. "You are such an asshole for heating the door." She knelt by his leg and gave him begging eyes back. "Walker, love, I don't want to hurt you."

"Do," he said. "It."

She stabilized his upper thigh with one hand and caught the calf of the other. "Oh, Gods, I don't think I can."

"Must."

In one movement, she straightened the leg, making a crunching sound. She screamed along with him for several moments. "I'm sorry. I'm sorry." She laid herself across his chest.

When his breathing steadied, she stood and ran to her bed, tearing off the covers with a snap, suddenly angry at him again. "That was an idiot move, Walker." She sprinted back and dumped the covers beside him in a heap. "You were beyond dumb to use up all your energy until you fell."

From a nearby chest, she grabbed a thermal tarp, spread it next to him, threw one of the blankets over it, and rolled him on.

He groaned.

"Hurt, huh? Well, you deserve it!" She unfastened his jumpsuit to the crotch, then stripped off all her clothes. Picking up the two remaining blankets, she laid next to him and formed a cocoon. Then she framed his face in her hands. "What else is hurt? I think you need to feel as much of my skin as possible for this to work. Am I right?"

He gave her a brief nod.

"I don't want to hurt you."

She climbed over him and gently lowered her body until her chest brushed his. He hummed, and she thought it might be approval.

"This wasn't worth it," she lectured in between kisses. "I would have dug my way out in a couple hours."

For a long while, he lay passive beneath her. She settled down more fully on top of him, tentatively at first, then with more weight when he didn't protest.

"Have I told you that I think you're an idiot?" she asked again, still shaken to her core from setting his leg.

"Yes, I think you have," he said, his voice weak, but at least he could speak.

She met his gaze. His face was ashen, but his eyes were clearer.

"I'm furious at you."

"I can tell." His lips tipped up in a brief smile.

She licked across his mouth, then deepened to run her tongue across his. Warmth, she thought. Heat. Liquid fire. His tongue felt rough and soft at the same time.

He gasped.

She grinned. "I can almost feel the heat transfer, if I concentrate."

"It's amazing. I've never known anyone could do anything like this." He licked his lips as if he wanted to taste her again. "My father never said it was possible."

Underneath her body, his erection had worked its way from between the flaps of his jumpsuit.

She rubbed across it with her own sex, enjoying the silky smooth feel of the head of his cock sliding across her clitoris.

He closed his eyes and groaned.

"Am I hurting you?" she asked, concerned because the sound could mean pleasure or pain.

"No."

Raine didn't think it would be polite to experiment, but she wondered if sex would speed his healing. It seemed to the first day she'd met him.

He whispered her name as she slid down his body, pressing kisses into his flesh.

"Gods, your body is amazing." She liked him with a sheen of sweat highlighting all his muscles, but he looked pretty damn good dry.

On impulse, she bit his hip. He arched up and groaned. She filed away the response for later thought. Right now, she wanted to run her mouth along other things. She loved the feel of his skin below her lips, the taste of his body—heat and hard muscle.

Using only the tip of her tongue, she licked up his long, straight shaft, all the way to the top. A small amount of liquid pooled on the head, and she sucked it off, interested to see what he tasted like. The liquid was hot and had a salty, sharp taste that was so very different from anyone else in any universe. She ran her tongue over the tip again.

"Woman, please," Walker said, but Raine wasn't exactly sure what he was asking for, except that he didn't want her to stop.

She'd done this before to other men, of course, but everything about

Walker was fresh and new. She worked her tongue into the hole at the tip of his cock to get another taste of him.

He writhed under her.

He tastes like summer. Like a beautiful summer morning, when you walk onto your porch and taste the beauty of a hot day. Crisp, fresh, with just the brief burn of heat underlying it.

He groaned, his eyes tightly shut.

She covered the head with her mouth and suckled him. Then she released and ran her tongue up his shaft once again.

Pressing a hand within his jumpsuit, she cupped the twin sacs below his erection. Rolling them gently between her fingers, she wondered why she hadn't done this before. *Because he's always been taking care of your pleasure.* The realization slammed into her and for a moment, she pulled away.

Walker whimpered at the loss, and she hastily took him into her mouth again.

In fact, he's always pleasuring you first, Raine. She'd been selfish in the extreme and hadn't even realized it.

She ran her mouth down his shaft, squeezing his balls at the same time. Using her free hand, she circled the bottom of his cock so he would feel totally covered and began a slow up and down glide.

She might have received more than she'd given in bed, but it wasn't too late to make it up to him, starting now.

Gradually, she increased the movement, flicking her gaze up to his face to judge her speed. She was careful not to touch his hurt leg.

A sheen of sweat covered his chest. Good. He'd gotten hot enough for that, at least.

She increased her speed when she tasted another drop of pre-come, watching as his thigh muscles became rock hard on either side of her. Every taste made her own desire climb that much higher.

"Raine." His whole body shuddered under her as he pumped deep inside her mouth. She drank him in, enjoying the burst of taste and the shivers of pleasure that tore through his body. Feeling powerful and pleased she could give him such pleasure, she was reluctant to move when he finished. But she knew the value of a hug after a person had climaxed. It felt like heaven to be held when your body was fulfilled.

As she curled into him, she was struck by the thought of what her life would be like once her plan for revenge on Malachi was fulfilled, and Walker would leave her.

Damn. She'd only known him for a handful of days and already it hurt to even think about losing him.

Chapter Six

"No." Walker tried to make it sound as final as possible. It had been three days since he'd broken his leg, but they had generated enough heat to heal it several times over.

His mate continued to work herself into the snowsuit.

"Raine," he growled.

"Use your head, Walker. You cannot travel to the trading station only wearing the clothes you came here with."

"I don't want you going without me." Anger raced through his bloodstream at the thought of her leaving. What if something happened to her while she was gone? He wouldn't be able to reach her. He'd be stuck here while she needed him. The thought twisted his guts into knots.

She rolled her eyes and stood up to bring the suit over her shoulders.

He crossed the room and grabbed her arms. "I'm being serious."

"You're not thinking this through."

"I'll go with you." He forced himself to sound reasonable.

"You'll freeze to death without a snowsuit."

"I didn't freeze on the way here," he pointed out, trying to gentle his voice.

"You were walking, which kept your blood circulating. I'll be sitting still in the Snow-doo." She shook her head. "I'm just going in to buy you clothes and arrange passage to Borrus for us with a freighter captain I know."

"I don't like it." He heard the snarl in his voice, made worse by the fact his teeth were clenched.

"Too bad." She smiled sweetly at him.

"I'm not letting you go."

"We have to get to Borrus."

"Forget Borrus." The words slipped out before he had a chance to stop them.

Her eyes narrowed.

He relented to cover his slip. "What if you are hurt, and I can't reach you?"

"I'm not the one who keeps getting injured," she pointed out.

She turned to walk to a nearby chest and stared at his hand when he didn't let her go. He debated the wisdom of holding her, then figured he still had a chance to talk her out of going. Finger by finger, he released her arm.

"What about when you hurt your back?"

She snorted. "Come on. That was two years ago." Opening the lid, she rummaged until she found whatever she sought.

"What if Delmundo is waiting for you at the trading station?"

She ambled back in his direction and laughed, the sound a little crazed. Grabbing her stomach with both hands, she doubled over, closing the distance between them.

"Are you all right?" He thought she seemed overly amused and tried to puzzle out this latest mood of hers.

She straightened, swept his feet right out from under him with one well placed kick and rolled him to his stomach.

It happened in seconds.

The restraints were in place by the time he tried to sit.

"You bitch!"

She *tsked* at him. "Such language," she purred, her husky alto sending tremors straight to his groin. Two pops sounded when she clamped on the leg restraints.

"You held them and pretended to laugh." When he worked his way free, he was going to tan her hide. Or screw her senseless.

"I'm going in to the trading station to buy you clothes." She turned him onto his back. "I'll return before night."

"Spend the time you're gone preparing yourself for my revenge." He tried to sit, but found it impossible with his hands shackled behind his back.

She batted her eyes at him. "I thought you didn't believe in vengeance."

He scowled at her. “I’m willing to make an exception.”

“Fantastic! I love a good retaliation.” She pecked his cheek quickly and stood. “I’ll be back.”

She had the gall to wink at him.

“You’re going to be very sorry.”

“I hope so,” she said, jogging across the room. At the table, she stopped and laid a set of keys down. “Just in case something happens, you can let yourself out once you make it over here.”

“When I get my hands on you—” He didn’t finish, because she disappeared into the entrance tunnel.

“Raine!” he shouted at the top of his lungs.

Staring up at the ceiling, he took five calming breaths and then another ten. He needed to control his worry for her. Otherwise, it would be a long day.

If something happened to her while she was gone, he would find the person responsible and kill them with his bare hands.

He hadn’t realized being in love would be such a pain in the ass.

Raine pulled the Snow-doo into the barn and shut off the engine. It was already dark, and she thanked the Gods it hadn’t snowed again while she was gone, because she’d had to follow her own tracks for the last ten leagues of the return trip.

She was bone weary, so tired she could drop. Cutting the engine, she opened the door and hopped down. She slung her packages over her shoulder and hiked back to the house, moving slow.

Driving the Snow-doo wasn’t difficult but the older model she’d been forced to buy when she’d gotten here vibrated to the point her spine jarred in agony with every bump. Her arms were jelly. She’d never gone to the trading station and back in one day before.

Sighing, she struggled through the snow to the upper entrance tunnel. She had to use the upper tunnel because of the recent snow fall, but the drift didn’t quite make it all the way to the top. Opening the portal, she tossed in the packages before hauling herself up. It took her two tries to heave herself inside.

She rolled far enough in so she could close the portal, then lay back panting for a few moments.

"Hard day?" Walker's voice filtered through the dark.

Raine jumped, catching her chest with her hand. "Gods, you scared me."

He moved closer, grabbing the shoulders of her snowsuit and dragging her down most of the hallway.

"Walker!" What in the hell was he doing?

"I can't lift you until you're far enough in for me to stand."

"I don't need to be carried!"

He didn't stop pulling her. "It's frustrating when somebody does something you don't like but you can't stop them, isn't it?" His voice sounded calm. Too calm.

Oh shit, she thought. *He's mad.*

"Shit is right. You are in so much trouble, I can't even begin to describe it to you."

With one heave, he had her over his shoulder. He strode across the room and dumped her on the bed, then went back into the hall. Raine started to sit up, but then fell back, too exhausted to make the effort.

He returned with her bags, shaking the clothing she'd purchased for him out onto the floor.

"I went to buy you clothes, you ungrateful wretch." Raine figured a good defense might be a good offense right about now.

He sorted through them. "Good. This way you won't be able to leave without me again," he said absently, his attention focused on the clothes. "What's this?" He held up a suit worn by visiting dignitaries on Borrus. She'd bought it second hand and was quite proud of the purchase.

"Your disguise. It's part of my plan."

His intense, green gaze flicked away from the cloth to her face. "Let's talk about this plan."

"I've booked passage for us tomorrow. We leave right before dusk." She blinked and realized she only had to look at him and need began to build inside her.

"The plan," he said, throwing down the suit and stalking over to her.

She couldn't do very much but watch him. Her body wasn't functioning properly. She groaned when she thought about the return trip in the morning.

"What?" he asked.

"I'm not looking forward to tomorrow's trip to the trading station."

"Why?"

"My body is beaten to pieces. The Snow-doo vibrates so hard, I feel like my spine is compressed into an excruciating mass."

He squatted beside the bed. "You're in pain."

She sniffed. She wasn't going to ask him to heal her, not with his attitude. Just because she'd restrained him, he'd gotten all fussy with her. "I'm fine."

"I'll drive us into town."

"You've driven a Snow-doo before?" She wondered when he'd have a chance. Certainly not in HeFO.

"No. You're going to teach me." He grabbed her snowsuit and parted it in one motion. "I'm not very happy with you."

"I did what I had to do." She infused her tone with righteousness.

"No, Raine, you took the easy way out."

"You were being unreasonable." She could hear the defensiveness in her voice.

He lifted her shoulders so he could take off the suit. "I'm not going to Borrus with you unless you agree right here and now that all decisions are going to be joint ones."

Raine felt her eyes grow wide. "Wait a second."

"No, you wait, Raine," he snapped, tightening his hold on her arm. "Agree that everything either of us does will be decided upon by both of us, or you can go to Borrus by yourself."

"But—" She couldn't believe how angry he sounded.

"No buts!" He hauled her up until she sat. "None."

He was being unreasonable, but then she realized that there wasn't any need to fight him on this. He was her team for this mission. Teams always communicated and agreed on the plan, or everything would blow into pieces at the crucial moment.

"Fine," she said, not being very gracious about it.

"You'll consult me in everything." He dragged the snowsuit to her waist.

"Yes."

"Swear it."

"What?"

"Swear and I'll believe you." The muscle in his jaw flexed and he pushed her onto her back. One by one, he removed her boots and threw them so hard, they bounced off the far wall. He dragged down the suit and flung it away as if it burned him. A thrill rode through her, tingles zinging in her veins even though his hands had just brushed her in a light sweep.

He was really worked into a snit.

"You won't take my word?" She tried to sound insulted, but it was hard around all the guilt she'd felt today. It must have been agony for him to have the cold eating into his skin while he slid across the ice floor to reach the keys on the table.

"No, I won't just take your word."

"What kind of oath are we talking about here?" They were tricky things, and she had to be careful. She didn't want to commit to something she couldn't stand by, no matter how much guilt she felt over leaving him locked up.

"Swear on your life you won't do anything without consulting me first."

She thought about her wording long and hard. "I promise on my life not to do anything without telling you first, unless it is a decision I have to make in the heat of the moment."

"Not good enough."

"It will have to be. I must be in a position to act if I need to."

"You're much too spontaneous." His face was hard.

"How do you figure that?" She dragged up a blanket from the bed, suddenly cold. She *was* too spontaneous. It was part of her charm.

"You didn't preplan locking me up."

"I needed to go and you weren't going to let me. I could tell." It was weird, fighting with him like this. As if they'd known each other so much longer than a week.

From behind his back, he pulled out her spare knife and threw it into the wall next to her.

"What in the hell are you doing!" Raine jumped to her feet, her mouth hanging open, the blanket dropping to the floor.

"That's how I feel when I deal with you, Raine." He closed the distance between them. "Like you're going to do some crazy thing any second."

For a moment, she couldn't speak, staring at the knife embedded in the wall. She just opened and closed her mouth, struggling for words. "You went through my trunks!"

He had put some serious skill behind the throw. The action had the appearance of something practiced and artfully done.

"I went through every trunk, drawer and bag in this place. You should think twice before you leave me here alone again." The satisfied gleam in his eyes showed he relished telling her that.

Her mouth dropped open. "How could you!"

"That's what I thought when you put the cuffs on me." He grinned like a space-pirate.

She closed her eyes and took a big breath. Okay, he had a right to do that, she told herself.

"Yes, I did." He narrowed his eyes and covered her hand with his. "We can talk things out, Raine."

Her eyes snapped open. "Look." She poked him in the chest. "I am sorry you forced me to lock you up, but we can't stay here for the rest of our lives, and you can't leave without clothes."

"Once I stopped fantasizing about wringing your neck for leaving me in shackles, I realized you had to go. I'm not the crazy one of our team."

Raine threw her hands in the air and walked a circle. "I didn't think you'd change your mind."

"I would have. I wouldn't have been happy, but you were right. You needed to go."

She strode to the knife and blew out a breath. It was buried half way up the blade. "Nicely thrown." She met his gaze. "You have talent."

He shrugged and seemed a little embarrassed. "Yeah, well, we're discussing your oath."

"If I give you my word, what do you give in return?"

He came to stand before her. His hand snaked into her hair, anchoring them together. "I promise to protect you with everything I have, heal you when you're hurt, and stand at your back no matter what mess you drag us into."

She blinked up at him for two heartbeats. It was the most beautiful thing anyone had ever said to her. "Then I give you my word." Her voice was hoarse around the odd lump growing in her chest. How could she have known him such a short time and already feel this gut-wrenching closeness to him?

"And I give you mine."

His lips crashed onto hers, his kiss so filled with passion, it took her breath away.

Chapter Seven

Walker was as nervous as a barefoot blind man in a room full of tacks. Dressed in a uniform which would allow him to blend in on Borrus as one of the many dignitaries that congregated there, and the snowsuit Raine had purchased for him, he paced by her side, his hood keeping him hidden. She had said they would be leaving on a transport an acquaintance of hers owned, but they had to walk through the trading station to reach the launch pad.

For a brief moment, he allowed himself to take stock of where he stood with Raine. He'd taken a grave risk forcing her to swear the night before, but he'd been lucky. It had paid off. With her agreement to include him in all her decisions, he had moved one step closer to binding her mind to him. She would now need to factor him into everything she did. Her body was already locked to his. He thought he might have woven some small threads between their hearts as well. He'd caught something in her eyes that told him she cared about him, both last night and when he'd broken his leg.

Walker sighed and forced himself to concentrate on his surroundings. He had a week left before they reached Borrus to work on her.

Inter-world Council troops marched between warming huts spaced around the station. His stomach tightened as they walked past them. He didn't want to be caught now that he had found his mate. He'd reached a point during his stay in HeFO when he'd just wanted to die, but now he wanted to live. With Raine. He touched his gloved hand to Raine's waist and smiled at her when she glanced his way.

They passed through an archway and spilled out to the launch pad. Raine guided them between transports until they arrived at one in the back corner.

"Trond," she said, flipping off her hood and extending her arm.

She didn't smile, and Walker had the feeling she didn't like the man, even though they shook hands.

"I thought you weren't gonna show, Stormy Weather." The man laughed, a huffing sound that matched his scarred and distorted face. He'd been born with one side wider than the other. Things had gone from bad to worse after that. Someone had carved him up on both cheeks, leaving raised white scars.

"We had to drive in this morning. It took longer than I had anticipated."

Raine didn't lie exactly. They had driven in, but they had also sold the Snow-doo and her icehouse. When he'd asked her why, she informed him she wasn't coming back to Sector 9. One way or another, she would live or die someplace else.

"Guess the weather held you up." He glanced at Walker. "Who are you?"

"Does it matter?" Raine asked him, bringing Trond's gaze back to hers. "We leaving now?"

"Yes." He waved them into the transport. "My co-pilot is sick with a hangover, so you probably won't see him this trip."

"Hold!" A guard marched towards them. "I need to see papers if you're leaving. We're checking for escaped prisoners."

The soldier stuck out his hand to Walker first.

Walker only had a fleeting moment to decide what to do. They needed to leave, and a quick glance around told him they were hidden by other transports. As a Healer, he'd sworn to use his powers only for good, but his need to protect his mate came before that vow. Raine would be sent to prison for aiding him. At all costs, he had to prevent that from happening. "Here you go," he said, and placed his own hand in the guard's. He was still reluctant to do harm, but made himself push power into the guard. Not too much, he didn't want to permanently harm him.

"What are you doing?" The guard tried to pull his hand away.

Walker tightened his fingers. From the corner of his vision, he could see Raine's mouth drop open.

He shoved heat and power through their connected hands, pushing past the gloves they both wore. The guard began to sweat profusely but was so confused, all he could ask was, “What are you doing?” over and over again.

Just a little bit more. He’d accidentally done this once before. He could cause a person to pass out by temporarily elevating their body temperature.

Sure enough, the guard’s knees buckled and he fell forward.

“What is going on?” Trond demanded.

“Shut up.” Raine’s voice held authority. She backed him despite the fact she must be as confused as the pilot. Walker’s heart warmed at the thought.

“What?” The guard slumped forward, passing out into the snow.

Walker dragged him behind the shelter of some crates, then strode back to the ship. “Let’s go.”

Raine closed her mouth and rounded on Trond. “You heard him. Get this heap into the atmosphere, pronto!”

“What did you do back on Sector 9?” Raine whispered to Walker. She was still reeling from what had happened and couldn’t get her mind around it.

They were sitting in Trond’s general room, which matched the rest of the ship’s run down, ill kept interior. Since Trond had cobbled together parts from different transports, the seats were different shades of green and gray and had a sticky, grimy sheen to them. Panels on the walls stood open, exposed wiring dripping out. Raine hadn’t had a lot of choices in transportation.

“Nothing,” Walker mumbled, not moving from where he’d sat when they’d gotten onto the transport.

Raine snapped off her shoulder harness and went to kneel beside him. Something was wrong. She hadn’t noticed it before because she was just too freaked out to concentrate on anything else but her own thoughts.

She had a sneaking suspicion she knew what the problem was. Flipping off her glove, she placed her hand onto his cheek, making him jump at the unexpected movement.

His skin was ice cold.

“That’s what I thought. You’re freezing.”

Walker snapped his head away, but she'd only needed a brief touch to figure out what she wanted to know.

"Every time you use your talent, you end up an ice cube."

"It's that damn planet," he murmured, lowering his head into his hands. "Gods, I just wish I could live someplace swelteringly hot."

"Well, there are easy ways to build your heat level."

He spread his fingers to stare at her with one eye. "I'm listening." Although his voice sounded tired, there was a thread of humor running through it.

"A few kisses should boost you, right?"

He dropped his hand. "You were exhausted last night so I left you alone. I'm not sure I can stop with just a few kisses, Raine."

His green eyes sparkled, and his gaze raked her from lips to breasts, narrowing as if he could see her nipples harden in reaction under her snowsuit.

"Sit back," she said, pushing in between his legs to kneel where she could reach him. "I'll make you warm again." Power swelled through her, not magic, but pride mixed with desire. That she could do this for him gave her a heady rush similar to the first time she'd returned from a mission with the team and she knew she'd done brilliantly.

She grabbed the top pockets of his snowsuit and pulled him forward, surprised at how much she wanted him. She'd only gone a day without, but it felt like much longer.

Their lips met and she forgot about warming him as her own desire began to build, heat pooling deep in her belly. She moved closer, restless and wanting. Tugging open his snowsuit in one sweep, she ached with the need to touch him, stroke the hard, corded muscles of his body.

She broke away to gasp for air. "What happened to the guard, Walker?" Pulling his shirt up, she ran her fingers across his flat abs, enjoying the feel of his body. The smell of summer heat curled around her.

Walker rested his face in the crook of her neck, his hands banded around her, his warm breath whispering across her skin. "It's one of the things I can do with my talent. I can warm to varying degrees, which can heal or hurt."

"Is he dead?"

"Just unconscious. He should have woken in time to watch us leave, although he'll be groggy for awhile."

She sighed. "You freaked Trond out. I hope he doesn't go run his mouth. I'll have to have a conversation with him." The pilot could turn out to be a large problem.

His lips whispered across the bare skin of her neck, making her shiver. "The situation seemed to call for fast action." Regret filled his voice.

"I'm not upset. We just need to deal with it." She considered the money she'd earned from the sale of the icehouse. It was enough to pay Trond off, or at least keep his mouth shut for awhile. The problem with buying silence was that people tended to get greedy and demand more.

"I don't suppose we can count on him to be discreet?"

She grinned and pressed her lips into his temple. Sometimes he was so naïve. She found it kind of cute. "No. He's an asshole of the first order, but we needed a transport and he's not one to ask questions."

"The incident with the guard may cause Sector 9 to communicate with the Council police on Borrus to warn them we're coming." He tangled his hands in her hair, raking his nails across her scalp.

She fought the urge to purr, placing a kiss onto the inside of his wrist instead. "We filed a flight plan going to Sector 12. We headed that direction until we were well out of Sector 9's tracking system, then turned. I seriously doubt they'll guess our destination."

He nodded, seeming to accept that. "What's our plan once we land?"

She'd been waiting for him to ask. "We need to talk to Rory Uslep," she murmured and licked across his pulse point.

He blinked several times, as if he struggled to keep his mind on the topic at hand. His eyelids had lowered, giving his dark green gaze the heavy, passion filled look she loved. "Who the hell is Rory Uslep?"

"One of the three representatives of Galaxy Grid 219. He's known as the man of the people. I figure he'll jump at the chance to prove your innocence, especially if he knows we'll give him all the credit, and he won't have to do any of the work."

Walker was speechless. He had no idea Raine planned to prove him innocent, only that she wanted revenge against Malachi Delmundo. He cupped her chin and studied her face. He knew she belonged to him. The way she responded to his power convinced him she was fated to be by his side. What she did to his body, heart and mind made him want to cradle her close for the rest of their lives.

On one level, there was intense desire and physical fulfillment, but underlying that was the respect he had for her courage, her discipline, and her brave heart. He enjoyed just sitting beside her, holding her hand with their fingers laced together. Earlier, when he'd thrown her knife into the wall, he'd loved it that he'd tilted her off balance, that he'd gained her admiration for his knife skills and brought her a step closer to seeing him as a mate worthy to stand by her side.

Her desire to prove his innocence made his heart constrict, even though he doubted it would be possible for her to succeed.

"Raine, I don't want you to take any risks for me. I think you're going to find that this revenge you plan isn't worth it." He had a sudden flash, a vision of her bloody and torn, lying on a floor, the red of the setting sun clashing with the pink marble under her and the blood on her chest. It made his fingers spasm on her chin.

She hissed in a breath.

"I'm sorry," he whispered and pressed a kiss on the red mark where his thumb had been. He blew a healing breath into her skin. Laving the spot with his tongue, he had the satisfaction of watching her tip her head so he could continue unimpeded down her neck.

He wanted to give her something wonderful, erase the vision he'd just seen in his mind. Pushing her back, he dropped to his knees, lowering her until she lay flat. His fingers made quick work of her snowsuit, then the blouse she wore beneath.

Resisting the temptation to use his power to bring her to orgasm, he used only his mouth in whispering touches. A lick here and suckle there, he savored the taste of his woman and the soft texture of her skin under his lips. He drew her nipple into his mouth and brushed the tip of his tongue softly across the tight bud.

"Oh, he's so good," she murmured. "Amazing. Better than anything I've ever had."

Walker grinned. He hoped she never stopped talking to herself out loud. He loved hearing her uncensored thoughts.

Nibbling down her stomach, he ran his tongue under the band to her panties. Raine arched and moaned below him.

"You make me feel like I'm going to explode inside, like the sky is twirling out of control." Her warm, wonderful hands tunneled in his hair as he eased the snowsuit off, taking her pants with it.

"Mmmm . . ." he hummed, always loving the look of her body. It was as if he saw it for the first time whenever he undressed her. She was slim, but totally in shape, a mixture of hard muscle and soft woman. Beautiful.

He pressed his face into her panties, nuzzling her clitoris lovingly with the tip of his tongue.

"Oh!" She started to sit up, but he pinned her down with his hands on her stomach and licked through the cloth of her underwear.

Her legs fell slack to the sides, and he took the opportunity to lie more comfortably between them. One hand traced up her body to roll a nipple with his thumb and forefinger.

He felt strong, his energy restored with only the touch of their bodies. His father had told him his mate could do this, but he was overwhelmed by the actual experience.

Keeping her panties in place, he moved his tongue over the fabric, wanting to heighten her pleasure with the rough texture of the cloth. She was soaking wet, her amazing scent wrapping about him, pulling at his own desire, but he ignored his needs.

She wanted to prove his innocence. The thought had his mind spinning in joy.

He knew she still planned to go her separate way when they finished this mission. But he was a step closer to winning her heart and mind. She cared enough to try to exonerate him.

He sucked her clit into his mouth through the white Moresung fabric. Raine almost levitated off the floor.

"Walker!" Her head tossed back and forth.

She was close. He could feel her orgasm just out of reach.

He swept aside her underwear and blew warm air on her wet sex.

She shivered and tried to close her legs at the sensation.

"Come for me, Raine," he murmured, before burying the tip of his tongue underneath the sensitive bud and fighting his way upwards.

Her hands tried to grab his hair, but it was too short for her to hang on.

"I," she said. But she didn't continue. Her orgasm shuddered through her on the word.

"Love," he whispered, gathering her limp body into his lap.

"Nice," Trond said from behind them.

Chapter Eight

Raine tried to surface up from the haze of complete satisfaction. Someone had spoken and it wasn't Walker.

Her man held her body on his lap, curling around to protect her from whomever stood in the doorway.

Her man? Well, he was kind of hers, she supposed. Certainly he wasn't anyone else's.

"Mind if we have a little privacy, Trond?" Walker's voice sounded deadly, even as his hand gently pressed her into his chest.

"I came to talk to you about that little scene on Sector 9." Trond didn't sound impressed with Walker's bravado, which didn't surprise Raine. Trond wasn't known for his brilliance.

Raine tried to put her mind in gear. Nudity had never really embarrassed her. She kept clothed because men tended to get out of hand around a naked woman. Fighting them had always been a pain in the rear.

She leaned against Walker's arm so she could sit. He didn't want to let her, but finally eased enough so he could meet her gaze.

"Let me handle him," she said, and kissed his full, masculine lips.

He hadn't lost his erection with their uninvited visitor, and the kiss caused his cock to jump under his clothes, brushing her thigh where she sat across his lap. He growled in her ear to let her know he wasn't pleased to let her up.

Her legs were shaky, but she managed to stand gracefully. This wouldn't work if she stumbled or tried to cover herself. At first, Walker's hands impeded her attempt to rise, then assisted her. She smiled, gathered her clothes in her hand and sauntered past Trond to the head. "Don't worry, Trond, we'll pay for your silence. Just don't get too greedy. I would hate to have to kill you to keep you quiet."

Trond's eyes snapped from her breasts to her face, and she could tell he believed her. It was in the frowning mouth, twitching eyelid, and narrowing eyes.

She wasn't surprised when he turned insulting. After all, in a way she'd insulted him by not caring if he saw her nude.

"You think you're man enough to kill me, Stormy Weather?" he sneered

"I don't have to be a man to kill you." As she walked past, she swept his feet out from under him and pushed his back so he fell face down on the floor. It happened so fast, he couldn't fully catch himself with his hands, and his forehead smashed into the floor with a thump.

Walker materialized beside her and rested a booted foot on Trond's shoulder. "I suggest you stay there and catch your breath. Bad things happen to people who threaten my woman."

Hmmm, Raine thought, careful to keep silent. Seems she wasn't the only one becoming a tad possessive.

Since Trond couldn't see her from his place on the floor, she put an added swing into her hips and smiled saucily at Walker as she left the room.

Trond yelled as Walker shifted his weight and leaned hard on his booted foot.

Borrus.

It was good to be back again, Walker thought. The atmosphere here was ideal for humans, the weather mild and the location centralized so that trade flowed in and out, bringing any item a man might want. It was perfect—so perfect that it was horribly crowded in certain parts of the Capital City.

He wasn't quite sure how they were going to pull off Raine's plan, even after she'd explained the whole thing through twice. But he had to admit, his woman was a mastermind at strategy. She'd casually thrown out that she had done all the planning for her team.

He'd also been impressed with the way she'd handled Trond. Just the right combination of force and negotiation had caused the pilot to accept their deal, when he clearly wanted more money. She'd been firm on the price, although she'd paid him more than Walker would have liked.

They went to one of the seediest hotels he'd ever stayed in, but Raine had told him it was in the factory district, one of the few parts of town Malachi didn't control. The air here was thick with smoke from the nearby factories, chasing away most people and making it a perfect hide out.

As they checked in, the desk clerk flirted with Raine until Walker leaned over the counter, grabbed his shirt front and pulled him forward. He smiled and said politely, "Room key, please."

The pimple-faced clerk nodded rapidly, and Walker set him down so he could follow his orders.

"El . . . Elevator's broken," the younger man stammered. "Gotta take the stairs." He pointed to the stairwell door.

Raine led the way, not saying anything until the door banged shut. "Nice he-man routine there, Walker."

"That imbecile deserved a scare. I think he would have flirted with you for as long as you let him."

She turned on the stair, brushing the wall with her shoulder. Peeling paint rained onto the floor. "Wait a second, you don't think I was encouraging him, do you?"

Walker laughed. He couldn't help it. Raine was so far out of the clerk's league, the thought was comical. "No, I thought you were being nice." In fact, she was way above Walker's league. But the Gods had matched them, for which he would be eternally grateful.

"Oh." She turned and climbed to the landing. "We'll need to meet with Rory at the Naked Lady tonight."

"We're going to a strip club to meet a Senator?"

"Yeah, well, he tends to hang there at night while the Senate's in session. It's kind of his home away from Galaxy Grid 219."

Walker held open the door for her to pass into the dimly lit corridor. "So it's a dive?"

She grinned. "How'd you know?"

Walker strode quickly down the hall to the room, afraid his feet might attach to the floor if he paused on the sticky carpet. "Just a guess."

Raine watched Walker close the bathroom door and stripped off her clothes as fast as she could. Time was tight but she had to have him before they left to meet Rory.

Just the thought of him inside her made her breasts heavy with desire and her panties soaking wet. She wiggled out of them, throwing her clothes onto the room's only chair.

When Walker opened the door, she stood casually posed against the dresser, half sitting on the edge. She gave him a challenging look, feeling like a temptress for the first time in her life. Every particle of her being was involved in this seduction. He had to come to her, touch her, love her. In only a few hours, their revenge would begin, and they wouldn't have time for love play.

Walker dropped a shoulder against the doorframe. "Gods, you're beautiful, Raine." His gaze wandered her body like a caress.

"I'm in the mood for you." She lowered her voice, infusing it with promise. She traced a circle around one breast, a thrill shooting through her when his eyes became heavy-lidded, his gaze following her hand.

She swept over the nipple, then squeezed it, sucking in a breath at how good it felt to see his erection strain against the front of his pants.

"Cup your breasts," he murmured.

When she did, he rewarded her by pulling off his shirt, revealing his muscled chest. He was perfectly formed, down to the swath of light brown hair that tapered into his pants.

"Brush your nipples with your thumbs."

She did as he asked, watching his reactions, and a zing ran straight to her clitoris when his hands balled into fists. She licked her lips against the physical ache to taste him.

The action made him unbutton his pants. "Sit on the dresser."

She had never known him to be so demanding before, although she'd seen flashes of this part of his personality. He might be laid back, but he certainly had moments when he could be forceful. It made her even hotter. She levered herself onto the cool metal of the dresser.

He toed off his boots and left them on the floor without taking his gaze off her. "Spread your legs so I can see how much you want me."

She widened them, cupping her breasts again. Liquid desire pooled inside her and slid past the lips of her sex.

His eyes flicked behind her, and she realized he watched in the mirror as well. For a moment, she was self-conscious about the scar on her back, but she pushed the feelings aside.

"Dip a finger inside yourself and tell me if you're ready."

Prolonging his anticipation, she pinched her nipples a second longer, then dropped a hand to meander down her stomach. She brushed the outside of her sex a few times.

"Raine," he growled.

His impatience turned her on even more. She pressed a finger inside her channel, sliding on her own wetness, then pulling out to stroke across her clit. Her gaze never left his body.

He ripped off his pants and stood trembling in the doorway. Sweat covered his skin, making her hum. She loved him hot like this, full of power and life.

Then he strode across the room, determination mixing with the lust in his eyes. "I was left unfulfilled on the ship." He grabbed her hand from between her thighs and licked across her wet fingers. "I don't want to be gentle."

She blinked at him, her brain slow and unfocused with desire. "Then don't be."

He growled low in his throat, whisking her off the dresser and turning her to face the mirror. "I'm going to take my pleasure," he rasped from between gritted teeth. "Keep up or I'll leave you behind."

She laughed at the thought, since she was on the edge of orgasm, but stopped when he bent her forward. His feet widened her stance until she stood on tiptoes, supporting herself with her hands on the dresser. He was so strong, he could easily overpower her. The thought made her hiss in a breath with need.

Keeping one hand on her back to pin her, he met her gaze in the mirror and prodded her entrance from behind. Her body shook with anticipation.

And then he was inside, penetrating with a slow glide that just kept going until he reached the top of her passage.

His eyes narrowed into slits of green, and he pulled his cock out half way. "Take all of me," he ordered, as if she hadn't on purpose.

She pushed her buttocks up and back as he came home again, slamming into her this time. A flash of painful pleasure shot through her.

"Yes," he praised, closing his eyes and tightening his hold on her hips.

Raine knew she only needed two more thrusts and she would climax. She inhaled a rough breath, his scent filling her lungs and adding to her desire.

He withdrew, then returned, picking up a rhythm that had nothing to do with her pleasure. His teeth bared in a silent growl.

It didn't matter, because she was coming.

Right.

Now.

She peaked and jerked through a soul splitting orgasm, but he continued to ride her.

Forcing her eyes open, she watched his face tighten into harsh planes and his arms bulge as his own release drew close. He was so magnificent, so absolutely male, covered in sweat and muscles, the smell of their mingled desire curling around her to clutch at her heart.

He tossed his head back, the muscles in his neck, arms and chest bunching with tension, and came on a shout. She could feel him pumping into her, and another orgasm ran through her body, catching her by surprise, making her scream his name.

Staring at her own reflection in the mirror, Raine watched her body shake uncontrollably with the after-shocks of pleasure. A painful sense of loss struck her at the thought of when they would part company. Squeezing her eyes shut against the image, her heart clenched and stuttered. She was too caught up in him, already too attached. How had this happened to her so quickly?

Chapter Nine

The owner of the Naked Lady didn't spend a lot of money on lighting. Everything was so worn down, the clientele might have turned around at the door if they had been able to see clearly. A long bar ran the length of the left wall, the seats taken by a boisterous crowd cheering the dancers on two stages. The front platform shimmied with a well-endowed blonde, the tiny silver disks adhered to her nipples blinking in the spotlights to match the patch of red, shiny fabric between her legs. The second stage held a nude redhead who spun upside down by her legs from a pole, her long hair sweeping the floor as she twirled.

Raine knew that the Naked Lady was only packed with patrons when the Senate was in Session. Since Rory used this as his home base while on Borrus, people had to wait to see him in the strip club, paying the two drink minimum.

They had been here for two hours, but Raine knew Rory would move her up to the head of the line as quickly as he could. For most of the time, he'd been speaking with a fat man who had the look of a fellow Senator. When that man had left, Rory had met her gaze, but another man ran to his table and started speaking, his words blurred but panicked.

Rory smiled at her and shrugged. She grinned back.

"You know him?" Walker had noticed the by-play.

"I did him a favor once. He owes me." She stirred her drink but didn't take a sip. She couldn't be the least bit distracted for the upcoming interview. She'd have to play her cards right to get everything she wanted.

"What kind of favor?" Walker's tone turned cold, and she focused on him.

"Are you asking if I've slept with him? Because if you are, the answer is no. The team took care of a problem for him." Was she irritated or glad at his possessiveness? Maybe a bit of both, she decided, not liking her conclusion.

He said nothing, but stared at her. Raine found it hard to concentrate on their conversation when her eyes lighted on a dancer standing between the legs of a man sitting at the next table. It appeared she planned to spend the whole evening wiggling her generous butt on his crotch.

Walker tapped her hand. "What problem?"

"I can't tell you, Walker."

"He wants you. I can feel it from here."

"You're getting a wee tad bit possessive, don't you think? First the clerk, then this." They were both getting out of control. It frightened her. They were moving too fast.

Green eyes danced in the dim lighting, capturing her as effectively as his hands did when they squeezed her wrists. Power pushed through his skin. It sizzled along her veins into her stomach, which did a crazy little flip-flop.

Raine forced herself to keep her face even.

"I am possessive, Raine, because you're mine. You might think it will be the end after this revenge of yours is over, but you won't be leaving me."

"Oh no?" Rebellion rose inside her. *Just who does he think he is, anyway?*

"Your mate, that's who."

She hummed in annoyance that she'd spoken her thoughts out loud again. "Don't try to boss me, Walker." *Mate.* She snorted.

"I'm not at all." He relaxed back into his chair and took a swallow of his drink. "I'm only telling you the truth."

Raine blinked and tried to figure out how she felt about that statement. She wasn't as angry as she should have been and if she were honest, she had been thinking similar thoughts about him only hours ago on the transport. She felt something for Walker beyond mere physical attraction, but what, she wasn't sure. The feelings were not only confusing but also overwhelming. She didn't like being out of control.

"Am I interrupting anything?" Rory Uslep sat at their table uninvited.

Raine forced herself to smile at him and focus on the business at hand, instead of dealing with her confusion. "We were debating what percentage of this place you own."

Rory barked a laugh, a free, open sound that was as fake as the rest of him. Not that Raine didn't like him. She did. When his daughter had been kidnapped, he'd spared nothing to get her back. It had been touching to see how much he loved his child.

Rory's smoothed, long, brown hair was worn in the Senator's queue, and he dressed with a polish he hadn't acquired in Galaxy Grid 219. Raine wouldn't be surprised to learn he'd moved there only because few people would run against him. After all, he just had to live in the middle of nowhere half the year. The rest of the time, he was here on Borrus.

To some, he might appear out of place in the Naked Lady, but Raine thought Rory tended to gravitate to situations where he was a diamond among pieces of coal.

"You know I don't own any of this place, Raine darling." He patted her arm as if he reassured her, but left his hand a second or two too long.

Beneath the table, Walker's foot pressed down on hers.

She removed her hand from under Rory's and picked up her drink. "I'm calling in that favor." No use messing around. Rory was a busy man, with important things pressing for his time, and all that.

"I figured you didn't show up with another man to take me up on my other offer from three years ago." Rory signaled the waitress for a drink, pointing first up in the air, then at his glass.

Raine was impressed Walker kept his face blank and, if she was completely truthful, she was impressed he'd seen Rory's desire through only a single exchange of glances. Walker was naïve about some things, not stupid.

"My friend here has been accused of a crime he didn't commit, and I need you to get him a Senate Pardon."

Rory snorted. "You don't ask for much, huh?"

Raine smiled and said sweetly, "We both know you have the juice to procure the pardon."

"I can get it. I just doubt he's innocent." He studied Walker. "You innocent?"

"Of the crime I'm accused of, yes." Walker's voice was pleasant enough, but there was something there that felt challenging and male, even to Raine.

"A comedian!" Rory barked another laugh. "What are the details?"

"I need you to send a note for me and witness the resulting discussion. When the criminal confesses, you are to have him arrested."

"Who will be your confessor?"

"Malachi Delmundo."

"Why am I not shocked?" Rory shook his head and took his drink from the waitress. "No wonder you're hanging out with this guy. You'll do anything to burn Delmundo."

"I've burned him quite a bit, but can you really have enough revenge?"

Walker shifted in disagreement.

"You most certainly cannot." Rory twirled the swizzle stick, making the liquid in his glass slosh over the side. "I'm not sure I want to get involved with Delmundo."

Raine's drink had come only half full. Rory's drinks were full and free. Looking at the waitress wiggle away, she didn't think that was all he received on the house. Raine was careful to remain silent unless she meant to speak. The last thing she needed was to have her opinions on Rory's sex life aired out loud.

"He'll jump at the chance to meet with you." Raine knew Malachi so very well.

"And then he'll hunt me down if this thing goes wrong." Rory's voice held no emotion.

"Tell him the note was forged." Raine didn't think Rory was really worried about Malachi. Killing a Senator wasn't a very smart move, especially since Rory could easily blame her if Malachi questioned him about this. Rory was trying to limit his effort as much as possible and still have the debt between them satisfied.

"This seems a little simplistic. Your plans are usually more complicated than this."

Raine nodded. He was right, they were. "The first rule in strategy is to keep it simple. The fewer moving parts, the less there is to go wrong. The most important thing is that I can't have Malachi figuring out I'm on the planet. He'll skip the meeting and hunt me down if he knows I'm on Borrus."

"What if he doesn't give the confession you're looking for?"

"Oh, he will." Raine had no doubt. Malachi's downfall would come from his uncontrollable bragging. "The minute he sees Walker and me together, he won't be able to stop himself. Anyway, what fun is sticking someone else with a crime if you can't tell anyone about it?"

"You better be right."

"Whether I am or not, your debt will be paid."

Rory shook his head. "You could have done so much more with this favor than save a stranger with it." He raised his arm in the air and snapped his fingers while still maintaining eye contact with her.

"You know, I'm a sucker for green eyes."

"No, I didn't know that." Rory leaned towards her. "I have green eyes." He fluttered his lashes, turning the words into a joke, but Raine knew on one level he was serious.

The pressure of Walker's foot on hers increased so suddenly, Raine jumped into the table, sloshing Rory's full drink onto his suit. He sprang away from her, and the waitress appeared with napkins to brush him off.

"Sorry about that. I'm a little space-sick from the long flight here."

Rory nodded, stilling the waitress's wandering hands and patting her ass to send her on her way. One of Rory's goons arrived bearing paper and a pen as if he'd overheard them. Raine wondered if he had.

"What do you want the note to say?"

"Meet me on top of the Senate Building tomorrow at the start of the afternoon session to discuss a mutually beneficial business proposition."

Rory wrote it and signed his name. "He could kill you, you know."

"Not there."

"You'll have to leave eventually."

"Theoretically, he'll confess, and you'll have him arrested." She raised an eyebrow.

"You better hope he confesses, Raine."

"He will." Raine stood before Walker did something to piss off Rory or she said something out loud best left securely in her head.

"I'll be there tomorrow. You and I should talk afterwards." There was a promise in his words.

Raine nodded and turned to the door.

"Talk, my ass," Walker fumed as they returned to their hotel. "I was about ten seconds away from laying hands on him." He stalked beside Raine, angry on more levels than he could count.

He wanted to tear Rory Uslep into pieces. How dare the pompous ass proposition his mate when he was sitting right there at the table? And he knew Rory would try to convince her again after they finished with Delmundo. Walker could see lust coming off the other man in waves every time he touched Raine.

This was the wrong moment to have another man vying for her affection. Raine hadn't committed to him, hadn't accepted yet that she was his mate. A growl rose in his chest filled with frustration.

He'd been sure that their lovemaking at the hotel had taken them to the next level, sure that he'd stamped his brand on her. It had been the first time she'd initiated sex like that, provoking him with her sexy body, adjusting her seduction to follow the images he'd had of her in his head, as if she'd truly connected with him on every plane.

The powerful feelings she'd invoked had made him insane.

Then in the Naked Lady, it had felt as if she'd taken a giant step back from him, all but promising she'd leave him when Malachi was defeated.

Walker gritted his teeth and tried to think around his growing anger and frustration. He wouldn't lose her.

Walker sounded bloodthirsty, but Raine didn't comment. She was too busy wondering why Rory's touch had caused her skin to crawl. She'd always considered having an affair with him. The only reason she hadn't was because at first, she'd been involved with someone else, then she'd been set on getting revenge. But tonight, she'd been physically repulsed by him.

"It's because I'm so far beneath you that he thinks he can easily steal you from me," Walker growled.

Raine grabbed his arm and hauled him to a stop in front of the hotel. "You aren't beneath me." What was he talking about?

Walker's jaw worked back and forth as if he ground his teeth. "Of course I am. You're beautiful, and I look like a thug."

Raine studied the pain in his eyes, hearing his unsaid insecurities over the fact he was a Breed. She tried to lighten his mood and reassure him. "You do look better without your clothes on."

His eyebrows went up so far, they hid under his short hair. She'd been right—it was wheat-colored and as it grew longer, it did help his appearance, softening the harsh planes of his face. Several times over the last couple days, she'd caught herself thinking his body wasn't the only part of him she liked.

"You think so?" He swooped her up and spun her around, the action filled with relief, but from what, she didn't know. "Maybe I should stay naked all the time."

"Maybe you should," she agreed, unable to figure out his swinging moods.

He let her slide down his body and tipped her head so he could meet her gaze. "Tell me you don't want him."

"I don't want him." She said it with so much conviction, she surprised even herself.

For a moment, Walker grinned at her, but then dropped his hands and strode away, scraping his fingers through his hair. "I have no idea what my problem is. I feel jealous if another man even looks at you, let alone touches you." He met her gaze. "I could have ripped him to shreds, Raine. That's how possessive I feel about you right now." He threw his hands out in a helpless gesture and stared off down the street.

Raine closed the distance between them to whisper, "Do you think this has anything to do with your father's blood?"

His jaw worked for a moment before he answered. "Maybe. Most likely. He was always overly protective of my mother."

"Walker." She rested her hand on his arm and felt his muscles bunch. "I don't want Rory."

"It was all I could do not to twist his arm off." He finally met her gaze. "I should be a bigger man and tell you to be with him. He's obviously rich and successful, even if he does hang out in a strip club." He stroked her arm, then gripped her hand. “But I won’t, for no other reason than I want you with every particle of my being.”

“It’s okay,” she soothed. And it surprised her that it was. She’d always been the cool one in every relationship she’d ever had. She’d been the one totally in control. She’d never felt this raw and scared.

But when she turned the tables and thought about what she would feel if a waitress had rubbed Walker’s arm as Rory had done hers, she was the one gnashing her teeth. Because she knew the other woman would touch what she did every night bunched muscles and warm, hair-dusted skin that smelled like summer and tasted like heaven.

She stepped close to him, then did something shocking, but she couldn’t stop herself. Pulling his head down, she bit his neck. Hard. So hard, she started to feel her teeth sink through his flesh but stopped herself in time before she broke the skin.

Walker growled and cradled her head in his hand, holding her tighter, instead of pushing her away as she expected.

Taking a shuddering breath, Raine tried to figure out what was going on. Her behavior since the moment she’d met him had been out of character. Walker had said they were fated to be together, but she knew that was craziness.

“What’s happening to me?” she murmured into his chest. Tearing herself from him was an agony, but she had to do it, since she couldn’t think clearly while she touched him. Stepping away, she rested her head in her hands.

She realized she’d turned to him for comfort when he was the very thing that confused her.

She hated this feeling. Hated it with a passion. It was as if she would soon need him just to breathe. She’d never been so out of control. “So vulnerable,” she whispered.

As much as she enjoyed him in bed, she didn’t want the attachment she now felt. It was stronger than even the bond she’d had with her team and it shook her.

Her mind reached overload, and her flight instinct clicked in place.

She would act out her revenge and run as fast and as far from Walker and these feelings as she could.

Chapter Ten

Raine had pulled away from him mentally as well as physically. She hadn't touched him since their conversation outside the hotel the night before. He'd tried to start her talking, but she'd told him she needed to think and had ended up sitting in the room's only chair staring out the window all night.

They were to meet Delmundo in only a few hours at the top of the Senate Building.

"We're assuming he'll show up." Walker broke the deadly silence that ruled the room.

"He'll show." Raine's voice came out flat. She stood and leaned her head against the glass, still gazing out the window.

Walker moved beside her to stare out the dirty glass. The Capital City stretched out in every direction, but the streets in this part of town were relatively unpopulated, a combination of the rain, which had started a few minutes ago and fell in sheets, and the seedy part of town. Warehouses and factories stretched in every direction, smoke pumping into the sky from forges, adding to the dreary skyline.

"Why are you so sure?" He wasn't trying to argue, just keep her talking. Walker's heart constricted in his chest, a deep ache that hurt with each beat of his pulse.

"He won't want to miss this opportunity."

"Rory or Delmundo?" He made sure he kept any inflection from his voice.

"Both. Malachi won't be able to help himself, and Rory will show to satisfy the debt he owes me."

He studied her reflection in the window. There was something sunken about her stance, as if she held a large weight on her shoulders. Her face had closed in on itself, her eyes listless, her body completely still. He wanted to reach out and cuddle her against his chest, rub her back, comfort her but he knew she wrestled with her feelings for him.

The bite she'd taken from his neck had shaken her as much as it had pleased him. It was not the right time to tell her she was acting out the mating ritual, branding him as hers. This was their destiny, but she had to come to him on her own, not because he told her it was their fate.

Without meaning to, he brushed his fingers across the bruise she'd left. Raine's eyes flicked to his in the window, and she winced.

"It's not a big deal, Raine. A love bite, nothing more."

She exploded a breath outwards, but instead of arguing as he'd expected, she said, "I was thinking that you shouldn't come with me today."

"Not a chance." He wanted to shake her and ask her what in the hell was wrong, but he kept his temper in check with effort.

She turned and leaned back against the window, hugging herself with her arms. "I don't know what Malachi might do and I'd rather you stay here."

"We both go or stay. We're not separating. You promised I got to agree to the plan before we put it into effect."

"You're not trained for these types of missions," she said, her voice reasonable.

"Fine then. We won't go." Walker crossed his arms and let his biceps bulge to emphasize his raw strength. He wasn't letting her go alone.

She narrowed her eyes. "We need to prove your innocence."

"By tricking Malachi into a confession? Come on. He won't fall for that."

"I'm telling you, he will. He's the biggest braggart in all of the Inter-worlds. He won't be able to help himself."

"He'll show up with twenty of his men and they'll simply kill us. You know that's a possibility."

"He's going to murder us on top of the Senate Building? He's not that stupid. We'll be safe, since we have to go through security before we reach the roof."

Walker sighed. "Raine, just talk to me about what's upsetting you. No matter what it is, we can work it out."

"I'm not sure we can, Walker. I don't like what I'm feeling right now."

Walker rested his hand above her head, caging her in. Maybe they needed to fight it out. She sure as hell wasn't going to tell him on her own. "Which is what?"

She gritted her teeth and stared at the wall opposite her, not meeting his gaze. "Out of control."

Walker laughed, he couldn't help it. "Of course you feel out of control. Love is like that, Raine."

She dropped her hands on her hips and stood on her tiptoes, her face turning stormy.

A knock cut their battle short. They both stared at the door in surprise.

Raine glided to one side of the portal, all signs of their fight replaced by intensity and focus. "Who is it?"

"The desk clerk. I have a message for you."

"Damn," Walker mumbled, shaking his head. At this rate, they'd never get this settled.

"Rory better not be backing out, the bastard," she snarled, but she pointed to the door for Walker to open it. Pulling a long knife from the top of her boot, she pressed herself against the wall.

Walker opened the door right as one of Malachi's men slashed the pimple-faced clerk's neck.

Raine saw the blood splatter first. It streaked across the front of Walker's shirt.

He stumbled back as if it were hot oil. "What the hell?"

She didn't have to guess who had come for a visit. Damn, how had he found out she was here?

Malachi and three men were inside their room within a heartbeat, dragging the dead clerk along with them.

"Nice, Malachi." Raine recovered as fast as she could from the shock of seeing her archenemy suddenly appear in her hotel room. "You've messed up the beautiful carpeting."

Malachi looked down at the sticky, thread-bare mess that passed for a rug. He grinned. "Oops." His brown-eyed gaze swept over her where she still stood pressed to the wall. "Close the door," he ordered one of his men without taking his eyes off her. "I received a note to meet your buddy, Uslep. I've known since you did that job for him that he was trying to jump into your pants. Took me all of five minutes to bribe one of the waitresses at the Naked Lady to find out you saw him last night." His tone took on a gloating singsong.

"You know what your problem is, Malachi?"

"Enlighten me."

"You are a braggart." She rolled her eyes. "Haven't you ever heard of mystery? Suspense?" Shrugging her shoulders to loosen the tension, she added, "Building anticipation?"

"You're insane." Malachi breathed the words as if they had just occurred to him. He blinked and seemed to force some emotion away.

If she didn't know better, she would have thought her sanity, or lack thereof, unnerved him.

Raine stared at him, taking in his stylish clothes and good looking face. Chocolate eyes and hair combined to create a breathtaking panorama. Beside him, Walker appeared coarse and unrefined.

And wonderful.

"What?" Malachi asked, his brows lowering in confusion.

Walker snorted, obviously fighting a laugh, drawing his gaze.

Shit, she'd spoken out loud. It was an annoyingly persistent habit that she was beginning to think was impossible to break.

"You," Malachi said, his lips tipping into a smile that didn't come from amusement. "Well, well, well. Look who has joined forces. The Breed and the Bitch."

"You should fit right in, since you're a Bastard." Raine made sure she gave the B a capital sound, mimicking him.

"Always sassy, even to the end, eh Raine?"

"I'm not afraid of you, Malachi." Raine thought fast. There were four of them. Walker was on the other side of the room from her. He met her gaze, arching one brow to show her he was waiting to follow her lead.

Her heart flipped. That he would trust her to make the call spoke of his respect for her planning ability. It wasn't the typical male thing to do. Most men would start fighting or try to talk their way out or do anything but follow a woman, especially one they'd slept with.

And right at that moment, with death standing only a few feet away, Raine fell totally, completely, one hundred percent in love with him.

"You should be afraid." Malachi turned to Walker. "I thought you were serving a life sentence on Sector 9?"

Walker shrugged, but didn't speak.

"Cat got your tongue, Healer?" Malachi stepped over the dead clerk towards him.

Raine controlled the urge to leap between them. She knew Malachi could be fast when it came to knife work.

"What do you want, Malachi?" Raine asked to distract him.

"I was wondering why you wanted to see me on top of the Senate building." He didn't turn around.

"I was trying to save some lives. I didn't think even you would be dumb enough to kill someone there." Raine stared at the clerk and shook her head. "You always were a bastard. Why kill this kid?"

That got his attention and he turned around. "Why not? He's nothing." He seemed genuinely confused.

"You know, you don't even understand that taking a human life is against the Gods." Raine had always pondered his ease with death. He'd had her team killed on a whim as far as she'd been able to find out. They hadn't been after him, even though he was on par with the usual scum they hunted.

"Human? An interesting word, Raine." He circled Walker, who stood in a relaxed pose, a blank look on his face. "Did you know the Healer here isn't human?"

"As far as I'm concerned he's more human than you are." Raine didn't like Malachi being this close to her man. Dammit, she wished she wasn't so far away. She glanced at the knife in her hand. She could throw it, but even if she killed Malachi, he had three guards here with him.

"Doogie, guard her with your blaster," Malachi said. "So, Walker, you escaped from the prison? I didn't think you had it in you."

"Blasters are illegal," Raine informed the man who pulled the gun.

"So's killing," the man said.

"True."

He had a point, that was for sure.

"So what's the story?" Malachi prompted. He obviously burned with curiosity, shifting from one foot to the other.

"Didn't you know that everything comes back to haunt you, Malachi?" Walker's voice was smooth and unconcerned, but his gaze flicked to the blaster, letting Raine know he was worried about it. "Even me."

If Malachi gave the word to kill her, she would throw the knife into his chest as a final goodbye. But she realized she didn't want to die. She wanted to feel the beautiful muscles of Walker's body one more time, run her hands along his amazing chest, her skin sliding in the sheen of sweat which showed her just how turned on she made him.

She knew one thing—all hell would break lose if they killed Walker first. Death would sweep through the room, and she would wield it. They would both live or both die.

Someone tapped twice on the door.

A man who looked like Doogie's twin went to let another person in. This time it was a woman. She was stunning, wrapped in a red dress that hugged all her curves to their best advantage. Her blond hair winged away from her heart-shaped face and baby-blue eyes.

"You remember your girlfriend, Merrium, don't you?" Malachi asked Walker.

Raine felt a pang of jealousy zip through her before she saw Walker's face. He actually growled at the blonde, baring his teeth. Merrium stepped back, placing a manicured hand on her chest, and Raine realized this must be the woman Malachi had used to betray Walker.

"The car's waiting," Merrium said and retreated to stand by the door, as far away from Walker as she could go.

"I didn't expect you to be coming along, Healer."

"Are we going someplace?" Raine asked.

"I have always wanted to kill Raine and drink her blood." Malachi sauntered over to tap Raine's cheek. "While it's tempting to do so here, I want to be able to take my time."

"I hope I poison you." Raine smiled at him and tightened her grip on the knife in her hand. *Closer, just get a little closer, you bastard.* Raine bit her lip to keep from speaking the words out loud.

They absolutely could not go back to Malachi's stronghold. She'd never been able to reach him there because he kept himself surrounded by so many people. It would be impossible to escape once they were there.

"Such bitterness." He shook his head. "If you had just let the whole thing drop, I would never have had to do this. But you had to have revenge."

"Yes. I did."

"Speaking of which, what did you do with my money?" Malachi leaned closer, his breath whispering across her face.

Raine rose up onto her tiptoes and whispered, "I spent it, you rat-bastard."

Chapter Eleven

Whatever Raine whispered in his ear made Malachi slap her hard. "I'll make you pay for that." Malachi's hand shook as if he wanted to slap her again. "I knew when your team signed that contract to terminate me that the seven of you would keep coming until all of you were dead."

Walker was so angry, he almost missed Raine's movement as she whisked Malachi's knife out of the sheathe behind his back and pitched it into the wall beside Walker's head.

The blade was a little closer to his face then he would have liked, but he didn't have time to think as he grabbed it.

Doogie fired right as Raine pushed Malachi into the blast. His body flew into the far wall as if swatted by the hand of a God.

Merrium stood beside the door, screaming.

Walker threw his knife at Doogie's chest. It ended up sticking out of his throat since he was also watching Raine fighting across the room. He launched himself at Doogie's look alike. Picturing his target several inches further back for maximum impact, he rammed his fist at the bad guy's nose. Walker might not be formally trained, but his cellmate at HeFO had taught him quite a bit during the long, long hours they had nothing to do but talk about the ins and outs of the criminal lifestyle.

Doogie's twin crumpled to the floor as his nose imploded like a piece of rotten fruit under Walker's fist. He wasn't going anywhere for a while.

Turning to Raine, he watched the beauty of her body as it flowed gracefully while she fought, her foot rounding to deliver a vicious kick. The man ended up in a heap on the ground.

With the last man's fall, Merrium went eerily quiet. For the first time, Walker analyzed his feelings for her. Nothing. No anger or desire or anything at all except maybe pity. Raine had healed the scars Merrium had left on his heart, and the anger faded with the realization that the Gods had sent him to Sector 9 for a higher purpose.

"You okay?" Walker asked Raine.

She nodded and wiped her knife on the fallen man's shirt. Taking a deep breath, she crossed the room to his side and touched the blood on his shirt.

"None of it's mine," he assured her.

"Good." She let out the breath as if she'd been holding it. "Gods, I was worried."

He caught her arm and started to pull her forward. "Don't be." Everything was going to be okay. He had her. She was safe. They would move to the hottest planet in the galaxies and raise magical children and live happily ever after.

Something moved in his peripheral vision, and Walker glanced up.

"Die, you Breed bastard," Merrium said, and fired Doogie's blaster.

Raine buckled backwards and crumpled so quickly, Walker didn't even have time to catch her as she fell. Merrium flung open the door and sprinted down the hall.

He dropped to Raine's side. If his mate died, he'd hunt Merrium and scrape her heart out with his bare hands. But there was time for that later, he promised himself. *This must be what Raine felt when Malachi killed her team—the burning urge for retaliation and retribution.*

Raine lay curled around her stomach, holding herself together with her hands. He pried her hands away to assess the damage.

What he saw stopped his heart and made him dig his fingernails into the flesh of her wrists before he controlled himself. She was dying and he knew it. A noise rose from his throat, a low growl of pain and fear.

"We," she blinked away the glaze from her eyes. "Have to move." She gasped and it sounded painful. "The Council police will be here soon."

"I can't move you. You might die." *Save her, dammit. Right now.* Hadn't his father once told him it was possible to exchange his life for hers? That he could transfer his life force to save his mate from death? He wasn't sure, couldn't think, couldn't remember.

"Do it." She gave him a hard stare, frowning with pain.

Walker gazed at her torn stomach, the wound not much smaller than his palm, the edges ringed with black. He would need a large amount of time to heal this kind of damage. Time he wouldn't have if he was back in prison.

He had no choice but to move her. Gods, she could die from the shock alone.

No!

He couldn't, wouldn't think that.

Get yourself under control. NOW!

He picked her up and grabbed their pack. Sprinting from the room, he burst through the hall door and jogged down the stairs. Each movement jarred her in his arms. Small, pain-filled cries escaped with each step, ripping at his soul and tearing at his own flesh as if he was the one bleeding to death.

He ran through the emergency exit at the bottom of the stairs, setting off the alarm, which wailed into the dark, rainy day.

"I'm sorry, baby," he whispered, scanning for a place to go.

His heart hammered so hard he couldn't hear anything but the rush of his own pulse.

Liquid slithered the length of his arm, thicker than rain, a drop hanging at his elbow for a moment before it fell. He refused to picture her life draining from her here on the sidewalk, and yet he had a sudden vision of the street filling with her blood, rising up to engulf him.

Shutting his eyes, he took a breath through his mouth and whispered, "I've spent years preparing for this moment. I will save her. I can do this." Calm settled over him, like a mantle from the Gods.

When he opened his eyes, he saw a factory ahead, the fence pried up so he could duck beneath it.

He felt the heat before he saw the open bay. Checking first to make sure no one was around, he slipped into the warehouse and slid behind some crates in time to avoid a man walking out.

Raine moaned from the pain.

"Shh," he whispered.

She fell silent, breathing rapidly through her mouth, and Walker's heart constricted.

He needed to get near the heat source he felt radiating close by. It would increase his chances to heal this kind of damage. Dodging behind some crates, he stopped at the edge of an immense room, staring in awe at the mechanized casting operation that poured red hot liquid of some kind into molds. There wasn't a single person to be seen; factory work was only done with humans on the less technically advanced Outer Worlds. The Inter-world Council had long ago banned these jobs as unskilled for everyone but the specialists who did repairs on the machines.

Stepping as close to the open pit as he could without being doused with sparks, he laid Raine down. She curled into her stomach, coughing convulsively.

"Don't die," he ordered, wiping off the foamy red substance that gathered at the edges of her lips. The calm mantle was still in place, and he felt strong, in control, and steady.

She wouldn't die because he willed it to be so.

He forced her hands away so he could press his own into her wound. She moaned in pain, then screamed when he pushed power into her.

Not too much. He had to be careful. Concentrating on repairing her wounds, he dove in and started to heal her.

Painstakingly, he moved through her core, mending torn muscles and healing her body.

He had no idea how much time had elapsed before he surfaced. Maybe minutes, but most likely long hours. He was exhausted, swaying in pain, having run his energy level lower than he'd ever pushed it.

The heat had sustained his temperature, allowing him to heal for much longer than he would have normally been able to. Raine's stomach still had a hole the size of his thumb, but he couldn't completely heal it. Not without re-energizing.

A flutter at his knee attracted his attention.

"You," Raine licked her dry lips. "You look like hell."

"So do you," he said, but that wasn't entirely true. Her color had returned, and he'd stopped the blood flow and healed most of the wound. "I'm out of energy, Raine. I've got nothing else to give you." He fell forward, barely catching himself with his hands. Stretching out alongside her body, he gathered her into his arms and held her close. Fear washed over him. He had no idea what would happen to her, since he'd never left someone half healed before.

The barrier he'd built around his emotions cracked; the feelings he'd held off coursed through him. Agony seized his heart and squeezed. He cradled her, rocking slightly to comfort his woman, while fear made him pant and bite his own lip to keep the pain from ripping free.

If he lost her, he would only live long enough to kill Merrium. Gnashing his teeth, he fought the urge to scream until tears spilled from his eyes to track down his cheeks.

Raine's hand came up to capture them. "It's okay, Walker. I just need to sleep." She moved her head a fraction closer to him, and he wrapped around her with the last bit of his strength.

"I love you," she whispered.

"I've always loved you, Raine, from the moment you first touched me back on Sector 9."

Raine woke when someone kicked her leg.

"What the hell are you two doing?" a gruff voice yelled at her. "This ain't no hotel."

She blinked up at a man with a toolbox in his hand.

"You've got until the count of five to get out of here or I'll call the guard."

Raine glanced back to find Walker staring at her. "How do you feel?" he asked.

"I said move!" The man with the toolbox flushed red in the face. "I'm two seconds away from turning you two in."

She sat up. Her stomach didn't protest, and she felt oddly rested, as if she'd been sleeping for days. She ran a hand along her skin. Perfect. There wasn't time to dwell on the miracle. "We're going."

Walker staggered to his feet and helped her stand, then shrugged on the pack. Like a pair of drunks, they lurched out of the factory into the sunny day, leaning on one another for support.

"What happened to my wound? The last thing I remember is that you couldn't heal it all."

"I didn't heal it completely." He shook his head and pulled up what remained of her shirt to stare at her stomach. "Perhaps the healing continued on its own while we slept. It shouldn't have, though. But everything seems to work differently with you than it does with others."

For a moment, they stood silent, taking that in. Raine rubbed her hand across her belly and realized they were *more* together than they were apart. Better. Stronger.

Magical.

She shivered as the importance of their relationship hit her. He had healed her. He had fought for her. But more than that, he had trusted and respected her.

Love made her knees feel wobbly and her body weak. She couldn't run now even if she wanted to. The thought brought relief. She threaded her fingers through his to lock him to her.

"How long do you think we were sleeping?" she asked, shading her eyes from the sun with her other hand.

"The night for sure. It was raining when we went in and close to dark."

Walker's face was still ashen, and Raine went up on her tiptoes to kiss him.

"What was that for?"

"Just because I love you, I guess."

"Just because, huh?" He smiled and she noticed some of his color had returned.

Malachi was dead. Her revenge was complete. Her whole life stretched out before her in an endless stream.

"What happened to the woman who shot me?"

Walker shrugged. "She escaped with her life." His tone sounded bloodthirsty.

She tipped her head to stare at him, surprised at the anger in his eyes. "We'll send a note to Rory and have him pick her up. He can put her in HeFO for her part in all this. Certainly a few years freezing on Sector 9 is revenge enough." She glanced up and down the street. "So what now?"

Walker squeezed her hand and she met his gaze. "I'm still a wanted man. We never proved my innocence."

"No," she said. "Maybe I can still get a pardon from Rory." She heard the doubt in her own words.

"You think that will work without proof?"

She wanted to say yes, but couldn't. "No, and I'd rather use him to put that bitch Merrium on ice."

He blinked at her candor and humor lines spread across his face. "You're the master planner. What do you suggest?" He became serious. "I'll follow your lead, Raine, as long as we stay together."

"I want to spend the rest of my life with you, wherever we end up."

"We'll be happy as long as we're together." He made it sound like a promise.

Her heart tumbled and love filled her.

Walkers mouth pulled into a sudden frown. "You know, I wonder why Malachi killed your team. That's what started this whole thing to begin with."

Raine had racked her brain for three years over the very same question. "Before Malachi died, he said he knew the team would keep coming for him when he heard we'd signed a contract to take him out." She blew out a breath. "The thing is, we turned down the contract we were offered. The team decided he was too well insulated and would be too hard to take out for the small amount of money we were offered. Malachi must not have known."

"All this death and pain and revenge over something that wasn't even true." He brought her hand up to kiss her knuckles. "I'm glad that part of your life is over."

"And a new life for both of us is beginning." She would come up with the perfect plan so they would live happily ever after. "First we find someplace to change clothes and clean up." She paused, thinking about the fact that Malachi would no longer be tracking her so she could freely spend his money. A slow smile of satisfaction spread across her face. "Then we're going to the One Bank to make a withdrawal."

"Why are you smiling?"

"We need to purchase fake papers for you, and then we're going on the trip of our lives."

"I think it will take more than fake papers to keep me free."

Her palm cupped his chin. "How do you feel about your face?"

"It's the one I was born with, so I suppose it's good enough." He pressed his lips onto her fingers. "Although I seem to remember you saying something about it not being exactly handsome."

"You heard that?" Raine felt a flush inch up her neck and cheeks.

He grinned, his green sparkling eyes telling her he was teasing.

Happiness bubbled inside her. "I've actually grown quite fond of it, but sadly it's the face of a wanted man."

"Yes."

"I was thinking we may need to change it." She gave his hair a playful yank. "And let your hair grow."

"Reorganizing my face and forged papers will take some serious balseems."

She skipped a happy circle around him, letting her hands touch his hard chest, bulging arms and sleek back.

Walker laughed. "Uh oh, you've got something up your sleeve."

"We're going to live the rest of our days spending Malachi's money, starting with buying you a new identity."

"You have that much?"

She looked at the love of her life, a slow smile spreading across her lips. "Oh, yeah." Raine flung out a hand. "Think of it, Walker. Sunsets on LackSui, taking luxury cruisers from planet to planet, staying in one of those hotels under Goda's oceans. We can go anywhere we want."

He shook his head. "If that will make you happy."

"It will."

Walker waved a hand and executed a perfect bow. "Then lead on. I'll be at your back, no matter where you take us."

She smiled because she knew he would.

About the Author:

Leigh Wyndfield spends her time away from writing reading anything she can get her hands on, watching movies, and skiing or hiking, depending on the season. Hooked on Battlestar Galactica *as a child, she often slipped away from her music lessons to sneak in the show after school. As she grew up, she realized she also loved romance novels. Unable to get her hands on romances that take place on other worlds, she started writing her own while working in the real world and obtaining her MBA from a top-tiered university. Installing software systems just didn't seem like any fun compared to writing, so she recently quit her job to create stories full time. Visit her website to learn about her other books at* www.leighwyndfield.com*!*

Summer Lightning

by Saskia Walker

To My Reader:

Picture this: you're totally alone and enjoying the summer sun on an isolated beach. What would make it even better for you—seeing a gorgeous hunk walking naked in the waves? And if he arrived at your door in the middle of a storm, offering to help you out of a fix? Well, what's a girl to do . . .

Chapter One

The sky roared overhead, the fluffy summer clouds fleeting across the expanse of bright blue. Sally spread her arms wide, closed her eyes and allowed her other senses to take over. Her skin warmed and prickled as the summer breeze danced over her. Against her back the solid shape of the sand dune molded her body, arching her as if offering her to the elements. The smell of ozone filled her nostrils, and the mesmerizing sound of the waves rolling up onto the shore washed over her. The sun broke through the racing clouds, and through her closed eyelids, the light dimmed and then brightened, charting its progress.

She sighed happily and rolled over onto her belly, folding her arms under her chin and exposing her back to the sun. It was idyllic; the small cove was so isolated she had pulled off her T-shirt and lay on the warm sand wearing only her shorts and deck shoes. Her nipples tightened when they made contact with the gritty sand; her skin tingled as her body responded to every stimuli that surrounded her.

It was just as she had imagined it would be—the secluded idyll fulfilling her desire to get closer to nature. Best of all, she still had another six days before she had to head home. She'd taken two weeks away from London and the office for much needed time to devote to her sculpture. She'd been busy working on a new cyber-warrior figurine when she decided to get out of the cottage and walk along the shore. Something about exposing herself to the elements made her feel closer to the clay when she returned, and this time would be no exception.

A strand of grass tickled her nose. She rubbed it away and opened her eyes, squinting, while she grew accustomed to the bright sunlight again. Much to her surprise, she saw a figure moving further down the cove.

"Damn," she whispered.

She hadn't seen another soul on the beach during the whole time that she had been there, and she snatched her T-shirt against her, lying flat against the ground. The clumps of beach grass lining the top of the dunes gave her cover, but she wanted her T-shirt nearby in case she needed it.

It was a man, and he seemed to be alone. *A very attractive man.* Perhaps she'd been away from people for too long, she thought. A few trips to the local village for supplies obviously wasn't enough contact to keep her in touch with the real world.

She smiled to herself, watching as he kicked off his sports shoes and walked barefoot towards the edge of the shore. He was tall and well built, with sun-streaked hair. He wore loud shorts and a T-shirt that was threadbare. His legs were corded with strong muscles, and she eyed them as an artist, and more, as a woman—a woman subconsciously hungry for such a sight.

He had the look of a beachcomber, but as she watched, he walked into the water and dipped a long plastic tube into the surf. He lifted it and looked at it in the light, then sealed it with a plastic cap. She wondered what he was doing.

He walked back to where he'd left his shoes and deposited the tube. Then he pulled his T-shirt over his head, giving her a look at his perfectly shaped torso as he did so.

"Wow," she whispered approvingly. If she was looking for inspiration, she had surely found it today. He was a handsome specimen all right, gorgeous looking and with a very impressive physique. The guy worked out, that much was obvious. He had amazing, powerful shoulders and a six-pack to match. He stood on the edge of the surf as if he owned it—it was as if Neptune himself had just walked out of the waves.

Sally's eyebrows shot up when she realized he wasn't stopping at the T-shirt. He was busy undoing the tie at his waistband and was about to drop his shorts. She glanced around, half expecting to see somebody else running over to accompany him. But, no, he appeared to be alone. And she was trapped there, clutching her T-shirt to her chest as she observed him, unseen. His shorts were kicked off unceremoniously and he walked, naked, towards the edge of the surf, giving her a look at his gorgeous backside. Sally was transfixed. Between her thighs a dense, humid heat rapidly built, and her sex clenched with appreciation and desire.

He waded into the water, unhindered by its temperature. She was amazed, because she knew how cold it was after a tentative paddle the week before. She had traveled up to Northumberland on the far north east of England, to get peace and solitude on this lonely coastline. The above average summer warmth was a lucky bonus, but the sea temperature was never going to get warm enough for her to consider a full-on paddlc.

She watched admiringly as he waded out until the water reached half way up his powerful thighs. He ran his fingers through his hair, arching his back, his face turned upwards and his eyes closed. Sally sighed longingly. She was willing to bet that running her hands over his physique would feel pretty darned good. He turned in the water, and she got a full frontal view of his masculinity, and she was very impressed. A purr of appreciation escaped her. The sound lifted and was swept away on the breeze as she lookcd at his cock, hanging heavy at the junction between his thighs. It was an imposing sight. He reached down and grasped it, his hand moving expertly as it grew and rose before her eyes.

Sally couldn't believe what was happening. At first she'd been alarmed to see someone there, and now she was enthralled. The most gorgeous hunk of man had stripped, right in front of her eyes and was now touching himself, completely without self-consciousness. What an incredible sight!

She was getting a secret show from an absolute sex god, and she was getting very horny as a result. Her clit was pounding, and her sex clenched as she eyed the magnificent tool he held in his hand.

He stroked his erection lazily up and down, and Sally felt an overwhelming urge to do the same. She pushed her hand inside her shorts, her fingers quickly sliding into her damp, sticky sex folds. She stroked her clit in time with his movements, her breathing speeding, her eyes riveted to the man standing in the waves, the water lapping against him as he unashamedly indulged himself. She wriggled and reached, her body beating out its own response.

What if he saw her, what if he caught her doing this, while watching him?

The sudden unbidden question brought about a rush of embarrassment and self-awareness. She couldn't believe she was doing this, out here in the open, but she couldn't shy away from the secret session of mutual self-loving. It was like a secret pagan ritual.

It was such a turn on.

His fist was moving faster, and his body tensed. His cock reached and then jerked an impressive stream of fluid into the air. She cursed under her breath, squeezed her hand over her pussy, crushing her clit and worked hard until she too came in a sudden rush. Her breathing rasped, and she felt stunned at the unexpected, deviant desire he had caused in her and the subsequent rush of sensations.

He turned around in the water. What if he came back towards her now? How was she going to get away without being seen? But then, much to her relief, she saw him dive and swim away. Taking advantage of the situation, she grabbed her T-shirt and pulled it on as she stood up. She shot off, jogging back towards the cottage, her mind already racing with ideas for a new sculpture, something pagan and sexy.

She glanced back over her shoulder. At the far end of the cove she saw a motorbike parked. A tent had been erected nearby. He was staying over. Would she see him again? A shiver of anticipation ran through her veins as she considered the question and then she darted inside her rented cottage, smiling to herself.

Julian Keswick lifted his boot a fraction, and his motorbike began to slow down. He had almost covered the five miles from the cove to the local village when he caught sight of Tom walking at the side of the road. He drew up alongside him. The old man started, as if alarmed, and Julian pulled off his helmet to reveal his identity.

"Oh, Mr. Keswick, it's you . . . got me old ticker going then, so you did."

"Sorry Tom, I didn't mean to spook you. Yes, it's me, back again. Anything new since my last visit?"

Julian had warmed to the old man from the first time he had come to this stretch of coast, five years earlier. On his visits he always made time for Tom, who many of the villagers referred to as "the local idiot." Not the case. Julian had many conversations with him and quickly found that Tom had a handle on everyone in the area and knew all the latest gossip. It helped Julian out when someone would willingly shed light on any changes or anything going on in the locality that might affect the local beaches.

The year before, Tom had given him the word on an illegal red diesel scam that could have had detrimental effects on the environment if the local fisherman hadn't been made aware of what exactly they were buying. As a marine conservationist on coastal duty, Julian's responsibility was to monitor the beaches of the area. It was a job he was not only dedicated to, but enjoyed immensely.

Tom pondered the question. "Come up to the pub with me and I'll tell you all," he offered, with a wink. That was his code for "buy me a pint and I'll spill the beans."

"Will do," Julian responded, pleased, and climbed off his motorbike. "Is there someone staying at the cottage in the cove?" He had noticed a Land Rover parked outside as he headed out and, earlier, when he'd been swimming; he thought he'd caught sight of movement at the cottage. It had never been occupied on his previous visits, and he was certainly surprised, and annoyed, if that was the case now.

"Aye, young woman up from London staying there now. Old man Greg came up from Newcastle and had it done out to be rented out as one of them holiday cottages. We didn't think anyone would come, you know, with the dirt track to navigate and all." He chortled. "But we was wrong. She's the third visitor; the other lots were families."

Julian gave an inward groan. *Tourists. Damn it.*

It was only a matter of time until it had to happen, he supposed. In his mind, it was *his* place. Isolated, hard to find, perfectly beautiful. Ramblers and coastal walkers sometimes happened by, but their kind had an innate respect for the environment. He had spent many hours alone at the cove, and he cared for it. He resented the idea of sharing it. Especially with a bunch of ignorant tourists who knew nothing about how precious the place was.

"Come on, I'll buy you a pint and we'll have a proper chat." He was about to push his bike on when he realized for the first time that Tom was without his bicycle. He was rarely seen without the archaic iron horse and even if he was walking, it was usually being pushed alongside him. "Where's your bike?"

Tom's mouth turned down at the corners. "The sea, *she* took it."

Julian grinned. As well as being a font of information, Tom shared Julian's appreciation of the ocean and thought of it as a woman, a very powerful woman—just as he did.

"I left it outside me cottage one night when I was late home from the pub, and she was mighty angry with me for some reason and came right up onto the sound and took it away. I've just about forgiven her now." He shook his head at Julian, forlornly.

Julian gave him a supportive pat on the back and gestured him on to the pub, some fifty yards ahead on the hillside. He often thanked his lucky stars that he had been stationed in this part of the world. Its strangeness never ceased to fascinate him, and the scenery along this stretch of coast was awesome. In particular, the cove where he had erected his tent was one of his favorite places.

He might be a scientist but he wasn't your live-in-a-lab type scientist. He liked to get back to nature; that's why he'd opted to study environmental science, to protect and support the earth's natural resources. That's also why he worked like he did, staying on location, instead of returning to base every day as was expected. He didn't want to be cooped up.

It was with a strange, longing feeling that he realized it was the first time he'd ever had to share the place with another human soul. He also realized, reluctantly, that he ought to go and introduce himself. He didn't want to scare the visitors while he went about his business, but he didn't relish the idea of the task. *Far from it.*

Sally refilled her dousing dish, set it down on the table and dipped one hand into the water. With the other hand, she pulled off the large, damp cloth that kept the clay workable, and then ran rivulets of water over the sculpture. She'd worked late into the night and slept until noon before waking, ravenous, and realized that she hadn't even eaten supper the night before. After a hearty breakfast, she'd pulled on an old shirt and jeans and returned to the sculpture.

When it was gleaming wet, she walked around the large kitchen table that she had covered with plastic sheets to use as her workstation while she was at the cottage. The torso was about half life-size. She wished she'd had enough clay to do a full size version, but then there would be the issue of getting it home, and she was very sure that she'd want to keep this one. She ran her fingers over the sculpture, possessively. It was well underway, and she was pleased with her progress. The rough clay at the base rose up just as the sea had, buffeting the strong columns of his thighs. There, she had already worked her magic, and the strong muscles were shaped and made hard and real by her fingers. She reached forward and stroked the outline of his cock, half formed from the clay. She was savoring that part for as long as possible, because she knew she would really enjoy molding it.

His abdomen, buttocks and hips had absorbed most of her time the night before, and she could already see something special emerging from her work. The cyber figurines she spent every moment of her spare time on had become very popular. She'd been selling them over the Internet for fourteen months already, but this was something different, more classical and yet earthy. She laughed at herself. Maybe it was because she felt possessive about the model. This was certainly one way to get her hands on him.

She moved to stand behind the figure, her hands against his buttocks, wondering what it would feel like to have the real man there, to have her hands on that glorious body of his. She stroked lightly around his hips to the front, where she touched the heavy, rising cock. It was only half formed—but in her mind? She remembered every glorious inch.

Smiling, she moved forward and rested against the back of the sculpture, not caring whether she stained her shirt. She always got herself into a complete mess when she worked. She sighed as she mentally planned working on the potent orbs of his testicles, and her fingers began to mark them out in the clay. This was so creative, she mused, and therapeutic, allowing herself to drift, her eyes still closed. *Very therapeutic indeed.*

When she heard the loud rap on the door, she leapt back, nearly overbalancing the table in the process, her eyes flashing open and her mouth opening in a silent exclamation. *Who the hell could that be?*

Maybe she could ignore it. When she leaned over and saw the dark shadow moving behind the glass door, she realized that it was too late and she couldn't hide. She'd probably already been seen. The only door into the cottage went straight into the kitchen, where she had set up her workstation. She cursed and took a regretful look at the torso, before stepping over and hauling the heavy door open.

She stared, in absolute horror, speechless. It was the man himself. He was right there, on her doorstep, looking gorgeous, despite the scowl on his face. He was wearing a bright, white T-shirt and blue jeans, a motorbike helmet hanging casually from one hand, his bike parked up a little way off. She gathered herself and moved quickly, edging herself into the open gap, holding the door as closed as she possibly could to block his view into the cottage.

"Well, hello," he said, his gaze traveling slowly from her face down to her bare feet and back up again. His expression morphed slowly from grumpy to friendly, and he shook his head and broke into a smile. "I've just popped over to introduce myself." He stuck out his hand. "I'm Julian Keswick, and I'm working along the coast here. I've set my tent up at the other end of the cove." He gestured over his shoulder. "Thought I'd better call by and say hello, to assure you the natives are friendly." He grinned at her again, his sensual mouth conveying so much in that simple, friendly gesture.

It was a totally gorgeous smile, warming her to the core, despite her awkwardness. Sally was transfixed, because he was even better looking close-up. He had startling green eyes, heavily fringed, and his hair was darker than she had originally thought, but sun-streaked from his time working outside. His skin was sun-kissed.

In fact, you know that he's sun-kissed all over, don't you, Sally?

She blushed at the memory, attempting to push it away. His bone structure was solid and strong, making her fingers twitch instinctively. The desire to reach out and trace the bones of his face was so great that she clutched her hands into fists.

Still standing with his hand extended, he looked down and noticed her reaction. "I'm sorry, have I caught you at a bad time?"

She felt as if she had been caught red-handed. She glanced down at herself and realized what a statc she must look. She had damp patches all over her clothes, and she hadn't even combed her hair. Not only that, but she was standing there with her hands in fists as if she was about to give the poor guy a black eye because he had dared to knock on her door.

With a great deal of effort she mustered up a smile, hoping that he wouldn't see past her and into the kitchen. If he caught sight of the sculpture and recognized something about it . . . well, that wasn't worth thinking about. She'd simply die of embarrassment.

"Sorry," she said, rubbing her hands on her shirt and taking his offered handshake. "I'm just surprised to see anybody around here. I've been here for a few days and the isolation has been great, but here you are now." It was coming out all wrong. Instead of trying to lure the guy in and have a go at chatting him up, which is what would have been ideal, she was literally chasing him off. All because she was so bloody nonplussed by his sudden appearance at the very moment that she had been fantasizing about him.

His smile faded somewhat, a small furrow developing between his eyebrows. Despite that, he gripped her hand, and when their eyes met over the contact, something instinctive passed between them. *Something very sexy and intimate.*

"I'm really sorry, but I can't invite you in," she blurted, trying to repair the damage of her less than hospitable welcome, and then bit her lip anxiously. Whatever the hell was she going to say next? She couldn't trust her own mouth. It was true enough that she couldn't invite him in though, but she would have to give a reason, or he'd assume she had something to hide. *And I don't have something to hide?*

Heat rose in her cheeks, and she silently cursed herself for not even thinking to cover the torso before answering the door. "I'm in the middle of something; it's nothing personal, really." *And now I am fibbing, because 'personal' is surely what it is.* She attempted to paste on another smile, regret at the missed opportunity already swamping her. Damn, the guy only presented himself at her door, and she practically had to chase him off with the broomstick. "Maybe another time?" *Feeble, still sounded like a brush off.* That was the last thing she wanted to give him.

"Sure, whatever." He looked her up and down again, as if regretful. "Shame," he murmured, and then shook himself slightly, saluted her and turned his back. "You know where I am if you need anything," he shouted over his shoulder, and pointed down the cove.

"Thanks," she called after him, her spirits lifting somewhat. Her heartbeat was still erratic, her nerve endings tingling. It was as if her whole body had grown acutely aware of the perfect male specimen who had been at such close hand. She blushed at her intense, animal response. Standing on the doorstep, watching him walk away, she suddenly became aware of the rising humidity in the atmosphere. That had to be partly to blame for the way she was feeling, surely?

She turned and went back into the kitchen, hands on hips, eyeing the torso accusingly. "You," she said, "are going to have find a new home!"

Chapter Two

Julian fidgeted restlessly. He was lying on top of his sleeping bag with his hands folded behind his head. The tent flap was open, and he stared out into the night. The sky was rumbling; a storm had been threatening for the past few hours. True to form for British weather, a few days of glorious heat was quickly followed up by humidity and sudden rainfall. The radio had reported a whammy-doozer of a storm hitting the north-east coast by midnight. He knew he ought to go check on the motorbike and secure the tent pegs. Instead, his mind kept wandering restlessly over to the woman at the cottage.

What a pleasant surprise she had turned out to be. He'd been unhappy about the visitor's presence, but his misgivings had vanished immediately when he had caught sight of her. It felt like a trick, though. A trick to make him forget his territorial attitude to the cove. He gave a wry smile at the idea of it. Perhaps Old Man Greg had put her there to distract him from his aggravation about the turn of events. Perhaps she was a gift from the sea, a symbolic gesture that would point out his ridiculous self-righteousness about the place. The sea had a way of showing Man he was but a small thing in nature's grand scheme.

Whatever it was, he couldn't shake off the woman's image. She was a sexy little thing and she'd been in his mind all day long. When she'd opened the door, she'd been embarrassed. He was convinced that he had caught her up to something—something sexy? She'd stood in the doorway, looking startled, as if he'd caught her *in flagrante delicto.* Her pupils had been dilated, her nipples hard and visible through that baggy shirt she'd been wearing. She'd been unmistakably aroused, but she was supposed to be alone. Tom had said she was staying there alone, and Tom's information had always been accurate.

He sat up and stuck his head out of the tent. On the distant horizon, the incoming storm was already visible, with flashes of lightning illuminating patches of cloud far away. Crackling electricity filled the air, and the humidity was at its most dense.

Over to the left, he could see the outline of the cottage. There was a light flickering at the window. It had to be a candle, or was he being overly symbolic and wishful? He'd certainly like to explore the resident by candlelight.

He'd definitely been without sex for too long, he decided. He used to have a relationship with a barmaid down the coast in Whitby, a nice uncomplicated sex thing, but Sandra had left for the city the year before, and since then he'd been self-sufficient. Until the woman at the cottage that morning—one look at her and his hunting instincts had instantly flared into action.

She had wild, long hair, bed-tousled and mahogany colored—the sort of hair a man could tangle his fingers in during a hot one-on-one session. He sighed. That wild hair, her dark brown eyes and the silver jewelry she wore gave her an untamed, gypsy look that was fascinating. *Untamed.*

Julian would readily admit to having a thing about wild, gypsy-looking women. The woman at the cottage was certainly that, and his imagination had been actively wondering what she looked like under that baggy shirt of hers. It was messy, like she'd just thrown it on to answer the door.

What *did* single women get up to, to satisfy their urges, he mused. Oh, he knew well enough, and it was a favorite topic to linger on. Assuming that she was single, he reasoned. She was certainly alone. He pictured her using a vibrator, and his cock instantly hardened as the image meandered through his mind, and then took up residence. Had that been what she was up to, when he had called by? *Maybe.* He could just picture her, lying back on her bed, a big silver vibrator humming in one hand, the other playing with her tits. In his mental image the vibrator slid easily in and out of her glistening pussy. He groaned, sat up, then climbed out of the tent and inhaled a deep draft of air. He really wasn't helping himself any.

Suddenly the sky cracked open, and a loud clap of thunder pealed overhead. Lightning flashed, lighting the area up as if it were daytime.

Julian turned back to the tent and quickly began to check the pegs, just as the sky opened and heavy torrents of summer rain began to pour down, breaking the humidity instantly. Before he climbed back inside, he glanced at the motorbike. It would fare better than the tent, and he rather wished he'd taken off and booked into the local B&B, but something had held him there, despite the incoming storm. And Julian knew exactly what—or rather *who*—that was.

Sally jumped when her mobile phone bleeped into action. Everyone had agreed that she needed a total break from business, and so far it had only rung a couple of times. Both times it had been traders who hadn't known she was out of the office.

"Hey, Sally, how's your sanity holding up?"

"Kitty! Oh, it is good to hear your voice." Kitty was her right hand woman and her best friend to boot. "My sanity is just fine."

"Excellent news, I know we said we'd leave you alone, but I was thinking that cabin fever might have set in by now."

Sally laughed in delight. "No, not at all, besides I've been busy with my cyber guys. How are things there? Are you coping?"

"We're coping well, so you just enjoy yourself. What's it like up there? Have you happened on any local talent?"

"It's beautiful and, well, actually, there is a guy."

"Oh, do spill, is he a hunk?"

Sally could practically see Kitty's face, avid with interest.

"Like you wouldn't believe, but it's probably just one of those things, you know, ships that pass in the night."

"Hey, girl, if his ship is passing, you make sure you jump it. A single woman can't pass up an opportunity like that, and you've been single for far too long."

She was right. Sally had sacrificed a potential love life to build her company. Relaxation time was infrequent, and when it did come along, she had her art to turn to. There hadn't been a man for a long time. *Too long.*

"Maybe." Sally smiled at the picture in her mind, of jumping Julian's ship in the night, but she didn't want to talk about it any more, in case it came to nothing. Kitty would grill her for details when she got back to London, and if there were none to tell, that line of conversation would get old and tired very quickly. "Anyway, tell me what I am missing."

She listened happily to Kitty relating the week's events as she sat up in bed, keeping an eye on the night sky out of the window. The storm had been going on for over an hour, and Sally had been trying to chill out and settle down in bed with a book when her friend rang. She was far too excited to sleep, and even after they had said their goodbyes, the electric atmosphere and the spectacle of the storm continued to fascinate her. The sky kept flashing into action, rain coming in off the sea in sheets that lit through each time the electricity in the atmosphere hit, brightening even the dark distant sea on the horizon and every surface between. The wilder elements and the force of nature surrounded her. She was wired.

When the storm had first begun, she had paced back and forth through the cottage, watching the summer lightning from the various windows, occasionally wondering about the man who was so close, yet so far away in his tent on the other side of the cove. Perhaps he'd gone home, wherever home was, when the storm hit, or earlier. She kind of wished she'd brought her binoculars, then she could have . . . what? *Spied on him? Sally, really!*

She chastised herself for even considering it, but it was an interesting idea. After all, hadn't that been what she had been doing when she first saw him? Inadvertently, of course. *Did that make it any better, or not?* She rolled on to her side on the bed, looking once again into the restless night sky. She'd left the curtains open so that she could watch it from the bed. The sash window was propped open, and she kept catching breaths of the fresh air that followed in the wake of the storm.

She couldn't understand why some people disliked storms. She found them entrancing, and being out here on the coast sure made it more intense. In the city, everything conspired to obscure the view. The feeling of being at one with the wilder side of the elements was lost when surrounded by high-tech city living.

The storm ran pure, liquid excitement through her veins, as real as if it had been tapped into her blood directly from the thunderous skies overhead. The wind had lifted substantially, and at that very moment, she heard a distant thudding sound, moving in time with the gusts through the tree. She sat up and strained to hear it again. Something was blowing in the wind, and it sounded like a door opening and closing. *The tool shed?* The letting agent had told her there was patio furniture in there, in case she fancied a barbecue. She hadn't even looked at it, because when she was outside she wanted to be on the dunes.

She switched on the bedside lamp, and listened again. When she heard the sound once more, she got out of bed to investigate, slipping on her deck shoes and a long, baggy T-shirt. As she went through the house, she flicked on all the lights, her city-girl upbringing making her more wary in the dark hours.

When she opened the door, the sky was mottled and streaked with moonlight edging between the clouds. The storm had started to move on, leaving a mournful wind in its wake and occasional incoming sheets of rain. She squinted out into the night. Why hadn't she thought to bring a light with her? Maybe there was one in the house. She was about to turn back inside when her eyes began to adjust, and she could see what was going on.

The tool shed was indeed open. It had a barn door affair, and the two large wooden panels had got unlatched and were flapping in the wind. About three feet out from the doors, a single white plastic garden chair lay on its back, edging along the ground, as if it were being tugged out of its housing on a piece of string. If it hadn't been such a nuisance, it would have been comical.

She took a deep breath and darted out, heading towards the escapee. As she did, she noticed another chair edging out behind it. What was it with these things? Busting to get out and get some sun, or what? The flapping motion of the doors had to be creating a draught that was catching them and sucking them out. If she didn't get them back in soon, the whole set would be out and partying.

Grabbing the farthest plastic runaway, Sally felt rather like a cowboy chasing an escaped herd. She smiled, undeterred by the latest sheet of rain that swept in and splattered against her. It was rather exhilarating, being out here in the thick of it, if a little cold. She flicked back her damp hair, wrestled the two chairs together into a stack and carried them back towards the outhouse. Pushing them inside, she grabbed at the nearest door, and turned around to see how to secure the doors. Suddenly, her blood curdled. Out of nowhere, a hand had reached over hers. A scream rose in her throat.

"Hey."

She jolted round. It was the man from the cove, Julian, and he was holding the door, helping her.

"Oh, it's you," she gave a slightly hysterical laugh, relief sinking through her veins.

"Seems that I've got quite a knack for disturbing people." He looked at her, concerned. "I saw all the lights going on, and I thought you might be in some kind of trouble, with the storm and all."

"Thanks, it's just that these doors have got loose." She looked up at him. His hair was so wet that it was stuck to his head, and there was a small gash on his forehead.

"What happened to your head?"

"I had a run in with a flying tent peg. It's nothing, really." He gave her a big smile, and she melted inside. He must have gotten soaked coming across the cove in this weather. Sure enough, his T-shirt and jeans were wet through.

"Oh, my, you're drenched!"

"Um . . . so are you, lady." She followed the line of his eyes and gasped, astonished, when she looked down at herself. Like the prize-winner in a wet T-shirt contest, her breasts were thoroughly exposed against the utterly translucent scrap of fabric that clung to her body in a most insistent way. She wrenched her shirt further down on the thigh, peeling it away from her body in an attempt at respectability, blushing to the roots of her hair.

"Watch out."

She heard his warning, and then felt herself being snatched in against his body, his arms quickly going around her. Winded by the sudden, intense strength of his physical embrace, she shut her eyes. She felt him kick out, batting against the loose door with one booted foot. The door would have crashed into her, would have injured her for sure. Her knees suddenly turned to jelly. Was it because of the near miss, or the proximity of her rescuer?

"Are you okay?"

They were welded together, both their damp clothes and the warm flesh beneath seemingly unwilling to part. She nodded and looked up into his eyes, shaking back the wet strands of hair encroaching on her view. His brow was drawn down, giving him a fierce, hungry look. A gust of wild sea air whipped up around them, buffeting them together as if colluding with the storm to unite them.

His hands moved to her upper arms, stroking her gently, possessively. Her breasts were chaffing against the hard outline of his chest. He had to be able to feel them; she could feel every ounce of him, every hard surface, every warm beat of his body, *everything*. The alert pulse throbbing inside her sex quickly stepped up its pace, beating out a fierce, erratic rhythm.

She shivered.

He blinked. "Why don't you go back inside," he whispered, his breath warm on her cheek. "I'll sort these doors out for you."

"No . . . I mean, yes, but what about you? Won't you come inside too?" She didn't want him to disappear. *No way.*

"I'll head off on my bike. My tent has perished in the storm." He shrugged it off.

"Look, please come in and let me see to that." She nodded at his forehead. "Let me say thanks for the help." He hesitated, and she swallowed her rising doubts. "I have brandy," she added.

He broke into a slow smile. "Okay, I'll come for the brandy. I don't need tending though. It's really nothing."

"We'll see."

Neither of them had moved, and after several more moments enjoying the mutual proximity, they finally eased apart. Sally stepped away and watched, her arms folded across her breasts, while he latched the doors closed and threw a large rock in front of them for good measure.

Inside the house, she noticed again how tall he was. What was she doing inviting a complete stranger into the house? Doubt mingled with the desire running in her veins. She wasn't in the habit of picking up men or taking risks with people she didn't know. *But,* her sensible side intervened, if he'd had dubious intentions, he would have made himself a nuisance earlier on, instead of helping her out, wouldn't he? She glanced back at him as she gestured to the sitting room. He was simply gorgeous. Her body flared immediately. There was no turning back. She needed to find out what might transpire.

He overwhelmed the tiny sitting room. Sally smiled as she set down the brandy glasses and bottle on the table next to the overstuffed armchair he was sitting on. *What was it Kitty had said, about jumping his ship?*

"Cheers," she whispered, as she offered him a glass and lifted her own, taking a long draught for courage. "Thanks for coming to my rescue." She peeled her T-shirt off her thigh again, flapping it lightly. His right eyebrow lifted, as if he was musing on a private joke.

"What is it?" she dared to ask.

"You're standing there half undressed, offering me brandy, like a fey woodland nymph tempting me into your lair, and *you* are thanking *me* . . . It just seems a bit ironic, that's all."

He was direct, that was for sure. And there was that humorous quirk in his eyebrow again. He gave her another slow, sexy smile. It was *so* suggestive. Sally felt warmed right through, and it wasn't just the brandy that was causing it. This certainly looked like it might be going somewhere interesting. She smiled at his blatant commentary on her appearance, set down her glass and picked up the small first aid kit she'd dug out of her wash bag.

"No arguments," she instructed, and moved closer to clean and dress his wound. The tension between them had barely lessened, and now, as she moved in against him, leaning closer, the tension began to creep higher again.

"I really appreciate you doing this," he said, looking up at her while she tended him.

Sally's gaze lowered from the band-aid she had just applied, to look into his eyes. They were devilish in their direct appraisal. Anticipation ran heavy and hot in her veins. The room suddenly felt stifling hot. She went to step away, but he grabbed her around the wrist with one strong hand.

"I don't even know your name."

"Sally, Sally Richards. I'm sorry. I was a bit preoccupied when you called by earlier." She blushed. He still held her in his grip, strong and firm. How strong might his arms feel around her, she wondered? His shoulders looked powerful—he'd be able to lift her easily. She'd be at his mercy, if he so desired. For some reason that notion made her cream.

"Sally . . ." He rolled the word around his tongue. "I like that." He was looking at her with a dark, roaming expression in his eyes, and she was very aware of her state of undress.

"You're not frightened, are you?"

She was surprised, but she shook her head. "I invited you in, didn't I?" She managed to get the words out and gave him a smile.

"You did, but now you are trembling." He fixed her with a determined gaze. "Your body is giving off some very strong signals, my dear, and my guess is that it's either fear, or arousal."

Sally trembled again. His words both shocked and thrilled her.

With one finger he stroked the tender, sensitive flesh on the inside of her wrist, as if encouraging her to confess to him, confess what it was that she was feeling.

"Yes," she whispered. "Yes, I am . . . aroused." *Be brave.* "I didn't want you to leave."

"And now?" he demanded, his voice controlled.

"Now, I . . . I still don't want you to leave." Her gaze dropped from his as she breathed out the words.

He let go of her wrist, rose to his feet and rested both hands on her waist, pulling her towards him. His face was millimeters from hers. The expression in his eyes told her he wanted her as much as she wanted him. She could see it; she could feel it. Her lips parted with the desire for his kiss.

"You're sure?" His hands stroked up over her waistline and caressed the sides of her breasts through the clinging wet T-shirt.

Sally groaned, nodding. She was quite willing to beg at that moment, beg for his body against hers. "Please . . ." she murmured. He reached down to slide her damp T-shirt up and over her head. She dutifully lifted her arms, allowing him to take control. He murmured appreciatively when her breasts bounced free, and he stroked their sides, lifting them and molding them gently in his hands. He ran a thumb over each nipple. A thread of electricity seem to spring from his fingertips and charge through her body, straight to her core, firing the dense heat there to fever pitch. Sally whimpered with sheer pleasure. He lowered his head to kiss her neck, his tongue darting out to taste her as he went the length of her throat.

"Oh yes, you look and taste just as good as I thought you would."

Somewhere his words registered. He had been imagining her naked too. Her body writhed in his arms at the very idea of it. He grabbed her and pinned her to the wall, his hips pressed hard against hers. The rigid, jutting outline of his cock inside his jeans pressed forcefully against her belly. She was swamped with lust, sheer, rampant lust, barely contained. It crackled between them, as palpable as the summer lightning that had sliced through the night sky minutes earlier.

Her hips moved against his, begging for him to take control of them. All she could focus on was the swell of his cock through his jeans. A gush of liquid heat had fired through her body when she felt the hard bulk of his erect cock. She wanted, badly. His eyes glinted, his hips rocking against hers, and then he glanced around.

"Where's the bed? I want to see you on your back."

Sally trembled at his directness. Her heart thudded out a violent rhythm.

"This way." She took his hand and led him through the cottage, to the oak and linen furnished bedroom, where the bedside lamp and the moonlight at the open window gave the room an eerie aura, the encroaching elements filling the atmosphere with tension. The curtains at the window lifted on the night air, the room swept through with the smell of the sea, as if the place were a cave on the shore.

She turned to him once they were inside, and her hands moved to his T-shirt of their own accord, eager to feel his chest. He grabbed the material and pulled it off, revealing the torso that had filled her mind since she'd first seen him on the beach. It was hard and defined, powerful, covered with a fine coat of hair, bleached golden. His biceps flexed as he moved to touch her. He put his hands into the niche of her waist, and walked her back towards the bed, easing her down onto it, before she could say or do another thing.

"What a picture," he murmured, looking down at her naked body. His hands went to undo his belt, his fingers moving deftly on the silver buckle, his muscular arms flexing. A draft of air from the open window lifted his hair, and the lamplight cast his face in shadows as he looked down at her. The muscles of his body seemed to unfurl as he moved, powerful and sexy. Like Neptune, a sea god stepped from the waves. Sally felt another pang of longing thrumming inside her.

He eyed her possessively as he undid his jeans and kicked his boots off. Her gaze dropped as he climbed out of his jeans, and she saw the bulge of his erection. His cock reared up, long and thick, its head beautifully defined and dark with blood. Her breath sucked into her lungs, as she wanted to suck the beautiful, hard thing into her body.

He reached down and kissed her deeply, his tongue teasing against hers. Her fingers twined around his neck, drawing him closer. His hands swept between her thighs, and her legs fell open. He climbed between them and rested over her. His hips were moving against hers, pressing his erection between them, and it was driving her wild. Every move he made sent a whirlwind of awareness through her senses. His closeness, his sheer maleness overwhelmed her with a rush of sensations.

"Please, Julian," she pleaded.

His eyes flashed at her. "Patience, my dear, or I might have to teach you some lessons in *restraint*."

Sally moaned at the idea of it.

"Oh, so we're not adverse to the idea, huh?"

No, I'm not.

But she couldn't form the words to answer. She pressed her lips together, her eyes flashing at him, her need overwhelming her.

He gave a dark chuckle and bent to tease each nipple with his tongue, moving from one to the other. His face pressed into the soft skin of her cleavage, absorbing her scent. His attention was too delicious; her nipples were tight knots of desire, and her breasts ached in his hands, sending rivers of heat through her body. When he moved lower, his mouth traveling over her belly, she couldn't hold back the whimper. His fingers stroked over the soft down on her pubis, then he opened her up, and she felt his breath hot on the tender, anxious skin between her thighs. When she felt his mouth touching her there, she clutched at the sheets, her lower lip caught between her teeth. She was helpless under his assault.

He teased her with his tongue, inviting her to enjoy his caresses. In the distance, the soft crash of the waves on the shore rolled in a rhythm as mesmerizing as his mouth on her sex. She heard the pleasured murmurs rise up from her own mouth, and then felt him as he followed the sounds, his tongue retracing her most sensitive places until she blossomed into climax, sweet and sudden. She was lost to it for a few moments, until she became aware of him moving. He snatched at his jeans and pulled a condom from the pocket. And then he was there, the weight of his body between her trembling thighs, and the hard nudge of his cock made her gasp, desire opening her up to him.

He locked her eyes with his, watching her expression as he eased inside her, slowly at first, then more forcefully. When he finally drove the full length of his shaft inside her, she gave a cry of pleasure. She felt him throbbing and clasped at him with her inner muscles. Holding him close, her hands absorbed the feel of the taut muscle of his backside. Their bodies locked together to fulfill the need that had been planted in them, thrusting and reaching, urging each other on. Each thrust inside her was so powerful and devastating, the sensitive flesh of her over-aroused sex was a riot of sensation, pumping and clasping at him. He had driven her to distraction and now he was moving so in tune with her body that Sally felt as if she was about to come, each and every time his cock stroked deep inside her.

As their movements grew increasingly feverish she bucked her body up against him. A blossom of that pleasure began to burst, to seep through her and her breath caught, her body arching. His hands roved feverishly through her hair. The heat of imminent climax flared up through her body.

His brows were drawn down, a bead of sweat sliding slowly down one side of his face. His mouth opened and each quick thrust drew a harsh breath from him. Sally cried out when the heat welled inside her. She felt his whole body arch and bow against hers. His cock heaved and lurched, their bodies clutching together in the moment of mutual climax. She was powerless to do anything but enjoy—she was in ecstasy.

"Oh yes . . . yes," he murmured, his eyes afire with passion. The wave of pleasure washed over her, lifting her on its crest, and then lingered, as if on the turn of the tide, before ebbing slowly away, leaving her panting and trembling with sensation, like a castaway clinging to the shore.

Chapter Three

Sally awoke to the distant sound of humming and the wafting aroma of breakfast. She stretched luxuriously and rolled over in the bed, opening her eyes. The sunlight poured in through the window, bathing everything in warm light. The storm had lifted the torrid atmosphere; the day was bright and clear. She sighed, her mind quickly recounting what had gone on the night before. They'd made love till dawn. Each time they thought themselves replete, they had begun to explore each other some more, testing the durability of the bed with their love-making all over again. And by the sounds of it, Julian was still here.

She got up, stretching, and pulled on another baggy T-shirt from the stack that she had brought with her. Checking the mirror to make sure her hair wasn't too mussed, she pulled the shirt straight and pushed her hair back. It occurred to her that she should have brought something a bit more interesting in the clothing department. He'd said he liked the way she looked naked, but she felt the urge to impress him dressed, too. She'd thought she was going to be on her lonesome sculpting all the time, not colluding with the local beachcombing stud. She smiled. Luckily, she had brought a couple of summer dresses with her; they may well be needed.

As she walked down the hall, she felt a wave of nerves hit her. She'd gone to bed with a complete stranger in the night. It was a heat of the moment thing; there was no holding back that kind of passion, but now they had to face each other.

Peeping around the corner of the kitchen door, she was delighted to see that he was indeed cooking breakfast. He was completely naked, apart from a cook's apron that he had donned for the task. The view was so spectacular and amusing that Sally wished she had her camera handy. The apron cord hung around his neck and high on his waist, leaving his muscular back and his gorgeous buttocks on full display for her eager eyes. There wasn't a woman on earth who wouldn't be pleased to find a sight like that in her kitchen first thing in the morning. And it put all thoughts of nervousness out of her head.

"Good morning, sexy," he said, when she entered the space, grabbing her into one arm for a slow, lingering kiss. The pulse point in the pit of her belly leapt into life. She would have to try to stay focused on rational behavior, at least for some of the time, or she'd be reduced to a puddle of lust every time he touched her. She sidled out of his arms, nonchalantly, pretending to be more interested in what he was cooking. She was hungry and her stomach was growling, but still she had to drag her gaze away from him to look at the food.

"I raided the fridge. I hope you don't mind."

"Of course not," she answered, looking up from the delicious meal he'd managed to conjure up with the few items she'd had in the fridge. The variety of flavors and textures made her mouth water. He clearly had more talents than the obvious ones that she had already discovered, and he was darned good at those. Apparently, he could cook as well.

"All this hot sex works up quite an appetite," he added, smiling a slow smile and winking at her.

She sat down, and he put a plate down in front of her. He'd made a fresh omelet, accompanied by strips of bacon that looked like he'd griddled them until crispy, then sautéed in butter with juicy cherry tomatoes and shallots. From somewhere he'd found what looked like fresh herbs. She took a mouthful of the succulent omelet, which he had mixed to the most amazing consistency, and it melted in her mouth. There were definitely chives in there, chives and fresh parsley.

"Where did you get the herbs?" she asked when he put a plate of warm bagels and a coffee pot on the table and then joined her, settling easily into the chair opposite her.

"There's a small herb patch in the back garden."

There is?

"It's gone wild because the house has been empty for years. But it's in a sheltered spot and some of them have survived."

"You know a lot about the place." She watched him butter a bagel and take a hearty bite. He nodded, wielding his fork over his portion of omelet. Everything he did only seemed to emphasize his strength and agility. He was like a prowling creature, always watchful, sleek and predatory.

"I approached the owner about buying the cottage, a year or so ago. It was his mother's house, and it had been empty since she passed on. I wondered what he had in mind for the place, but all has now become clear." He gestured around the recently refurbished kitchen. "Not bad, but I had better plans for it than letting it to a never ending stream of tourists." The last words were ejected with feeling, and it was grim.

Tourists? Is that how he saw her? An annoying tourist on his patch?

He gave her a quick, reassuring smile when he noticed the growing tension in her expression.

"I'm sorry, I don't mean you. You're a very welcome sight." He winked. "I just worry about the area getting overpopulated, you know."

His smile was still tight, she noticed. She had begun to wonder if he had been upset about her presence in the property, which he obviously had a hankering for. But it seemed more than that; it was the cove itself. She could have guessed that, she realized, if she'd thought back to her first sighting of him. She frowned, wondering where she stood in all this. And how would he feel if he knew the agent had advertised the property as if the cove was the exclusive domain of the tenant? When she'd read about it, she knew it was just a sales pitch. The beaches were national property. But what would other visitors make of it? And more importantly, what would Julian make of it? That kind of news might be better coming from her than anyone else. She mentally shelved the task. She'd get to it later on; why spoil the current mood any further than it had been already?

"Don't worry," he added. "I got over it. I have a flat I use as a base instead, down the coast in Hull. It's close to the waterside and to the conservation unit, my HQ. I have to go back there at the end of every week to report anyway . . ." His voice drifted off as he tucked into the food.

"What is it that you do?"

"Beach patrol, conservation, up and down the coast from Hull to the border of Scotland. I cover a lot of miles so I camp out when the weather's good."

That explained the test tube. It was part of his work.

"And if you get caught out by the weather, you can take advantage of the local *tourists*?" she teased, trying to lighten the underlying attitude she felt to her presence.

"Only if they're attractive brunettes with come-to-bed eyes."

Well parried, she reflected, smiling at his remark.

"And what is it that you do? Something to do with these guys?" He nodded over at her latest cyber warrior, who stood by on the far work surface.

Thank God she had tidied everything away after his last impromptu visit. The new piece that he had inspired was safely hidden in the broom cupboard. "Yes and no. That's more of a personal project, but I have sold a few. I'm an importer, figurines too, but oriental mass-market stuff. I studied sculpture at art college, and I felt I knew enough about it to become a buyer. At first I worked for a major fancy goods importer, then my dad encouraged me to start my own business and things went from there."

"Corporate lady, are you?" He eyed her up and down.

"Not really. It's a specialist market, and I mostly supply hotel chains. I've been in the business for five years, and it's gotten easier as I've gotten more experience. Things are changing for me all the time. When I started out, I had to go over to Singapore to shop for samples. Now, because so many companies worldwide are selling their goods over the net, I don't really have to leave my office, except if I'm looking for new outlets. My reputation is built to the extent I don't have to do as much of that. In fact it's ticking over so well that I was able to take my first proper holiday and take time for my own sculpture." She gestured over at the cyber figurine.

He nodded, looking thoughtful. "Do you have staff?"

"Yes, all part timers, working mothers mostly. It's me doing my bit for womankind."

"The politically-correct city girl, huh?"

"I guess I try to be, although I don't label myself that way." She stuck her tongue out at him.

"And is there a partner knocking about?" He looked a bit awkward, and a hint of color rose on his angular cheekbones. The man was almost blushing.

"No partner, business or otherwise." She smiled, showing him she wasn't concerned by his question.

He nodded. "Do you have to wear a suit and high heels and all that?"

He looked perturbed as he asked. That amused her greatly. He was such a man of the shore, so unlike any man she'd ever met before. Was that why she was so attracted to him? Because he was so unlike all the stuffed suits and smart-mouthed city lads she met in London?

"Sometimes. Why, does it bother you?"

"It doesn't bother me. I was just trying to picture it."

His hot stare made her feel restless, and she wriggled on her seat, and then set down her knife and fork. She picked up her coffee cup to distract herself. She glanced out of the window, away from his sexy expression. Could she stop thinking about sex at all with him around?

"I'll have to head to Morpeth, the nearest big town, to pick up a new tent." He smiled across at her.

"It might sound selfish, but I'm kind of glad you didn't have a tent to go back to last night."

"I couldn't wish for better hospitality, but I'll be out of your hair soon."

An instant objection to his words rose up inside her. She quelled it, trying to stay cool. *Why not, though?* He was the perfect companion, the perfect man for a wild holiday affair. "You're welcome to stay in the cottage, with me." Her gaze lifted to meet his. "For the rest of the week. I'm here until Friday." She could see he was interested.

"Well, if you're sure I wouldn't get under your feet . . ."

Nothing could be further from the truth. "There may be some sort of forfeit . . . sexual of course." *Did I really say that?*

He laughed. "Of, course. I'll take you up on your offer, but if you change your mind, just say. I have to be back in Hull on Friday anyway. I can pick up a new tent then."

"Good, that's sorted." *Bliss, three more days of hot sex!* "What do you have to do today?"

"I need to survey two beaches about twenty miles up the coast, take samples, check the wildlife numbers and make notes on any changes. When I'm in this neighborhood, I usually stay here on the cove all week and use it as a base. Both spots are within easy reach. One's a cliff edge shore; the other is a small harbor beach, both terrific places. You should check them out while you're up here."

"Well, I need to get out, so if you're up for it, we could go in my Land Rover. I haven't seen enough of the coast. You could be my guide."

He nodded, smiling that sexy smile. "Sure, it's a great idea." He reached for his coffee cup and took a sip, still looking at her over the rim. His hands were strong—she felt the urge to sketch them. He put the cup down and frowned. "Do you have any sugar?"

"No, sorry, I don't take sugar so I didn't bring any with me, although there might be some in a cupboard somewhere."

Sally rested back in her seat and watched him moving along the cupboards, quickly glancing in each. He was so nonchalant about the fact he was naked, all but for an apron! How could she not love that? In fact, he seemed totally unaware of his body, completely lacking in self-consciousness. He was certainly unaware of the effect he had on her. She crossed her legs, savoring the rhythmic, tickling sensation deep between her thighs. She'd never met a man so at ease with himself. He was every artist's dream model. She wondered if he would model for her during his stay. Just as the question permeated through her consciousness, he crossed the kitchen towards the far work surface, glancing approvingly at the cyber figurine as he went past.

"He's cool, I like the little man."

"Thank you."

She got the words out and then the smile on her face froze and she watched, horror struck, when his hand reached for the handle on the broom cupboard. She clapped her hand over her mouth. She'd completely forgotten about the torso when he'd started hunting through the cupboards on his quest for sugar.

"Hello, what have we here?"

She prayed he was talking about the broom. The dustpan and brush? *Let it be the feather duster, please.* But, no, he was bending into the cupboard, looking at what had to be her latest sculpture.

"This looks interesting."

Maybe he wouldn't recognize it.

He squatted down on his haunches and slid out the thin chipboard plinth it was resting on to get a better look. "Why have you got it hidden away in the cupboard?" he asked, and turned back to her before she had a chance to do anything about composing her features.

She dropped the hand from her mouth, and laughed, nervously.

His brow furrowed, a half-smile still hovering. He glanced from her to the sculpture and back, a curious expression on his face. He turned the plinth slowly, looking at the clay.

She was speechless. What could she say? All she could do was hope that he wouldn't realize the sculpture was of him. Maybe the floor would open up and swallow her.

"This is me, isn't it?" he said, still puzzled, but fascinated too.

Damn. She couldn't bring herself to deny it.

"But you certainly didn't have time to get up and do this between dawn and breakfast . . . so, when . . . ?" He turned the plinth again, and looked at the hand, which rested on the rising cock, the thumb obviously working against it.

Oh no! That was such a huge clue.

He stared at it for what seemed an age and then pushed it back into its hidey-hole in the cupboard. She realized she was holding her breath, and her lungs were about to burst.

He shook his head, and stood up, closing the cupboard, and turned to her. His expression was dark but controlled, and his eyebrows were drawn down as he considered her.

She bit her lip. *How upset was he going to be?* How would she feel, if the tables were turned? She had intruded on his privacy, and she shouldn't have worked on the model without his permission. What had she been thinking of?

"You were watching me on the beach the other day, weren't you?" His tone was stern, and he folded his arms across his chest while he contemplated her.

She felt like a naughty schoolgirl. "I couldn't help it." *That sounded so lame.* She'd made a conscious choice here. "I'm sorry, I just . . . well, you inspired me." She adopted what she hoped was an imploring expression. He took a step closer, his fingers tapping against his folded arms, his mouth tight. She'd blown it with him already. He was upset with her. She stood up as he approached.

She swallowed. "I'm really sorry," she added.

"That's not good enough." He frowned. "You'll have to be punished."

"Punished?" Her voice faltered. What had she got herself into here?

He grabbed at her wrist, drawing her in close against him. His eyes were gleaming, his hand strong and controlling on her wrist.

"Yes, punished."

She stared up at him, in disbelief. Then she saw it. Despite his deadpan features, she caught a glimpse of the dark, expectant twinkle in his eyes. His mouth twitched to one side in a sardonic smile.

"Your face is a picture," he commented, and then broke into a laugh, the timbre deeply amused and satisfied. But he didn't let her go.

"You devil!" She gave a nervous laugh, her eyes wide with incredulity. He was teasing her!

"That's as may be, but you've still got to be punished."

She stared at him, disbelief spiraling inside her. Whatever did he mean by it, to punish her? Then, somewhere inside her an instinctive pang of anticipation suggested an answer to the question: did he mean to have her, for her naughtiness? On his terms, whatever they might be. Her heart began to race. He was having fun with her, but he also seemed intent on following it through.

He eyed her up and down with deliberation, as if the idea of it was very appealing to him. Clasping her waist, he drew her whole body up against him. If she had any doubt about his sheer physical strength before, it was all erased. She was easily captured in his grasp. For some reason it made her legs tremble, and she felt the heat building between her thighs. He ran his hands over the outline of her breast, where her nipple jutted hard through the fabric of her T-shirt.

"I'll give you a thirty second head start, but I have to warn you, I'm fast on my feet."

As he said the words, he set her aside. He flexed his arms and knotted his fingers in a stretch, as if preparing to work her over. He nodded at the door.

She stared at him. *He couldn't be serious!*

"Thirty . . . twenty-nine . . . you're wasting time. Anyone would think you wanted to be punished!" And then he smiled again, and the urge to spar rose up alongside the flood of anticipation inside her.

"*If* you can catch me. I'm pretty fast on my feet too," she retorted. She turned and headed for the door.

"Twenty-eight!"

She heard his voice as she bolted out across the grass bank that linked the cottage grounds to the edge of the cove. The grass was deep and springy beneath her bare feet, damp and lush from the overnight rain. Where she was headed, she didn't know; she just wanted to make space between them, to outrun him, to show him she was game as much as he was.

Punish her indeed.

She glanced back over her shoulder, to see him nonchalantly leaning up against the doorframe, watching her with that smile on his face. He was an absolute devil, taunting her like that! She turned back to her path and ran as fast as her feet would carry her, her breath catching in her lungs, her emotions flying somewhere between elation and trepidation. She squinted into the distance where she could make out the outline of his motorbike on the far end of the cove. If she could make it that far . . . she'd have proved a point. She dug deeper and found more resources, moving faster than she thought she could. Behind her, she heard him shouting after her.

He was on his way.

She didn't pause to look back, but noted that the grass beneath her feet had first become thicker and heavier, and now it was sparser, where the earth turned to sand at the edge of the cove. She had a good start on him.

But not good enough.

She heard him thundering up behind her and couldn't resist taking a glance. That was fatal. The sight of a gorgeous hunk ripping off an apron as he ran after her put a massive obstacle in front of her determination.

"Damn!" She'd tripped and landed with a thud on the first sand dune she'd had to mount. Struggling to her knees, she pulled her T-shirt down over her exposed bottom, suddenly realizing she was in as much of a state as him. What if someone saw the pair of them running around half naked?

"Perfect," he declared, as he descended to his knees beside her, and grabbed her into his arms. She struggled hopelessly, wriggling in his arms in an effort to get free. He lifted her easily, flipping her over onto her hands and knees.

"You have the sexiest bottom I've ever seen. You can't expect a man to watch you running around like that and not have the urge to give you a good seeing to."

Sally giggled, her head hanging down as he pushed her T-shirt up over her hips and shoulders, letting it to drop down her arms and pool on the sand in front of her. She was totally naked, out here in the bright sunshine. It felt strange, but somehow right.

He rested his hand around the curve of her buttock. She leaned into his touch, quickly forgetting her attempt at escape. He moved his hand, stroking her gently in circular motions. It felt deliciously naughty, his movements warming the surface of her bare bottom. Her pussy was flooded with arousal and her entire nether region tingled with sensation.

"Are you ready to accept your punishment?"

Her head swung around just as he lifted his hand away from her bottom and held it aloft. When she realized he was serious, her amusement faded. Her mouth opened and she attempted to move, but he had her in a firm grip. He didn't keep her contemplating the situation for long, his hand quickly slapping down onto each of her buttocks in turn, making quick bursts of contact on her buttocks. The sting and the sudden shock of it made her gasp, but very soon a warm, tingling glow spread from the point of contact and quickly keyed into her body, as if each slap was triggered to make contact with the pounding pulse raging inside her. She wriggled, rubbing her thighs together and arching her back, quickly becoming addicted to the beautiful mixture of pain and pleasure he was arousing.

"You're enjoying this, aren't you, you naughty girl," Julian said, and gave a dark chuckle.

She felt her cheeks color but she nodded her head, unable to deny it. She'd never been spanked before, and she was shocked at the hot, tingling sensation it brought about. Her hair trailed on the sand as her head hung down. He was spanking her naked bottom, here, out in the open on the beach. Pleasure, pain and shame engulfed her. He gave her another round of slaps. The heat spread quickly from her backside, heightening the points of arousal in her body, each sting quickly interacting with the need for some overt, sexual activity that her body desired. Her breasts swung down, swaying with every movement of her body, her nipples sticking out like totems of lust. Her sex was creaming; she could smell her own desire mounting all around them. Her whole body was on fire and trembling from the quick fire contact on her buttocks, and she was aching for more.

As if he knew what she was thinking he paused, and thrust his hand lower, sliding his fingers along the folds of her sex. Sally's head lifted and she bit her lip to stop herself from crying out. She watched the sea moving, rhythmic and strong, making its way surely into the cove, as surely as the liquid signs of her arousal were spilling down her inner thighs and over his inquisitive fingers.

"Oh yes, you are so wet, you little sexpot." He shoved his thumb inside her, drawing a sudden gasp from her. He flexed his hand, rocking it so that his index finger caressed her clit, and his thumb rubbed inside the entrance to her sex, where her sensitive flesh swelled and throbbed under his touch. Within seconds she was teetering on the edge of climax. She cried out and thrust her hips back onto his hand in the moment of her release.

She panted for several long moments, her eyes shut, trying to regain her equilibrium. Then she swung her head around to look at the man who had mastered her senses so thoroughly. He was kneeling beside her, looking down at her body with a satisfied half smile. Self-assured and totally lacking in self-awareness, he was fisting his cock in one strong hand, riding the stiff shaft hard, its head gleaming with a creamy drop of his semen. She stared, transfixed, absorbed by the experience, her responses instinctive.

"You want it, don't you?"

She nodded and crawled nearer to him, her body burning up with arousal. She had never been overtly submissive before. Sometimes in her fantasies, yes, but she'd never met anyone like Julian before. It was only him that made her feel this way, like it was right and she didn't have to hide it. His total male virility and his prowess as a lover overwhelmed her. And she was so goddamn hot as a result!

He smelt delicious, and she breathed him in, running her nose against his thigh. She opened her mouth, her tongue licking up the underside of his cock.

"Oh yes, that's good. Do it, Sally, suck me."

His cock was long and dark, fit to burst. Her fingers closed on its girth, and she stroked its velvety smooth surface. She leaned into him, her tongue tracing the crown of his cock. He groaned, his body taut with restraint. She licked the length of him, reveling in the taste of his body and the effect it had on her, sending wild frissons of delight through her entire body. She looked up at him from below as her mouth closed over the crown of his cock.

"Yes, yes, let me see it sliding into your pretty mouth." His eyes were glazed, his lips parted as he watched her moving on him. "That looks so hot," he groaned. "I'll remember that image forever."

Under her tongue and hands she could feel his tension building. She began to move faster, sensing his need. His hands moved through her hair and stroked at the back of her neck, cupping her then letting her slip away again when she took him deep. Suddenly she could taste him, the first salty offerings of his climax. His cock reached, seemingly growing even larger. He panted loudly, his voice hoarse. Then his head went back, and he bellowed at the sky. Under her fingers his balls contracted. A moment later, he was spilling into her mouth.

His body shuddered. She glanced down at the spilled drops on her breasts, slowly rubbing them into her skin. There was something very pagan and earthy about doing that, which left her unable to resist.

"You are one sexy woman," he said, when he caught sight of her massaging her breasts with his come.

She didn't know what she liked best, seeing him roaring at the sky like a beast unleashed, or when, afterwards, he grinned and grappled her into his arms, rolling her across the sand, laughing and kissing her face while singing her praises.

She hadn't had so much pleasure and so much fun since . . . well, *ever.* No, she admitted to herself, purring as he came in for another kiss, she'd never had so much fun. Ever. He kissed her tenderly, and then he gave a deep sigh.

"You have the most gorgeous bottom I have ever seen, but I think you enjoyed your punishment far too much. You were on fire, you little harlot."

"Should I apologize?"

"No," he commented, smiling. "I'll just have to keep thinking of ways to get even with you."

"I can't wait to see what you come up with," she replied, teasingly.

"The tide is coming in," he commented, as he lifted her easily into his arms and began to walk away from the spot where they had been nestled for some time.

She gazed up at him, spellbound. She was convinced she was dreaming. At any moment she would wake, and it would be the night of the storm, but she'd be alone. Or, worse still, she'd be at home in her South Kensington apartment, alone. She shunned the idea but prayed that she wouldn't wake up, not yet.

"This might help," he murmured, his face in shadow, the sun fanning out behind his head.

"What?" She smiled up at him, idly, and then she felt the lap of water around her dangling toes. She jumped. *What on earth?*

"You got so hot when I was trying to give you a spanking, I think you need a bit of a cooling off. This will surely do it."

She gasped, snapped back into reality, and looked around to see where they were. He'd waded out into the water, and she hadn't even realized. She'd been so enamored with him, so lost in her reverie that she hadn't even noticed where he'd been headed. The water was rising up around her legs, icy cold and getting deeper all the time. His grip slackened. She knotted her fingers around his neck, shaking her head at him, emphatically, but he grinned and peeled them off easily and swung her in his arms, hoisting her out into the water.

"But Julian . . . I . . ."

It was too late. *I can't swim.* Sally gasped and cried out, her heart leaping as the icy water enveloped her.

Chapter Four

Julian froze.

What the hell have I done?

". . . I can't swim." He caught the words just as he saw her slip under the water, her expression filled with fear.

Within a heartbeat, he ducked down under the water to lift her back out, easily capturing her arms as they thrashed against the water. She gasped and coughed when he stood up, lifting her out of the water.

"Sorry, sweetheart, sorry," he soothed, holding her close to him.

"Silly," she gulped. "It's silly of me, I know. It's only shallow water, but it's just that I had a bad experience as a kid and I . . . panic."

"Shh, don't say anything. There's no need to explain. I should have thought about it before I pulled the prank. I shouldn't have assumed you'd be okay with it."

He carried her back towards the shore and frowned when she began shivering in his arms. It was stupid of him—he hated himself for being so ignorant.

Setting her down against the first dune they reached, he dropped down beside her and began to rub some heat back into her body. It was mostly fright and she snuggled up in his arms, taking the comfort he offered.

"What a pity you aren't going to be here long enough for me to teach you to swim." Already he felt annoyed that their time was limited. He was enjoying her company. *In so many ways.*

"I ought to learn," she replied, vaguely.

He pushed her wet hair back and wrapped himself around her back, positioning her between his thighs to maximize the shared warmth.

"God, that feels good," she murmured, when he started to massage her shoulders, releasing the tension knotted there.

"Pleased to be of service."

Her shoulders and the delicate beauty of her spine were exquisite, and he traced them with his fingers, gently massaging her. Just when she seemed to be totally at ease in his arms, she stiffened again. He stopped rubbing her and followed her gaze. She was looking out into the bay.

"Oh my god, there's someone out there. They must have seen us!"

He looked over where she was pointing, at the figure on the horizon, just visible on the edge of the next cove. Julian wasn't concerned; he knew that it was most likely to be Tom, collecting his shrimps. He shielded his eyes to get a better look.

Sally tried to hide herself under him.

"That's Tom from the village, and he's very short sighted, so your honor is safe, Missy." He turned back to her. "Although . . . as you were such a bad girl earlier . . . maybe I should call him over for a second opinion on whether I've punished you enough."

Her mouth opened, her eyes widening. He growled at her and dipped down to nibble on her collarbone, tickling her with his warm breath.

"No," she wailed, giggling and squirming against him.

He lifted his head. "So, I have to take care of it all by myself. A man's life is hard one."

There was a beatific smile on her face. He looked down at her, shaking his head, but he was smiling too. It felt good; it felt easy and comfortable, being around her. She responded so well to his teasing ways. And she was a wildcat in the sex department.

She reached over and ran her fingers through his hair. "So you're not really upset about the sculpture? That I saw you . . . ? I mean, it wasn't my fault you were frolicking around naked in my cove."

"*Your* cove . . . ?!"

"Sorry, I meant . . ." She blushed.

"It's okay, I know what you meant," he said. "It makes you feel that way when you're here alone, doesn't it?" She nodded and something deeply intimate passed between them, like a silent acknowledgement about the place and its special aura. "And, no, I'm not upset about the sculpture."

"In that case, would you be prepared to model for me again?"

"Again? I wasn't aware that I had ever modeled for you before."

She pouted up at him. "I mean, would you please model for me . . . for the first time?"

"Yeah, why not? I'll give it a go, but if I feel you're taking artistic license with me, I may have to punish you again."

Her eyes brightened with interest. Whatever this was that had been triggered between them, he liked it. *A lot.*

"I'll try to remember to behave appropriately," she murmured, as his mouth descended to hers, and he kissed her with a possessive, consuming force that swept everything away, leaving just the two of them, clinging together in the sand, as hungry for each other as they were for life itself.

Julian couldn't keep his eyes off her when she stepped down from her Land Rover that evening. She looked like a dream date, and she was his for the night and for the rest of the week. That felt good, really good.

Her hair tumbled past her shoulders in a burnished, sable curtain. She was wearing a gauzy summer dress that looked as if it might slip off her shoulders at any moment, and she seemed to float rather than walk. It had been hard to get his job done that day, with her along, but luckily she had wandered off occasionally and gave him a minute here and there to compose his thoughts, take his samples and make notes. Even then, thoughts of their escapade on the beach that morning came to mind far too readily.

She smiled when she saw him watching her tuck her keys into her bag, and her eyes were glowing with the hidden secrets they shared. He couldn't help thinking what a treat the inhabitants of the village pub were in for.

He stopped her just as he was about to open the door and usher her inside. "Are you ready for this?"

"Ready for what?"

He loved that look she gave him. There was an openness about her expression that he found entrancing. Especially when it revealed to him how hot she was for him. That had him wanting to capture her into his arms—and keep her there.

"The Lobster Pot." He nodded up at the sign over the pub. "The social hotbed of a small village pub. You'll be the focus of everyone's attention. I've seen others backing out of the door because of the scrutiny they received in this place."

She lifted one eyebrow at him.

"Have you ever seen that film, *An American Werewolf in London,* where they go to the pub on the moors?"

She gave a nervous laugh. "Stop it! You're teasing me again!"

"Wait and see." He shrugged her comment off.

"Actually, they did rather give me the once over at the shop." She nodded across the street. The one and only convenience store slash post office was stationed right opposite the pub on the main street, two vital lifelines for the village close at hand. The pub also doubled up as the local eatery, and the store was stocked with everything from fishing tackle to frozen food, and stamps to stationery.

"I just thought the shopkeeper was a bit odd, you know."

"No, believe me; the whole village will be enthralled." He nodded at the pub. "And there will be a fair few of them in here right now." He was looking forward to it. He loved observing the locals and it was going to be fun watching them with an out-of-towner in their midst, especially one who was such a beautiful, gypsy-looking woman.

Sure enough, when they stepped inside, a sudden silence descended over the interior of the pub. The bar was lined with six stools upon which the usual six customers sat, a group of men of varying age groups who did little but argue over the course of their evenings spent together. At the far end of the room a mixed group were playing snooker. When Sally walked through the door, all heads turned to silently observe her. The only movement was a lone snooker ball rolling across the table.

Julian rested his hand around her shoulders and led her towards the near end of the bar.

"What would you like to drink?"

"I'll try the local ale, whatever you recommend." She smiled up at him in the most disarming way. There was a twinkle in her eyes, and he knew that she was acknowledging his previous remarks. She coped with it well, he noticed. But then he supposed that being an international importer who had to present herself and her wares at business meetings meant that she would have to have the requisite confidence.

The pub slowly began to revert back into its usual hum of conversation, but Sally continued to be the subject of speculative glances and whispered conversations throughout their visit.

Brenda, the motherly, friendly landlady, took their order with a smile and winked. "Just you ignore them ones that stare, sweetheart." Brenda offered conspiratorially.

"We're going to eat, so I'll take a menu over to the snug." He indicated a cozy booth nested into a bay window overlooking the street outside. Brenda nodded and deposited their ale on the bar.

"I have to ask," Sally said, after they had put in their order and reflected on the day's visits. "Why do you call him Old Man Greg?"

"You'll find that everyone gets a nickname around here and they really stick. When he was a young man, I understand that he was called that because of his build and posture." Julian sipped his beer, wondering what a city girl would make of it all.

"I see." Her eyebrows had lifted, but she didn't comment further. "And what do they call you?"

He shuffled his feet under the table. He was beginning to regret the line of conversation.

"I guess you'll find out anyway . . . they call me Double O Beach-patrol, you know, like 007."

As one would expect, she burst out laughing. "That would be because you are spying on behalf of the government?"

He nodded.

"I'd love to know what they might call me if I were a regular." She had such a naughty smile, Julian couldn't hold back his grin.

"I can think of a suggestion or two, very flattering, of course."

She idly studied the various boat related objects and fishing tackle that decorated the walls of the pub. "Where are you from, originally?" she asked.

"Well, much as I hate to admit it, I'm sort of a city boy, much like yourself." Her eyebrows went up again. He knew she'd be surprised. He tried not to be too self-righteous about the difference between the city and countryside because the spotlight usually ended up on him as a result.

"So, let me get this right. You teased me about being a city girl, when you're 'sort of' a city boy yourself?"

"Yes, I suppose you've got a point there."

It was she that tutted at him then.

"I was brought up in Surrey, just outside Guildford. Home Counties stock. My dad is a high-court judge, my mum runs the local Women's Institute." He wasn't surprised when she giggled. People often did because it didn't hold with the image he had carved for himself.

The food arrived but he carried on. "Let me get this over with. The whole family are city dwellers. I have two older brothers who are lawyers and one who is a schoolteacher. I used to take my younger sister off to the coast rambling and collecting pebbles and shells when we were kids, but to no avail. She's a DJ and a part time psychology student."

"So you're like the black sheep or the *wild* sheep or something?"

"That's exactly it. The whole family thought I was mad. On weekends they'd head to the theatre, museums and concerts while I'd head the other way to the coastline."

"Do you have to do the family thing and visit at Christmas time?" She was biting her lip, trying not to giggle. "I mean, it must really be difficult for you having to go to there."

"You can tease all you like, Madame, but as it happens I don't have to go down at Christmas time because the family have always traditionally rented a cottage in the Lake District, and I meet up with them there. In fact I blame that yearly event for the way I have turned out." He gave a smug smile.

"Well, I guess that is some sort of reason." She pouted mockingly. "Shame I won't see you down in London at Christmas time though."

Julian hitched up on taking a mouthful of his fish pie. He was so surprised, he grabbed his pint to give himself a moment to compose a suitably open-ended answer. He realized he certainly wouldn't mind seeing her again, if he did happen that way.

"You never know, things might change," he offered. With her there, the city was looking a whole lot more inviting.

She smiled and continued with her meal, but he could tell she had another question in mind.

"Go on, what else did you want to ask? I can see you're busting to ask another question."

"I was just thinking about the fact that you are so attached to this place, to the cove."

"It's always felt like home to me. I don't know why, it just does. Can you understand that?"

She nodded, but he noticed that she had grown serious.

"You feel very strongly about the cottage drawing tourists, don't you?"

"I feel strongly about the fact it has brought you, so much so that I had to act."

She smiled but the concerned look didn't disappear. "You're avoiding the issue."

"I am. Okay . . . I can't say I am pleased about it." He knew he was being self-righteous, but he wasn't in the habit of lying. Besides, he had already made his feelings known earlier that day. She was a clever lady, and he was worried above all that he had offended her. All he could do was hope to explain. "It's nothing personal. It's just that I've seen other places suffer simply because people don't follow the rules and show no respect."

She nodded, again looking very thoughtful. "Julian, there is something you should know. The cottage is being advertised as having a private beach nearby."

What the hell? It was as if someone had tripped a switch in his head.

"They've got no right." His volume control was quickly flying up and several curious stares came in his direction. He attempted to drop his voice a notch. "I bet that's Old Man Greg cashing in. Why should he care? He doesn't live here any more. But he should have more sense. It won't be worth it in the long run."

"I doubt he had anything to do with it. It's just an advertising slant," Sally reasoned. "It will be whoever is marketing it."

"Damn them. It is *not* a private beach . . . although I wish it bloody well was!" Through his indignation, he realized he was taking out his concerns for the cove on her.

Thankfully someone put money into the jukebox and the atmosphere between them began to ease up. "I'm sorry," he said and reached out for her hand.

She gave him a weak smile. "Did we just have our first disagreement?"

"I guess so. Forgive me, please?"

"Yes, of course. I understand, I just thought you should know."

"You were right. I need to lighten up and do something positive about it. I'll look into getting the place signposted with local information and arrange refuse collection and all the rest."

Just then he felt a tap on his shoulder. Glancing round he saw that it was Tom, and he was pointing over at Sally's plate.

"The shrimps are good. Did you like the shrimps?"

Sally looked up at him and smiled. "Oh yes, of course. The shrimp was delicious."

"I caught them fresh this morning." Tom beamed. "You must be the lady staying at the cottage, the one that he was asking about."

"This is Tom," Julian interrupted. "A font of knowledge on all things local."

Sally looked at Julian with an accusing expression. "Well, I don't feel so bad about spying on you now, Mr. Double O Beachpatrol, since you were busy asking about me," she commented when Tom finally ambled off.

"Guilty as charged. I saw your car and did some snooping."

"I'm glad you did . . ." She gave him a smile that recalled last night's lovemaking. This morning's. Just looking into her eyes made him hard.

"So am I."

"Let's forget about the tourist thing," she said decisively. "I want us to enjoy our time together. Let's just go with the flow," she added, suggestively.

"I'm not arguing."

"Besides, you promised to model for me."

Why did that sound like it was going to be a difficult task, Julian wondered? *Because she gets you going every time she looks at you with those curious, sexy eyes, idiot.*

"Hmm, so I did," he eventually replied, wondering what he was letting himself in for. Every time she looked at him with those sexy gypsy eyes, he got aroused. Would he be able to rein in his natural urges and cope with the scrutiny?

Chapter Five

Sally pulled the curtains shut in the kitchen window and turned back to her subject. *Oh boy, her subject.* Julian was standing in the middle of the rustic kitchen, looking possibly the most self-aware that she'd ever seen him, awaiting her instructions. She'd changed into her work gear, a tank top and jeans, and had brought in a couple of lamps from the sitting room to spotlight him.

"Right. I've got my sketchbook, so if you'd like to . . ." She indicated his clothes. "Undress."

She could tell that he tried not to look amused or surprised, but both reactions were there in his expression.

"This is purely work for you, isn't it? I mean I'm not going to be treated like some sort of sex object?"

How did he manage to make that question sound more like a suggestion? She chuckled. "Would it bother you if I was thinking about sex while I measured you?"

There was a moment's hesitation before he came right back at her. "Well, you were the one who first mentioned forfeits of a sexual nature in return for your hospitality, and as I'm your guest, I aim to fulfill my obligation."

He winked at her and began to undress, not once breaking eye contact with her, as if daring her to look down at his body instead.

She realized she ought to distance herself from him, but she couldn't help herself. Apart from the little disagreement that they'd had back at the pub, the teasing, sexy atmosphere between them hadn't really let up since their first morning together. If anything, it had increased as the moments passed, just waiting to peak into something much more specific and physical when the time was right.

She busied herself setting the lamps up on either side of him, taking care to throw his body in relief, casting shadows into the areas that fascinated her artist's eye the most—the dips in his buttocks, the curve of his lower back, the chiseled plane where his abdomen veered into his groin.

"I'm all yours," he said, arms outstretched.

She flexed her fingers. "May I get more closely acquainted with my subject matter?"

He nodded and watched quietly, letting her do as she wished with him. Stepping closer, she gave a sigh of pleasure and ran one finger down the muscle between his neck and shoulder. She stroked the back of her hand down his chest. The sensation of skin against skin only seemed more electric through the fine covering of hair on his pecs.

With her hands on his shoulders, she moved slowly down to trace the powerful line of his biceps, memorizing them in three dimensions with her inner eye, storing away the information for future use. She glanced over at the torso that she had set nearby for comparison. One thing was for sure; she would be reworking it in a life size version when she got home.

"Do I measure up to your satisfaction?" he asked, flexing. He gave her a half smile, as if he was amused by her attentions.

She only nodded in response. She was trying to ignore her body's signals, but it was futile. She had quickly bypassed simmering and was well on her way to boiling point. *Must concentrate.* At least for a little while. She had to show him she had some iota of self-control.

Her hands trailed around his hipbone and across his back as she walked around him. She splayed her palms over his shoulder blades, noting the shape and strength of each part of him, memorizing each bone and the way it was sheathed in muscle. Her hand slipped down into the dip of muscle on his buttock. She smiled to herself when she remembered that just a couple of days earlier, when she had molded him in clay, she'd wished then that he were real. She closed her eyes when she recalled the wish, and thanked the goddess of wishes, who must surely be looking over her.

With curious fingers, she caressed his fit backside. It was so bloody sexy! She'd never understood the obsession some women had with the male posterior—until now. Now it all made perfect sense. Instinctively, her body told her that muscle was what drove him hard inside her during lovemaking. Feeling the muscle flex under her hand was almost too much. Her sex was alive with sensation. She sighed again and ran her hands down the back of his taut thighs, bending to get the measure of him with her hands.

She turned away and picked up her sketchbook, attempting to make some quick charcoal images. His physical reality was soon too much of a distraction. She meandered up and down around him, considering him from all angles, the sketchbook dangling in her hand. There really wasn't much hope of getting any serious work done here. Maybe in time she could relax around him enough to concentrate on his body as purely art subject, but right now, all this was doing was sending her hormones into overdrive.

"You're not drawing." He had an amused look on his face.

"No, I am finding it hard to concentrate, but . . ." She tried to look professional. "My visual memory is being stoked." She dropped the sketchbook on the table and briefly pressed her arm across her breasts, quelling their need for contact.

He gave her a slow grin that teased and taunted.

She blushed furiously. *Am I that obvious?*

The tension between them was ratcheting up. Stepping in front of him, she looked pointedly at his hips.

"Besides, for the purposes of this session, you are supposed to be in a state of *partial* arousal . . ." She eyed his upright cock with a mocking smile.

Not only was he as hard as steel, but his gaze was so hot that she began to feel restless with tension. The atmosphere between them crackled with anticipation.

"What do you expect," he murmured. "You were touching me . . . and I enjoyed it."

He suddenly reached over and grabbed her by the neckline of her tank top, pulling her closer to him. With the fabric fisted in one hand, he ripped it right down the middle with the other.

She gasped, astounded and yet wickedly thrilled by his unexpected, outrageous action. His eyes were on her breasts as they bounced free of the tight fabric.

"I'll buy you a new one," he said. "I couldn't resist." With one finger, he pushed open the torn material and circled the dark areole of one nipple. "Your nipples were digging through the material, I had to see them. You've been tormenting me, Sally; everything about you is made to torment me. Even this little top you're wearing was designed to get me hot and bothered."

"I couldn't help being aroused, with you so . . ." she swallowed, "hard."

"You're complaining about my physical state and yet it's all . . . your . . . fault."

He bent and circled her breast with his hand, caressing it then taking the nipple that he had teased into his mouth, tonguing it, then grazing it with his teeth. Sally felt weak at the knees; her head was spinning. He turned his attention to the other breast. She felt his cock brushing against her leg.

After he'd all but reduced her to a puddle of lust on the floor, he pushed her toward the nearest wall, running his hands all over her body, pressing the crease of her jeans into her hot niche. Her clit was crushed, pounding and swollen. Then he flipped her round and spread-eagled her against the wall, his foot pushing her legs apart. He explored her, urgent and demanding, molding and stroking her breasts from behind, his cock hard against her.

"I think you've been a very naughty girl," he murmured against her ear, one hand reaching down to rub her pussy through her jeans while he rocked his entire body against her back. "And you know there can only be one outcome in a situation like this. You'll have to be shown what a bad girl you've been. I'll have to demonstrate it to you . . . physically."

Sally's fingers clutched at the surface of the wall. Her heart was thudding, her body weak and her mind running feverishly. *Does he mean to spank me again?*

He lifted her and carried her into the bedroom. He could manhandle her so easily. She was like a doll to him, something he could toy with at will. And that notion sent her into overdrive!

"Take off your jeans," he said. "Then kneel on the bed."

She did as he instructed, pulling open her belt and zipper with trembling fingers. She crawled onto the bed, the tug of war between fear and desire making her both willing, and ashamed for wanting it so much. She was learning about the delights of submission, and there was so much more to discover.

Even though she knew what was coming, she flinched when she felt his hand against her bottom. But he slid his hand easily between her thighs and tisked when he felt the moisture that oozed from inside her.

"You are so bad."

"Yes, I am." Admitting it aloud sent a shudder through her body, as if she'd opened herself up to him even more, somehow.

He gave a dark chuckle. "I believe that you knew what you were doing to me in there," he added. His hands were soothing her buttocks, warning her, readying her.

No, I can't possibly enjoy what is to come, a voice in her head interjected. He gave a single slap on each cheek and let the fire spread through her, before returning to deliver a quick burst of short, sharp shocks across her buttocks. The sting was almost too much; she whimpered. Then the delicate strands of pleasure began to weave amongst the pain, and her cries soon became much more pleasured in nature. She bit her lip and hung her head. Yes, she did enjoy this beautiful, strange punishment. Her whole nether region was throbbing, and her core was on fire. She arched her back and pushed her bottom upward, exposing more of her pussy, and as she did, the palm of his hand slapped up against her swollen sex folds. Sheer ecstasy flooded her body and she was close to coming when he suddenly lifted her and rolled her over on the bed.

"Sally . . . Sally . . . you are enjoying that far too much. I'm going to have to think of some other way to punish you."

The linen cover on the bed felt rough against her buttocks, sending an after tremor of pleasurable pain through her.

"Oh no, I'm not done with you yet," he said, when she reached up for him. "In fact your new punishment is that you're going to have to wait, my dear. You are such a randy little sexpot, I can't think of a better way to make you suffer. I think I will have to teach you some self-restraint. *Forcibly.*"

He grabbed both her wrists into one strong hand and then snatched up the belt from her abandoned jeans on the bedside chair with the other. He quickly tethered her to the oak struts on the headboard.

It made her feel even more aroused. *Did he know that it would?* It was as if he knew instinctively what would drive her wild in bed, and Sally inwardly cursed the overwrought feeling that realization brought about.

"Please, Julian, I beg you. Don't make me wait . . ."

That just made him smile.

She writhed within the constraints. She was on fire. Her lust was fast becoming primitive, animalistic. She struggled against the belt. She wanted to free herself and force him to take her. Hard.

Julian stood running his hand up and down the length of his cock, an almost lazy stroke, while he watched her futile struggle. "I could look at you all evening. It suits you to be displayed like that." He nodded at her body, the way her breasts rolled and jiggled as she struggled against the restraints.

With his free hand, he leaned over and squeezed and molded the flesh of her breasts. Each touch caused her to moan aloud and tremble. He ran his hand lower and pushed her legs apart. Her legs were completely splayed, her ankles out toward the edge of the bed. Cool air ran over her burning pussy. Sally felt her face coloring. Somehow being displayed so thoroughly made her feel so exposed. And aroused. Even though he'd seen it all before, it was so blatant. She had so little control. He could do whatever he wanted to her. That was at the core of her lust, and she was becoming more desperate for him as each moment passed.

He walked to the end of the bed, and stared at her, while he continued to pump his cock.

"Your pussy is beautiful."

He was a master of torment. She knew that her clit was swollen and pounding, her sex gaping. She began to wonder if she would come without even being touched, just from being exposed under his devilish, watchful eyes while he continued his manly display.

The sensation of his gaze lingering on her breasts, her beaded nipples and the folds of her sex, brought her arousal to a fevered pitch. Yet still he did not touch her, did not bring her relief. He kept her waiting for so long, craving him and the thrust of him between her thighs. And when he finally rose up over her, she wanted him so badly that her juices were dribbling down between her buttocks. She couldn't stop herself lifting her hips and opening herself up to him.

"Please, I beg you, Julian, please."

He cursed under his breath, as if her comment had shredded his final bit of self-control. He reached for the bedside table, snatching up a condom and ripping it open. Kneeling over her, he rolled it on quickly and rammed his erect cock deep inside her, claiming her to the core and beyond.

She cried out. Tears of relief blurred her vision.

He started to thrust hard and fast, knocking up against the core of her, sending deep spasms of pleasure through her body. She moaned aloud, even though she bit her lip to try and hold back, it was too much. Her whole body had been tenderized and made ready for this and now that he was inside her, she couldn't help shouting her joy.

"Yes, Sweetheart, you can let go now," he said, with a wicked smile.

"You bastard," she accused and thrust up against him, laughing with delight when his face contorted with pleasure. She held him deep inside her and squeezed his cock hard with her inner muscles.

"God . . . you're . . . so hot!" he said, between gritted teeth, and he sounded as if the words had been wrenched from his lungs.

"You better believe it," she replied and rammed hard onto him again, using the struts on the bed head to gain more purchase.

She felt wild, as if being tethered up and at his mercy had unleashed some primitive urge to do combat. The truth was she'd never been this keyed up before. She had never been so close to coming, nor held off for so long.

They went at each other hard and fast, and when she finally came, her whole body jerked with the force of it. He groaned and spilled, his cock spurting inside her. She bit his shoulder, moaning loudly as ripple after ripple of pleasure soared through her, arresting her every nerve ending in the experience and making her body shudder, seize and, finally, grow limp and sanguine.

Chapter Six

Sally climbed up the bluff at the end of the cove and turned to look back at the view. Breathtaking. The day was blustery, the coolest since she arrived, and the breeze whipped through her hair, dancing amongst the skirts of her dress before it swept on. It was her last day with Julian. *The last day.* They'd shared such wonderful days, and nights . . . *oh, the nights.*

But all good things must come to an end, she supposed, especially holiday romances.

She had spent the morning alone, letting him go about his business while she brooded over her sculpture and wondered about the fact that she was becoming so attached to him. She finally decided she'd better be alone for a few hours, or it would be a complete shock to her system when they had to part the next day.

The relationship had been so highly sexually charged, and when she tried to think with a level head the best she could do was question her capability to analyze her own emotions at all. How could she have grown so attached to him so quickly? It had happened far too fast, and it was frightening her to death. He had keyed into a sexual side of her that she hadn't known existed. But that wasn't all; the distinction between lust and love had become a whole lot more fuzzy over the past few days. She just knew that she was going to pine for him when she got back to London, like some dreadful, lovesick teenager just back from a holiday romance. *I am a grown woman, for goodness sakes!*

She sighed and pushed her hands into the deep pockets on her dress. Just as she did her mobile phone started to vibrate, and she lifted it out of her pocket. It was Julian.

"I thought you were supposed to be back by now."

"I'm nearly there; I had to stop for petrol, so I thought I'd give you another quick call."

"You just want to keep me crazy with anticipation for your return, don't you?" She couldn't keep the stupid grin off her face, despite her attempt at levelheaded thinking just moments before.

"Oh, yes, I want you to be ready for me when I arrive back, because I'm hungry for you." There was a deeply suggestive tone to his words, and Sally gave a delighted laugh. He'd phoned her at least once an hour, and it was very easy to flirt back when his warm, deep voice tickled her every nerve ending. She turned her back on the breeze and stepped along the bluff.

"Oh, don't you worry. I am absolutely dripping with anticipation . . ." She let that one sink in and was gratified to hear him give a low groan. "It's been a constant and inevitable state when you're around. Besides, I want to make the most of our last night together."

She noticed the hesitant pause at the other end of the line. Their last night together was important to him, too. That much had been obvious this morning when he'd had a hard time leaving for his daily duties. She tried to redirect the conversation, secretly vowing not to mention the fact that it was their last night again.

"In fact, I was getting so hot with anticipation over the thought of your return, that I had to take a walk over to the bluff." She lifted her chin and looked up the coast, wondering how far away he was. As she did a movement caught her eye, a figure out in the bay. "Hey . . . it looks like that fisherman is busy again. Tom?"

"Probably, I imagine he'll be working on the turn of the tide," Julian commented.

She noticed that the figure was waving. She lifted her hand to return the greeting and chuckled into the phone. "There you go, Mr. Keswick, you were wrong when you said that we couldn't be seen on the cove. Your friend is busy waving at me as I speak." She chuckled again.

The sound of the engine revving up at the other of the phone dropped off.

"You sure? If it is Tom, he's short sighted, so even if you're standing on his side of the bluff, I doubt he could see you."

Sally looked back towards the figure in the water. It was then that she realized that he was waving with both hands, and he had begun to look as if he was distressed. "Oh my God, Julian, I think he's in trouble. In fact, the tide is coming in fast now and he's not moving. He's waving for help!"

As she spoke, the wind lifted again, weaving her hair across her face. She pulled it back and looked at the froth on the incoming tide with wide eyes. The surf was up.

"I thought it didn't sound right," Julian commented, then she heard the motorbike revving up again, and his voice was all but drowned out.

"What should I do?" she shouted into the phone.

"Call the police and tell them to alert the Coastguard. Be sure to tell them the tide is on the turn. I'll be there in a matter of minutes."

With that, the line went dead. Sally punched 999 into the phone and followed his instructions, moving down the other side of the bluff as she did so, her breath catching in her lungs. Her body started to tremble. As she got closer to the shore edge she could see all too clearly that he was floundering, but seemed unable to move. He had to be trapped in some way. She described the location as best as she could to the police operative, and kept waving to the figure in the hope that he would see her and know that help was on its way.

It was the longest five minutes of Sally's life. She felt completely useless and once again rued her inability to swim. By the time she heard Julian's bike roaring along the dirt track behind her, she was knee deep in the freezing cold water. She kept shouting to Tom, trying to encourage him. The tide had come in rapidly, and it scared her the way the wind whipped up the waves. She turned to watch as Julian clambered off the bike and threw off his helmet and jacket. She became aware of another noise and saw the Coastguard's boat roaring along the coast towards them.

"He's in no man's land," Julian shouted, as he shoved off his boots.

"What do you mean?"

He ran into the water. "It's too shallow for the boat to come in. I'll have to go get him."

Julian.

Her stomach knotted with fear. She watched as he dove into the water, his muscular shoulders quickly whipping into action as his arms cleaved through the waves.

Julian!

Whatever it was that had trapped Tom might endanger Julian as well. Her heart beat hard in her chest, her voice trapped in her throat. One hand covered her mouth. What if he got injured too? What could she do to help? She reached into the pocket of her skirt and punched in 999 again. She updated the police operator on what was happening and then watched as the Coastguard's boat drifted to a halt some twenty yards out from where Tom's head was visible in the water. The surf was up to his chin now and his head kept bobbing down beneath the water as if he was weakening. His hands had long since stopped waving.

"Julian, be careful!"

She got the plaintive cry out but the sound was whipped away on the wind. The two men were barely visible in the water. She could see that the Coastguard was leaning over the side of the launch, shouting instructions. She watched as Julian finally reached the man struggling in the water. He exchanged a few words. Sally gasped when she saw him flip under the water and dive. She barely registered that she was wading in the water and it was up to her hips. A smattering of relief hit her when she saw that Julian's head had emerged from the water again and within seconds he had maneuvered Tom into the life-saving position and had begun to slowly swim back towards the shore.

When they got closer to her, she assisted Julian, helping to bring Tom the last few yards to the shore's edge. He was wearing a threadbare sweater that was water logged, and his trousers were rolled up to knee level, as if he'd only been that deep to begin with.

"Oh my God," Sally cried, when she saw the trail of blood on the sand. On one foot Tom was wearing a thin, worn, sports shoe. The other foot was bare; it was swollen and bleeding.

"Got me foot stuck in the rocks, lost me shoe. Bastards got me on the way back in," mumbled Tom, in between chattering teeth as he dropped to the ground.

"Stay quiet," Julian insisted and bent down to examine the wounds. "Weaver fish," he mumbled beneath his breath.

"What's happened to him?" Sally asked.

"If you're shrimping, you have to protect your feet because it stirs up other fish along the way, fish that are less easy to handle. The weaver fish have got him. See there?" He indicated the bare foot that was bleeding.

She leaned over and saw a nasty looking object embedded in Tom's foot.

"Weavers have spines on their backs. Their spines get stuck in and break off, poisoning the local area. It's not overly dangerous but it is very painful," he added, looking back at Tom, whose eyes were closed, his expression frozen and his complexion pale. "The foot then swells up with the incoming tide."

Sally stared in horror at the poor man. She dropped to her knees and stroked his forehead, offering encouragement.

"I tried to ask the Coastguard if he'd called an ambulance," Julian added. "But I don't know if they heard me."

"The police are sending one," she answered. "I phoned them again when I realized the boat couldn't get in."

"Good girl." Julian muttered the reply but he was focused on tracing the number of wounds.

Sure enough, a few minutes later the ambulance arrived and Tom was soon wrapped in a silver foil sheet and lifted onto a stretcher. Sally was shivering but relief began to surface when she saw the paramedics taking charge.

It was short lived.

Julian leaned over to say his good byes to Tom, and she saw the old man mumble something to him. Julian laughed loudly and gave the man an encouraging pat on the hand. The stretcher went into the ambulance, and the doors were slammed shut. Julian jogged back to the spot where she was standing. He peeled off his wet T-shirt and hauled the belt from his jeans. His nipples were nut-hard from cold, his upper arms covered in goose bumps. A shiver shook her entire body when she noticed.

"Will he be okay?"

He nodded, dropping the heavy belt to the ground. "I'm going back in."

"You're doing *what*?" She stared at him, aghast. *He can't be serious!*

"His shrimping gear is still out there. It's his livelihood." He broke into a grin when he saw her worried expression and leaned over to kiss her, briefly but passionately, on the mouth.

"Don't worry, gorgeous. It will only take a couple of minutes and it will mean a lot to Tom. I promise my feet won't touch the bottom if you promise you'll warm me up when I get back." He flickered his eyebrows at her and then slapped her on the behind.

How dare he be so nonchalant?

"I'll warm you up with a good tongue-lashing for going back in there, is what I'll do!" She was fuming at him for taking another risk.

He grinned at her and ran off, quickly cutting a path through the waves and disappearing towards the deeper water.

He was a liability, that man!

Even though he had promised her he wouldn't set foot down, her heart rate had notched up a number of levels. She knew that if she hadn't been so bloody cold, she'd have broken out in a sweat. Hadn't he seen Tom's injuries? How dare he take risks like that? The ambulance was a good quarter of a mile away, and her phone was probably dead or waterlogged by now.

She was scared to death in case anything would happen to him. She stretched her arms up in the air in an effort to relieve the tension coursing through her body, and put both hands on her head, biting her lip and trying to reason through his words. He shouldn't need to set foot down. He was right. He was strong. She couldn't help herself though.

I'll just die if anything happens to the man!

That's when it hit her. She was in love with him!

The water ran torrents over him and with his eyes closed he looked like a classical sculpture in the rain, mighty and powerful but still. The steam from the shower was building and she moved closer, her hands roaming up his chest, soaping him as she went, working heat back into both their bodies. She pushed back her wet hair and moved slowly, edging around him in the cubicle as best she could, adoring the feeling of him safe and warm again.

God he felt good. She wanted to keep her hands on him, always. A possessive streak had taken hold of her and she was struggling to make sense of that, and all the other thoughts and feelings tumbling through her mind. She gripped his arms and looked up at him. "I was so worried about you," she murmured.

"No need, but I appreciate it." He reached down for her hand, drew her fingers up to his lips and kissed them gently, watching her as he did so. He wasn't teasing this time and the connection between them had intensified.

"You crazy man."

"Yeah, crazy," he replied, his stare direct but deeply thoughtful, his eyes on her mouth. He bent his head to kiss her, moving her under the stream of water, forcing her to close her eyes and blinding her to his intense stare. His tongue probed into her mouth, his hands going to the tiles behind her head.

She felt his cock grow hard against her hip and reached for it. The possessive streak reared up again inside her and she pumped him hard in her soapy hand, moaning against his mouth while he kissed her with fire, with passion and urgency. She rode his cock hard with her fist, her other hand reaching down to grasp his balls, already high and tight against his body. She wanted him, she needed him, she loved him.

He hauled his head back and exclaimed loudly, letting out a great beast of a shout, his hips reaching each time as she slid her hand up and down his length. "I'm crazy for this, for you," he blurted, between gritted teeth, his eyes wild.

"And me for you, I want more, I want more of you, Julian. Let me see you come."

"Oh, you will," he replied with a hoarse laugh, shaking his head in disbelief, "any second now."

She looked down at his cock reaching in her hand. Her body clenched inside, but she wanted to see him come and worked him harder, ignoring his mumbled pleas for time. The head of his cock was dark with blood and oozing, each splash of water sending a jerk through him. He gave another shout, fierce and primal, and then she felt him rising in her hand. She held her breath. He spurted quick and hard, powerful to the last.

A moment later she felt his hand go around her neck, one thumb pushing her chin up so he could look into her eyes.

"Why do you have to feel so . . . perfect?" he mumbled, leaning into her, his mouth against her hair, his arm drawing her close and locked in against him.

"Why do you?" she replied.

"Here you go."

Sally glanced around, she was miles away and was surprised to hear his voice. She'd left him, gone out into the garden and hadn't realized that time had gone by quite so much. He had brought out two mugs of hot tea and set them down on the garden wall, then clambered up beside her. She crossed her legs, smoothing her jeans down, before picking up the mug by her side.

"Thanks, I couldn't resist watching the sunset." The sky was molten golds and reds. The wind had streaked amber threads through the atmosphere, bathing the cottage in the glorious light unique to that time of day. Despite the nip in the air, the light reflected warmly off the old stones of the house and she sighed deeply, wrapping her hands round the cup for comfort.

"Are you warm enough? Can I get you a sweater?"

"No, thanks." She smiled over at him and noticed how much warmer and relaxed he looked after the hot shower. "Are you feeling better now?"

"Yes. It didn't bother you did it, today?" He reached out to stroke her back through the soft fabric of her shirt. His expression was marked with concern.

She took a moment to allow his features to etch on her memory, to notice the way his hair lifted on the breeze and how the color of his eyes became luminescent in the outside light. "It was just a bit of a shock, and I'm still worrying about Tom." She forced a smile. She was feeling emotional after the events of the day, but that wasn't all.

"I phoned the hospital. He's fine. Mostly suffering from the effects of the cold but he'll be fine." Julian looked out at the sea. "And he'll be back out there shrimping again as soon as he can."

"Couldn't he do something else, something . . . safer?" She frowned and looked down into her tea before sipping at it.

"He could, but he won't. The sea is his challenge, and it's also a part of him, kind of like his wife, you know?" He smiled at her. "The nagging wife he has to pacify. It's in his blood, and I think even for people like us, who aren't born and bred here, it gets that way a bit too."

She nodded; she understood what he meant.

"It didn't put you off visiting again did it? I mean . . . I assumed you might want to visit again?" The question was cautiously asked.

"Yes, I want to visit again and, no, it didn't put me off. There are dangers in city life, too. It's just different here and being so close to nature, well, it's got problems as well as joys, just as anything in life. Part of what is special about the place is learning its ways and dealing with them."

"I couldn't have put it better myself." He leaned over and kissed her cheek, sliding his arm further around her. "I'll miss you," he added quietly a moment later. "I'll have to leave early in the morning."

"I know."

"I want to stop off at the hospital in Morpeth to visit Tom as I pass by, and I need to be back in my office in Hull by midday." He looked reluctant. "I could stay later but I'd agreed to have a report on the director's desk by three."

"Julian," she said and rested one hand on his chest, looking up at him with an earnest expression. "Please don't say another word. I understand. I have to go, too. I have to leave and . . . I have to get on with my life." It was true. It was the unavoidable truth of the matter. Her idyll was coming to an end and that brought such a sense of loss.

Julian gazed at her for a moment and then he winked and grabbed her against him possessively.

"I should keep you with me, take you back to my flat and tie you up so you can't escape." He kissed the top of her head and held her close.

He had said it in a light, joking way, but she felt the tension in him and wondered if he was putting the suggestion forward to check out her reaction.

"There are laws against that sort of thing," she retorted, but she was smiling.

"They can send me down. It would be worth it to keep you with me for a while longer." His arm was possessive around her shoulders.

Her heart gave a funny flip and she closed her eyes for a moment. This was a holiday romance, she reminded herself, but she didn't want it to end.

"If I could stay longer, I would." She opened her eyes and raised her head to look at him. *Oh yes,* he looked hopeful too. Her spirits were lifting by the moment.

"You promise to visit the cove again?"

She nodded. She didn't want it to be just a fling. And now it felt as if he didn't want that either. Could she dare to believe it could be more?

"Yes, I will, of course I will. And in the meantime . . . would you like to come down to visit with me, sometime?" she asked, tentatively.

"In the big city?" His sudden, warm smile told her she hadn't been wrong to ask.

"Do you think you can bear it?"

"To be with you, yes. I'd travel to the depths of hell for an hour in your company."

That made her heart soar. Knowing that he wanted to be with her again simply filled her with joy. And she believed he meant it. He was willing to endure the city just to see her again. She could no longer fight it; she had to admit just how much he had come to mean to her, so much more than a holiday romance. In her relief, the emotion that had welled in her heart finally spilled over and she was flooded with it. "As soon as you can then?"

"The summer is our busy time, but late September should be a good time to work in some leave."

Nearly three months. "I'll count the days."

"Me too."

"And can I call you when I need to?" She winked at him, suggestively.

"Oh, yes. I'll be expecting regular doses of phone sex to keep me from going mad. You know, I think I'm addicted to you."

And then he kissed her, hungrily, deeply, and passionately. He cupped her face, his fingers meshing in her hair. She melted against him, her body liquid with desire and with the need to be close to him. Their tongues rasped, their bodies acknowledging the mutual draw and the image of a possible future that had all their barriers melting.

He drew back, pushing strands of her hair back from her face and looking at her with bright eyes. "Right, now that's settled, and I know I'm going to see you again sometime soon, I can relax . . ." He paused to watch her reaction and she smiled, an echo of heat, pleasure and recognition running through her. "So, I'm going to take you to the village for dinner at The Lobster Pot. That's if you think you can stand the extra attention?"

"*Extra* attention?"

"It will be much worse than last time, I assure you, because by now the whole village will know that you alerted the authorities about Tom. You were simply a curiosity before. Now you're a heroine. I reckon you'll be there for at least the next ten years, maybe longer if no one else beats your record."

"Oh, Julian, it wasn't me. It was you. You're the hero." She nudged him away, smiling, and blushing too. She was flattered by his remarks, but she would always remember his courage and bravery when he rescued Tom.

"Nope, you're the one who spotted him. You're the one who took action, so you're going to have to carry the responsibility of being the superstar." He lifted his hands, as if it was nothing to do with him, then winked and hauled her closer again. "Okay, I promise I'll act like a good bodyguard and fight off your adoring fans if it gets to be too much for you."

How could she not adore that humor and that generosity of spirit?

"Thank you. You're a true hero," she mocked and rested her head on his shoulder.

And how could she not adore the feeling of bliss that his very proximity gave her?

That night they made love slow and gentle. Julian wanted to savor every moment. He couldn't get enough of her. In his imagination she was the wandering gypsy woman who'd taken up residence in his special place, but in his heart he knew that she was a city girl, a woman with a vibrant career pulling her back, a woman with friends and a life outside of this. What they had was magic, but soon it would be gone until the distant day when they might see each other again. The thought had gnawed at him insistently and he tried to lay it to rest so that they could have one last night to remember, but there was a knot in his chest that he just couldn't ignorc. A knot of hard, raw emotion.

He led her to the bedroom and undressed her slowly, taking time to observe her beautiful, lush femininity. He savored her responsiveness, the building anticipation that was so evident in her expression. She seemed happy to let him undress her but she wasn't submissive tonight. No, they weren't playing that game. Tonight they expressed themselves as equals in their naked, physical union.

Her eyes sparkled, and she stroked his face, whispering affectionate words when he lifted her into his arms, carrying her to the bed. He rested her down against the covers, marveling at her curves, her warm, inviting body.

In the soft light from the bedroom lamp her skin seemed pale, almost delicate. It belied the athletic little tyke that he had witnessed running naked across the beach the other day. It also belied the tensile strength and determination he had witnessed earlier today when she had helped to haul Tom from the ocean. She was a chameleon, at once soft and feminine, yet strong and resilient. The contrast was one of the many aspects of her that fascinated him.

He touched one finger against her collarbone and drew it down between her breasts, noticing how she trembled in response. The knowledge that he could affect her that way made his blood roar. He wanted to crush her with his body; he wanted to thrust himself inside her until relief came. He ran his fingers lower, over the gentle curve of her belly. When she whimpered and her legs parted, he could only feast his eyes on her. Patches of color marked her cheekbones. She lifted an arm over her head, her breasts rolling in the most languid way. Everything about her was so feminine; she called to every atom of his being. His cock had never felt so engorged, so rigid and hot for contact. But he wanted to savor each and every inch of her body, every flavor, every texture.

He undressed. She leaned back against the pillows, watching, her gaze sweeping over him and coming to rest on his cock. Her eyes were wide and dark, her lips parted. He sat next to her, and when his hand touched between her thighs, she grabbed his hand and guided him deeper, a muffled plea in her voice. He didn't resist. His fingers stroked the soft down of her mons and then slipped easily into the damp channel below. Liquid heat trickled from her pussy. His pulse beat like a drum inside his head. Her skin there was so soft, wet and inviting, that he had to pause, close his eyes for a second, and swallow down the urge to rush.

She arched against him, and when his finger dipped into the slippery niche of her sex, his cock bounced against his belly, eager and demanding for her. She leaned up against him, her breasts rubbing against his skin. Her nipples were so hard they grazed against his bare skin. Each touch threatened to squander his self-control. He dropped down and lapped hungrily at the salty folds of her sex and when the taste and her scent washed over him, he shuddered with pleasure.

Sally, beautiful, luscious Sally.

He ran his tongue back and forth over her clit. She gave a strange, tortured cry, and her fingers tugged on his hair, pulling him up. It had to be soon. He pulled on a condom and her hand followed his, moving quickly to the base of his cock. He groaned with feral pleasure. She was begging for him to be inside her. And he wanted that above all else.

Easing the crown of his cock inside her, he let out a low growl, his thighs trembling with the effort to restrain himself. Easing slowly deeper, he felt her clutching at him with her sweetness and her moisture slid down around his balls. Her legs latched around his hips and her nails scraped over his back, sharp and possessive. They began to move in unison, reaching for the prize.

The tension built, thundering hooves of intense pleasure building speed in the base of his cock each time he rode high and tight inside her lush body. Each slow thrust of their bodies was bringing him on, the clutch of her body on him, milking him until finally he couldn't hold back any longer. His whole body reached, his back arching, every muscle in his arms cording with tension. His cock jerked, the climax roaring through him, flooding his every sense. For a moment he lost touch with reality. Dazzling white light blazed through his mind. And then her name: *Sally.*

He felt her hands clutching at him and her body was shuddering in release. Her head pushed back in the pillows, her lips parted, her eyes slits of darkness. Pleasure speared through him all over again as he watched her climax.

"Sally, yes love. Oh, yes."

Chapter Seven

Julian stomped through his lab and into the office space he shared with George MacIntyre, his lab-based colleague, and shifted a stack of papers so that he could dump his briefcase on his desk.

George stared at the shiny new leather object Julian had deposited on the desk. His glance slowly lifted to focus inquiringly on his colleague.

Julian tugged at the already skewed knot on his tie and undid the top button of his crisp, new linen shirt. "Come on then, say it. Get it over with," he said, beckoning to George with one hand while he fiddled with the shirt collar.

George smiled silently.

"Look, I'm making an effort. What's the problem?"

George shrugged. "I'm not saying there is a problem. I just haven't seen you in a suit before. How do you expect me to react?" He grinned. "She's had quite an effect on you, this Sally woman, hasn't she?"

Julian harrumphed loudly and dropped into his chair, pushing his fingers through his hair in a distracted gesture, undoing what efforts he'd made there in the process. "No. Well, yes. Actually, I have to give my termly talk to the pollution research students over at the University," he commented, vaguely. "I just thought I'd play the part, for a change."

There *was* more to it than that. But he was finding it hard to verbalize, even to George, who'd been a close friend for many years since back when they were matched up on the North-East coast workload.

"I can't wait to see Jeffrey's face," George commented.

Jeffrey, the director of their conservation unit, lived in designer suits but had long since given up trying to impose some regulation smartness on either George—who lived in a scruffy lab coat—or Julian, whose best efforts were usually jeans and a short sleeved, open neck shirt. "When is it you are off to London?" George added, glancing at the wall planner.

Julian looked back to his friend. Perhaps George knew him better than he had thought; he didn't seem overly surprised by what was a significant change in behavior. And he wasn't shying away from the cause, either. Julian had sworn he'd be in a coffin before he'd ever be seen dead in a suit and had threatened to have it written into his will that should not be the case, even then. But if he were to fit into Sally's world, change would be necessary.

"Not for another month. The wait is killing me, but I had to work it into the summer schedule." He shook his head. Yes, he had it bad. In fact he'd gone beyond that. Now he was trying to think of ways to make this long-distance relationship thing work. He'd spent restless nights going through his options, of which there weren't many.

"When you met Catherine," he said, and drummed his fingers on the desk, fighting the urge to leave the room or change the topic of conversation to the latest football results. "How did you know that she was the one? You know, the one you wanted to spend the rest of your life with?"

George sat back into his chair. "Well, it had to happen to you eventually, Mister free and easy," he said. "But the fact that you're even asking me that question . . ." he looked at Julian meaningfully, "tells me that she probably is 'the one.' "

Julian was about to declare the uselessness of his advice when the message began to sink in. Yes, the fact that he was asking himself that question had to be significant in itself. He'd certainly never considered the notion before.

"So what are you going to do about it?"

"Damned if I know." That was the knee-jerk response. He'd been thinking, and he'd been thinking hard. The only feasible option would have to be discussed with George anyway, because it might affect him. Why not now, Julian asked himself? The conversation was going down that road, and he'd had more than enough lonely contemplation.

"Do you remember Tony Foster?"

George chortled and leaned over to tickle the mouse on his computer so that his beloved seascape screensaver wouldn't black out. Then the smile began to disappear from his face and his head snapped back to look at Julian. His eyebrows shot up. "Ah, I see."

Tony had transferred to a post in the south the year before, much to the amusement of the whole division. He had sacrificed duties along one of the most interesting estuaries in England for somewhat more stressful work overseeing the team who dealt with the Thames area. Last they heard, Tony was engaged to a Swedish au pair and expecting twins.

Julian had wondered how George would react. To distract himself from the ominous silence coming across the desk, he opened his briefcase, lifted out the notes he was working on for his talk at the University, and the carefully bubble-wrapped package he had brought with him. Setting it on his desk, he unwrapped the cyber warrior Sally had sent to keep him company. He was a cute little guy with a cheeky grin, a harpoon and a bullet belt filled with test tubes hanging low on his hips. He was like some futuristic beach warrior and she had to know he'd love it. He set it up next to his computer and looked at it thoughtfully.

"Right," George said, eyeing the sculpture and giving a deep, heartfelt sigh. He turned back to his computer and clicked on the government home page. "We'd better take a look at the transfer possibilities, hadn't we?"

When Julian looked at him, he found George's smile wasn't, as he might have expected, mocking. Instead, it was marked with a kind of resigned sadness.

Sally drummed her fingers on her desk and wedged the phone between her shoulder and jaw so she that could continue stuffing envelopes with the latest catalogue during the phone conversation.

"Believe me, I'm in business myself, and I am well aware that you are contravening the Trades Description Act with both the information on your web site and in the brochure. The beach is *not* the exclusive domain of the cottage or its tenants."

At the other end of the phone the agent muttered on about wording and how the public could read too much into the description of the cottage.

"Excuse me, I have more to do with my valuable time than to debate wording and interpretation. It's quite obvious to me and anyone else who might read it what you are trying to do, and it's wrong. If you don't change the information immediately, I will get in touch with the Advertising Standards Agency and then you'll not only be forced to change it, but you'll have to deal with them as well."

When the agent grunted relinquishment down the phone, Sally offered her good byes and triumphantly hung up. She looked at Kitty, who had been standing watching her for the past two minutes.

"What?"

Kitty walked over to the desk and collected the stack of mail from the post tray. "I was just recognizing the signals, the pattern that is emerging."

"What pattern?" Sally asked, a creeping sense of unease rising up inside her. Kitty often second-guessed her, and she didn't know if she was ready to share her thoughts yet.

"When you start complaining about things and getting on your high-horse, it usually means you are in one of your action phases. And the last time that happened, we had a major reshuffle in the working practices here. I want to know if we have to expect something like that again, or is this just about you and the fact that you're missing your hunk?"

Sally stared at her friend, mouth open. Kitty really did have a handle on her. She knew she'd been talking about Julian incessantly since she got back, because Kitty kept pointing it out. But Kitty's analysis of her behavior was too uncanny.

"It's not just about him," she retorted. "It's the place, the cottage and the cove. It's special and I miss the place."

"You're only saying that because you don't know for sure if Julian feels the same as you do. It's displacement theory in action. You are focusing on the cove and acting on it, because if you get sidelined by him, you still have the cove to fixate on, to help you through."

"Kitty, do you have to be right about everything?"

Kitty grinned, proud of her deductions, and tucked the stack of mail under one arm.

"Well, I don't think you have to worry about your beach hunk, because he calls you so often he's obviously just as infatuated as you are. Besides, if it was the place that meant so much to you, you'd be telling me my job is at risk, and you're going to pack up and do a runner to the north."

Sally stared down at her desk, color climbing into her cheeks. "Your job isn't at risk," she replied.

Silence followed. She forced herself to look up. Kitty was staring at her, her expression somewhat more subdued.

"I see. Is it too soon to ask what your action phase might involve this time around?"

"It is too soon, because I haven't decided on anything definite yet, but, trust me, your job is safe and so are those of the rest of the girls. I promise you that."

Kitty shuffled the mail from arm to arm and shook her head. When she turned to leave the room, Sally shouted after.

"And you're wrong about the cove. I do love the place."

I love the place and I love Julian. Desperately.

Julian stood at the edge of the cove, his arms folded across his chest, scowling at the sea. His mood was just about as grumpy as it could get. Being back at the cove only served to remind him that he'd had heaven for a few days and, more importantly, that he didn't have it any more. It didn't help that a god-awful brat pack had taken up residence in the cottage the last time he had passed through. They had left signs of their presence not only at the cottage but also on the beach itself. He'd had to collect their barbecue debris and their environmentally unfriendly litter. He'd have to remember to order in some friendly environment reminder signposts, which had never been needed here before. It seemed such an atrocity to him, and no matter how he reasoned it out in his mind he couldn't come to terms with it. He daren't even look over at the cottage this time, in case some similar atrocity was going on. The only person he wanted to see there was Sally. Sally whose presence had felt right there.

Sally, who had felt right in every way.

He was counting the moments until they could be together again, just living for those two weeks they had promised each other in London. It was only days away now. He loved her far too much to be apart like this. Long distance was simply not going to work. He had decided to talk seriously to her, and, if she felt the same way, he would definitely try to transfer to a location nearer her. He'd do anything, even live in the city for her—he'd decided it was the only way. He'd been happy with his life before, but it was never going to feel right again, not without her. He felt as if he'd had part of himself taken away, and it hurt, bad. *Really bad.*

He was just about to pitch his tent when his mobile bleeped at him from the pocket of his leather jacket.

"Julian?"

"Sally!" Some elemental force inside him leapt with pride and longing. Just hearing her voice brought such a rise of emotion in him; there wasn't any denying it.

"I know you're busy, and I know I called you this morning, but I had to dash for a flight, and I really wanted to tell you something."

Flight? Where was she going, and with whom?

There was a deep breath being drawn in at the other end of the line and for a split second Julian wondered if she was going to cancel his trip down, if she was going to dump him.

"What is it . . . ?"

"Julian, I love you."

"Oh." Relief swamped him. "Thank goodness for that," he blurted. He laughed.

She laughed too. "Um, what is so funny?"

"Nothing, I'm just relieved. I love you too." They'd been so close to saying it, so many times. It was always there, silent but palpable between them. And he was so godamn relieved that it was out now. "In fact, I love you so much that I can't wait until I have you in my arms, so that I can tell you—and show you—in the flesh."

She purred into the phone. "Well, it won't be long now."

"No, and just as well."

"Are you sitting down?" she quizzed.

"No, I'm standing on the edge of the cove, looking over at our old love nest."

She chuckled. It was a gorgeous sound and it did strange, tormenting things inside his chest.

"That's even better. I've got a surprise for you. Are you looking at the cottage?"

"Yes."

"Well, I wanted you to know that I bought it."

What? She had to be kidding. "Sally, are you crazy? Stop kidding me. Old Man Greg would never sell. You know that I tried to buy the cottage from him."

"I gave him an offer he couldn't refuse."

"Sally . . ." Both doubt and hope trickled inside him. Was this a joke, or a daydream?

"Darling, I'm loaded. I never told you, but the oriental figurine market went mad just after I got into it, and I'm the top British importer. I tracked him down and . . . well, he accepted my offer. I've got heaps to sort out, and the move will have to be spread over the next year or maybe more. I'll have to keep going up and down but eventually I'm going to do the majority of my work from the cottage. The actual mechanics of the business will still be based in London, but I can do all the paperwork at a distance and fly down from Newcastle when I need to."

She burbled on enthusiastically while Julian tried to make sense of it all.

"I've looked into getting planning permission for an office outbuilding, and I've been sorting it all out over the past few weeks. I'll need your help because it has to be designed to fit in with the landscape, and the stone has to be right, but it looks like it's all going to go through."

"Sally, slow down!" He couldn't keep up with her stream of enthusiasm because he was so thrown by the whole thing.

"Okay, I know it's a lot to take in. I just didn't want to tell you about it until I knew I could pull it off."

"You really own the cottage?" That much had just about sunk in.

"Yes, you don't mind do you? I mean . . . I wanted it so that it would be our place."

"Ours?" The doubt that he'd felt had withered away, and hope had lodged itself inside his heart. Her words were slowly sinking in, but he still couldn't come to terms with it. He'd been lecturing himself on staying focused on visiting her in London, and now she was talking about owning the cottage? Living here? Even if it was only part-time . . . what bliss it would be. His beautiful sexy, clever Sally, here, close by when he needed her? And he did need her.

"Yes, darling, *ours,* although I want you to be friendly to any other visitors to the area. No growling or scaring them off. I'll be around to make sure of that." She laughed again. "And I want you to help me convert the attic into a studio for me, so I can see the cove . . . and watch Double O Beachpatrol frolic in the waves while I sculpt." She gave another delighted chuckle.

"I can't believe you're saying this, I can't believc it's true."

"I'll prove it's true for you. Tell me, can you still see the cottage?" Her voice had grown somehow more intimate.

"Yes, and it's so beautiful, I wish you could see it now, in the sunset."

He looked over at it, the old stone walls warm and mellow, so inviting in the light of the setting sun. A movement caught his eye. The door opened. Standing in the doorway was Sally, wearing a floating purple dress. And she was beckoning to him, like a gypsy woman calling her wandering man home for the night.

Julian whooped. She giggled in the phone.

"Sally, you are in *big* trouble for tricking me like this," he said. "So you better start running now, because when I catch you . . . !" And with that he dropped the phone and began to run down the cove towards her.

But Sally didn't run. She switched her phone off and stayed put, and when he arrived at her door, she walked into his arms, forever.

About the Author:

Saskia is British and lives on the edge of the Yorkshire moors, close to the home of the famous romance writing sisters, the Brontë's. There's heaps of inspiration in the beautiful windswept countryside nearby and in her most wildly romantic moments, Saskia swears she can feel the spirits of Cathy and Heathcliff out there on the moors!

Saskia has had short fiction published on both sides of the pond and is thrilled to be the first British author writing for **Secrets.** *Visitors are welcome at* www.saskiawalker.co.uk *and she loves to hear from readers, so send her an email at* saskia@saskiawalker.co.uk.